THE

PARTISAN:

A

ROMANCE OF THE REVOLUTION.

BY W. GILMORE SIMMS,

AUTHOR OF "THE YEMASSEE," "GUY RIVERS," "MARTIN FABER,"
"RICHARD HURDIS," "BORDER BEAGLES," ETC.

"And Liberty's vitality, like Truth,
Is still undying. Like the sacred fire
Nature has shrined in caverns, still it burns
Though the storm howls without.

New and Revised Edition.

CHICAGO AND NEW YORK:
BELFORD, CLARKE & CO.
1886.

AMS PRESS
NEW YORK

Reprinted from the edition of 1886, New York
First AMS EDITION published 1968
Manufactured in the United States of America

Library of Congress Catalogue Card Number: 68-55650

AMS PRESS, INC.
New York, N.Y. 10003

INTRODUCTION

TO RICHARD YEADON, ESQ., OF SOUTH CAROLINA.

My Dear Yeadon:

When, in 1835, I first inscribed this romance with your name
we neither of us could have imagined the long list of other volumes which
have followed from the same pen. That I have continued a profession in
which so few of our people of the South have found it prudent to engage,
is in proof of a certain degree of success in my case. Of this it is
scarcely proper that I should make any boast; but it will not be denied
that I should express myself quite satisfied with the encouragements
which have attended my career. These have not been so great, in pecu-
niary respects, as yours. You have grown to fortune. You are one of
her favourites; and it is some satisfaction, that, though her bounties have
been withheld from me, they have been so lavishly bestowed on those who
are worthy, and whom I rank among my friends—friends who have not
changed from the beginning, and with whom I mostly bear the same
grateful relations which cheered me in the opening of my career of life.

A portion of what was said in the preface to the first edition of "The
Partisan," may be properly included in what I have to say now, when,
after a lapse of nearly twenty years, I am called upon to revise its pages,
for the eyes of a wholly new generation. The work was originally
planned as the first of a Series devoted to the illustration of the war of
the Revolution in South Carolina. With this object, I laid the founda-
tions of this work more deeply and broadly than I should have done, had
I purposed merely the single story. I designed, in fact, a trilogy. Seve

ral of the persons of the story were destined to be the property of the Series. But, with a perfect knowledge of the danger which usually attends such an experiment, I so arranged my *material* as to make each of the stories independent of the others. Each was to be wrought out to its separate conclusion. But the preparation of the successors of " The Partisan," was necessarily to depend upon the degree of favor with which that story was received. I need not tell you that I had no reason to complain of this. The work was treated with indulgence by the critics, and was welcomed with kindness by its readers. It is impossible to enumerate the copies circulated and the number of editions through which it passed. It was successful far beyond its merits. Its pages were charged with many crudities—there were some serious faults of design and development—the style was careless, and the incidents charactarized by coarseness, and an ambitious effort at effect—which declared sufficiently for the unpractised hand, and the imperfect tastes of youth. The censures of criticism, on these points, were all very soon justified to my own mind, by my own growing experience; and I have in this, as in most cases where my writings were the subject, been compelled to recognize the justice of the most severe judgments uttered by my critics—I mean by those who were at the pains to examine, and who approached their tasks with equal conscientiousness and capacity.

It was while spending part of a summer with a friend in the neighborhood of the once beautiful, but now utterly decayed town of Dorchester, that I availed myself of the opportunity to revisit the ancient ruins of the place. When a boy I had frequently rambled over the ground, and listened to its domestic chronicles, from the lips of one—now no more—who had been perfectly conversant with its local history, as with a large body of revolutionary and traditional history besides.

Many of its little legends were impressed upon my memory, and the fortunes of more than one of its families, of whom no record now remains, but that of the place of burial, were deeply scored upon my mind. These, together with the melancholy transitions through which the place itself had gone—finally exchanging all the hum of busy life, for the bleak silence and speaking desolation of the tomb—were well calculated to inspire me with sentiments of veneration. It was with the revival of old memories, and the awakening of new impulses and sentiments, that I rambled. My aim has been to give a story of events, rather than of persons. The one, of course, could not well be done without the other; yet it has been my object to make myself as greatly independent as possible of the necessity which would combine them. A sober desire for history—the unwritten, the unconsidered, but veracious history—has been with me, in this labor, a sort of principle. The phases of a time of errors and of wrongs—of fierce courage—tenacious patriotism—yielding, but struggling virtue, not equal to the pressure of circumstances, and failing for a time, Antæus-like, only for a renewal and recovery of its strength—it has been my aim to deliniate, with all the rapidity of one, who, with the mystic lantern, runs his uncouth shapes and varying shadows along the gloomy wall, startling the imagination and enkindling curiosity. The medium through which we now look at these events is, in some respects, that of a glass darkened. The characters rise up before us grimly or indistinctly. We scarcely believe, yet we cannot doubt. The evidence is closed—the testimony now irrefutable—and imagination, however audacious in her own province, only ventures to embody and model those features of the Past, which the sober History has left indistinct, as not within her notice, or unworthy her regard. History, indeed, as we style it somewhat complacently, is quite too apt to overlook the best essentials of society—such as constitute the moving impulses of men to action—in order to dilate on great events,—scenes in which men are nearly massed, while a single favorite overtops all the rest, the Hero rising to the Myth, and absorbing within himself all the consideration which a more veracious and philosophical mode of writing would distribute over states and communities, and the humblest walks of life.

Nor is "The Partisan" merely a local chronicle, embodying traditionary heroes only. The persons of the drama, many of them, are names of the nation familiar to our daily reading. Gates, Marion, DeKalb, Cornwallis, Tarleton, and others, are all the property of our histories. In illustrating the career of these persons, and endeavoring to delineate their characteristics, I have followed the best authorities. I have had some before me, besides, which have never been in print. The severity with which I have visited the errors of Gates, and the traits which I have given of his character may be thought harsh, but they are sustained by all the best authorities—by Otho Williams, Lee,

Johnson, and, to a certain extent, the ancient histories. Something
has been said of the questionable propriety of thus reviving these facts,
however true, and dwelling upon the faults and foibles of a man conspicuous in our history, and one, too, whose name is associated inevi-
tably with one glorious event in our history. We have been reminded
also of the benevolent maxim of the Latins—" *De mortuis nil nisi
bonum.*" But we must take the case out of the application of
the maxim in regard to the great necessities of future generations.
The individual must be made the example for the benefit of the
race. I am decided that a nation gains only in glory and in greatness, as it is resolute to behold and pursue the truth. I would
paint the disasters of my country, where they arose from the obvious
error of her sons, in the strongest possible colors. We should then
know—our sons and servants, alike, should then know—how best to
avoid them. The rock which has wrecked us once should become the
beacon for those who follow. It is only by making it so, that the
vicissitudes of life—its follies or misfortunes—can be made tributary to
its triumphs. For this reason I have dwelt earnestly upon our disasters; and, with a view to the moral, I have somewhat departed from
the absolute plan of the story, to dilate upon the dangerous errors of
the leading personages in the events drawn upon. The history of the
march of Gate's army, I have carefully elaborated with this object;
and the reflecting mind will see the parallel position of cause and
effect which I have studiously sought to make obvious, wherever it
seemed to me necessary for the purposes of instruction. It is in this
way, only, that the novel may be made useful, when it ministers to
morals, to mankind, and to society.
    But—

> " Next to singing the most foolish thing,
>   Is gravely to harangue on what we sing."

and I have surely said enough for the purposes of explanation. It remains only to add that my proposed trilogy is now complete, and the
Partisan warfare of Carolina, which constitutes one of the most brilliant chapters in our revolutionary history, will be found illustrated
in this volume, and that of the two works by which it will be followed
—Mellichampe and Katharine Walton.

THE PARTISAN.

CHAPTER I.

"Oh, grievous desolation! look, and see
Their sad condition! 'Tis a piercing sight:
A country overthrown and crushed—the scythe
Gone over it in wrath—and sorrowing Grief
Dumb with her weight of woe."

Our narrative begins in South Carolina, during the summer of 1780. The arms of the British were at that time triumphant throughout the colony. Their armies overran it. Charleston, the chief city, had stood a siege, and had fallen, after a protracted and honourable defence of eight weeks; succumbing finally to famine, rather than the force of arms. One-half of the military strength of the lower country, then the most populous region, had become prisoners of war by this disaster; and. for the present, were thus incapacitated from giving any assistance to their brethren in arms. Scattered, crushed, and disheartened by repeated failures, the whigs, in numerous instances, hopeless of any better fortune, had given in their adhesion to the enemy, and had received a pledge of British protection. This protection secured them, as it was thought, in their property and persons, and its condition simply called for their neutrality. Many of the more firm and honourably tenacious, scorning all compromise with invasion, fled for shelter to the swamps and mountains; and, through the former, all Europe could not have tracked their footsteps. In the whole State, at this period, the cause of American liberty had no head, and almost as little hope: all was gloomy and unpromising. Marion, afterwards styled the "Swamp Fox," and Sumter, the "Game Cock"—epithets aptly descriptive of their several military attributes—had not yet properly risen in arms, though both of them had been engaged already in active and successful service. Their places of retreat were at this time unknown; and, certainly, they were not then looked to, as at an after period, with that anxious reliance which their valour subsequently taught their countrymen to entertain. Nothing, indeed, could be more deplorably prostrate than were the energies of the colony. Here and there only did some little partisan squad make a stand, or offer a show of resistance to the incursive British or the marauding and malignant tory—disbanding, if not defeated, most usually after the temporary object had been obtained, and retreating for security into shelter and inaction. There was no sort of concert, save in feeling, among the many who were still not unwilling for the fight : they doubted or they dreaded one another; they knew not whom to trust. The next door neighbour of the staunch whig was not unfrequently a furious loyalist—as devoted to George the Third as the other could have been to the intrinsic beauty of human liberty. The contest of the Revolution, so far as it had gone, had confirmed and made tenacious this pirit of hostility and opposition, until, in the end, patriot and loyalist had drawn the sword against one another, and rebel and tory were the degrading epithets by which they severally distinguished the individual whose throat they strove to cut. When the metropolis fell into the hands of the British, and their arms extended through the State, the tories alone were active and formidable. These, hitherto outlawed in all the provinces, had mostly sought shelter in Florida; whence they emerged as soon as the British arms had established their ascendency in Georgia and Carolina. They now took satisfaction for their own previous trials ; and crime was never so dreadful a monster as when they ministered to its appetites. Mingled in with the regular troops of the British, or forming separate bodies of their own, and officered from among themselves, they penetrated the well known recesses which gave shelter to the fugitives. If the rebel resisted, they slew him without quarter ; if he submitted, they hung him without benefit of clergy : they spoiled his children of their possessions, and not unfrequently slew them also. But few sections of the low and middle country escaped their search It was only in the bald regions o

North Carolina that the fugitives could find repose; only where the most miserable poverty took from crime all temptation, that the beaten and maltreated patriots dared to give themselves a breathing-space from flight. In the same manner the frontier-colony of Georgia had already been overrun and ravaged by the conquerors: and there, as it was less capable of resistance, almost all show of opposition had been long since at an end.

The invader, deceived by these appearances, declared, in swelling language, to his monarch, that the two colonies were properly subjugated, and would now return to their obedience. He knew not that,

> "Freedom's battle once begun,
> Bequeathed from bleeding sire to son,
> Though baffled oft, is ever won."

But, though satisfied of the efficiency of his achievements, and himself convinced of the truth of the assurances which he had made to this effect, the commander of the British forces did not suffer the slightest relaxation of his vigilance. Earl Cornwallis, one of the best of the many leaders sent by the mother-country to the colonies in that eventful contest, had taken charge of the southern marching army soon after the fall of Charleston. He was too good a soldier to omit, or to sleep in the performance of any of his duties. He proceeded with due diligence to confirm his conquests; and, aptly sustained by the celerity and savage enterprise of the fierce legionary, Colonel Tarleton, the country was soon swept from the seaboard to the mountains. This active but cruel commander, who enacted the Claverhouse in South Carolina with no small closeness of resemblance to his prototype, was as indefatigable as unsparing. He plunged headlong into fight, with a courage the most unscrupulous, with little reflection, seeming rather to confide in the boldness and impetuosity of his onset than to any ingenuity of plan, or careful elaborateness of manœuvre. Add to this that he was sanguinary in the last degree when triumphant, and we shall easily understand the sources of that terror which his very name was found to inspire among the undrilled, and, in half the number of instances, the unarmed militia which opposed him. "Tarleton's quarters" was the familiar and bitterly-derisive phrase by which when the whigs had opportunities of revenge, his bloodthirsty treatment of the overthrown and captive was remembered and requited.

The entire colony in his possession—all opposition, worthy the name, at an end—the victor, the better to secure his conquest, marched an army throughout the county. His presence, for the time, had the desired effect. His appearance quelled disaffection, overawed all open discontents, and his cavalry, by superior skill and rapidity of movement, readily dispersed the little bands of Carolinians that here and there fell in his way. Nor was this exhibition of his power the only proceeding by which he laboured to secure the fruits of his victory. With an excellent judgment, he established garrisons in various eligible points of the country, in order to overawe by his continual presence: these stations were judiciously chosen for independent and co-operative enterprise alike; they were sufficiently nigh for concert—sufficiently scattered for the general control of an extensive territory. Rocky Mount, Ninety-Six, Camden, Hanging Rock, Dorchester, and a large number of military posts besides, were thus created; all amply provided with munitions of war, well fortified, and garrisoned by large bodies of troops under experienced officers.

These precautions for a time compelled submission. The most daring among the patriots were silent—the most indulgent of the loyalists were active and enterprising. To crown and secure all, Sir Henry Clinton, who was at this period commander-in-chief of the southern invading army, proclaimed a general pardon, with some few exceptions, to all the inhabitants, for their late treasonable offences—promising them a full re-instatement of their old immunities; and requiring nothing in return but that they should remain quietly in their homes. This specious and well-timed indulgence had its due effect; and, in the temporary panic produced by Lincoln's defeat, the fall of the metropolis, the appearance of an army so formidable as that of the British, and the establishment of military posts and fortresses all around them, the people generally put on a show of acquiescence to the authority of the invader, which few in reality felt, and which many were secretly but resolutely determined never to submit to.

Thus much is necessary, in a general point of view, to the better comprehension of the narrative which follows. The reader will duly note the situation of the colony of South Carolina ; and when we add, that the existing condition of things throughout the Union was only not so bad, and the promise of future fortune but little more favourable, all has been said necessary to his proper comprehension of the discouraging circumstances under which the partisan warfare of the South began. With this reference, we shall be better able to appreciate that deliberate valour, that unyielding patriotism, which, in a few spirits, defying danger and above the sense of privation, could keep alive the sacred fires of liberty in the thick swamps and dense and gloomy forests of Carolina—asking nothing, yielding nothing, and only leaving the field the better to re-enter it for the combat. Let us now proceed to the commencement of our proper narrative.

CHAPTER II.

" Sweet flow thy waters, Ashley, and pleasant on thy banks
The mossy oak and massy pine stand forth in solemn ranks ;
They fringe thee in a fitting guise, since with a gentle play,
Through bending groves and circling dells thou tak'st thy mazy way—
Thine is the summer's loveliness, save when September storms
Arouse thee to the angry mood that all thy face deforms;
And thine the recollection old which makes thee proudly shine,
When happy thousands saw thee rove, and Dorchester was thine."

THE scene is very much altered now. Dorchester belongs to
Ashley no longer. It is a name—a shadow. The people are gone;
the site is distinguished by its ruins only. The owl hoots through
the long night from the old church-tower, and the ancient woods
and the quiet waters of the river give back, in melancholy echoes,
his unnoted cries. The Carolinian looks on the spot with a saddened
spirit. The trees crowd upon the ancient thoroughfare ; the brown
viper hisses from the venerable tomb, and the cattle graze along the
clustering bricks that distinguish the ancient chimney-places. It
is now one of those prospects that kindle poetry in the most insensible observer. It is one of the visible dwelling-places of Time ; and
the ruins that still mock, to a certain extent, his destructive pro
gress, have in themselves a painful chronicle of capricious change
and various affliction. They speak for the dead that lie beneath
them in no stinted number ; they record the leading features of a
long history, crowded with vicissitudes.

But our purpose now is with the past, and not with the present.
We go back to the time when the village of Dorchester was full of
life, and crowded with inhabitants ; when the coaches of the wealthy
planters of the neighbourhood thronged the highway ; when the
bells from the steeple sweetly called to the Sabbath worship ; and
when, throughout the week, the shops were crowded with buyers,
and the busy hammer of the mechanic, and the axe of the labourer,
sent up their crowding noises. imaging, upon a small scale, many of

the more stirring attributes of the great city, and all of its life
Dorchester then had several hundred inhabitants. The plan of the
place lies before us now—a regularly laid out city, of perfect
squares, with its market-place, its hotels, and its churches; its busy
wharves, and its little craft of sloop and schooner, lying at anchor,
or skimming along the clear bosom of the Ashley. It had its garrison also, and not the smallest portion of its din and bustle arose
from the fine body of red-coated and smartly-dressed soldiers then
occupying the square fort of tapia-work, which to this day stands
upon the hill of Dorchester—just where the river bends in with a
broad sweep to the village site—in a singular state of durability and
preservation.

This fort commanded the river and village alike. The old bridge
of Dorchester, which crossed the Ashley at a little distance above it,
was also within its range. The troops at frequent periods paraded
in the market-place, and every art was made use of duly to impress
upon the people the danger of any resistance to a power so capable
to annoy and to punish. This being the case, it was amusing to
perceive how docile, how loyal indeed, are those inhabitants, who, but
a few weeks before were in arms against their present rulers and who
now only wait a convenient season to resume the weapons which
policy had persuaded them to lay aside.

None of the villagers were more dutiful or devout in their allegiance than Richard Humphries—Old Dick, sly Dick—Holy Dick,
as his neighbours capriciously styled him—who kept the " Royal
George," then the high tavern of the village. The fat, beefy face of
the good-natured Hanoverian hung in yellow before the tavern
door, on one of the two main roads leading from the country through
the town. The old monarch had, in this exposed situation, undergone repeated trials. At the commencement of the Revolution, the
landlord, who, after the proverbial fashion of landlords in all
countries, really cared not who was king, had been compelled by
public opinion to take down the sign and replace it with another
more congenial to the popular feeling. George, in the mean time,
was assigned less conspicuous lodgings in an ancient garret. The
change of circumstances restored the venerable portrait to its place;
and under the eyes of the British garrison, there were few more

thorough-going loyalists in the village than Richard Humphries.
He was a sociable old man, fond of drink, who generally filled his
own glass whenever called upon to replenish that of his customer.
His house was the common thoroughfare of the travelling and the
idle. The soldier, not on duty, found it a pleasant lounge; the
tory, confident in the sympathies of the landlord, and solicitous
of the good opinion of the ruling powers, made it his regular resort; and even the whig, compelled to keep down his patriotism,
in order to keep up his credit, not unwisely sauntered about in
the same wide hall with the enemy he feared and hated, but whom
it was no part of his policy at the present moment to alarm or irritate. Humphries, from these helping circumstances, distanced all
competition in the village. The opposition house was maintained
by a suspected whig—one Pryor—who was avoided accordingly.
Pryor was a sturdy citizen, who asked no favors; and if he did
not avow himself in the language of defiance, at the same time
scorned to take any steps to conciliate patronage or do away with
suspicion. He simply cocked his hat at the ancient customer,
now passing to the other house; thrust his hands into the pockets
of his breeches, and, with a manful resignation, growled through
his teeth as he followed the deserter with his eyes—"The white-
livered skunk! He may go and be d—d."

This sort of philosophy was agreeable enough to Humphries,
who, though profligate in some respects, was yet sufficiently world-
ly to have a close eye to the accumulation of his sixpences.
His household was well served; for, though himself a widower,
his daughter Bella, a buxom, lively, coquettish, but gentle-natured
creature, proved no common housekeeper. She was but a girl,
however, but sixteen, and as she had long lacked the restraining
presence of a matron, and possessed but little dignity herself, the
house had its attractions for many, in the freedoms which the old
man either did not or would not see, and which the girl herself
was quite too young, too innocent, and perhaps too weak, often to
find fault with. Her true protection, however, was in a brother
not much older than herself, a fine manly fellow, and—though
with the cautious policy of all around him suppressing his predi-
lections for the time—a staunch partisan of American liberty.

It was on a pleasant afternoon in June, that a tall, well made youth, probably twenty-four or twenty-five years of age, rode up to the door of the " Royal George," and throwing his bridle to a servant, entered the hotel. His person had been observed, and his appearance duly remarked upon, by several persons already assembled in the hall which he now approached. The new comer, indeed, was not one to pass unnoticed. His person was symmetry itself, and the ease with which he managed his steed, the unhesitating boldness with which he kept on his way and gazed around him at a period and in a place where all were timid and suspicious, could not fail to fix attention. His face too, was significant of a character of command, besides being finely intelligent and tolerably handsome ; and hough he carried no weapons that were visible, there was something exceedingly military in his movement ; and the cap which he wore, made of some native fur and slightly resting upon one side of his thickly clustering brown hair, imparted a daring expression to his look which gave confirmation to the idea. Many were the remarks of those in the hall as, boldly dashing down the high road, he left the church to the right, and moving along the market-place, came at once towards the tavern, which stood on the corner of Prince and Bridge streets.

" A bold chap with his spurs, that," exclaimed Sergeant Hastings, of the garrison, who was a frequent guest of the tavern, and had found no small degree of favour with the landlord's daughter. 'A bold chap, that—do you know him, Humphries ?"

This question brought the landlord to the window. He looked intently upon the youth as he approached. but seemed at fault.

"Know him ? why yes, I think I do know him, sergeant : that's—yes—that's—bless my soul, I don't know him at all !"

" Well, be sure now, Humphries," coolly spoke the sergeant. "Such a good-looking fellow ought not to be forgotten. But he 'lights, and we shall soon know better."

A few moments, and the stranger made his appearance. The landlord bustled up to him, and offered assistance, which the youth declined for himself, but gave directions for his horse's tendance.

" Shall be seen to, captain," said the landlord.

" Way do you call me captain ?" demanded the youth, sternly.

" Bless me, don't be angry, squire; but didn't you say you was a captain ?" apologetically replied Humphries.

" I did not."

" Well, bless me, but I could have sworn you did—now didn't gentlemen ?—sergeant, did'nt you hear—"

" It matters not," the stranger interrupted ; " it matters not. You were mistaken, and these gentlemen need not be appealed to. Have my horse cared for, if you please. He has come far and fast to-day, and will need a good rubbing. Give him fodder now, but no corn for an hour."

" It shall be done, captain."

"Hark'ee, my friend," said the youth angrily, " you will not style me captain again, unless you would have more than you can put up with. I am no captain, no colonel, no commander of any sort, and unless you give me the troops, am not willing to wear the title. So, understand me."

" Ask pardon, squire; but it comes so common—ask pardon, sir ;" and the landlord shuffled off, as he spoke, to see after his business. As he retired, Sergeant Hastings made up to the new comer, and with all the consequence of one having a certain portion of authority, and accustomed to a large degree of deference from those around him, proceeded to address the youth on the subject matter of his momentary annoyance.

" And with your leave young master, where's the harm in being captain or colonel ?   I don't see that there's any offence in it."

" None, none in the world, sir, in being captain or colonel, but some, I take it, in being styled such undeservedly. The office is good enough, and I have no objections to it ; but I have no humour to be called by any nickname."

" Nickname—why, d—n it, sir—why, what do you mean ?   Do you pretend that it's a nickname to be called an officer in his majesty's troops, sir ?   If you do, sir—" and the sergeant concludes his swaggering speech with a most stormy stare.

" Pistols and daggers ! most worthy officer in his majesty's troops do not look so dangerous," replied the youth very coolly.   He saw at a glance the sort of Hector with whom he had to deal, and would have answered him with his boot, but that his policy demanded forbearance. He continued, pacifically : " I have no sort of intention to offend captain or sergeant. I only beg that, as I am neither one nor the other, nobody will force me into their jackets."

" And why not, young master ?" said the sergeant, somewhat pacified, but still, as he liked not the *nonchalance* of the stranger, seemingly bent to press upon him a more full development of his opinions. " Why not ? Is it not honourable, I ask you, to hold his majesty's commission, and would you not, as a loyal subject, be very glad to accept one at his hands ?"

There was no little interest manifested by the spectators as this question was put, and they gathered more closely about the bewel stranger, but still keeping at a deferential distance from the sergeant. He, too, looked forward to the reply of the youth with some interest. His head was advanced and his arms akimbo, and, stationed in front of the person he examined, in the centre of the hall, his clumsy compact person and round rosy face looked exceedingly imposing in every eye but that of the person for whose especial sight their various terrors had been put on. The youth seemed annoyed by the pertinacity of his assailant, but he made an effort at composure, and after a brief pause replied to the inquiry.

" Honourable enough, doubtless. I know nothing about the employment, and cannot say. As for taking a commission at his majesty's hands, I don't know that I should do any such thing."

The declaration produced a visible emotion in the assembly. One or two of the spectators slid away silently, and the rest seemed variously agitated, while at the same time, one person whom the stranger had not before seen—a stout, good-looking man, seemingly in humble life, and not over his own age—came forward, and, with nothing ostentatious in his manner, placed himself alongside of the man who had so boldly declared himself. Sergeant Hastings seemed for an instant almost paralysed by what appeared the audacity of the stranger. At length, detaching his sword partially from the sheath, so that a few inches of the blade became visible, he looked round with a potential aspect upon the company, and then proceeded—

"Ha! not take a commission from the hands of his majesty ! This looks suspicious ! And pray, sir, tell us why you would not accept his majesty's commission ?"

Unmoved by the solemnity of the proceeding, the youth with the utmost quietness replied—

"For the very best reason in the world—I should scarcely know what to do with it."

"Oh, that's it !" said the sergeant. "And so you are really not an officer ?"

"No. I've been telling you and this drinking fellow, the land-lord, all the time, that I am no officer, and yet neither of you seems satisfied. Nothing will do, but you will put me in his majesty's commission, and make me a general and what not, whether I will or no. But where's the man ?—Here, landlord !"

"Father's out, can I serve, sir ?" said a soft voice, followed by the pretty maid of the inn, the fair Bella Humphries, whose person was now visible behind the bar.

"Yes, my dear, you can ;" and as the stranger youth spoke, and the maid courtesied, he tapped her gently upon the cheek, and begged that he might be shown his apartment, stating, at the same time, the probability that he would be an inmate for several days of the tavern. The sergeant scowled fiercely at the liberty thus taken, and the youth could not help seeing that the eye of the girl sank under the glance that the former gave her. He said nothing, however, and taking in his hand the little fur valise that he carried, the only furniture, besides saddle and bridle, worn by his horse, he followed the steps of Bella, who soon conducted him to his chamber, and left him to those ablutions which a long ride along a sandy road had rendered particularly necessary.

The sergeant meanwhile was not so well satisfied with what had taken place. He was vexed that he had not terrified the youth— vexed at his composure—vexed that he had tapped Bella Humphries upon her cheek, and doubly vexed that she had submitted with such excellent grace to the aforesaid tapping. The truth is, Sergeant Hastings claimed some exclusive privileges with the maiden. He was her regular gallant—bestowed upon her the greater part of his idle time, and had flattered himself that he stood alone in her esti mation; and so, perhaps, he did. His attentions had given him a large degree of influence over her, and what with his big speech, swaggering carriage, and flashy uniform, poor Bella had long since been taught to acknowledge his power over her fancy. But the girl was coquettish, and her very position as maid of the inn had contributed to strengthen and confirm the natural predisposition. The kind words and innocent freedoms of the handsome stranger were not disagreeable to her, and she felt not that they interfered with the claims of the sergeant, or would be so disagreeable to him, until she beheld the scowling glance with which he surveyed them.

In the hall below, to which the landlord had now returned Hastings gave utterance to the spleen which this matter had occasioned.

"That's an impudent fellow—a very impudent fellow. ı don't like him, at all!"

The landlord looked up timidly. "And what, sergeant—what!"

"I say, I don't like him. I suspect him!"

"Suspect! God ha' mercy; and who do you think—who do you think he is, sergeant?"

"How should I know? I asked you: you know every thing; at least, you pretend to. Why are you out here? Who is he?"

"Bless me, I can't say; I don't know."

"What do you *think* he is?"

"Think! I think! oh! no! no! I don't think."

"He certainly is an impudent—a very suspicious person."

"Do you think so, sergeant?" asked one of the persons present, with an air of profound alarm.

"I do—a very suspicious person—one that should be watched narrowly."

"I see nothing suspicious about him," said another, the same individual who had placed himself beside the stranger when the wrath of the sergeant was expected to burst upon him, and when he had actually laid his hand upon his sword. "I see nothing suspicious about the stranger," said the speaker, boldly, "except that he doesn't like to be troubled with foolish questions."

"Foolish questions—foolish questions! Bless me, John Davis, do you know what you're a saying?" The landlord spoke in great

2

trepidation, and placed himself, as he addressed John Davis, between him and the sergeant.

" Yes, I know perfectly what I say, Master Humphries ; and I say it's very unmannerly, the way in which the stranger has been pestered with foolish questions. I say it. and I say it again ; and I don't care who hears it. I'm ready to stand up to what I say."

" Bless me, the boy's mad ! Now, sergeant, don't mind him— he's only foolish, you see."

" Mind him—oh no ! Look you, young man, do you see that tree ? It won't take much treason to tuck you up there."

" Treason, indeed ! I talk no treason, Sergeant Hastings, and I defy you to prove any agin me. I'm not to be frightened this time o' day, I'd have you to know ; and though you are a sodger, and wear a red coat, let me tell you there is a tough colt in the woods that your two legs can't straddle. There is no treason in that, for it only concerns one person, and that one person is your own self, and I'm as good a man as you any day."

" You d—d rebel, is it so you speak to a sergeant in his majesty's service ? Take that "—and with the words, with his sword drawn at the instant, he made a stroke with the flat of it at the head of the sturdy disputant, which, as the latter somewhat anticipated the assault, he was prepared to elude. This was done adroitly enough, and with a huge club which stood conveniently in the corner, he had prepared himself without fear to guard against a repetition of the attack, when the stranger, about whom the coil had arisen, suddenly made his appearance, and at once interposed between the parties.

CHAPTER III.

" It is a written bondage—writ in stripes,
    And letter'd in our blood. Like beaten hounds,
    We crouch and cry. but clench not—lick the hand
    That strikes and scourges."

HASTINGS turned furiously at the interruption ; but the stranger though entirely unarmed, stood his ground firmly, and looked on him with composure.

" That's a bright sword you wear," said he, " but it is scarcely a good stroke, and anything but a gallant one, Master Sergeant, which you make with it. How now, is it the fashion with British soldiers to draw upon unarmed men ?"

The person addressed turned upon the speaker with a scowl which seemed to promise that he would transfer some portion of his anger to the new comer. He had no time, however, to do more than look his wrath at the interruption ; for among the many persons whom the noise had brought to the scene of action was the fair Bella Humphries herself. The maid of the inn—accustomed probably to quell such conflicts by her beauty and persuasions— waited not an instant to place herself between the parties, and, as if her own interest in the persons concerned gave her an especial right in the matter, she fearlessly passed under the raised weapon of Hastings, addressing him imploringly, and with an air of intimacy, which was, perhaps, the worst feature in the business. So, at least, the individual appeared to think to whose succour she had come. His brow blackened still more at her approach, and when she interfered to prevent strife, a muttered curse, half-audible, rose to his lips. Brandishing the club which he had wielded with no little readiness before, he seemed more than ever desirous of renewing the combat, though with all its disadvantages. But the parties around generally interfered to prevent the progress of the strife :

and Bella, whose mind seemed perfectly assured of Hastings' invincibility, addressed her prayers only to him, and in behalf of the other.

"Now don't strike, Sergeant—don't I pray! John is only foolish, and don't mean any harm. Strike him not, I beg you!"

"Beg for yourself, Bella Humphries—I don't want any of your begging for me. I'm no chicken, and can hold my own any day against him. So don't come between us—you in particular—you had better keep away."

The countryman spoke ferociously; and his dark eye, long black hair, and swarthy cheek, all combined to give the expression of fierce anger which his words expressed, a lively earnestness not ill-adapted to sustain them. The girl looked on him reproachfully as he spoke, though a close observer might have seen in her features a something of conscious error and injustice. It was evident that the parties had been at one period far more intimate than now; and the young stranger, about whom the coil began, saw in an instant the true situation of the twain. A smile passed over his features, but did not rest, as his eye took in at a glance the twofold expression of Bella's face, standing between her lovers, preventing the fight—scowled on furiously by the one, and most affectionately leered at by the other. Her appeal to the sergeant was so complimentary, that even were he not half-ashamed of what he had already done in commencing a contest so unequal, he must have yielded to it and forborne. Some of his moderation, too, might have arisen from his perceiving the hostile jealousy of spirit with which his rival regarded her preference of himself. His vanity was enlisted in the application of the maiden, and with a becoming fondness of expression in his glance, turning to the coquette, he gave her to understand, while thrusting his sword back into the scabbard, that he consented to mercy on the score of her application. Still, as Davis held out a show of fight, and stood snugly ensconded behind his chair defying and even inviting assault, it was necessary that the sergeant should draw off honourably from the contest. While returning the weapon to the sheath, therefore he spoke to his enemy in language of indulgent warning, not unmixed with the military threats common at the period—

" Hark you, good fellow—you're but a small man to look out for danger, and there's too little of you, after all, for me to look after I let you off this time; but you're on ticklish territory, and if you move but one side or the other, you're but a lost man after all. It's not a safe chance to show rebel signs on the king's highway, and you have an ugly squinting at disaffection. My eyes are on you now, and if I but see you wink, or hear you hint, treason,—ay, treason, rebellion—I see it in your eyes, I tell you,—but wink it o look it again, and you know it's short work, very short work and a shorter journey, to the tight rope and the branching tree."

The speaker looked round significantly upon the company as he uttered a warning and threat, which, though addressed particularly to the refractory countryman, were yet evidently as much meant for the benefit of the rest. Not that the worthy sergeant had any reason for uttering language which, in all respects, seemed so gratuitous; but this was of a piece with the wantonly injudicious habit of his superiors, from whom, with the readiness of inferiority and sycophancy, he made free to borrow; and, with as little discrimination, quite as frequently employed·it, not less for 'he gratification of his vanity than for the exercise of his power. The speech had something of its usual effect,—keeping in silence those whose love to talk might have prompted to occasional remark, though without any serious feeling in the matter; and subduing thoroughly all demonstrations of dislike on the part of the few, who, feeling things more deeply, might be disposed rather to act than to speak, when under such provocation. Whatever the persons around may have felt at the moment, they were generally prudent enough to be silent. Old Humphries alone, with uplifted hands, now somewhat touched with liquor, and seeing all danger over, came forward, and hobbling up to the sergeant, cried out, in reply—

" Why, bless us, sergeant, you talk as if you were among the enemies of his majesty, and not among his good friends and well-wishers. Now, I'm sure I can answer for all here. There's Jones and Baxter, Lyons and Tom Walker there—all for the crown,—right loyal good fellows, who drink the health of King George—God bless him!— whenever they can get a drink; and as for Jack Davis, bless us, ser

2

geant, there's no better boy in Goose Creek, though he is cross and snappish when his fit's on, and no chicken either, as he says himself. He'll fight for his majesty any day, I know. There's no mistake in him—there's no mistake in any of the boys—I can answer for all that's here except—" and here the landlord paused in one of the longest speeches he had ever made, and his eye rested doubtfully upon the person of the stranger.

"Except me," said the latter, coming forward, looking Hastings attentively in the face as he spoke, and at the same time placing his hand with some little emphasis upon the shoulders of old Humphries, —"except me, Master Humphries, for whom you can say nothing— of whom you know nothing—but about whom you are excessively curious. You only know I am not a captain, nor yet a colonel ; and as I have not satisfied your desires on these subjects, of course you cannot answer for my loyalty."

"Bless me, no ; that I can't, stranger."

" But I can answer for myself and prefer to do so, Master Humphries, and that's enough for all parties ; and I can say, as you have already said for these gentlemen, that my loyalty is quite as good as that of any around me, as we shall all see in due season. And now that this quarrel is ended, let me only beg of the worthy sergeant here, that he may not be so quick to draw his weapon upon the man that is unarmed. The action is by no means so creditable to the soldier, and one that he may, most probably, in time, come to be ashamed of."

The perfect coolness and self-possession of the stranger, in this brief interlude, confounded Hastings not less than it did the rest. He knew not in what character to behold him, and, but that he was rather stolid than otherwise, might have exhibited traces of that confusion which his mind certainly felt. But the air of superiority which the other manifested, annoyed him too greatly to give way to doubt or indetermination ; and he was about to answer roughly, when a remark which Davis made, of a churlish nature, to the coquettish Bella Humphries, who still lingered beside the sergeant, attracted the latter's attention, and giving a glance to the speaker, he threw his collected spleen in that quarter, while addressing the girl—

"See now, that's the good you get for saving him from punishment. He doesn't thank you at all for what you've done."

"No, that I don't!" cried the incorrigible Davis: "I owe her as little thanks as I owe you kindness,—and I'll pay off both some day. I can hold my own without her help; and as for her begging, I don't want it—I won't have it—and I despise it."

"What's that?" cried Hastings, with a show of returning choler.

"Nothing, sergeant, nothing; don't mind what he says; he's only foolish, and don't mean any harm. Now take your hand away from the sword, I beg you."

The girl looked so prettily, as she prayed him to be quiet, that the soldier relented. Her deferential solicitude was all-influential, and softened much of the harsh feeling that might have existed in his bosom. Taking her arm into his own, with a consequential strut, and throwing a look of contempt upon his rival as he passed, the conqueror moved away into the adjoining apartment, to which, as his business seems private at present, we shall not presume to follow him.

His departure was the signal for renovated life in several of those persons who, in the previous scene, seemed quiescent enough. They generously came forward to Davis with advice and friendly counsel to keep himself out of harm's way, and submit, most civilly, like a good Christian, to the gratuitous blow and buffet. The most eloquent among them was the landlord.

"Now, bless me," said he, "John, my dear boy, why will you be after striving with the sergeant? You know you can't stand against him, and where's the use? He's quite too tough a colt for you to manage, now, I tell you."

"So you think, Master Humphries—so you think. But I'm not so sure of it, now, by half. I can stand a thump as well as any man—and I haint lived so long in Goose Creek not to know how to give one too. But how you stand it—you, I say, Dick Humphries —I don't altogether see."

"Eh, John—how I stand it? Bless us, what do you mean, boy? He don't trouble me—he don't threaten me—I'm a good subject to his majesty."

The youth laughed irreverently, and the stranger who had been standing apart, but still within hearing, noted the incident with considerable show of interest in his countenance.

"And what do you laugh at, John? Don't boy—I pray you, don't. Let's have a glass together, and don't trouble yourself to be laughing again; there's danger in it. Come: a glass.—Good old Jamaica! Won't you join us, stranger?"

The youth declined, and Davis proceeded—

"Why do I laugh, Master Humphries,? In truth I ought not to laugh when I see "——

Here he paused, and with a praiseworthy delicacy, he whispered in the old man's ear his objections to the large degree of intimacy existing between the British sergeant and his pretty daughter.

"Oh, go, John! there's no harm boy. You'se only jealous 'cause she turned you off."

"Turned me off, indeed!" responded the other, indignantly and aloud—"turned me off! No, master Humphries—not so bad neither. But it's no use talking—you'll know all in time, and will wish you had minded what I told you. But go your own gait, you'll grow fatter upon it;" and with this not very nice proverb the disappointed lover turned away without taking the proffered Jamaica.

This scene had not been lost on the stranger youth, though little regarded by the other personages, who had each made his speech and taken his drink and departure. There was much more spoken that we do not care to record, but which, duly noted by the one observer to whom we have made especial reference, was held not unworthy in his mind of proper consideration. He had seen a dogged disposition on the part of Davis to break and quarrel with the British sergeant; and though he clearly saw that much of this disposition arose, as old Humphries had asserted, from a jealous dislike of the intimacy between Bella and the person in question, he yet perceived that many of the phrases made use of by the countrymen indicated anything but respect or good feeling for the British authority. There was a sturdy boldness in his air and manner, when the other spoke to him of treason, which said that the crime was, after all, a venial one in his mind; and this disposition, perceptible as it must have been to the sergeant, not less than to stranger, might doubtless have prompted much of that violence on his part which had been so happily and in time arrested. Nor was there anything precipitate or uncommon in what the sergeant had done. Such exhibitions were frequent in the bitter and unscrupulous warfare of the south. The word and the blow, and usually the blow first, was the habitual mode of silencing, not treason merely, but all manner of opposition; and this was the injudicious course by which the British, regarding South Carolina as a conquered province, revolted the popular feeling from all sympathy with their authority, and provoked that spirit of determined resistance and hostility which, in a few weeks only after this event, blazed up throughout the whole colony, from one end to the other, and commenced that series of harassing operations, the partisan warfare, which, in spite of frequent defeats, cut off the foraging parties of the British army destroyed its resources, diminished its exercise, contracted its sphere of operations daily, and in the end, drove the invader to the seaboard, and from thence to his departing vessels.

Old Humphries followed Davis to the door, and again renewed his exhortation. The landlord seemed to have a good feeling for his guest, who had probably been a crony of his own, and a favoured lover of his daughter, before the British army had made its appearance to compel a change of political sentiment in the one, or a British sergeant, in his red coat and round face, to effect as great a revolution in the bosom of the other. His object seemed to be to persuade Davis into a more cautious utterance, when speaking of the existing powers; and he warned him of the unhesitating nature of the enemy when punishing what they held rebellion, and of the severe kinds of punishment put in exercise on such occasions. But, whether it was that the youth really felt sorely, too sorely for calm reflection, the loss of his sweetheart—or whether the assault of the sergeant had opened his eyes to the doubtful tenure by which the American held his security under the rule that now prevailed throughout the land—may not well be said; but there was a reckless audacity in his replies to the friendly suggestions of the landlord, which half frightened the latter personage out of his wits.

"I'd rather eat acorns, now, Master Humphries, I tell you, and sleep in the swamps in August, than hush my tongue when I feel it's right to speak. They shan't crow over me, though I die for it; and let them look out; for I tell you now, Dick Humphries, flesh and blood can't stand their parsecutions. There's no chance for life, let 'lone property. Look how they did Frampton's wife, and she in such a way; and only three days ago they tied up Tom Raysor's little boy Ben, and gave him a matter of fifty lashes with hickories thick as my thumb, and all because the boy wouldn't tell where his father was hiding."

"But you see, John, that all came of the hiding. If Frampton and Raysor had not taken to the swamp, the old lady would have been let alone, and the boy wouldn't have been whipt. Aint they in arms now against his majesty?"

"Yes; and if his majesty goes on after this fashion there will be a few more, I can tell you. Now, you yourself, Dick Humphries, I put it to yourself, whether the thing's right, and whether we ought to stand it. Now, I know you of old, and know you're no more a loyalist than—"

"Hush! Bless us, John Davis, how you talk, boy! hush, hush!" and with an air of the greatest trepidation, looking round and perceiving that, though the stranger appeared to be reading very earnestly from the pages of the "Royal (Charleston) Gazette," he was yet within hearing, the landlord led his companion farther from the door, and the conversation, as it proceeded to its conclusion, was entirely lost to all ears but their own. It was not long before Humphries returned to the hall, and endeavoured to commence a sort of desultory dialogue with the stranger guest, whose presence have produced the previous quarrel. But this personage seemed to desire no such familiarty, for scarcely had the old man begun, when throwing down the sheet he had been reading, and thrusting upon his head the rakish cap which all the while had rested on his knee, he rose from his seat, and moving rapidly to the door of the apartment, followed the steps of Davis, whom he beheld pursuing his way along the main bridge road and towards the river. The path was clear in this quarter; not a solitary being but themselves was to be seen—by them at least. In the centre of the bridge—a crazy structure of ill-adjusted timber thrown over a point of the stream where it most narrowed—the pursuing stranger overtook the moodily-wandering countryman. He stopped him in his progress till he could come up with him by a friendly hail; and, freely approaching him, tendered him his open hand in a cordial salutation. The other grasped it with honest pleasure.

"Master Davis, for such I believe is your name," said the stranger, frankly, " I owe you many thanks for so readily, though I must say rashly, taking up my quarrel. I understand that your brush with that soldier-fellow was on my account; and though, like yourself, I need nobody to fight my battles, I must yet thank you for the good spirit which you have shewn in this matter."

" No thanks, stranger. I don't know what name to call you—"

" No matter; names are unnecessary, and the fewer known the better in these doubtful times. I care not to utter mine, though it has but little value. Call me what you please." The other looked surprised, but still satisfied, and replied after this fashion—

" Well, stranger, as I said, you owe me no thanks at all in this affair; for though I did take up the matter on your hook, it was because I had a little sort of hankering to take it up on my own. I have long had a grudge at that fellow, and I didn't care much on whose score it began, so it had a beginning."

" He has done you wrong?" half affirmatively, half inquiringly, said his companion.

" Reckon he has, squire, and no small wrong neither; but that's neither here nor there, seeing there's little help for it."

" How! no help for it! What may be the nature of this injury, for which a man with your limbs and spirit can find no help? "

The countryman looked at the speaker with a curious expression, in which a desire to confide, and a proper hesitancy in entrusting his secret thoughts to a stranger, were mingled equally. The other beheld the expression, and readily defining the difficulty, proceeded to remove it.

" This man has wronged you friend Davis: you are his match—more than his match; you have better make and muscle, and manage your club quite as well as he his broadsword:—why should you not have justice, if you desire it? "

" If I desire it!" cried the other, and his black eye sparkled,

'J do desire it, squire; but there's odds against me, or we' a ~~ at it afore this."

" What odds ?"

" Look there !" and as Davis replied, he pointed to the fortress upon the opposite hill, a few hundred yards off, where the cross of Great Britain streamed high among the pine-trees, and from the entrance of which, at that very moment, a small body of regulars were pouring out into the street, and proceeding with martial music to the market-place.

" I see," replied the other—" I see; but why should they prove odds against you in a personal affair with this sergeant ? You have justice from them surely."

" Justice !—such justice as a tory captain gives when he wants your horse, and don't want to pay for it."

Davis replied truly, in his summing up of British justice at that period.

" But you do not mean to say that the people would not be protected, were complaints properly made to the officers ? "

" I do; and what's worse, complaint only goes after new hicko ries. One man was strapped up only yesterday, because he complained that Corporal Townes kicked his wife and broke his crockery. They gave him a hundred lashes."

" And yet loyalty must have its advantages, more than equal to this usage, else "—and a smile of bitter scorn played upon the lips of the speaker as he finished the sentence—" else there would no: be so many to love it so well and submit to it so patiently."

The countryman gazed earnestly at the speaker, whose eyes were full of a most searching expression, which could not be misunder stood.

" Dang it, stranger," he cried, " what do you mean—who are you ? "

" A man !" answered the speaker boldly;—" one who has not asked for a British protection, nor submitted to their hickories ;" and the form of the stranger was elevated duly as he spoke. and his eye was lighted up with scornful fires, as his reference was so is sarcastically to the many in the neighbourhood who had done both. The face of Davis was flushed when he heard this reply the tears gathered in his eyes, and with a bitter emphasis, though in low tones, as if he felt all the shame of his acknowledgment, he replied—

"God help me, but I did! I was one of those who took a protection. Here it is—here's the paper. Here's where I sold my country, and put myself down in black and white, to be beaten like a dog with hickories. But it's not too late; and look you, stranger, I believe you're true blue, but if you aint, why it's all the same thing—I care not—you may go tell quick as you please; but I will break the bargain."

"Ha!—speak!" and the form of the stranger was advanced and his eyes dilated, as he watched the earnest glow in every feature of his companion.

"By tearing up the paper: see,"—and, as he spoke, he tore into small bits the guaranty of British protection, which, in common with most of his neighbours, he had been persuaded to accept from the commandant for his security, and as a condition of that return, which he pledged, at the same time, to his duty and his allegiance

"Your life is in my hands," exclaimed his companion, deliberately. "Your life is in my hands."

"Take it!" cried the countryman, and he threw himself upon his guard, and while his right hand threw up the cudgel which he carried, the fingers of his left clutched fiercely and drew forth the hunting knife which was concealed in his bosom. His small person, slight but active, thrown back, every muscle in action and ready for contest; his broad-brimmed white hat dashed from his brow; his black, glossy hair dishevelled and flying in the wind, lips closely compressed, while his deep, dark eye shot forth fires of anger, fiercely enlivening the dusky sallow of his cheek—all gave to him a most imposing expression of animated life and courage in the eye of his companion.

"Take it—take the worthless life!" he cried, in low but emphatic accents. "It is worthless, but you will hev' to fight for it."

The other regarded him with a look of admiration sobered into calm.

"Your life is in my hands, but it is safe. God forbid, Master Davis," said he, with solemnity. "God forbid that I should assail it.

2*

I am your friend, your countryman, and I rejoice in what you have done. You have done well and nobly in destroying that evidence of your dishonour; for it is dishonour to barter one's country and its liberties for dastardly security—for one's miserable life. You have done well; but be not rash. Your movements must be in quiet. Nothing rash, nothing precipitate. Every step you now take must be one of caution, for your path is along the steeps of danger. But me with me—you shall know more. First secure those scraps; they may tell tales upon you; a quick hand and close eye may put them together, and then your neck would be fit game for the halter yon sergeant warned you of. But what now—what are the troops about?"

The countryman looked, at his companion's question, and beheld the troops forming in the market-place, while the note of the bugle at intervals, and an occasional sullen tap of the drum, gathered the crowd of the village around them.

" It's a proclamation, squire. That's the market-place, where they read it first. They give us one every two or three days, sometimes about one thing, sometimes another. If the cattle's killed by the whigs, though it may be their own, there's a proclamation; but we don't mind them much, for they only tell us to be quiet and orderly, and, heaven knows, we can't be more so. They will next go to the church, where they will again read it. That's nigher, and we can get round in time to hear what it is. Shall we go, squire?" The other expressed his willingness, and leaving the bridge, they proceeded in the direction of the crowd.

CHAPTER IV.

"— ——————Keep thy counsel well,
And fear not. We shall mate with them a true
And spoil them who would strike us. We are free,
And confidently strong—have arms and men—
Good fellows in the wood, that will not fly
When blows are to be borne."

By a short path the stranger and his companion moved from the bridge to the place of gathering. It was not long before they found themselves in the thick of the crowd, upon the green in front of the church, from the portals of which the heavy roll of the drum commanded due attention from the populace. The proclamation which the commander of the garrison at Dorchester now proceeded to read to the multitude, was of no small importance. Its contents were well calculated to astound and terrify the Carolinians who heard it. It was one of the many movements of the British commander, unfortunately for the cause of royalty in that region, which, more than anything besides, contributed to arouse and irritate that spirit of resistance on the part of the invaded people, which it should have been the studious policy of the invaders to mollify and suppress. The document in question had been just issued by Sir Henry Clinton, declaring all paroles or protections granted hitherto to be null and void, and requiring the holders of them, within twenty days, to resume the character of British subjects—taking up arms in the promotion of his majesty's cause against their brethren, under pain of being treated as rebels to his government.

The motive of Sir Henry for a movement so exceedingly injudicious, may be only conjectured from the concurrent circumstances of the time. The continental army, under De Kalb, was on its way to the South—Gates had been ordered to command it—and this intelligence, though not generally known to the people of Carolina,

ould not long be withheld from their possession. It was necessary
to keep them from any co-operation with their approaching friends
and no more effectual mode, simply considered by itself, could have
been suggested to the mind of the Briton than their employment
under his own banners. This apart, the invasion of the adjoining
states of Virginia and North Carolina had been long since determined upon, and was now to be attempted. Troops were wanted
for this purpose, and no policy seemed better than to expend one
set of rebels upon another. It was also necessary to secure the conquered province; and the terrors of the hangman were providently
held out, in order to impel the conquered to the minor risks of
the bayonet and shot.

The error was a fatal one. From that hour the declension of
British power was precipitately hurried in Carolina, the people losing confidence in those who had already so grossly deceived them
for the condition of the protection or parole called for no military
service from the citizen who took it. He was simply to be neutral
in the contest; and, however unworthy may have been the spirit
consenting even to this condition, it cannot be denied that a foul
deception had been practised upon them. The consequences were
inevitable; and the determined hostility of the foe was coupled, on
the part of the Carolinians, with a wholesale scorn of the want of
probity manifested by the enemy they were now not so unwilling to
encounter.

From the church-porch the proclamation was again read to the
assembled multitude. The crowd was variously composed, and
various indeed was the effect which it produced among them. The
stranger and his companion, at a little distance, listened closely to
the words of the instrument; and a smile of joy, not unmarked by
Davis, played over the features of the former as he heard it read.
The latter looked his indignation: he could not understand why
such a paper should give pleasure to his comrade, and could not
forbear, in a whisper, demanding the occasion of his satisfaction.

" It pleases you, stranger? I see you smile!"

" It does please me—much, very much," responded the other
quickly, and with emphasis, but in a whisper also.

" What!" with more earnestness, said the countryman—" wha

does it please you to listen to such villainy as this ? I do not understand you."

" Not so loud, comrade ; you have a neck, and these fellows a rope ; besides, there's one to the left of us whose looks I like not."

The other turned in the direction signified, and saw the propriety of his companion's caution, as he beheld within a few feet the harsh features of the notorious Captain Huck, a furious and bloody tory-leader, well-known, and held in odious estimation, throughout the neighborhood. The stranger went on, still whispering :—

" Look pleased, friend Davis, if you can ; this is no time to show any but false colors to the enemy. I am pleased, really, as you think, and have my reason for being so, which you shall know in good time. Take breath and listen."

The paper was finished, and the detachment moved on its way to the " Royal George Tavern," the crowd generally following ; and there it was again read. Our two friends kept together, and proceeded with the multitude. The stranger was eminently watchful and observant ; he noted well the sentiment of indignation which all faces manifested ; there could be no doubt of that expression. The sober farmer, the thoughtless and gay-hearted planter of the neighborhood, the drudge, the mechanic, the petty chapman—all had in their looks that severe soberness which showed a thought and spirit, active, and more to be respected, as they were kept so well restrained.

" God save the king !" cried the officer, as he concluded the instrument, from the steps of the tavern.

"Ay, God save the king, and God bless him, too !" echoed old Humphries, at the entrance. A few only of the crowd gave back the cry, and even with them the prayer was coldly uttered ; and there was nothing like that spirit which, when the heart goes with the decree of the ruler, makes the welkin ring with its unregulated rejoicings.

" You are silent ; you do not cry with the rest," said one at the elbow of the stranger. He turned to behold the features of the tory captain, of whom we have already spoken, who now, with a scrutinizing glance, placed himself close beside the person he had addressed. The mean cunning—the low, searching expression of

his look—were eminently disgusting to the youth, who replied,
while resuming his old position :—

"What? God save the king? Did I not say it? It's very
natural; for I am so used to it. I'm quite willing that God should
save his majesty—God knows he needs it."

This was said with a very devout countenance, and the expression was so composed and quiet, that the tory could say nothing,
though still not satisfied, seemingly, with much that was in the language. It sounded very like a sneer, and yet, strictly speaking, it
was perfectly unexceptionable. Baffled in this quarter, the loyalist,
who was particularly desirous of establishing his own claims to
British favour, now turned with a similar inquiry to Davis; but the
countryman was ready, and a nudge in the side from his companion,
had anything been wanting, moved him to a similar answer. Huck
was not exactly prepared to meet with so much willingness on the
part of two persons whose movements he had suspected, and had
been watching; but, concluding them now to be well affected, he
did not scruple to propose to them to become members of the troop
of horse he was engaged in raising. To the stranger he first
addressed himself, complimenting him upon his fine limbs and
figure, and insisting upon the excellent appearance he would make,
well mounted and in British uniform. A smile of sovereign contempt overspread the youth's features as he listened to the tory
patiently to the end. Calmly, then, he begged permission to decline
the proposed honour.

"Why, you are loyal, sir?" he asked, seeming to doubt.

"Who denies it?" fiercely replied the stranger.

"Oh, nobody; I mean not to offend: but, as a loyal subject, you
can scarce withhold yourself from service."

"I do not contemplate to do so, sir."

"And why not join my troop? Come, now, you shall have a
lieutenancy; for, blast me, but I like your looks, and would be
devilish glad to have you. You can't refuse."

"But I do," said the other, coolly—almost contemptuously.

"And wherefore?" Huck inquired, with a show of pique in his
countenance and manner—"wherefore? What better service? and
to a soldier of fortune, let me ask you, what better chances may

now of making every thing out of these d—d rebels, who have gone into the swamps, leaving large estates for confiscation ? What better business ? "

" None< I fully agree with you."

" And you will join my troop ? "

" No ! "

The man looked astonished. The coolness and composure with which the denial was made surprised him not less than the denial itself. With a look of doubt and wonderment, he went on—

" Well, you know best ; but, of course, as a good citizen, you will soon be in arms ; twenty days, you know, are all that's allowed you."

" I do not need so many ; as a good citizen, I shall be in arms in less time."

" In whose troop ?—where ? "

" Ah, now we come to the point," was the sudden reply ; " and you will now see why I have been able to withstand the tempting offers you have made. I am thinking to form a troop of my own, and should I do so, I certainly should not wish so much success to yours as to fall into your ranks."

" Indeed ! Well, I'm glad, anyhow, that his majesty is likely to be so well served with officers. Have you yet applied for a commission to the commandant ? "

" No ; nor shall I, till my recruits are strong enough to make my appearance respectable."

" That's right ! I know that by experience. They never like you half so well as when you bring your men with you ; they don't want officers so much as men ; and some of the commands, if they can choose you out of your recruits, will not stop to do so ; and then you may whistle for your commission. I suppose your friend, here, is already secured for your squad ? "

The tory referred to Davis, who did not leave his companion to reply ; but, without scruple, avowed himself as having already been partially secured for the opposition troop.

" Well, good luck to you. But I say comrade, you have commanded before—of course you are prepared to lead ? "

" I have the heart for it," was the reply ; and as the stranger spoke, he extended his arms towards the tory captain, while elevating his figure to its fullest height; "and you can say yourself for the limbs. As for the head, it must be seen if mine's good for anything."

"I doubt it not; and service comes easy after a brush or two. But wouldn't you like to know the major?"

"Who?—the officer in command of the garrison here?"

"The same."

"In time, I'll trouble you, perhaps, to help me to that knowledge. Not yet; not till I get my recruits."

"You are right in that; and, talking of the recruits, I must see after mine; and, so, a good-evening to you, and success. We shall meet again."

The tory moved among the separate groups as he spoke, and the stranger turned to Davis while he muttered—

"Ay, we shall meet again, Master Huck, or it will be no fault of mine. If we do not, Old Nick takes marvellous care of his own. But, ha! comrade, keep you here awhile; there is one that I would speak with."

At a little distance apart, at one wing of the tavern, stood a man, attired in the blue homespun garments of the country, among the humbler classes; and with nothing particular to distinguish him, if we except a face somewhat more round and rosy than belongs usually to the people dwelling in Dorchester and its neighbourhood. He was like them in one respect—having a sidelong, indirect movement, coupled with a sluggish, lounging, indifferent gait, which is a general feature of this people, unless when roused by insult or provocation. In his hand he carried a whip of common leather, which he smacked occasionally, either for the sharp, shot-like sounds which it sent forth, or when he desired to send to a greater distance that most grumbling of all aristocrats, the hog, as it approached him. The quick eye of the stranger had singled out this personage; and, leaving Davis where he stood, and moving quickly through the straggling groups that still clustered in front of the tavern, he at once approached him confidently as an old acquaintance. The other seemed not to observe his coming, until our first acquaintance speaking as he advanced, caught his notice. This had no sooner been done, than the other was in motion. Throwing aside his sluggishness of look, he recognized by a glance the stranger, and his head was bent forward to listen, as he saw that he was about to speak. The words of our old acquaintance were few, but significant—

"I am here before you—say nothing—lead on, and I will follow."

With a nod, the person addressed looked but once at the speaker; then, without a word, moving from his easy position against the tavern, and throwing aside all show of sluggishness, he led the way for the stranger. Taking an oblique path, which carried them in a short time into the neighboring woods, they soon left the village behind them.

Davis had been reluctant to separate from the companion to whom he had so readily yielded his confidence. He had his doubts —as who could be without them in that season of general distrust? But when he remembered the warm, manly frankness of the stranger —his free, bold, generous, and gentle contenance—he did not suffer himself to doubt, for a moment more, that his secret would be safe in his possession. This, indeed, was the least of his difficulties. The fair coquette of the inn had attracted him strongly, and with a heavy heart, he turned into the " Royal George," and, throwing his form at length upon a bench, he solaced or vexed, himself with an occasional glance at Bella Humphries, whose duties carried her to and fro between the bar and the sitting-room; and with thoughts of that vengeance upon his enemy which his new relation with the stranger seemed to promise him.

Meanwhile, following the steps of the individual he had so singled out, the stranger kept on his way until the village had been fairly passed; then plunging down a little by-path, into which the former had gone, he soon overtook him, and they moved on closely together in their common progress. The guide was a stout able-bodied person, of thirty years, or perhaps more—a rough-looking man, one seemingly born and bred entirely in the humble life of the country. He was powerful in physical development, rather stout than high, with a short thick neck—a head round and large, with eyes small settled, and piercing—and features even solemn in their general expression of severity. He carried no visible weapons, but he seemed the man to use them; for no one who looked in his face could doubt that he was full of settled purpose, firm in his resolve, and reckless, having once determined, in the prosecution of the most desperate enterprise.

The route they were pursuing grew more and more tangled as they went, gradually sinking in level, until the footing became slightly insecure, and at length terminated in the soft oozy swamp surface common to the margin of most rivers in the low country of the south. They were now close on the banks of the Ashley, which wound its way, perceptible to the two in occasional glimpses, through the close-set foliage by which they were surrounded. A few more strides through the copse and over the miry surface, brought them again to a dry elevation, isolated by small sluices of water, and more closely wrapped in brush and covering. Here their progress was self-arrested, for they were now perfectly secure from interruption. In all this time, no word had been exchanged between the parties; but the necessity for farther caution being now over, they came to a pause, and the silence was broken as follows by our last made acquaintance:

"We are safe here, Major Singleton, and can now speak freely. The sharpest scout in the British garrison could not well come upon us without warning, and if he did, would do so by accident."

" I'm glad of it, for I'm heartily tired, and not a little impatient to talk with you. But let us be at ease."

They threw themselves upon the ground—our elder acquaintance, whom we now know as Major Singleton, with an air of superiority which seemed familiar, choosing the most favorable spot, while the other remained standing until his companion had adjusted himself; and then took his seat respectfully on the ridgy roots of the pine-tree spreading over them.

"And now, Humphries," said Singleton, "what of my sister—is she safe, and how did she bear the journey?"

"Safe, major, and well as could be expected; though very feeble. We had some trouble crossing the Santee, but it did not keep us long, and we got on tolerably well after. The whole party are now safe at ' The Oaks.'"

" Well, you must guide me there to-night, if possible; I know nothing of the place, and but little of the country. Years have passed since I last went over it."

" What! have you never been at 'The Oaks,' major? I was told you had."

" Yes, when a boy; but I have no distinct memory on the subject, except of the noble trees, the thick white moss and the dreamy quiet of all things around. The place, I know, is beautiful."

" You may well say so, major; a finer don't happen often in the low country, and the look at it from the river is well worth a journey."

" Ah! I have never seen it from that quarter. But you said my uncle was well, and "—here the voice faltered a little—" and my cousin Katharine—they are all well? "

"All well, sir. The old squire is rather down in the mouth, you see, for he's taken a protection, and he can't help seeing the troubles of the county. It's this that makes his trouble; and though he used of old time to be a dashing, hearty, lively, talkative gentleman, always pleasant and good-humoured, yet now he says nothing; and if he happens to smile at all, he catches himself up a minute after, and looks mighty sorry for it. Ah, major, these cursed protections— they've made many a good heart sore in this neighbourhood, and the worst is to come yet, or I'm mistaken."

"A sore subject, Humphries, and not very necessary to speak on. But what news—what stirring, and how get on our recruits? "

" Slowly enough, major; but that is to be expected while the country is overrun with the red-coats. The folk are afraid to move, and our poor swamp-boys can't put their noses out yet—not until the enemy turns his back on them for a while, and gives them chance for a little skirmish, without the risk of the rope. But things would change, I'm certain, if the great general you spoke of, with the continentals, would only come south. Our people only want an opportunity."

" And they shall have it. But what intelligence here from the city ? "

" None, sir, or little. You heard the proclamation? "

" Yes, with joy—with positive delight. The movement is a

grand one for our cause: it must bring out the ground-rats—those
who skulked for safety into contracts, measuring honour by acres,
and counting their duty to their country by the value of their
crops."

"True—I see that, major, but that's the thing I dread. Why
should you desire to bring them out?"

"Why, because, though with us in spirit and sentiment, they yet
thought to avoid danger, while they believed themselves unable to
serve us by their risk. Now, forced into the field—compelled to
fight—is it not clear that the argument is all in favour of our side?
Will they not rather fight in conformity with their feelings and
opinions than against them? particularly when the latter course must
place them in arms against their friends and neighbours—not to speak
of their countrymen—in many instances to their relatives, and the
members of their own families. By forcing into the field those who
were quiet before, Sir Henry Clinton has forced thousands into our
ranks, who will be as slow to lay down their weapons as they were to
take them up."

"I hope so, major; but I fear that many will rather strike for what
seems the strongest, and not ask many questions as to which is the
justest side."

"No—this I fear not. The class of people on whom I rely are
too proud to suffer this imposition, and too spirited not to resist the
indignity which it puts upon them. They must be roused by the
trick which has been practiced, and will shake off their sleep. Let us
hope for it, at least."

"I am willing, sir, but fear it. They have quite too much at
stake: they have too much plate, too many negroes, and live too comfortably to be willing to stand a chance of losing all by taking up
arms against the British, who are squat close alongside of them."

"So should I fear with you, Humphries, and for like reasons, if
the protections protected them. I doubt not that they would be willing to keep quiet, and take no part in this struggle, if the conquerors
were wise enough to let them alone; but they kick and cuff them on
all occasions, and patriots are frequently made by kicking. I care
not for the process, so it gives us the commodity. Let them kick on,
and may they get extra legs for the purpose!"

" Amen," said Humphries, gravely. " If it makes them stand up to the rack, as you think it will. But—" changing somewhat abruptly, he said to Singleton—

" You were with Jack Davis, of Goose Creek, major, when you first came up—I thought you were unknown in these parts ? "

" You thought rightly ; I am still unknown, but I learned to know something of him you speak of, and circumstances threw us together." Here Singleton related the occurrences at the tavern, as already known to us. Humphries, who was the son of the landlord, gave close attention, and with something more than ordinary interest. He was not at any time a man to show his feelings openly, but there was an increased pressure of his lips together as that portion fell upon his ear which described the enterference of his sister, the fair coquette Bella, for the protection of her cast-off lover. His breathing was far less free at this point of the narrative ; and when Singleton concluded, the listener muttered, partly in solilquy and partly in reply—

" A poor fool of a girl, that sister of mine, major ; loves the fine colors of the jay in spite of his cursed squalling, and has played upon that good fellow, Davis—Prickly Ash, as we sometimes call him in the village—till he is half out of his wits. Her head, too, is half turned with that red coat ; but I'll cure her of that, and cure him too, or there's no virtue in twisted bore. But, major, did you do anything with Davis ? "

The answer was affirmative, and Humphries continued—

" That's a gain, sir , for Davis is true, if he says it, and comes of good breed he'll fight like a bull-dog, and his teeth shall meet in the flesh. Besides, he's a great shot with a rifle, like most of the boys from Goose Creek. His old mother kept him back, or he'd a-joined us long ago, for I've seen how his thoughts run. But it's not too late, and if the word's once out of his mouth, he's to be depended on—he's safe."

" A few more will do. You have several others, have you not, gathering in a safe place ! " said Singleton.

" In the swamp—thirteen, true as steel, and ready for fight. They're only some some six miles off, and can be brought up in two hours, at notice. See, this river comes from the heart of the Cypress

Swamp, where they shelter ; and if there be no tory among us to show them the track, I defy all Proctor's garrison to find us out."

" We must be among them to-morrow. But the evening wears and the breeze freshens up from the river : it is sweet and fresh from the sea—and how different, too, from that of the forests ! But come—I must go back, and have my horse in readiness for this ride to ' The Oaks,' where you must attend me,"

" Your horse ! Where is he ?" asked the other quickly.

" In your father's stable."

" He must not be suffered to stay there ; if he is, you will not have him long. We must hide him out, or that black-hearted tory, Huck, will be on his quarters before three days ; he's beating about the country now for horses as well as men."

" See to it then for I must run no such risk. Let us return at once," said Singleton.

" Yes ; but we take different roads : we must not know each other. Can you find the way back alone, major ? "

" Yes—I doubt not."

" To the left now—round that water ; keep straight up from the river for a hundred yards, and you fall into the track. Your horse shall be ready in an hour, and I will meet you at supper."

They parted—Singleton on his way as directed, and Humphries burying himself still deeper in the copse.

CHAPTER V.

"It needs but to be bold—be bold—be bold—
Everywhere bold.—'Tis every virtue told;
Courage and truth, humanity and skill,
The noblest cunning that the mind can will,
As the best charity we do but kill,
Not succour, when we shudder at the ill:
The loathing and the sorrow that not strives
Were sorry proof of manhood."

It was not long before Singleton reached the tavern, which he now found crowded. The villagers of all conditions and politics had there assembled, either to mutter over their doubts or discontents, or to gather counsel for their course in future, from the many, wiser than themselves, in their own predicament. There, also, came the true loyalist, certain to find defference and favour from those around him, not so happy or so secure as himself in the confidence of the existing powers. The group was motley enough, and the moods at work among them not less so. Some had already determined upon submission,—some of the weak—the time-serving—such as every old community will be found to furnish, where indolent habits, which have become inveterate, forbid all sort of independence. Some fluctuated, and knew not what to do, or even what to think. But there were others, Singleton imagined, as he looked into their grave, sullen features, full of thought and pregnant with determination, who felt nothing so strongly as the sense of injustice, and the rebel-daring which calls for defiance at every hazard.

"Vengeance! my men!" he muttered to himself, as passing full into the apartment, he became at once visible to the group. The old landlord himself was the first person who confronted him, speaking still after that familiar fashion which had already had its rebuke from the same quarter.

"Ah, captain! (the brow of Slngleton darkened)—squire, I mean. I ask pardon, squire; but here, where every man is a captain, or a

51

colonel, or something, it comes natural to captain or colonel all, and is not often amiss.   No offense, squire—it's use only, and I mean no harm."

"Enough, enough! good Master landlord!   Least said, soonest mended.   Shall we soon have supper?"

The ready publican turned to the inner door of the apartment and put the same question to his daughter, the fair Bella; then, without waiting for her reply, informed the inquirer that many minutes would not elapse before it would be on table.

"Six o'clock's the time of day for supper, squire—six for supper—one for dinner—eight for breakfast—puntual to the stroke, and no waiting.   Heh! what's that you say, Master Dickenson?—what's that about Frampton?" said old Humphries, turning to one of the villagers who had just entered the apartment.   The person so addressed came forward; a thin-jawed, sallow countryman, whose eyes were big with the intelligence he brought, and who seemed anxious that a well-dressed and goodly-looking stranger, like Singleton, should have the benefit of his burden.

"Why, gentlemen, the matter with Frampton's strange enough. You all know he's been out several days, close in the swamp.   He had a fight, stranger, you see, with one of Huck's dragoons; and he licked the dragoon, for all the world, as if he'd a licked him out of his skin.   Now the dragoon's a strong fellow enough; but Frampton's a horse, and if ever he mounts you the game is up, for there's no stopping him when he gets his hand in.   So, as I tell you, the dragoon stood a mighty slim chance.   He first brought him down with a back-handed wipe, that came over his cheek for all the world like the slap of a water-wheel—"

"Yes, yes, we all heard that; but what was it all about, Dickenson?—we don't know that, yet," cried one of the group which had now formed around the speaker.

"Why, that's soon told.   The dragoon went to Frampton's house when he was in the swamp, and made free with what he wanted. Big Barney, his eldest son, went off in the meanwhile to his daddy, and off he came full tilt, with Lance, his youngest lad along with him.   You know Lance, or Lancelot, a smart chap of sixteen; you've seed him often enough."

"Yes, yes, we know him.

"Well, as I tell you, the old man and his two boys came full
tilt to the house, and 'twas a God's mercy they came in time, for
the doings of the dragoon was too rediculous for any decent body
to put up with, and the old colt couldn't stand it no how; so, as I
tell you, he put it to him in short order. He first gave him a back-
handed wipe, which flattened him, I tell you; and when the
sodger tried to get up, he put it to him again so that it was easier
for him to lie down than to stand up; and lie down he did, without a word, till the other dragoons tuk him up. They came a few
minutes after, and the old man and the youngest boy, Lance, had
a narrow chance and a smart run for it. They heard the troops
coming down the lane, and they took to the bush. The sodgers
tried hard to catch them, but it aint easy to hook a Goose-Creeker
when he's on trail for the swamp, and splashing after the hogs
along a tussock. So they got safe into the Cypress, and the dragoons had nothing better to do than go back to the house. Well,
they made Frampton's old woman stand all sorts of treatment, and
that too bad to find names for. They beat her too, and she as
heavy as she could go. Well, then, she died night afore last, as
might be expected; and now the wonder is, what's become of her
body. They laid her out; and the old granny that watched her
only went into the kitchen for a little while, and when she came
back the body was gone. She looked out of the window, and sure
enough she sees a man going over the rail with a bundle all in
white on his shoulder. And the man looked, so she swears, for all
the world like old Frampton himself. Nobody knows anything
more about it; and what I heard, is jist now what I tell you."

The man had narrated truly what he had heard; and what, in
reality, with little exaggeration, was the truth. The company had
listened to one of those stories of brutality, which—in the fierce
civil warfare of the South, when neighbours were arrayed against
one another, and when, on one side, negroes and Indians formed
allies, contributing, by their lighter sense of humanity, additional
forms of terror to the sanguinary warfare pursued at that period—
were of almost daily occurrence. Huck, the infamous tory captain,
of whom we have already obtained a slight glimpse in the progress
of our narrative, was himself a character well fitted, by his habitual

3

cunning and gross want of all the softening influences of humanity, to give countenance, and even example, to crimes of this nature. His dragoons, though few as yet in number, and employed only on marauding excursions calling for small parties, had already become notorious for their outrages of this description. Indeed, they found impunity in this circumstance. In regular warfare, under the controlling presence of crowds, the responsibility of his men, apart from what they owed or yielded to himself, would have held them certainly in some greater restraints; although, to their shame be it said, the British generals in the South, when mortified by defeat and vexed by unexpected resistance, were themselves not always more tenacious of propriety than the tory Huck. The sanguinary orders of Cornwallis, commanding the cold-blooded execution of hundreds, are on record, in melancholy attestation of the atrocities committed by the one, and the persecutions borne by the other party, during this memorable conflict.

It could easily be seen what was the general feeling during this recital; and yet that feeling was unspoken. Some few shook their heads very gravely, and a few, more daring yet, ventured to say, that " it was very bad, very bad indeed—very shocking !"

" What's very bad, my friends? what is it you speak of as so shocking?" was the demand of one just entering. The crowd started back, and Huck himself stood among them. He repeated his inquiry, and with a manner that left it doubtful whether he really desired to know what had been the subject of their remarks, or whether, having heard, he wished to compel some of them to the honest utterance of their sentiments upon it. Singleton, who had listened with a duly-excited spirit to the narrative of the countryman, now advanced deliberately towards the new-comer, whom he addressed as in answer to his question—

" Why, sir, it is bad, very bad indeed, the treatment received, as I learn, by one of his majesty's dragoons, at the hands of some impudent rebel a few nights ago. You know, sir, to what I allude. You have heard, doubtless."

The bold, confident manner of the speaker was sufficiently imposing to satisfy all around of his loyalty. Huck seemed completely surprised, and replied freely and with confidence—

" Ay, you mean the affair of that scoundrel, Frampton. Yes, I know all about it; but we're on his trail, and shall soon make him sweat for his audacity, the blasted rebel."

" Do you know that his wife is dead ?" asked one of the country-men, in a tone subdued to one of simple and inexpressive inquiry.

" No—and don't care very greatly. It's a bad breed, and the misfortune is, there's quite too many of them. But we'll thin them soon, and easily, by G—d ! and the land shall be rid of the reptiles."

" Yes, captain, we think alike," said Singleton, familiarly—" we think alike on that subject. Something must be done, and in time, or there will be no comfortable moving for a loyalist, whether in swamp or highway. These rascal rebels have it in their power to do mischief, if not taken care of in time. It is certainly our policy to prevent our men from being ill-treated by them, and to do this, they must be taken in hand early. Rebellion grows like joint-grass when it once takes root, and runs faster than you can follow. It should be seen to."

" That is my thought already, and accordingly I have a good dog on trail of this lark, Frampton, and hope soon to have him in. He cannot escape Travis, my lieutenant, who is now after him, and who knows the swamp as well as himself. They're both from Goose Creek, and so let dog eat dog."

" You have sent Travis after him, then, captain ?" inquired a slow and deliberate voice at Huck's elbow. Singleton turned at the same moment with the person addressed, and recognised in the speaker his own lieutenant, the younger Humphries, who had go back to the tavern almost as soon as himself. Humphries, of whose Americanism we can have no sort of question, had yet managed adroitly to conceal it; and what with his own cunning and his father's established loyalty, he was enabled, not only to pass without suspicion, but actually to impress the tories with a favourable opinion of his good feeling for the British cause. This was one of those artifices which the necessities of the times imposed upon most men, and for which they gave a sufficient moral sanction.

" Ah, Bill, my boy," said Huck, turning as to an old acquaint-ance, " is that you ! Why, where have you been ?—haven't seen

you for an age, and didn't well know what had become of you—
thought you might have gone into the swamps too with the skulk
ing rebels."

"So I have," replied the other calmly—"not with the rebels,
though. I see none of them to go with—but I have been skirting
the cypress for some time, gathering what pigs the alligators found
no use for. Pigs and poultry are the rebels I look after. You may
judge of my success by their bawling."

In confirmation of what Humphries had said, at that moment the
collection of tied pigs with which his cart had been piled and the
tethered chickens undergoing transfer to a more fixed dwelling, and
tumbled from the mass where they had quietly but confusedly lain
for an hour or two before—sent up a most piteous pleading,—which,
for the time, effectually silenced the speakers within. A moment's
pause obtained, Humphries reverted, though indirectly, to the question which he had put to the tory captain touching the pursuit of
Frampton by Travis; and, without exciting his suspicion by a positive inquiry, strove to obtain information.

"Travis will find Frampton if he chooses,—he knows the swamp
quite as well—and a lean dog for a long chase, you know,—that is,
if you have given him men enough."

"I gave him all he wanted: ten, he said, would answer: he could
have had more. He'll catch him, or I'm mistaken."

"Yes, if he strikes a good route. The old paths are washed now
by the freshet, and he may find it hard to keep track. Now, the
best path for him to take, captain, would have been up over Terrapin Bridge by Turkey Town. That will bring him right into the
heart of the swamp, where it's most likely Frampton hides."

"Terrapin Bridge—Turkey Town," said the other, seeming to
muse. "No, he said nothing of these places: he spoke of—"

"Droze's old field," exclaimed Humphries, somewhat eagerly.

"Yes, that's the name; he goes that route; and I remember he
spoke of another, where he said the waters were too high."

"Ay—and does he think to find Frampton on the skirts?—and
then, what a round-about way by Droze's! eh! neighbours?—he
can't be there before midnight. But of course he went there in
time," said Humphries, insinuating the question.

"Only two hours gone," replied the other, giving the desired intelligence; "but he won't do more than stretch to the swamp to-night. He wants to be ready to make a dash with the daylight upon them, when he hopes to find the fellow not yet out of his nest."

Humphries looked approvingly as he heard the plan. He ex changed glances of intelligence at intervals with Singleton, who listened attentively to this dialogue, which had wormed out the secret of one of those little adventures of Huck's party, in which his command was most generally employed. The look of Singleton spoke clearly to Humphries his desire to have a hand in the performance which was now naturally suggested to both. The lieutenant, eager like his superior, was yet prudent enough to keep his countenance. They both looked unconcerned enough, and now remained silent.

Huck, in the meantime, who had long been desirous of securing Humphries for his troop, now pressed the latter more earnestly than ever upon that subject. Taking him aside, he detailed to him in an undertone the thousand advantages of profit and position which must result to him from coming out in arms for his majesty, and in his, Captain Huck's, particular command of cavalry. It was amusing to observe how much stronger became his anxiety whenever his eye rested upon the form of Singleton, whom he now regarded in the light of a rival leader. The eye of young Humphries, also, glanced frequently in the same direction, as, from a previous knowledge of the character of Singleton, he felt how impatient he would be until he could make the attack, which he saw he contemplated, upon the marauding party which had been sent out under Travis. It was in such little adventures that the partisan warfare of Carolina had its origin.

Humphries, closely pressed by Huck, had yet ingenuity enough to evade his application without offending his pride or alarming his suspicions. He made sundry excuses, simply as to time, leaving the tory to infer that in the end the recruit would certainly be his.

"You will soon have to come out, Bill, my boy; and dang it, out there's no better chance than you have in my troop. You shall be my right-hand man, for I know you, old fellow—and blast

me, but I'd sooner trust you than any chap of the corps. I may
as well put you down."

"No, not yet: I'll be ready to answer you soon, and I can easily
make my preparations. You have arms a-plenty?"

"Soon shall have. Three wagons are on their way from Charleston with sabres and pistols especially for us."

"I shall, no doubt, want some of them, and you shall then hear
from me. There is time enough in all next week."

"Yes; but be quick about it, or there will be no picking; and
then you have but twenty days, remember. The proclamation
gives but twenty days, and then Cornwallis has sworn to treat as
rebels, with the utmost severity of the law, all those who are not
in arms for his majesty—just the same as if they had fought
against him. See, I have it here."

He took from his pocket the proclamation, and with it a private
order, which was issued by the commander-in-chief to all the subordinate commands, giving directions for the utmost severity, and
prescribing the mode of punishment for the refractory, nearly in the
language, and to the full effect, of Huck's representations. Humphries looked grave enough at these crowding evidences, but
resisted, by well urged evasions, the exhortations of the tempter.
The tory captain was compelled to rest satisfied for the present,
assured that he had held forth especial inducements to the countryman which must give his troop a preference over any claims that
might be set up by the rival recruiting officer, as he considered
Singleton. With a hearty shake of the hand, and a few parting
words in whisper to his companion, he left the hotel to make his
way—a subtle sycophant with his superiors—to the presence of
Major Proctor of the Dorchester garrison, from whom he had
received his commission.

Singleton, while this episode of Humphries and the tory had
been going on, employed himself in occasional conversation with
the landlord and sundry of the villagers in another end of the
apartment. In this conversation, though studiously selecting topics
of a nature not to startle or offend the fears or the prejudices of
any, he contrived, with no little ingenuity, to bring about, every
now and then, occasional expressions of their feelings and opinions

He saw, from these few and brief evidences, that their feelings were not with their rulers—that they subscribed simply to a hard necessity, and would readily seek the means of relief, did they know where to find it. He himself took care, while he uttered nothing which could be construed into an offence against loyalty, to frame what he did say in such a guise that it must have touched and ministered largely to the existing provocations. He could see this in the burning indignation strong in every countenance, as he dwelt upon the imperative necessity they were now under of taking up arms in obedience to the proclamation. His urging of this topic was, like that of Huck, ostensibly the obtaining of recruits for his contemplated troop. His policy was one frequently acted upon in that strange warfare, in which the tories, when defeated, found few conscientious scruples to restrain them from falling into the ranks and becoming good soldiers along with their conquerors. Such devices as that which he now aimed to practise were freely resorted to; and the case was not uncommon of a troop thus formed under the eye of the enemy, and, in his belief, to do the battles of the monarch, moving off, *en masse*, the first opportunity, and joining with their fellow-countrymen, as well in flight as in victory. Such, however, was scarcely now the object of the stranger: he simply desired that his loyalty might pass unquestioned; and he put on a habit, therefore, as a disguise, which but too many natives wore with far less scruple, and perhaps with some show of grace. It may be said, as highly gratifying to Singleton, that in the character thus assumed he made no converts.

But the bell for supper was now ringing, and, taking his way with the rest, he passed into the inner apartment. Bella Humphries presided, her brother taking a seat at the other end of the table, and ministering to the guests in that quarter. Singleton was assigned a seat, possibly by way of distinction, close to the maiden, who smiled graciously at his approach. Still she looked not so well satisfied. Neither of her squires was present, and her eye wandered from side to side among unattractive countrymen at the table, resting at last, as with a dernier hope, upon the manly and handsome face and person of our adventurer. The coquette must be busy. It is her necessity. She has smiles to circulate

and, like the counterfeiter with false coin, she is ever on the look
out for the *flat*. While she watched Singleton with ready smiles,
he had an opportunity of scanning her features more narrowly.
She was very girlish, certainly very youthful in appearance, and
her face was decidedly handsome. He saw, at a glance, that she
was incapable of any of that settled and solemn feeling which
belongs to love, and which can only exist along with a strongly
marked character and truly elevated sentiments. Her desire was
that of display, and conquest made the chief agent to this end. It
mattered not how doubtful was the character of her captives, so
that they were numerous; and Singleton felt assured that his
simple Goose Creek convert, Davis, but for the lack of red coat and
command, stood quite as good a chance in the maiden's heart as
the more formidable sergeant. How long he would have scanned
the features which seemed not unwilling to attract his eye, we may
not say; but his gaze was at length disturbed by the entrance of
Davis, who, taking his seat at the opposite corner of the table, now
appeared in a better and a more conciliatory humour. He addressed
some country compliment to Bella, which she was not displeased to
listen to, as she was perfectly satisfied to have a swain, no matter
who, in the absence of the greater favourite. She answered some
few remarks of Singleton and Davis with a pretty, childish simplicity, which showed that, after all, the misfortune of the girl was
only a deficiency in the more interesting points of character, and
not the presence of any improper or wanton state of feeling.

Meantime the supper proceeded. Towards its conclusion,
Humphries, the brother, giving Davis a look and a sign, which the
latter seemed to comprehend, left the apartment. Davis followed
him. They were gone about a quarter of an hour, which time
was spent by Singleton in a lively chat with the girl, when, through
the window, he saw the face of a man, and the motion of a hand,
which beckoned him. In a moment after the person was gone;
and, suffering some few seconds to elapse, Singleton also rose and
obeyed the signal. He took his way into the yard, and under the
shadow of a tree, at a little distance from the house, distinguished
the person of the younger Humphries. Singleton at once approached him—the other motioned silence, seeing him about to

speak, and led him to the stable, where all was perfectly in shadow.

"We are safe now," said he. Singleton immediately addressed him, and with some show of impatience, on a subject which had much employed his thoughts during the past hour.

"Well, Humphries, say, can we not strike at that fellow Tracy? Is it possible to do anything with his detachment?"

"Travis, not Tracy, major," replied the other. "It is possible, sir; and there is a strong chance of our success if we manage well, and if you can postpone going to ' The Oaks' to-night."

"True," said the other; "I should like very much to go there; but this movement of Tracy—or Travis, you say—gives us a good beginning, which we ought on no account to miss. Besides, we should put your men on their guard. Are they not in some danger?"

"Not if they watch well; but there's no answering for new hands. They must have practice before they can learn, and down here, they've had but little yet. They're not like your Santee boys I've heard you tell of."

"Willing soon will!" said the other. "But let us move. I'll say no more of ' The Oaks' to-night at least. We can move there to-morrow. Of course you lead the route, for I know nothing about it."

"Trust to me; and, major, go back to the house quietly. Wait till you hear my whistle three times—thus. It's an old signal, which you'll have to learn here, as our little squad all knows it, and knows nothing else by way of music. Meantime I'll get things in readiness, and set Davis to carry out the horses to the bush."

"Is he resolved to go with us?" was Singleton's question.

"True as steel. A little weak o' heart, sir, about that foolish girl—but that's all the better, for it makes him hate the British the more. Here he comes. You had better go now, major, and let us be as little seen together as may be. You'll mind the whistle —thus, three times;" and in a low tone Humphries gave him the signal. Singleton went towards the house, in the shadow of which he was soon lost from sight, while Humphries and Davis proceeded to the farther arrangement of the enterprise.

It was not long before this was completed, and with a rush of pleasure to his heart, Major Singleton heard the thrice-uttered note —the signal agreed upon—directly beneath his chamber window. He rose at the sound, and silently descending the stairs, passed through the hall, where, in something like uncomfortable solitude, the fair Bella sat alone. She looked up as she heard his footsteps, and the gracious smile which her lips put on, was an invitation to make himself happy in a seat beside her. But he resisted the blandishment, and lifting his hat as he passed, with a smile in return, he soon disappeared from her presence, and joined the two who awaited him. All was ready for departure, but Davis craved a few minutes' indulgence to return to the house.

" Why, what should carry you back, Davis ?" asked Humphries, peevishly.

" Nothing, Bill; but I must—I will go," said the other.

" I see, I see: you will be as foolish as ever," exclaimed the former, as the lover moved away.

" The poor fellow's half mad after my sister, major, and she, you see, don't care a straw about him. She happened to smile on him at supper-table, and he takes it for granted he's in a fair way. We must wait for him, I suppose; and if I know Bella, he won't keep us long."

Meanwhile, the seat beside her, which her smile had beckoned Major Singleton to occupy, had been eagerly filled by Davis. The girl was not displeased to see him : she was lonesome, wanted company, and liked, as all other coquettes do, to have continually in her presence some one or other of the many subjects of her daily conquest. It did not much concern her which, so that she was allowed to carry on her pretty little practice. Her graciousness softened very greatly the moody spirit of her swain, so that he half-repented of that rashness which was about to place him in a position calculated, under every probability, to wrest him, for a time at least, from the enjoyment of that society which he so much coveted. Her gentleness, her good-nature, her smiles—so very unfrequent to him for so long a time—almost turned his brain, and his professions of love grew passionate, and he himself almost eloquent in their utterance. Surely, there is no tyranny like that of love, since it puts us so completely in subjection to the character which deliberate reason would teach us to despise.

But in the midst of his pleading, and while she regarded him with her most gracious smile, the voice of the obtrusive Sergeant Hastings was heard in the tap-room, and the sweet passages of love were at once over between the couple.

"As rocks that have been rent asunder" was their new position. The maiden drew her chair a foot back from its place, and when Davis looked into her face, and beheld the corresponding change in its expression, he rose up, with a bitter curse in his throat, which he was nevertheless too well behaved to utter. He wanted no better evidence of her heartlessness, and with a look which said what his tongue could not have spoken, he seemed to warn her that he was lost to her for ever. His determination was at length complete, and rapidly passing the luckier sergeant, who now entered the apartment, he was soon again in company with the two he had left in waiting. Humphries smiled as he saw the desperate manner of his comrade, but nothing was said, and the three together made their way on foot, till, leaving the village, they entered the forest to the right, and found the clump of trees to which their horses had been fastened. In a moment they were mounted and speeding with the wind towards the close and scarcely penetrable estuary known as the Cypress Swamp, forming a spacious reservoir for the Ashley, from which, by little and little, winding as it goes, it expands at length, a few miles below, into a noble and navigable river.

CHAPTER VI.

"Stretch out thy ward before thou set'st thy foot
'Tis a dim way before thee, and the trees
Of byegone centuries have spread their arms
Athwart thy path. Now make thy footing sure
And now, God cheer us, for the toil is done."

NIGHT had fairly set in—a clear starlight night— before the three set forth upon their proposed adventure. To Majo. Singleton, who was a native of the middle country, and had lived heretofore almost exclusively in it, the path they now travelled was entirely unknown. It was necessary, therefore, to move on slowly and with due circumspection. But for this, the party would have advanced with as much speed as if they were pursuing the common highway; for, to the other two, accustomed all their lives to the woodland cover and the tangled recesses of the swamps, their present route, uncleared, in close thicket growth, and diverging as it continually did, was, nevertheless, no mystery. Though necessarily somewhat slow in their progress, the delay was much less than might have been expected; for Singleton, however ignorant of the immediate ground over which they sped, was yet thoroughly versed in forest life, and had traversed the larger and denser swamps of the Santee, a task, though similar, infinitely more difficult and extensive than the one now before him. After a little while, therefore, when his eye grew more accustomed to the peculiar shades about him, he spurred his good steed forward with much more readiness than at their first setting out, and it was not long before the yielding of the soil beneath his hoofs and the occasional plash of the water, together with the more frequent appearance of the solemn and ghostly cypresses around them, gave sufficient indication of the proximity of the swamp recesses.

They had ridden some five miles, and in all this time no word had been spoken by either of the three, except when, here and there, an increased difficulty in the path led Humphries to the utterance of some caution to his companions. They were now close upon the cypress causeway, and the swamp was gathering around them. Their pace grew slower and more fatiguing, for the freshet had swept the temporary structure over which they rode, and many of the rails were floating in their path. Little gaps were continually presenting themselves, many of which they saw not, but which, fortunately for their safety, were generally avoided by the horses without any call for interference on the part of their riders. Stumbling sometimes, however, they were warned not to press their animals; and picking their way with as much care as possible, they went on in single file, carefully and slowly, over the narrow and broken embankment. It was at this part of their progress that Humphries broke out more freely into speech than he had done before, for his usual characteristic was that of taciturnity.

"Now I do hate these dams and causeways; our people know nothing of road-making, and they ridge and bridge it, while our bones ache and our legs go through at every step we take in going over them. Yet they won't learn—they won't look or listen. They do as they have done a hundred years before, and all your teaching is of no manner of use. Here is this causeway now—every freshet must break its banks and tear up the poles, yet they come back a week after, and lay them down just as before. They never ask if there's a way to build it, which is to make it lasting. They never think of such a thing. Their fathers did so a hundred years ago, and that's reason enough why they should do so now."

"And what plan have you, Humphries, by which to make the dam solid and strong against the freshets, such as we have, that sweep every thing before them, and sometimes give us half a dozen feet of water for a week, over a road that we have been accustomed to walk dryshod?"

"To be sure there is a way, major, and with far less labour. There's no use in building a road unless you give it a backbone. You must run a ridge through it, and all the freshets make it stronger, for they wash the refuse and the mud up against it, instead of washing it away. You see all good roads rise in the centre. The water run off and never settle, which they always do in the hollows between these poles. You fell your tree, always a good big one, to make your ridge—your backbone; and if it be a causeway like this, running through a swamp, that you would build, why you fell your dozen trees, or more, according to the freshet's call for them. You lay them side by side, not across, but up and down the road, taking care to put the big ones in the cen tre. So you may run it for miles, heaping the earth up to the logs. A road made after that fashion will stand a thousand years, while such a thing as this must always be washing away with every freshet. It takes, in the first place, you see, a great deal more of labour and time, and a great deal more of timber, to build it after this fashion; then, it takes more dirt to cover the rails—a hundred times the quantity—and unless they're well covered, they can't be kept down; they will always come loose, and be floating with every rain, and then the water settles heavily in their places and between them. This can't be the case where you lay the timber up and down, as I tell you. It must stand fast; for the rain can't settle, and the earth gathers close to the ridge, and hugs it tighter the more the water beats on it. Besides, building it this way, you use heavy timber, which the waters can't move at any season. But here we stop; we have no further use for the causeway to-night; there's our mark. See to that white tree there; it's a blasted pine, and it shines in a dark night as if it was painted. The lightning peeled it from top to toe. It's a'most two years since. I was not far off in the swamp, catching terrapins, when it was struck, and I was stupified for an hour after, and my head had a ringing in it I didn't get rid of for a month."

"What, do we go aside here?" inquired Davis, who did not seem to relish the diversion, as the first plunge they were required to make from the broken causeway was into a turbid pond, black, and almost covered with fragments of decayed timber and loose bundles of brush.

"Yes, that's our path," replied Humphries, who resolutely put his horse forward as he spoke.

"This is about one of the worst places, major, that we shall have to go through, and we take it on purpose, so that we may not be tracked so easily. Here. when we leave the causeway, we make no mark, and few people think to look for us in the worst place on the line. No, indeed; most people have a love to make hard things easy, though they ought to know that when a man wants to hide, he takes a hole, and not a highway, to do it in. Here, major, this way—to your left, Davis—through the bog."

The party followed as their guide directed, and after some twenty minutes' plunging, they were deep in the shadow and the shelter of the swamp. The gloom was thicker around them, and was only relieved by the pale and skeleton forms of the cypresses, clustering in groups along the plashy sides of the still lake, and giving meet dwelling-place to the screech-owl, that hooted at intervals from their rugged branches. Sometimes a phosphorescent gleam played over the stagnant pond, into which the terrapin plunged heavily at their approach; while on the neighbouring banks the frogs of all degrees croaked forth their inharmonious chant, making the scene more hideous, and certainly adding greatly to the sense of gloom which it inspired in those who penetrated it. A thousand other sounds filled up the pauses between the conclusion of one and the commencement of another discordant chorus from these admitted croakers—sounds of alarm, of invitation, of exulting tyranny—the cry of the little bird, when the black-snake, hugging the high tree, climbs up to the nest of her young, while, with shrieks of rage, flapping his roused wings, the male flies furiously at his head, and gallantly enough, though vainly, endeavours to drive him back from his unholy purpose—the hum of the drowsy beetle, the faint chirp of the cricket, and the buzz of the innumerable thousands of bee, bird, and insect, which make the swamps of the South, in mid-summer and its commencement, the vast storehouse, in all its forms, of the most various and animated life—all these were around the adventurers, with their gloomy and distracting noises, until they became utterly unheeded at last, and the party boldly kept its onward course into their yet deeper recesses.

"Well, Humphries," said Major Singleton, at length breaking the silence, "so far, so good; and now what is our farther progress, and what the chances for trapping this Travis? Will he not steal a march upon us, and be into the swamp before daylight?"

"Never fear it, major," replied the other, coolly enough, while keeping on his way. "You remember, sir, what Huck gave us of his plan. He will place himself upon the skirts of the swamp, high above the point at which we struck, and keep quiet till morning. He will be up betimes, and all that we must do is to be up before him. We have a long ride for it, as it is one part of our work to stop him before he gets too far into the brush. I know his course just as if I saw him on it."

"Yes; such, indeed, may have been the plan; but is there no chance of his departing from it? A good leader will not hold himself bound to a prescribed course, if he finds a better. He may push for the swamp to-night, and I am very anxious that we should be in time to strike him efficiently."

"We shall, sir," replied the other, calmly; "we shall have sufficient time, for I know Travis of old. He is a good hound for scent, but a poor one for chase. He goes slow to be certain, and is always certain to be slow. It's nature with him now, though quick enough, they say, some twenty years ago, when he went out after the Cherokees. Besides, he has a long sweep to make before he gets fairly into the swamp, and the freshet we have had lately will throw him out often enough, and make his way longer. We shall be in time."

"I am glad you are so sure of your man, Humphries. I would not like to lose a good chance at the party. A successful blow struck in this quarter, and just at this moment, would have a fine effect. Why, man, it would bring out those fellows handsomely, whose ears are now full of this protection business, which troubles them so much. If they must fight, they will see the wisdom of taking part with the side which does not call upon them to strike friends or brethren. They must join with us to a man, or go to the West Indies, and that, no doubt, some of the dastards will not fail to do in preference. God help me, but I can scarce keep from cursing them, as I think on their degradation."

"Bad enough, major, bad enough when it's the poor man, without house and home, and nothing to live for and nothing to lose, who takes up with the enemy and fights his battles; but it's much worse when the rich men and the gentlemen, who ought to know better, and to set a good example, it's much worse when they're the

first to do so. Now I know and I feel, though I expect you won't
be so willing to believe it, that, after all, it's the poor man who is
the best friend of his country in the time of danger. He doesn't
reckon how much he's to lose, or what risk he's to run, when there's
a sudden difficulty to get through with. He doesn't think till it's
all over, and then he may ask how much he gains by it, without
getting a civil answer."

"There's truth in what you say, Humphries, and we do the poor
but slack justice in our estimation of them. We see only their
poverty, and not their feelings and affections; we have, therefore,
but little sympathy, and perhaps nothing more than life and like
wants in common with them."

"That's a God's truth here, major, where the poor man does the
fighting and the labour, and the rich man takes protection to save
his house from the fire. Now, it's just so with this poor man
Frampton. He was one of Buford's men, and when Tarleton came
upon them, cutting them up root and branch, he took to the swamp,
and wouldn't come in, all his neighbours could do, because the man
had a good principle for his country. Well, you see what he's
lost;—you can't know his sufferings till you see him, major, and I
won't try to teach you; but if there's a man can look on him, and
see his misery, and know what did it, without taking up sword and
rifle, I don't want to know that man. I know one that's of a different way of thinking, and willing to do both."

"And I another!" exclaimed Davis, who had been silent in their
ride hitherto.

"Is Frampton here in the swamp—and shall we see him to-night?"
asked Singleton, curious to behold a man who, coming from the
poorest class of farmers in the neighbourhood, had maintained such
a tenacious spirit of resistance to invasion, when the more leading
people around him and indeed the greater majority, had subscribed
to terms of indulgence, which, if less honourable, were here far more
safe. The sufferings of the man himself, the cruel treatment his
wife had undergone, and her subsequent death, also contributed
largely to that interest which, upon hearing his simple but pathetic
story, the speaker had immediately felt to know him.

"We shall see him in an hour, major, and a melancholy sight it is ; you'll be surprised, and if you aint very strong of heart, it will go nigh to sicken you.   But it does good to see it for one's self ; it makes one strong against tyranny."

" It grows very dark here."

" That's water before you, and a good big pond, too," said Davis.

" This is the track, major ;" and Humphries led the way to the left, inclining more in the direction of the river.   A sullen, child-like cry, succeeded by a sudden plunge into the water, indicated the vicinity of an alligator, which they had disturbed in his own home ; the rich globules of light, showering over the water around him, giving a singular beauty to the scene, in every other respect so dark and gloomy.   They kept continually turning in a zigzag fashion almost at every step, to avoid the waving vine, the close thicket, or the half-stagnant creek, crowded with decayed fragments of an older and an overthrown forest.

A shrill whistle at this moment, thrice repeated, saluted their ears. It was caught up in the distance by another, and another, in a voice so like, that they might almost have passed for so many echoes of the same.

" Our sentries watch closely, major ; we must answer them, or we may sup on cold lead," said Humphries.   As he spoke, he responded to the signal, and his answer was immediately followed by the appearance of a figure emerging from behind a tree that bulged out a little to the left of the tussock upon which they were now standing.   The dim outline only, and no feature of the new-comer, was distinguishable by the group.

" Ha ! Warner, you watch ?—All's well ; and now lead the way. Are all the boys in camp ?"

" All !" was the reply ; " and a few more come in from Buford's corps who know Frampton."

" And how is he ?—does he know them ?"

" He's in a bad fix, and knows nothing.   You can hardly get a word out of him since his wife's come."

" His wife !   Why, man, what do you think of?—his wife's dead !" exclaimed Humphries with surprise.

" Yes—we know that ; but he brought her, all the same as if she was alive, on his shoulders, and he won't give her up.   There he sits, close alongside of her, watching her all the time, and brushing the flies from her face. He don't seem to mind that she's dead."

"Great God!" exclaimed Singleton, "the unhappy man is mad. Let us push on, and see what can be done for him."

"Ah! nothing can be done for him, I'm afeared," answered Humphries. But, without a word farther, following their new guide, Warner, they advanced upon their way, until the blaze of a huge fire, bursting as it were out of the very bosom of the darkness, rose wavingly before them. The camp of the outlawed whigs, or rebels as they were styled by the enemy, lonely and unattractive, on a little island of the swamp, in a few moments after rose fully in their sight; and plunging into the creek that surrounded it, though swimming at that moment, a bound or two carried them safely over and they stood in the presence of their comrades.

CHAPTER VII.

"Do I not live for it? I have no life,
But in the hope that life may bring with it
The bitter-sweet of vengeance"

THE gloomy painter would have done much with the scene before
us. The wild and mystic imagination would have made it one of
supernatural terrors ; and fancy, fond of the melancholy twilight,
would have endowed the dim shadows, lurking like so many spectres
between the bald cypresses, with a ghostly character, and most
unhallowed purpose. Though familiar with such abodes, Singleton,
as he looked upon the strange groupings thrown along the sombre
groundwork, was impressed with a lively sense of its imposing felicity. They stood upon an island in the very centre of the swamp—
one of those little islands, the tribute ooze of numerous minor water-
courses, hardening into solidity at last. These, beating their feeble
tides upon a single point, in process of time create the barrier which
is to usurp their own possessions. Here, the rank matter of the
swamp, its slime and rubbish, resolving themselves by a natural but
rapid decomposition into one mass, yield the thick luxuriance of soil
from which springs up the overgrown tree, which throws out a
thousand branches, and seems to have existed as many years—in
whose bulk we behold an emblem of majesty, and, in whose term
of life, standing in utter defiance of the sweeping hurricane, we
have an image of strength which compels our admiration, and
sometimes the more elevated acknowledgment of our awe. Thus,
gathering on this insulated bed, a hundred solemn cypresses mingled
their gaunt, spectral forms with the verdant freshness of the water-
oak—the rough simplicity and height of the pine—all intertwined
and bound together in the common guardianship of the spot, by the
bulging body of the luxuriant grape-vine, almost rivalling in thick-
ness, and far surpassing in strength, the trees from which it

depended—these formed a natural roof to the island, circumscribing its limits even more effectually than did the narrow creek by which it had been isolated, and through which the tribute waters of this wide estuary found their way, after a few miles of contracted journeying, into the bed and bosom of the Ashley.

A couple of huge fires, which our party had seen in glimpse while approaching, were in full blaze upon the island; one, the largest, near its centre; the other somewhat apart, upon a little isthmus which it thrust forth into the mouth of the creek. Around the former lay a singular assemblage of persons, single, or in groups, and in every position. These were not more than twenty in all, but so disposed as to seem much more numerous to the casual spectator. Three, in the glare of the fire, sat upon a log at cards, one at either end, and the third, squat upon the ground beside it. A few slept; some were engaged in conversation, while one, more musical than his neighbours, broke into a song of some length, in which the current situation of the things around him underwent improvisation. A stout negro prepared the evening meal, and passed between the card-players and the fire to their occasional inconvenience; their sharp but unheeded denunciations being freely bestowed at every repetition of the offence. The dress and accoutrements of this collection were not less novel, and far more outré, than their several positions and employments. Certainly, taste had but little share in their toilet arrangements, since the hair of some of them flew dishevelled in the wind, or lay matted upon their brows, unconscious of a comb. The faces generally of the party were smeared, and some of them absolutely blackened, by the smoke of the pine-wood fires which at night were kept continually burning around them. This had most effectually begrimed their features, and their garments had not failed to partake of the same colouring. These, too, were as various as the persons who wore them. The ragged coat, the round-jacket, and sometimes the entire absence of both, in the case of some individual otherwise conspicuous enough, destroyed all chance of uniformity in the troop. There was but one particular in which their garb seemed generally to agree, and that was in the coonskin cap which surmounted the heads of most of them—worn jauntily upon the side of the head, with slips that flapped over the ears, and the tail of the animal depending from front or rear, tassel-fashion, according to the taste of the wearer. Considering such an assemblage, so disposed, so habited, in connection with the situation and circumstances in which we find them, and we shall form no very imperfect idea of the moral effect which their appearance must have had upon the new comers. The boisterous laugh,the angry, sharp retort, the ready song from some sturdy bacchanal, and the silent sleeper undisturbed amid all the uproar, made, of themselves, a picture to the mind not likely to be soon forgotten. Then, when we behold the flaming of the torch in the deep dark which it only for a moment dissipates, and which crowds back, as with a solid body, into the spot from which it has been temporarily driven—the light flashing along and reflected back from the sullen waters of the creek;—and listen, at the same moment, to the cry of the screech-owl as the intruder scares him from his perch—the plaint of the whippoorwill, in return, as if even the clamour of the obscene bird had in it something of sympathy for the wounded spirit,—these, with the croaking of the frogs in millions, with which the swamp was a dwelling-place among a thousand, were all well calculated to awaken the most indifferent spectator, and to compel a sense of the solemn-picturesque even in the mind of the habitually frivolous and unthinking.

With the repeated signals which they had heard from their sentries on the appearance of the new comers, the scattered groups had simultaneously started to their feet, and put themselves in a state of readiness. The signals were familiar, however, and spoke of friends in the approaching persons ; so that, after a few moments of buzz and activity, they generally sank back sluggishly to their old occupations,—the card-players to finish their game, and the less speculative, their sleep. Their movement, however, gives us a better opportunity to survey their accoutrements. The long, cumbrous rifle seemed the favourite weapon, and in the hands of the diminutive, sallow, but black-eyed and venturous dweller in the swamps of the lowlands, across whose knee we may here and there see it resting, it may confidently be held as fatal at a hundred yards. A few of them had pistols—the common horse-pistol—a weapon of little real utility under any circumstances. But a solitary musket, and that, too, without the bayonet, was to be seen in the whole collection; and though not one of the party present but had his horse hidden in the swamp around him, yet not one in five of the riders possessed the sabre, that most effective weapon of cavalry. These were yet to be provided, and at the expense of the enemy.

The immediate appearance of Major Singleton, as he followed Humphries up the bank, once more called them to their feet. He had been expected, yet few of them personally knew him. They knew, however, that he was high in favour with Governor Rutledge, and bore his commission. Of this they had been apprised by Humphries, who had been the recruiting officer of the troop. They now crowded around him with a show of curious examination, which was narrow and close without being obtrusive.

With that manly, yet complaisant habit which distinguished him, he soon made himself known to them, and his opening speech won not a little upon their hearts. He unfolded his commission, delivered an address from the executive, in which a direct and warm appeal was made to their patriotism, and concluded with some remarks of his own to the same effect, which were all enthusiastically received. His frank, fearless manner, fine eye, and manly, though smooth and youthful face, took admirably with them, and at once spoke favourably to their minds in support of his pretensions to govern them. This command they at once tendered him; and though without the material for a force called for by the commission which he bore, yet, in those times, it was enough that they loved their leader and were not unwilling to fight with an enemy. Major Singleton was content to serve his country in an humbler command than that which his commission entitled him to hold. Acting, therefore, as their captain for the present, he made Humphries his lieutenant. Him they had long known, and he was a favourite among them. He, indeed, had been chiefly instrumental in bringing together their scattered elements, and in thus forming the nucleus of a corps, which, in the subsequent warfare, contributed in no slight degree to the release of the country from foreign thraldom. In Humphries they had a good officer and every confidence, though it was obvious enough, that, while full of courage, calm, collected, and not easily moved, he yet lacked many of those essentials of superior education and bearing, without which militia-men are not often to be held in order. He was not sufficiently their superior to stand apart and to command them; and the inferior mind will never look to its equal in the moment of emergency. Though ready and acute enough in the smaller details of military adventure—the arrangement of the ambuscade, the rapid blow at the rear, or the plan for striking at the foragers of an enemy—he was yet rather apt to go forward with, than to command, his party. He trusted rather to his presence than to the superior force of his character, to urge upon them the performance of their duties; and, conscious of this, though ready at all times to lead, he yet shrank from the necessity of commanding. This capacity can only result successfully from an habitual exercise of authority. It was with no small satisfaction, therefore, that he placed his recruits under the control of Major Singleton, although, it may be said, that such a transfer of his command was rather nominal than real; Humphries still counselling, in great part, the particular business of adventure which Singleton was the better able to direct. The latter had yet to acquire a knowledge of localities and men, which could only be obtained by actual experience.

"And now, major, soldiers without arms are not apt to fight well. Come, sir, with me, and see our armory. It's a queer one, to be sure, to those used to a better; but it must serve where there's no choice. This way, sir—to the left. Here, Tom, bring a chunk."

The black led the way with a blazing brand, until their farther progress was arrested by the waters of the creek. In the centre of the stream grew a cypress of immense size, much larger than any of its surrounding companions. Motioning Singleton to wait, Humphries waded into the water almost up to his middle, until he reached the tree, into which, taking the blazing brand from the black, he entered, returning in a few moments with half a dozen fine sabres, which, one after the other, he threw from him to the bank.

"This is all our stock in trade, major; and you have your choice of them till we can get a better. This, if I know the signs of the weather, we shall do before long. Meanwhile, as the stuff's good, they will answer our present purpose."

Singleton pressed the points of the weapons severally to the earth, testing the elasticity of the steel, then accommodating the hilt to his grip, declared himself suited. Humphries made a selection after him, and the remaining four were subsequently distributed among chosen men, to whom commands in the little corps were assigned. As rebels, heretofore, the short-shrift and sure cord must have been their doom, if taken. The commission of the state, and a due register of their names in the books of the orderly, now secured them in the immunities of regular warfare, and made that comparatively innocent which before was obnoxious to doom and degradation.

We have spoken of two several fires as conspicuous upon the island at the approach of Singleton, the one upon the centre, the other, and smaller one, at its remotest extremity. Of the use made of the former, we have already seen something; the other, while it had caught the eye of Major Singleton, had been too remote to enable him to distinguish the employment or character of the various persons who yet closely encircled it. He could see that there were several figures sitting around the brands, which seemed to have been but loosely thrown together, as they had now fallen apart, and only gave forth a flickering blaze at intervals, denying that constant light, without which he could not hope to gain any knowledge of the persons, even at a far less distance. These persons had not moved at his approach, and had remained stationary all the while he was employed in making himself known to those who were to be his comrades. This alone would have been enough to attract his attention; and, in addition, he saw that those around him, when bending their glances off in the direction of his own, shook their heads with an air of solemnity, and, though saying nothing, were yet evidently influenced by a knowledge of some circumstances connected with the mysterious group, of a painful character. Observing the inquiring look of Major Singleton, Humphries approached, and whispered him that the party at the opposite fire consisted of Frampton, his two sons, and the dead

4

body of his wife, and proposed that they should go to him. The major at once consented.

"You'll see a sad sight, Major Singleton—a sad sight!—for the man is crazy, let them say what they may. He don't know half the time what he says or does, and he scarcely feels anything."

They moved over in the prescribed direction, and approached without disturbing the chief personage of the group. The elder son, a youth of twenty, looked up at their coming, but said nothing. It was evident that he, and he alone, had been weeping. The other son, a tall fine-looking lad of sixteen, seemed inspired with harsher feelings as his eye gazed from the face of the father to that of the mother, whose dead body lay between the two, her head on the lap of the elder son, over whose arms her hair streamed loosely —long, and delicately brown and glossy. She had evidently been a woman of some attractions. Her person was well formed and justly proportioned, neither masculine nor small. Her features were soft and regular. The face was smooth, but had been bruised, seemingly as if she had fallen upon it; and there were blotches upon the cheek and forehead, which may have been the conse- quence of blows, or might be the natural evidence of that decay which was now strongly perceptible The face of the chief mourner, who sat silent at her feet, looking forward into her face, was a fine one, as well in its mould as in its expression. It was that of a splendid savage. There was enough of solemn ferocity in it for the murderer, enough of redeeming sensibility to soften, if not to sub- due, the other more leading attributes of its character. His skin was dark like that of the people generally of that neighbourhood His eyes were black and piercing; and a burning spot on each cheek seemed to have borrowed from the red glare of the fire at his side a corresponding intensity of hue. His lips were parted; and the lower jaw seemed to have been thrown and kept down spasmodically. Through the aperture glared the tips of the small and white teeth, sometimes closed together by a sudden convulsive jerk, but immediately relaxing again and resuming their divided position.

He took no sort of notice of the new-comers, until, throwing himself alongside of the younger boy, Humphries took the hand of the mother into his own, and gazed over upon her face. Frampton then gave him a look—a single look; and as their eyes met, those of Humphries intuitively filled with water. The bereaved wretch, as he saw this, laughed sneeringly and shook his head. There was no misunderstanding the rebuke. It clearly scorned the sympathy, and called for the sterner tribute of revenge. The elder son then carried on a brief conversation in an under tone with the lieutenant, which was only audible in part to Singleton, who sat on the root of a tree opposite. He gave the particulars of his mother's removal in this dialogue, and of the resolute doggedness with which his father had hitherto resisted the burial of the body.

" It must be buried at once," said Humphries more earnestly to the youth. The father heard him, and glaring upon him with the eye of a tiger, the desolate man bent forward and placed his hand resolutely upon the body, as if determined not to suffer its removal.

" Nay, but it must, Frampton ;—there's no use in keeping it here : and, indeed, there's no keeping it much longer. Hear to reason, man, and be persuaded."

The person addressed shook his head, and maintained his hold upon the corse for a moment in silence; but all on a sudden, half rising to his feet, he shook his fists fiercely at the speaker, while his expression was so full of ferocity, that Humphries prepared for, and every moment expected, an attack.

" You have lied to me, Humphries !" he exclaimed with difficulty, as if through his clenched teeth.—" You have lied to me ;— you said he should be here,—where is he ? why have you not brought him ?"

" Who ? brought who ?" demanded the other earnestly.

" Who !"—and as the maniac half shrieked out the word in sneering repetition, he pointed to the body, while he cried, with a fierce laugh, between each pause in his words—" who !—did he not strike her—strike her to the ground—trample upon her body —great God !—upon her—my wife ?" And, as the accumulated picture of his wife's injuries rose up before his mind while he spoke, his speech left him, and he choked, till his face grew livid

in their sight, and yet he had no tears. He soon recovered suffi
ciently to speak again with something like a show of calmness.

"You said you were my friend—that you would bring him to
me—that I should kill him here—here, even while mine eyes yet
looked upon her. Liar! where is he! Why have you not brought
him?"

"I am no liar, Frampton, and you know it. I never promised
to bring the dragoons to you; but I am willing to lead you to
them."

"Do I want a leader for that?—you shall see:" and he relapsed
after this reply, into the same solemn stupor which had marked his
looks at the first coming of the two. Humphries proceeded with
temper and coolness—

"It is time, Frampton, to be a man—to bear up against your
losses, and think how to have revenge for them."

"I am ready. Speak not to me of revenge—speak not; I am
thirsting—thirsting for blood!" was the reply.

"Yet, here you sit moping over your losses, while the red-coats
are in the swamp—ay, hunting us out in our own grounds—Huck's
dragoons, with Travis at their head."

The man was on his feet in an instant. There was a wild glow
now visible in his face, which completely superseded the sombre
fixedness of its previous expression. All now was summary im
patience.

"Come!" said he, waving his hand impatiently, and convulsively
grasping his bosom with his fingers—"come!"

"It is well. I now see you are in the right mood for vengeance.
and I have made all arrangements for it. Here is a sword; and
this, Frampton, is our commander, Major Singleton. He is now
our leader, and will put us on the dragoons' tracks in short order."

The maniac turned stupidly to Singleton, and bending his head
with a strange simper on his lips, simply repeated the word
"Come!" with which he showed his willingness for the adventure.
Humphries whispered Major Singleton to take him at his word.
and move him off to the rest of the party, while he gave directions
for the interment of the body. Singleton did so, and without any
show of reluctance, Frampton followed him. Once did he stop

suddenly, turn quickly round, and seem about to retrace his steps; but seeing it, Singleton simply observed, as if to himself—

"We shall soon be upon the dragoons, and then—"

The object was gained, and the distracted, desolate creature followed, like a tame dog, the lead of his commander. He listened in gloomy silence to the arrangements, as they were agreed upon, for the encounter with Travis. He knew enough of that sort of fighting to see that they were judiciously made; but for this he did not care. All plans are necessarily slow and tedious to the mood that craves for vengeance; and Frampton, satisfied with the promise which they conveyed to his mind of the revenge which he desired, offered no suggestion, nor interfered in the slightest degree with any of their plans. Still, not a word which had been uttered among them escaped his appreciation. He was now fully awakened to a single object, and the reasoning faculties grew tributary to the desire of his mood when that became concentrated. He saw that the proposed operations were the best that could be devised for the encounter, and he looked to that now for the full satisfaction of his thirst.

Humphries having given his directions duly for the interment of the body, now returned to join in the deliberations with the rest. His opinion was adopted by Major Singleton, who, giving orders that all things should be in readiness, himself saw to the execution of certain minor resolves; then, dispersing his sentries, he proceeded, with the coolness of an old soldier, to enjoy the three hours of slumber which had been allotted before the necessary start to intercept Travis.

It was an hour after midnight when the guards aroused them with the preparations for their movement. The night was still, clear, and calm. The winds were sleeping, or only strove with a drowsy movement along the tops of the trees, the highest above the swamp. Sweetly the murmurs of the creek around them, swollen by the influx of the tide from the sea, which is there quite perceptible, broke upon the ear, as the waters, in feeble ripples, strove against the little island, and brought with them a sense of freshness from the deep, which none feels more pleasantly than he who has been long wandering in the southern forests. Not a lip had yet spoken among the troops, and, save the slight cry of the capricious insect, and the sound produced by their own early movement in bustling into action, there was nothing in that deep stillness and depth of shadow calculated in the slightest degree to impair the feelings of solemnity which, in his own abode, Silence, the most impressive of all the forest divinities, exacts from his subjects. With a ready alacrity, obeying the command of their leader, the troopers were soon in saddle, forming a compact body of twenty men, Frampton and his two sons included; the very boys being thus early taught in the duties of the partisan. Following in such order as the inequalities of the swamp would permit, they were soon advanced upon their route through bog and through brier, slough, forest, and running water—a route, rugged and circuitous, and not always without its peril. In three hours, and ere the daylight yet dappled the dun east, they skirted the narrow ridge where the arrangement of Singleton placed them, and over which the scouting party of Travis was expected to pass. There, with hostile anxiety, and well prepared, they confidently awaited the arrival of the enemy.

CHAPTER VIII.

" There shall be joy for this. Shall we not laugh—
Laugh merrily for conquest, when it takes
The wolfdog from our throats, and yields us his."

TRAVIS, the faithful coadjutor of the tory Huck, was on his march into the swamp before daylight. As Humphries had anticipated, he took the path, if so it might be called, on which the ambuscade had been laid for him. He might not have done so, had he dreamed for an instant of the existence in this quarter of such a body of men as that now preparing to receive him. Looking on his object, however, simply as the arrest of Frampton, and the scouring of the swamp of such stragglers besides as might have been led for shelter into its recesses, he adopted the route which was obviously most accessible, and most likely, therefore, to be resorted to by the merely skulking discontent. The half-military eye, looking out for an enemy in any respect equal in strength, would have either studiously avoided the ridge over which Travis now presumed to ride, or would have adopted some better precautions than he had troubled himself to take. It was naturally a strong defile, well calculated for an easy defence, as only a small force could possibly be of use upon it. But two persons could ride abreast in the prescribed direction, and then only with great difficulty and by slow movement; for little gullies and fissures continually intersected the path, which was circuitous and winding, and, if not always covered with water and swamp, quite as difficult to overcome, from its luxuriant growth of umbrage.

Though an old traveller in such fastnesses, these obstructions were in no sort pleasant to the leader of the British party, who, being a notorious grumbler, accompanied every step which he took with a grunting sort of commentary by way of disapprobation.

" Now, may the devil take these gullies, that go as deep when you get into them as if they were made for him. This is a day's

chase, and the next time Huck wants a hunt, he shall enjoy it himself. I like not this service. It's little less than a disparagement of
the profession, and speaks not well for an old soldier."

The leader spoke with feeling, and no little emphasis, as his steed
scrambled up the bank from the slough in which his legs had been
almost fastened, the slimy ooze of which, left by the now-receding
tide, rendered the effort to release himself a matter of greater difficulty than usual. The grumbling continued, even after he had
gained the tussock.

"Thou a soldier!" cried one who rode up behind him, and who
spoke in terms of familiarity indicating close companionship—"thou
a soldier, Travis, indeed! What should make thee a soldier?"

"Am I not, Clough?" was the reply.

"And wherefore dost thou grumble, then?"

"Wherefore? Because, being a soldier, I am sent upon any but
a soldier's service. A dog might do this duty—a dog that you had
well beaten."

"And what better service, Travis, couldst thou have to keep thee
from grumbling? Art thou, now, not a sorry bear with a sore
head, that kindness annot coax, and crossing only can keep civil!
Send thee on what service Huck may, it is all the same; thou wilt
grumble at the toil, even when it likes thee best. What wouldst
thou have—what would please thee?"

"By Saint Jupiter, but he might ask, at least! He might give a
man his choice," responded the other, gruffly. "It's but a small
favour I ask, to be suffered to choose for myself whether I shall work
for my master on hill or in hole—with a free bit, or hand to hand,
close struggle with a hungry alligator in his wallow."

"And thou wouldst choose the very service he now puts thee to.
What! do we not all know thee—and who knows thee better than
Huck? He sees thou art the best man for the swamp; that thy
scent is keen with the bloodhound, thine eye like the hawk's, and
thou art quick for fight as the major's bull-pup. It is because he
knows thou art fond of this sort of venture that he puts thee upon
it; and what thou grumblest at, therefore, it will be out of thine
own wisdom to show, even if thou wert really discontented with
the duty, which I believe not."

"It's a dog's life only, this scenting swamps for the carrion they had better keep—wearing out good legs and horses, and making soldiers do the duty of a hungry dog. Rot it, but I'll resist after this! Let them send others that are younger, and like it better. I'll give it up—I'll do no more of it."

"Say so to Huck, and lose command of the scouts—the best game thou hast ever played at, if the baggage-wagons speak true," was the reply. "What! shalt thou grumble to do what thou art best fitted for? What wouldst thou be after—what other service would please thee?"

"Thou mayst see me in a charge yet, Sergeant Clough," replied Travis, boastfully, "provided thou hast blood enough to stop until it's over. When thou hast seen this, thou wilt ask me no child's questions. What! because I am good at the swamp, am I therefore worth nothing on the highway? It were a sorry soldier that could not take clear track and bush and bog alike, when the case calls for it, and do good service in all. But thou shalt see, some day, and grow wiser."

"Well, thou dost promise largely, like an old debtor; but, to my mind, thou art just now where thou shouldst be—in the swamps; for, truth to speak, thou lovest them—thou lovest the wallow and the slough—the thick ooze which the alligator loves, and the dry fern-bank where he makes his nest; thou lovest the terrapin because of his home, not less than of the good soup which he gives us; and the ugly moccasin, and the toad, and the frog—the brown lizard and the green—the swamp-spider, with its ropy house and bagging black body—all these are favourites with thee, because thy spirit craves for thee a home like that which they abide in."

"It is a goodly place, with all that company thou speakest of: the air is pleasant to the sense, and the noises—there is no music like the concert the frogs make for one at sunset."

"Said I not? Why, man, thou quarrellest with kindness, when thou ravest at Huck for sending thee to the swamp. Thou wert feverish and impatient this morning until thou wert fairly in it, with its mud and water plashing around thee; and now thou art here, with the trees crowding upon us so thickly that the sun looks not

4*

under them once in the whole year, thou creepest like a terrapin
upon thy journey, as if thou didst greatly fear thou wouldst too
quickly get through it. A barren fear, this, for we see but the
beginning : the bog deepens, and the day grows darker as we go.
Thou art slow, Travis."

"Saint Jupiter, Master Clough, wouldst thou lead ? Thou art a
better swamp-sucker than Ned Travis, and he born, as I may say, in
a bush and cradled in a bog, and his first breeches, like mother Eve's
petticoat, made out of bulrushes ! Go to, friend, and be modest !"

"Ay, when thou art wise, and can go without counsel. Once
more, Travis, but I do think thy snail's pace were better mended."

"Teach Goose Creek, would you ? Talk not so loudly, Sergeant
Clough, of running through the Cypress, or the gray-squirrel will
look down and laugh. He's up betimes this morning, and knows
more of a long leap through a broad swamp like this of the Ashley
than comes to thy wisdom. Speak before him with becoming reve
rence, for he watches thee from the pinetop above thee."

The sergeant, who was an Englishman, looked upward with due
simplicity, and received in his face the dismembered and decayed
branch which the playful animal threw down, as he leaped away
from the tree they were passing.

"Now, d—n the rebel ! That were a hanging matter for one of
Washington's cavalry."

"Ay, could you catch him !" replied Travis, with a laugh at the
discomfiture of his companion, who busied himself in freeing his
face from the dust of the decayed branch.

"See what thou gettest for thy stupidity. Think you gray-jacket
knew not all you were saying ? He did : not a word escaped him ;
and, believe it or not, his tribe have quite as much understanding as
we, though, to be sure, they have not the same tongue to make it
known. It's a God's truth, now, that squirrel has been outstanding
sentinel for his company, just as ours watches for us ; and look
where they go, all around us, and all in the same direction ! See
to yon pine, how full of them ! It bends and shakes, big as it is,
as they leap off to the next tree. They are all off, just as the sentinel gave them notice. Every now and then, as we drew nigh, he
barked away—bark after bark—' bow-wow,' though thou never

heard'st a syllable, all the time as good as saying: 'Now they come—nigher, nigher, nigher!'—and when he thought it time to move, he tumbled the dry branch into your open mouth, and made off with his last signals."

"Pshaw! what nonsense you talk!"

"Nonsense! Saint Jupiter, but it's true as turpentine! There's no truth, if that be not. Why, man, I go farther: I do believe, in my conscience, that they understand arithmetic and navigation. Don't you think he told his fellows how many we were, and what route over the water we were going to take? You see they have taken a different direction altogether."

"You think I swallow your fool's stories?" said Clough.

"Quite as easy to swallow, and better food than the branch the squirrel threw thee: but if thou believe not, I care not.—Rot thee, for an infidel, having as little belief as brains! Thou art worse than Turk or Hebrew, and should have no water from me wert thou famishing."

"Thou canst scarce deny it here," was the reply, as the squad, one after the other, struggled through a quagmire that spread across the path.

"Nor would I here; I am charitable: take thy fill of what is before thee.—But hold up, men; we are on the broad track. This tussock runs for a hundred yards, widening to a fork; and I've a mind that you shall go through the worst part of it, Sergeant Clough, that you may get more wisdom in swamp-sucking. Close up, men—close up!"

They passed over the broad path in a few moments, until they reached a point from which ran out another route, clearly indicated upon the sky by an opening through the trees, which let in, for the first time after their entrance, the unobstructed sunlight.

"To the right now, men—to the right! It's the worst track. but carries us soonest to the heart of the swamp, and we can pass it now without swimming: the waters are going down, and it will not be so bad, after all."

"Is it worse, Travis, than what we have passed?" inquired Clough, rather anxiously.

"Worse!" exclaimed Travis, turning shortly upon the speaker,

with a sneer; "Saint Jupiter! said I not you should learn swamp-
sucking? You'll drink before you come out. But the water's fresh."

"Fresh, here in the swamp?"

"Ay, fresh enough—fresh from the sea, unless the tide's gone
clean down. But on; do not fear; it looks worse than it tastes.
On, and follow me close!"

They dashed after their leader as he gave the word, but their
progress was much slower than before.

In the mean while, let us turn our eyes upon the party in waiting for them. Following the suggestions of his lieutenant, Humphries, Major Singleton had disposed of his men at convenient
distances for mutual support along the more accessible ridge which
the party of Travis had originally pursued. The design had been
a good one; for it was not to be supposed that one who had shown
himself so careful in selecting the least obstructed route, would
willingly leave it, in preference for another, so indirect and difficult
of passage as that upon which Travis had now turned his horse.
The ambuscade had been well laid, and must have been successful,
but for this circumstance. Major Singleton himself, being in
advance, was the first to perceive this change of movement, which,
taking place just when his anxieties were most aroused, was productive of an exaggerated degree of disappointment. He cried
out to Humphries, who lurked in a low bush on the opposite bank,
and saw not so readily,—

"They leave the track, Humphries! they have turned off to the
right—we are foiled!"

The lieutenant rose from his recumbent position, and saw the
truth of his commander's suggestion. To effect a change of ambuscade at this moment was hopeless; and there remained but one
mode, and that was, to persuade them to return to the path from
which they departed. At first, the lieutenant thought to throw
himself immediately in their way; and, being well known, and
looked upon as loyal by all the dragoons, he believed that he might
lure them back by misrepresentations of one kind or another.
This thought he abandoned, however, as he still desired to keep
himself from present detection, which he could not hope, should
any of them escape to tell the story.

"There is but one way, major," he exclaimed, while smearing nis visage with the mud around him, and leaping boldly forth on foot upon the broad path—" there is but one way, sir : keep your men fast, while I make myself visible to Travis. I will run upon the bank, and make them hear me. They will follow the tussock, and, by the time I am in cover, you will have them between you. The rest of the work is yours."

He waited not for an answer, but the next instant was seen by Singleton coursing along the tussock towards the route taken by Travis. When upon the highest point, and perceptible to them, he broke a dried stick, with a sharp, snapping sound, which reached the quick ear of their leader. Travis turned instantly, and ordered a halt.

"Hold up, men—hold up a moment! See you nothing to the left?"

All eyes were turned in the required direction, but they failed to distinguish any object in particular, other than belonged to the region.

"Look, Clough, your eyes are younger than mine—look to the left, beyond the big water-oak, close by the blasted pine—the very highest point of the tussock we just left."

"I see, I see!" cried one of the troopers ; "it's a man."

"Now I have it! You are right, Wilkins—it's a man—a stout fellow, and must be Frampton," cried Clough ; "the very dog we seek."

"No, 'tis not the man we seek," was the reply of Travis, who had been watching intently. "This is a short, stout man, not of more inches than myself; Frampton, though stout, is tall. But he is our game, be he who he may. All are outlaws here, and rebels for the rope. Here, Corporal Dricks, have your string in readiness ; we shall doubtless need a cast of your office, and the noose should be free for service. Ride close, and be ready. Ha! he scents—he sees us! He is on the wing, and we must be quick and cautious. After him, Clough, to the left—right, Wilkins ! Get upon the tussock, and, if he keeps it, you have him. Ride, boys ! To the left, Clough—to the left ! He can't clear the pond, and we are sure of him !"

Half of the troops dashed after the suspicious person, who was our acquaintance Humphries; the other half, slowly returning, re-entered the old trail, and kept their way towards the flying object and the pursuit. The lieutenant found no difficulty in misleading his pursuers, having once drawn them back to their original route. They urged the chase hotly after him, but he knew his course, and was cool and confident. Doubling continually through bog and through brier—now behind this, now under that clump of foliage or brush—he contrived to boggle them continually in perpetual intricacies, each more difficult than the other, until he not only led them into the very thick of the ambuscading party, still maintaining his original lead upon them, but he scattered them so far asunder, that mutual assistance became impossible.

It was then that, gathering himself up for breath along the edge of a bank, he coolly wiped the moisture from his brow, looking from side to side, as he heard the splashing in the water or the rustling in the brush of his bewildered pursuers. He, meanwhile, fairly concealed from their sight by a thick cluster of laurels that rose out of the bay before him, conceiving the time to have arrived for action, gave the shrill whistle with which his men were familiar. The pursuers heard it reverberate all around them from a dozen echoes of the swamp; they gave back, and there was a pause in the chase, as if by common consent. The sound had something supernatural and chilling in it; and the instinct of each, but a moment before so hot upon the heels of the outlaw, was now to regain his starting-place, and recover his security with his breath.

But retreat was not so easy, and prudence counselled too late. They made the effort, however; but to succeed was denied them. The word of command reached their ears in another voice than that of their own leader, and in the next instant came the sharp cracking reports of the rifle—two, three, four.

Travis went down at the first shot; they beheld his fall distinctly, as he stood upon the highest point of the ridge, which was visible for a hundred yards round. For a moment more. the enemy remained invisible; but Major Singleton now gave his orders shrilly and coolly:—

"Steady, men—in file, open order—trot!"

And then came the rush of the charge, and the stragglers beheld the flashing sabres dealing with the few troopers who held the broad ridge of the tussock. The tories fought well; but the surprise was too sudden, and too little prepared for, and they fought at disadvantage. Still, as they remembered the unsparing character of their own warfare, and were conscious of innumerable outrages, such as had driven Frampton to outlawry, they stood their ground bravely enough. Parrying the first strokes of their assailants, who had every advantage, they dashed aside from the path, and strove to escape by plunging in every direction through the swamp. But with the loss of the ridge, which Singleton with his few troopers now traversed in all directions, they lost all chance of extrication. They floundered from slough to slough, while, dismounting and on foot, the whigs pursued them. The cry for quarter on all hands ended the combat, and the survivors were drawn forth to become prisoners. They threw down their arms, generally, and were spared; one who resisted was cut down by Davis, who had shown himself a true man in close contest; and one strove to escape by turning back upon his path, and plunging on through the swamp in an opposite direction to that taken by the rest; but there was an eye upon him, quickened by hate, and a deadly hostility which nothing could blind—a footstep which he could not evade.

The fugitive was the sanguinary corporal of Tuck—a wretch who always carried the cord at his saddle-bow for sudden executions, and enjoyed nothing so well as its employment. His pursuer was the maniac Frampton. That fierce man had singled out this one antagonist, and throughout the brief struggle, in which he bore an active part, had never once withdrawn his glance from him. But for this, the wretch might have escaped; and even then, had not guilt or fear paralysed his energy or judgment, his chances might have been good; but he held too long to his horse, and lost that time, in trying to urge him along the track he had taken, which, on foot, he might have pursued much more effectually. The animal became entangled in some water-vines, and before he could get him free, or even get from his back, the pursuer was charging into the swamp, with drawn sword waving overhead, and but a few paces from him. Leaping from his steed, which he left struggling, the fugitive made for the opposite bank, and reached it before Frampton had yet got through the slough. But even this advantage did not serve him long. Though brave enough, the corporal seemed at that moment to lack much of his wonted firmness. Probably he knew the pursuer, had heard his story, and dreaded his vengeance. It was not improbable, indeed, that he himself had been one of those concerned in the assault upon Frampton's wife. If so, the flight of the one and the concentrated pursuit of the other were both natural enough. Guilt is apt to despair, and to sink into imbecility, in its own consciousness of crime, and in the presence of the true avenger. Still, for a moment, there was a show of spirit. He wheeled, and confronted the pursuer with a word of defiance; but the moment after, he turned again in flight. He ran over the tussock upon which both of them now stood, and, bounding through a pond that lay in his way, made off for a close cover of cypresses that grew at a little distance.

Should he gain that cover, his safety would most probably be certain, as he would then have gained on Frampton, and had long since been out of reach of the rest. But if the one ran with the speed of fear, madness gave wings to the other. The fugitive looked over his shoulder once as he flew, and he could see in the eye of his pursuer that there was no pity, nothing but death; and utterly vain must be his cry for quarter. Perhaps he felt this conviction only from a due consciousness of what he deserved from his own atrocities. The thought increased his speed; but, though capable and elastic enough, he could not escape the man who rushed behind him. Defying wood, water, and every obstruction, the fierce wretch pressed close upon the fugitive. The corporal felt the splashing of the water from his adversary's feet; he knew that the next moment must be followed by the whirl of the sabre; and he sank motionless to the ground. The blow went clean over him; but though it carried Frampton beyond him, yet he did not fall. The maniac soon recovered, and confronted the corporal, who now found it impossible to fly; his hope was in fight only. But what was his lifted weapon against that of his opponent, wielded by his superior strength, made terrible by madness! The sword was dashed aside—dashed down in the heavy sweeping stroke with which the other prefaced the conflict.

"Mercy! mercy!" cried the corporal, as he saw that it was all over. A howl like that of the wolf was the only response, and the weapon bit through the bone as the arm was unavailingly thrown up to resist it. The stricken member hung only by the skin and a part of the coat-sleeve. The steel was already in the air—

"Mercy, Frampton! have mercy—"

The speech was silenced, as, crushing through bone and brain, the thick sword dug its way down into the very eyes of the pleader. The avenger knelt upon the senseless body, as it lay at his feet, and poured forth above it a strain of impious thanksgiving to Heaven for so much granted and gained of the desired vengeance. His wild, wolfish laugh, at intervals while he prayed, taught the rest of the party where to look for him.

CHAPTER IX.

*" It is all dim—the way still stretches out
Far in the distance. We may nothing see,
Till comes the season in the dawning light."*

IT was an easy victory, and won without loss. Wiping his
bloody sword upon the mane of his steed, Major Singleton rode up
to his captives, who, by this time, were all properly secured.
Four persons had fallen in the conflict, and among these was their
leader, Travis. He was shot dead upon the spot. Clough was
severely wounded in the breast, though perhaps not mortally, and
lay gasping, but without a groan, upon the ground where he had
fallen, and around which the surviving prisoners were grouped.
Three others had fallen, either killed outright or mortally wounded:
two of these by the sabre, not including the corporal, who fell by
the hand of Frampton, and who was at once rolled into the swamp.
The prisoners, five in number, were natives, generally of the very
lowest class, and just the sort of men to fight, according to the
necessity of the case, on either side. Such, indeed, were a large
proportion of the tories residing in the province. There were
many who were avowedly monarchists; who had no sympathy
with the revolutionary movement, and no belief in its necessity or
propriety; many who were of foreign birth, Scotch, German, and
English; and these were frequently persons of great worth, and
conscientious in the adoption of their cause, and of these, the
unprejudiced judgment of our times has determined that there
can be no proper ground for reproach. But with the class of
whom we write, and whom we find engaged in such warfare as that
which we describe, the case is different. For them, there can be no
apology. They were desperates of the worst description—outcasts
from several of the provinces,—who, taking refuge at first in
Florida—which still remained loyal to the British crown—had

seized the moment of British ascendency in the South, to inundate Carolina and Georgia with their masses. Without leading principles and miserably poor—not recognised, except as mercenaries, in the social aristocracies which must always prevail in slaveholding nations—they had no sympathy with the more influential classes,—those who were the first to resist the authority of England. The love of gain, the thirst for rapine, and that marauding and gipsy habit of life which was now familiar to them, were all directly appealed to in the tory mode of warfare. They were ready on any side which offered them the greatest chance for indulging in these habits. The tories forming Huck's cavalry were all of this sort; and the small detachment just overthrown by Singleton had no sympathy with their leader, only as his known character promised them plunder. Defeat had no attraction in their eyes; and, as that is always the true cause which is triumphant, they now freely tendered themselves, with clamorous tongues, and to the no small chagrin of the wounded Clough, as recruits for Singleton. The Briton denounced their perfidy in fearless language, and threatened them terribly with the vengeance of Huck and Tarleton ; but the remote fear is no fear with the vulgar. They seldom think in advance of the necessity, and the exhortation of their wounded officer had no visible effect. They persisted in their determination to fight on the right side, and earnestly asserted their love of country, alleging that force only had placed them in the ranks of the enemy. Major Singleton conferred with Humphries on the course to be taken in this matter. The latter knew most of the parties, but had been prudent to keep from sight, and they had not seen him, only in the brief glimpse which they had of him in the pursuit, when, at such a distance, perpetually moving, and with his face well smeared with the rank ooze from the creek around him, he must have been unknown, except upon the narrowest examination, even to the mother that had borne him. It was still his policy to keep from sight in connexion with his whig partisans; for, passing in Dorchester as a loyal citizen—a character in part obtained through his father's loudly-voiced attachment to the existing powers—he was of far greater advantage to the cause of the country than he possibly could have been even in active military service. He obtained intelligence with singular adroitness, conveyed it with despatch, and planned enterprises upon the facts he thus gathered, with no little tact and ingenuity. To remain unknown, therefore, or only known as he had been heretofore, in close connexion with loyalty alone, was clearly the policy of our lieutenant.

There was one man from whom Humphries seemed willing to withhold his confidence. He counselled his commander to accept the services of the remaining four, recommending that they should be so distributed among the men who had been tried, as to defeat any concert between them, should they feel any impulse to disaffection. In this manner it was also thought that a proper bias would be given to their minds, which, as they both knew, were sufficiently flexible to find but little difficulty in conforming to any circumstances which should for a moment take the shape of a necessity.

"But the fifth—the other fellow—the blear-eyed—what of him? You say nothing of him, Humphries."

Singleton pointed through the copse as he spoke, where the individual referred to leaned against a tree, a little apart from the rest; his head cast down, his arms relaxed beside him, one leg at ease, while the whole weight of his body rested upon the other. The features of his face were dark and unprepossessing—dark and sallow; his cheeks lank and colourless; a small nose; retreating forehead, covered with long thin black hair, that streamed from under a broad white hat, something the worse for wear. A strange protrusion of his eyes gave his face a gross and base expression, which was not before lacking to produce distrust, or even dislike, in the mind of the observer. Humphries gazed on him a moment before he spoke, then, as if satisfied, he proceeded to reply—

"I know nothing against the chap, major; but the truth is, I don't like him. Indeed, I know nobody that does. His right name is Blonay, but we all know him better by the name of Goggle—a nickname which he got on account of his eyes. Something has hurt them when young, which, you see, makes him stare when he looks at you."

"Well, but we must not refuse him because he has got a blear eye; we are too much in need of men to stand upon trifles. Know you nothing against him?"

"The blood's bad that's in him. His father was a horse-thief, and they do say, a mulatto or an Indian. As for himself, the worst is, that we know nothing about him; and that's no good sign, major, in a country where everybody knows the business of everybody. How he lives, and where and by what means he gets his bread, is a secret. He will not work; but see him when you will, you see him as you see him now—one half of him sleeping while the other half takes the watch. Not that he can't move when the time comes for it—or rather when he's in the humour for it. Touch him close upon his goggle eye, and he's up in arms in a moment. He will fight like a wildcat, too, and that's in his favour; but the worst is, he fights with a bad heart, and loves to remember injuries. I do believe they keep him from sleep at night. He's not like our people in that; he can't knock away at once, and have done with it, but he goes to bed to think about it, and to plan when to knock, so as never to have done with it. He loves to keep his wrongs alive, so that he may always be revenging."

"Still, I see nothing, lieutenant, that should make us discourage his desires; and, truth to say, it is far easier for us now to keep doubtful friends in our ranks, moving with us, and continually under our eye, than positive enemies in our camp in the form of prisoners, whom we are bound to keep guard over. We can manage our allies if they show signs of bad faith, although we risk something, doubtless, even by the partial confidence. Better do this than break up our little force watching those who profess themselves friends, and may yet prove so."

"You may be right, major, and I only speak perhaps from an old prejudice; but keep an eye upon him, for he certainly will keep one on you. Even now he is looking slyly to this bush, although he can't see or hear either of us, but after the old fashion, to find out what he can. If he were only honest, he'd be a spy among a thousand."

"I will see to him in particular, and if it be possible to drill honesty into him, something may be got out of him yet. We must take him."

"Very good, sir;—and you now go back into the camp?"

"Yes: we must put the wounded man into some sort of care, though he will suffer, wanting attendance."

"Leave that to me, sir. You take him into camp, and I have two men to come out this very day, one of whom is a sort of doctor—good as any one hereabout. He used to drench horses in Dorchester; and some of the grannies did say, that there were no drinks like those made by Doctor Oakenburg. But that, I'm thinking, was because he put more brandy in them than anything else; and if a Dorchester granny loves one thing more than another, after opium, it is brandy; and sometimes, liking them equally well, she takes both together. He, major, and the old negro, with some one of the troop, will be guard enough, and Frampton's son Lance can stay with them in the swamp. He's quite too young to be of much service, and will only learn what's bad, going with the troop."

"I have thought better of that, and shall endeavour to attach the lad to myself, and probably, in the end, place him at 'The Oaks' with my uncle. But time wears, and we must move for the camp. I shall take these men into service, and place the wounded man under the charge of one of the troopers, and your doctor can relieve him."

"Well, the doctor will be here to-day with Lieutenant Porgy"—

"Porgy—an ancient and fishlike name."

"Yes, but Lieutenant Porgy is not a fish—though you may call him a strange one. He is more fleshy than fishy; for that matter he has flesh enough for a score of dragoons. He's a perfect mountain of flesh."

"He will never suit for a dragoon, Humphries."

"Well, Sir, if I didn't know the man, I should think so too; but he rides like the devil, and fights like blazes. He's been fighting from the very beginning of the war down in the south. He comes from the Ashepoo, and is a mighty smart fellow, I tell you. You'll like him. Lord, how he can talk. You'll like him, I know. He's been a rich planter in his time, but he's ate and drank and talked

everything away, I reckon, but his horse, his nigger servant, and
his broadsword."

"And he's one of our lieutenants, you say."

"Yes, he joined us, saying he had been a lieutenant from the
beginning, with Harden and Moultrie, and he wasn't going to be
less with anybody else. You'll like him, Sir, he's a man; though
he's a mountain of flesh."

"Very good. I suppose you know him well, and now to other
matters."

Counselling thus, the two continued to confer apart upon other
matters connected with their enterprise. To visit "The Oaks"
during the day, where his uncle and sister resided, was the object
of Singleton; out his desire was also to intercept the supply of
arms and ammunition of which Huck had spoken as on their way
to Dorchester. They were looked for hourly, and could not be
very remote. It was determined, therefore, to intercept them, if
practicable, as an acquisition of the last importance. To arrange
their route, plan the place of their next meeting, provide the means
of intelligence, and concert what local measures might seem necessary in future, was the work of but little time between the two;
and this done, Humphries, withdrawing silently from the cover in
which the conference had been carried on, unperceived by the rest,
made his way by a different route out of the swamp, and keeping
the forest all the way, was, after no long time, safely in Dorchester
—looking for all the world as pacific and quiet as ever—without
weapon of any kind, as, with a wonted precaution, he had left his
sword in the woods, safely hidden, and his hands now grasped only
the common wagon-whip, which he handled with a dexterity which
seemed to indicate but little acquaintance with any more dangerous or deadly instruments.

Major Singleton, in the mean while, had returned to his troop.
They had been busied during his absence in collecting the scattered
horses and arms, and repairing their own little losses. The captives
were loud in the profession of their new faith, as patriots; and as
rebellion loves company, the whigs were not unwilling to receive
an accession, even from their late enemies. Major Singleton declared his acceptance of their services, taking care to address him

self particularly to the man Blonay, or, as they styled him more familiarly, Goggle. An awkward touch of the hat acknowledged this last courtesy, and one eye of Goggle, as he made the movement, peered up into that of Singelton with a searching and doubtful glance. The major did not appear to notice him or them any farther, but, giving directions for the disposal of the wounded sergeant, Clough, so as to spare him as much pain as possible, he led the way once more to the cover of the secluded place, in the centre of the swamp, which had been chosen as their camping-ground.

Here the whole party arrived at length, and having completed his arrangements, placing Clough in charge of one of his dragoons, and in as much comfort as possible, Major Singleton gave the word, and the squad moved forward on their way out of the swamp, and in the direction of the village. But this course was only kept while he yet remained in the swamp. As soon as he emerged from it, he drew up his men, and then, for the first time, perceived the absence of the elder Frampton. The two sons had kept with the troop, and seemed to know nothing of their father. The younger had ridden close beside his commander, who had so willed it. Nobody could give him any account of the absent man after his removal from the body of the corporal whom he had slain. He had disappeared suddenly, it was thought at that juncture, and there were not wanting those who insisted upon his absence from that moment; but Singleton remembered to have seen him after they had reached the camp, and to have noted the singular composedness of his features. But few farther inquiries were made after the absentee, as the major well knew that with a man in such a mood but little could be done. He was, perhaps, perfectly satisfied that nothing could have happened to him, from the composure of the two sons, who, doubtless, were acquainted with all the father's movements. Conjecture succeeded to inquiry, but was interrupted by the order to move on.

The course of the troop lay now towards the Goose Creek road. Major Singleton dared not carry his squad along the Ashley without exposing himself, unnecessarily, to unequal encounter; and, at Dorchester, with a force far superior to his own. Pursuing a northerly direction for a while, therefore, he placed himself at equal distances between the Wassamasah and Dorchester roads; then striking to the left, he passed over an untravelled surface of country, broken with frequent swamps, and crowded with luxuriant undergrowth. In a few hours, however, he had gone over the ground almost unseen, and certainly unobstructed. Davis was his guide in this quarter, and he could not have had a better. The discarded lover had given sufficient earnest of his truth and valour, in the courage and perfect coolness of his conduct in the preceding struggle; and he now led the party with all the caution of the veteran, and all the confidence of a thorough-bred soldier.

The road, like all in that country, was low and miry; and the path taken for greater security, being little travelled, was still more troubled with natural obstructions. They reached the desired point at length, which was the Goose Creek Bridge; then leaving it to the left, they once more departed from the beaten track, and throwing themselves directly across the country, were, after a few hours, again upon the Dorchester road, and some two or three miles below the garrison. They covered themselves in the close forest by Archdale Hall, and Singleton then proceeded to inspect the road. To his great satisfaction, he saw that the wagons had not yet made their appearance, and must be still below them. Cheered with this conviction, he despatched scouts to bring him intelligence, and then proceeded to arrange an ambush for the entrapping of the looked-for detachment.

The road, at the spot chosen for this purpose, was narrow—but a single track, and that raised into a causeway from a ditch on either side, at that time filled with water, and presenting natural advantages for the forming of an ambush. The woods, growing close and thickly, formed a natural defile, of which Singleton, with the eye of experience, soon availed himself. He divided his little force into two equal bodies; and giving the command of one of them to Davis, placed him upon the right of the road in the route from Charleston, while he himself occupied the left. The former division lying in covert some fifty yards below, was ready, in the event of a struggle between the baggage guard and Singleton's troop—to which it was to be left—to secure the precious charge which the guard had undertaken to defend, and at the same time

5

to cut off their retreat. Thus arranged, and with the plan of con-duct properly understood on all hands, the parties lay close hidden, impatiently awaiting the approach of the enemy.

They had not long to wait; for, scarcely had their arrangements been well completed, before the scouts came at full gallop along the path, crying loudly that the enemy was at hand. A shot or two whistled over the heads of the fugitives at the same moment, giving full confirmation to their intelligence ; and a few seconds after, the rush of half a score of British dragoons was heard upon their footsteps. Passing through the ambuscade without pausing for an instant, the scouts kept on their flight, bringing the pursu-ers fairly between the two parties. Once enclosed, a shrill whistle from Singleton announced the charge which, he led in person ; and dashing out from his cover, he threw his men quickly between the flying scouts and the assailants. In the same moment the squad of Davis obeying the same signal, as repeated by their leader, followed him as he charged upon the force left in possession of the munition wagons. The guard in this quarter, seeing the superi-ority of the force opposed to them, and struck with surprise, offered but a feeble resistance, and were soon put to flight. Davis fol-lowed them a little distance, and then returned to the aid of Sin-gleton. His approach and attack upon the rear of the party with which his commander had been contending, put an end to the fight—the dragoons having lost three men killed and two wounded. With the charge of Davis, they threw down their arms and were made prisoners.

CHAPTER X

"I see the shape of murder, with red hand,
That through the night creeps to his victim's couch."

THE whole affair was over in the space of ten minutes. In as little time the wagons were sacked. The swords and pistols were strewn upon the ground, and each trooper made his selection without stint or limit. In addition to this, each soldier was required to carry an extra sword, and holsters with their contents; and in this manner supplies were secured for a much larger force than that which Singleton now commanded. The rest were broken against the trees—muskets, pistols, and swords sharing the same fate—while the wagons themselves, carefully tumbled from their axles, and their wheels torn apart, were thrown into the slough by the road-side. There was no concealing their spoils, under the circumstances, and with prisoners to take care of; and the necessity which called for this destruction of property, so valuable at the time, was the subject of no small regret with the troopers. Even Davis muttered to the major his desire that the wagons, or at least one of them, should be preserved and filled with spoils so highly important to the enterprise. But Singleton knew better than to encumber his party, whose utility consisted chiefly in the rapidity of its movement, with such burdens, and peremptorily enforced the order which destroyed the valuable residue. This done, he gave orders to mount; and having carefully secured his prisoners, the party moved at a brisk pace along the road downward until they came within ten miles of the city; then moving to the right, they crossed Ashley ferry without molestation, and towards evening had placed themselves in safety, with all their spoils, in the close swamp thickets of the river, on the western side, and but a short distance from Dorchester itself.

Here Singleton made his camp, within a few miles of his uncle's plantation. He now felt secure for a brief period, as he was taught to believe that the affections of the people were with his cause, and the rapidity of his proceedings must baffle any pursuit. Still he knew that he could not hope to maintain this security for any time. The audacity of the two efforts which he had made that day, so nigh the garrison, could not long be concealed, and must soon call out a superior force sufficient for his annihilation. This he well knew; yet he required but a few days for all his purposes.

His object was twofold—the attainment of recruits, and the arousing of his uncle, whose bravery was well known, and whose influence in the country was considerable, to a proper sense of his duty. The first of these objects promised well, so far as opportunity had been given him to judge;—of the second, he did not despair, particularly as he well knew what must be the influence upon Colonel Walton of the recent proclamation of Sir Henry Clinton. He knew the stern sense of integrity which the colonel insisted upon with the tenacity of a professional moral disciplinarian; and he did not err in the thought, that his sense of humanity was sufficiently alive to prompt a due indignation at the many atrocities hourly committed by the tory leaders under the especial sanction of the British. Other motives for the contemplated visit might not be wanting to his mind, as he thought of his lovely cousin—the stately and the beautiful Katharine Walton—one of those high-souled creatures that awe while they attract; and, even while they invite and captivate, control and discourage. His sister, too—she was there; a meek, sad, but uncomplaining girl, perishing of disease, without having lived—one of the unrepining sufferers, whose melancholy fortunes, so much at variance with what we know of their deserts, would lead us sometimes improperly to doubt of that justice which we assume to mark all the decrees of Providence. But let us not anticipate.

Having placed his camp in such security as he thought necessary and which was practicable, Major Singleton towards sunset rode forth in the direction of Dorchester Bridge to meet Humphries, as had been agreed upon between them. The lieutenant was in waiting at the time appointed, and came forward to meet his superoir.

" Ride aside, Major Singleton, if you please. The brush is best for us just now. There are strange birds on our road that we must sheer from."

" What mean you, Humphries—what birds ?"

" British officers ! Major Proctor, himself, and another have just gone by ; and if I mistake not, on a visit to ' The Oaks.' They say he looks hard upon your cousin, sir, the beautiful Miss Katharine."

" Ha ! do they say that ?" responded Major Singleton, with something like a start—" and she ?" he continued, inquiringly.

" They say nothing of her, whether she likes it or not ; but young ladies will be young ladies, major ; and a smart officer, with a king's commission in his pocket, and a showy red coat on his back, is no small danger to an easy heart."

" No, indeed !" replied the other, in a tone which seemed to have found nothing consolatory in his companion's reflection, and in which there may have been something of latent bitterness— " no, indeed !—such attractions are at all times sweet with the sex, and seldom utterly unsuccessful. They love the conquest, always, even when they may despise the game. 'Tis with most of them after this fashion, and the goodly outside is a fair offset to worth and good manners. But how shall we know, of a certainty, the destination of Proctor ?"

" Only by dogging his footsteps, major. We may do that with some safety, however, as I happen to know the back track which hugs the river, and is seldom travelled. This brings us close on the park, yet gives us a good shelter all the way along the copse. We shall take our watch, and yet be all the time hidden ; and where I shall carry you shall give us a fair peep at all the grounds as well as the river."

" That is well. And now of Dorchester ; what stirs in the village ? and what of Huck ? Do they know yet of the affair of the swamp, or are they ever like to know ?"

" They know not yet, certainly ; but Huck musters strong, and talks of a drive to Camden. There is news, too, which moves the garrison much. They talk of the continentals from Virginia."

" Do they ? they must be De Kalb's. And what do they say on the subject ? do they speak of him as at hand ?"

" Nothing much, but they look a deal, and the whigs talk a little more boldly. This provokes Huck, who threatens a start on the strength of it, and is hurrying his recruits for that purpose. There is also some talk of a force from North Carolina under Sumter, and they have got wind of the last move of our Colonel Marion, there-away among Gainey's corps of tories, where you cut them up in such fine style; but there's nothing certain, and this I get out of Huck in curses now and then. He's mighty anxious that I should join him, and I'm thinking to do so, if it promises to give me a better hold on him."

" Think not of it, Humphries ; it will be twice putting your neck in the halter, and the good that it may do is too doubtful to justify such a risk."

" He presses me mighty hard, major, and I must keep out of his way or consent. He begins to wonder why I do not join his troop, and with some reason too, believing me to be a loyalist, for certainly, were I to do so, it would be the very making of me."

" Thou wouldst not turn traitor, Humphries ?" replied the other, looking sternly upon the speaker.

" Does Major Singleton ask the question now ?" was the reply, in a tone which had in it something of reproach.

" I should not, certainly, Humphries, knowing what I do. Forgive me ; but in these times there is so much to make us suspect our neighbours, that suspicions become natural to every mind. You I know, however, and I have trusted you too long not to continue in my confidence now. But how come on our recruits ?"

" Tolerably ; as you say, these are suspicious times, major, and they are slow to trust. But the feeling is good with us, and they only wait to see some of the chances in our favour before they come out boldly in the cause."

" Now, out upon the calculating wretches ! Will they dare nothing, but always wait for the lead of others ? Chances, indeed ! as if true courage and a bold heart did not always make their own.

But what of the villagers ? How of that old tavern-keeper of whom you spoke—your father's rival ?"

" But so no longer. Old Pryor, you mean. He is a prime piece of stuff, and will not scruple to do what's wanted. He was always true with us, though kept down by those about him ; yet he only wants to see others in motion to move too. He'll do any thing now—the more readily, as the Royal George, being entirely loyal, does all the business; and poor Pryor, being all along suspected, has not a customer left. He'd burn the town, now, if we put it into his head !"

" Well, just now we lack no such spirit. May not his rashness prompt him to too much speech ?"

" No, sir ; that's the beauty of rebellion with old Pryor. It has hands and a weapon, but it wants tongue. If he felt pain, and was disposed to tell of it, his teeth would resist, and grin down the feeling. No fear of him ; he talks too little : and as for blabbing, his wife might lie close, and listen all night, and his dreams would be as speechless as his humour. He locks up his thoughts in close jaws, and at best only damns a bit when angered, and walks off with his hands in his breeches pocket."

" A goodly comrade for a dark night ! But let us move. Dusk closes upon us, and we may travel now with tolerable security. Our course is for the river ?"

" Yes ; a hundred yards will take us in sight of it, and we keep it the whole way. But we must hug the bush, as much out of sight there as if we were upon the high-road. There are several boats, chiefly armed, upon it now ; besides the galley which runs up and down—some that have brought supplies to the garrison Their shot would be troublesome did they see us."

They rode down the hill, entered a long copse, and the river wound quietly on its way a little below them. They were now on a line with the fortress of Dorchester; the flag streamed gaudily from the staff, and they could see through the bushes that several vessels of small burden were passing to and fro. They sank back again into the woods, and kept on their course in comparative silence, until, close upon sunset, they found themselves at a few hundred yards from " The Oaks ;" the spacious and lofty dwelling rising dimly out of the woods before them, while from their feet the extensive grounds of the park spread away in distance and final obscurity.

Leaving them to amuse themselves as they may, let us now re turn to the Cypress Swamp, where we left the wounded Clough under the charge of the dragoon and negro. The injury he had received, though not, perhaps, a fatal one, was yet serious enough to render immediate attention highly important to his safety; but in that precarious time surgeons were not readily to be found, and the Americans, who were without money, were not often indulged with their services. The several corps of the leading partisans, such as Marion, and Sumter, Pickens, Horry, &c., fought daily in the swamps and along the highways, with the painful conviction that, save by some lucky chance, their wounds must depend entirely upon nature to be healed. In this way, simply through want of tendance, hundreds perished in that warfare of privation, whom, with a few simple specifics, medical care would have sent again into the combat, after a few weeks' nursing, hearty and unimpaired. The present circumstances of Clough's condition were not of a character to lead him to hope for a better fortune, and he gave himself up despondingly to his fate, after having made a brief effort to bribe his keeper to assist in his escape. But attendance was at hand, if we may so call it, and after a few hours' suffering, the approach of Doctor Oakenburg was announced to the patient.

The doctor was a mere culler of simples, a stuffer of birds and reptiles, a digger of roots, a bark and poultice doctor—in other words, a mere pretender. He was wretchedly ignorant of every thing like medical art, but he had learned to physic. He made beverages which, if not always wholesome, were, at least, sometimes far from disagreeable to the country housewives, who frequently took the nostrum for the sake of the stimulant. Doctor Oakenburg knew perfectly the want, if he cared little for the need, of his neighbours; and duly heedful of those around him who indulged in pipe and tobacco, he provided the bark and the brandy. A few bitter roots and herbs constituted his entire stock of medicines; and with these, well armed at all points and never unprovided, he had worked out for himself no small reputation in that section of country. But this good fortune lasted only for a season. Some of his patients took their departure after the established fashion; some more inveterate, with that prejudice which distinguishes the bad subject, turned their eyes on rival remedies; many were scattered abroad and beyond the reach of our doctor by the chances of war; and, with a declining reputation and wofully diminished practice, Oakenburg was fain, though a timid creature, to link his own with the equally doubtful fortunes of the partisan militia. This decision, after some earnest argument, and the influence of a more earnest necessity, Humphries at length persuaded him to adopt, after having first assured him of the perfect security and unharming character of the warfare in which he was required to engage.

With a dress studiously disposed in order, a head well plastered with pomatum, and sprinkled with the powder so freely worn at the time, a ragged frill carefully adjusted upon his bosom to conceal the injuries of time, and an ostentatious exhibition of the shrunken shank, garnished at the foot with monstrous buckles that once might have passed for silver, Oakenburg still persisted in exhibiting as many of the evidences of the reduced gentleman as he possibly could preserve. His manner was tidy, like his dress. His snuff-box twinkled for ever between his fingers, one of which seemed swollen by the monstrous paste ring which enriched it; and his gait was dancing and elastic, as if his toes had volunteered to do all the duty of his feet. His mode of speech, too, was excessively finical and delicate—the words passing through his lips with difficulty; for he dreaded to open them too wide, lest certain deficiencies in his jaws should become too conspicuously notorious. These deficiencies had the farther effect of giving him a lisping accent, which not a little added to the pretty delicacies of his other features.

He passed through the swamp with infinite difficulty, and greatly to the detriment of his shoes and stockings. Riding a small tackey (a little, inconsiderate animal, that loves the swamp, and is usually born and bred in it), he was compelled continually to be on the look-out for, and defence against, the overhanging branches and vines clustering about the trees, through which his horse, in its own

5*

desire to clamber over the roots, continually and most annoyingly bore him. In this toil he was compelled to pay far less attention to his legs than was due ·to their well-being, and it was not until they were well drenched in the various bogs through which he had gone, that he was enabled to see how dreadfully he had neglected their even elevation to the saddle skirts—a precaution absolutely necessary at all times in such places, but more particularly when the rider is tall, and mounted upon a short, squat animal, such as our worthy doctor bestrode.

Dr. Oakenburg was in the company—under the guidance in fact—of a person whose appearance was in admirable contrast with his own. This was no other than the Lieutenant Porgy, of whom Humphries has already given us an account. If Oakenburg was as lean as the Knight of La Mancha, Porgy was quite as stout as Sancho—a shade stouter perhaps, as his own height was not inconsiderable, yet showed him corpulent still. At a glance you saw that he was a jovial philosopher—one who enjoyed his bottle with his humours, and did not suffer the one to be soured by the other. It was clear that he loved all the good things of this life, and some possibly that we may not call good with sufficient reason. His abdomen and brains seemed to work together. He thought of eating perpetually, and, while he ate, still thought. But he was not a mere eater. He rather amused himself with a hobby when he made food his topic, as Falstaff discoursed of his own cowardice without feeling it. He was a wag, and exercised his wit with whomsoever he travelled; Doctor Oakenburg, on the present occasion, offering himself as an admirable subject for victimization. To quiz the doctor was Porgy's recipe against the tedium of a swamp progress, and the fertile humours of the wag perpetually furnished him occasions for the exercise of his faculty. But we shall hear more of him in future pages, and prefer that he shall speak on most occasions for himself. He was attended by a negro body servant—a fellow named Tom, and of humours almost as keen and lively as his own. Tom was a famous cook, after the fashion of the southern planters, who could win his way to your affections through his soups, and need no other argument. He was one of that class of faithful, half-spoiled negroes, who will

never suffer any liberties with his master, except such as he takes
himself. He, too, is a person who will need to occupy a considerable place in our regards, particularly as, in his instance, as well as
that of his master—to say nothing of other persons—we draw our
portraits from actual life.

Porgy was a good looking fellow, spite of his mammoth dimensions. He had a fine fresh manly face, clear complexion, and
light blue eye, the archness of which was greatly heightened by its
comparative littleness. It was a sight to provoke a smile on the
face of Mentor, to see those little blue eyes twinkling with treache-
rous light as he watched Doctor Oakenburg plunging from pool
to pool under his false guidance, and condoling with him after.
The doctor, in fact, in his present situation and imperfect experience, could not have been spared his disasters. He was too little
of an equestrian not to feel the necessity, while battling with his
brute for their mutual guidance, of keeping his pendulous members
carefully balanced on each side, to prevent any undue preponder-
ance of one over the other—a predicament of which he had much
seeming apprehension. In the mean time, the lively great-bodied
and great-bellied man who rode beside him chuckled incontinently,
though in secret. He pretended great care of his companion, and
advised him to sundry changes of direction, all for the worse, which
the worthy doctor in his tribulation did not scruple to adopt.

" Ah! Lieutenant Porgy," said he, complaining, though in his
most mincing manner, as they reached a spot of dry land, upon
which they stopped for a moment's rest—" ah! Lieutenant Porgy
this is but unclean travelling, and full too of various peril. At one
moment I did hear a plunging, dashing sound in the pond beside
me, which it came to my thought was an alligator—one of those
monstrous reptiles that are hurtful to children, and even to men."

" Ay, doctor, and make no bones of whipping off a thigh-bone,
or at least a leg : and you have been in danger more than once
o-day."

The doctor looked down most wofully at his besmeared pedes-
als ; and the shudder which went over his whole frame was per-
eptible to his companion, whose chuckle it increased proportion-
ably.

"And yet, Lieutenant Porgy," said he, looking round him with a most wo-begone apprehension—"yet did our friend Humphries assure me that our new occupation was one of perfect security. 'Perfect security' were the precise words he used when he coun selled me to this undertaking."

"Perfect security!" said Porgy, and the man laughed out aloud. "Why, doctor, look there at the snake winding over the bank be fore you—look at that, and then talk of perfect security."

The doctor turned his eyes to the designated point, and beheld the long and beautiful volumes of the beaded snake, as slowly crossing their path with his pack of linked jewels full in their view, he wound his way from one bush into another, and gradually folded himself up out of sight. The doctor, however, was not to be alarmed by this survey. He had a passion for snakes; and admiration suspended all his fear, as he gazed upon the beautiful and not dangerous reptile.

"Now would I rejoice, Lieutenant Porgy, were yon serpent in my poor cabinet at Dorchester. He would greatly beautify my collection." And as the man of simples spoke, he gazed on the retiring snake with envying eye.

"Well, doctor, get down and chunk it. If it's worth having, it's worth killing."

"True, Lieutenant Porgy; but it would be greatly detrimental to my shoes to alight in such a place as this, for the thick mud would adhere—"

"Ay, and so would you, doctor—you'd stick—but not the snake. But come, don't stand looking after the bush, if you won't go into it. You can get snakes enough in the swamp—ay, and without much seeking. The place is full of them."

"This of a certainty, Lieutenant Porgy? know you this?"

"Ay, I know it of my own knowledge. You can see them here almost any hour in the day, huddled up like a coil of rope on the edge of the tussock, and looking down at their own pretty figures in the water."

"And you think the serpent has vanity of his person?" inquired the doctor, gravely.

"Think—I don't think about it, doctor—I know it," replied the other, confidently. "And it stands to reason, you see, that where there is beauty and brightness there must be self-love and vanity. It's a poor fool that don't know his own possessions."

"There is truly some reason, Lieutenant Porgy, in what you have said touching this matter; and the instinct is a correct one which teaches the serpent, such as that which we have just seen, to look into the stream as one of the other sex into a mirror, to see that its jewels are not displaced, and that its motion may not be awry, but graceful. There is reason in it."

"And truth. But we are nigh our quarters, and here is a soldier waiting us."

"A soldier, squire!—he is friendly, perhaps?"

The manner of the phrase was interrogatory, and Porgy replied with his usual chuckle.

"Ay, ay, friendly enough, though dangerous, if vexed. See what a sword he carries—and those pistols! I would not risk much, doctor, to say, there are no less than sixteen buckshot in each of those barkers."

"My! you don't say so, lieutenant. Yet did William Humphries say to me that the duty was to be done in perfect security."

The last sentence fell from the doctor's lips in a sort of comment to himself, but his companion replied—

"Ay, security as perfect, doctor, as war will admit of. You talk of perfect security: there is no such thing—no perfect security any where—and but little security of any kind until dinner's well over. I feel the uncertainty of life till then. Then, indeed, we may know as much security as life knows. We have, at least, secured what secures life. We may laugh at danger then; and if we must meet it, why, at least we shall not be compelled to meet it in that worst condition of all—an empty stomach. I am a true Englishman in that, though they do call me a rebel. I feel my origin only when eating; and am never so well disposed towards the enemy as when I'm engaged, tooth and nail, in that savoury occupation, and with roast-beef. Would that we had some of it now!"

The glance of Oakenburg, who was wretchedly spare and lank, looked something of disgust as he heard this speech of the gour-

mand, and listened to the smack of his lips with which he con
cluded it.

He had no taste for corpulence, and probably this was one of
the silent impulses which taught him to admire the gaunt and
attenuated form of the snake. Porgy did not heed his expression
of countenance, but looking up overhead where the sun stood just
above them peering down imperfectly through the close umbrage,
he exclaimed to the soldier, while pushing his horse through the
creek which separated them—

"Hark you, Wilkins, boy, is it not high time to feed? Horse and
man—man and horse, boy, all hungry and athirst."

"We shall find a bite for you, lieutenant, before long—but
here's a sick man the doctor must see to at once: he's in a mighty
bad way, I tell you."

"A sick man, indeed!" and the doctor, thrusting his hands into
his pocket, drew forth a bottle filled with a dark thick liquid,
which he shook violently until it gathered into a foam upon the
surface. Armed with this, he approached the little bark shanty
under which reposed the form of the wounded Clough.

"You are hurt, worthy sir?" said the mediciner, inquiringly;
"you have not been in a condition of perfect security—such as
life requires. But lie quiet, I pray you; be at ease, while I look
into your injuries," said the doctor, condolingly, and proceeded to
the outstretched person of the wounded man with great deliberation.

"You need not look very far—here they are," cried Clough,
faintly, but peevishly, in reply, as he pointed to the wound in his
side.

The doctor looked at the spot, shook his head, clapped on a
plaster of pine gum, and administered a dose of his nostrum, which
the patient gulped at prodigiously, and then telling him he would
do well, repeated his order to lie quiet and say nothing. Hurrying away to his saddle-bags after this had been done, with the
utmost despatch he drew forth a pair of monstrous leggings, which
he bandaged carefully around his shrunken shanks. In a moment
after he was upon his tackey, armed with a stick, and hastening
back upon the route he had just passed over.

Porgy, who was busy urging the negro cook in the preparation of his dinner, cried out to the dealer of simples, but received no answer. The doctor had no thought but of the snake he had seen, for whose conquest and capture he had now set forth, with all the appetite of a boy after adventures, and all the anxiety of an inveterate naturalist, to get at the properties of the object he pursued. Meanwhile the new comer, Porgy, had considerably diverted the thought of the trooper from attention to his charge ; and laying down his sabre between them, the sentinel threw himself along the ground where Porgy had already stretched himself, and a little lively chat and good company banished from his mind, for a season, the consideration of his prisoner.

His neglect furnished an opportunity long watched and waited for by another. The shanty in which Clough lay stood on the edge of the island, and was one of those simple structures which the Indian makes· in his huntings. A stick rested at either end between the crotch of a tree, and small saplings, leaning against it on one side, were covered with broad flakes of the pine bark. A few bushes, piled up partially in front, completed the structure, which formed no bad sample of the mode of hutting it, winter and summer, in the swamps and forests of the South, by the partisan warriors. In the rear of the fabric stood a huge cypress, from the hollow of which, at the moment when the sentinel and Porgy seemed most diverted, a man might have been seen approaching. He cautiously wound along on all-fours, keeping as much out of sight as possible, until he reached the back of the hut ; then lifting from the saplings a couple of the largest pieces of bark which covered them, he introduced his body without noise into the tenement of the wounded man.

Clough was in a stupor—a half-dozy consciousness was upon him—and he muttered something to the intruder, though without any fixed object. The man replied not, but approaching closely, put his hand upon the bandagings of the wound, drawing them gently aside. The first distinct perception which the prisoner had of his situation was the agonizing sense of a new wound, as of some sharp weapon driven directly into the passage made by the old one. He writhed under the instrument as it slanted deeper **and** deeper into his vitals; but he had not strength to resist, and but little to cry out. He would have done so; but the sound had scarcely risen to his lips, when the murderer thrust a tuft of grass into his mouth and stifled all complaint. The knife went deeper— the whole frame of the assailant was upon it, and all motion ceased on the part of the sufferer with the single groan and distorted writhing which followed the last agony. In a moment after, the stranger had departed by the way he came; and it was not till he had reached the thick swamp around, that the fearful laugh of the maniac, Frampton—for it was he—announced the success of his new effort at revenge.

The laugh reached Porgy and the dragoon—they heard the groan also, but that was natural enough. Nothing short of absolute necessity could have moved either of them at that moment— the former being busied with a rasher of bacon and a hoe-cake hot from the fire, and the latter indulging in an extra swig of brandy from a canteen which Porgy, with characteristic providence, had brought well filled along with him.

CHAPTER XI.

" Now, this were sorry wisdom, to persuade
   My sword to mine own throat. If I must out,
   Why should I out upon mine ancient friend
   And spare mine enemy ?"

" THE OAKS," the dwelling-place of Colonel Walton, was one
of those antique residences of the Carolina planters to which, at
this day, there attaches a sort of historical interest. A thousand
local traditions hang around them—a thousand stories of the olden
time, and of its associations of peril and adventure. The estate
formed one of the frontier-plantations upon the Ashley, and was
the site of a colonial barony. It had stood sieges of the Indians
in the wars of the Edistoes and Yemassees ; and, from a blockhouse station at first, it had grown to be an elegant mansion,
improved in European style, remarkable for the length and deep
shade of its avenues of solemn oak, its general grace of arrangement, and the lofty and considerate hospitality of its proprietors.
Such, from its first foundation to the period of which we speak,
had been its reputation ; and in no respect did the present owner
depart from the good tastes and the frank, manly character of his
ancestors.

Colonel Richard Walton was a gentleman in every sense of the
word ; simple of manner, unpretending, unobtrusive, and always
considerate, he was esteemed and beloved by all around him. Born
to the possession of large estates, his mind had been exercised
happily by education and travel ; and at the beginning of the
revolutionary struggle, he had been early found to advocate the
claims of his native colony. At the commencement of the war
he commanded a party of horse, and had been concerned in some
of the operations against Prevost, in the rapid foray which that
general made into Carolina. When Charleston fell before the arms

of Sir Henry Clinton, overawed as was the entire country below
the Santee by the immediate presence in force of the British army,
he had tendered his submission along with the rest of the inhabitants, despairing of any better fortune.   The specious offers of
amnesty made by Clinton and Arbuthnot, in the character of com-
missioners for restoring peace to the revolted colonies, and which
called for nothing but neutrality from the inhabitants, had the
effect of deceiving him, in common with his neighbours.   Nor was
this submission so partial as we have been taught to think it.   To
the southward of Charleston, the militia, without summons, sent in
a flag to the British garrison at Beaufort, and made their submission.   At Camden, the inhabitants negotiated their own terms of
repose.   In Ninety-Six the submission was the same ; and, indeed,
with the exception of the mountainous borders, which were unin-
vaded, and heard only faint echoes of the conflict from afar, all
show of hostility ceased throughout the colony—the people, generally, seeming to prefer quiet on any terms to a resistance which,
at that moment of despondency, seemed worse than idle.

This considerate pliability secured Walton, as it was thought, in
all the immunities of the citizen, without subjecting him to any
of those military duties which, in other respects, his majesty had
a perfect right to call for from his loyal subjects.   Such, certainly,
were the pledges of the British commanders—pledges made with
little reflection, or with designed subterfuge, and violated with as
little hesitation.   They produced the effect desired, in persuading
to easy terms of arrangement the people who might not have been
conquered but with great difficulty.   Once disarmed and divided,
they were more easily overcome ; and it was not long, after the
first object had been obtained, before measures were adopted well
calculated to effect the other.

Colonel Walton, though striving hard to convince himself of
the propriety of the course which he had taken, remained still
unsatisfied.   He could not be assured of the propriety of submission when he beheld, as he did hourly, the rank oppression and
injustice by which the conquerors strove to preserve their ascendency over the doubtful, while exercising it wantonly among the
weak.   He could not but see how uncertain was the tenure of his

own hold upon the invaders, whom nothing seemed to bind in the shape of solemn obligation. The promised protection was that of the wolf, and not the guardian dog ; it destroyed its charge, and not its enemy ; and strove to ravage where it promised to secure. As yet, it is true, none of these ills, in a direct form, had fallen upon Colonel Walton ; he had suffered no abuses in his own person or family ; on the contrary, such were his wealth and influence, that it had been thought not unwise, on the part of the conquerors, to conciliate and soothe him. Still, the colonel could not be insensible to the gradual approaches of tyranny. He was not an unreflecting man ; and as he saw the wrongs done to others, his eyes became duly open to the doubtful value of his own securities, whenever the successes of the British throughout the state should have become so general as to make them independent o. any individual influence. So thinking; his mind gave a new stimulus to his conscience, which now refused its sanction to the decision which, in a moment of emergency and dismay, he had been persuaded to adopt. His sympathies were too greatly with the oppressed, and their sufferings were too immediately under his own eyes, to permit of this; and sad with the consciousness of his error—and the more so as he esteemed it now irremediable—vexed with his momentary weakness, and apprehensive of the future— his mind grew sullen with circumstances—his spirits sank ; and, gradually withdrawing from all the society around him, he solaced himself in his family mansion with the small circle which widowhood, and other privations of time, had spared him. Nor did his grief pass without some alleviation in the company of his daughter Katharine— she, the high-born, the beautiful, the young—the admiration of her neighbourhood, revelling in power, yet seemingly all unconscious of its sway. The rest of his family in this retirement consisted of a maiden sister, and a niece, Emily Singleton, whom, but a short time before, he had brought from Santee, in the hope that a change of air might be of benefit to that life which she held by a tenure the most fleeting and capricious.

He saw but few persons besides. Studiously estranging himself, he had no visitors, unless we may except the occasional calls of the commanding officer of the British post at Dorchester. This visitor, to Colonel Walton, appeared only as one doing an appointed duty, and exercising, during these visits, that kind of surveillance over the people of the country which seemed to be called for by his position. Major Proctor had another object in his visits to " The Oaks." He sought to ingratiate himself in the favour of the father, on account of his lovely daughter ; and to the charms of one, rather than the political feelings of the other, were the eyes of the British officer properly addressed. Katharine was not ignorant of her conquest, for Proctor made no efforts to conceal the impression which she had made upon his heart. The maiden, however, gave him but small encouragement. She gloried in the name of a rebel lady, and formed one of that beautiful array, so richly shining in the story of Carolina, who, defying danger, and heedless of privation, spoke boldly in encouragement to those who yet continued to struggle for its liberties. She did not conceal her sentiments ; and whatever may have been the personal attractions of Major Proctor, they were wanting in force to her mind, as she associated him with her own and the enemies of her country. Her reception of her suitor was coldly courteous ; and that which her father gave him, though always studiously considerate and gentle, Proctor, at the same time, could not avoid perceiving was constrained and frigid—quite unlike the warm and familiar hospitality which otherwise marked and still marks, even to this day, the gentry of that neighbourhood.

It was drawing to a close—that day of events in the history of our little squad of partisans whose dwelling was the Cypress Swamp. Humphries, who had engaged to meet Major Singleton with some necessary intelligence from Dorchester, was already upon his way to the place of meeting, and had just passed out of sight of Ashley River, when he heard the tramp of horses moving over the bridge, and on the same track with himself. He sank into cover as they passed, and beheld Major Proctor and a Captain Dickson, both on station at the garrison, on their way to " The Oaks." Humphries allowed them to pass ; then renewing his ride, soon effected the meeting with Major Singleton. As we have already seen, their object was " The Oaks " also ; but the necessity of avoiding a meeting with the British officers was obvious, and they

kept close in the wood, leaving the ground entirely to their oppo-
nents.

Though, as we have said, rather a frequent visitor at "The
Oaks," the present ride of Major Proctor in that quarter had its
usual stimulus dashed somewhat by the sense of the business which
occasioned it. Its discharge was a matter of no little annoyance
to the Englishman, who was not less sensitive and generous than
brave. It was for the purpose of imparting to Colonel Walton, in
person, the contents of that not yet notorious proclamation of Sir
Henry Clinton, with which he demanded the performance of military duty from the persons who had been paroled ; and by means
of which, on departing from the province, he planted the seeds of
that revolting patriotism which finally overthrew the authority he
fondly imagined himself to have successfully re-established.

Colonel Walton received his guests with his accustomed urbanity:
was alone when he received them; and the eyes of Proctor looked
round the apartment inquiringly, but in vain, as if he desired
another presence. His host understood the glance perfectly, for
he had not been blind to the frequent evidences of attachment
which his visitor had shown towards his daughter ; but he took no
heed of it ; and, with a lofty reserve of manner, which greatly
added to the awkwardness of the commission which the Englishman came to execute, he simply confined himself to the occasional
remark—such only as was perfectly unavoidable with one with
whom politeness was habitual, and the predominant feeling at
variance with it, the result of a calm and carefully regulated principle. It was only with a steady resolution, at last, that Proctor
was enabled to bring his conversation into any thing like con-
sistency and order. He commenced, despairing of any better
opening, with the immediate matter which he had in hand.

"Colonel Walton does not now visit Dorchester so frequently as
usual, nor does he often travel so far as the city. May I ask if he
has heard any late intelligence of moment."

Walton looked inquiringly at his guest, as if to gather from
his features something of that intelligence which his words seemed
to presage. But the expression was unsatisfactory—perhaps that
of care—so Walton thought, and it gave him a hope of some

better fortune for his country than had usually attended its arms heretofore.

"I have not, sir; I ride but little now, and have not been in Dorchester for a week. Of what intelligence do you speak, sir ?"

"The proclamation of Sir Henry Clinton, sir—his proclamation on the subject of protections granted to the militia of the province, those excepted made prisoners in Charleston."

Colonel Walton looked dubious, but still coldly, and without a word, awaited the conclusion of Proctor's statement. But the speaker paused for a moment, and when he again spoke, the subject seemed to have been somewhat changed.

"I am truly sorry, Colonel Walton, that it has not been heretofore in your power to sympathize more freely and openly with his majesty's arms in this warfare against his rebellious subjects."

"Stay, sir, if you please: these subjects, of whom your phrase is rather unscrupulous, are my relatives and countrymen; and their sentiments on this rebellion have been and are my own, though I have adopted the expedient of a stern necessity, and in this have suspended the active demonstration of principles which I am nevertheless in no haste to forget, and do not suppress."

"Pardon me, sir; you will do me the justice to believe I mean nothing of offence. However erring your thought, I must respect it as honest; but this respect does not forbid that I should lament such a misfortune—a misfortune, scarcely less so to his majesty than to you. It is my sincere regret that you have heretofore found it less than agreeable to unite your arms with those of our army in the arrest of this unnatural struggle. The commission proffered you by Sir Henry—"

"Was rejected, Major Proctor, and my opinions then fairly avowed and seemingly respected. No reference now to that subject need be made by either of us."

"Yet am I called upon to make it now, Colonel Walton; and I do so with a hope that what is my duty will not lose me, by its performance, the regard of him to whom I speak. I am counselled to remind you, sir, of that proposition by the present commander in-chief of his majesty's forces in the South, Earl Cornwallis. The proclamation of Sir Henry Clinton to which I have alluded,

is of such a nature as opens fresh ground for the renewal of that
offer ; and in this packet I have instructions to that end, with a
formal enclosure of seal and signature, from his excellency himself,
which covers the commission to you, sir, in your full rank, as
engaged in the rebel army."

" You will keep it, sir; again it is rejected. I cannot lift arms
against my countrymen; and though I readily understand the
necessity which requires you to make the tender, you will permit
me to say, that I hold it only an equivocal form of insult."

" Which, I again repeat, Colonel Walton, is foreign to all
intention on the part of the Commander-in-chief. For myself, I
surely need make no such attestation. He, sir, is persuaded to the
offer simply as he knows your worth and influence —he would
secure your co-operation in the good cause of loyalty, and at the
same time would soften what may seem the harsh features of this
proclamation."

" And what is this proclamation, sir ? Let me hear that : the matter has been somewhat precipitately discussed in advance of the text.'

" Surely, sir," said Proctor, eagerly, as the language of Colonel
Walton's last remarks left a hope in his mind that he might think
differently, on the perusal of the document, which he now took
from the hands of his companion, Dickson—" surely, sir, and I
hope you will reconsider the resolve which I cannot help thinking
precipitately made."

The listener simply bowed his head, and motioned the other to
proceed. Proctor obeyed ; and, unfolding the instrument, proceeded
to convey its contents to the ears of the astonished Carolinian.
As he read, the cheek of Colonel Walton glowed like fire—his eye
kindled—his pulsation increased—and when the insidious decree,
calling upon him to resume the arms which he had cast aside when
his country needed them, and lift them in behalf of her enemies,
was fairly comprehended by his sense, his feelings had reached that
climax which despaired of all utterance. He started abruptly from
his seat, and paced the room in strong emotion ; then suddenly
approaching Proctor, he took the paper from his hand, and read it
with unwavering attention. For a few moments after he had been
fully possessed of its contents, he made no remark; then with a

strong effort, suppressing as much as possible his aroused feelings, he addressed the Briton in tones of inquiry which left it doubtful what, in reality, those feelings were.

" And you desire that I should embrace this commission, Major Proctor, which, if I understand it, gives me command in a service which this proclamation is to insist upon—am I right ?".

" It is so, sir ; you are right. Here is a colonel's commission under his majesty, with power to appoint your own officers. Most gladly would I place it in your hands."

" Sir—Major Proctor, this is the rankest villany—villany and falsehood. By what right, sir, does Sir Henry Clinton call upon us for military service, when his terms of protection, granted by himself and Admiral Arbuthnot, secured all those taking them in a condition of neutrality ?"

" It is not for me, Colonel Walton," was Proctor's reply—" it is not for me to discuss the commands of my superiors. But does not the proclamation declare these paroles to be null and void after the twentieth ?"

" True. But by what right does your superior violate his compact ? Think you, sir, that the Carolinians would have made terms with the invader, the conditions and maintenance of which have no better security than the caprice of one of the parties ? Think you, sir, that I, at least, would have been so weak and foolish ?"

" Perhaps, Colonel Walton—and I would not offend by the suggestion," replied the other with much moderation—" perhaps, sir, it was a singular stretch of indulgence to grant terms at all to rebellion."

" Ay, sir, you may call it by what name you please ; but the terms, having been once offered and accepted, were to the full as binding between the law and the rebel as between the prince and dutiful subjects."

" I may not argue, sir, the commands of my superior," rejoined the other, firmly, but calmly.

" I am not so bound, Major Proctor ; it is matter for close argument and solemn deliberation with me, and it will be long, sir, before I shall bring myself to lift arms against my countrymen."

" There is a way of evading that necessity, Colonel Walton," said Proctor, eagerly.

The other looked at him inquiringly, though he evidently did not hope for much from the suggested alternative.

"That difficulty, sir, may be overcome: his majesty has need of troops in the West Indies; Lord Cornwallis, with a due regard to the feelings of his dutiful subjects of the colonies, has made arrangements for an exchange of service.. The Irish regiments will be withdrawn from the West Indies, and those of loyal Carolinians substituted. This frees you from all risk of encountering with your friends and countrymen, while at the same time it answers equally the purposes of my commander."

The soldier by profession saw nothing degrading, nothing servile in the proposed compromise. The matter had a different aspect in the eyes of the southern gentleman. The proposition which would send him from his family and friends, to engage in conflict with and to keep down those to whom he had no antipathy, was scarcely less painful in its exactions than to take up arms against his immediate neighbours. The sugges·ion, too, which contemplated the substitution of troops of foreign mercenaries, in the place of native citizens, who were to be sent to other lands in the same capacity, was inexpressibly offensive, as it directly made him an agent for the increase of that power which aimed at the destruction of his people and his principles. The sense of ignominy grew stronger in his breast as he heard it, and he paced the apartment in unmitigated disorder.

" I am no hireling, Major Proctor; and the war, hand to hand with my own sister's child, would be less shameful to me, however full of pain and misery, than this alternative."

"There is no other, sir, that I know of."

" Ay, sir, but there is—there is another alternative, Major Proctor; more than that, sir—there is a remedy."

The eyes of the speaker flashed, and Proctor saw that they rested upon the broadsword which hung upon the wall before them.

"What is that, sir?" inquired the Briton.

"In the sword, sir—in the strife—to take up arms—to prepare for battle!" was the stern reply.

6

Either the other understood him not, with an obtuseness not common with him, or he chose not to understand him, as he replied—

"Why that, sir, is what he seeks—it is what Lord Cornwallis desires, and what, sir, would, permit me to say, be to me, individually, the greatest pleasure. Your co-operation here, sir, would do more towards quieting discontent than any other influence."

The manner of Walton was unusually grave and deliberate.

"You have mistaken me, Major Proctor. When I spoke of taking up the sword, sir, I spoke of an alternative. I meant not to take up the sword to fight your battles, but my own. If this necessity is to be fixed upon me, sir, I shall have no loss to know my duty."

"Sir—Colonel Walton—beware! As a British officer, in his majesty's commission, I must not listen to this language. You will remember, sir, that I am in command of this garrison, and of the neighbouring country—bound to repress every show of disaffection, and with the power to determine, in the last resort, without restraint, should my judgment hold it necessary. I would not willingly be harsh; and you will spare me, sir, from hearing those sentiments uttered which become not the ears of a loyal subject."

"I am a free man, Major Proctor—I would be one, at least. Things I must call by their right names; and, as such, I do not hesitate to pronounce this decree a most dishonest and criminal proceeding, which should call up every honest hand in retribution. Sir Henry Clinton has done this day what he will long be sorry for."

"And what, permit me to add, Colonel Walton—what I myself am sorry for. But it is not for me to question the propriety of that which my duty calls upon me to enforce."

"And pray, sir, what are the penalties of disobedience to this mandate?"

"Sequestration of property and imprisonment, at the discretion of the several commandants of stations."

"Poor Kate!—But it is well it is no worse." The words fell unconsciously from the lips of the speaker: he half strode over the floor ; then, turning upon Proctor, demanded once more to look upon the proclamation.   He again read it carefully.

"Twenty days, Major Proctor, I see have been allowed by Sir Henry Clinton for deliberation in a matter which leaves so little choice.   So much is scarcely necessary ; you shall have my answer before that time is over.   Meanwhile, sir, let us not again speak of the subject until that period."

"A painful subject, sir, which I shall gladly forbear," said Proctor, rising ; "and I will hope, at the same time, that Colonel Walton thinks not unkindly of the bearer of troublesome intelligence."

"God forbid, sir ! I am no malignant.   You have done your duty with all tenderness, and I thank you for it.   Our enemies are not always so considerate."

"No enemies, I trust, sir.   I am in hopes that, upon reflection, you will not find it so difficult to reconcile yourself to what, at the first blush, may seem so unpleasant."

"No more, sir—no more on the subject," was the quick, but calm reply.   "Will you do me honour, gentlemen, in a glass of Madeira—some I can recommend ?"

They drank ; and seeing through the window the forms of the young ladies, Major Proctor proposed to join them in their walk— a suggestion which his entertainer answered by leading the way. In the meanwhile, let us go back to our old acquaintance, Major Singleton, and his trusty coadjutor, Humphries.

CHAPTER XII.

"We meet again—we meet again, once more,
We that were parted—happy that we meet,
More happy were we not to part again."

KEEPING close in cover, Major Singleton and his guide paused
at length in the shelter of a gigantic oak, that grew, with a hundred others, along the extreme borders of the park-grounds. The
position had been judiciously taken, as it gave them an unobstructed view of the Mansion House, the lawn in front, and a portion of the adjacent garden. They were themselves partial occupants of the finest ornament of the estate—the extensive grove of
solemn oaks, with arms branching out on every side, sufficient each
of them for the shelter of a troop. They rose, thickly placed all
around the dwelling, concentrating in a beautiful defile upon the
front, and thus continuing for the distance of a full mile until they
gathered in mass upon the main road of the country. In the rear
they stretched away singly or in groups, artfully disposed, but
without regularity, down to the very verge of the river, over which
many of them sloped with all their weight of limbs and luxuriance
upon them; their long-drooping beards of white moss hanging
down mournfully, and dipping into the river at every pressure of
the wind upon the boughs, from which they depended. Under
one of these trees, the largest among them, the very patriarch of
the collection, the two adventurers paused; Singleton throwing
himself upon a cluster of the thick roots which had risen above
and now ran along the surface, while his companion, like a true
scout, wandered off in other parts of the grove with the hope to
obtain intelligence, or at least to watch the movements of the British officers, whose presence had prevented their own approach to
the dwelling.

As Singleton gazed around upon the prospect, the whole scene grew fresh under his eye; and though many years had elapsed since, in the buoyancy and thoughtlessness of boyhood, he had rambled over it, yet gradually old acquaintances grew again familiar to his glance. The tree he knew again under which he had formerly played. The lawn spread freely onward, as of old, over which, in sweet company, he had once gambolled—the little clumps of shrub trees, here and there, still grew, as he had once known them ; and his heart grew softened amid its many cares, as his memory brought to him those treasures of the past, which were all his own when nothing of strife was in his fortunes.

What a god is memory, to keep in life—to endow with an unslumbering vitality beyond that of our own nature—its unconscious company—the things that seem only born for its enjoyment—that have no tongues to make themselves felt—and no claim upon it, only as they have ministered, ignorant of their own value, to the tastes and necessities of a superior ! How more than dear—how precious are our recollections ! How like so many volumes, in which time has written on his passage the history of the affections and the hopes ! Their names may be trampled upon in our passion, blotted with our tears, thrown aside in our thoughtlessness, but nothing of their sacred traces may be obliterated. They are with us, for good or for evil, for ever ! They last us when the fath r and the mother of our boyhood are gone. They bring them back as in infancy. We are again at their knee—we prattle at their feet—we see them smile upon, and we know that they love us. How dear is such an assurance ! How sweetly, when the world has gone wrong with us, when the lover is a heedless indifferent, when the friend has been tried and found wanting, do they cluster before our eyes as if they knew our desire, and strove to minister to our necessities ! True, they call forth our tears, but they take the weight from our hearts. They are never false to us,—better, far better, were we more frequently true to them !

Such were the musings of Singleton, as, reclined along the roots of the old tree, and sheltered by its branches, his eye took in, and his memory revived, the thousand scenes which he had once known of boyish frolic, when life wore, if not a better aspect of hope to his infant mind, at least a far less unpleasant show of its many privations. Not a tree grew before him which he did not remember for some little prank or incident; and a thousand circumstances were linked with the various objects that, once familiar, were still unforgotten. Nothing seemed to have undergone a change—nothing seemed to have been impaired. The touches of time upon the old oak had rather mellowed into a fitting solemnity the aspect of that to which we should scarcely ever look for a different expression.

While he yet mused, mingling in his mind the waters of those sweet and bitter thoughts which make up the life-tide of the wide ocean of memory, the dusk of evening came on, soft in its solemnity, and unoppressive even in its gloom, under the sweet sky and unmolested zephyr, casting its pleasant shadows along the edges of the grove. The moon, at the same time rising stealthily among the tree-tops in the east, was seeking to pale her ineffectual fires while yet some traces of the sun were still bright in waving lines and fragments upon the opposite horizon. Along the river, which kept up a murmur upon the low banks, the breeze skimmed playfully and fresh; and what with its pleasant chidings, the hum of the tree-tops bending beneath its embrace, and the still more certain appreciation by his memory of the genius of the place, the feeling of Singleton's bosom grew heightened in its tone of melancholy, and a more passionate phase of thought broke forth in his half-muttered soliloquy :—

"How I remember as I look; it is not only the woods and the grounds—the river and the spot—but the very skies are here; and that very wind, and the murmuring voices of the trees, are all the same. Nothing—nothing changed. All as of old, but the one— all but she—she, the laughing child, the confiding playmate ; and not as now, the capricious woman—the imperious heart, scorning where once she soothed, denying where she was once so happy to bestow. Such is her change—a change which the speechless nature itself rebukes. She recks not now, as of old, whether her word carries with it the sting or the sweet. It is not now in her thought to ask whether pain or pleasure follows the thoughtless slight or the scornful pleasantry. The victim suffers, but she recks not of his grief. Yet is she not an insensible—not proud, not scornful

Let me do her justice in this. Let me not wrong her but to think
it. What but love, kindness, and all affection is her tendance upon
poor Emily. To her, is she not all meekness, all love, all forbearance? To my uncle, too, no daughter could be more dutiful, more
affectionate, more solicitously watchful. To all—to all but me!
To me, only, the proud, the capricious, the indifferent. And yet,
none love her as I do; I must love on in spite of pride, and scorn,
and indifference—I cannot choose but love her."

It is evident that Major Singleton is by no means sure of his
ground, as a lover. His doubts are, perhaps, natural enough, and,
up to a certain period, must be shared by all who love. His musings, as we may conjecture, had for their object his fair cousin,
the beautiful Kate Walton—according to his account, a most capricious damsel in some respects, though well enough, it would appear,
in others. We shall see for ourselves as we proceed. Meanwhile,
the return of Humphries from his scouting expedition arrests our
farther speculations upon this topic, along with the soliloquy of our
companion, whose thoughts were now turned into another channel, as he demanded from his lieutenant an account of his discoveries.

"And what of the Britons, Humphries? are they yet in saddle,
and when may we hope to approach the dwelling? I have not
been used to skulk like a beaten hound around the house of my
mother's brother, not daring to come forward; and I am free to
confess, the necessity makes me melancholy."

"Very apt to do so, major, but you have to bear it a little longer.
The horses of the officers have been brought up into the court, and
the boy is in waiting, but the riders have not made their appearance. I suppose they stop for a last swig at the colonel's Madeira.
He keeps a prime stock on hand, they say, though I've never had
the good fortune to taste any of it."

"You shall do so to-night, Humphries, and grow wiser, unless
your British major's potations exceed a southern gentleman's capacity to meet them. But you knew my uncle long before coming
down from Santee with him."

"To be sure I did, sir. I used to see him frequently in the village · but since the fall of Charleston he has kept close to the plan

ation. They say he goes nowhere now, except it be down toward Caneacre and Horse Savannah, and along the Stono, where he has acquaintance. I 'spose he has reason enough to lie close, for he has too much wealth not to be an object, and the tories keep a sharp look-out on him. Let him be suspected, and they'd have a pretty drive at the old plate, and the negroes would soon be in the Charleston market, and then off to the West Indies. Major Proctor is watchful too, and visits the squire quite too frequently not to have some object."

"Said you not that my cousin Kate was the object? Object enough, I should think, for a hungry adventurer, sent out to make his fortune in alliance with the very blood he seeks to shed. Kate would be a pleasant acquisition for a younger son."

There was something of bitterness in the tone of the speaker on this subject, which told somewhat of the strength of those suspicions in his mind, to which, without intending so much, Humphries, in a previous remark, had actually given the direction. The latter saw this, and with a deliberate tact, not so much the work of his education as of a natural delicacy, careful not to startle the nice jealousies of Singleton, he hastened to remove the impression which unwittingly he had made. Without laying any stress upon what he said, and with an expression of countenance the most indifferent, he proceeded to reply as follows to the remark of his companion :—

"Why, major, it would be a pleasant windfall to Proctor could he get Miss Walton; but there's a mighty small chance of that, if folks say true. He goes there often enough, that's certain, but he doesn't see her half the time. She keeps her chamber, or takes herself off in the carriage, when she hears of his coming ; and his chance is slim even to meet with her, let 'lone to get her."

There was a tremulous lightness in Singleton's tone as he spoke to this in oblique language—

"And yet Proctor has attractions, has he not? I have somewhere heard so—a fine person, good features, even handsome. He is young, too."

"Few better-looking men, sir, and making due allowance for an enemy, a clever sort of fellow enough. A good officer, too, that knows what he's about, and quite a polite, fair-spoken gentleman."

" Indeed ! attractions quite enough, it would seem, to persuade any young lady into civility. And yet, you say—"

" Hist, major ! 'Talk of the ——' Ask pardon, sir ; but drop behind this bush. Here comes the lady herself with your sister, I believe, though I can't say at this distance. They've been walking through the oaks, and, as you see, Proctor keeps the house."

The two sank into cover as the young ladies came through the grove, bending their way towards the very spot where Singleton had been reclining. The place was a favourite with all, and the ramble in this quarter was quite a regular custom of the afternoon with the fair heiress of Colonel Walton in particular. As she approached they saw the lofty carriage, the graceful height, and the symmetrical person of our heroine—her movement bespeaking for her that degree of consideration which few ever looked upon her and withheld. Her dress was white and simple, rather more in the fashion of the present than of that time, when a lady's body was hooped in like a ship's, by successive layers of cordage and timber ; and when her headgear rose into a pyramid, tower upon tower, a massy and Babel-like structure, well stuccoed, to keep its place, by the pastes and pomatums of the day. With her dress, the nicest stickler for the proper simplicities of good taste would have found no cause of complaint. Setting off her figure to advantage, it did not unpleasantly confine it ; and, as for her soft brown hair, it was free to wanton in the winds, save where a strip of velvet restrained it around her brows. Yet this simplicity indicated no improper indifference on the part of the lady to her personal appearance. On the contrary, it was the art which concealed itself—the felicitous taste, and the just estimate of a mind capable of conceiving proper standards of fitness—that achieved so much in the inexpressive yet attractive simplicity of her costume. She knew that the elevated and intellectual forehead needed no mountainous height of hair for its proper effect. She compelled hers, accordingly—simply parting it in front—to play capriciously behind ; and, " heedful of beauty, the same woman still," the tresses that streamed so luxuriantly about her neck, terminated in a hundred sylph-like locks, exceedingly natural to behold, but which may have cost her some half-hour's industrious application daily at the toilet. Her eye was dark and richly

6*

brilliant in its expression, though we may look into its depths vainly
for that evidence of caprice, and wanton love of its exercise, which
Singleton had rather insisted upon as her characteristic. Her face
was finely formed, delicately clear and white, slightly pale, but
marked still with an appearance of perfect health, which preserved
that just medium the eye of taste loves to rest upon, in which the
rose rises not into the brilliant glow of mere vulgar health, and is
yet sufficiently present to keep the cheek from falling into the opposite extreme, the autumnal sickness of aspect, which, wanting in the
rose, it is so very apt to assume.

Not so the companion beside her. Pale and shadowy, the young
girl, younger than herself, who hung upon her arm, was one of the
doomed victims of consumption—that subtle   death that sleeps
with us, and smiles with us—insidiously winds about us to lay
waste, and looks most lovely when most determined to destroy.
She was small and naturally slight of person, but the artful disease
under which she suffered had made her more so ; and her wasted
form, the evident fatigue of her movement, not to speak of the pain
and difficulty of her breathing, were all so many proofs that the
tenure of her life was insecure, and her term brief. Yet few were
ever more ready for the final trial than the young lady before us.
The heart of Emily Singleton was as pure as her eyes were gentle.
Her affections were true, and her thoughts had been long since
turned only to heaven. Her own condition had never been concealed from her, nor was she disposed to shrink from its consideration. Doomed to a brief existence, she wasted not the hours in
painful repinings at a fate so stern ; but still regarding it as inevitable, she prepared as calmly as possible to encounter it. Fortunately, she had no strong passions aroused and concentrated, binding her to the earth. Love—that quick, angry, and eating fever of
the mind—had never touched the heart that, gentle from the first,
had been restrained from the indulgence of such a feeling by the
due consciousness of that destiny which could not admit of its
realization. Her mood had grown loftier, sublimer, in due proportion with the check which this consciousness had maintained upon
her sensibilities. She had become spiritualized in mind, even as
she had grown attenuated in person ; and with no murmurings, and

but . . . . . . , her thoughts were now only busied with those heavy award contemplations which take the pang from death, and disarm parting of many of its privations. Singleton looked forth from his cover upon the form of his sister, while the tears gathered in big drops into his eyes.

"So pure, so early doomed! Oh, my sweet sister!—and when that comes, then, indeed, am I alone. Poor Emily!"

Thus muttering to himself, as they came near, he was about to emerge into sight and address them, when, at the instant, Humphries caught his wrist, and whispered :—

"Stir not—move not. Proctor approaches, with Colonel Walton and another. Our hope is in lying close."

The ladies turned to meet the gentlemen. The two British officers seemed already acquainted with them, since they now advanced without any introduction. Proctor, with the ease of a well bred gentleman, placed himself beside the fair heiress of the place, to whom he tendered his arm ; while his companion, Captain Dickson of the Guards, made a similar tender to Emily. The latter quietly took the arm of Dickson, releasing that of her cousin at the same moment. But Kate seemed not disposed to avail herself of her example. Civilly declining Proctor's offer, with great composure she placed her arm within that of her father, and the walk was continued. None of this had escaped the notice of Major Singleton, whose place of concealment was close beside the path ; and, without taking too many liberties with his confidence, we may say that his feelings were those of pleasure as he witnessed this proceeding of his cousin.

"I take no aid from mine enemy, Major Proctor," said the fair heiress, half apologetically, and half playfully,—"certainly never when I can do without it. You will excuse me, therefore ; but I should regard your uniform as having received its unnaturally deep red from the veins of my countrymen."

"So much a rebel as that, Miss Walton! It is well for us that the same spirit does not prevail among your warriors. What would have been our chances of success had such been the case ?"

"You think your conquest then complete, Major Proctor—you think that our people will always sleep under oppression, and return you thanks for blows, and homage for chastisement. Believe so—it is quite as well. But you have seen the beginning only. Reserve your triumph for the end."

" Do the ladies of Carolina all entertain this spirit, Miss Walton ? Will none of them take the aid of the gallant knight that claims service at their hands ? or is it, as I believe, that she stands alone in this rebel attitude, an exception to her countrywomen ?"

" Nay ; I cannot now answer you this question. We see few of my countrywomen or countrymen now, thanks to our enemies ; and I have learned to forbear asking what they need or desire. It is enough for me that when I desire the arm of a good knight, I can have him at need without resorting to that of an enemy !"

" Indeed !" replied the other, with some show of curiosity— " indeed, you are fortunate ; but your reference is now to your father ?"

" My father ?—Oh, no ! although, as now, I not unfrequently claim his aid in preference to that of my foe."

" Why your foe, Miss Walton ? Have we not brought you peace ? There is no strife now in Carolina."

" Peace, indeed ! the peace of fear, that is kept from action by chains and the dread of punishment ! Call you that peace ! It is a peace that is false and cannot last. You will see."

" Be it as you say. Still we are no enemies—we who serve your monarch as our own, and simply enforce those laws which we are all bound in common to obey."

" No monarch of mine, if you please. I care not a straw for him, and don't understand, and never could, the pretensions of your kings and princes, your divine rights, and your established and immutable systems of human government, humanity itself being mutable, hourly undergoing change, and hourly in advance of government."

" Why, this is to be a rebel ; but we shall not dispute, Miss Walton. It is well for us, as I have said before, that such are not the sentiments of your warriors ; else, stimulated, as they must have been, by the pleadings of lips like yours, they must have been invincible. It will not indicate too much simplicity, if I marvel that their utterance hitherto has availed so little in bringing your men into the field. We have not easily found our foes in a country in which, indeed, it is our chief desire to find friends only."

" It follows from this, Major Proctor, that there is only so much more safety for his majesty's more loyal subjects."

" You are incorrigible, Miss Walton."

" No, sir ; only too indulgent—too like my countrymen—dreading the combat which I yet see is a necessity."

" If so, why has there been so little opposition ?"

" Perhaps, sir, you will not always ask the question."

" You still have hopes, then, of the rebel cause."

" My country's cause, Major Proctor, if you please. I still have hopes; and I trust that his majesty's arms may not long have to regret the continuance of a warfare so little stimulating to their enterprise, and so little calculated to yield them honour."

The British colonel bowed at the equivocal sentiment, and after a pause of a few moments the lady proceeded—

" And yet, Major Proctor, not to speak too freely of matters of which my sex can know so little, I must say, knowing as I do the spirit of some among my countrymen—I must say, it has greatly surprised me that your conquests should have been usually so easy."

" That need not surprise you, Miss Walton ; you remember that ours are British soldiers"—and with a smile and bow, the British major made his self-complacent, but only half serious answer.

" By which I am to understand, on the authority of one of the parties, its own invincibility. It is with your corps, I believe, that the sentiment runs—though they do not—' we never retreat, we die.' Unquestionable authority, surely ; and it may be that such is the case. Few persons think more highly of British valour than the Carolinians. Father, you, I know, think extravagantly of it ; and cousin Robert, too : I have heard you both speak in terms which fully sustain you, Major Proctor, in what might be called the self-complaisance which just now assigned the cause of your success."

Colouring somewhat, and with a grave tone of voice that was not his wont, Proctor replied—

" There is truth in what I have told you, Miss Walton ; the British soldier fights with a perfect faith in his invincibility, and this faith enables him to realize it. The first lesson of the good officer is to prepare the minds of his men with this confidence, not only in their own valour, but in their own good fortune."

" And yet, Major Proctor, I am not so sure that the brave young men I have known, such as cousin Robert—the major, for he, too, is a major, father—so Emily says—I am not so sure that they will fight the less against you on that account. Robert I know too well to believe that he has any fears, though he thinks as highly of British valour as anybody else."

" Who is this Robert, Miss Walton, of whom you appear to think so highly ?"

There was something of pique in the manner and language of Proctor as he made the inquiry, and with a singular change in her own manner, in which she took her loftiest attitude and looked her sternest expression, Katharine Walton replied—

" A relative, sir, a near relative ; Robert Singleton—Major Robert Singleton, I should say—a gentleman in the commission of Governor Rutledge."

" Ha ! a major, too, and in the rebel army !" said the other. " Well, Miss Walton, I may have the honour, and hope some day to have the pleasure, to meet with your cousin."

The manner of the speaker was respectful, but there was a slight something of sarcasm—so Katharine thought—in his tones, and her reply was immediate.

" We need say nothing of the pleasure to either party from the meeting, Major Proctor ; but if you do meet with him, knowing Robert as I do, you will most probably, if you have time, be taught to remember this conversation."

Proctor bit his lip. He could not misunderstand the occult meaning of her reply, but he said nothing ; and Colonel Walton, who had striven to check the conversation at moments when he became conscious of its tenor, now gladly engaged his guest on other and more legitimate topics. He had been abstracted during much of the time occupied by his daughter and Proctor in their rather piquant dialogue ; but even in the more spirited portions of it, nothing was said by the maiden that was not a familiar sentiment in the mouths of those Carolinian ladies, who were proud to share with their countrymen in the opprobrious epithet of rebel, conferred on them in no stinted terms by their invaders.

Meanwhile Major Singleton, in his cover, to whose ears portions of the dialogue had come, was no little gladdened by what he heard, and could not forbear muttering to himself—

" Now, bless the girl ! she is a jewel of a thousand."

But the dark was now rapidly settling down upon the spot, and the dews, beginning to fall, warned Kate of her duty to her invalid cousin. Withdrawing her arm from her father, she approached Emily, and reminded her of the propriety of returning to the dwelling. Her feeble lips parted in a murmured reply, all gentleness and dependence—

" Yes, Kate, you are right. I have been wishing it, for I am rather tired. Do fix this handkerchief, cousin, higher and close about my neck—there, that will do."

She still retained Dickson's arm, while she passed one of her hands through that of her cousin. In this manner, followed by Colonel Walton and Major Proctor at a little distance, the three moved away and returned to the dwelling.

Glad of his release from the close imprisonment of his bush, Singleton now came forward with Humphries, who, after a brief interval, stole along by the inner fence, in the close shadow of the trees, and with cautious movement reached a position which enabled him to see when the British officers took their departure. His delay to return, though not long protracted—for the guests only waited to see the ladies safely seated and to make their adieus— was, however, an age to his companion. Singleton was impatient to present himself to his fair cousin, whose dialogue with Proctor had given him all the gratification which a lover must always feel, who hears from the lips of her whom he loves, not only those sentiments which his own sense approves, but the general language of regard for himself, even so slight and passing as that which had fallen from his cousin in reference to him. She had spoken in a tone and manner which was common, indeed, to the better informed, the more elevated and refined of the Carolina ladies at that period ; when, as full of patriotic daring as the men, they warmed and stimulated their adventurous courage, and undertook missions of peril and privation, which are now on record in honourable evidence of their fearlessness, sensibility, and love of country. It was not long after this when the trusty lieutenant returned to his superior, giving him the pleasing intelligence of the departure of Proctor and his companion. Waiting for no messenger, Singleton at once hurried to the dwelling of his uncle, and, leaving Humphries in the hall, he was hurrying forward when, in the passage-way leading to the upper apartments, the first person he met was Kate herself.

" Why Robert, cousin Robert, is it you !"

The heart of the youth had been so much warmed towards her by what he had heard in the previous dialogue, that his manner and language had in them much more of passionate warmth than was altogether customary even with him.

" Dear, dear Kate, how I rejoice to see you !"

" Bless me, cousin, how affectionate you have become all at once ! There's no end to you—there—have done with your squeezing. Hold my hand quietly, as if you had no wish to carry off the fingers, and I will conduct you to Emily."

" And she, Kate !"

He urged the question in an under-tone, and the eyes of his cousin were filled with tears as she replied hastily—

" Is nigher heaven every day—but come."

As they walked to an inner apartment, he told her of his previous concealment, and the partial use he had made of his ears while her chat with Proctor had been going on.

" And you heard—what !"

" Not much, Kate ; only that you have not deserted your country yet, when so many are traitors to her."

The light was not sufficient to enable him to see it, but there was a rich flush upon the cheek of his companion as he repeated some portions of the conversation he had heard, which would have made him better satisfied that her supposed caprice was not so very permanent in its nature.

In a few moments they were in the apartment, where, extended upon a sofa, lay the slight and shadowy person of Emily Singleton. Her brother was beside her in an instant, and she was wrapped in his arms.

"Emily—my dear, dear sister!" he exclaimed, as he pressed his lips warmly upon her cheek.

"Dear Robert, you are come! I am glad, but there now, dear Robert—there!—Release me now."

She breathed more freely, freed from his embrace, and he then gazed upon her with a painful sort of pleasure—her look was so clear, so dazzling, so spiritual, so unnaturally life-like.

"Sit by me," she said. He drew a low bench, and while he took his seat upon it, Katharine left the room. Emily put her hand into that of her brother, and looked into his face without speaking for several minutes. His voice, too, was husky when he spoke, so that, when his cousin had returned to the apartment, though all feelings between them had been perfectly understood, but few words had been said.

"Sit closer, brother—closer," she said to him, fondly, and motioned him to draw the bench beside her. He did so, and in her feeble tones many were the questions which the dying girl addressed to her companion. All the domestic associations of her home on the Santee—the home of her childhood and its pleasures, when she had hopes and dreams of the future, and disease had not yet shown itself upon her system. To these questions his answers were made with difficulty; many things had occurred, since her departure, which would have been too trying for her to hear. She found his replies unsatisfactory, therefore, and she pressed them almost reproachfully—

"And you have told me nothing of old *mauma*,* Robert: is she not well? does she not miss me? did she not wish to come? And Frill, the pointer—the poor dog—I wonder who feeds him now. I wish you could have brought mauma with you, Robert—I should like to have her attend on me, she knows my ways and wishes so much better than anybody else. I should not want her long."

And though she concluded her desire with a reference to her approaching fate, the sigh which followed was inaudible to her brother.

* Probably a corruption of mamma, an affectionate term of endearment which the southern child usually addresses to its negro nurse.

"But you are well attended here, Emily, my dear. Cousin Kate—"

"Is a sister, and all that I could desire, and I am as well attended as I could be anywhere; but it is thus that we repine. I only wished for mauma, as we wish for an old-time prospect which has grown so familiar to our eyes that it seems to form a part of the sight: so indeed, though every thing is beautiful and delightful about 'The Oaks,' I still long to ramble over our old walks among the 'Hills.'"

The brow of Singleton blackened as she thus passingly alluded to the beautiful estate of his fathers; but he said nothing, or evaded, in his answer, the demand,—and she proceeded in her inquiries—

"And the garden, Robert—my garden, you know. Do, when you go back, see that Luke keeps the box trimmed, and the hedge; the morning I left it, it looked very luxuriant. I was too hurried to give him orders, but do you attend to it when you return. He is quite too apt to leave it to itself."

There was much in these simple matters to distress her brother, of which she was fortunately ignorant. How could he say to the dying girl, that her mauma, severely beaten by the tories, had fled into the swamps for shelter?—that her favourite dog, Frill, had been shot down, as he ran, by the same brutal wretches?—that the mansion-house of her parents, her favourite garden, had been devastated by fire, applied by the same cruel hands?—that Luke the gardener, and all the slaves who remained unstolen, had fled for safety into the thick recesses of the Santee?—how could he tell her this? The ruin which had harrowed his own soul almost to madness, would have been instant death to her; and though the tears were with difficulty kept back from his eyes, he replied calmly, and with sufficient evasion successfully to deceive the sufferer.

At this moment Katharine re-entered the apartment, and relieved him by her presence. He rose from the bench, and prepared to attend upon his uncle, who, as yet unapprised of his arrival, remained in his chamber. He bent down, and his lips were pressed once more upon the brow of his sister. She put her hand into his, and looked into his face for several minutes without speaking; and that look—so pure, so bright, so fond—so becoming of heaven, yet so hopeless of earth !—he could bear the gaze no longer; the emotion rose shiveringly in his soul—the tears could be no longer kept from gushing forth, and he hurried from her sight to conceal them.

"Oh, why—why," he said, in a burst of passionate emotion, as he hurried below—" wherefore, great Father of Mercies, wherefore is this doom? Why should the good and the beautiful so early perish—why should they perish at all? Sad, sad, that the creature so made to love and be beloved, should have lived in affliction, and died without having the feelings once exercised or compensated, which have been so sweet and innocent. Even death is beautiful and soft, seen in her eyes, and gathering in words that come from her lips like the dropping so much music from heaven My poor, poor Emily!"

CHAPTER XIII.

"The time is come ; thy chances of escape
Grow narrow, and thou hast, to save thyself,
But one resolve. Take oath with us and live."

COLONEL WALTON, upon the departure of his guests, retired to an inner apartment. His spirits, depressed enough before, were now considerably more so. Mingled feelings were at strife in his bosom—doubts and fears, hopes and misgivings—a sense of degradation—a more unpleasant consciousness of shame. The difficulties of his situation grew and gathered before his eyes the more he surveyed them; they called for deliberate thought, yet they also demanded early and seasonable determination. The time allowed him for decision by the ruling powers was brief, and the matter to be decided involved, in addition to the personal risks of life and liberty, the probable forfeiture of an immense estate, and the beggary, in consequence, of an only and beloved daughter. To save these, in part, from what he conceived otherwise to be inevitable ruin, he had originally laid aside his arms. He was now taught, in the most impressive manner, the error of which he had been guilty in yielding so readily to circumstances—placing himself so completely, not only in the power of his enemy, but in the wrong ; in having foregone that fine sense of national, to say nothing of personal honour, without which the citizen merits not the name, and has no real claim upon the protection of his country. This sacrifice he had made without realizing, in its place, that very security of person and property, its pledged equivalent, which had been the price of its surrender. Bitterly, in that moment of self-examination, did he reproach himself with the unmanly error. Truly did he feel, by his present situation, that he who submits to tyranny arms it ; and by not opposing it, weakens that power,—better principled, or with better courage than himself,—which battles with it to the last.

The exigency grew more and more involved the more he thought upon it. He could see but one alternative left him,—that which he had already hinted at to Major Proctor, of again lifting his sword ; and, if compelled to use it, of doing so for the only cause which he could consider legitimate—that of his country. Yet, how hopeless, how rash and ill-advised, at that moment, seemed the adoption of such an alternative ! The people of the colony had all submitted ; so it seemed, at least, in the absence of all opposition to the advancing armies of the British. They scoured the country on every side. They planted posts, the better to overawe the dis-affected, and confirm their conquests, in every conspicuous or popu-lous region ; and though tyrannizing everywhere with reckless rule and a rod of iron, the people seemed to prefer a lot so burdensome and wretched, rather than exchange it for a strife having not one solitary hope to recommend it. Such was the condition of things in Carolina at the time of which we write, just after the parting proclamation of Sir Henry Clinton, when, upon transferring the southern command to Lord Cornwallis, he adopted this mode of strengthening his successor by the employment of the native militia.

Colonel Walton was not a coward, but he deliberated carefully upon all adventure involving peril in its progress. The circum-stances in which the colony stood at that period were too obvious not to force themselves upon his consideration ; and desperate and degrading as were the requirements of the proclamation, he saw no mode of escape from them. What if he drew the sword ? would he not draw it alone ? Where should he find support ! To what spot should he turn—where strike—where make head against the enemy ?—where, except in the remoter colonies, where a doubtful struggle was still maintained—doubtful in its results, and only exposing its defenders there to the same fate he was now about to encounter in his native soil ? The prospect grew brighter a short time after, when Sumter came plunging down from North Carolina with the fierce rapidity of flame ; when Marion emerged from his swamps on the Peedee and Black River, with the subtle certainty which belongs to skill and caution mingled with determined and fearless valour : and when, like our hero, Major Singleton, a hundred brave young partisan leaders, starting suddenly up, with their little squads, on every side throughout the country, prepared to take terrible vengeance for the thousand wantonly inflicted sufferings which their friends and families had been made to bear at the hands of their enemies.

Leaving his companion, Humphries, comfortably cared for in the hall, along with Miss Barbara Walton, the maiden sister of the colonel, Major Singleton proceeded at once to the apartment where his uncle continued to chafe in his many bewilderments of situation. He found him pacing hurriedly along the room, his strides duly increasing in length with the increasing confusion of his thoughts. These occasionally found their way to his lips in soliloquizing speech, and now and then took on them a shape of passionate denunciation. Too much absorbed for the time to notice the appearance of his nephew, he continued to mutter over his discontents, and in this way conveyed to the major a knowledge of his precise feelings. The latter stood quietly at the entrance, for a few moments, survey-ing his uncle (himself unseen), and listening to the angry ejacula-tions, with which, from time to time, he broke the silence, to give expression to his words. He listened with real pleasure. Familiar as he was with his uncle's character, Major Singleton had properly estimated the effect upon him of Clinton's proclamation, and he now came forward seasonably to his assistance. The colonel turned as he drew nigh, and, for a moment, the pleasurable emotion with which he met the son of his sister, and one who had long been a very great favourite with himself, drove away many of the trouble some thoughts which had been busy with his mind.

"Ah, Robert!—my dear boy! when did you arrive, and how ?"

"On horseback, sir. I reached Dorchester yesterday."

"Indeed? so long—and only now a visitor of 'The Oaks?' You surely mean to lodge with us, Robert?"

"Thank you, uncle ; but that I dare not do. I should not feel myself altogether safe here."

"Not safe in my house! What mean you, nephew? Whence the danger—what have you to fear?"

"Nothing to fear, if I avoid the danger. You forget, sir, that I have not the security of British favour—I have not the talisman of

Clinton's protection—and if suspected to be Major Singleton, I should risk the rope as a rebel."

"True, true—but how left you things at Santee? What are the prospects of a crop?"

"Such as the storm leaves us, good uncle. The tories have been sowing fire in my fields, and left it to ripen in lieu of corn and provender."

"God bless me, Robert!—how was that?"

"They suspected me, hearing that I was from home—made free with my plate, burnt the mansion, barn, and a few other of the buildings, drove the negroes into the swamp, and sent their horses first, and then the fire, into the cornfields. They have done some business there after their usual fashion."

The colonel strode over the floor, his hands upon his brows, speechless for a time, but looking his deep interest in the narrative he had heard, probably with more earnestness, as he darkly saw the destiny of his own fine dwelling and plantation in it. His nephew surveyed him with exemplary composure before he continued the dialogue.

"Yes ; it was fortunate that poor Emily came away in season. A week later, and Heaven only knows what might have been her sufferings at the hands of the wretches."

"And where is this to end, Robert? What is to be done? Are we to have no relief from Congress?—will Washington do nothing for us?"

"Can you do nothing for Washington? Methinks, uncle, Hercules might give you some advice quite as fitting as that he gave to the wagoner. There is no helping one's neighbour to freedom. Men must make themselves free—they must have the will for it. The laws and the strong arm, unless they grow out of their own will, never yet gave, and never will give, any people their liberty. Have you not thought of this before, good uncle?"

"Why, what would you have us do?—what can we do, hemmed in as we are, wanting arms and ammunition, and with a superior force watching us?"

"Do?—ay, you may well ask what can you do. What has anybody ever yet done, that set forth by asking such a question? But come, we will to supper first ; there stands our summoner. We will try aunt Barbara's coffee, of which I have an old memory, and after that we will talk of what we can do in this matter. Coffee is a good stimulant, that wonderfully helps one's courage."

Following the black, who had thrice summoned them without receiving any attention, they descended to the supper-table, spread out after the southern fashion, with the hundred dainties of the region, —rice-waffles and johnny-cake, hominy, and those delicacies of the pantry in the shape of sweetmeats and preserves, which speak of a wholesome household economy, the fashion of which is not yet gone from the same neighbourhood. There, presiding in all the dignity of starched coif, ruff, and wimple, sat stiffly the antique person of Miss Barbara Walton, the maiden sister of the colonel; there, also, in his homespun coat, turned up at the sleeves, and with hands that were not idle, our old acquaintance, Humphries, listening patiently, all the while, to a bitter complaint of Miss Barbara about the diminished and daily diminishing number of her brother's best cows, the loss of which could only be ascribed to the tories. Beside him sat the fair Kate Walton, amused with the efforts which Humphries made, while equally desirous to do the supper justice, and to appear attentive to the ancient lady. And there, reclining on a sofa at some little distance from the table, lay the attenuated figure of Emily Singleton—pale as a white rose, and, as if her thoughts were fast claiming kindred with heaven, almost as silent as one. Major Singleton had a seat assigned him fronting his cousin; and the little chit-chat which followed his and his uncle's entrance was duly suspended with the progress of the repast. To travellers who had toiled so much during the day as Singleton and his lieutenant, the supper was an item of importance, and we need not say that it received full justice at their hands. It was only when roused into consciousness by the very absence of all speech around them, that the soldiers looked up, in a brief pause in their progress, and found that they alone had been busy. This fact offered no stop, however, to their continued industry—to that of Humphries, at least.

" Them are mighty nice waffles, now, major; they'd please you, I reckon."

Cuffee, one of the black waiters, with the proper instinct of a good house-servant, at once placed the dish before the speaker himself and his plate received a new supply. Singleton kept him company, and the host trifled with his coffee, in order to do the same. Tea was anti-republican then, and only the tories drank it. Finding that a cessation had really taken place, Miss Barbara commenced her interrogatories, which, with sundry others put by his cousin Kate, Major Singleton soon answered. These matters, however, chiefly concerned old friends and acquaintances, little domestic anecdotes, and such other subjects as the ladies usually delight to engage in. More serious thoughts were in Colonel Walton's mind, and his questions had reference to the public and to the country— the war and its prospects.

" And now, Robert, your news, your news. You look as if you had much more in your budget of far more importance. Pray, out with it, and refresh us. We are only half alive here, good nephew."

" Do you live at all here, uncle, and how? How much breath is permitted you by your masters for your daily allowance? and, by-the-way, the next question naturally is—how go on the confiscations? You still keep 'The Oaks,' I see ; but how long—how long ?"

The nephew had touched the key to a harsh note ; and bitter indeed was the tone and manner of Colonel Walton, as he replied—

" Ay, how long—how long, indeed, am I to keep the home of my fathers—the old barony, one of the very first in the colony ? God only knows how soon the court of sequestration will find it better suited to a stranger rule ; and I must prepare myself, I suppose, for some such change. I cannot hope to escape very long, when so many suffer confiscation around me."

" Fear not for ' The Oaks,' uncle, so long as you keep cool, submit, swear freely, and subscribe humbly. Send now and then a trim present of venison and turkey to the captain's quarters, and occasionally volunteer to hang a poor countryman, who loves war to the knife better than degradation in a foreign chain. There can be no difficulty in keeping ' The Oaks,' uncle, if you only continue to keep your temper."

" Nay, Robert, sarcasm is unnecessary now, and with me : I need no reproaches of yours to make me feel in this matter."

7

"What, uncle, are you in that vein? Have your eyes been opened to the light at last?"

"Somewhat, Robert—but a truce to this for the present. Let us have your intelligence from Santee. They talk here of some risings in that quarter, but we have no particulars, and know nothing of the success of either party. There is also some story of approaching continentals. Has Congress really given us an army? and who is to command it? Speak, boy; out with your budget."

"Thank you, good mine uncle; but how know I that I unfold my budget to a friend, and not to an enemy? What security do you give me that I talk not with a devout and loyal subject of his majesty—so very much a lover of the divine right of kings, that he would freely lend a hand to run up his own nephew to a swinging bough, the better to compel the same faith in others?"

"Pshaw! Robert, you speak idly: you mean not to suppose me a tory?"

The brow of Colonel Walton darkened awfully as he spoke.

"I have little faith in neutrals," was the calm reply; "I hold to the goodly whig proverb, 'He who is not for me, is against me.' Pardon me, therefore, uncle, if I prefer—I who am a whig—to speak to you, who are neither whig nor Englishman, after such a fashion as shall not make you the keeper of unnecessary secrets, and expose a good cause to overthrow, and its friends to injury."

The taunt thus uttered with a most provoking and biting dryness of phrase, operated strongly upon the mind of the colonel, already acted upon, in no small degree, by his own previous rebukings of conscience to the same effect. He exclaimed bitterly, as, rising from the supper-table, he strode away under the momentary impulse—

"Ay, by heaven! but your words are true. Who should esteem the neutral, when his country is in danger, and when her people are writhing under oppression? True, though bitter—more bitter, as it is too true. Robert Singleton, thou hast given me a keen stroke, boy, but I have deserved it. Thou hast spoken nothing but the truth."

"Now, indeed, uncle, I rejoice to see you, and in this humour. You have felt the stroke at last, but it is not my speech that has done it, uncle of mine. It is the proclamation of Sir Henry Clinton."

The youth fixed his eye keenly, as he spoke, upon the face of Colonel Walton, while his glance indicated a sort of triumphant joy, finely contrasted with the disquietude and vexing indignation strongly legible upon the face of his uncle.

"You are right there, too, Robert. I confess not to have thought so seriously upon this matter—not, certainly, so much to the point —as after hearing the contents of that dishonourable instrument of Sir Henry Clinton—God curse him for it!"

"God bless him for it, I say, if for nothing else that he has done," immediately rejoined the nephew. "My prayers have been heard in that; and this proclamation of the tyrant is the very best thing that he could have done for our cause and country, and the very thing that I have most prayed for."

"Indeed! Major Singleton, you surprise me. What should there be so very grateful to you—so worthy of your prayers and acknowledgment—in this proceeding of Sir Henry Clinton?" inquired the other, with something more of stiffness and hauteur in his manner.

"Much, Colonel Walton, very much. As a true patriot, and a lover of his country at every hazard, I prayed that the time might soon come, when the oppressor should put his foot, aye, and the foot of his menials, too—on the necks of those selfish or spiritless, those too little wise, or too little honourable, who have been so very ready to hug his knee, and yield up to a base love for security their manly character and honest independence. Verily, they meet with their reward. Let them feel the scourge and chain, until, beaten and degraded, the stern necessity shall stimulate them to the duties they have so neglected. I rejoice in their desperation—I rejoice when I hear them groan beneath the oppression—not only because they merit such reward but because it makes them stronger in our cause."

"How know you that?" quickly said the other.

"How know I that? Let me answer that question by another more direct. Will Colonel Walton be able any longer to keep the quiet security of his plantation, to hug his grounds, save his crops, and keep his negroes from the West Indies, without military service—active military service, and against his countrymen too—against his avowed principles?"

The colonel strode the room impatiently. The other continued—

" No, no, good uncle, you have no help. Earl Cornwallis compels you to your duty. You must buckle on the sword—you must take up arms for or against your people, and in either case at the expense of all that comfortable quiet for which you have already made quite too many sacrifices. I know you too well to suppose that you can fight against our people—your people ; and I am glad therefore that you are forced into the field. How many thousands are in your condition ! how many that look up to you, influenced by your example ! Will these not be moved in like manner and by like necessities ? You will see—we shall have an army of native citizens before many days."

" Perhaps so, Robert, and I am not too timid to wish that such may be its effect. But is it not a dishonourable deception that he has practised in this movement ? Did not the protections promise us immunity in this particular ?"

" No, sir—I think not. I see nothing that Clinton has done in this so very grievous. Your protection secured you, as a citizen, to conform to the duties of the citizen, and to protect you as such. One of the duties of the citizen is the performance of militia service."

" Granted, Robert—but commutable by fine. I am not unwilling to pay this fine; but Clinton's proclamation insists only on the duty."

" And I am glad of it. Uncle, uncle, do you not see the dishonourable character of such an argument ? Your conscience forbids that you should serve against your country, but you avoid this actual service in your own person, by paying the money which buys a mercenary to do the same duty. You will not do murder with your own hand, but you pay another to perform the crime. Shame ! shame, I say !"

" Not so, Robert ; we know not, and I believe not, that the money is so appropriated. It becomes the spoil of the leaders, and simply helps them to fortune."

" Granted, and the sterner argument against you is yet to come.

You are wealthy, and avail yourself of your good fortune to buy yourself out of a danger to which the poor man must submit. By what right would you escape from and evade your duties, when he, as a citizen, having the same, must submit to their performance! His conscience, like your own, teaches him that to fight for his country and against her invaders is his first duty. You evade your duty by the help of your better fortune, and leave him, as in the present instance, either to perish hopelessly in unequal contest— unequal through your defection—or to take up arms in a battle to which his principles are foreign. Such is the effect of this most unpatriotic reservation, which, on the score of your money, you have presumed to make. You sacrifice your country doubly, when you contribute to violate the conscience of its citizens. The duties of the rich man—the leading, influential man—are those chiefly of example. What is our safety, and where would be the safety of any nation—its freedom or its glory—if, when danger came, its rich citizens made terms with the invader which sacrificed the poor? Such is your case—such your proceeding exactly. There is now, thank Heaven, but one alternative that Clinton's proclamation has left you."

"That is the sword—I know it, I feel it, Robert."

" Touch it not, touch it not, dear uncle, I pray you. Forbear the sword—the bloody smiting sword. Submit rather to the oppression. Touch it not."

Such was the adjuration of the feeble girl who lay gasping on the sofa. Her eyes were illuminated with a holy fire ; her cheeks, pale, almost transparent, shone, white and glittering, with a spiritual glory, from the pillow on which her head was resting; while one of her long, taper fingers was stretched forward with an imploring earnestness. She had been a silent listener with the rest to the warm and deeply important dialogue which had been going on. The novelty of the difficulty—for they had not heard of the proclamation before —had kept them dumb until that moment, when Colonel Walton, as one having come to a settled conclusion, had referred to the sword as a last alternative. The gentle spirit of Emily Singleton, quick, sensitive, though frail and fleeting, then poured forth its feeble notes, in order to arrest the decision.

" Oh, touch not the sword, uncle, I pray you—the keen sword, that cuts away the happy life, and murders the blessed, and the blessing, peace—the peace of the innocent, the peace of the young and good. Oh, Robert, wherefore have you come with these fierce words ? Is there to be no end to strife—the bloody and the brutal strife—the slaying of men—the trampling of God's creatures in the dust ?"

" Why, sister—dear Emily—but how can we help it ? We must fight our enemies, or they will trample on us the more."

" I see not that : better let them rob and plunder; but take not life, risk not life. Life is holy. None should take life but him who gives it, since to take life takes away from man, not only the privilege to breathe, but the privilege to repent of sins, to repair injustice, to make himself fit for immortality. When you slay your enemy, you send him not merely from one world—you send him into another—and which ? Oh, brother, dear brother, wherefore would you engage in this horrid war ? What blessing so great will it bring you, as to take from you the thought of the butchery you must go through to secure it ? Oh, turn not away, Robert, but hear me ! I would not vex you, nor would I now speak of things beyond my poor ability ; but can you not avoid this fighting, this hewing down of man, this defacing of God's image, this defiling and death of the goodliest work of Heaven ? I know, Robert, you have a true heart, and love not such an employment—say to me, and I will believe you—can you not avoid it ?"

She sank back nearly exhausted. Her breath flickered, and the glow which now overspread her cheek was, if possible, more threatening in its aspect than the death-like paleness which habitually rested there. Her prostration called for the quick attention of her cousin, and as Katharine Walton bent over her, and her brother knelt beside her, a momentary fear came upon them both, that the effort she had made had destroyed her. But a deep sigh indicated the returning consciousness, and the strange, spiritual light ascended once more into and rekindled her eyes. She saw who were immediately beside her ; and there was something of a smile of joy, as she beheld the two, so closely associated in her love, whom, of all the world, she desired to see more immediately linked together. Katharine understood the glance, and rising from her kneeling position, extricated her hand, which lay partly under that of Robert, on the back of the sofa. The movement recalled the thoughts of Emily from the new direction which they had taken, and she now recurred to the unfinished topic.

"I will trust your assurance, brother, as I know your gentleness of feeling. May you not escape this bloody employment? for my poor thought fails to perceive the good or the glory which can come of the distresses of humanity."

"It would be shame, Emily, deep shame and dishonour to avoid it; and, indeed, it may not be avoided. The persecutor pursues when you fly, and he tramples even more freely when you resist not. It is in the nature of injustice and wrong to grow insolent with impunity; and the dishonour must rest on him, who, being himself strong, looks unmoved on the sufferings of the weak, and withholds his succour. Believe me, dear Emily, I love not this strife; but defence of our country is war under God's own sanction, since it seeks to maintain free from blood and from injustice the home which he has given to the peaceful."

"You shall not persuade me of it, Robert," was the reply of the dying maiden. "You will have your arguments, I know, and they will seem wise on your lips, and I may not be able to answer them from mine. But shall I believe in any argument of man, however plausible, when the words of God are so positive? He has forbidden strife, forbidden life. Vengeance is mine, saith the Lord."

"But self-defence and vengeance, dear Emily, are very different things."

"Yes, you are right there; and I did not use the right word, nor refer to the proper command. 'Thou shalt do no murder.'"

"But self-defence is not murder," was the answer to this.

"Ah! still I err! I am too poor in wit and wisdom to maintain this or any argument. But strife is forbidden, and war and violence; and smitten on one cheek, we are commanded to submit the other."

"Ah! Emily, you only prove how impossible it is, in the present state of the world, to be a Christian."

"Alas! for the world, that it should be so! Yet I fear that you are right. But I must cease. I can only pray for you, Robert.

God prosper you, my brother, in your cause, and keep you from danger beneath the shelter of his holy arm.   If you err, my brother I know that you err humanly, and may Heaven be indulgent to all our errors."

She motioned to Katharine Walton, and pointed to the Bible upon the table.   Katharine opened it, and prepared to read.   The company was instantly hushed.   A lesson from the Psalms formed the exercise for the night.   Sweetly, softly, unaffectedly, yet very clearly, the tones of Katharine's voice rose, and filled the apartment, while she gave due effect to the earnest lyrics of the inspired psalmist.   At the close, the brief sentence, so soft, so solemn—"Let us pray!"—from the same sweet speaker, brought the whole family in silence to their knees.   And the humble prayer was offered up, from sweet lips and a gentle spirit, in behalf of the wild and erring.

Yielding a kiss to the fond pressure of her brother's lips, Emily Singleton was assisted to her chamber on the arms of her lovel cousin.

CHAPTER XIV.

"I may not listen now. How should we hea
The song of birds, when, in the stormy sky,
Rolls the rude thunder?"

THE ladies had retired, but it was not easy for Singleton and his uncle to resume the topic which had previously engaged them. There was a visible damp upon their spirits—the elastic nephew, the hesitating colonel, the rough, honest, and direct Humphries, all felt the passionate force of Emily's exhortation, though its argument necessarily failed upon them. There had been quite too much that was awing in her speech and manner—as if death were speaking through the lips of life. Their thoughts had been elevated by her language to a theme infinitely beyond the hourly and the earthly. The high-souled emphasis with which she had insisted upon the integrity of human life, as essential to the due preparation for the future immortality, had touched the sensibility of those whose vocation was at hostility with the doctrine which she taught; and though, from the very nature of things, they could not obey her exhortations, they yet could not fail to meditate upon, and to feel them.

Thus impressed, silent and unobserving, it was a relief to all, when Major Singleton, shaking off his sadness with an effort, reminded Humphries of the promise which he had presumed to make him, touching the old Madeira in his uncle's garret. He briefly told the latter of the circumstance alluded to, and the prompt orders of Colonel Walton soon brought the excellence of his wines to the impartial test to which Humphries proposed to subject them.

The lieutenant smacked his lips satisfactorily. It was not often that his fortune had indulged him with such a beverage. Corn whiskey. at best, had been his liquor in the swamps; and, even in

7*

his father's tavern, the tastes were not sufficiently high, of those who patronized that establishment, to call for other than the cheapest qualities. A brief dialogue about the favourite wines—a sly reference on the part of Singleton to the drinking capacities of his British guests, and a hypocritical sort of condolence upon the privations to which his uncle must be subjected, in consequence of the proclamation, soon brought the latter back to the legitimate topic.

"But what news, Robert, do you bring us? What of the continentals—is it true that we are to have an army from Virginia, or is it mere rumour?—a thing to give us hope, only the more completely to depress and mortify? Speak out, man, and none of your inuendoes—you know well enough that I am with you, body and soul."

"I believe you will be, uncle, but you certainly are not yet. With the hope, however, to make you so more completely, I will give you news that shall cheer you up, if you have the heart to hope for a favourable change of things. It is no mere rumour, sir, touching the northern army. Congress has remembered us at last, and the continentals are actually under way, and by this time must be on the borders of North Carolina."

"Indeed! that is well," cried the colonel, chuckling, and rubbing his hands—"this is good news, indeed, Robert, and may help us somewhat out of our difficulties."

"Not so, Colonel Walton, if it please you. It will help *you* out of no difficulties, if you are not willing to lend a hand for that purpose. Congress cannot afford an army—it can only give us the nucleus for one; some fifteen hundred men at the utmost, and but half of these continentals. We have the Delaware and Maryland lines—brave troops, indeed—among the very bravest that Washington commands—but few, too few for our purpose, unless we ourselves turn out."

"Who commands them, Robert?"

"De Kalb while on the march; but, if we need men, and if our arms are few, the name of our commander is a host for us. The conqueror of Burgoyne at Saratoga has been ordered from Virginia to lead them."

"What, Gates! that is brave news, truly—brave news—and we shall do well to wish him success in another glass of Madeira. Come, Mr. Humphries—come, sir—you see Proctor has left us some of the genuine stuff yet—enough for friends, at least."

"Ay, sir," said Humphries, drinking, "and this news of the continentals promises that we have enough also for our enemies."

"Bravo! I hope so; I think so. Nephew, drink; drink—and say, what has been the effect of this intelligence upon the people? How has it wrought upon the Santee?"

"Everywhere well, uncle, and as it should, unless it be immediately in your neighbourhood, where you breathe by sufferance only. Everywhere well, sir. The people are roused, inspirited, full of hope and animation. The country is alive with a new sentiment. Nor is its influence confined only to the hopes of friends: it has had its effect upon the fears of enemies. Rawdon already feels it, and has drawn in all his outposts. He keeps now those of Ninety-Six, Camden, and Augusta only. He is concentrating his force against the coming of Gates, whose first blow must be against his lordship. This concentration has given opportunity to our people, and opportunity gives them courage. The Santee and the Pedee countries are full of whigs, only wanting embodiment to prove effective. Colonel Sumter has returned from North Carolina, with a growing troop which threatens Ninety-Six itself."

"And Marion?"

"Aye, Marion—from him I bring you better news yet, when I tell you that I left him on Briton's Neck, where we stood upon the bodies of half of Gainey's tories, whom we had just defeated with bloody slaughter —Gainey himself wounded, and his troop for the time dispersed."

"Better and better, Robert; and I rejoice that you had a hand in the business. But what, in all this time, of that sanguinary rider, Tarleton? What keeps him quiet—what is he doing? Surely, with a taste like his, the very knowledge of these risings should be grateful."

"Doubtless they will be, when he gets wind of them; but he is now with the cavalry of the legion, somewhere in the neighbourhood of Rocky Mount, where Sumter is said to be looking after him.

Thus, you see, we are all engaged or preparing—all but you, of the parishes. You either hug the knees of your invaders, or sleep on, to escape the sense of shame : all but your Washington, who, I am told, still contrives to keep his horse together, though sadly cut up while under White and Baylor."

" True, true,—our people here are but too much disposed to sub mission. They have given up in despair long since."

" I reckon that's a small mistake, colonel," said Humphries, inter rupting—" I beg pardon, sir, but I rather think it's not exactly as you say. I don't think our people any more willing to submit than the people on Black River and Pedee, but it's all because we han't got leaders ; that's the reason, colonel. I know, of my own know ledge, there's any number will turn out, if you'll only crook a finger and show 'em the track ; but it's not reasonable to expect poor men, who have never ruled before, to take the lead of great people in time of danger."

Humphries spoke up, and spoke justly for the honour of his neighbours. Singleton continued, when his lieutenant concluded—

" He speaks truly, Colonel Walton, as I can testify. What if I tell you that your people—here, under your own eye—are not only ready to take up arms, but that many of them are in arms !—more, sir,—that they have already done service in your own neighbour hood, and are ready to do more—that a promising squad, under my command, now lies upon your own river, and that, in a few days, I hope to join Colonel Marion with a troop of fifty men, gathered from among your own parishioners ! These are the people who are so willing to submit, according to your account ; pray you, uncle, never write their history."

" Robert, you surprise me."

" Pleasantly, I hope, mine uncle—it is the truth. The whole was planned by Colonel Marion, from whom I have this duty in charge. Disguised, he has been through your parish. Disguised, he sat at your board, in the character of a tory commissary, and your scorn ful treatment persuaded him to hope that you might be brought into action. Are you staggered now ?"

The colonel was dumb when he heard this narrative ; and Major Singleton then proceeded to give a brief account of the little events of recent occurrence in the neighbourhood, as we have already narrated them, subsequently to his assumption of command in the Cypress Swamp. The story, though it gave him pleasure, was a sad rebuke to Colonel Walton's patriotism. He scarcely heard him to the end.

" Now, Heaven help me, Robert, but I take shame to myself that you, almost a stranger upon the Ashley, should have thus taken the lead out of my own hand, as I may say, and among my own people."

" It is not too late, uncle, to amend the error. You may yet help greatly to finish what has been tolerably well begun."

" No—it is not too late. I can do much with Dorchester and Goose Creek. I have influence throughout St. Paul's, and great part of St. George's. Cane Acre will come out to a man."

Rapidly moving to and fro along the apartment, Colonel Walton enumerated to himself, in under tones, the various sections of country in his knowledge which he thought might be moved at his instigation. His nephew did not suffer the mood of his uncle to relax.

" Now is the time, uncle—now is the time, if ever. Your name will do everything in this quarter ; and you may conjecture for yourself, what the shame must be, if others achieve the work which you touched not. You have now a glorious opportunity at this season ; Tarleton, whom they so much dread, being absent; Wemyss in another direction, and your garrison so weak in Dorchester that they cannot easily spare a detachment. Besides, the approach of Gates promises sufficient employment to all the force which Rawdon and Cornwallis can bring up."

" The thing looks well," said Walton, musingly.

" Never better, if the heart be firm. Now is the time, if ever— beat up recruits—sound, stimulate your neighbours, and dash up with as smart a force as you can possibly muster to join with the army from Virginia. They will receive you joyfully, and your corps must increase with every mile in your progress."

" Would I were on the way ; but the beginning is yet to be made, and on what plea shall I seek to persuade others, without authority myself, and known as one having taken protection ?"

"That latter difficulty is cured by the assumption of a new character. Destroy the one accursed instrument, and, in its place, I am proud to hand you a badge of honour and of confidence. Look on this paper and peruse this letter. The one is from his excellency, Governor Rutledge—the other from Colonel Marion. Read—read!"

Walton unfolded the envelope, and the commission of Governor Rutledge as colonel of state militia met his eye: the letter from Colonel Marion was an invitation to the service—a brief, manly, modest letter; such as could only come from Marion—so calm, so unassuming, yet so conclusive in its exhortations.

"You see, uncle," said the major, when he saw that the other had concluded the perusal of the documents—"you see, I come not unprovided. Both Rutledge and Marion hold your name of sufficient importance to our cause to desire its influence; and they would have you, on any terms, emancipate yourself from the villanous bondage—for it is no less—into which you have fallen. Here, now, you have an opportunity, by an honourable, and, let me add, an atoning transaction, of returning to the service of your country. Do not let it pass you. Let me not think, my dear uncle, that my word, pledged for you to Marion, when I undertook and craved this commission, was pledged in vain, and is now forfeited."

This warm appeal of Singleton, in the utterance of which he had discarded all that asperity which had kept pace with much of his share in the previous dialogue, was soothing to his uncle's spirit. He was moved; and slowly again, though unconsciously, he read over the letter of Marion. So high a compliment from the gallant partisan was flattering in the extreme; and the trust of Governor Rutledge, tendered at a moment when he was suffering from the smitings of conscience, was healing and grateful. For a few moments he spoke not; but at length approaching his nephew, he seized his hand, and at once avowed the pleasure it gave him, to avail himself of the privileges which the commission conferred upon him.

"I will be no longer wanting to my country, Robert. I will do my duty. This paper gives me power to enrol men, to form troops, and to act against the enemy, and find my sanction in the commission of the executive. I will do so. I will pause no longer, and, spite of the sacrifice, will act as the occasion requires."

The countenance of Major Singleton, and that of Humphries, no less, glowed with an honest pleasure, as the former replied—

"Spoken as it should be, Colonel Walton—spoken as it should be. The decision comes late, but not too late. It is redeeming, and God grant that it be as prosperous to all as it is surely proper and praiseworthy."

"So I believe it, or I would not now adopt it: but, Robert, know you not that such a decision makes me a beggar? Sequestration—"

"Now, out upon it, uncle! why will you still ballast your good works with a weight which shall for ever keep them from heaven's sight? You are no niggard—you live profusely—care not for money: wherefore this reference to wealth in comparison with honour and honourable duty?"

"The wealth is nothing, Robert; but I have a strange love for these old groves—this family mansion, descended to me like a sacred trust through so many hands and ancestors. I would not that they should be lost."

The youth looked sternly at the speaker for a few moments in silence, but the fierce emotion at length found its way to his lips in tones of like indignation with that which sparkled from his eyes.

"Now, by heaven, uncle, had I known of this—had I dreamed that thou hadst weighed, for an instant, the fine sense of honour in the scales against thy love of this thy dwelling-place—my own hand should have applied the torch to its shingles. Dearly as I have loved this old mansion, I myself would have freely kindled the flame which should have burned it to the ground. I would have watched the fire as it swept through these old trees, scathing and scattering the branches under which I had a thousand times played—I would have beheld their ruin with a pleasurable emotion; and as they fell successively to the earth which they once sheltered, I would have shouted in triumph, that I saved you from the dishonourable bargain which you have made for their protection so long."

"But Kate, Kate, Robert; my sweet child—my only child!"

It was all that the father said, but it was enough, if not to con
vince, at least to silence, the indignant speaker. Her good was,
indeed, a consideration; and when Singleton reflected upon the
tender care which had kept her from privation and sorrow all her
life hitherto, he could not help feeling how natural was such a consideration to the mind of such a father.

But the emotion had subsided—the more visible portions of it,
at least; and Colonel Walton, his nephew, and Humphries, engaged in various conversation, chiefly devoted to the labours that
lay before them. Having gained his object, however, Major Singleton was in no mood to remain much longer. His duties were
various; his little squad required his attention, as he well knew
how little subordination could be had from raw militia-men, unless
in the continued and controlling presence of their commander.
The hour was growing late, and some portion of his time was due
to his sister and the ladies, who awaited his coming in the snug
back or family parlour, into which none but the select few ever
found admission.

Leaving Humphries in the charge of Colonel Walton, our hero
approached the quiet sanctuary with peculiar emotions. There
was a soft melancholy pervading the little circle. The moral influence of such a condition as that of Emily Singleton was touch-
ingly felt by all around her. The high-spirited, the proud Katharine Walton grew meek and humble, when she gazed upon the
sufferer, dying by a protracted and a painful death, in the midst of
youth, rich in beauty, and with a superiority of mind which might
well awaken admiration in the other, and envy in her own sex.
Yet she was dying with the mind alive, but unexercised; a heart
warm with a true affection, yet utterly unappropriated; sensibilities touching and charming, which had only lived, that memory
might mourn the more over those sweets of character so well known
to enjoyment, yet so little enjoying.

It was a thought to make the proud heart humble; and Kate
looked upon her cousin with tearful eyes. She sat at her feet,
saying no word, while the brother of the dying girl, taking a place
beside her, lifted her head upon his bosom, where she seemed

pleased that it should lie, while he pressed his lips fondly and frequently to her forehead. In murmured tones, unheard by the rest, she carried on with him a little dialogue, half playful, half tender in which she pressed him on the subject of his love for her cousin. The mention of Kate's name, a little louder than she usually spoke, called for the latter's attention, who looked up, and a suffusion of her cheek seemed to show a something of consciousness in her mind of what was the subject between them. The eye of Emily caught the glance, and a smile of archness playèd over her lips for an instant, but soon made way for that earnest and settled melancholy of look which was now the habitual expression of her face. They continued to converse together, the others only now and then mingling in the dialogue, on those various little matters belonging to her old home and its associates, which a young and gentle nature like hers would be apt to remember. Sometimes, so feeble was her utterance that Robert was compelled to place his ear to her lips the better to take in what she said.

It was at one of these moments that a severe clap of thunder recalled the major to a sense of his duties. The sudden concussion startled the nervous maiden, and Kate came to her assistance, s·· that his hand was brought once more in contact with that of the woman he loved, in the performance of an office almost too sacredly stern to permit of the show of that other emotion which he yet felt—how strangely!—in his bosom. The blood tingled and glowed in his veins, and she, too—she withdrew her fingers the moment her service could well be dispensed with. Another roll of the thunder and a message from Humphries warned Singleton of the necessity of tearing himself from a scene only too painfully fascinating. He took an affectionate leave of his aunt, and pressing the lips of his sister fondly, her last words to him were comprised in a whisper—

"Spare life—save life, Robert, when you can: God bless you! and come back to me soon."

Kate encountered him in the passage-way. Her look was something troubled, and her visible emotion might have been grateful to the vanity of our hero, did he not see how unusually covered with gloom were the features of her face.

"Dear Kate—sweet cousin—I must leave you now."

"I know it, Robert—I know more: you have persuaded m,
father to break his parole."

"I have done my best towards it, Kate; but if he has resolved,
the impulse was as much his own as from me. He could not well
have avoided it in the end, situated as he was."

"Perhaps not, Robert; still, your persuasions have been the most
immediately urgent; and though I dread the result, I cannot well
blame you for what you have done. I now wish to know from
you, what are the chances in favour of his successful action. I would
at least console myself by their recapitulation when he is absent,
and perhaps in danger."

Major Singleton gave a promising account of the prospects before them; such, indeed, as they appeared at that time to the sanguine Americans, and needing but little exaggeration to persuade.
She seemed satisfied, and he then proceeded to entreat her upon a
subject purely selfish.

"Speak not now—not now on such a matter. Have we not
enough, Robert, to trouble us? Danger and death, grief and many
apprehensions hang over us, and will not suffer such idle thoughts,"
was the reply.

"These are no idle thoughts, Kate, since they belong so closely
to our happiness. Say to me, then, only say that you love me."

"I love you, indeed—to be sure I do, as a cousin and as a
friend; but really you ask too much when you crave for more. I
have no time, no feeling, for other love in these moments."

"Nay, be serious, Kate, and say. We know not how soon our
situation may change. I am hourly exposed in a hazardous service
—I may perish; and I would, before such an event, be secure in
the hope that I may look to you for that love which would make
me happy while living, or—"

She stopped him with a cool, sarcastic speech, concluding the
sentence for him in a manner most annoying—

"Drop a tear for me when I am dead."

She saw that he looked displeased, and immediately after, with
an art peculiarly her own, she diverted his anger.

"Nay, dear cousin, forgive me; but you looked the conclusion, ana so pathetically, I thought it not improbable that its utterance would find you speechless. Be not so tragic, I pray you. .I am serious enough as it is—soberly serious, not tragically so. Be reasonable for a while, and reflect that these very vicissitudes of your present mode of life should discourage you from pressing this matter. I do not know whether I love you or not, except as a relation. It requires time to make up one's mind on the subject, and trust me I shall think of it in season. But, just now, I cannot —and hear me, Robert, firmly and honestly I tell you, while these difficulties last, while my father's life is in danger, and while your sister lies in my arms helpless and dying, I not only cannot, but will not, attempt to answer you. Forbear the subject, then, I pray you, for a better season ; and remember, when I speak to you thus, I speak to you as a woman, with some pretensions to good sense, who will try to think upon her affections as calmly as upon the most simple and domestic necessity of her life. Be satisfied, then, that you will have justice."

Another summons from Humphries below, and a sudden rush of wind along the casement, warned him of the necessity of concluding the interview. He had barely time to press her hand to his lips when she hurried him down to her father. A few brief words of parting, a solemn renewal of their pledges, and, in a few moments, the two partisans were on horse, speeding down the long avenue on the way to their encampment.

CHAPTER XV.

" 'Tis a wild night, yet there are those abroad
   The storm offends not. 'Tis but oppression hides,
   While fear, the scourge of conscience, lifts a whip
   Beyond his best capacity to fly."

THE evening, which had been beautiful before, had undergone a change. The moon was obscured, and gigantic shadows, dense and winged, hurried with deep-toned cries along the heavens, as if in angry pursuit. Occasionally, in sudden gusts, the winds moaned heavily among the pines; a cooling freshness impregnated the atmosphere, and repeated flashes of sharpest lightning imparted to the prospect a splendour which illuminated, while increasing the perils of that path which our adventurers were now pursuing. Large drops, at moments, fell from the driving clouds, and every thing promised the coming on of one of those sudden and severe thunder storms, so common to the early summer of the South.

Singleton looked up anxiously at the wild confusion of sky and forest around him. The woods seemed to apprehend the danger, and the melancholy sighing of their branches appeared to indicate an instinct consciousness, which had its moral likeness to the feeling in the bosom of the observer. How many of these mighty pines were to be prostrated under that approaching tempest! how many beautiful vines, which had clung to them like affections that only desire an object to fasten upon, would share in their ruin! How could Singleton overlook the analogy between the fortune of his family and friends, and that which his imagination depicted as the probable destiny of the forest?

"We shall have it before long, Humphries, for you see the black horns yonder in the break before us. I begin to feel the warm breath of the hurricane already, and we must look out for some smaller woods. I like not these high pines in a storm like this, so use your memory, man, and lead on to some thicket of scrubby

oaks—if you can think of one near at hand. Ha!—we must speed
—we have lingered too long. Why did you not hurry me? You
should have known how difficult it was for me to hurry myself in
such a situation."

This was spoken by Singleton at moments when the gusts permitted him to be heard, and when the irregularity of the route
suffered his companion to keep beside him. The lieutenant answered promptly—

"That was the very reason why I did not wish to hurry you,
major. I knew you hadn't seen your folks for a mighty long spell,
and so I couldn't find it in my heart to break in upon you, though
I felt dub'ous that the storm would be soon upon us."

"A bad reason for a soldier. Friends and family are scarcely
desirable at such a time as this, since we can seldom see them, or
only see their suffering. Ha!—that was sharp!"

"Yes, sir, but at some distance. We are coming to the stunted
oaks now, which are rather squat, and not so likely to give as the
pines. There aint so much of 'em, you see. Keep a look out, sir,
or the branches will pull you from your horse. The road here is
pretty much overgrown, and the vines crowd thick upon it."

"A word in season," exclaimed Singleton, as he drew back before an overhanging branch which had been bent by the wind, and
was thrust entirely across his path. A few moments were spent
in rounding the obstruction, and the storm grew heavier; the winds
no longer laboured among the trees, but rushed along with a force
which flattened their elastic tops, so that it either swept clean
through them, or laid them prostrate for ever. A stronger hold,
a positive straining in their effort, became necessary now, with both
riders, in order to secure themselves firmly in their saddles; while
their horses, with uplifted ears, and an occasional snort, in this
manner, not less than by a shiver of their whole frames, betrayed
their own apprehensions, and, as it were, appealed to their masters
for protection.

"The dumb beast knows where to look, after all, major: he
knows that man is most able, you see, to take care of him, though
man wants his keeper too. But the beast don't know what. He's like
the good soldier that minds his own captain, and looks to him only,

though the captain himself has a general from whom he gets his orders. Now, say what you will, major, there's reason in the horse —the good horse, I mean, for some horses that I've straddled in my time have shown themselves mighty foolish and unreasonable."

Humphries stroked the neck of his steed fondly, and coaxed him by an affectionate word, as he uttered himself thus, with no very profound philosophy. He seemed desirous of assuring the steed that he held him of the better class, and favoured him accordingly. Singleton assented to the notion of his companion, who did not, however, see the smile which accompanied his answer.

"Yes, yes, Humphries, the horse knows his master, and is the least able or willing of all animals to do without him. I would we had our nags in safety now: I would these five miles were well over."

"It's a tough ride; but that's so much the better, major—the less apt we are to be troubled with the tories."

"I should rather plunge through a crowd of them, now, in a charge against superior cavalry, than take it in such a night as this, when the wind lifts you, at every bound, half out of your saddle, and, but for the lightning, which comes quite too nigh to be at all times pleasant, your face would make momentary acquaintance with boughs and branches, vines and thorns, that give no notice and leave their mark at every brush. A charge were far less difficult."

"Almost as safe, sir, that's certain, and not more unpleasant. But let us hold up, major, for a while, and push for the thicket. We shall now have the worst of the hurricane. See the edge of it yonder—how black! and now—only hear the roaring!"

"Yes, it comes. I feel it on my cheek. It sends a breath like fire before it, sultry and thick, as if it had been sweeping all day over beds of the hottest sand. Lead the way, Humphries."

"Here, sir,—follow close and quick. There's a clump of forest, with nothing but small trees, lying to the left—now, sir, that flash will show it to you—there we can be snug till the storm passes over. It has a long body and it shakes it mightily, but it goes too fast to stay long in its journey, and a few minutes, sir—a few minutes is all we want. Mind the vine there, sir; and there, to your left, ' a gully, where an old tree's roots have come up. Now, major, the sooner we dismount and squat with our horses the better."

They had now reached the spot to which Humphries had directed his course—a thick undergrowth of small timber—of field pine, the stunted oak, black-jack, and hickory—few of sufficient size to feel the force of the tempest, or prove very conspicuous conductors of the lightning. Obeying the suggestion and following the example of his companion, Singleton dismounted, and the two placed themselves and their horses as much upon the sheltered side of the clump as possible, yet sufficiently far to escape any danger from its overthrow. Here they awaited the coming of the tempest. The experienced woodman alone could have spoken for its approach. A moment's pause had intervened, when the suddenly aroused elements seemed as suddenly to have sunk into grim repose. A slight sighing of the wind only, as it wound sluggishly along the distant wood, had its warning, and the dense blackness of the embodied storm was only evident at moments when the occasional rush of the lightning made visible its gloomy terrors.

" It's making ready for a charge, major: it's just like a good captain, sir, that calls in his scouts and sentries, and orders all things to keep quiet, and without beat of drum gets all fixed to spring out from the bush upon them that's coming. It won't be long now, sir, before we get it; but just now it's still as the grave. It's waiting for its outriders—them long streaky white clouds it sent out an hour ago, like so many scouts. They're a-coming up now, and when they all get up together—then look out for the squall. Quiet now, Mossfoot—quiet now, creature—don't be frightened—it's not a-going to hurt you, old fellow—not a bit."

Humphries patted his favourite while speaking, and strove to soothe and quiet the impatience which both horses exhibited. This was in that strange pause of the storm which is its most remarkable feature in the South—that singular interregnum of the winds, when, after giving repeated notice of their most terrific action, they seem almost to forget their purpose, and for a few moments appear to slumber in their inactivity.

But the pause was only momentary, and was now at an end. In another instant, they heard the rush and the roar as of a thou

sand wild steeds of the desert ploughing the sands; then followed
the mournful howling of the trees—the shrieking of the lashed
winds, as if, under the influence of some fierce demon who enjoyed
his triumph, they plunged through the forest, wailing at their own
destructive progress, yet compelled unswervingly to hurry forward.
They twisted the pine from its place, snapping it as a reed, while
its heavy fall to the ground which it had so long sheltered, called
up, even amid the roar of the tempest, a thousand echoes from the
forest. The branches of the wood were prostrated like so much
heather, wrested and swept from the tree which yielded them without a struggle to the blast; and the crouching horses and riders
below were in an instant covered with a cloud of fragments. These
were the precursors merely: then came the arrowy flight and form
of the hurricane itself—its actual bulk—its embodied power, pressing along through the forest in a gyratory progress, not fifty yards
wide, never distending in width, yet capriciously winding from
right to left and left to right, in a zigzag direction, as if a playful
spirit thus strove to mix with all the terrors of destruction the
sportive mood of the most idle fancy. In this progress, the whole
wood in its path underwent prostration—the tall, proud pine, the
deep-rooted and unbending oak, the small cedar and the pliant
shrub, torn, dismembered of their fine proportions; some, only by
a timely yielding to the pressure, passed over with little injury, as if
too much scorned by the assailant for his wrath. The larger trees
in the neighbourhood of the spot where our partisans had taken
shelter, shared the harsher fortune generally, for they were in the
very track of the tempest. Too sturdy and massive to yield, they
withheld their homage, and were either snapped off relentlessly and
short, or were torn and twisted up from their very roots. The poor
horses, with eyes staring in the direction of the storm, with ears
erect, and manes flying in the wind, stood trembling in every joint,
too much terrified, or too conscious of their helplessness, to attempt
to fly. All around the crouching party the woods seemed for
several seconds absolutely flattened. Huge trees were prostrated,
and their branches were clustering thickly, and almost forming a
prison around them; leaving it doubtful, as the huge terror rolled
over their heads, whether they could ever make their escape from

the enclosure. Rush after rush of the trooping winds went over them, keeping them immovable in their crowded shelter and position—each succeeding troop wilder and weightier than the last, until at length a sullen, bellowing murmur, which before they had not heard, announced the greater weight of the hurricane to be overthrowing the forests in the distance.

The chief danger had overblown. Gradually the warm, oppressive breath passed off; the air again grew suddenly cool, and a gush of heavy drops came falling from the heavens, as if they too had been just released from the intolerable pressure which had burdened earth. Moaning pitifully, the prostrated trees and shrubs, those which had survived the storm, though shorn by its scythes, gradually, and seemingly with painful effort, once more elevated themselves to their old position. Their sighings, as they did so, were almost human to the ears of our crouching warriors, whom their movement in part released. Far and near, the moaning of the forest around them was strangely, but not unpleasantly, heightened in its effect upon their senses, by the distant and declining roar of the past and far travelling hurricane, as, ploughing the deep woods and laying waste all in its progess, it rushed on to a meeting with the kindred storms that gather about the gloomy Cape Hatteras, and stir and foam along the waters of the Atlantic.

"Well, I'm glad it's no worse, major," cried Humphries, rising and shaking himself from the brush with which he was covered. "The danger is now over, though it was mighty close to our haunches. Look, now, at this pine, split all to shivers, and the top not five feet from Mossfoot's quarters. The poor beast would ha' been in a sad fix a little to the left there."

Extricating themselves, they helped their steeds out of the brush, though with some difficulty—soothing them all the while with words of encouragement. As Humphries had already remarked in his rude fashion, the horse, at such moments, feels and acknowledges his dependence upon man, looks to him for the bridle, and flies to him for protection. They were almost passive in the hands of their masters, and under the unsubsided fear would have followed them, like tame dogs, in any direction.

The storm, though diminished of its terrors, still continued; but

8

this did not discourage the troopers. They were soon mounted and once more upon their way. The darkness, in part, had been dissipated by the hurricane. It had swept on to other regions, leaving behind it only detached masses of wind and rain-clouds sluggishly hanging, or fitfully flying along the sky. These, though still sufficient to defeat the light of the moon, could not altogether prevent a straggling ray which peeped out timidly at pauses in the storm; and which, though it could not illumine still contrived to diminish somewhat the gloomy and forbidding character of the scene. Such gleams in the natural, are like the assurances of hope in the moral world—they speak of to-morrow—they promise us that the clouds must pass away—they cheer, when there is little left to charm.

The path over which the partisans journeyed had been little used, and was greatly overgrown. They could move but slowly, therefore, in the imperfect light; and, but for the frequent flashes of lightning it might have been doubtful, though Humphries knew the country, whether they could have found their way. But the same agent which gave them light, had nearly destroyed them. While Humphries, descending from his steed, which he led by the bridle, was looking about for a by-path that he expected to find in the neighbourhood, a sudden stroke of the lightning, and the over-whelming blaze which seemed to kindle all around them, and remained for several seconds stationary, drove back the now doubly terrified steeds, and almost blinded their riders. That of Singleton sank upon his haunches, while Mossfoot, in her terror, dragged Humphries, who still grasped firmly his bridle, to some little distance in the woods. Sudden blackness succeeded, save in one spot, where a tree had been smitten by the fluid, and was now blazing along the oozy gum at its sides. The line of fire was drawn along the tree, up and down—a bright flame, that showed them more of the track they were pursuing than they had seen before. In the first moment following the cessation of the fiercer blaze made by the lightning, and when the tree first began to extend a certain light, Singleton thought he saw through the copse the outline of a human form, on foot, moving quickly along the road above him. He called quickly to Humphries, but the lieutenant was busy with his steed, and did not seem to hear. Again was the object visible, and Singleton then cried out—

"Who goes there ?—ho !"

No answer; and the fugitive only seemed to increase his speed, turning aside to the denser woods, as if he strove to elude observation. The challenge was repeated.

"What, ho! there—who goes? Speak, or I shoot."

He detached one of his pistols from the holster as he spoke, and cocked it to be in readiness. Still no answer, the person addressed moving more quickly than ever. With the sight, with an instinct like lightning, the partisan put spurs to his steed, and drove fearlessly through the bush in pursuit. The fugitive now took fairly to his heels, leaping over a fallen tree, fully in sight of his pursuer. In a moment after, the steed went after him—Humphries, by this time in saddle, closely following on the heels of his commander. For a moment the object was lost to sight, but in the next he appeared again.

"Stand !" was the cry, and with it the shot. The ball rushed into the bush which seemed to shelter the flying man, and where they had last seen him—they bounded to the spot, but nothing was to be seen.

"He was here—you saw him, Humphries, did you not?"

"A bit of him, major—a small chance of him behind the bush, but too little a mark for them pistols."

"He is there—there !" and catching another glimpse of the fugitive, Singleton led the pursuit, again firing as he flew, and, without pausing to wait the result, leaping down to the spot where he appeared to them. The pursuit was equally fruitless with the aim. The place was bare. They had plunged into a hollow, and found themselves in a pond, almost knee deep in water. They looked about vainly, Humphries leading the search with unusual earnestness.

"I like not, major, that the fellow should escape. Why should he stand a shot, rather than refuse to halt, and answer to a civil question ? I'm dub'ous, major, there's something wrong in it; and he came from the direction leading to our camp."

"Ha! are you sure of that, Humphries?—think you so?"

"Ay, sir—the pine that was struck marks the by-path through which I should have carried you in daylight. It is the shortest, though the worst; and he could not have been far from it when you started him. Ah! I have it now. A mile from this is the house of old Mother Blonay, the dam of that fellow Goggle. We will ride there, major, if you say so."

"With what object, Humphries? what has she to do with it?"

"I suspect the fugitive to be Goggle, the chap I warned you not to take into the troop. Better we had hung him up, for he's not one to depend upon. All his blood's bad : his father—him they call so, at least—was a horse-thief; and some say, that he had a cross in his blood. As for that, it's clear to me, that Goggle is a half-breed Indian, or mestizo, or something. Anybody that looks on Goggle will say so ; and then the nature of the beast is so like an Indian—why, sir, he's got no more feeling than a pine stump."

"And with what motive would you ride to his mother's?"

"Why, sir, if this skulking chap be Goggle, he's either been there, or is on his way there; and if so, be sure he's after mischief. Proctor or Huck at the garrison will soon have him among them, and he'll get his pay in English guineas for desertion. Now, sir, it's easy to see if he's been there, for I s'pose the old hag don't mind to tell us."

"Lead on ! A mile, you say?"

"A short mile; and if he's not been there yet, he must be about somewhere, and we may get something out of the old woman, who passes for a witch about here, and tells fortunes, and can show you where to find stolen cattle; and they do say, major, though I never believed it—they do say," and the tones of his voice fell as he spoke—"they do say she can put the bad mouth upon people ; and there's not a few that lay all their aches and complaints to her door."

"Indeed !" was the reply of Singleton ; "indeed ! she is a sight worth seeing; and so let us ride, Humphries, and get out of this swamp thicket with all possible speed."

"A long leap, major, will be sure to do it. But better we move slowly. I don't want to lose our chance at this rascal for something ; and who knows but we may catch him there. He's a great skunk, now, major, that same Goggle; and though hanging's much too good for him, yet them pistols would have pleased me better had they lodged the ball more closely."

CHAPTER XVI.

"A hag that hell has work for—a born slave
To an o'ercoming evil—venomous, vile,
Snake-like, that hugs the bush and bites the heel."

The troopers had not been well gone, before the fugitive they had so vainly pursued stood upon the very spot which they had left. He rose from the mire of the pond, in which he had not paused to imbed himself when the search was hottest and close upon him. The conjecture of Humphries was correct, and Goggle or Blonay was the person they had chased. He had left his post in the bivouac when the storm came on, and was then upon his way to his mother's cabin. From that spot his farther course was to the British garrison with his intelligence. His determination in this respect, however, underwent a change, as we shall see in the progress of the narrative.

Never had better knowledge of character been shown than in the estimate made by Humphries of that of the deserter. Goggle was as warped in morals as he was blear in vision; a wretch aptly fitted for the horse-thief, the tory, and murderer. His objects were evil generally, and he had no scruples as to the means by which to secure them. Equally indifferent to him what commandment he violated in these practices; for, with little regard from society, he had no sympathy with it, and only obeyed its laws as he feared and would avoid their penalties. He hated society accordingly as he was compelled to fear it. He looked upon it as a power to be destroyed with the opportunity, as a spoil to be appropriated with the chance for its attainment; and the moods of such a nature were impatient for exercise, even upon occasions when he could hope no addition to his pleasure or his profit from their indulgence.

Squat in the ooze and water of the creek, while the horse of Singleton at one moment almost stood over him, he had drawn breath with difficulty through the leaves of a bush growing upon the edge of the ditch in which his head had found concealment ; and in this perilous situation his savage spirit actually prompted him to thrust his knife into the belly of the animal. He had drawn it for this purpose from his belt, while his hands and body were under water. Its point was already turned upward, when Singleton moved away from the dangerous proximity. Here he listened to the dialogue which the two carried on concerning him ; and, even in that predicament of dirt and danger in which he lay, his mind brooded over a thousand modes by which he should enjoy his malignant appetite, that craved for revenge upon them both. When they were fairly gone, he rose from the mire and ascended cautiously to the bank ; shook himself like a water-dog, while he almost shivered in the saturated garments which he wore ; then rubbed and grumbled over the rifle which he had taken with him into the mire, and which came out as full of its ooze and water as himself.

" So ho !" said he, as he shook himself free from the mud—" So ho ! they are gone to old Moll's to look after me, eh ! Now would I like to put this bullet into that Dorchester skunk, Humphries, d—n him. I am of bad blood, am I !—my father a horse-thief and a mulatto, and I only fit for hanging ! The words must be paid for ; and Moll must answer for some of them. She is my mother, that's clear—she shall tell me this night who my father is ; for, Blonay, or Goggle, or the devil, I will know. She shall put me off no longer. No ! though she tells me the worst—though she tells me that I am the spawn of Jack Drayton's driver, as once before I've heard it."

Thus muttering, he looked to his flint and inspected the priming of his rifle. With much chagrin he found the powder saturated with water, and the charge useless. He searched his pockets, but his flask was gone. He had purposed the murder of Humphries or Singleton had this not been the case. He now without hesitation took the track after them, and it was not long before he came in sight of the miserable clay and log hovel in which his mother, odious and dreaded as she was, passed fitly her existence. This spot was dreary in the extreme : an old field ; a few cheerless pines rose around it, and the thick broom straw waved its equally bald, though more crowded forms in uncurbed vegetation among them. The hovel stood in a hollow, considerably below the surrounding level, and the little glimmer of light, stealing from between the logs, only made its location seem more cheerless to the observer.

Blonay—or, as we shall hereafter call him, according to the fashion of the country, Goggle—cautiously approached a jungle, in which he hid himself, about a stone's throw from the hovel. There he watched, as well as he might, in the imperfect light of the evening, for the appearance of the troopers. Though mounted, they had not yet succeeded in reaching the spot, which, familiar to him from childhood, he well knew to find in the darkest night, and by a route the most direct. He was there before them, snug in his cover, and coolly looking out for their coming. More than once he threw up the pan of his rifle, carefully keeping it from its usual click by the intervention of his finger, and cursed within himself his ill fortune, as he found the powder saturated with water, a soft paste beneath his touch. He thrust his hand into his pocket, seeking there for some straggling grains, of which in the emergency he might avail himself; but he looked fruitlessly, and was compelled to forego the hope of a shot, so much desired, at one or other of the persons now emerging from the wood before him.

The barking of a cur warned the indweller of visiters, but without offering any obstacle to their advance. Humphries proceeded first, and motioning his companion to keep his saddle, fastened his horse to a bough, and treading lightly, looked through the crevices of the logs upon the old crone within. Though in June, a warm season at all times in Carolina, the old woman partook too much of the habits of the very poor in that region to be without a fire; and with the taste of the negro, she was now bending over a huge light wood blaze, with a pipe of rude structure and no small dimensions in her mouth, from which the occasional puff went forth, filling the apartment with the unpleasant effluvia of the vilest leaf-tobacco; while her body and head swung ever to and fro, with a regular seesaw motion, that seemed an habitual exercise. Her thin, shrivelled, and darkly yellow features, were hag-like and jaundiced. The skin was tightly drawn across the face, and the high cheek-bones and the nose seemed disposed to break through the slender restraints of their covering. Her eyes were small and sunken, of a light grey, and had a vicious twinkle, that did not accord with the wretched and decayed aspect of her other features. Her forehead was small, and clustered with grisly hair of mixed white and black, disordered and unbound, but still short, and with the appearance of having but lately undergone clipping at the extremities. These features, repulsive in themselves, were greatly heightened in their offensive expression by the severe mouth and sharp chin below them. The upper lip was flat, undeveloped entirely, while the lower was thrust forth in a thick curl, and, closely rising and clinging to the other, somewhat lifted her glance into a sort of insolent authority, which, sometimes accompanying aroused feeling, or an elevated mood of mind, might look like dignified superiority. The dress which she wore was of the poorest sort, the commonest white homespun of the country, probably her own manufacture, and so indifferently made, that it hung about her like a sack, and gave a full view of the bronzed and skinny neck and bosom, which a regard to her appearance might have prompted her to conceal. Beside her a couple of cats of mammoth size kept up a drowsy hum, entirely undisturbed by the yelping of the cur, which, from his little kennel at one end of the hovel, maintained a continuous clamour at the approach of Humphries. The old woman simply turned her head, for a moment, to the entrance, took the pipe from her mouth, and discharging the volume of smoke which followed it, cried harshly to the dog, as if in encouragement. Her call was answered by Humphries, who, rapping at the door, spoke civilly to the inmate.

"Now open the door, good woman. We are friends, who would speak with you. We have been caught in the storm, and want you to give us house-room till it's over."

"Friends ye may be, and ye may not. Down by the dry branch, and through the old road to mother Blonay's, is no walk that friends often take; and if ye be travellers, go ye on, for there's no accommodation for ye, and but little here ye would eat. It's a poor country y'are in, strangers, and nothing short of Dorchester, or it may be Rantowle's, will serve your turn for a tavern."

"Now, out upon you, mother! would you keep a shut door upon us, and the rain still pouring?" cried Humphries, sharply.

8*

"Ye have been in it over long to mind it now, I'm thinking, and ye'd better ride it out. I have nothing for ye, if ye would rob. I'm but a lone woman, and mighty poor; and have no plate, no silver, no fine watch, nor rings, nor anything that is worth your taking. Go to 'The Oaks,' or Middleton Place, or the old hall at Archdale, or any of the fine houses; they have plenty of good picking there."

"Now," said Humphries to his superior—"how pleasantly the old hag tells us to go and steal, and she looking down, as a body may say, into the very throat of the grave that's gaping after her."

The old woman, meanwhile, as if satisfied with what she had done, resumed her pipe, and recommenced her motion, to and fro, over the blaze. Humphries was for a smart application of the foot to the frail door that kept him out, but to this his companion refused assent.

"Confound the old hag, major; she will play with us after this fashion all the night. I know her of old, and that's the only way to serve her. Nothing but kicks for that breed; civility is thrown away upon them."

"No, no—you are rash; let me speak. I say, my good woman, we are desirous of entrance; we have business, and would speak with you."

"Business with me! and it's a gentleman's voice too! Maybe he would have a love-charm, since there are such fools; or he has an enemy, and would have a bad mouth put upon him, shall make him shrivel up and die by inches, without any disease. I have worked in this business, and may do more. Well, there's good wages for it, and no danger. Who shall see, when I beg in the rich man's kitchen, that I put the poison leaf in the soup, or stir the crumbs with the parching coffee, or sprinkle the powder with the corn flour, or knead it up with the dough? It's a safe business enough, and the pay is good, though it goes over soon for the way it comes."

"Come, come, my good woman," cried Singleton impatiently, as the old beldam thus muttered to herself the various secrets of her capacity, and strove to conjecture the nature of the business which her visiters had with her. "Come, come, my good woman, let us in; we are hurried, and have no little to do before daylight."

" Good woman, indeed ! Well, many's the one has been called good with as little reason. Yes, sir, coming : my old limbs are feeble ; I do not move as I used to when I was young."

Thus apologizing, with her pipe in one hand, while the other undid the entrance, Mother Blonay admitted her visiters.

" So, you have been young once, mother ?" said Humphries, while entering.

The old woman darted a glance upon him,—a steadfast glance from her little grey eyes, and the stout and fearless trooper felt a chill go through his veins on the instant. He knew the estimate put upon her throughout the neighbourhood, as one possessed of the evil eye, or rather the evil mouth ; one whose word brought blight among the cattle, and whom the negroes feared with a superstitious dread, as able to bring sickness and pestilence—a gnawing disease that ate away silently, until, without any visible complaint, the victim perished hopelessly. Their fears had been adopted in part by the whites of the lower class in the same region, and Humphries, though a bold and sensible fellow, had heard of too many dreadful influences ascribed to her, not to be unpleasantly startled with the peculiar intensity of the stare which she put upon him. Though a soldier, and like his fellows, without much faith of any kind, he had not altogether survived his superstitions.

" Young !" she said, in reply ; " yes, I have been young, and I felt my youth. I knew it, and I enjoyed it. But I have outlived it, and you see me now. You are young, too, Bill Humphries ; may you live to have the same question asked you which you put to me."

" A cold wish, Mother Blonay ; a bitter cold wish, since you should know, by your own feelings, how hard it will be to outlive activity and love, and the young people that come about us. It's a sad season that, mother, and may I die before it comes. But, talking of young people, mother, reminds me that you are not so lonesome as you say. You have your son, now, Goggle."

" If his eye is blear, Bill Humphries, it's not the part of good manners to speak of it to his mother. The curse of a blear eye, and a blind eye, may fall upon you yet, and upon yours—ay, down to your children's children—for any thing we know."

" That's true, mother—none of us can say.   I meant no harm, but as everybody calls him Goggle—"

" The redbug be upon everybody that so calls him!   The boy has a name by law."

" Well, well, mother, do not be angry, and wish no sores upon your neighbours' shins that you can't wish off.   The redbugs and the June-flies are bad enough already, without orders ; and people do say you are quite too free in sending such plagues upon them, for little cause, or for no cause at all."

" It's a blessing that I can do it, Bill Humphries, or idle rowdies, such as yourself, would harry the old woman to death for their sport.   It's a blessing and a protection that I can make the yellow jacket and the redbug leave their poison stings in the tender flesh, so that the jester that laughs at the old and suffering shall learn some suffering too."

" Quite a hard punishment for such an offence.   But, mother, they say you can do more ; that you have the spell of the bad mouth, that brings long sickness and sudden death, and many awful troubles ; and some that don't wish you well, say you love to use it."

" Do they say so ?—then they say not amiss.   Think you, Bill Humphries, that I should not fight with him who hates me, and would destroy me if he could ?   I do ; and the bad mouth of Mother Blonay upon you, shall make the bones in your skin ache for long months after, I tell you."

" I beg, for God's sake, that you will not put your bad mouth upon me then, good mother," exclaimed Humphries, with ludicrous rapidity, as if he half feared the immediate exercise of her faculty upon him.

The old woman seemed not displeased with this tacit acknowledgment of her power, and she now twisted her chair about so as to place herself directly in front of Singleton.   He, meanwhile, had been closely scrutinizing the apartment, which was in no respects better than those of the commonest negro-houses of the low country.   The floor was the native soil.   The wind was excluded by clay, loosely thrust between the crevices of the logs ; and an old scaffolding of poles, supporting a few rails crossing each other, sustained the mattress of moss, upon which the woman slept. She dwelt unassisted, seemingly, and entirely alone. A few gourds, or calabashes, hung from the roof, which was scantily shingled : these contained seeds of various kinds, bunches of dried thyme, sage, and other herbs and plants ; and some which, by a close analysis of their properties, would be found to contain a sufficient solution of the source from whence came her spells of power over her neighbours, whether for good or evil.

Singleton had employed himself in noticing all these several objects, and the probability is, that the quick eye of the old woman had discovered his occupation. She turned her chair so as to place herself directly before him, and the glance of her eye confronting his, compelled him to a similar change of position. The docile cats, with a sluggish effort, changed their ground also ; and after circling thrice about their new places of repose, before laying themselves down upon it, they soon resumed their even and self-satisfied slumberous hum, which the movement of their mistress had interrupted. A moment of silence intervened, during which Dame Blonay employed herself in examining Singleton's person and countenance.

He was, of course, quite unknown to her, and a curious desire to make the acquaintance of new faces is, perhaps, as much the characteristic of age as its garrulity. Memory, in this way, becomes stirred up actively, and the decaying mind delights in such a survey, that it may liken the stranger to some well known individual of former days. It is thus that the present time continually supplies with aliment the past from which it receives so much of its own. The close survey of the woman did not please Singleton, who at length interrupted it by resuming the subject where Humphries had discontinued it. With becoming gravity, he asked her the question which follows, in respect to the extent of her powers—

"And so, dame, you really believe that you possess the power of doing what you say you can do?"

"Ay, sir, and a great deal more. I can dry up the blood in the veins of youth; I can put the staggering weakness into the bones and sinews of the strong man; I can make the heart shrink that is brave—I can put pain there instead of pleasure."

"Indeed! if you can do this, dame, you can certainly do much more than most of your neighbours. But is it not strange, mother, that these powers are all for evil? Have you no faculty for con ferring good—for cheering the heart instead of distressing it, and giving pleasure instead of pain?"

"Ay! I can avenge you upon your enemy!" As she spoke, her form suspended its waving motion, was bent forward in eagerness, and her eye glistened, while her look seemed to say, "Is not that the capacity you would have me serve you in?"

"That, also, is a power of evil, dame, and not of good. I spoke of good, not evil."

"Not that!" she muttered, with an air of disappointment, while drawing herself back and resuming her croning movement.

"Not that! is not revenge sweet, young master—very sweet, when you have been robbed and wronged for years; trampled in the dust; laughed and sneered at; hunted and hated: is not the moment of revenge sweet? When you see your enemy writhing in pain, you put your ear down and listen to his suffering, and your heart, that used to beat only with its own sorrow, you feel is throbbing with a strange, sweet joy at his—is it not sweet, my master?"

"Ay, sweet perhaps to many, dame, but I fear me, still evil; still not good; still harmful to man. Have you no better powers in your collection? none to give strength and youth, and bring back health?"

She pointed to a bunch of the smaller snake-roots which lay in the corner, but with much seeming indifference, as if the cure of disease formed but an humble portion of her mystery and labours.

"And your art gives you power over affections, and brings pleasure sometimes, mother?"

"Is it love?—the love of the young woman—hard to please, difficult to soothe, cold to sweet words—that you would win my young master?"

She again bent her head towards him, and suspended her motion, as if now hopeful that, in this reference, she had found out the true quest of the seeker. A warm glow overspread the cheek of Singleton, as, in answering the inquiry correctly, he must necessarily have confessed that such a desire was in his bosom,

though certainly without any resort to such practices as might be
ooked for in her suggestion.

"Ay, indeed, such an art would be something to me now, could
it avail for any purpose—could it soften the stern, and warm the
cold, and make the hard to please easy—but I look not for your
aid, mother, to do all this."

"I can do it—fear me not," said the old woman, assuringly.

"It may be, but I choose not that thou shouldst. I must toil
for myself in this matter, and the only art I may use must be that
which I shall not be ashamed of. But we have another quest,
dame; and upon this we would have you speak honestly. You
have a son?"

The old woman looked earnestly at the speaker; and, as at that
moment the sabre swung off from his knee, clattering with its end
upon the floor, she started apprehensively, and it could be seen that
she trembled. She spoke after the pause of an instant:

"Sure, captain—Ned, Ned Blonay is my son. What would you
tell me? He has met with no harm?"

"None, mother—none that I can speak of," said Humphries
quickly; "not that he may not happen upon it if he does not
mind his tracks. But tell us—when was he here last, mother?
Was he not here to-night? and when do you look for him again?"

The apprehensions of the woman had passed off; she resumed
her seesaw motion, and answered indifferently:

"The boy is his own master, Bill Humphries; it is not for an
old woman like me to answer for Ned Blonay."

"What! are you not witch enough to manage your own son?
Tell that to them that don't know you both better. I say to you,
Mother Blonay, that story wont pass muster. You have seen Gog-
gle to-night."

"And I say, Bill Humphries, that the tongue lies that says it,
though it never lied before. Go—you're a foul-spoken fellow, and
your bones shall ache yet for that same speech. Goggle—Goggle
—Goggle! as if it wasn't curse enough to be blear-eyed without
having every dirty field-tackey whickering about it."

"Our object is not to offend, my good woman," said Singleton,
interposing gently; "but to ask a civil question. My companion

only employs a name by which your son is generally distinguished among the people. You must not allow him to anger you, therefore, but answer a question or two civilly, and we shall leave you."

"You have smooth words, captain, and I know what good-breeding is. I have lived among decent people, and I know very well how to behave like one if they would let me ; but when such ill-spoken creatures as Bill Humphries ask me questions, it's ten to one I don't think it worth while to answer them ; and answer I will not, except with curses, when they speak nicknames for my child. I know the boy is ugly and blear-eyed. I know that his skin is yellow and shrivelled like my own, but he has suckled at these withered paps, and he is my child ; and the more others hate and abuse him, the more I love him—the more I will take up for him."

"Now, Mother Blonay, you needn't make such a fuss about the matter. You know I meant no harm. Confound the fellow, I don't care whether he has eyes or not ; sure I am, I know the name which people give him without minding the blear. I only want you to say what you've done with him—where he is now ?"

"You are too quick—too violent, Humphries, with the old woman," said Singleton in a whisper.

"Major, don't I know her ? The old hag—I see through her now, jist as easy as I ever saw through any thing in my life. I'll lay now she knows all about the skunk."

"Perhaps so, but if she does, this is not the way to get at her information."

"But little hope of that now, since she's got her back up. Confound Goggle ! if I had him under a stout hickory I reckon I'd make her talk to another tune."

This was loud enough for the old woman, who replied :—

"Yes—you'd beat with blows and whips a far better man than yourself. But go your ways, and see what will come of this night's work. I have curses, have I ?—if I have, you shall hear them. I have a bad mouth, have I ?—you shall feel it. Hearken, Bill Humphries ! I am old and weak, but I am strong enough to come to you where you are, and whisper in your ears. As what I say will do you no pleasure, you shall hear it."

And, tottering forward from her seat, she bent down to the chair upon which he sat, and though he moved away in an instant, he was not quick enough to avoid the momentary contact of her protruded and hag-like lip with his ear, that shrunk from the touch as with an instinct of its own. She whispered but two words, and they were loudly enough uttered for Singleton to hear as well as Humphries.

" Your sister—Bella Humphries !"

The trooper started up as if he had been shot ; staggered he certainly was, and his eyes glared confusedly upon those which she piercingly fixed upon him with a fiendish leer. She shook her long bony finger at him, and her body, though now erect, maintained its waving motion just as when she had been seated. Recovering in a moment, he advanced with threatening action, exclaiming :—

" You old hag of hell ! what do you mean by that ? What of Bella ?. what of my sister ?"

" Goggle—Goggle—Goggle—*that* of her ! *that* of her !" was all the reply ; and this was followed by a low chuckling laugh, which had in it something exceedingly annoying even to Singleton himself. The trooper was ferocious, and with clenched fist seemed about to strike. This, when she saw, seemed to produce in her even a greater degree of resolution. Instead of shrinking, she advanced, folded her arms upon her breast, and there was a deep concentrated solemnity in her tone as she exclaimed :—

" Now may the veins dry up, and the flesh wither, and the sinews shrink, and the marrow leave the bones ! Strike the old woman, now, Bill Humphries—strike, if you dare !"

Singleton had already passed between the parties, not, however, before he had been able to see the prodigious effect which her adjuration had produced upon the trooper: His form was fixed in the advancing position in which he stood when she addressed him. His lips were colourless, and his eyes were fastened upon her own with a steadiness which was that of paralysis, and not of decision. She, on the other hand, seemed instinct with life—a subtle, concentrated life. The appearance of decrepitude had gone, the eye had stronger fire, the limbs seemed firm on the instant, and there was something exceedingly high and commanding in Ler position. A moment after, she sank back in her chair almost exhausted—the two cats anxiously purring about her, having stood at her side, as if bent to co-operate in her defence, on the first approach of Humphries. He now recovered from the superstitious awe which had momentarily possessed him ; and heartily ashamed of the show of violence to which her mysterious speech had provoked him, began to apologize for it to Singleton.

" I know it's wrong, major, and I wasn't exactly in my sober senses, or I wouldn't have done it. But there's no telling how she provoked me ; and the fact is, what she said worries me no little now ; and I must know what she meant. I say, mother—Mother Blonay !"

Her eyes now were fixed upon his with a dull, inexpressive glare, that seemed to indicate the smallest possible degree of consciousness.

" She is now exhausted, and cannot understand you ; certainly not to satisfy your inquiries," said Singleton.

The trooper made one or two efforts more, but she refused all answer, and showed her determination to be silent by turning her face from them to the wall. Finding nothing was to be got out of her, Singleton placed beside her upon the chair a note of the continental currency, of large amount but for its depreciated value ; then, without more words, they left the hovel to its wretched tenant, both much relieved upon emerging into the open air. The severity of the storm had now greatly subsided ; the rain still continued falling, however, and, hopeless of any farther discoveries of the fugitive they had pursued, and as ignorant of his character as at first, they moved onward, rapidly pushing for their bivouac upon the Ashley.

CHAPTER XVII.

THEY had scarcely gone from sight, when Goggle entered the dwelling. The old hag started from her seeming stupor, and all her features underwent a change. She fondled upon her son with all the feeble drivelling of age ; called him by various affectionate diminutives, and busied herself, in spite of her infirmities, waddling about from corner to corner of the hut, to administer to his desires, which were by no means few. He, on the other hand, manifested the most brutal indifference to all her regards, shook her off rudely as she hung upon his shoulders, and, with a boisterous manner, and a speech coupled with an oath, demanded his supper, at the same time throwing himself, with an air of extreme indolence, along the bed.

"And, Neddy dear, what has kept you so late ? Where have you been, and whence come you last ?" were the repeated questions of the old woman.

"A'drat it! mother—will you never be done asking questions ? It's not so late, I'm sure."

"Later than you said ; much later, by two hours, boy."

"Well, if it is, what then ? It's well you have me at all, for I've had a narrow chance of it. Swow ! but the bullets sung over my ears too close for comfort."

"You don't say so, Ned ! What ! that stark, bull-head Humphries, has he shot at you, Ned, my son ?"

"Him or Singleton, d—n em. But I have a hitch on him now that shall swing him. He plays 'possum no longer with Huck, if you have a tongue in your head, mother."

"Who—I ! What am I to do, Ned, boy ! Is it to put Bill

Humphries in trouble? If it's that, I have the heart to do it, if it's only for his talk to-night."

" Yes, I heard it."

" You! Why, where were you, Ned?"

" There."

He pointed to the end of the hovel, where, snugly concealed on the outside, his eye, piercing through a hole between the logs, had witnessed all that had taken place in the apartment while the partisans held it.

" And you heard and saw all?" said the old woman. " You heard his foul speech, and you saw him lift his hand to strike me because I spoke to him as he deserved! But he dared not—no, he dared not! 'Twas as much as his life was worth to lay hands on me. His arm should have withered! That it should."

" Psho! Psho! withered!" exclaimed the son scornfully. She might deceive herself, but not him.

" But who was the other man, Neddy—the Captain?"

" His name's Singleton, and he's a major of the continentals—that's all I know about him. He took me prisoner with some others of Travis's, and I joined his troop, rather than fare worse. This gives me pickings on both sides; for since I've joined we've had smart work in skirmishing; and down at Archdale Hall we made a splash at Huck's baggage-wagons, and got good spoil. See, here's a watch—true gold!—was this morning in a red-coat's fob, now in mine."

" It's good gold, and heavy, my son;—will give you yellow-boys enough."

" Ay, could we sell—but that's the devil. It comes from a British pocket, and we can't venture to offer it to any of their colour. As for the continentals, they haven't got any but their ragged currency, and that nobody wants. We must keep the watch for a good chance, for that and other reasons. I took it from a prisoner by sleight of hand, and it must not be known that I have it, on either side. Proctor would punish, and the young fellow Singleton, who has an eye like a hawk, he would not stop to give me a swinging bough if he thought I took it from one of his prisoners."

" Give it to me, boy: I'll save you that risk."

"You shall do more, mother; but first get the supper. I'm hellish hungry, and tired out with the chase I've had. A'drat it! my bones are chilled with the mud and water."

"There's a change in the chest, boy, beside you. Put the wet clothes off."

"It's too troublesome, and they'd only get wet too; for I must start back to the camp directly."

"What camp?"

"Singleton's—down upon the river—five miles below the Barony. I must be there, and let him see me, or he'll suspicion me, and move off. You will have to carry the message to Proctor."

"What, boy! will you go back and put your neck in danger? Suppose he finds you missing?"

"Well, I'll tell him the truth, so far as the truth will answer the purpose of a lie. I'll say that I came to see you, and, having done so, have come back to my duty. They cannot find fault, for the troopers every now and then start off without leave or license. I'm only a volunteer, you see."

"Take care, boy; you will try the long lane once too often. They suspect you now, I know, from the askings of that fellow Humphries; and him too, the other—what's his name?—he, too, asked closely after you."

"Singleton. I heard him."

"What Singleton is that, boy? Any kin to the Singletons hereaway in St. Paul's?"

"No, I believe not. He's from the 'High Hills,' they say, though he has friends at 'The Oaks.' It was there he went to-night. But the supper, mother—is it all ready?"

"Sit and eat, boy. There's hoecake and bacon, and some cold collards."

"Any rum?" he inquired, rising sluggishly from the bed, and approaching the little table which, while the preceding dialogue had been going on, his mother had supplied with the edibles enumerated. She handed him the jug, from which, undiluted, he drank freely, following the stronger liquid with a moderate draught from the gourd of water which she brought him at the same moment. While he ate, he muttered occasionally to his mother, who hung around him all the while in close attendance, regarding the besmeared, sallow, and disfigured wretch with as much affection as if he had been the very choicest of all God's creatures.   Such is the heart, erring continually in its appropriation of sympathies, which, though intrinsically they may be valueless, are yet singularly in proof of that care of nature, which permits no being to go utterly unblest by its regard, and bestows on every homestead, however lowly, some portion of its soothing and its sunshine.

Goggle had eaten, and now, like a gorged snake, he threw himself once more at length upon the couch that stood in the corner, grumbling, as he did so—

"A'drat it! I hate to go out again! But I must—I must go back to camp, to blind Singleton ; and as for that fellow Humphries, hear you, mother—I was in the pond by Coburn's corner when he came upon me, and just about to cross it. They called out, and crack, crack went their pistols, and the balls both times whizzed close above my head.   It was then they gave chase, and I lay close, and hugged the hollow. Singleton's horse stood right across me, and I expected his hoofs every moment upon my back."

"You don't say so, Neddy ?"

"Ay, but I do—but that's not it. The danger was something, to be sure, but even then I could listen—I could hear all they said ; and I had reason to listen, too, for it was of me Humphries spoke. The keen chap suspected me to be the man they chased, though they could not make me out ; and so he spoke of me. Can you count up what he said, mother ?"

"No, Neddy ; how should I ?"

"What! and you tell fortunes, too, and bewitch, so that all of them call you cattle charmer, yet you can't tell what Bill Humphries spoke about me, your own son! For I reckon I am *your* son, no matter who was my right father!—Can you not tell,—eh ?"

"No, sure not: some foul speech, I reckon, considering who spoke it."

"Ay, foul speech enough, if you knew. But the long and short of it, mother, is this, and I put the question to you plainly, and expect you to answer plainly—"

"What do you mean, my son ?"

" Ay, that's it—I'm your son, I believe that; but tell me, and tell me truly—who was my father ? It was of that that Humphries spoke. He spoke for all the country round, and something, too, I've heard of before. He said I was no better than my father ; that he was a horse-thief, and what was worse, that I had a cross in my blood. Speak, now, mother—speak out truly, for you see I'm in no passion ; for, whether it's true or not, I will have it out of him that spoke it, before long, some way or other. If it's true, so much the worse for him, for I can't cut your throat, mother—I can't drink your blood ; but what I can do, I will, and that is, have the blood of the man that knows and speaks of your misdoings."

That affectionate tenderness of manner which she had heretofore shown throughout the interview, passed away entirely after this inquiry of Goggle. She was no longer the mother of her son. A haggard scorn was in every feature—a hellish revival of angry passions, of demoniac hate, and a phrensied appetite. As she looked upon the inquirer, who, putting such a question, yet lay, and seemingly without emotion, sluggishly at length upon her couch, her ire seemed scarcely restrainable—her figure seemed to dilate in every part—and, striding across the floor with a rapid movement, hostile seemingly to the generally enfeebled appearance of her frame, she stood directly before, and looking down upon him—

" And are you bent to hearken to such foul words of your own mother, bringing them home to my ears, when your bullet should have gone through the head of the speaker ?"

" All in good time, mother. The bullet should have gone through his head but for an accident. But it's well it did not. He would have died then in a moment. When I kill him now, he shall feel himself dying, I warrant."

" It is well, boy. Such a foul speaker should have a death of terror—he deserves it."

" Ay, but that's neither here nor there, mother,—you have not answered my question. Speak out; was I born lawfully ?"

" Lawfully!—and what care you, Ned Blonay, about the lawfulness or the unlawfulness of your birth—you who hourly fight against the laws—who rob, who burn, who murder, whenever a chance offers, and care not ? Is it not your pleasure to break the laws—to live on the profits and the property of others? Whence came the purse you brought here last week, but from the red-coat who travelled with you as a friend, and you, all the time receiving pay from his people? Whence came this watch you just now put into my hands, but from your prisoner? and the hog of which you ate for supper, your own rifle shot it in the swamp, although you saw the double fork in the ear, and the brand on its quarter, which told you it belonged to Squire Walton, at 'The Oaks?'—what do you care about the laws, then, that you would have me answer your question?"

" Nothing; I don't care *that* for all the laws in the country—not that! But still I wish to know the truth of this matter. It's for my pleasure. I like to know the truth; whether I mind it or not is another thing."

" Your pleasure, boy—your pleasure! and what if I tell you that Humphries spoke true—that you are—"

" A bastard! speak it out—I want to hear it; and it will give me pleasure—I love that which provokes me. I can smile when one does me an injury—smile all the time I bear it quietly, for I think of the time when I'm to take pay for it. You don't understand this, perhaps, and I can't give you any reason to make it more plain. But so I do—and when Humphries had done speaking, I would have given something handsome to have had him talk it over again. When I have him in my power, he shall do so."

" The Indian blood! It will show itself anyhow!"—was the involuntary exclamation of the old woman.

" Ha! what's that, mother!"

" Ask me not."

" Ay, but I will—I must; and hear me once for all—you tell me the truth, on the instant, or you never see my face again. I'll go to the Indies with Sir Charles Montague, that's making up a regiment in Charleston for that country."

" Beware, boy—ask me not—any thing else. You will hate me if I tell you. You will leave me for ever."

" No—don't be afraid. Come, speak out, and say—was my father's name Blonay?"

"Blonay was my lawful husband, boy, when you were born," said the woman, evasively.

"Ay, that may be well enough," he exclaimed, "yet I be no son of his. Speak the truth, mother, and no two bites of a cherry. Out with it all—you can't vex me by telling it. Look here—see this wound on my arm—when it begins to heal, I rub it until it unscars and grows red and angry again. I like the pain of it. It's strange, I know, but it's my pleasure; and so I look to be pleased with the story you shall tell me. Was Blonay my father?"

"He was not."

"Good!—who was?"

"Ask no more."

"Ay, but I will—I must have it all—so speak on."

"I will not speak it aloud—I will not. I have sworn it."

"You must unswear it. I cannot be trifled with. You must tell me the secret of my birth, and all. I care not how dark, how foul, how unlawful—you must suppress nothing. This night must give me the knowledge which I have wanted before—this night you speak it freely, or lose me for ever."

The woman paced the apartment convulsively, undergoing, at every moment, some new transition, from anger and impatience, to entreaty and humbleness. Now she denounced the curiosity of her son, and now she implored his forgiveness. But she cursed or implored in vain. He lay coolly and sluggishly, utterly unmoved, at length, upon the bed; heedless of all her words, and now and then simply assuring her that nothing would suffice but the true narrative of all that he wished to know. Finding evasion hopeless, the old woman seemed to recover her own coolness and strength with the resolve which she had taken, and after a little pause for preparation, she began.

"Ned Blonay, it is now twenty-nine years since you were born—"

"Not quite, mother, not quite,—twenty-eight and some seven months. Let's see, November, you remember, was my birthday, and then I was but twenty-eight; but go on, it's not important—"

"Twenty-eight or twenty-nine, it matters not which—you were born lawfully the son of John Blonay, and as such he knew and

9

believed you. Your true father was an Indian of the Catawba nation, who passed through the Cypress the year before on his way to the city."

"Go on—the particulars."

"Ask not that—not that, boy; I pray ye—"

"All—all."

"I will not—I cannot—it was my wickedness—my shocking wickedness! I will not speak it aloud for worlds."

"Speak it you must, but you may whisper it in my ears. Stoop—"

She did so, passively as it were, and in a low tone, broken only by her own pauses and his occasional exclamations, she poured into his ear a dark, foul narrative of criminal intercourse, provoked on her part by a diseased appetite, resulting, as it would seem, in punishment, in the birth of a monster like himself. Yet he listened to it, if not passively, at least without any show of emotion or indignation; and as she finished, and hurrying away from him threw herself into her old seat, and covered her skinny face with her hands, he simply thrust his fingers into the long straight black hair depending over his eyes, which seemed to carry confirmatory evidence enough for the support of the story to which he had listened. He made no other movement, but appeared, for a while, busy in reflection. She every now and then looked towards him doubtfully, and with an aspect which had in it something of apprehension. At length, rising, though with an air of effort, from the couch, he took a paper from his pocket which he studied a little while by the blaze in the chimney, then approaching her, he spoke in language utterly unaffected by what he had heard—

"Hark ye, mother; I shall now go back to the camp. It's something of a risk, but nothing risk, nothing gain; and if I run a risk, it's for something. I go back to blind Singleton, for I shall tell him all the truth about my coming here. He won't do anything more than scold a little, for the thing's common; but if he hould—'

"What, my son?—speak!"

"No," he muttered to himself, "no danger of that—he dare not. But you come, mother,—come to the camp by sunrise, and see what you can. You'll be able to prove I was with you after the storm, and that'll clear me; then you can go to Dorchester, make all haste, and with this paper, see Proctor, and put it in his own hands yourself. There's some news in it he will be glad to pay for. It tells him something about the camp; and that about Col. Walton, shall make him fly from 'The Oaks,' as an old owl from the burning cypress. You can also tell him what you see at camp, and so use your eyes when you come there. Mind, too, if you see Huck or any of his men, keep dark. He would chouse you out of all the pay, and get the guineas for himself; and you might whistle for your share."

He gave her a dirty paper as he spoke, in which he had carefully noted down every particular relating to his new service, the force, the deeds, and the camp of Singleton—all that he thought would be of value to the enemy. She heard him, but did not approve of his return to the camp. The conference with Singleton and Humphries, together with the undisguised hostility of the latter, had filled her mind with troublesome apprehensions; and she warned her son accordingly; but he took little heed of her counsel.

"I'm bent upon it, mother, for it's a good business. You come —that's all, and say when and where you've seen me to-night. Come soon—by sunrise, and I'll get off clear, and stand a better chance of being trusted by the commander."

" And Bill Humphries ?"

"Ah! he must have his swing. Let him. The dog swallows his legs at last, and so will he. I only wait the time, and shall then shut up his mouth in a way shall be a lesson to him for ever—in a way he shan't forget, and shan't remember. He shall feel me before long."

" And he shall feel me too, the reprobate; he shall know that I have a power, though he laughs at it."

" A'drat it, but it's dark, mother; a thick cloud's yet over the moon, and but a sloppy path for a shy foot, but it must be done. There's some old hound yelping yonder in the woods; he don't like being out any more than myself."

" You will go, Ned !" and the old woman's hand was on his

shoulder. He shoved it off with something of hurry, while he answered—

"Yes, yes; and be sure you come, and when you have helped me out of the scrape, go, off-hand, to Proctor. See him, himself; —don't let them put you off. He will pay well and not chouse you, for he's a true gentleman. Good-night—good-night."

She watched him from the door-way until he was completely lost from sight in the adjacent forest.

CHAPTER XVIII.

"Oh cruel! and the shame of such a wound
Makes in the heart a deeper gash than all
It made upon the form"

SINGLETON and Humphries were hailed as they approached the patrols by the voice of Lance Frampton, the younger son of the maniac. He had volunteered to fill the post which had been deserted by Goggle. He reported the absence of the half-breed, and was gratified by receiving from his commander a brief compliment upon his precision and readiness. Such approval was grateful to the boy, coming from Singleton; for the gentle manner of the latter had already won greatly on his affections. Young Frampton, though but sixteen, was manly and fearless, full of ambition, and very promising. He rode well, and could use his rifle already with the best shots of the country. The unsettled life of the partisan warrior did not seem to disagree with his tender years, so far as he had already tried it; and his cheerless fortunes, indeed, almost denied him the choice of any other. Still, though manly in most respects, something of sadness rested upon his pale countenance, which was soft like that of a girl, and quite unlike the bronzed visages common to the sunny region in which he had been born and lived. In addition to the leading difference between himself and the people of his own condition around him, his tastes were naturally fine, his feelings delicate and susceptible, his impressions acute and lasting. He inclined to Major Singleton intuitively; s the manly freedom and ease of deportment for which his commander was distinguished, were mingled with a grace, gentleness, and pleasant propriety, to which his own nature insensibly beguiled him. He saluted them, as we have already said, with becoming modesty, unfolded his intelligence, and then quietly sank back to his position.

Humphries did not seem much surprised at the intelligence.

9*

"As I expected," he said; "it's the nature of the beast. The fellow was a born skunk, and he will die one. There's no mending that sort of animal, major, and there's little use, and some danger, to waste time on it."

"How long is it, Lance, since his departure became known to Lieutenant Davis?" was the inquiry of Singleton.

"Not a half-hour, sir. When Lieutenant Davis went the rounds, sir, to relieve him, the place was empty, and he said Goggle must have gone before the storm came up."

"Had you the storm here, Lance?" inquired Humphries.

"Not much of it, sir. It swept more to the left, and must have been heavy where it went, for the roaring of the wind was louder here than it felt. The trees doubled a little, but didn't give—only some that had the hearts eaten out. They went down, sir, at the first push of the hurricane."

Singleton conferred briefly with Humphries, and then despatched the boy to Davis, with instructions to place the party in moving order by sunrise—the two officers, riding more slowly in the same direction, conferred upon future arrangements.

"That fellow's absence, Humphries, will compel us to change our quarters, for his only object must be to carry the news to Dorchester."

"That's it, for certain, major; and the sooner we move the better. By midday to-morrow, Proctor and Huck, and the whole of 'em would be on our haunches, and we only a mouthful. A start by the time the sun squints on the pine tops, sir, would do no harm; and then, if you move up to Moultrie's old camp at Bacon's bridge, it will be far enough to misguide them for the present. From the bridge, you see, you can make the swamp almost at any moment, and yet it's not so far but you can get to 'The Oaks' soon as ever Proctor turns back upon Dorchester."

"What force has he there, think you?"

"Not enough to go far, sir, or stay out long. The garrison's but slim, and Huck is for the up country, I heard him say. He may give you a drive before he goes, for he is mighty ready to please Proctor; but then he goes by Monk's corner, and so on up to Nelson's ferry; and it will be out of his way to set upon you at Moultrie's."

"Why does he take that route, when his course is for the Ca-tawba?"

"Ha! sir, you don't know Huck. He's an old scout, and knows where the best picking lies. He goes along that route, sir, skimming it like so much cream as he goes; and woe to the housekeeper, loyalist or whig, that gives him supper, and shows him too much plate. Huck loves fine things; and for that matter, plunder of any kind never goes amiss with a tory."

"True; and the course he takes through Sumter gives him spoil enough, if he dares touch it; but Marion will soon be at Nel son's, where we hope to meet him. Let us ride on now, and see to our movement."

"With your leave, now, major, I'll go back to Dorchester."

"With what object?"

"Why, sir, only, as one may say, to curse and quit. That rascal Goggle will be in Proctor's quarters by daylight, and will soon have a pretty story for the major. I must try and get there before him, so as to stop a little the blow. Since it must come, it needn't come on anybody's head but mine; and if I can keep my old father 'rom trap, why, you see, sir, it's my born duty to do so."

"How will you do that?"

"I'll tell you, sir. Dad shall go to Proctor before Goggle, and shall denounce me himself. He shall make something out of the Englishman by his loyalty, and chouse Goggle at the same time. Besides, sir, he will be able to tell a truer story, for he shall say that we've gone from the camp, which, you know, will be the case by that time. So, if he looks for us here, as Goggle will advise him, the old man will stand better than ever in the good graces of the enemy; and will be better able to give us intelligence, and help our cause."

"But will your father like such a mission?"

"Like it, major! why, aint I his son—his only son—and won't he do, think you, what I ask him? To be sure he will. You will see."

"The plan is good, and reminds me of Pryor. You will see him, and hurry his recruiting. Say to him, from me, how much Colonel Marion expects from him, is, indeed, the letter I gave him has already persuaded him. Remind him of that letter, and let him read it to you. This will please him, and prompt to new efforts, should he prove dull. But let him be quiet—nothing impatient, till Colonel Walton is prepared to start. Only keep in readiness, and wait the signal. For yourself, when you have done this, delay nothing, and risk nothing in Dorchester. You have no plea if found out; and they will hang you off-hand as soon as taken. Follow to Bacon's bridge as soon as possible, and if you find me not there, I am either in the swamp, or in the south towards the Edisto; possibly on the road to Parker's ferry. I wish to keep moving to baffle any pursuit."

Protracted but little longer, and only the better to perfect their several plans, the conference was at length concluded, and the two separated; the one proceeding to his bivouac, and the other on his journey of peril, along the old track leading to the bridge of Dorchester.

Singleton had scarcely resumed command of his squad before the fugitive Goggle stood before him, with a countenance cold and impassive as ever, and with an air of assurance the most easy and self-satisfied. The eye of the partisan was concentrated upon him with a searching glance, sternly and calmly, but he shrank not beneath it.

"You have left your duty, sir—your post; what have you to say ?"

The offender frankly avowed his error, but spoke in extenuation.

"The storm was coming up, sir; nobody was going to trouble us, and I thought a little stretch to the old woman—my mother, sir, that is—would do no harm."

"You were wrong, sir, and must be punished. Your duty was to obey, not to think. Lieutenant Davis, a corporal's guard !"

Goggle looked somewhat astounded at this prompt movement, and urged the measure as precipitate and unusual.

"But, major, the troopers go off continually from Colonel Washington's troop, when they want to see their families—"

"The greater the necessity of arresting it in ours; but you will make your plea at morning, for with the sunrise you shall be examined."

The guard appeared, and as the torch flamed above the head of the fugitive, Singleton ordered him to be searched narrowly. With the order, the ready soldiers seized upon and bound him. His rifle was taken from his grasp—a measure inexpressibly annoying to the offender, as it was a favourite weapon, and he an excellent shot with it. In the close search which he underwent, his knife, and, indeed, everything in his possession, was carefully withdrawn, and he had reason to congratulate himself upon the timely delivery of the stolen watch to his mother ; for the prisoner from whom it had been taken had already announced its loss ; and had it been found upon the thief, it would have been matter, under the stern policy pursued by Singleton, for instantly hurrying him to some one of the thousand swinging boughs overhead. With the clear daylight, a court-martial at the drum-head sat in judgment on the prisoner. He told his story with a composure that would have done credit to innocence. There was no contradiction in his narrative. Singleton proposed sundry questions.

" Why did you not stand when called to ?"

" I was but one, major, and you were two ; and when the British and tories are thick about us, it stands to reason that it was them calling. I didn't make out your voice."

" And why did you not proceed directly to your mother's ? Why let so much time elapse between the pursuit and your appearance at her cabin ?"

" I lay close after they had gone, major, for I didn't know that they had done looking after me."

Prompt and ready were his several responses, and, apart from the initial offence of leaving his post, nothing could be ascertained calculated to convict him of any other error. In the meantime he exhibited no more interest in the scene than in the most ordinary matter. One side of his body, as was its wont, rested upon the other ; one leg hung at ease, and his head, sluggish like the rest of his person, was bent over, so as to lie on his left shoulder. At this stage of the proceedings, his mother, whose anxieties had been greater on the subject than those of her son, now made her appearance, tottering towards the group with a step in which energy and feebleness were strangely united. Her first words were those of reproach to Singleton :—

"Now, wherefore, gentlemen, do you bind the boy ?   Is it because he loves the old woman, his own mother ?   Oh, for shame ! it's a cruel shame to do so !   Will you not loose the cord ?"

She hobbled over to the place where her son stood alone, and her bony fingers were for a moment busied with the thongs, as if she strove to release him.   The prisoner himself twisted from her, and his repulse was not confined to his action.

"A'drat it, mother ! have done.   Say it out what you know, and done with it."

"What can you say, dame, in this matter ?" inquired Singleton.

"It's my son you tie with ropes—it's a good son to me—will you not loose him ?"

"He has done wrong, dame ; he has left his post, and has neglected his duty."

"He came to see his mother—his old mother ; to bring her comfort, for he had been long away, and she looked for him—she thought he had had wrong.   Was there harm in this ?"

"None, only as he had other duties, not less important, which he sacrificed for this.   But say what you know."

She did so, and confirmed the fugitive's story ; was heard patiently through a somewhat tedious narrative, in which her own feelings; and a strange show of love for the indifferent savage, were oddly blended with the circumstances which she told.   Though unavailing to save him from punishment, the evidence of his mother, and her obvious regard, had the effect of modifying its severity.   The court found him guilty, and sentenced him to the lash.   Twenty lashes, and imprisonment in the discretion of the commander, were decreed as his punishment.

A long howl—a shriek of demoniac energy—from the old woman, as she heard the doom, rang in the ears of the party.   Her long skinny finger was uplifted in vain threatenings, and her lips moved in vague adjurations and curses.   Singleton regretted the necessity which made him sanction the decree, but example was necessary in the lax state of discipline at that time prevailing throughout the country.   Marion, who was himself just and inflexible, had made him a disciplinarian.

"You will not say 'Yes' to this," cried the old woman to Singleton "You are a gentleman, and your words are kind. You will forgive the boy."

"I dare not, my good woman. Your son knew his duty, and neglected it. We must make an example, and warn other offenders. The punishment is really slight in comparison with that usually given for an offence so likely to be fatal as this of which your son has been guilty. He must submit."

The old woman raved furiously, but her son rebuked her. His eyes were thrown up obliquely to the commander, and the expression of his face was that of a sneaking defiance, as he rudely enough checked her in her denunciations.

"Hold tongue, mother—a'drat it! Can't you thank the gentlemen for their favour?"

A couple of soldiers strapped him up; when, having first taken off his outer jacket, one of them, with a common wagon-whip, prepared to execute the sentence, while the old woman, almost in danger from the lash, pressed closely to the criminal, now denouncing and now imploring the court; at one moment abusing her son for his folly in returning to the camp, and the next, with salt tears running down her withered cheeks, seeking to soothe and condole with him in his sufferings. They would have removed her from the spot before the punishment began, but she threw herself upon the earth when they attempted it, and would only rise when they forbore the effort. He, the criminal, was as impassive as ever. Nothing seemed to touch him, either in the punishment he was to receive, or the agonizing sensations which he witnessed in his mother, and which were all felt in his behalf. He helped the soldiers to remove his vest, and readily turned his back towards them, while, obliquely over his shoulder, his huge staring eyes were turned to the spot where Singleton stood, with glance somewhat averted from the scene of ignominy.

The first stroke was followed by a piercing shriek from the old woman—a bitter shriek and a curse; but with that stroke she began counting the blows.

"One"—"two"—her enumeration perpetually broken by exclamations of one sort or another—now of pity, now of horror, denunciation, and the most impotent expressions of paralytic rage—in some such phrases as the following:—"The poor boy!—his mother never whipped him!—they will murder him!—two—for he came to see her—three—was ever the like to whip a son for this!—four —God curse them! God curse them!—five—I can curse, too, that I can—they shall feel me, they shall hear me!—six, seven—that is eight—nine. Oh, the wretches! but bear up, Ned, bear up—it is half over—that is ten—my poor boy! Oh, do not strike so hard! Look! the red on the shirt—it is blood! Oh, wretches! have you no mercy?—it is most done—there, there—stop! Hell blast you for ever!—that was twenty. Why did you strike another? I curse you with a black curse for that other stroke! You ragged imp!— you vile polecat!—I curse you for that stroke!"

The execution was over. Unflinching to the last, though the strokes were severely dealt, the criminal had borne them. He looked the very embodiment of callosity. His muscles were neither composed nor rigid during the operation; and though the flesh evidently felt, the mood of the wretch seemed to have undergone no change. Before he could yet be freed from the cords, his mother's arms were thrown around him; and though he strove to shake her off, and shrank from her embraces, she yet persisted, and, with a childish fondness, she strove, with kind words, while helping him on with his jacket, to console him for his sufferings.

"And you will go with me now, Neddy—you will go from these cruel men?"

"I cannot, mother; don't you know I'm to be under guard so long as the major chooses?"

"He will not—you will not tie him up again; you will let him go now with his mother."

She turned to Singleton as she spoke; but his eye refused her ere his tongue replied—

"He will be in custody for twelve hours; and let me say to you, dame, that for such an offence his punishment is a very slight one. Marion's men would suffer two hundred lashes, and something more restraint, for the same crime."

"God curse him!" she said bitterly, as she again approached her son, with whom she conversed apart. He whispered but a word in her ear, and then turned away from her. She looked after him a moment, as the guard marched him into the rear but her finger was uplifted towards Singleton, and the fierce fire shooting out from her grey eye, and moving in the direction of the pointed finger, was long after remembered by him. In a few moments more, she was gone from the camp, and, with a degree of elasticity scarcely comporting with her years, was trudging fast on her way to Dorchester.

Waiting until she had fairly departed, Singleton at length left his camp on the Ashley, and leaving no traces of his sojourn but the dying embers of his fires, he led the way towards the designated encampment at Bacon's Bridge. This was a few miles above Dorchester, on the same river, and immediately contiguous to the Cypress Swamp. An old battery and barracks, built by General Moultrie, and formerly his station, prior to the siege of Charleston, furnished a much more comfortable place of abode than that which he had just vacated. Here he took that repose which the toils of the last twenty-four hours rendered absolutely necessary.

CHAPTER XIX.

'Let aer pulse beat a stroke the more or less
And she were blasted. I will stand by this ,
My judgment is her fear."

LEAVING Singleton, as we have seen, as soon as the absence of
Goggle from the camp was certainly known, Humphries hurried on
his returning route to the village of Dorchester. Cool and calculating, but courageous, the risk which he ran was far from inconsiderable. How could he be sure he was not already, suspected:
how know that some escaping enemies had not seen and given
intelligence of his presence among the rebels; and why should not
the fugitive be already in the garrison with Proctor preparing the
schemes which were to wind about and secure him ? These questions
ever rose in his mind as he surveyed his situation and turned over
his own intentions; but, though strong enough as doubts, they were
not enough as arguments, to turn him from a purpose which he
deemed good and useful, if not absolutely necessary. He dismissed
them from his thoughts, therefore, as fast as they came up. He was
a man quite too bold, too enterprising to be discouraged and driven
from his plans by mere suggestions of risk; and whistling as he
went a merry tune, he dashed forward through the woods, and was
soon out of the bush and on the main road of the route—not far
from the spot where, in the pause of the storm, they had stumbled
upon the half-blood, Blonay.

The tree which the lightning had stricken just beside the path,
was still in flame. The rain could not quench it, as the rich lightwood, traced through every cavity of the bark by the greedy fire,
furnished a fuel not easily extinguishable. The flame licked along
the sides, at intervals, up and down, from top to trunk; at one
moment, lost from one place—the next, furiously darting upon another. Its blaze showed him the track through the hollow to old

Mother Blonay's, and, as he beheld it, a sudden desire prompted him once more to look into the dwelling of the old woman. He was strangely fascinated in this direction, particularly as he remembered the equivocal nature of the threat which she had screamed in his ear in regard to his sister. " Goggle, Goggle, Goggle !" But that he already entertained much anxiety in respect to the girl, he would have attached no importance to the unmeaning syllables. But now, a shiver ran through his frame while he thought upon them !

" She shall tell me what she means !" he muttered as he went.

Alighting from his horse, he approached the hovel, hitched the animal to a hanging bough, and, with as light a footstep as possible, quietly approached the entrance. Peeping through an aperture between the loose logs he gazed upon the inmate. There, still in her seat beside the fireplace, she kept up the same croning movement, to and fro, maintaining her balance perfectly, yet fast asleep all the while. Sometimes her rocking would be broken with a start, but sleep had too far possessed her ; and though her dog barked once or twice at the approach of the stranger, the interruption in her seesaw was but for a moment, and an incoherent murmur indistinctly uttered, only preceded her relapse into silence and slumber as before. Beside her lay her twin cats—twin in size though not in colour—a monstrous pair, whose sleep emulated that of their mistress. On a bench before her, clearly distinguishable in the firelight, Humphries noted her travelling bundle with a staff run through it. This indicated her itinerant habits, and his conclusion was, that the old hag, who wandered usually from plantation to plantation, from hovel to hovel, pretending to cure or charm away disease, and taking large collections in return from the charitable, the ignorant, and superstitious alike—had made her preparations for an early journey in the morning. While he looked, his own superstitious fancies grew active ; and, a cold shiver which he could not escape, but of which he was heartily ashamed, came over him, and, with a hurried step, he darted away from the contemplation of a picture he could not regard in any other light than as one horrible and unholy.

Humphries was not the slave of a feeble and childish superstition ; but the natural influences which affect the uneducated mind commonly, had their due force on his. The secret cause is always mysterious, and commonly produces enervating and vague fears in the bosoms of all that class of people who engage in no thoughts beyond those called for by their everyday sphere and business. So with him. He had doubts, and in proportion with his ignorance were his apprehensions. Ignorance is of all things the most apprehensive in nature. He knew not whether she had the power that she professed, or that any one could possess such power, and his active imagination gave her all the benefit of his doubt. Still he did not fear. No one who knew his usually bold character, his recklessness of speech and action, would deem him liable to any fear from such influences as were supposed to belong to the withered tenant of that isolated hovel. And yet, when he thought upon the cheerless life which she led and seemed to love—when he asked himself what might be its pleasures or its solace—he could not avoid feeling that in its anti-social evidences lurked the best proof of its evil nature. Wherefore should age, poverty, and feebleness, fly so far, and look so harshly upon, the whole world around it ? Why refuse its contiguity ?—why deny, why shrink away from the prospect of its comforts and its blessings ? Why ? unless the mood within was hostile—unless its practices were unfriendly to the common good, as they were foreign to the common habit, of humanity ? He knew, indeed, that poverty may at all times sufficiently account for isolation—that an acute sensibility may shrink from that contact with the crowd which may, and does, so frequently betray or wound it ; and he also well knew that there is no sympathy between good and bad fortune, except as the one is apt to desire that survey of the other which will best enable it to comprehend the superior benefits of its own position. But that old woman had no such sensibilities, and her poverty was not greater—not so great, indeed, as that of many whom he knew besides, who yet clung to, and sought to share some of the ties and regards of society, though unblessed by the world's goods, and entirely out of the hope of a redeeming fortune. Did he not also know that she exulted in the thought that she was *feared* by those around her, and studiously inculcated the belief among the vulgar, that she possessed attributes which were dangerous and unholy! Her very pride was an abomination to humanity, as her chief source of satisfaction seemed to lie in the exercise of powers unwholesome and annoying to man. No wonder the blood grew cold and curdled in the veins of the blunt countryman as he thought upon these matters. No wonder that he moved away to his horse, with a rapidity he would not his enemy should see, from a spot over which, as his mind dwelt upon the subject, such an infernal atmosphere seemed to brood and gather. The bark of the dog as the hoofs of his charger beat upon the ground while he hurried along his path, startled more completely the old hag, who half rose from her seat, threw up her head to listen, then, pushing the dismembered brands of her fire together, composed herself once more in her chair to sleep.

The evening of the day upon the history of which we have been engaged, had been rather remarkable in the annals of the " Royal George." There had been much to disturb the waters, and, we may add, the spirits in that important domain. There had been a partial sundering of ancient ties—a violation of sometime sacred pledges, an awkward collision of various interests.

On the ensuing Monday, Sergeant Hastings, of whom we have already seen either too much or too little, was to take his departure with the notorious Captain Huck to join Tarleton on the Catawba. The interval of time between the present and that fixed for this, so important, remove, was exceedingly brief; but a day, and that a holiday, intervened—and then farewell to the rum punch, the fair coquette, and the pleasant company of the " Royal George."

The subject was a melancholy one to all parties. The sergeant preferred the easy life, the good company, the cheering liquor of the tavern, and there were other and less honourable objects yet in his mind, unsatisfied, and as far from realization as ever. Bella Humphries had too little regard for him really to become his victim, though he had spared no effort to that end. On the contrary, the girl had latterly grown peevish in some respects, and he could clearly perceive, though the cause remained unknown, that his influence over her was declining. His assumption of authority, his violence, and perhaps his too great familiarity, had wonderfully lessened him in her regard ; and, if the truth must be known, John Davis was in reality more potent in her esteem than she had been willing to acknowledge either to that personage or to herself.

While Davis kept about the tavern, a cringing and peevish lover, contributing to her conceit while acknowledging her power, she was not unwilling, with all the thoughtlessness of a weak girl, to trifle with his affections ; but now that he had absented himself, as it seemed for ever, she began to comprehend her own loss and to lament it. Such a consciousness led her to a more close examination of Hastings's pretensions, and the result of her analysis was quite unfavourable to that worthy. His many defects of disposition and character, his vulgarity, his impudence, all grew remarkably prominent in her eyes, and he could now see that, when he would say, in a manner meant to be alluring :—

"Hark'ee, Bell, my beauty—get us a swig, pretty particular, and not too strong o' the lemon, and not too weak o' the Jamaica, and not too scant considering the quantity"—there was no sweet elasticity in the utterance of—

"Yes, sergeant, certainly,—you shall have it to your liking ;" coupled with a gracious smile and a quickness of movement that left the time between the order and its instant execution a space not perceptible even to that most impatient person, himself. He could feel the change now, and as the time allowed him was brief, and opportunities few, he hurried himself in devising plans for the better success of a design upon her, long entertained, of a character the most vile and nefarious.

But his bill remained unpaid ; and this was the worst feature in the sight of our landlord. That evening (Saturday) the worthy publican had ventured to suggest the fact to the disregarding memory of the sergeant, who had, with the utmost promptness, evaded the demand. Some words had passed between them—old Humphries had been rather more spirited, and Hastings rather more insolent than usual ; and the latter, in search of consolation, made his way into the inner room where Bella officiated. To crown his discontent, his approach was utterly unnoticed by that capricious damsel. He dashed away in dudgeon from the house at an early hour, certainly less regretted by the maid than by the master of the inn.

Such had been the transactions of the evening of that night, when, at a late hour, Humphries approached the dwelling of his father. The house lay in perfect shadow as he drew nigh the outer buildings, in the rear of one of which he carefully secured his horse. The moon, obscured during the early part of the evening, and dim throughout the night, had now sunk westering so far, that it failed to touch entirely the close and sheltered court in front of the house. As he drew nigh, moving along in the deeper shadow of the fence to the rear of the dwelling, for which he had a key, he started. Was it a footstep that reached his ear ? He squatted to the ground and listened. He was not deceived. The indistinct outline of a man close under the piazza, was apparent. He seemed busied in some labour which he pursued cautiously, and in perfect silence. Humphries could see that he stooped to the ground, and that in the next moment, his arms were extended. A few seconds after and the person of the man seemed to rise in air. The watcher could no longer be mistaken. Already had the nightstalker taken two steps upon the ladder which he had placed against the house, when Humphries bounded forward from his place of watch. His soul was on fire, for he saw that the object of the stranger was the chamber of his sister, the windows of which looked out upon the piazza, and were all open, as was usual in the summer nights.

The look of the old hag, her strange words uttered as a threat, grew strong in his mind, and he now seemed to understand them. Drawing his dirk from his bosom, the only weapon he had ventured to bring with him from the stable, in the fodder of which he had hidden his sabre and pistols, he rushed furiously towards the burglar But his movement had been too precipitate for success ; and with the first sound of his feet, the marauder had dropped from the ladder, and taken to his heels. The start in his favour being considerable, gave him a vast advantage over his pursuer, for, though swift of foot, active, and spurred on by the fiercest feelings, Humphries failed to come up with him. A moment after the fugitive had leaped the fence, the dirk of the former was driven into that part of it over which his body had passed. The villain had escaped.

Gloomy and disappointed, the brother returned to the spot, and calmly inspected the premises. Painfully and deeply apprehensive were his thoughts, as he surveyed the ladder, and the open windows above. But for his timely arrival there would have been little or no difficulty in effecting an entrance. Did the wretch seek to rob? That was the hope of Humphries. Could it be possible that his sister had fallen? was she a victim, privy to the design of the felon? or did he only now, for the first time, seek her dishonour? He knew that she was weak and childish, but he also believed her innocent. Could she have looked for the coming of a paramour? The unobstructed windows, the unbroken silence, the confident proceeding of the man himself—all would seem to strengthen the damning idea which now possessed his mind; and when his perpetually recurring thought brought to him the picture of the old hag, her hellish glare upon him, and her mysterious threat—a threat which now seemed no longer mysterious—the dreadful apprehensions almost grew into certainty. There was but one, and that a partial mode, of ascertaining how far the girl was guilty of participation in the design of the stranger; and, with the thought, Humphries at once ascended the ladder which he threw down after him. From the piazza he made his way to the girl's chamber.

A light was burning in the fireplace, dimly, and with no power to serve him where it stood. He seized it, almost convulsively, in one hand, while the uplifted dagger was bare in the other; and thus he approached the couch where she lay. He held the light above, so that its glare touched not her eyes, and he looked down into her face. She lay sleeping, soundly, sweetly, with a gentle respiration like a sigh swelling equally her bosom. There was no tremor, no start. Her round, fair face wore a soft, smiling expression, showing that the consciousness within was not one of guilt. One of her arms hung over the pillow, her cheek resting upon it; the other pressed slightly her bosom, as naturally as if there had been a throbbing and deeply feeling heart under it. The brother looked, and as he looked, he grew satisfied. He could not doubt that sleep; it was the sleep of innocence. A weight of nameless, of measureless terror, had been taken from his soul in that survey; and nature claimed relief in a flood of tears. The drops fell on the cheek of the sleeper, and she started. With the movement, he put aside the dagger, not, however, before her eyes had beheld it.

" Oh, William ! brother, dear brother ! is it you ? and—the knife ?"

She had caught his hand in her terror, and amaze and bewilderment overspread her features.

" Sleep on, Bell, sleep on ; you are a good girl, and needn't fear."

He kissed her as he spoke, and, with the fondness of a sister, and the thoughtlessness of a girl, she began to prattle to him ; but he bade her be quiet, and, taking the light with him, descended to the lower apartment, adjoining the bar-room, where his father usually slept. To his surprise he was not there, but a gleam through the door led the son to the place where the old man usually served his customers. The picture that met his eye was an amusing one. There, at length upon the floor, the landlord lay. A candle placed beside him, with a wick doubled over and blazing into the tallow, lacked the friendly aid of the snuffers. The old man was too deeply engaged in his vocation to notice this. His head, resting upon one hand, was lifted upon his elbow, and before him were sundry shingles, covered with tallies in red chalk and in white, against his sundry customers. The landlord was busily engaged in drawing from these chronicles, the particular items in the account of Sergeant Hastings, which he transcribed upon a sheet of paper which lay before him. A tumbler of Jamaica, of especial body, stood conveniently close, from which he occasionally drew strong refreshment for his memory. He was too earnest in his labour, to notice the entrance of his son at first ; but the other had too little time to spare, to scruple much at disturbing his father at his unusual labour.

" Ah, bless me, Bill—that you ? Why, what's the to-do now ? What brings you so late ?"

" Business, business, father, and plenty of it. But get up, rouse you and bustle about, and get away from these scores, or you won't understand a word I tell you."

The landlord rose immediately, put his shingles aside, picked up the sheet containing the amount in gross charged against Sergeant Hastings, which he sighed deeply to survey, and, in a few moments, was prepared to listen to what his son could say. He heard the narrative with horror and astonishment.

" God bless us and preserve us, Bill ! but this is awful hard ; and what are we to do—where shall we run—how ?—"

" Run nowhere, but listen to what I tell you. You can't help it now, but you may make something out of it. If Proctor must hear the truth, he may as well hear it from you."

" From me !—bless me, Bill, my boy—from me ?"

" Yes, from you. Set off by daypeep to the fort, and see Proctor yourself. Tell him of your loyalty, and how you love the king; and you can cry a little all the time, if it comes easy to you. I don't want you to strain much about it. Tell him that you have an unworthy son, that's not of your way of thinking. Say he's been misguided by the rebels, and how they've inveigled him, till he's turned rebel himself; and how he's now out with Marion's men, in Major Singleton's squad. When you've done this, you can cry again, and do any thing to throw dust in his eyes. Say it's all owing to your loyalty that you expose your own flesh and blood, and mind you don't take any money for telling."

" Bless me, my dear boy, but this is awful to think on."

" It must be thought on, though, and the sooner the better. Coming from you, it will help you ; coming from that skunk, Goggle, and you silent, and they pack you off to the Charleston provost, or maybe draw you over the swinging bough. Tell Proctor our force is thirty ; that we lay at Slick pond last night, and that we push for Black river by daypeep, to join with the Swamp Fox. This, you see, will be a truer story than Goggle can tell, for if he sends Proctor after us to Slick pond, he'll have a journey to take back."

" Bless me, what's to become of us all, Bill, I don't see. I am all over in a fever now, ever since you tell'd me your story."

" Shake it off, and be comfortable, as you can be. Thinking about it never cured the shaking ague yet, and never will. You must try."

" And I will try—I will, boy ; but bless me, Bill, wouldn't it be better for us all to take to the swamp—eh ?"

" No—stay where you are ; there's no need for you to go out, and you can do good where you are. Besides, there's Bell, you know."

" True, true."

" Lead out trumps, that's the way, and mind how you play 'em ; that's all you've got to do now, and if so be you try, you can do it. Don't burn daylight, but be with Proctor as soon as sunrise lets you. Don't stop to talk about Edisto catfish, or what's for dinner, and whether it's like to rain or shine, but push through the crowd, and don't mind your skirts. All depends on you, now."

" Bless us, bless us ! what times, what times ! Oh, Bill, my boy, what's coming to us ! Here was Huck, to-day, and says Continental Congress is to make peace with Great Britain, and to give up Carolina and Georgia."

" Oh ! that's all a fool notion, for it's no such thing. That's all a trick of the tories, and you needn't mind it. But what of Huck ?"

" He goes a-Monday to join Tarleton."

" Good !—and now I must leave you. I've got a mighty deal to see to afore daylight, and I won't see you for a smart spell, I reckon, as I shall have to hug the swamp close after this. Don't be slow now, father, 'cause every thing hangs on your shoulders, and you must tell your story straight."

In their dialogue the son had taken care to omit nothing which a shrewd, thinking mind might suggest, as essential to the successful prosecution of the plan advised. This done, he took his way to the dwelling of old Pryor, and tapping with his knife-handle thrice upon one of the small, but ostentatious, pine pillars of the portico, the door was unclosed, and he was at once admitted, as one who had been waited for. There we shall leave him, conferring closely with a select few, busy, like himself, in preparations for a general uprising of the people.

CHAPTER XX.

She is lost !—
She is saved !—GOETHE.

HUMPHRIES, poor old man, placed himself at an eastern window, the moment his son had departed, to watch for the first glances of the daylight. What a task had he to perform ! what a disclosure to make ! and how should he evade the doubt—though complying with the suggestion of reason and his son alike—that he should, by the development he was about to make, compromise the safety of the latter. Should he be taken, the evidence of the father would be adequate to his conviction, and that evidence he was now about to offer to the enemy. He was to denounce him as a rebel, an outlaw, whom the leader of a single troop might hang without a trial, the moment he was arrested. The old man grew miserable with his reflections, and there was but one source of consolation. Fortunately, the supply of old Jamaica in the " Royal George" was still good ; and a tumbler of the precious beverage, fitly seasoned with warm spices and sugar, was not ineffectually employed to serve the desired purpose.

And with this only companion, whose presence momently grew less, the worthy landlord watched for the daylight from his window ; and soon the grey mist rose up like a thin veil over the tops of the tall trees, and the pale stars sped, retreating away from the more powerful array which was at hand. The hum of the night insects was over—the hoarse chant of the frog family was silent, as their unerring senses taught them the coming of that glorious and beautiful presence which they did not love. Fold upon fold, like so many variously shaded wreaths, the dim curtain of the night was drawn gradually up into heaven, and once more the vast panorama of forest, river, and green valley came out upon the sight, rising, by little and little, into life, in the slowly illumined distance.

The moment old Humphries saw the approach of daylight, he finished his tumbler of punch, and, with a sad heart, he set out for Proctor's quarters. Some little delay preceded his introduction to the commandant of the garrison, who received him graciously, and civilly desired to know his business. This was soon unfolded, and with many pauses, broken exclamations of grief and loyalty, the landlord gave a brief account, as furnished him by his son, of all the events which had occurred to Singleton and his squad since his assumption of its command. The affair of the tories and his troop in the swamp—the capture of the baggage and arms—the delay of which, a matter of surprise to Huck, was now accounted for—and the subsequent bivouac upon the Ashley, were quickly unfolded to the wondering Briton. He immediately despatched a messenger for Huck, while proceeding to the cross-examination of his inform ant—a scrutiny which he conducted with respect and a proper consideration.

All was coherent in his story, and Proctor was inly troubled. A piece of daring, such as the formation of Singleton's squad, so near the garrison, so immediately in the neighbourhood and limits of the most esteemed loyalty, was well calculated to annoy him. The name of Major Singleton, too, grated harshly on his ears. He could not but remember the meaning reference of Katharine Walton to her cousin of the same name; and he at once identified him with his rival in that young lady's regard. Huck came in while yet he deliberated; and to him the narrative which Humphries delivered, who stood by all the while, was also told. The tory was not less astounded than Proctor; and the two conferred freely on their news before Humphries, whose loyalty was properly confirmed in their opinion, by his unscrupulous denunciation of his own son. To Huck, the commandant of the garrison was compelled to apply, and the troop of the former was required to disperse the force of Singleton. The garrison guard was too small, under the doubtful condition of loyalty in the neighbourhood, to spare a detachment; and it was arranged, therefore, that Huck should depart from his original plan and route, which was to start on the ensuing day for Camden, and immediately to make a circuit through the country by the Ashley, and having done so, go forward by Parker's Ferry, and gain, by a circuitous

10

sweep, the course which had been formerly projected, and which, indeed, the orders received by him from Cornwallis, compelled him to pursue. It was hoped that he would overhaul the little force of Singleton, in which event it must have been annihilated.

In the mean time, Proctor prepared his despatches for Charleston, calling for a supply of troops—a call not likely to be responded to from that quarter, as the garrison there had been already drawn upon by the interior, to such an extent as to leave barely a sufficient force within the walls of the city for its own maintenance. This Proctor knew, but no other hope presented itself, and glad to use the troop of Huck, he contented himself with the consciousness of having done all that could be done by him, under existing circumstances. Civilly dismissing Humphries, he would have rewarded him, but the old man urged his simple and sincere loyalty, and naturally shrank back at the idea of receiving gold as the reward of his son's betrayal. He did his part shrewdly, and leaving the two conferring upon the particulars of the tory's route, hurried away to the tavern in no enviable state of feeling.

His son, whom we have seen entering the dwelling of old Pryor, was glad to meet with several sturdy whigs in close conference. They had been stimulated by the whispers of an approaching army of continentals, and the vague intelligence had been exaggerated in due proportion to the thick obscurity which at that time hung about the subject. The host himself—who was a sturdy patriot, and more than usually bold, as, of late days, he was more than usually unfortunate—presided upon this occasion. The party was small, consisting of some half dozen persons, all impatient of the hourly wrongs, which, in their reckless indifference to the feelings of the conquered, the invaders continually committed. The reduction of the British force in the lower county, in the large draughts made upon it for the upper posts, had emboldened disaffection; and the people, like snakes long huddled up in holes during the severe weather, now came out with the first glimpses of the sunshine.

The arrival of Humphries with the intelligence which he brought, gave them new spirits. The successes of Marion at Britton's Neck, and Singleton in the swamp, of which they had not heard before, though small, were yet held an earnest of what might be anticipated, and what was hoped for. The additional news that the approaching continentals were to be commanded by Gates, whose renown was in the ascendant—so far in the ascendant, indeed, that the star of Washington almost sank before it—went far to give hope a positive body and a form. Doubt succeeded to bold prediction, and the conspirators were now prepared—those reluctant before—to begin properly the organization of their section, as had been the advice of Marion.

Still, they were not altogether ready for the field. Property was to be secured, families carried beyond reach of that retribution which the enemy usually inflicted upon the feeble in return for the audacity and defiance of the strong; arms were to be procured, and, until the time of Sir Henry Clinton's indulgence—the twenty days —had expired, they determined to forbear all open demonstration. To these, Humphries had already designated their leader, in the person of Colonel Walton, whom they all knew and esteemed. His coming out they were satisfied would, of itself, bring an active and goodly troop into the field. Popular as he was, both in St. Paul's and St. George's, it was confidently believed that he would bring both the parishes out handsomely, and his skill as a leader had been already tried and was highly estimated. The spirits of the little knot of conspirators grew with every enumeration of their prospects and resources, and they looked up, as daylight approached, full of hope and mutual assurances. Two of the party agreed to come out to Humphries, in the contiguous wood, by the first ringing of the bell for sabbath service—for the day was Sunday—and there, at a given spot, the lieutenant was to await them.

Before the daylight he took his departure, and leading his horse into the close swamp thicket on the river, where his first conference with Singleton had taken place, he fastened him carefully, took his seat at the foot of a tree which overhung the river, and there mused, half dozing, for the brief hour that came between the time and the dawning. But soon the light came winding brightly and more brightly around him; the mists curled up from the river, and the breeze rising up from the ocean, with the dawn, refreshed and animated him. He sat watching the mysterious separation of those twin agents of nature, night and day, as the one rolled away in fog along the river, and the other burst forth, in gleams from the sky and bloom upon the earth.

But these sights were not such as greatly to amuse our lieutenant, and the time passed heavily enough, until about eight o'clock, when, from the river's edge, he distinguished, crossing the bridge at Dorchester, the time-worn, bent figure of old dame Blonay. She was on her way to the garrison for the revelation of that intelligence which his father had by this time already unfolded. The lieutenant now understood a part of the design, and readily conceived that such was the purport of her visit to the village. Yet why had not her son undertaken the task himself? Why depute to an infirm old woman the performance of an object so important? The question puzzled him; and it was only a dim conjecture of the truth, which led him to believe that Goggle had made his way back to camp with the view to some farther treachery.

As the hag grew more distinct to his eye, in the increasing light, her sharp features—the subtle cast of her eye—the infirm crazy motion—bent shoulders, and witch-like staff which she carried, brought many unpleasant fancies to the mind of the observer; and the singular, and, to him, the superstitious fear which he had felt while gazing upon her, through the crevices of her hut the night before, came back to him with increased influence. He thought of the thousand strange stories of the neighbourhood, about the witchcraft practised by her and others. Indian doctors were then, all over the country, renowned for their cures, all of which were effected by trick and mummery, mixed up with a due proportion of forest medicines—wild roots and plants, the properties of which, known through long ages to the aborigines, were foreign to the knowledge, and therefore marvellous in the estimation of the whites. To their arts, the Gullah and the Ebo negroes, of which the colony had its thousands furnished by the *then* unscrupulous morality of the mother country and the northern colonies, added their spells and magic, in no stinted quantities, and of the foulest and filthiest attributes. The conjuration of these two classes became united in the practice of the cunning white, of an order little above them, and mother Blonay formed the representative of a sect in the lower country of South Carolina, by no means small in number or trifling in influ-

ence, and which, to this day, not utterly extinguished, remains here
and there in the more ignorant sections, still having power over the
subject minds of the weak and superstitious.

As we have said, Humphries was not one, if the question were
to be asked him, to say that he believed in the powers thus claimed
for the old woman before us. But the bias of years, of early education and associates, was insurmountable; and he felt the influence
which his more deliberate reflection was, nevertheless, at all times
disposed to deny. He felt it now as she came towards him ; and
when, passing along, he saw her move towards the dwelling of his
father, he remembered her mysterious speech associated with the
name of his sister, and his blood grew cold in his veins, though, an
instant after, it again boiled with a fury naturally enough arising
from the equivocal regard in which that speech had seemed to place
the girl. As the wretch passed along the copse to the edge of which
his feet had almost followed her, he placed himself in a position to
observe the direction which she would pursue in entering the village, and was satisfied of her object when he saw her bending her
way to the fortress.

We need scarcely add that the old woman told her story to Proctor, and was listened to coldly. She had brought him no intelligence, and, indeed, he knew rather more than herself. But one
point of difference existed between the account given by old Humphries and the woman. The one stated that Singleton's band had
withdrawn from the Ashley, and had pushed for Black river—the
other affirmed it to be there still.

The difference was at once made known to Huck, a portion of
whose troopers were even then getting into saddle. The residue
were soon to follow, and the whole were expected to rendezvous that
night at Parker's ferry. Mother Blonay was mortified that she
brought no news to the garrison ; but, as her story confirmed that of
Humphries, Proctor gave her a reward, small, however, in comparison
with what had been expected. She left the garrison in bad humour,
and was soon joined on her way by Sergeant Hastings, whose orders
required him to march with the detachment which was to follow
Huck that afternoon. His chagrin, on this account, was not less
than hers. A bitter oath accompanied the information which he

gave her of the orders he had just received. The two then spoke
of another matter.

" Far off as ever, mother, and without your help there's nothing
to be done now. Last night I was in a fair way enough, but up
comes that chap her brother—it could be nobody else—and I had
to cut for it. I went over the fence then a thought quicker than I
should be able to do it now."

" It was not Bill Humphries you saw, for he was at my cabin
long time after hours last night; and then he'd not venture into
this quarter now. No—no. 'Twas the old man, I reckon."

" Maybe, though he seemed to run too fast for the old fellow.
But no matter who 'twas. The thing failed, and you must chalk
out another track."

" I will : dont fear, for I've said it ; and come fire, come storm,
it must be done. Goggle—Goggle—Goggle ! He must pay for that,
and he shall ; *she* shall—they shall *all* pay for that, and old scores
besides. It's a long-standing account, sergeant, and you can help
me to make it up and pay it off ; and that's the reason I help you
to this. I shall go about it now, and—" After a pause, in which
she seemed to meditate a while—" Yes ; meet me in the swamp
thicket above the bridge, just after you pass the Oak Grove."

" When ?"

" This morning—soon as the bells strike up for church, and before the people begin to come in freely. Don't be backward, now,
but come certain, and don't wait for the last chimes."

The worthy pair separated, and the glimpses of a previous connexion, which their dialogue gives us, serve a little to explain some
portions of our own narrative.

While this matter had been in progress, two sturdy troopers
joined Humphries in the swamp. Their horses were carefully hidden, and they determined to await the time when the roads should
be free from the crowd on their way to church, before they ventured abroad. They amused themselves as well as they might,
keeping close in cover themselves, by watching the people as they
crossed the bridge, hurried along the highway leading to the village, or lounged on the open ground in front of the church ; for all
of these points might easily be commanded from different places

along the thicket. There came the farmer on his plough-horse, in his coarse striped breeches, blue homespun coatee, and broad-brimmed hat; there, the whirling carriage, borne along by four showy bays, of the wealthy planter; there the trudging country girl in her huge sunbonnet and short-waisted cotton frock; and there, in little groups of two or three, the negroes, male and female, with their own small stock of eggs, chickens, blackberries, and sassafras, ploughing their way through the heavy sands to occupy their places in the village market.

While Humphries looked, he saw, to his great vexation, the figure of Dame Blonay approaching, accompanied by his sister. All his suspicions were reawakened by the sight. The girl was dressed as for church. Her dress was simple, suited to her condition, and well adapted to her shape, which was a good one. Her bonnet was rather fine and flaunting, and there was something of gaudiness in the pink and yellow distributed over her person in the guise of knots and ribands. But still the eye was not offended, for the habit did not show unfavourably along with the pretty face, and light, laughing, good-natured eye that animated it. What a contrast to the old hag beside her! The one, capricious enough, was yet artless and simple—the other old, stern, ugly, poor, was even then devising plans for the ruin of the child.

"Come, my daughter, come farther—I would not others should hear what I say to you; and I know it will please you to know. The wood is cool and shady, and we can talk there at our ease."

"But, mother, wasn't it a strange dream now—a very strange dream, to think that I should be a great lady, and ride in my coach like the ladies at 'Middleton Place,' and 'The Oaks,' and 'Singletons,' and all the rich people about here?—and it all seemed so true, mother—so very true, I didn't know where I was when I woke up this morning."

There was a devilish leer in the old hag's eye, as she looked into that of the vain-hearted but innocent girl beside her, and answered her in a speech well calculated to increase the idle folly already so active in her mind. Humphries heard nothing of the dialogue—he was quite too far off; but he felt so deeply anxious on the subject of the old woman's connexion with his sister, that he had actually given some directions to the two troopers along with him, and was about to emerge from his cover, and separate them at all hazards, when the bells from the village steeple struck up, and warned him of the extreme risk which he must run from such an exposure of his person. The same signal had the effect of bringing Bella and Mother Blonay more closely to the copse, to which the old woman, now, by various suggestions, contrived to persuade her companion. While they approached the thicket, Humphries changed his course and position, so as to find a contiguous spot, for the concealment of his person, the moment they should stop, which would enable him to gather up their dialogue ; and it was not long before they paused, at the old woman's bidding, in a well shaded place, completely unseen from the road and quite out of hearing from the village. Here the conversation between them was resumed —Mother Blonay leading off in reply to something said by Bella, the purport of which may be guessed from the response made to it.

"A bad dream, do you say, my daughter? I say it is a good dream, and you're a lucky girl, if you don't stand in the way of your own fine fortune. There's good coming to you : that dream's always a sign of good ; it never fails. So mind you don't spoil all by some foolish notion."

"Why, how shall I do, mother? what shall I say? Dear me! I wouldn't do any thing to spoil it for the world!"

And the two seated themselves upon the green turf in the thicket, the right hand of the girl upon the knee of the hag, while her eyes looked up apprehensively and inquiringly into the face of the latter. She gave her some counsel, accordingly, in answer to her questions, of a vague, indefinite character, very mysteriously delivered, and the only part of which, understood by Bella, was a general recommendation to her, quietly to receive, and not to resist her good fortune.

"But, mother, I thought you said you would show him to me— him, my true-and-true husband, that is to be. Now I wonder who it can be. It can't be John Davis, for he's gone away from the village, and they say he's out in the swamp, mother—can you tell?"

"No, Bella ; and it's no use : he's nothing at all to you. You are not for such a poor scrub as John Davis."

"You think so, mother? Well, I'm sorry; for I do believe John had a true-and-true love for me in his heart, and he often said so. I wonder where he is."

"John Davis, indeed, my child! how can you speak of such a fellow? Why, what has he to show for you? A poor shoat that hasn't house, nor home, nor any thing to make a wife comfortable, or even feed her when he gets her. No, no, girl, the husband that's for you is a different sort of person—a very different sort of person, indeed."

"Oh, do, mother! can't you tell me something about him, now? —only a little: I do so want to know. Is he tall, now, or short? I hope he's tall—eh?—middle size, and wears—oh, speak, mother! and don't shake your head so—tell me at once!"

And the girl pressed forward upon the old woman, and her eye earnestly watched the features of her countenance, heedless of the ogre grin which rested upon her lips, and the generally fiendish expression of her skinny face. The old woman did not immediately answer, for her thoughts seemed to wander, and her eye looked about her, as if in search of some expected object.

"What do you look for, mother?—you don't mind what I say, do you?"

"I was looking and thinking, my daughter, how to answer you best. How would you like, now, instead of hearing about your husband that is to be, to see him?"

"What! can you make him come, mother, like a picture, with a big frame round him? and shall I see him close—see him close? But I mustn't touch him, I suppose; for then he'd vanish, they say."

"Yes,—how would you like to see him, now, Bella?"

"Oh, dear me, I should be frightened! You'd better tell me who he is, and don't bring him; though, indeed, mother, I can't think there would be danger."

"None—none at all," said the old woman in reply, who seemed disposed to prolong the dialogue.

"Well, if he only looked like John Davis, now!"

"John Davis, indeed, Bella! I tell you, you must not think of John Davis You are for a far better man. What do you say,

10*

now, of the sergeant, Sergeant Hastings ? suppose it happened to be him, now ?"

"Don't talk to me of Sergeant Hastings mother; for I was a fool to mind him. He don't care *that* for me, I know : and he talks cross to me ; and if I don't run myself out of breath to serve him, he says ugly things. Besides, he's been talking strange things to me, and I don't like it. More than once I've been going to tell brother William something that he once said to me : and I know, if I had, there would have been a brush between them ; for William won't stand any thing that's impudent. Don't talk of *him* to me."

"But I must, my daughter, for it cannot be helped. If I see that he's born to be your husband, and you his wife, it must be so, and I must say it."

"No—no—it's not so, mother, I know. It shan't be so," said the girl, firmly enough. " I won't believe it, neither, and you're only plaguing me."

" It's a truth, Bella, and neither you nor I can help it, or keep it off. I tell you, child, that you were born for Sergeant Hastings."

"But I won't be born for him, neither. I can't, and I won't, for you don't know what he said to me, and it's not good for me to tell it again, for it was naughty ; and I'm sorry I ever talked cross to poor John Davis, and I did so all because of *him*."

The change in her regards from Hastings to her old lover, was a source of no small astonishment to the old hag, who knew not how to account for it. It gave less satisfaction to her than to Humphries, who, in the neighbouring bush, heard every syllable which had been uttered. The secret of this change is easily given. As simple as a child, the mere deference to her claims of beauty, had left her easily susceptible of imposition ; and without any feeling actually enlisted in favour of Hastings, she had been on the verge of that precipice—the gulf which passion or folly so often prepares for its unheeding votaries. His professions and flatteries had gradually filled her mind, and when his continued attentions had driven all those away, from whom she had, or might have received them, it followed that she became a dependant entirely upon him, who, in creating this state of subservience, had placed her, to a certain degree at least, at his mercy. She felt this dependence now, and it somewhat mortified her ; her vanity grew hurt, when the tone of deference formerly used by her lover, had been changed to one of command and authority ; and she sometimes sighed when she thought of the unremitting attentions of her old lover from Goose Creek, the indefatigable Davis. The gaudy dress, and imposing pretensions of the sergeant, had grown common in her eye, while, at the same time, the inferiority of the new lover to the old, in delicacy of feeling, and genuine regard, had become sufficiently obvious. She had, of late, instituted the comparison between them more than once, and the consequence was inevitable. There was no little decision in her manner, therefore, as she refused to submit to the fate which Mother Blonay desired to impose upon her.

" But, Bella, my daughter—"

" No, no, mother—don't tell me of Sergeant Hastings any more, —I won't hear of him any longer."

" And why not, Bella, my dear ?" exclaimed the redoubtable sergeant himself, coming suddenly into her presence, and speaking to her with a mixed expression of pride and dissatisfaction in his countenance—" why not, I pray, my dear ?"

The poor girl was dumb at this intrusion. She scarcely dared to look up, as, with the utmost composure, Hastings took a seat beside her. The old hag, who had arranged the scheme, at the same moment rose to depart. Quick as thought, Bella seized her hand, and would have risen also, but with a decided force the sergeant prevented her, and retained his hold upon her wrist while compelling her to resume the seat beside him.

" I must go, sergeant—father is waiting for me, I'm sure—and the bells are 'most done ringing. Don't leave me, mother."

But the old woman was gone, moving out of sight, though still keeping within hearing, with all the agility of a young person. The poor girl, left alone with her danger, seemed for the moment stupified. She sat trembling beside the strong man who held her, speaking, when she did, in a tremor, and begging to depart.

But why dwell on what ensued ? The brutal suitor had but one object, and did not long delay to exhibit its atrocious features. Entreaties were succeeded by rudenesses ; and the terrified girl, hrieking and screaming to the old hag who had decoyed and left her, was dragged recklessly back into the wood by the strong arms of her companion.

"Cry away—Goggle now—Goggle now—Goggle now—scream on, you poor fool—scream, but there's no help for you."

And as the old beldam thus answered to the prayers of the girl, she was stricken aside and hurled like a stone into the bush, even while the fiendish soliloquy was upon her lips, by the raging brother who now darted forward. In another instant, and he had dashed the ravisher to the earth—torn his sister, now almost exhausted, from his grasp—and with his knee upon the breast of Hastings, and his knife bared in his hands, that moment would have been the last of life to the ruffian, but for the intervention of the two troopers, who, hearing the shriek, had also rushed forward from the recesses in the wood where the providence of Humphries had placed them. They prevented the blow, but with their aid the sergeant was gagged, bound, and dragged down into the copse where the horses awaited them.

"Oh, brother—dear brother William!" cried the terrified girl— "believe me, brother William, but it's not my fault—I didn't mean to do wrong! I am innocent—that I am!".

She hung upon him as if she feared his suspicions. He pressed her to his arms, while weeping like a very child over her.

"I know it—I know it, Bella! and God knows how glad I am to know it! Had I not heard all between you, and that old hag of hell, I'd ha' put this knife into you, just the same as if you were not my own flesh and blood. But go now—run to church, and pray to have some sense as well as innocence; for innocence without sense is like a creeping baby that has not yet got the use of its arms and legs. Go now—run all the way—and mind that you say nothing to the old man about it."

Throwing her arms about his neck and kissing him, she hurried upon her way with the speed of a bird just escaping, and narrowly, from the net of the fowler.

CHAPTER XXI.

' Unfold—unfold—the day is going fast,
And we must read this ancient history "

THE clouds were gathering fast—the waters were troubled—and the approaching tumult and disquiet of all things in Carolina, clearly indicated the coming of that strife, so soon to overcast the scene—so long to keep it darkened—so deeply to empurple it with blood. The continentals were approaching rapidly, and the effect was that of magic upon the long prostrated energies of the South. The people were aroused, awakened, stimulated, and emboldened. They gathered in little squads throughout the country. The news was generally abroad that Gates was to command the expected army—Gates, the conqueror at Saratoga, whose very name, at that time, was a host. The successes of Sumter in the up-country, of Marion on the Pedee, of Pickens with a troop of mounted riflemen—a new species of force projected by himself—of Butler, of Horry, James, and others, were generally whispered about among the hitherto desponding whigs. These encouraging prospects were not a little strengthened in the parishes by rumours of small successes nearer at hand. The swamps were now believed to be full of enemies to royal power, only wanting embodiment and arms ; and truly did Tarleton, dilating upon the condition of things at this period in the colony, give a melancholy summary of those influences which were crowding together, as it was fondly thought by the patriots, for the overwhelming of foreign domination.

" Discontents"—according to his narrative—" were disseminated —secret conspiracies entered into upon the frontier—hostilities were already begun in many places, and every thing seemed to menace a revolution as rapid as that which succeeded the surrender of Charleston."

The storm grew more imposing in its terrors, when, promising himself confidently a march of triumph through the country, Gates, in a swelling proclamation, announced his assumption of command over the southern army. It was a promise sadly disappointed in the end—yet the effect was instantaneous; and, with the knowledge of his approach, the entirè Black river country was in insurrection.

This was the province of Marion, and to his active persuasion and influence the outbreak must chiefly be ascribed. But the influence of events upon other sections was not less immediate, though less overt and important in their development. The fermenting excitement, which, in men's minds, usually precedes the action of powerful, because long suppressed, elements of mischief, had reached its highest point of forbearance. The immediately impelling power was alone wanting, and this is always to be found in that restless love of change, growing with its facilities, which forms so legitimate a portion of our proper nature. There is a wholesome stir in strife itself, which, like the thunderstorm in the sluggish atmosphere, imparts a renewed energy, and a better condition of health and exercise, to the attributes and agents of the moral man.

Let us turn once more to the region already somewhat familiar through these pages. We are again in the precincts of the Ashley. These old woods about Dorchester deserve to be famous. There is not a wagon track—not a defile—not a clearing—not a traverse of these plains, which has not been consecrated by the strife for liberty; the close strife—the desperate struggle; the contest, unrelaxing, unyielding to the last, save only with death or conquest. These old trees have looked down upon blood and battles; the thick array and the solitary combat between single foes, needing no other witnesses. What tales might they not tell us! The sands have drunk deeply of holy and hallowed blood—blood that gave them value and a name, and made for them a place in all human recollection. The grass here has been beaten down, in successive seasons, by heavy feet—by conflicting horsemen—by driving and recoiling artillery. Its deep green has been dyed with a yet deeper and a darker stain—the outpourings of the invader's veins, mingling with the generous streams flowing from bosoms that had but one hope—but one purpose—the unpolluted freedom and security of home; the purity of the threshold, the sweet repose of the domestic hearth from the intrusion of hostile feet;— the only objects for which men may brave the stormy and the brutal strife, and still keep the " whiteness of their souls."

The Carolinian well knows these hallowed places ; for every acre has its tradition in this neighbourhood. He rides beneath the thick oaks, whose branches have covered regiments, and looks up to them with heedful veneration. Well he remembers the old defile at the entrance just above Dorchester village, where a red clay hill rises abruptly, breaking pleasantly the dead level of coun- try all around it. The rugged limbs and trunk of a huge oak, which hung above its brow, and has been but recently overthrown, was itself an historian. It was notorious in tradition as the " *gal- lows oak ;*" its limbs being employed by both parties, as they seve- rally obtained the ascendency, for the purposes of summary execu- tion. Famous, indeed, was all the partisan warfare in this neigh- bourhood, from the time of its commencement, with our story, in 1780, to the day, when, hopeless of their object, the troops of the invader withdrew to their crowded vessels, flying from the land they had vainly struggled to subdue. You should hear the old housewives dilate upon these transactions. You should hear them paint the disasters, the depression of the Carolinians ! how their chief city was besieged and taken ; their little army dispersed, or cut to pieces ; and how the invader marched over the country, and called it his. Anon, they would show you the little gathering in the swamp—the small scouting squad timidly stealing forth into the plain, and contenting itself with cutting off a foraging party or a baggage wagon, or rescuing a disconsolate group of captives on their way to the city and the prison-ships. Soon, emboldened by success, the little squad is increased by numbers, and aims at larger game. Under some such leader as Colonel Washington, you should see them, anon, well mounted, coursing along the Ashley river road, by the peep of day, well skilled in the management of their steeds, whose high necks beautifully arch under the curb while, in obedience to the rider's will, they plunge fearlessly through brake and through brier, over the fallen tree, and into the suspicious water. Heedless of all things but the proper achievement of their bold adventure, the warriors go onward, while the broadswords flash in the sunlight, and the trumpet cheers them with a tone of victory.

And goodlier still is the sight, when, turning the narrow lane, thick fringed with the scrubby oak and the pleasant myrtle, you behold them come suddenly to the encounter with the hostile invaders. How they hurrah, and rush to the charge with a mad emotion that the steed partakes—his ears erect, and his nostrils distended, while his eyeballs start forward, and grow red with the straining effort; then, how the riders bear down all before them, and, with swords shooting out from their cheeks, make nothing of the upraised bayonet and pointed spear, but, striking in, flank and front, carry confusion wherever they go—while the hot sands drink in the life-blood of friend and foe, streaming through a thousand wounds.

Hear them tell of these, and of the "Game Cock," Sumter; how, always ready for fight, with a valour which was too frequently rashness, he would rush into the hostile ranks, and, with his powerful frame and sweeping sabre, would single out for inveterate strife his own particular enemy.

Then, of the subtle "Swamp Fox," Marion, who, slender of form, and having but little confidence in his own physical prowess, was never seen to use his sword in battle; gaining by stratagem and unexpected enterprise those advantages which his usual inferiority of force would never have permitted him to gain otherwise. They will tell you of his conduct and his coolness; of his ability, with small means, to consummate leading objects—the best proof of military talent; and of his wonderful command of his men; how they would do his will, though it led to the most perilous adventure, with as much alacrity as if they were going to a banquet. Of the men themselves, though in rags, almost starving, and exposed to all changes of the weather, how cheerfully, in the fastnesses of the swamp, they would sing their rude song about the sapacity of their leader and their devotion to his person, in some

WARFARE OF THE WOODS.

such strain as that which follows, and which we owe to brave and generous George Dennison!

George Dennison was himself a follower of Marion. He belonged to the race of troubadours, though living too late for the sort of life which they enjoyed, and for the fame which crowned their equally eccentric lives and ballads. He sang for the partisans, the gallant feat even in the moment when performed, and taught to the hearts of a rude cavalry, the lurking hope of remembrance in song when they themselves should never hear. In the deep thickets of the wood, in the wild recesses of the swamp, when the day's march was over, when the sharp passage at arms was ended, whether in flight or victory,—his ballads, mostly extempore, cheered the dull hours and the drowsy bivouac, while his rough but martial lyrics inspired the audacious charge, and prompted the bold enterprise and the emulous achievement. Ah brave and generous George Dennison, we shall borrow of the songs of thy making. We shall prolong for other ears the echoes of thy lively lays, and the legends which we owe to thee, who art thyself unknown. For verily, thou hadst the heart and courage of true and gallant partisan ; and thou couldst sing with the natural voice of a warm and passionate poet ; and thou couldst share the sufferings, and soothe the sorrows of a comrade, with the loyalty of a knightly friendship ; and thou couldst love with all the tende sweetness that lies in the heart of woman ; and thou couldst cling in fight to thy enemy, with the anger of a loving hate ; and thou didst not love life too much for honor; and thou didst not fear death so much but thou couldst brave him with a laugh and a song, even in the crossing of the spears ! Verily, George Dennison, I will remember thee, and preserve thy rude ballads, made by thee for thy comrades' ears in the swamps of Carolina, so that other ears shall hear them, who knew thee not. Thou shalt tell them now, of the life led by thee and thy comrades, for long seasons, when thou hast followed the fortunes of the famous Swamp Fox :

THE SWAMP FOX.

I.

" We follow where the Swamp Fox guides.
 His friends and merry men are we,
And when the troop of Tarleton rides,
 We burrow in the cypress tree.
The turfy hammock is our bed,
 Our home is in the red-deer's den,
Our roof, the tree-top overhead,
 For we are wild and hunted men.

II.

" We fly by day, and shun its light,
 But, prompt to strike the sudden blow,
We mount, and start with early night,
 And through the forest track our foe.
And soon he hears our chargers leap,
 The flashing sabre blinds his eyes,
And ere he drives away his sleep,
 And rushes from his camp, he dies.

III.

" Free bridle-bit, good gallant steed,
 That will not ask a kind caress,
To swim the Santee at our need,
 When on his heels the foemen press—
The true heart and the ready hand,
 The spirit, stubborn to be free—
The twisted bore, the smiting brand—
 And we are Marion's men, you see.

IV.

"Now light the fire, and cook the meal,
 The last, perhaps, that we shall taste;
I hear the Swamp Fox round us steal,
 And that's a sign we move in haste.
He whistles to the scouts, and hark!
 You hear his order calm and low—
Come, wave your torch across the dark,
 And let us see the boys that go,

v.

We may not see their forms again,
  God help 'em, should they find the strife
For they are strong and fearless men,
  And make no coward terms for life:
They'll fight as long as Marion bids,
  And when he speaks the word to shy,
Then—not till then—they turn their steeds,
  Through thickening shade and swamp to fly.

VI.

Now stir the fire, and lie at ease,
  The scouts are gone, and on the brush
I see the colonel bend his knees,
  To take his slumbers too—but hush!
He's praying, comrades: 'tis not strange;
  The man that's fighting day by day,
May well, when night comes, take a change,
  And down upon his knees to pray.

VII.

'Break up that hoecake, boys, and hand
  The sly and silent jug that's there;
I love not it should idly stand,
  When Marion's men have need of chee
'Tis seldom that our luck affords
  A stuff like this we just have quaffed,
And dry potatoes on our boards
  May always call for such a draught.

VIII.

Now pile the brush and roll the log:
  Hard pillow, but a soldier's head,
That's half the time in brake and bog,
  Must never think of softer bed.
The owl is hooting to the night,
  The cooter crawling o'er the bank,
And in that pond the plashing light,
  Tells where the alligator sank

II.

"What—'tis the signal! start so soon,
  And through the Santee swamp so deep,
Without the aid of friendly moon,
  And we, Heaven help us, half asleep!
But courage, comrades! Marion leads,
  The Swamp Fox takes us out to-night;
So clear your swords, and spur your steeds,
  There's goodly chance, I think, of fight.

X.

"We follow where the Swamp Fox guides,
  We leave the swamp and cypress tree,
Our spurs are in our coursers' sides,
  And ready for the strife are we—
The tory camp is now in sight,
  And there he cowers within his den—
He hears our shout, he dreads the fight,
  He fears, and flies from Marion's men."

Thus sang the native warrior of the Ashley, gallant George Dennison, long after the war was over. He told the story truly of the Partisan, and he did not sing amiss. He had a rough and native vigour—a talent all his own—and did not smoothe his song to the loss of spirit, and did not shape his applauses to please the ears the pretender. He made no man the hero of his song who had not made himself a hero in his performances. Truer historian o. the deeds which he beheld, never put fact on record; more faithful bard never sang in honour of brave spirits. Verily, he was not unworthy to chant the praises of our forest rangers.

And gallant men were the warriors whom he honoured by his songs. They owe, perchance, but little to his rustic muse, and they have had the fortune to secure the homage of others who have better guaranties of Fame. Sharing the glories of Marion, their own deeds have grown famous in song and story—while poor George Dennison remains unknown. Yet, could he now survive to describe their progress—to paint their deeds—to give us the lively details of those wild and picturesque adventures, in which day and night found them perpetually engaged—he would show us such

scenes as imagination cannot well conceive, or poetry of herself depict. He would show us the rude forester, as, passing from his
farmstead to the swamp, flying from the marauder, he became, in
time, the adroit partisan, under the ablest leaders. How the neces
sity, ever present, and usually in the aspec of a pressing danger,
brought out all the resources of a natural art, and taught him in a
thousand stratagems. How he grew, in time, to be as stealthy as
the fox, and as subtle as the serpent. How he grew, in time, to
practise all the arts of all the natural inhabitants of swamp and
thicket : to imitate the cry of the bird, the stealth of the beast, the
speed of the eagle, the fierce valour of the tiger ! How to snare and
circumvent the foe ! How, imbedding himself in the covering
leaves and branches of the thick-limbed tree, he would lie in wait
till the fall of evening ; then, dropping suddenly upon the shoulders
of the sentry as he paced beneath, would drive the keen knife into
his heart, before he could yet recover from his panic. How he
would burrow in the hollow of the miry ditch, and crawling, Indian
fashion, into the trench, wait patiently until the soldier came into
the moonlight, when the silver drop at his rifle's muzzle fell with
fatal accuracy upon his button, or his breastplate, and the sharp
sudden crack which followed almost invariably announced the victim's long sleep of death. And a thousand legends besides would
he teach us, making them live to our eyes, and work like passion in
our souls, of which tradition and history speak but faintly, and of
the arts and valour by which our partisans grew enabled to neutral·
ize the superiority of European force and tactics. Often and again
have they lain close to the gushing spring, and silent in the bush,
like the tiger in his jungle, awaiting until the foragers had squatted
around it for the enjoyment of their midday meal ; then, rushing
forth with a fierce halloo, seizing upon the stacked arms, and beating down the surprised but daring soldiers who might rise up to defend them. And this sort of warfare, small though it may appear,
was at last triumphant. The successes of the patriots, during the
whole period of the revolutionary contest in the south, were almost
entirely the result of the rapid, unexpected movement—the sudden
stroke made by the little troop, familiar with its ground, knowing
its object, and melting away at the approach of a superior enemy,

like so many dusky shadows, secure in the thousand swamp recesses which surrounded them. Nor did they rely always on stratagem in the prosecution of their enterprises. There were gleams of chivalry thrown athwart this sombre waste of strife and bloodshed, worthy of the middle ages. Bold and graceful riders, with fine horses, ready in all cases, fierce in onset, and reckless in valour, the southern cavalry had an early renown. The audacity with which they drove through the forest, through broad rivers, such as the Santee, by day and by night, in the face of the enemy, whether in flight or in assault the same, makes their achievements as worthy of romance as those of a Bayard or Bernardo. Thousands of instances are recorded of that individual gallantry— that gallantry, stimulated by courage, warmed by enthusiasm, and refined by courtesy—which gives the only credentials of true chivalry. Such, among the many, was the rescue of the prisoners, by Jasper and Newton; the restoration of the flagstaff to Fort Moultrie, in the hottest fire, by the former; and the manner in which he got his death-wound at Savannah, in carrying off the colours which had been intrusted to him. Such were many of the rash achievements of Sumter and Laurens, and such was the daring of the brave Conyers, who daily challenged his enemy in the face of the hostile army. These were all partisan warriors, and such were their characteristics. Let us now return to the adventures we have undertaken to relate, borrowing freely from George Dennison, and relate the deeds which distinguish the lives of others, less known, b it not unworthy to be ranked honourably among the bravest.

CHAPTER XXII.

"Now, yield thee up thy charge—delay and die—
I may not spare thee in a quest like this,
But strike even while I speak."

WE have witnessed the sudden capture of the truculent British sergeant, by the brother of the damsel whom he had destined for his prey. Aided by his new recruits, Humphries brought his prisoner to the camp with little difficulty. The worthy sergeant, it is true, did at first offer resistance; he mouthed and struggled, as the bandages compressed his mouth, and the ligatures restrained his arms; but the timely application of hand and foot, which his captors did not hesitate to employ to compel obedience, not to speak of the threatening aspect of the dagger—which the much roused lieutenant held more than once to his throat—brought him to reason, and counselled that wholesome resignation to circumstances, which, though not always easy and pleasant of adoption, is, at least, on most occasions, well becoming in him who has no alternatives. He was, therefore, soon mounted on horseback, along with one of the troopers, and in a state of most commendable quietness, he reached, after an hour's quick riding, the encampment at Bacon's Bridge. There, well secured with a stout rope, and watched by the guard assigned for the other prisoners, close in the thick and knotty wood which girded the swamp, we will at present leave him.

Singleton had well concealed his little squadron in the same shelter. Like a true partisan, he had omitted no precautions. His scouts—men that he could trust—were out in all directions, and his sentries watched both sides of the river. The position which he had chosen was one established by General Moultrie in the previous season. It had been vacated when that brave old warrior was called to league his troops with those of Lincoln, in defence of the city. The entrenchments and barracks were in good order, but Singleton studiously avoided their use; and, to the thoughtless wayfarer passing by the little fort and the clumsy blockhouse, nothing could possibly have looked more pacific. The partisan, though immediately at hand, preferred a less ostentatious position. We find him accordingly, close clustering with his troop in the deep wood that lay behind it. Here, for a brief period at least, his lurking-place was secure, and he only desired it for a few days longer. Known to the enemy, he could not have held it, even for a time so limited; but would have been compelled to rapid flight, or a resort to the deeper shadows and fastnesses of the swamp.

At this point the river ceased to be navigable even for the common poleboats of the country; and this was another source of its security. Filled up by crowding trees—the gloomy cypresses striding boldly into its very bosom—it slunk away into shade and silence, winding and broken, after a brief effort at a concentrated course, into numberless little bayous and indentures, muddy creeks, stagnating ponds, miry holes; constituting, throughout, a region only pregnable by desperation, and only loved by the fierce and filthy reptile, the ominous bird, the subtile fox, and venomous serpent. This region, immediately at hand, promised a safe place of retreat, for a season, to the adventurous partisan; and in its gloomy recesses he well knew that, unless guided by a genuine swamp-sucker, all Europe might vainly seek to find the little force, so easily concealed, which he now commanded.

Humphries soon furnished his captain with all the intelligence he had obtained at Dorchester. He gave a succinct account of the affair of Mother Blonay, and her visit to the village—of the movement of Huck to assail him on the Stono—and of the purpose of the tory to proceed onward, by the indirect route already mentioned, to join with Tarleton on the Catawba. The latter particulars had been furnished the lieutenant by the two troopers who had joined him.

The whole account determined Singleton to hurry his own movement to join with Marion. That part of the narrative of Humphries relating to Mother Blonay, decided the commander to keep Goggle still a prisoner, as one not to be trusted. Giving orders, therefore, for his continued detention, he proceeded to put things in readiness for the movement of the squad, with nightfall, to their old and better shelter on the little island in the Cypress Swamp. This done, Singleton commanded his horse in readiness, and bidding the boy Lance Frampton in attendance, despatched him to prepare his own. To Humphries he now gave charge of the troop—repeated his orders to move with the dusk to their old quarters—and having informed the lieutenant of the true object of his own adventure, he set forth, only attended by the boy Frampton, taking an upper road leading towards the Santee.

That object may as well be told now as ever. Singleton had been for some time awaiting intelligence of Marion's movement to Nelson's ferry. A courier had been looked for daily, since he had left his leader; and as, in these suspicious times, every precaution in the conveyance and receipt of intelligence was necessary, it followed that many difficulties lay in the way of its transmission. Men met on the highways, to fear, to avoid, and frequently to fight with one another. They assumed contrary characters in the presence of the stranger, and the play at cross-purposes, even among friends, was the natural consequence of a misunderstood position.

There were signs and phrases agreed upon between Marion and his trusted men, mysterious or unmeaning to all besides, which Singleton was not permitted to impart to others. This necessity prompted him forth, if possible, to meet with the expected courier, bearing him his orders. He attached the younger Frampton to his person. He chose him as too young for treason, and, indeed, he wanted no better companion to accompany him on his ramble. Setting forth by noonday, he kept boldly along the common Ashley river or Dorchester road, as, winding in accordance with the course of the stream it carried him above and completely around the spot chosen for his camp in the Cypress.

The two saw but little, for some time, to attract them in this ramble. They traversed the defile of thick oaks, which form so large a part of the growth of that region; then fell into a monotonous pine-land track, through which they pushed their way. Cheerless quite, bald of home and habitation, they saw nothing throughout the melancholy waste more imposing than the plodding

21

negro, with his staff in hand, and with white teeth peering through his thick, flagging lips, in a sort of deferential smile, at their approach. Sometimes, touched with the apprehensions of the time, he too would start away as he beheld them, and they might see him, as they looked backward, cautiously watching their progress from behind the pine-tree, or the crumbling fence. Occasionally they came to a dwelling in ruins, or burnt—the cornfield scorched and blackened with the recent fire, the fences overthrown, and the cows, almost wild, having free possession, and staring wildly upon them as they drew nigh.

" And this is war !" said Singleton, musingly. " This is war— the merciless, the devastating war ! Oh, my country, when wilt thou be free from invasion—when will thy people come back to these deserted dwellings—when will the corn flourish green along these stricken and blasted fields, without danger from the trampling horse, and the wanton and devouring fire ? When—oh, when ?"

He spoke almost unconsciously, but was recalled to himself, as, wondering at what he heard, the peering eyes of Lance Frampton, as he rode up beside him, perused keenly the unusually sad expression of his countenance. Singleton noted his gaze, and, without rebuking it, addressed him with a question concerning his father, who had been missing from the troop ever since the affair with Travis.

" Lance, have you heard nothing of your father since I last asked you about him ?"

" Nothing, sir; nothing at all, since we left the Cypress."

" You did not see him then, at our departure ?"

" No, sir ; but I heard him laugh long after I missed him from the troop. He couldn't have been far off, sir, when we came out of the swamp; though I didn't see him then, and—and—I didn't want to see him."

" Why not, boy ?—your father, too !"

" Why, sir, father is very strange sometimes, and then we never talk to him or trouble him, and he don't want people to see him then. We always know how he is when he laughs, sir, and then we go out of his way. We know he is strange then, for he never ᴧughs at any other time."

" What do you mean by strange—is he dangerous ?"

" Sometimes, sir, he plays dangerously with you. But it's all in play, for he laughs, and doesn't look in earnest; but he is apt to hurt people then. He once threw me into the tree when he was so : but it wasn't in earnest, he didn't mean to do me hurt, I'm sure ; but he didn't know ; he can't tell what he does when the strange fit is on him."

" And where do you think he is now ?—in the swamp ?"

" Yes, sir ; he loves to be in the swamp."

" And how long, boy, is it since he became strange ?"

" Oh, a very long time, sir ; ever since I was a little child. But he has been much stranger since my mother's death !"

" No wonder ! no wonder ! That was enough to make him so— that cruel murder; but we will avenge it, boy—we will avenge it."

" Yes, sir ; that's what I want to do, as soon as you'll let me. I long to have a chance to cut a man over the head."

The boy stopped and blushed—half fearing that he had said too much ; but the kindled fire of his eye was unshadowed, and there was a quiver of his lips, and an increasing heave of his breast, that did not escape the keen glance of Singleton. The latter was about to speak, when suddenly the boy stopped him, bent forward upon his horse, and pointing with his finger to an opening from the roadside, called the attention of his commander in that direction.

" I'm sure, sir, it's a man—a white man ; his back was to us, sir ; he's in there."

At the word, Singleton drove the spur into his steed, and the boy followed him. In a few moments, he was at the designated spot, and there, sure enough, even as his companion had said, in the little break of the woods, on the hillock's side, a strange man stood before them.

The person, thus surprised, now evidently beheld them for the first time. He had been tightening the saddle-girth around his horse, that stood quietly cropping the grass at their approach ; and his eyes were turned over his shoulder, surveying the new-comers. He hesitated, and his manner had in it something of precipitation. This was the more evident to Singleton, as, on their appearance, he began to whistle, and obviously assumed a degree of composure which he did not feel. He had been taking his midday repast at the spring, which trickled from the hillside below them; and the remains of his meal, consisting of a bit of dried venison, cold ham, and corn hoecake, were still open upon the grass, lying on the buckskin wrapper which contained them. The man was certainly a traveller and had ridden far; the condition of his horse proved that; though his dress and appearance were those of the plain farmers of the neighbourhood. A coarse blue homespun coatee, with thin, whity-brown pantaloons, loosely made, and a quaker hat, in the riband of which a huge pipe was stuck ostentatiously, formed his habit. But Singleton saw that the pipe had never been smoked, and his infer-ence was not favourable to the traveller, from this simple circum-stance.

Throwing his bridle to Lance Frampton, the partisan alighted, and approached the stranger, who turned to meet him. There was quite a show of good-humour in his countenance, as Singleton drew nigh, and yet the latter saw his real trepidation; and the anxious looks which, more than once, he cast upon the stout animal which had borne him, seemed to say how glad he would have been to use him in flight, could he possibly have thought to do so in safety.

"Good-day, my friend, good-day. You have ridden far," said Singleton, "and your horse tells it. May I ask what quarter you come from?"

"Oh yes, to be sure you may, stranger; there's no harm that I can see in the question, only as it happens to want an answer. It's no safe matter, now-a-days, stranger, to tell one's starting and stop-ping, since, you see, it mayn't altogether please them that hears."

There was evidently a disposition on the part of the countryman to feel his way, and see how far he could bully the new-comer, in this equivocal sort of speech. But he was mistaken in the man before him, and though he had spoken his evasive reply in a man-ner meant to be conciliatory while it remained unsatisfactory, he was soon compelled to see that his questioner was by no means to be trifled with.

"Safe or not, my friend," said Singleton, gravely. "there are some questions that a man must answer, whether he likes it or no:

there is a school proverb that you must remember, about the bird that can sing and will not."

The man turned his tobacco in his jaws, and though evidently annoyed and disquieted, replied—

"Why, yes, stranger, I reckon I know what you mean, though I haint had much schooling; three months one year, and three another, and then three years without any, don't teach a body every kind of larning. But the saying you p'int to I remember well enough; Many's the time I've hearn it. 'The bird that wont sing must be made to sing.'"

"I see your memory may be relied upon for other matters," said Singleton; "and now, taking care not to forget the proverb, you will please answer me a few questions."

"Well, stranger, I'm willing enough. I'm all over good-natur, and never fail to git vexed with myself afterward, when the devil drives me to be oncivil to them that treats me well. Ax your questions straight off-hand, and Pete Larkin is the boy to answer, far as his larning goes."

"I am glad, Mr. Larkin, for your own sake, that you have this temper. You will please to say, now, where you are from."

"Well, now, stranger, I'm only come from a little above—and as you say, I've had a tough ride of it; but it's a good critter, this here nag of mine, and does one's heart good to go on him. So, you see, when I'm on him, I goes it. I hate mightily to creep, terrapin fashion, in a dogtrot; for you see, stranger, it's a bad gait, and sickens a short man, though the horse that travels stands it best of any."

Singleton had no disposition to interrupt the speaker, though he saw that he meant to be evasive. He watched his features attentively, while he spoke, and when he had done, proceeded in his inquiries.

"From above! but what part? I would know precisely, Mr. Larkin."

"Well, now, stranger, as I haint got no secrets, I 'spose I may as well tell you 'xactly how 'tis. I'm from cl'ar across the Santee I live 'pon the Santee, or thereabouts."

"Indeed! and is it true, as we hear below, that the wolves have grown troublesome in that quarter?"

"Wolves, stranger? Well, now, that can't be; for, you see, 1 come from all about, and nobody that I seed along the road, or in any settlement, made complaint. I reckon you aint hearn very particular right, now."

"It must be the owls, then—yes, it is the owls; have you seen any of them on your way?"

This question, urged with the utmost gravity by the partisan, completed the fellow's astonishment. Revolving the huge quid of tobacco—for such it seemed—which from the commencement of the dialogue had been going to and fro between his jaws, it was some seconds before he could recover sufficiently from his astonishment to reply.

"Owls! God bless me, stranger, but that's a queer question, any-how. To be sure thar's owls all along the Santee. You may hear them in the swamp any time o' night, and an ugly noise they makes all night long, but nobody thinks o' minding them. They troubles nobody, and sometimes, when there's going to be a death in the family, the white owls comes into the bedroom, and they won't drive 'em out, for you see it's no use; the sick body will die after that, whether they drive the owl off or no."

"Yes, yes—true;" said Singleton musingly, while watching the other's countenance with a circumspect regard. He saw that the countryman was not the man he expected, but even with this discovery there had grown other suspicions as to his real character, the more particularly as he perceived how disquieted the examina-tion and restraint had made him. After a moment's pause, he proceeded to put a more direct inquiry.

"Where do you live upon the Santee?"

"Well, now, stranger, I don't know if you'll know the place when I tell you, seeing it's a little out of the way of the settlement; but I live close upon the left hand fork of the White Oak Branch, a leetle above the road that runs to Williamsburg. I come down that road when I crossed the Santee."

"And where did you cross the Santee?"

"At Vance's ferry :—I 'spose you know where that is?"

"I do; but why did you not cross at Nelson's—why go out of your way to Vance's?"

The countryman stammered, hesitated for a moment, and while he replied, his eye sank beneath the penetrating glance of Singleton.

"Well, stranger, to say truth, 'twas beca'se I feared to come bv Nelson's; I was afeard of the inimy?"

"And whom do you call the enemy?"

"Them that's not a friend to me and my friends; them's my inimies, stranger, and I reckon them's your inimies too."

" Perhaps so; but I must first know who they are, before I can say. Speak out, my good fellow, and let your answers be a little more to the point, if you please."

The mass of tobacco, in the fellow's jaws, performed a more rapid revolution before the man replied; and he then did so only as he saw the hand of Singleton upon the pistol in his belt.

"Well, stranger, if I must, I must: so, by the inimy I means the rebels; them that aint friendly to the king's government—them's the inimy; and there was plenty to spare of them at the nighest track. The river swamp at Nelson's was chock full of Marion's men, and there was no passing; so I took the road across, down by Wright's Bluff, that lets you into the Vance's ferry track, and—"

"You stopped at Watson's? *

Singleton put the question affirmatively, and the other looked surprised; the tobacco was about to be revolved from the one jaw to the opposite side, as had been the case at almost every interval made between his sentences, when, quick as lightning, and with a grasp of steel, Singleton seized him by the throat. The fellow strove to slip away, but never did finger more tenaciously gripe the throat of an enemy. The partisan was a man of immense strength, and the stranger was short and small. His powers were far inferior. He strove to struggle, and laboured, but in vain, to speak. The fingers were too closely compressed; and, still maintaining his hold with more tenacity than ever, the assailant bore him down to earth, and with his knee fixed firmly upon his breast, in spite of

---

* At that time one of the chain of military posts which the British had established throughout the country.

very effort for release by the man beneath him, he choked him until his tongue hung out upon his cheek, and his jaws were sufficiently distended to enable him to secure the game for which he toiled so desperately. Turning the bearer of despatches—for the prisoner was such—upon his side, the silver bullet which contained them rolled forth upon the grass, and in a moment after was secured by the ready hands of Lance Frampton.

CHAPTER XXIII.

" Ye blight the sense when ye do wound the heart—
Reason is feeling's best and born ally,
And suffers with her kindred."

" STIR not—move a foot, and you die !"

Such were the brief words of Singleton, as, with foot upon his breast. he kept the bearer of despatches prostrate upon the earth. The man saw the peremptory look, the ready pistol, and he doubted not that the words were sternly earnest. His struggles ceased with the command ; and the partisan handing his cocked pistol to the attentive boy Frampton, proceeded to examine the prize which he had gained. The screw bullet soon yielded up its trust, and the intelligence was important. The courier showed symptoms of disquiet, and the foot of his conqueror was pressed, in consequence, more firmly upon his bosom.

" Shoot him if he stirs," said Singleton to the boy, who looked his readiness to obey the command.

The former then quietly perused the cramped document which the bullet had contained.

Its contents were valuable, and greatly assisted our hero in his own progress. Though from an enemy, it contained desirable intelligence ; and, taken in connexion with the verbal narrative which the courier had given of the presence of Marion's men on the Santee, it at once determined Singleton to make an early movement in that quarter. The despatch was from Lord Rawdon, in command at Camden, to Earl Cornwallis at Charleston. It claimed the immediate attendance of the commander-in-chief in Camden, to quell discontents, and prepare for the enemy—announcing the approach of Gates with a formidable army of seven thousand men. This was the alleged force of the continentals ;—very greatly exaggerated beyond the truth, but at this time confidently believed and insisted

11*

upon by both parties in the state. The express contained, in addition to this highly interesting matter, the heads of other subjects not less interesting to the partisan, and scarcely less important to the cause. It described, in brief, numerous risings in every quarter; the defection of the militia *en masse*, under Lyle, who had carried them over to Sumter; the union of Sumter with the Waxhaw whigs; and the affairs on the Catawba, at Williams's, and the Rocky Mount: in all of which the "Game Cock" had handled the enemy severely. The despatch betrayed great anxiety, and its contents were of the most stimulating tendency to Singleton. It now impressed upon him the necessity of that early movement to join with Marion which he had already contemplated.

"You may rise, sir," said the partisan, moving his heel from the breast of the courier, who had lain quietly enough but uncomfortably under it.

"You may rise, but you are my prisoner—no words, but prepare to submit. See to your animal—make no effort to fly, or I shoot you down on the instant."

The man rose tamely enough, but sullenly. After a few moments he found his speech, which was now more agreeable and less broken than when the bullet was revolving to and fro in his jaws.

"Well, now, captain, this is mighty hard, I do think. You won't keep me, I reckon, seeing I'm no fighting man, and haint got any we'pons. I'm a non-combatant, so I am, and I aint free to be taken prisoner. It's agin the laws, I reckon."

"Indeed! but we'll see. Mount, sir, and no talking."

"Well, it's a tough business, and I do think, after all, that it's only joking with me you are—you're two good loyalists, now, I'm certain."

"You mistake, sir, I'm an American—one of Marion's men, and no traitor. To horse, and no more of this—no trifling."

"God help me, cappin, but you're not in airnest, sure? It's no small difficulty, now, this express, and it's a matter to be well paid for; and if so be you are, for certain, one of Marion's men, you mought let'n have a free pass up, for a smart chance of the guineas. Afore God, cappin, if you'll only clear the road you shall have one half—"

The pistol was at his head.

" Another word, scoundrel, and I send the bullet through your skull. Mount quickly—quickly !"

With the back of his hand he smote the tory upon his mouth as he spoke, and the fire of insulted patriotism flashed from his eye, with a threatening brightness that silenced at once, and most effectually, all farther solicitations from the bearer of despatches. Reluctantly, but without farther pause, he got into saddle, taking the place assigned him by his captor, between himself and the boy. In this manner they took their way to the Cypress Swamp, and it was not long before they were, all three, lodged in its safe and deep recesses.

There we find our almost forgotten friends, the sentimental gourmand, the philosophic Porgy, and the attenuated naturalist, Doctor Oakenburg ; the one about to engage in his favourite vocation, and hurrying the evening meal ; the other sublimely employed in stuffing with moss the skin of a monstrous " coachwhip," which, to his great delight, the morning before, he had been successful enough to take with a crotch stick, and to kill without bruising. Carefully skinned, and dried in the shade, the rich colours and glossy glaze of the reptile had been well preserved, and now carefully filled out with the soft and pliant moss, as it lay across the doctor's lap, it wore to the eye of Singleton a very life-like appearance. The two came forward to meet and make the acquaintance of the partisan, whom before they had not seen. Porgy was highly delighted, for, like most fat men, he liked company, and preferred always the presence of a number.

" There's no eating alone," he would say—" give me enough for a large table, and a full company round it : I can then enjoy myself."

His reception of Singleton partook of this spirit.

" Major Singleton, I rejoice to see you ; just now particularly, as our supper, such as it is, is almost at hand. No great variety, sir— nothing much to choose from—but what of that, sir ? There's enough, and what there is, is good—the very best. Tom, there— our cook, sir, he will make the very best of it—broils ham the best of any negro in the southern country, and his hoe-cake, sir, is absolutely perfection. He does turn a griddle with a dexterity that is re-markable. But you shall see—you shall see for yourself. Here, Tom!"

And rolling up his sleeves, he took the subject of his eulogy aside, and a moment after the latter was seen piling his brands and adjusting a rude iron fabric over the coals, while the epicure, with the most hearty good-will for the labour, busily sliced off sundry huge collops from the convenient shoulder of bacon that hung suspended from a contiguous tree.

The labours of Porgy were scarcely congenial either with the mood of Singleton or the quiet loveliness of the scene. Evening was fast coming on—all the swamp was in a deep shadow, save where, like a wandering but pure spirit, a rose-like effusion, the last dying but lovely glance from the descending sun, rested flicker-ingly upon the top of one of the tallest pines above them. A space between the trees, opening to the heavens in one little spot alone, showed them a sprinkling of fleecy white clouds, sleeping quietly under the sky, their western edges partaking slightly of the same last parting glance of the sinking orb. A slight breeze stirred fitfully among the branches; and the occasional chirp of the nimble sparrow, as it hopped along on the edge of the island, was the only sound, other than that made by the hissing fire, and the occa-sional voice of Porgy, which came to the ears of Singleton. He threw himself upon the green bank, under a tree, on the opposite side of which the boy Lance had already placed himself, a little behind him. Suddenly, the boy started to his feet. The wild, unearthly laugh of his father, that eldritch scream which chilled to the very bones of the hearer, was heard on the skirts of the island. Looking to the quarter whence the cry proceeded, they beheld the huge figure of the elder Frampton peering from behind a tree—his eyes staring forth vacantly upon them, while his hands were uplifted to a stretching branch above him, which he grasped firmly. He laughed repeatedly, and Singleton at length arose, beckoned and called to him. But he gave no heed to the call, and when the latter offered to approach him, the maniac moved away rapidly, with another eldritch laugh, that seemed to mock pursuit. At this moment the boy came up in sight of his father, and the wild man seemed to recognise his son.

"He will come now, sir," said Lance to Major Singleton; "he will come now, sir: but we must not seem to urge or to watch him."

They fell back accordingly, took their old places along the bank, and awaited the result of their experiment. As the boy had predicted, the maniac in a few moments after was beside them. He came forward with a bounding motion, as if now only satisfied with an inordinate extreme of action, corresponding to the sleep-less impulse and the fierce fever preying upon his mind. Without a word, but with a perpetually glancing movement of the eye, which seemed to take in all objects around, he squatted down quietly beside his son. He stared for an instant curiously into the boy's eyes, then extending his hand, his fingers wandered uncon-sciously in his long black hair. The latter, all the time, with a proper caution, arising from his previous intimacy with his father's habits, took care neither to move nor speak. He sat patiently, unmoved, while the fingers of the maniac played with his hair, lifted curl after curl with affectionate minuteness, and wound par-ticular locks about his finger. Then he stroked down, once or twice, the thick volumes of hair together; and at length, laughing again more wildly than ever, he withdrew his hand entirely, and turning his face from the two, his eyes became fixed with a strange intensity upon the extended form of the tory whom Singleton had taken, and who now lay tied beneath a tree at a little distance. Soon the maniac slowly rose and moved towards the captive—walked all around and examined him in every particular; the latter all the while, with no little anxiety, turned his glance in every quarter, following the movement of the observer. The fingers of the maniac kept a motion as restless as his person—now grasping, and now withdrawn from, the handle of the unsheathed knife that was stuck in the folds of a thick red handkerchief, ragged and soiled, which was strapped about his waist. At length, leaving the object of his inspection, he approached Singleton, and, with something more of coherence than usual, and a singularly calm expression, he proposed an inquiry about the person whose presence appeared so much to trouble him.

"He is not a red-coat—not a dragoon?"

"No; a tory, but a prisoner. He is a bearer of dispatches— a non-combatant."

The reply of Singleton, which was immediately made to the maniac, brought forward another party in the person of Doctor Oakenburg, who now—having first, with the utmost tenderness, hung his snake over a limb above him—joined the group.

"A prisoner, and yet a non-combatant, Major Singleton? Sir, oblige me, and explain. Is that possible?—have I not heard imperfectly? I too, sir, am a non-combatant, sir; that was understood, sir, when Master Humphries first spoke to me in this behalf. My engagements, sir, required no risk at my hands, and promised me perfect safety."

"Is he not safe enough?" was the calm inquiry of Singleton, as, with a smile, he pointed to the corded courier, and thus answered the doctor's question. Just at his ears, in the same moment, the maniac, who, unperceived by the doctor, had stolen close behind him, now uttered one of his most appalling screams of laughter; and the non-combatant did not seek to disguise the apprehensions which prompted him to a hasty retreat in the rear of Singleton. The partisan turned to him, and changing his topic somewhat, inquired—

"You are the doctor, sir? Doctor—"

"Oakenburg, sir; of an old German family of high descent, and without stain of blood. They came over, sir, with the Elector."

In a whisper, Singleton inquired if his skill could reach the case of Frampton; but the suggestion was productive of quite too much alarm in the mind of the adventurer. He seemed nowise desirous of martyrdom in the prosecution of the healing art; and, when he found his tongue, in reply to the demand of Singleton, he gave his opinion in a half-unintelligible jargon, that the case was confirmed and hopeless. The savage, in the meanwhile, had drawn nigher to his son, one of whose hands he had taken into his own. But he said nothing all the while; and at length, having made all arrangements for the evening repast, the provident Porgy came forward, with the lofty condescension of a host accustomed to entertain with princely bounty, and announced things in readiness. Singleton then spoke to the maniac, and endeavoured to persuade him to the log on which the victuals had been spread, and around which the party had now gathered ; but his application was entirely unheeded.

" He won't mind all you can say to him, major; we know him, for he's been several times to eat with us; that's the way with the creature. But put the meat before him, and his understanding comes back in a moment. He knows very well what to do with it. Ah, Providence has wisely ordained, major, that we shall only lose the knowledge of what's good for the stomach the last of all. We can forget the loss of fortune, sir, of the fine house, and goodly plate, and pleasant tendance—we may even forget the quality and the faces of our friends ; and, as for love, that gets out of our clutches, we don't know how ; but, major, I wont believe that anybody ever yet lost his knowledge of good living. Once gained, it holds its ground well; it survives all other knowledge. The belly, major, will always insist upon so much brains being preserved in the head, as will maintain unimpaired its own ascendency."

As the gourmand had said, the meat was no sooner placed before the maniac, than seizing it ravenously in his fingers, he tore and devoured it with a fury that showed how long had been his previous abstinence. His appetite was absolutely wolfish; and while he ate, Singleton watched him with mingled emotions of pity and disgust. His garments were in tatters about him, torn by the thick woods in which he had ranged with as little scruple as the wild beasts whom he now resembled. His face had been scratched with briers, and the blood had congealed along the seams upon his cheek, unremoved and unregarded. His thick, black hair was matted down upon his forehead, and was deeply stained with the clayey ooze of the swamp through which he had crawled. His eyes had a fiery restlessness, and glared ever around him with a baleful, and malignant sort of light, which was full of evil omen. When he had eaten, he, without a word, dashed off from the place where he had been seated, plunged into the creek, and the fainter and fainter echoes of his wild laugh declared his rapid progress away into the thick recesses of the neighbouring cypress. Over these, darkness now began to consolidate ; and at length, impatient of farther delay in a purposed object, Singleton rose from his place and gave orders to Lance to get his own and the horse of his superior in readiness.

"Shall we ride to-night, sir?" inquired the boy.

"Instantly : I shall put you on a new duty to-night, Lance, and hope that you will perform it well. Speed now with the horses, for the dark gathers."

The bosom of the youth thrilled and throbbed with a new emotion of pleasure, as he heard the promise, and the feeling gave a degree of elasticity to his movement, which enabled him to place the steed before his leader instantaneously.

Singleton sprang the pan of his pistols, renewed the priming, gave several orders touching the prisoner, and some parting directions ; then leaping into saddle, bade Lancelot find the track. Porgy waved a blazing torch over the creek, giving them a brief light at starting, and the two were soon plunging through the gloomy pathway, if by any stretch of courtesy it may be called a pathway, and taking a direction which Singleton thought most likely to give them a meeting with the now approaching troop under the command of Humphries.

CHAPTER XXIV.

" The game is lost, and needless to pursue,
hrough such a waste, m such a night as this."

THE course of Singleton lay for " the Oaks." He was about to
pay a parting visit, and to seek, if possible, to persuade his uncle
to set forth with him for the Santee, with whatever force might
have been procured by him from among his neighbours. This was,
indeed, his only opportunity. He had arrested one courier, it is
true ; but others must succeed in giving to Cornwallis the important intelligence which, for the present, he had stayed. The movement of Cornwallis towards Camden, in compliance with the necessity of the case, and Rawdon's solicitations, would have the effect
of breaking up communication throughout the intervening country,
and making any effort to pass it dangerous to the partisan. This
was a consideration which he necessarily concluded must influence
Colonel Walton's conduct ; and the opportunity of passing at Nelson's, now filled with Marion's men, was one not to be disregarded.
His hopes were, that his uncle would carry with him a decent
number of sturdy fellows into the camp of the continentals. Nor
was this hope an unreasonable one. Colonel Walton, though slow
in taking up the cause of his country, had, at last, set heartily about
it. By his earnestness and industry, since his determination had
been made to resume his arms, he strove to appease his consci
ence, and do away with any reproach that might have been due to
his past forbearance. He had made some progress with his recruits,
and was night and day indefatigable. He rode through his neighbourhood among all sorts of people, and played his game with skill
and coolness. He knew that Proctor watched him, and he was
circumspect accordingly. But, though cautious, he did not relax.
In the little interval which followed his resolve to come out, and
the moment under our view, he had secured some twenty pledges

—pledges of stout, honest woodsmen,—men who had been chaied by the insolence of their oppression, borne down by wrongs, and were impatient for redress. He was now, even while Singleton rode with his attendant towards the river, engaged in close council with a little band at Johnson's house, on Cane Acre, to whom he was successfully urging such considerations as did not fail, in the end, to effect the object he desired. Let us there leave him, for the present, and return to the camp at Bacon's Bridge.

With the close of day, Humphries made his preparations for moving to the Cypress in obedience to the command of Singleton. The horses were saddled quickly, the arms prepared, the surplus baggage put upon pack-horses, the prisoners were mounted, and all appearance of a camp broken up in that quarter. The prisoners were placed under the immediate surveillance of Davis, who brought up the rear of the troop.

The custody of Hastings placed the rivals in a novel sort of relationship to one another; and the sturdy Goose Creeker did not feel less of his bitterness of spirit because he was compelled to suppress its utterance. His old love for Bella Humphries grew active with the feeling of jealousy which the presence of the sergeant necessarily provoked. He really loved the girl, and his hate for the dragoon was, in consequence, entirely without qualification. He felt that he was getting angry, as, while arranging the prisoners, his eye continually fell upon Hastings. But he knew and respected the situation of the enemy too much to give utterance to his feelings at large; feelings which, at the same time, were sufficiently evident to the eye of the dragoon.

He, on the other hand, conscious of his danger, and apprehensive of punishment corresponding to the outrageous character of his last offence, strove to be very conciliatory, and addressed some soothing and gracious speech to his rival, as the latter approached him; but the other was not to be soothed in this fashion. A glance of contempt, mingled with hate, was the only response given to the obsequious remark of Hastings ; and, in a few minutes after, when he could do so unobserved, Davis came back to where his prisoner stood, and in a low tone thus addressed him—

" Look ye, Sergeant Hastings, there's no love lost between us, and it's no use for you to make sweet speeches. You're in no fix to help yourself now; but I've got sich a grudge agin you, that must be satisfied, and I'll be on the look-out, though it's agin orders, to work a clear way for you out of this hobble, if so be you'll only promise to give me satisfaction when I've done so. Say the word now that you will cross swords with me, if I help you to a clear track, and here's my hand upon it, that you shall have a fair fight and free passage."

" Well—but, Davis, my friend—"

"No friend, if you please. I'm your deadly enemy, and f so be I can, as God shall help me, I'll cut your heart out of your hide, or there's no snakes."

" Well, well—but I've no weapon."

" I'll bring you one—only say the word," was the pertinacious and quick reply. Finding there was no escape, the sergeant readily enough closed with the terms, and Davis then promised to seek him out in the swamp, conduct him to a clear ground, and make the terms of fight equal between them. This done, he turned away from the prisoner with something more of light-heartedness than usual, as he anticipated the pleasure of that strife with his enemy which promised to revenge him for so many wrongs.

The prisoners were soon all mounted, Goggle along with them, and so disposed as to ride between alternate files of the troopers. In this order they set forth for the recesses of the swamp, and a route was chosen by Humphries which enabled him to keep away from all beaten roads; the necessity still existing, while in the neighbour-hood of a superior force, for the utmost caution, as the objects of the partisan required security from observation even in preference to any successes which so small a party might obtain.

It was not long before they began to enter the swamp, and to meet with its obstructions. The twilight gradually ceased to glim-mer, the trees crowded more closely on the path, and the shades stalking about them incessantly grew incorporated into huge masses, from which the trees themselves were scarce distinguishable. Then came the varieties of the swamp; the black and stagnant puddle, the slimy ooze, the decayed and prostrate tree, and the hanging vine swinging across the route. The night came down shortly after they had penetrated the morass, and, though a clear starlight evening, it was only now and then that glimpses could be obtained of the pale and melancholy watchers suddenly peering down into the openings of the trees overhead.

A closer order of march was now imposed upon the troop, as, carefully leading the way, Humphries guided them through one little creek, and along the banks of another. The earth between the two parallel waters lay tolerably high, and formed a defile, as it were, through which they continued to move with no other obstructions than such as were presented by the occasional morasses formed in the curves of the creek, and the close trees, that suffered them to move only in single file. Once fairly in the swamp, Humphries had a torch lighted and carried by a trooper in front with himself. This serving sufficiently to pick the path, though yielding no assistance to those who came after, they were compelled simply to keep close, and follow the leader.

The lieutenant kept unrelaxing watch during all this period, and the utmost order was observed during the progress. His ear was keenly observant of every sound that reached his ears, though deceived by none of them. He was skilled in woodcraft, and knew well how to decoy the bird, and to deceive the reptile, by his various imitations. At this time, however, he permitted himself no exercise of his powers in this respect; but watchful in the highest degree, he gave his orders briefly, in a low tone, and without the employment of unnecessary words.

At length the defile narrowed, the undergrowth thickened about the trees in luxuriant vegetation, and so dark was the place that the figure of each individual horse could only be made out by the rider immediately behind it. To the instinct and better vision of the animals themselves the movement was in great part left; the trooper and his prisoner, alike, only taking care not to fall far behind the steed in advance. This being the case, and heedful of his charge—while Davis was directed closely to watch and bring up the rear—Humphries stationed himself at the mouth of the defile, having first led the way through which they were yet to pass. There, with uplifted torch, he numbered one by one the steeds of all that came through and passed before him; and in this way with a precaution which he considered the most complete that could be adopted, confidently thought that there could be no risk of losing any of his prisoners. And, indeed, with the ordinary prisoner, the man only skilled to fight bulldog fashion, without ingenuity, and solely relying upon his teeth, the precaution would have been enough.

But Goggle was not of this description. He had the gift, along with Indian blood, of Indian subtlety. He had kept his course quietly and patiently with the rest, and there was no gloom, no dulness, no flagging of spirits about him. All was coolness in his mood, and he knew his ground. He had heard the orders of Humphries, readily understood the route, and prepared to avail himself of circumstances as they might occur in his favour. There was a cry which the troops were heard to utter successively, as they advanced through a certain point of the defile, the meaning of which he clearly enough understood. A ragged pine had thrust an arm directly over the path, and so low as to endanger the head of a tall man moving along too erectly. The cry of each rider, therefore, as he passed under it, was to his immediate follower—

"Stoop low !—heads down !"

Goggle heard this cry before he reached the obstruction. He coolly prepared himself for a little scout practice,—buttoned his jacket closely, and freed his feet from his stirrups as he proceded. He did this without the slightest precipitation or impatience. In order to accustom his horse to the relaxation of the bit, so that his movement might not undergo any change at the trying moment, he gradually yielded up the bridle, until the animal failed entirely to feel its restraints upon his mouth ; then, dropping the reins altogether as he heard the cry of his predecessor to "stoop," instead of doing so, he threw his arms upwards, caught the overhanging branch firmly with both hands, and with the activity of an ape, lifted himself fairly out of the saddle, and for a moment swung in air The horse passed from under him, and, with his old habit, followed the lead to which he had been accustomed. The succeeding steed approached, Goggle gave the cry, in the most measured language and as he did so he whirled himself over, out of the trooper's way, upon the top of the branch, where he sat with all a squirrel's sense of security.

Here he remained in quiet as the troop proceeded. He knew the length of the defile, and could see in the distance the glimmering of the torch by which Humphries enumerated the troopers as they came forth from the avenue; and as the rear of the party with Davis was at hand, he felt secure that all would have passed him some time before his empty saddle would warn the lieutenant of his departure.

A moment after, the voice of Davis, as he passed under the tree where the fugitive sat chuckling at his success, apprised him of the proper time to commence his flight. The ground was free, and dropping from his perch, the fugitive crossed the path, and took the water of the creek as soon as possible, following its course towards the river for a brief space, then turning aside and shrouding himself, while still keeping his onward way, in a close-set forest of small saplings.

Here he had scarcely entered when the alarm was given. The vigilant Humphries had discovered the absence of the prisoner, as the untrammelled animal came forth from the defile. A confused shouting, a rush as of one or more in search, reached the ears of the fugitive; but he was safe, and laughed at all pursuit.

The sounds finally died away; and Goggle, who had lain quiet while the confusion lasted, now resumed his flight. Davis and some of the troopers had dashed back when the alarm was given; but in the thick darkness which shrouded the region, there was no prospect of retaking the prisoner so long as he kept silent. This was soon evident to Humphries, and, sore and chagrined, he hurried on the progress of the party, swearing vengeance against the tory, his hostility to whom naturally underwent due increase and animation, as he found himself outwitted by the subtle enemy in so simple a manner. Humphries got back to camp late at night without farther incident, and without meeting with Singleton, as the latter had proposed. They had taken different routes; and when the commander emerged from the swamp, he took the road back to the bridge, only accompanied by his youthful protégé. He reached the river just as the fugitive Goggle was about to emerge from the swamp. The latter heard at a distance the feet of the horse, and lay snug beside the road as they passed. The unobstructed starlight was now around them, and he was enabled to distinguish their persons. He conjectured what would be the route of Singleton, and he now beheld the opportunity of finding his reward with the British, and of gaining his revenge upon one, at least, of his American enemies. Toil and fatigue were at once forgotten, fear was discarded from his mind ; and, now, running, now walking, with an Indian pertinacity of spirit, he took the directest course leading to Dorchester.

CHAPTER XXV.

"Her words are so much music, caught from heaven
When clouds are parting, and the rosy eve
Comes to her sway."

THE hour was late when the Half Breed reached the village. The sentries were all set, and Proctor had retired for the night; but, aware of the value of his intelligence, the fugitive did not scruple to disturb him. He told his story at full, and had the satisfaction to find that he told it to a willing ear. Proctor at once proceeded to arm a party, and heading it himself, prepared to surprise the rebel partisan in the quiet dwelling to which Goggle had seen him pursuing his way. The British major was the more willing to move in this business now, than he otherwise might have been, as he had been troubled with some doubts whether the suspicious attitude of Colonel Walton had not already called for his attention. He was glad of an opportunity, therefore, of proving his alacrity in the cause, and making amends for what might be construed into previous neglect. Something of his stimulus to present action, may also, not unjustly, be ascribed to the jealous instincts which coupled Robert Singleton with his fair cousin. We leave him, with a little troop of half a score, getting into saddle, and about to move in the direction of "The Oaks." Goggle remained behind, at the suggestion of Proctor, who needed not his assistance farther, and saw that his fatigued condition craved for immediate rest.

Let us now return to Singleton and his attendant. Having reached the neighbourhood of "The Oaks," they took the back track leading to the river, which carried them immediately into the rear of the dwelling-house. There, dismounting and carefully concealing their horses in the brush, Singleton placed his pistols in his belt, and leaving the boy in charge of the animals, with instructions to watch closely, proceeded to the mansion.

Proud of the trust, Lance Frampton promised his commander to watch well, and approve himself a worthy sentinel. In a few moments the partisan was once more treading the well known path, covered with those grave guardians of a century, the spreading and moss-bearded oaks, and on his way to the presence of those well beloved beyond all, and dearer to him than the life-blood at his heart. Many minutes had not elapsed before he was at the side of the frail and attenuated form of her, the sister and the playmate of his boyhood; feeble to prostration, sustained by pillows, and scarcely able to turn upon him those lovely eyes, still bright, and brightening to the last, as if the reluctant soul had concentrated within all its heavenward fires; and thence, though clinging still to mortality, was already evolving some of that divine light which it was so soon to be mingled with for ever.

"Dear, dear Emily!" he exclaimed; "my sister, my sweet sister!"—and his lips were pressed to her forehead; and, though he strove hard for their suppression, the tears gathered in his large sad eyes. Her's were the only unclouded ones in the chamber. On one side sat Kate Walton, while his aunt moved around the couch of the sufferer, heedful of all her wants. They too were in tears, and had evidently, before this, been weeping. It was a scene for tears; in which smiles had been irreverent, and joy an unbecoming and most impious intruder.

Yet, though the dying girl wept not herself, and though her eye had in it that glorious effulgence which is so peculiarly the attribute of the victim to the deadly form of disease under which she laboured, yet the brightness of her glance was no rebuke to the tearfulness of theirs. It was a high and holy brightness; a deep expression, full of divine speech, and solemnizing even while it brightened with an aspect not of the earth. The light might have streamed from the altar, a halo from heaven around the brow of its most favourite apostle.

She spoke to him of the commonest affairs of life; yet she knew that death was busy at her heart. Whence was this strength of mind—this confidence? Is there, indeed, a moment before the

12

hour of dissolution when the mortal is vouchsafed communion, a close communion and converse with its God. Are there glimpses of the future from which, at such moments, the sufferer draws his hope, his consolation? It is, it must be so. The dim confine, the heavy earth, cannot always be around us. The soul must sometimes employ the wings of a divine prescience, and shaking off human care with human feeling, forget for a while the many pains, along with the humble pleasures, of humanity, and be only alive to the immortality of the future. The dark mansions of the coming time, and the huge and high barriers which control it, must then be thrown aside; and faith and the pure spirit, in their white garments, already on, must be suffered to take a momentary survey of the world which is to be their own.

But the spirit had come back to earth, and now grew conscious of its claims.

"Dear, dear Robert!" she replied, as she motioned to be free from those caresses which he bestowed upon her; and which, though studiously light and gentle, were yet too much for a frame spiritualizing so fast: "you are come, Robert, and with no ill news. You have no harshness on your brow, and the vein is not swollen; and by this I know you have not been engaged in any war and violence. Is it not so?"

He did not undeceive her, and suppressed carefully every allusion to his late adventures; spoke of indifferent things, and encouraged in her that idea of the national peace, which, from a hope, had already grown into a constant thought within her mind.

"Oh, would that I could only hear of it, Robert, ere I leave you! Could I know that you were safe, all safe, before I die—you, dear aunt, and you, sister, my more than sister—and you, Robert, who have been to me father and brother, and all, so long; would I could know this, and I should die happy—even with joy! But death will have its sting, I feel, in this. I shall go to peace—I feel that; while all the strifes, and all the cares, the wounds, and the dangers, will be left for you!"

Her eyes now filled, as her earthly sorrows were renewed. Her brother strove to console her in the usual commonplace. Alas! there is no language for such a time and occasion, but the common-place and fruitless, and silence then is the only fruitful speech.

"Fear not for us, dear Emily; and let not our afflictions fill your mind. Be calm on that subject; you have pains and sufferings enough of your own, my dear sister, to keep you from desiring any share in ours."

"I have no sufferings now, Robert; I have long ceased to have sufferings of my own. Have I not long survived the hope of life? have I not long laboured to sustain myself against the coming and the fear of death? God be praised! for I think I have succeeded. These were my afflictions once, and they are now over. Yet I have sorrows not my own, and they are, that I must leave you to sorrows—griefs of an unnatural time, and horrors that come with the disease, as it would seem, of nature. For war is her disease—her most pestilent disease. The sharp sword, the torturing scourge, the degrading rope, the pining and the piercing famine—these are the horrible accompaniments of war; and oh, brother, soldier as you are, when I leave you to the dangers of these, I carry with me all my human sorrows. I may die, but my soul must bear along with it those thousand fears which belong to my sympathies with you."

"Ah, too considerate of us, so unworthy such consideration!" was the exclamation of Kate beside her. "Do not, dear Emily, oppress yourself by reflections such as these. You leave us to no difficulties; for though the country still be at war, yet our quarter is free from its ravages; and though under hostile control, it is still quiet, and not now a dangerous one. We are all here at peace."

"Why seek to deceive me, Kate, when but a glance at Robert tells a different story? Look at the sword by his side—the pistols in his belt, and say why they are there, if war be not around us—if there be no occasion for strife, and if he is not exposed to its dangers? You cannot persuade me out of my senses, though in this I am quite willing that you should. Would that it could be so? I would not believe these truths if I could help it."

"And you need not, Emily, my sister; for though there be war, and though I may be engaged in it, yet the present prospect is, that it will soon be over, and as we all wish it—giving us peace and freedom alike, and securing honourable station for our country among the nations of the earth. This last thought, my Emily, ought to make you better satisfied with the risks our people are compelled to run."

" It does not, brother. I have not that vain ambition, which, for the sake of a name, is content with the bloodshed and the misery of mankind ; and I hold the doctrine hateful to one professing the Christian faith. How it may be upheld, this warfare in which life is taken as a worthless thing, and man's blood shed like water, for any pretence, and with any object, by a believer in the Saviour, and the creed which he taught, I can never understand."

" You would not have us submit to wrong and injustice ?"

" No ; but the means employed for resistance should be justly proportioned to the aggression. But, alas for humanity ! the glory and the glare of warfare, under false notions of renown, are too often sufficient, not only to conceal the bloodshed and the horror, but to stimulate to undue vengeance, and to make resistance premature, and turn the desire of justice into a passion for revenge. Then, for the wrong done by one captain, all the captains conspire to do greater wrongs; and the blazing dwelling by midnight, the poor woman and her naked children escaping from the flames to perish of hunger ; the gibbeted soldier on the nighest tree ; the wanton murder of the shrieking babe, quieted in its screams upon the bayonet of the yelling soldiers—these are the modes by which, repairing one wrong, war does a thousand greater. Oh, when, calling things by their right names, shall we discover that all the glory of the warrior is the glory of brutality ?"

The picture which the enthusiastic girl had given of the terrors of war, was too felicitously just, as it had occurred in Carolina, to be denied by her auditor; and as she had herself made the right distinction between war as an absolute necessity, forced upon a people in their defence, and pursued only so far as adequately to obtain the mere object of justice, and war as a means of national or individual aggrandizement or fame, there was no legitimate answer to her exhortation. A momentary silence ensued, which was due to the exhaustion following her effort at speech. In a little while she again addressed her brother—

"And how long, Robert, do you stay in our neighbourhood?"

"But a few days more, Emily: I linger now somewhat over my time; but my objects are various and important."

"And where then do you go?"

"Either to the Santee or the Peedee; wherever there is a chance of finding Colonel Marion, to whose brigade I am attáched."

"And not so easy a matter," said Kate Waton, "if reports speak truly of your colonel. He is here, there, and everywhere, and they say cannot often be met with either by friend or foe, except when he himself pleases. What is it Colonel Tarleton calls him?"

"The Swamp Fox: and a good name, for certainly he knows more of the navigation of the thick swamps of the Santee and Peedee, than ever seaman of the broad ocean. In a circuit of five miles he will misguide the whole force of Tarleton for as many days; then, while he looks for him in one quarter, Marion will be cutting up his foragers or the tories in another. He is fearless, too, as well as skilful, and in the union of these qualities he is more than a match, with an equal force, for any score of the captains they can send against him."

As the major spoke with that warm enthusiasm of his commander, which distinguished the men of Marion generally, an audible sigh from his sister recalled him to his consideration, and he turned to her with some observation on an unimportant subject. She did not seem to heed what he said, but, after a moment's pause, asked, rather abruptly, if he should not move first for the Santee.

"I think so," was the reply; "the probability is that I shall there find my orders, if, indeed, I do not find my commanding officer. I wait but to fulfil some important duties here, when I shall move direct in that quarter."

"And when, Robert, do you expect to return?" was the farther inquiry, put with considerable earnestness of manner.

"In three or four weeks, Emily; not before, and probably not even then; for I may be ordered to join the continentals, on Gates's arrival, and shall then have a more limited range and exercise than now."

"That will be too late, too late!" murmured the maiden with an expression of deep regret.

"Too late for what, dear Emily?" said the major, quickly, in reply; but when he met her glance, and saw the mournful utterance which it looked, he needed no answer to his question. Never did eye more explicitly speak than hers, and he turned his own away to conceal its tears.

"Too late to see me die!" she murmured, as he bent his head downward, concealing his face in the folds of her encircling arms. " Ah, Robert! I leave you, but not lonely I hope—not altogether alone." Her eye rested upon the face of Kate Walton, as she uttered this hope; and though her brother saw not the look, yet the cheeks of the conscious Kate, so silently yet expressively appealed to, were deeply crimsoned on the instant. She turned away from the couch and looked through the window opening upon the waters of the Ashley, which wound at a little distance beyond them, stealing off, like a creation of the fancy, under the close glance of the observer. Her fingers played all the while with the branches of the oak that rose immediately beside the window.

Emily then intimated to her brother her increasing debility, the necessity of her own repose and of his departure, with a calmness which was perfect, and painfully appalling to him in consequence.

"But come to me to-morrow, to-morrow night, Robert; come early—I would speak with you; I have much to say to you, and I feel that I have but little time to say it in. Fail me not, unless there be hazard, and then heed not my desire. You must risk nothing, Robert; your life is more valuable to me, strange to say, as my own is leaving me. I know its value, as I am now about to be taught its loss. But go now—and remember, to-morrow."

His grief and her farewell were alike voiceless. He pressed her cold cheek with his lips at parting; then, like one who had left behind him all his consciousness, he descended with his beautiful cousin from that sad but sacred apartment, where life still lingered, neutralizing decay with its latent freshness, but where immortality already seemed to have put on some hue of that eternal morning, whose bloom and whose freshness speak not only for its lasting existence, but for its holy purity.

CHAPTER XXVI.

"I cannot list thy pleading, though thou plead'st
In music which I love."

HER father being absent, Kate did the honours of the household, and we need not say how much gratification Major Singleton felt when he found himself alone with his sweet cousin in the parlour below. He loved—he had much to say, and the present was an opportunity which he had long desired. We have already seen him urging those claims upon her closest regards which she continued to evade. He now determined to press them; and, handing her to the sofa with a degree of rigid solemnity in his manner which led her to conclude that his object was any thing but what it really was, she willingly took the seat to which he conducted her.

Singleton was no sentimentalist, but a man of sterling character, and deep, true feeling. He was one of those who never trifle; and the prompter at his heart, though taking the name of that capricious mood which is always fair game for the arch jest and playful satire, was yet altogether a more lofty and dignified sentiment. His love was of his life a vital part; it made up his existence, and embodied in its own the forms of a thousand strong obligations to society and man. It was now prominent to his own view in the form of a sacred duty—a duty to others not less than to himself. Perhaps, too, as he was something of an idealist, and strove to believe in attributes which are not always found profusely in the world, there may have been something of the spiritualizing character of poetry mixed up in his devotions—giving dignity to a purpose which is usually urged with timidity, but which, in the present case, was treated with all the straightforward singleness of aim which belongs to the man of mere business.

"Katharine," he said, after a brief pause, during which his eyes gazed on her with a calm deep earnestness which at length sent the glance of hers downward beneath them—"Katharine, my cousin, months have passed since you were taught to know my feeling towards you. Since I have known you, that feeling has been hourly on the increase. I loved, the more I knew ; and though changes have come over us both—changes of fortune, of condition, of appearance—yet I have only admired you the more with every change. You have always seemed to me the one—the one only—whom I could truly love and cherish as a wife ; and this thought, my cousin, has not been because of your beauty, which, though great, has never called forth, and shall never call forth, so long as I think you what I think you now, one single encomium from me."

She would have interrupted him, but he simply placed his finger upon her arm, and proceeded.

"Nay, fear not, and do not interrupt me. I know you too well, and think of you too highly, to endeavour now to fill your ears with praises of that beauty of which neither of us can be utterly unconscious. I shall speak of other qualities which have recommended you to me, not in praise of them now, but only as, in urging my pretensions to your hand, I would prove to you that I have studied your character, and am so far satisfied with the results as to be willing now to adventure all my affections—and they are concentrated very closely now, and will soon be more so—in the offer which I shall make you. I think now that I know your character. I have seen its firmness, its masculine good sense, and its unostentatious delicacy. Such a character will not be apt to misunderstand mine, and in this lies one chief security of domestic bliss. Such, for a long season, has been my thought, and I must now act upon it, or never. I have reasons for desiring it now, which your own reflections may not teach you, but which you must know hereafter. Cousin, dear Kate, forgive me if my speech be less than gentle—if it seem abrupt or harsh. I am not apt at professions ; and with you I would rather avoid that show of sentiment which I know makes up, most commonly, the language of the lover. To you I would rather that my words should be of the most simple and least equivocal character. To your good sense, not your weak

nesses, the proffer of my hand is now made. Let me hope that
your good sense will determine the question, which I would not
willingly submit to any other tribunal."

He took her hand, at the conclusion of his remarks, and she suffered it to rest passively in his grasp. She did not immediately
answer, but appeared lost in reflections, which were not, however,
the less pleasing because they exhibited themselves in doubt and
indecision. Her eye, meanwhile, did not fall beneath the searching gaze of his: its deep and beautiful blue met his own unshrinkingly; nay, with something of a sympathizing fondness in its expression, which the tenor of her uttered reply did not, however,
confirm. The pause of the moment over, she turned to her suitor.

"Robert, you have but this moment come from the chamber of
sickness—soon to be the chamber of death. You cannot deceive
yourself as to the condition of Emily; she is sinking fast."

"I know it—I feel it," he answered, gloomily.

"How can you know it—how can you feel it, Robert, when you
come from the presence of one already linked as it were with heaven, and thus immediately after urge to me so earthly a prayer?
How can I, so filled as my thoughts should be, and are, with considerations of gloom and the grave, thus give ear to any less sanc-
tified consideration? Pardon me, dear cousin; but it seems to me
almost irreverent that we should discourse of any other themes at
this moment than those of sorrow."

"At another time, and with an affliction less severe than this,
your rebuke would have been felt. But this to me is no common
affliction. It leaves me alone—unaccompanied—desolate in all the
wide world of man. You know our history. For years that girl
has been all to me: I had her to love; I was her brother—her
protector—her all; and upon her I expended a thousand strong
feelings and warm affections which, when she goes, must crowd
back upon, and overwhelm me. We must have something in life
giving us the right to love—something which we can make our
own exclusive altar-place, which our loves and cares may hallow to
themselves, sacred from all intrusion, all rivalry, all denial from
another. While she lived—while there was hope for her—there
was always one sacred to me—of whose sympathies, when others

12*

were cold or stern, I could be certain. When she leaves me, Kate, I am alone ; there is but one to whom I may turn with confidence and trust—but one, and of that one I would be secure in the proffer which I now make to you : it is for you to say, and to say freely, with what hope."

" Robert, you know well how I esteem you—"

" Utter no professions, Kate—not so coldly, at least—if you really have any regard for me."

" You mistake—you do me injustice, cousin—I would not be cold or inconsiderate. I do esteem you—"

" Esteem !"

" Well, well—love you, then, if you like the word better."

He pressed her hand.

" I do love you, and too well ever to be cold to your claims, or indifferent to your affection. I have heard you with a degree of regard of which I shall not speak ; and I feel, deeply feel, the high compliment which you have paid me, in the offer of your hand. But let me ask of your reason—of your own good sense—if the present be the season for engagements of this nature ? I speak not now of the condition of your sister, but of the country. What is the hope of repose, of domestic felicity, at such a period, when the strong arm of power, at its caprice, invades every sanctuary ?— when the family mansion of the wealthy planter shares the fate of the loghouse of the squatter ?—and when a renewal of injury only meets your application for redress ? You will see that this is no season for thoughts such as those belonging to the offer which you make me."

" It is, then, to the time—to the consummation, at this period—of my proposal, and not to the proposal itself, which you object ? Do I understand you thus, dear cousin ?"

" Not exactly, Robert. I object to *all* at this season. I object to a consideration of the proposal at this moment, as unseemly and improper, for many reasons; and I beg, therefore, that you would withdraw your application, and not exact from me any answer *now*."

" And why not answer for the future, Kate ? Why not speak conditionally in answer, and with reference to the period when peace shall be restored to the country ?   I would not, indeed, that we should marry now.   I would only be assured that I have in you, whatever may be the chances of war or the vicissitudes of life, one to love me, and who could meet me with an affection like my own.   I would have you ever as an ark to me, shrining and preserving my best affections, however the storms raged and the billows rolled around us."

" I will not deny to you, Robert, that, were I disposed to make at this moment a pledge of my heart to any, I know not one to whom I would sooner make it than to you.   If my character has been your study, I too have been somewhat observant of yours.   I have long regarded you as one to whom honour is dear, and manliness habitual—as one delicate and true in feeling, gentle in deportment, and properly sensible of that consideration of the claims of others, without which no man can possibly be the gentleman.   These, I hold, in addition to your acknowledged bravery and good sense, to be your characteristics; and they are such as all sensible women must esteem, and such as, in you, my cousin, I have long been accustomed to esteem and—love.   Is not this enough ?   Wherefore press me to say that I will not, at this time, make pledges of affection to *any* man—that I will not bind myself or my affections for the future—that in this season of peril, owing as I do the duty of a child to her parent, I will not, while he may need my attendance, bind myself to other duties, which may be inconsistent with those which I owe to him ?   Such must be my answer, Robert, to the proffer which you make me."

" Ah, Kate ! your pledge would be everything to me, amid the dangers of the war we wage."

" Nothing !" she replied quickly ; " nothing more than I would be to you, Robert, even now, were those dangers to come home to you.   Were you wounded, believe me, cousin, or brother, or lover, I should watch by your bedside, bathe your head, bring you refreshment ; ay, dress your wounds—I pledge it as a true woman— with as little scruple as if you were even now my wedded husband. Nay, shake not your head !   You know me not, Robert, if you doubt me in this.   I may not have the strength, but I have the heart, I am sure, to do all this that I promise."

"And wherefore not say more ?   Why, if you are willing to per
form such duties, will you not give me the right to claim them at
your hands ?"

" Because such a pledge may prove inconsistent with the duties
which I owe to another. Urge me no more, Robert. Be content
with what I have said. At this moment I cannot make the pledge
that you require. I *dare* not ! Wait the due season : when the
war is over ; when Carolina shall be free from hostile footsteps ; and
when the land is cleansed of its pollution ;—come to me then, if
you hold this same temper, and then, if there be no change in me
—nay, there can be no change—I shall give you my hand, perfectly and all your own, as fully as I give it to you this moment in
sisterly regard. There, take it, and leave me, for the hour is growing late."

He carried the extended fingers to his lips, and without farther
word was about to hurry from the apartment, when he was arrested
in his progress by the sudden appearance of his aunt bringing a
message from his sister, requiring to see him again, if he had not
already departed. An unlooked-for change had come over her, according to the old lady's representations ; she had grown sensibly
weaker, and she thought her mind incoherent and slightly wandering.

With palpitating heart and trembling footsteps, followed by the
two ladies, Singleton again ascended the stairs leading to the chamber of death ; but, remembering the reference of Emily to his sword
and pistols, and how their presence had disturbed her, he took them
from his belt and placed them upon a table which stood in the passage. The next moment, he resumed his seat beside the shadowy
person of the maiden.

CHAPTER XXVII.

"How the flame flickers in the lamp!—how bright,
With a strange beauty—and now, dim for ever."

AND two opposing and mighty principles were at fearful strife in
that chamber. Death was there with power not to be withstood
and there life vainly endeavoured to combat him. Yet there were
no shows of terror or of violence in the struggle—no exhibition of
the torturing pain, and of the spirit vainly resisting and striving to
escape. All was gentleness, even in the murmurs which occasionally fell from the lips of the dying girl. Her cheek was transparent—her eye wore a sublimated light, as it quivered in its socket,
and flickering in changing directions, seemed in search of some
expected presence. Her pale lips were slightly parted, and the
even tops of the pearly teeth below were just perceptible. The
gauze of her drapery was scarcely lifted by the heave of her bosom;
and as her hand lay partially upon it, you might even trace out the
smallest of her blue veins, like so many fibres of the flower, shining through the delicate skin. She was dying—dying without
seeming pain; and well might her brother fancy, from the pleasant
smile upon her countenance, that the whispering sound which
reached his ears on entering the apartment, had fallen from the
sister angels already busy around her.

He sat beside her, took her hand, pressed his lips upon her forehead, and for a few seconds remained without attracting her notice.
Her eye at length glanced wildly upon him, and the lips, which
had fallen apart, were reclosed as she recognised him. At last a
faint smile enlivened them—a fond effulgence filled her eye—she
laid one of her hands upon that with which he had already clasped
her own, and murmured something faintly which he could not
understand. It was a strong effort which her mind had made to

concentrate itself upon a single object, and some minutes elapsed before it was quite successful. At length she spoke :—

" Oh, Robert, I sent for you. I'm so glad you were not yet gone, for I feel that I am dying. I am not mistaken now. I know it to be death. This darkness — these shades that come across my eyes are its cloud, and it presses momently closer and closer upon them. It must be so; and I have been afraid—very much afraid since you left me, that my thoughts were crowding and confused. They were strangely mixed up together—very strangely; and once I felt that they were escaping me ; and then I grew terrified. I would not lose my senses—I would have them to the last; for I would speak to you and to Kate, even with my parting breath. It is sweet to die so. I could bear it then : but not to know, not to say farewell, and pray for you in the moment of parting, would be terrible indeed—terrible, terrible !"

Her eyes closed, and her hands were clasped, as she concluded the sentence, while her lips separated, and her voice was heard in whispers, as if in prayer. When her eyes again opened, there was a wildness in their expression—a misty gleaming, that seemed to confirm to those around her, the fear which she had expressed. The mind was evidently wandering; but the strong will, still pre-eminent, enabled her to bring back the forgetting thoughts, and to fix them in expression. Her words now were in broken murmurs.

" Not my will, not my will, but thine, Father !—yet for him— for Robert, my poor brother—could it only be—for him—for Robert !"

The name recalled her more vividly to him who sat beside her, and her eyes were again fixed upon his face.

" Old mauma !—is she here, Robert—where ?"

He shook his head negatively, but made no other reply.

" Be good to her for me ; tell her—ah !"

She closed her eyes, and a slight distortion of the lips declared the pang which she felt at that moment, and from which it was several minutes before she was so far recovered as to be able to speak again. When she did, it was with a sweet smile of patient resignation.

" Strange that death cannot take his prey without inflicting pain! I am willing to go with him. I offer no resistance; yet he strikes and rends, the same as if I did. Life struggles still, even when you desire it not; but it does its duty—it holds on to its trust, and I must not complain. But, dear Robert, forget not old mauma! Give her all my things; and there is a new frock which I have made for her. Kate will give you the message that is to go along with it. And, Robert—the garden—the—ah, how cloudy, cloudy—so very dark; and that is through sin—sin—"

The lips continued to mutter, though the words grew indistinct. The, mind was again wandering—the soul was anxiously seeking to escape its earthly tabernacle; but the flesh as tenaciously strove to detain its prisoner. Singleton on one side, and Kate upon the other, bent speechlessly over the dying maiden. The eyes of Kate were full of tears; but Singleton choked with the grief to which tears could give no utterance. She started while he lay in this position, and her head, with unusual vigour, was lifted from the pillow; while her eye, glancing with a strong light, looked down upon him with a bewildered glance, as if terror and astonishment prompted its expression. He was roused less by her movement, of which, as his face was buried in the pillow, he had been unconscious, than by the words which followed it.

"Oh, you are here? Well, take it; but it's a sin, and you know that it is a sin. There were but two, and they both died; and —yes, yes,—they both died—one in the morning and the other in the evening, but all on the same day, and that was God's blessing. It's—"

She shook her head, as she checked herself in her wandering expressions, and, with a sad look, remarked upon it—

"It is so—I feel it—I feel how uncertain my thoughts are; they are continually going from me, or putting on strange forms, and I only get them back with an effort which is painful."

She raised her right hand as she concluded, gazed upon it attentively, and then begged Kate to hand her a mirror. She looked in it for a few moments, and then put it away from her, with a melancholy but sweet smile.

"I shall not look in it again, I think. I do not wish it; for it tells me how young I am—how very young to die: but the less sorrow, the less sin! I have loved you all—you, Robert—you, and you, Kate—and you, too dear aunt, I have indeed loved you very much; yet sometimes I have pained and angered you."

"Oh! no! no! no!"

"Yet, it could not have been otherwise; but I know that you will forgive me all. Forgive me, if I have said a cross word, or done any thing unkindly. Forgive me—will you not?—for indeed I would not thinkingly have pained you."

"Forgive you! ay, that we do, my child; if there be any thing you have done needing forgiveness from us, or anybody—which I believe not—I forgive you from my soul, my blessed angel—God almighty bless and forgive you!"

Her aunt was the only one about her who could reply; she understood the speechless sorrow in the faces of her brother and cousin, and the pressure of her hand in theirs had a sufficient answer. This pressure seemed to prompt a new feeling and desire; and with an eye turned pleadingly to Kate, she strove to carry her hand towards that of her brother. Without scruple, Kate freely extended it, and the hands of the cousins were clasped above the form of the sufferer. She nodded her head, and smiled in approbation. At this moment a servant from below beckoned Kate away, and she left the room. A sudden stir—a commotion, rather louder than usual, and certainly not desirable at such a place and hour, reached the ears of Singleton; and while he was wondering, Kate reappeared. Her face was full of alarm, and, hurriedly, she informed Singleton of the approach of enemies.

"Oh, Robert, you must fly! A troop is below from the garrison, with Major Proctor at their head. They are now moving rapidly down the avenue, and will soon be here. Fly to the back balcony, while I keep the door closed in front."

He bowed his head slightly in reply, but took no other heed of her information; while, proceeding to do as she had said, Kate descended to the hall below. With head bent down upon the pillow, Singleton gave way to that abstraction of the soul which belonged to a sorrow so trying as his own. He seemed utterly to have forgotten the words of his cousin, and made no movement, and showed no disposition to heed the warning. Seeing this, his aunt now came towards him, and endeavoured to arouse him to a sense of his danger.

"You waste time, Robert, that is precious. For God's sake fly, my son; fly while the chance is allowed you."

It was a moment when he seemed not to comprehend. His thoughts were not with himself. He answered inconsequentially—

"Why do you tell me this? Wherefore?"

"Why, Robert, why? It will soon be too late. Why not do as Kate advised you? Take the back piazza, and delay no longer."

"Ah,—leave her?" was the melancholy reply, as he gazed down with a look of self-abandonment upon the scarce conscious girl before him.

"What is it—what is it, aunt?" she cried, starting up from the pillow, as the entreaties of the old lady, rather loudly expressed, reached her senses, and aroused them.

"He is in danger—the British are coming; and he won't fly, though he knows they will hang him without judge or jury."

"Robert, Robert!" said the girl, turning to him quickly—all her thoughts coming back to their proper activity. "Delay not an instant, my dear brother. Delay not, delay not—but fly."

"Urge me not, Emily; there is little danger, and I would much rather remain here with you."

"Deceive me not, brother—I warn you, deceive me not!" she exclaimed, with a sterner tone of expression than heretofore.

"There is danger, and your stay involves your safety. Do I not know the doom which they hold for him whom they call the rebel —do I not? Leave me, and go at once—I implore, I command you."

"I cannot—"

"You must not vex me now—chafe me not, dearest brother, in these moments which should be sacred to peace. Do not embitter my thoughts by uselessly exposing yourself to danger. Ha! they come—they come! Fly, I command you—fly—fly from me, or I will leave you in anger. Fly, fly!"

He turned to press his lips to her forehead, but she motioned him away.

"Say that you will go—yes!" was her brief sentence.

"I will—I will, my poor Emily—I will."

She turned to him with affectionate fondness, gave him her hand, and his lips were glued to her own.

"God bless you—God bless you, and keep you safe for ever. Fly now, and delay not."

A noise from below of approaching feet, warned him of the necessity of a rapid flight; but as he was about to leave the chamber, the little black girl who attended upon it, informed him that a guard had been posted at both the doors, in the front and rear of the building. There was but one resource, and that was suggested by his aunt. She pointed to the chamber window, against which the shrouding branches of the massive oak from below had lifted themselves, as with a friendly offer of succour. He returned to the chamber—his lips were once more hurriedly pressed to those of his sister, whom he was never more to see; but now she repulsed him impatiently. He obeyed her sadly; tearing himself at length away, he passed through the window and was soon descending the tree, which fortunately stood on the side of the dwelling, remote from the two entrances, and hiding every thing in the deepest shadow.

"Look, look down, aunt, and say if he is safe," said Emily, panting with the impatient effort. The old lady gazed attentively, as the rustling of the tree indicated his progress down.

"He is now at the bottom, my child. He is safe down."

"Does he fly—unseen?"

"No, my child, he stands at the bottom."

"Oh, call to him to go—bid him not delay—does he go now?"

"Yes; now he moves; he moves towards the big walnut-tree."

"Oh heavens! he will be seen by others, if you can see him so far. Say, dear aunt, where is he now?"

"He moves from tree to tree, my child. Be patient, they see him not. Now I lose him, he goes behind the kitchen. Now he moves along the fence—he is over it, and in the shadow. They cannot see him now, and he will soon be at the river. He is safe I'm sure—he must be safe!"

"Thank God, thank God—ah!—mercy!—What is that, what is that?—They have slain him, they have slain him!"

A sudden rush of feet, loud voices in dispute, and the discharge of a pistol, were the sounds which had so acted upon the senses of the dying girl. These circumstances require an attention to the progress of the party under Proctor, and their success in entering the house before the doors could be closed against them, according to the original design of Katharine. Finding her purpose hopeless when she descended to the hall, she met Major Proctor at the threshold. His manner was studiously respectful ; how could it be otherwise, when met by the majestic form of a woman like the one who stood before him ?—her figure erect—her high forehead seeming to expand with the swelling veins upon it—her eye kindling with intensest light, and the whole expression of her face that of dignified rebuke.

"Major Proctor chooses strange hours for doing honour to my father's household ; but when he learns that the master of the house is from home, I trust that, as a gentleman, he will forbear to trespass farther upon the privacy of ladies. I doubt not that my father will freely see him in any seasonable visit he may think fit to make."

She stood directly before him in the passage-way, and it was not so easy to pass by her. He had previously given orders to a couple of soldiers to secure the back entrance ; and feeling himself, accordingly, perfectly secure in his hold upon his prey, having himself the command of the front, there was no necessity for any precipitation which might seem to diminish his respectful deportment towards her who addressed him, and whom he was so desirous to conciliate. Lifting his cap with a modest and even humble air, while speaking in the most cautious and gentle accents, he replied—

"The hour is certainly an unseasonable one, Miss Walton, and nothing but an imperative sense of duty to my king and command could prompt me, in this manner, to any trespass upon the privacy of those whom I so much respect as the family of Colonel Walton. It is my deep regret that any thing should occur rendering such an assurance on my part necessary."

"Mere compliment, Major Proctor, contrasts oddly with the violation of that sacred privacy which should be conceded to our sex, when unprotected by the presence of any one of yours."

"I knew not of your father's absence, Miss Walton," returned the Englishman, quickly. Her reply was instant.

" And the knowledge of it now, sir, secures us, I trust, from any farther intrusion ?"

The retort annoyed him, since his previous remark led obviously to the inference which she had made from it. There was a flush upon Proctor's cheek as he replied, with an air of decision—

"I am sorry, Miss Walton, to say that it does not. I know the unamiable light in which I must appear to you from such a declaration, but I must be content to rely for my justification on your own knowledge of what is most becoming in a soldier. I must do my duty."

" You are imperative, Major Proctor—but I am yet to know what part of your duty it is that brings you to our poor abode at midnight."

" The arrest, Miss Walton, of a rebel—a traitor to his king and country—a disloyal citizen, who has been skulking about the swamps, coming forth only to murder, and who, I am informed on good authority, is even now in this dwelling."

The epithets conferred so freely upon her cousin, awakened all the indignation of the high-spirited maiden. Her eye shot forth angry and brighter fires, and the curling hauteur of her lip looked a volume of contempt upon the speaker. She suppressed much of this in her language, and subdued the fever of her fierce thought to something like a quiet expression of unconcern.

" Your rebel has a name, Major Proctor ?"

" He has, Miss Walton; regard for your family has alone prevented me from giving it utterance."

" Ha! indeed—you are considerate. But, sir, you will please me not to constrain yourself too far. I would know this brave rebel who gives you so much annoyance. Thank God! there are some still in Carolina, like myself, who owe no allegiance to the king of England: who hate his rule as they despise the slaves who obey it."

Major Proctor, with a flushing face, simply bowed as he replied—

" The rebel, Miss Walton, now supposed to be in this house, is one Robert Singleton, one of Marion's men, and ranking as a major in the army of rebellion. You will suffer me, I hope, to proceed in searching for him, since it is my duty, and one that I am resolute to perform. Your language, Miss Walton, is such as to render any scruples unnecessary; but I was a gentleman, Miss Walton, before I became a soldier. As a lady, I cannot be your enemy, whatever may be the wrong which I may suffer at your hands."

The respectful, manly deportment of Major Proctor could not fail to exercise its full force upon a woman of so much character as Katharine Walton. She replied almost instantly, making at once a dignified acknowledgment of the undue severity of her speech, yet insisting upon the provocation which she had received.

"Robert Singleton is my relative, my friend, Major Proctor—one whom I dearly love. You knew much of this, if not all, yet your epithets were unscrupulous and unqualified in connection with his name. I am a Southron, sir; one of a people not apt to suffer wrong to their friends or kindred, without resenting and resisting it; and though a woman, sir—a weak woman—I feel, sir, that I have the will and the spirit, though I may lack the skill and the strength, to endeavour to do both."

"It is a spirit which I honour, Miss Walton, and my speech to you, in reference to your relative, my own sense of propriety has already taught me was highly unbecoming. You will forgive me, if I rightly understand your nature, Miss Walton, much more readily than I will forgive myself for the error. Meanwhile, I trust that you will permit me to pursue this search, since you have *not* assured me that its object is not here."

"I trust that Major Proctor, aware of my father's absence, will leave us unmolested until his return."

"I cannot—I dare not, Miss Walton—my duty forbids it."

"Your duty gives you no command here, Major Proctor, and your troops must be withdrawn, though I call upon my father's slaves with a view to their expulsion."

"Will they obey you, Miss Walton?"

"Ay, sir, to the last! I have but to say the words and they will rush upon your bayonets."

"I am wasting time, Miss Walton—permit me to pass onward."

And he advanced as he spoke. She stood resolutely fixed in the spot where she had first encountered him, and he saw that he would be compelled to employ some gentle force to put her aside.

Annoyed and chagrined at the idea of any such necessity, he sought by farther exhortation to gain his object, but she refused to hear him. At length, as a last resort, he said—

" Miss Walton, I have no desire to press this matter. Give me your word that the person I seek is not here, and I withdraw my men instantly."

" Withdraw your men, sir—you keep them here at your peril—give no assurances."

Finding his efforts unavailing, Proctor at once advanced, and, resolute to put her aside and proceed in his search, his hands were already extended for that purpose, when, seeing his object, she hastily drew back.

" Touch me not, sir, if you please. If you are resolute to intrude upon us, you do so at your own risk."

And before he could pass she had withdrawn herself from his presence, and hastily ascended the staircase. Placing a guard at the entrance, he quickly followed her, and as he entered the upper passage-way he found her standing firmly in front of the door leading to Emily's chamber.

" Major Proctor," she said, solemnly, "this is the chamber of sickness—soon to be the chamber of death! I charge you not to approach it."

" Miss Walton, I will do my duty, if you will allow me, with as much forbearance as possible; but I *must* do it."

" At your peril, sir ;" and as he approached she presented one of the pistols of Singleton which she had seized from a neighbouring table. The sight of it only impelled the soldier in his forward progress.

" Back, sir ! I command—I implore you! I would not use this weapon if I could avoid it; but I certainly shall use it, if you dare to approach. Force me not to do so, I entreat you."

" I cannot hesitate—I cannot hear you ;" and with the words he resolutely advanced. She thrust the weapon forward, fixed its aim as nearly as possible upon him, and with the single words—

" God forgive me, if I err in this," resolutely drew the trigger.

In the next moment Proctor put her aside with the utmost gentleness.

"You are spared a crime, Miss Walton. The spilling of blood is not always grateful to man; what should it be to woman?"

He turned from her to the handle of the chamber door, and she was too much stunned to seek to arrest him further. But, as he entered the appartment, he started back in horror. The picture that met his sight was too unexpected—too imposing—too unlike any thing he had ever looked upon or seen. He had beheld the field of battle, strewn with dead and wounded; but the sublimer powers of death, in which he effects his conquest without visible stroke or weapon, had never met his eyes till now; and he gazed with something like stupefaction upon his features, as the spectacle rose vividly before him.

There, rising from her couch, and partially erect under the sudden convulsion, as well of physical pang as of mental excitement, Emily Singleton met the first glance of the intruder. Her face was ghastly pale, but still how beautiful! her eye was glazing fast, but still how expressive! and the look which she addressed to the intruder—a look which seemed to signify that she understood his purpose—was that of some angry ghost rising from its shroud for the purposes of solemn rebuke. A wan, spectral light from her eye, seemed to fall in rays about the wasted cheek below it; and the slight exhibition of her teeth, which the lips, parting as in speech had developed, contributed still more strongly to the awful, spell like expression which her whole countenance wore at that moment She murmured, but incoherently—it might be an imprecation—and so the Englishman thought it. Her arm was slightly moved and her fingers separated, as she strove to lift them; but the fingers closed again feebly, and the lifted arm sank back again beside her He stopt to see no more, but rushed from the apartment. Kate took her place beside the dying maiden, and her hand adjusted the pillows while supporting her. A sweet smile now overspread her features, and her hand sank upon one shoulder. Gradually the glaze overspread her eyes, as a cloud shutting in the blue skies, and she fell silently into the sacred slumber.

"Go up, go up, my blessed angel!—the heavens are open for you!"

These were the words of the aunt, while Kate lay beside the life-less girl immersed in a sorrow which was speechless. The spirit had gone for ever from the trying and troubling earth; the silver cord had been loosed—the golden bowl was broken.

CHAPTER XXVIII.

"The courage that looks up, though numbers press,
And takes a newer vigour from the storm."

PUSHING hastily from the chamber of death, Major Proctor proceeded to the court below, where he assembled his men for the pursuit. Though profoundly impressed with the solemn event which he had witnessed—so far different from any thing he had expected to see in the apartment—he was too good a soldier, and too mindful of his duty, to lose time in those now idle regrets at his own abruptness, which he yet properly felt. A few brief words, directing his men upon different routes—having equally divided them, and the party dispersed in obedience to his commands. One of them, consisting of four men, he himself led, and in the very direction taken by our flying partisan.

Singleton knew his danger if taken, and at once, as soon as he reached the horses, prepared for the most rapid flight. He was weaponless, and there was no other alternative for safety; otherwise he would most willingly have stood his ground, for his was the spirit prompt always to extricate itself from its difficulties by the boldest daring. The strife with Proctor also promised him a large degree of satisfaction, apart from that which the exercise itself might yield. It was with some vexation, therefore, that, feeling for his pistols in his belt, he remembered where he had left them. It was too late to retrieve, and idle to lament the misfortune. It was only in flight that it could be lessened; and he took his measures accordingly.

"Tighten your girth, Lance, and mount quickly; we shall be pursued shortly, and I am without weapon of any sort. I have left my sword and pistols behind me."

"Here are mine, sir; they are small, but they've got a good charge, and new flints both."

13

" Give me one of them, quickly now, and mount. We must get into the main road, if we can, before they come out of the avenue; so hasten, hasten but hurry not; cool, boy—cool."

He tightened his own saddle-girth as he spoke; took off the handkerchief that encircled his neck, and thrust it into his pocket then seeing that the boy was mounted and ready, he was soon in saddle himself.

" Now pick the way, Lance; speak nothing, but keep cool and silent: gently, gently at first; let us send them as few sounds as possible."

The boy, with goodly promptitude, obeyed to admiration. Starting with an easy, slow motion, they emerged from the heavy oaks by the water's side, ascended the rising ground, and skirted along the low fence which girdled one corner of the estate, and led directly to the main road. The track was simply a negro foot-path; but the evening was sufficiently clear to enable them to trace it out perfectly and keep it with little trouble. " We shall escape them! A few hundred yards more will give us a fine start, boy, and that is all I care for. How far is it now to the main track ?"

" Not far, sir; just ahead. I think I see the opening in the trees. We shall soon be in it. Ha! did you hear a noise, sir—now ?"

" Yes: they are in saddle; they are after us. Push on, push on; we have little time to waste."

" Yes, sir, that they are; and if I'm not very much mistaken, they are after us from two sides—down on our trail, and coming out from the avenue. You hear, sir? somebody cried out from the quarter of the road, and we hear the horses' feet from the river, at the same time."

" More reason for speed, far more, boy; we shall have to trust entirely to that. There is the main road, and they will soon see us on it. You know your horse, Lance—you are not afraid of him ?"

" Afraid of him! no, sir, that I'm not; never was afraid of any horse yet."

" Then go ahead; strike in your rowel, and spare not. There's no danger in front of you, so drive on."

This little dialogue was all over in a few moments. The boy

put spurs to his animal as soon as the main road was entered, and, with an easy mastery of his own steed, Singleton kept his place close beside him. The road was a heavy sand, over which they had to speed for the few minutes succeeding their first entrance upon it; but soon they got upon a tough, pine land ridge, upon which the beating of their hoofs might clearly be distinguished at some distance by a heedful ear; and it was not long, accordingly, before a loud shout from the pursuers announced their discovery.

"We could turn down here, sir, into the woods; and there's a sort of wagon track somewhere about here, I think I could find, sir, leads to the Stono. That would lose them, certain, from our trail," said the boy.

"No matter, no matter, keep on as you are; if they come no nigher we are safe."

"But I think they gain on us, sir; shall I go faster? My nag can do much more."

"No, keep his strength; they don't gain much now, and we shall find it more useful—What is that?"

A sound—a rushing motion in the woods they had but recently left, warned them of new pursuers: the crackling of the dry sticks under feet was distinctly heard, as the enemy moved over the same ground with more haste and less caution than had been observed by them.

"Ha, we have them there, have we! and they will soon be on the road. They hear us, and know our route. Push on, boy, a little, but not much faster; a breath more of speed only, is all we want—so, so."

The coolness with which Singleton spoke and acted took from the flight most of the terrors which it otherwise might have occasioned in the mind of the boy. His figure grew more and more upright with the feeling of confidence, as it swelled in his bosom; he began to imagine the events of a struggle; he began to fancy the features of the collision; and, with all its disadvantages, to hope for the strife. There was much of the same mood at work in the mind of his leader; and his chagrin may not be expressed, when, under its stimulus, he reflected upon his want of his weapons. There was an air of vexatious indifference, a sort of reckless hardihood in his demeanour, which, looking occasionally behind him, the boy could not avoid perceiving. Singleton caught the movement once or twice; and, at length, in sharper tones than usual, addressed him—

"Why do you look around, sir? are you afraid?"

"No, sir—oh no!—I don't think I am—that is to say——but I never tried."

"Tried what?"

"To fight with men, sir, and to shoot them; and I don't know, sir, whether I should be afraid or not."

Singleton smiled; the feeling of the boy rebuked his own, as it was somewhat boyish also.

"Go on, sir; look not behind you again, unless you would have your own shoulders rise up to frighten you. And you may urge your nag a little faster; those fellows are now out of the bush, and in the heavy sand; you will soon hear them on the ridge, and then they will have the same clear track with ourselves; go on, now, and to keep you from looking behind you more frequently than is needful, remember that I am between you and danger. Touch up your nag; let him feel the thorn, and be lively."

The boy felt mortified that Singleton should think that he looked round from apprehension; and thought how happy he should be to show his superior that he was not afraid; but without a word, he did as he was directed—struck the spur quickly into the yet unbreathed animal, which bounded away under the keen impulse with a far more generous movement.

As the partisan had said, the pursuers were soon upon the pine-land track, over which they had themselves passed but recently. Proctor led them with an earnestness which arose, not less from his own estimate of the value of the game, than from a personal feeling, if not interest, which he seemed to entertain in the arrest of Single ton. He had preserved his temper, under great provocation, dealing with Katharine Walton; but he remembered with bitterness that her sharp sarcasms had been uttered in defence of the very person he pursued. This quickened his eagerness.

As he entered the little negro trail running by the fence, he heard the shout of the party from the avenue below; and, as this seemed to say that the fugitive was within his reach, a new impetus wa: given to his exertions. By dint of hard riding he soon got up with the party which led off the pursuit; and the spur was not spared in order to diminish the vantage ground which the partisan had already won, in the space thrown between them. The composure and coolness of the flight tended to this object not less than the speed of the pursuers; and it was with no small satisfaction that Proctor was now enabled to distinguish the regularly recurring tread of the flying horses. He readily imagined that Singleton would put his animal to its fullest speed, and so thinking, he did not doubt that a little more effort must result in their overhauling him; believing this, he shouted encouragingly, crying out to his men, while bending forward with all speed in the chase himself—

"Five guineas to the man who first lays hands on the rebel! so to it, men—he cannot now escape us. We gain on him at every leap, his horse will soon be breathed. Heed not the boy, but see that the other is secure at all hazards—alive if you can take him, dead if he resist you: we must have him, dead or alive; and the reward is the same. On—on!"

A cheer—a hearty cheer—thoroughly English, followed this speech. Five guineas! The spell was potent. Fiercely did they urge the rowel in the warming flanks of their chargers. They dashed headlong through the thicket; they wound about following the sinuous pathway, and at length found themselves upon the broad trace over which Singleton and the boy were riding. Their horses' feet were heard, but they themselves remained unseen. The thick shadow of the forest lay over the road ahead, and under its friendly shelter the two fugitives were then speeding, with a pace somewhat quickened in obedience to the necessity. The boy wondered at Singleton's coolness as their pursuers drew more nigh. He knew not the recklessness of danger which follows habitual strife. He heard the cries of the pursuers to their steeds. He remembered that their own had not been forced, and he felt more assured.

"Now, boy—now is the time; they are drawing nigher, and we may as well leave them for a while. Bend to it and keep beside me."

The boy did as he was bidden, and the difference was soon perceptible the noble animals sprang off with all the elasticity of freshness, while those of their pursuers, which had been ridden rapidly to " The Oaks," and then as rapidly after them, failed, in spite of the repeated urging of their riders, to increase their speed a second. Gradually, the sounds grew less and less distinct upon their ears, and were nearly lost, when all on a sudden, and quite unexpectedly, the steed of Singleton stumbling along the ground, precipitated his rider clean over his head. The boy instantly gathered up his reins, and leaped from his animal beside him.

" Oh, sir ! you are hurt ! I'm afraid you are hurt !" was his passionate exclamation, as he approached the partisan.

" A little, Lance—a little ; but I'm afraid Sorrel is hurt a great deal more. He moves with difficulty."

Singleton rose with some effort from the ground. He had been slightly stunned and somewhat bruised by the fall ; but not so much as to incapacitate him from movement. He approached his horse, which had also risen to his feet, and now remained trembling upon the spot where he had fallen. Singleton took the bridle in hand, and led him off a few paces. This was sufficient to satisfy him that the animal was too much lamed to yield him much if any service in the flight that night. The danger was pressing, as in the brief time occupied by the event recorded, the pursuing party had regained the ground, and something more, which, in the increased speed of the partisan, they had previously lost. Singleton at once adopted his decision.

" Lance, you must mount instantly and fly ; I'll take the bush and try to get into safe cover. There's no time to waste, so at once about it. To horse, boy ; why do you stand ?"

" Why, sir, it's you that's wanted in camp, not me. I can hide in the bush just as well as you, sir ; I'm not afraid !"

" Go to, my poor boy ; go to, and be not foolish ; do as you're told, and no trifling. Know you not that if they take you they'll hang you to the tree as a rebel ?"

"But, sir, they will hang you too—I know that ; and I'm small —I can hide better in the bush than you."

" Answer not, but do as I have told you. Mount at once and fly, or I shoot you down on the spot. Go. I shall save myself."

The boy obeyed reluctantly, and it was high time that he should

He had barely time to remount, which he did with a sad, slow motion when he heard the voices of the pursuers, who in all this while had failed to hear the tread of the fugitives. The boy sped quickly on his way, while Singleton, leaving the lamed horse in the road, not having time to remove him, plunged into the thick woods alongside, just in season to avoid the immediate observation of the pursuers. They came up to the spot, and though his horse, with a native instinct, hobbled forward feebly, as it were to escape them, they quickly surrounded him, and, perceiving his condition, at once conjectured that the rider was in the neighbouring woods.. The voice of Proctor was at once heard with the promptest order—

"Dismount, fellows—dismount, and search the wood—he must be close at hand, and cannot escape us if you look well. The woods are thin and open. Five guineas, you know, dead or alive, to the man that first takes him."

"Ah! there's a chance then, for a choice of death, at least," said Singleton to himself, bitterly, as, standing immediately beside the road, he heard the sanguinary order. His hands fingered his belt unconsciously, where the pistols had been placed, and he cursed the thoughtlessness which had brought him off from the dwelling without having first secured them. But he made up his mind to resist at all hazards, weaponless or not, if once encountered. He had his hope of escape, however, and one that did not seem so very unreasonable. Instead of rushing off into the woods, where, from the lack of undergrowth, he might have been discovered readily, he clung to the luxuriant brush, the product of a vigorous sun acting freely upon it, that skirted the road. The troopers dismounted, all but Proctor himself, and a single corporal. Supposing, very naturally, that the fugitive would seek to embower himself as far in the woods as possible, the troopers scattered themselves over too large a surface; and the cries and clamour of the search gradually receded from the highway.

Proctor, meanwhile, accompanied by his single companion, kept moving to and fro along the road; and as he moved down the path, a new prospect of escape was suggested to the active mind of the partisan. The horses of the troopers were fastened to the swinging boughs of a tree only a few paces distant. Could he reach them unheard?   He looked out, and waited until the forms of the two mounted men grew more indistinct upon the road, then cautiously skirting the track, and still behind the bush, he approached the tree.   The horses heard him, but did not whinny or show alarm as he drew nigh ; and before emerging from cover, he sought with his eye to determine the nag of best speed and bottom.   He did so—one a few yards distant pleased him best, and he anxiously awaited until the two riders, who were now returning, should again wander away from the spot, to rush out and secure him.   In the mean while the hunt of the troopers continued in the wood.   The dancing shadows of the starlight occasionally deceived them into hopes of the fugitive—sometimes the persons of one another ; and on these occasions their hurras and encouraging shouts were prodigious.   Proctor passed close beside the tree as he came up, in the rear of which Singleton had sheltered himself. He was chafed at the delay, and shouted to his men as laggards, repeating the reward offered, and in his tone and language showing an anxiety to capture the fugitive which could not well be ascribed to his love for his king.

" He must be there, Corporal Turner—he could not have gone far, sir—but a moment before he was mounted, and we heard both horses distinctly.   This beast is Singleton's, for so the fellow Blonay described him—a bright sorrel, with long tail, and a white blaze on his right shoulder.   This is the animal."

" It is, sir—the very nag ; and, as you say, sir, he cannot have gone far into the bush, if he went in at all ; but may he not, sir, have gone double with the boy on the other horse ?"

" The devil !—yes—I did not think of that ; and if so, we have lost him.   Damnation !—it must be so."

And in his chagrin Proctor resumed his sauntering ride to and fro along the high-road, followed by the corporal at a little distance. How impatiently, yet cautiously, did the partisan look forth from the bush, watching their movements !   Satisfied at length with the distance thrown between them, and impelled the more readily to action by the increasing and approaching clamour from the wood, he resolutely advanced from his cover, and with a most marvellous composure undid the loop of the bridle from the bough, and led out the steed which his eye had already chosen. It was a broad chested, strong-shouldered, and well built animal, that, under ordi nary circumstances, would have been admirably well calculated both for flight and burden. But he had been hardly ridden that night, and there was no erectness n his head and neck—nothing elastic in his tread—as Singleton led him out from the group. But there was no time to be lost in lamenting this misfortune. Besides, his condition was that of all the rest, and the prospect of the escape now was quite as good as that of the pursuit. In an instant more the partisan was mounted—the head of his animal turned up the road, and, with a single glance behind him to note the distance of his enemy, he plied the spur, and once more resumed his flight.

"What is that?" cried Proctor to the corporal. "Ha! it must be the rebel; and, by Heaven! upon one of our own horses. Ride— ride, sir—after him with me, and he shall not escape us yet—my horse is too good for any he could get from that pack, and I can soon overhaul him. Sound, sir, sound for the men to saddle; and follow—sound, sir, and follow."

His orders were given with a rapidity almost emulating his horse's speed. Vexation at being so foiled, anger at the cause, and a sense of his duty—to say nothing of motives and feelings working in his bosom, which Proctor did not dare to analyse—all combined to stimulate the Briton to the most hearty endeavours. His steed went over the ground like an arrow, while the corporal wound his bugle, calling up the wandering troopers dispersed about the wood. His animal failed utterly to keep up with that of his commander, and Proctor had the satisfaction to perceive that he gained upon the fugitive. Singleton was soon conscious of this fact, and seeing there was but one enemy, he began to calculate the necessity of a conflict at all hazards, almost without a weapon, and trusting only to a proper management of his steed to foil and overthrow that of his pursuer. He was a famous horseman, and knew most of the arts by which this might be accomplished. His calculations became momently more and more necessary. The closer tramp of the pursuing steed was now sharply in his ears, and he had already meditated a sudden turn upon him as soon as he should reach the top of that slight elevation of land to which he was fast speeding.

18*

This would give him an advantage in descending upon the uptoil-
ing charger. With this purpose, he gathered up the reins with
a firm but not a close grasp upon the animal, as his object was not
by any means to restrain him; he placed his feet firmly in the
stirrups, which he threw close under the belly of the steed, wrap-
ping his legs, as it were, around him; then, crouching forward
upon the saddle, he awaited the proper moment for the contemplated evolution. The pursuer came on with a reckless, unrestrain-
able motion, and had already begun to move along the elevation,
when he drew the curb so suddenly upon his horse's mouth as
almost to throw him back upon his haunches.

Both parties were suddenly arrested in their plans and pro-
gresses. The rush of a troop in front was in their ears, with the
cry of many voices. The partisan looked forward, and wondered,
dreading to find himself between two enemies; but the next
moment reassured him, as he heard the voice of the boy, Frampton,
who was evidently in advance of the new-comers.

"Here they are! here they are, Colonel Walton! They have
killed the major! shew 'em no quarter!—cut 'em down—cut 'em
down! There's not many of them."

"Back, boy! keep from the track!—to the rear, to the rear!"
cried the individual in command of the new-comers, while waving
his sword and advancing towards Singleton. The partisan cried
out to his uncle in the next moment—

"Ha! a friend in need, good uncle! I shall remember the proverb." And, without a word farther, he wheeled in with the
advancing troop, which consisted of a little party of volunteers
pledged to go out with Walton.

Proctor was near enough to hear the dialogue and to understand
the danger. It was now his turn to fly, and he delayed not a moment in the endeavour to do so. But the troop of Walton, comparatively fresh—for they had just started forth from their place of
assemblage near the Cross Roads when they met with Lance—was
down upon him in an instant. Proctor bravely threw himself forward upon the first trooper that approached him, and his sword
flashed back defiance upon them, while his voice shouted encouragingly—as if it could have been heard—to his men, who were now

approaching, though not yet in sight. They certainly could not have come up in time to save him, had Walton pressed the assault; but that gentleman disdained the advantages which were in his grasp.

"Forbear, Major Proctor," he said, mildly and respectfully, as he rode up in front of his enemy. "We purpose you no harm at this moment. You are free to return to your troop. When we meet, sir, again in strife, there will be no surprise on either side, and our several positions will then be understood."

"Colonel Walton," replied the Briton, "I bitterly regret to see you thus—espousing a cause so indefensible and hopeless."

"Neither indefensible nor hopeless, sir, as you shall see in time. But there is no need of comment here. I forbear all the advantages of the present moment, as I am unwilling that you should think I have played the hypocrite to deceive you thus to your ruin. You have forborne, sir, heretofore, in your treatment of my house—your intentions have been friendly : permit me, sir, to requite them as I do now. You are at liberty. Farewell, sir. The terms of our meeting, henceforward, must accord with those existing between my country and yours—peace or war ! peace or war . Farewell, sir."

Proctor, chagrined at his disappointment, was nevertheless highly touched with the courtesy of his new enemy. In a few brief words he uttered his acknowledgments, and turned back to meet his troop, with a bitter spirit, sore on many accounts. His present hope of Katharine was evidently at an end ; and, feeling towards her as he did, how painful was the new position in which he stood to her father! The subject distressed him ; and he strove, by a motion as rapid as that of the pursuit, to escape from thoughts too little calculated to yield him satisfaction to win him to their indulgence. The parties were separated ; the one on its way back to the garrison ; the other, somewhat more imposing from its new acquisition of force, speeding boldly for the Cypress Swamp.

CHAPTER XXIX.

"I take the hand of my fierce enemy
In a true pledge—a pledge of earnest faith
I fain would seal in blood—his blood or mine."

WHILE the events which we have just recorded had been going on in one quarter, others not less imposing, though perhaps less important to the partisans, had taken place in the swamp. There, as we remember, Humphries, after the escape of Goggle, had be stowed his men in safety. Deeply mortified by that occurrence, the lieutenant had been more than usually careful of his remaining prisoners, as well as of his appointments at the camp. The fires had been well lighted, the several watches duly set, and all preparations were in even progress for the quiet passage of the night.

To John Davis much of these matters had been given in charge, and, in their proper execution, he approved himself the same trusty soldier that we have elsewhere found him. The prisoners were put entirely and particularly under his direction; and having placed them separately, each securely tied, in the little bark huts which were scattered about the island, through the co-operation and continued presence of the sentries closely set around them, their custody was quite as complete as, under existing circumstances, it could possibly have been made.

Such, among others, was the condition of the luckless Hastings. His hut was isolated from the rest, and stood, on the very edge of the island, upon a slight elevation. Tied, hand and foot, with cords too stout for his strength, he lay upon a pile of rushes in the corner of his cabin, musing, doubtless, like most of his fellows who have experienced a sudden reverse, upon the vexatious instability of fortune. Nor did his musings prompt him at all times to that due resignation which a proper course of reflection, in such a case, would be most usually apt to occasion. He suffered himself to be too much disquieted by his thinking; and, at such moments, seeking to

elevate himself from his prostrate condition, he would lose his balance, and roll away from his place, like a ball under some foreign
compulsion. A few feeble efforts at release, resulting always in the
same way, taught him at last to remain in quiet, though, had he
known the fate of Sergeant Clough, upon whose bed of death he now
lay at length, his reflections, most probably, would have been far
less satisfactory than even now he found them.

They were far from agreeable. The sergeant chewed but the cud
of bitter fancy; the sweet was all denied him in his dungeon of bark.
He could not misunderstand or mistake the dangers of his position.
He was the prisoner of the man he had striven to wrong in the
tenderest part; he beheld the authority which that man exercised
over those around him; he well knew the summary character of the
times, which sanctioned so frequently the short shrift and sudden
cord; and, considering himself reserved for some such fearful mode
of exit, as the meditative vengeance of Humphries might best determine, he bitterly denounced his own evil fortune, which had thus
suffered him to be entrapped. He writhed about among his rushes,
as these thoughts came more vividly to his mind; and despair of
escape at length brought him a certain degree of composure, if not
of resignation. He drew up his knees, turned his face to the dark
wall, and strove to forget his predicament in the kindly arms of
sleep.

Yet there was hope for him at hand—hope of a change of condition; and any change was full of promise to Hastings. The hope
which had been partially held out to him by Davis, before con-
ducting him to the swamp, was now about to be realized. The
watches had all been set, Humphries himself had retired; and, apart
from the sentries, but a single trooper was visible upon the island,
in the centre of which, by a blazing fire, he stood, with one foot of
his horse over his knee, from the quick of which he was striving
hard, with hook and hammer, to extract a pebble.

From his couch of pine brush, under the dark shadow of a tree,
Davis looked forth, momently and anxious, upon the horseman.
At length the latter proved successful. The horse was led away to
the end of the island, and, after a little while, the trooper himself
had disappeared. With the exception of the sentries, all of whom

Davis himself had placed, the partisans had each taken the shelter of his greenwood tree. Some were pillowed here, some there, in little clusters of two or three, their heads upon their saddles, their hands clutching fast the rifle or broadsword, and the bridle hanging above, ready for sudden employment. Sometimes, a solitary trooper stretched himself alone, under a remoter shelter, and enjoyed to himself those solacing slumbers which it is always so pleasant to share.

With the perfect quiet of all things around him, Davis rose from his own place of repose. He cautiously surveyed the course he proposed to take, and stealing carefully from the inclining shadow of one tree to that of another, he approached unobserved the hut of Sergeant Hastings. The sentinel was prompt.

" Ho !—stand—the word !"

" Continental Congress ! It's a big word, Ralph Mason, and hard to come at; the more so when it's a quick sentry like you, that doesn't give a body time to look it up. But that aint much of a fault, any how, in a soldier. Better too quick than too slow, and the good sentry is more to the troop than the good horse, though the one may carry him off when the tories are upon him in double quick time. You can go now, Ralph ; go to my straw, and you can lie down till I come to wake you up. I'm to ax the prisoner here some questions."

Glad of this relief, the sentinel made his acknowledgments to his superior, and did not hesitate to avail himself of the proposed luxury. Taking his place for a moment, to and fro before the door of the hut, the Goose Creeker employed the time between the departure of the sentinel, and his probable attainment of the bed of rushes to which he had assigned him, in the meditation of that plan which his mind had partially conceived, while escorting his prisoners to the swamp, and of which he had given a brief hint to Hastings himself;—a plan which promised him that satisfaction for his previous injuries at the hands of Hastings, which his excited feelings, if not a high sense of honour, had long insisted upon as necessary to his comfort. The present time seemed a fitting one for his purpose; and the opportunity which it offered, as it might not occur again, was quite too good to be lost.

Having properly deliberated, he put aside the bushes which hung partially across the entrance, and at once passed into the hut of the prisoner. Hastings was not asleep, and started hastily at the intrusion. His vorst fears grew active, as he saw the figure of one before him, whom, in the dimness of the place, he could not distinguish. He could only think of Humphries, and his breathing was thick and rapid, as he anticipated, each moment, some fearful doom at the hands of the avenger. His tones were hurried, as he demanded—

" Who's there ?—speak !—what would you ?"

" Don't be scared, Sergeant Hastings ; it's me, John Davis—him they call Prickly Ash, of Goose Greek. Mayhap you may remember sich a person. I 'm that man."

Hastings rather freely avowed his recollection.

" Well, I 'm mighty glad you're not asleep, as I didn't want to put hands on you for any business but one, and that's the one I come to see you about now. You're sure, now, Sergeant Hastings, you're wide awake, and able to talk about business."

The reply was in the gentlest and most conciliatory language. The tones were singularly musical, indeed, for a throat so harsh as that which Davis formerly knew in possession of the same person ; and the sigh-like utterance which told the partisan that he was all attention, contrasted oddly, in the thoughts of Davis, with those notes which he had been taught hitherto to hear from the same quarter.

" Well, if you're wide awake, Sergeant Hastings, I 've some talk for you that maybe you'll be glad enough to hear, for it consarns both you and me a little."

" Any thing, Mister Davis—any thing you have to say, I shall be happy, very happy, to listen to."

" Very good," said the other ; " that's very good, and I 'm mighty glad to see you've got your mind made up as to what's to come ; and so, since you're ready to hear, I 'm cocked and primed to speak, and the sooner I begin the better. Now, Sergeant Hastings, mind what I say, and don't let any of my words go into one ear and out of the other. Thev're all words that cost something, and some thing's to be paid for them in the eend.   I give you this warning, as it aint fair to take a man onawares."

Hastings modestly promised due heedfulness, and the other pro ceeded as follows:—

" You see, then, Sergeant Hastings, you're not in garrison now; you're not at the Royal George, nor in any of them places where I used to see you, with the red-coats, and them lickspittles the tories, all about you, ready to back you agin their own countrymen, whether you're right or wrong.   You're turned now, as I may say, on the flat of your back, like a yellow-belly cooter, and nobody here to set you on your legs agin, but me, and me your inimy."

Hastings sullenly and sadly assented to the truth of this picture, in a groan which he accompanied by a writhing motion of the body that turned his face completely away from the speaker.

" You needn't turn your back, Sergeant Hastings; it's no part of a gentleman to do so: but jist listen a bit to the God's truth, and you'll larn a little civility, if so be it's in your skin to larn any thing that's good.   You see, now, the game goes agin you— the cards is shuffled, and trumps is changed hands.   You're in as bad a fix, now, as if you was at old sledge, and all seven up was scored down agin you.   You're not cock of the walk any longer: you aint where you can draw sword agin a man that's got none, and have a gang of chaps to look on, and not ax for fair play. There's some chance now for a small man, and I reckon you feels the difference."

A sullen response from Hastings, who—though irritated greatly, thought it the wiser policy not to appear so—acknowledged the correctness of what his companion had said.

" But don't think," the other proceeded—" don't think, Sergeant Hastings, that I come to crow over you in your misfortunes.   No ! dang it, I'm not the lad to take advantage of any man in his troubles, even though I despise him as I despise you.   I'm for fair play all the world over, and that's the reason why I come to you now."

" What would you have, Mister Davis?" inquired the sergeant, with something of his old dignity of manner.

"Well, that's a civil question enough, and desarves a civil answer. You ax me what I will have. I'll tell you after a bit; but there's something, you see, that's like a sort of history, and, if you'll listen, I'll take leave to put that afore it."

"Go on, Mister Davis; I shall be glad to hear you."

"Well, I don't know that for certain; but we'll see how glad you are as we git on in the business. What I've got to say won't take long, though I must begin at the beginning, or you mightn't so well understand it. It's now going on nine or ten years since old Dick Humphries—that's the father of Bella—first come into our parts, and made acquaintance with our people. Bella was a little girl at that time; but from that time I took to her, and she sort-a-took to me. The more we know'd, the more we liked one another. I can say for myself, I never liked anybody half so well as I liked her. Well, everybody said it was a match, and Bella seemed willing enough till the war broke out, and you came into our parts, with your red coats, and flashy buttons, and topknots; and then everything was at odds and ends, and there was no living with the gal at all. Her head got turned with your flummery, and a plain lad like myself stood no chance."

"Well, but, Mister Davis, that was no fault of mine, if the girl was foolish."

"Look you,—no ill words about the gal; becase, dang it, I don't stand it. She may be foolish, but you ha'vnt any right yet, that I can see, to call her so; and it's more shame if you do, seeing that it's all on your account that she is so."

"I mean no harm—no offence, Mister Davis."

"Well, well, I aint taking any harm and any offence at that. I only want to 'mind you to keep a civil tongue in your head when you talk of Bella; for, though she shies away from me, and I stand no chance with her, and the game's all clear done atween us, I won't hear anything said to her disparagement; and it will be mighty ridiculous for you if you say it. I'm trying to speak to you civilly, and without getting in a passion—and it's not so easy—for you're my prisoner, you see; and it's not the part of a gentleman to say ugly things to a man that can't help himself; but it's in the way of what I've got to tell you, and you'll be good-natured and excuse it, if I sometimes graze upon a part of you that's sore, and say sich words in your hearing, as makes you feel like a rascal, and if I don't stop to pick what words I shall say it in. But that's neither here nor there; and I may as well go on with what I was saying. Bella took a liking to you, and to your coat, and buttons —monstrous little else, Sergeant Hastings, now, I tell you, for the gal has sense enough to see that you're not the properest looking chap, nor the finest, nor the best-natured, that comes into these parts. But it was the showy buttons and the red clothes—the big feather, and—I don't want to say it, Sergeant Hastings, becase, as I said before, you're my prisoner, and it's not genteel to say ugly things to one's prisoner; but my mother always trained me to have an ambition for truth, and a man's not a gentleman if he doesn't speak it; so that's the reason, you see, that makes me tell you that it was partly because you were so flashy, and so impudent, and had such a big way about you, that took in the poor gal at first, and that takes in so many that ought to know better. It was your impudence, you see, sergeant—that was it; and, as sure as there's snakes, she'll get tired of you, you can't reckon how fast, if she once gets you for a husband."

"But that she'll never do, Mister Davis;—oh, no, leave me alone for that. I'm no fool, I can tell you. It's the young bird only that's to be caught by the chaff."

"Chaff!—well, you can't mean to say that Bella Humphries is chaff; but do you mean that you won't marry her—and the gal so loves you too?" The astonishment of Davis was conspicuous in his emphasis.

"Marry her, indeed! No, I thank ye! I never thought of such a thing!" was the contemptuous reply of the prisoner.

"Now, dang it, Sergeant Hastings, but I do despise you more than a polecat. You're a poor, mean skunk, and a dirty varmint, that's only fit for killing; and I've the heart to do it now, on the spot, I tell you; but I won't, for you're my prisoner."

The indignation of Davis was kept down with difficulty; and Hastings, lacking entirely that delicacy which should have taught him that the considerations of his rival, in what he had said, had been singularly unselfish, only made the matter worse by undertaking to assure him that his determination had been made, the better to open the way for himself in the renewal of his addresses. This assurance neither deceived nor satisfied the lieutenant; and his words, though cool, were very bitter, and solemnly urged.

"You're a shoat, a mean shoat, Sergeant Hastings; and if I had nothing else to hate you for, I should hate you mighty long and heartily for that. But it's no use talking; and the sooner we stop the better. Now, can you guess what I come to you for to-night?"

"I cannot—no—what?"

"To set you free; to cut your ropes; put you on a clear track, and mount you on a nag that'll take you into Dorchester in a short hour and a half, free riding. I told you I would do it. I will keep my word."

"Indeed! Do I hear you, Mister Davis? my dear friend—"

"No friend, I thank you—no friend, but a bitter inimy, that won't do nothing for you without the pay. I will do all this for you, as I have said, but there's something I ax for it in return."

"What! speak! aye! What price? name your reward, sir, and—"

"I will—only be quiet and keep a civil tongue in your head while I tell you. You've put the flat of your sword to my shoulder, Sergeant Hastings, when I had none to lift up agin you; that's to be paid for. You've come between me and the gal I had a liking for, ever since I was a boy; that's to be paid for. You tried to git her to like you, and then you laugh at her liking; and that's to be paid for too. Now, can you reckon up what'll best pay for these matters?"

The sergeant was silent; the other continued—

"I'll tell you. A fair fight, as you promised me—a fair fight with broadswords, in a clean track, and no witnesses but them there bright stars, and the round moon that'll soon be rising up to give us enough light to do our business."

"I'm willing, Mister Davis; but I've no sword, and I'm tied here as you see."

"Never be a bit afeard. I'll come in an hour, and I'll cut your cords. I'll carry you out to the skairts of the swamp, where the clear moon will look down upon us. I'll hitch a stout horse to the hanging bough ; and it shall stand in sight waiting for you, the moment you get clear from me. I'll give you the pick of a pair of swords, which shall lie flat upon the airth before you ; and you shall then give me satisfaction for all them there matters that I tell ye of. You're a bigger man than me ; you're used to the broadsword : I can handle it too, though I does it rough and tumble, and had no schooling in the we'pon ; and you shall have as fair a chance as ever you had in all your born days before. And that's the offer I make you. Only say the word, and I'll go to the spot—carry out the horse—carry out the swords, and send the sentries off from the track where I shall take you."

The proposition took Hastings by surprise. He was no coward ; but, under existing circumstances, he would rather have avoided the encounter in the novel shape which it now put on. Yet, as he reflected, he grew more and more satisfied with the plan. He had manifestly all the advantages of strength, and personal knowledge and practice of the weapon ; and his apprehensions of Humphries were too great not to desire to escape at all hazards from his clutches. Guilt made a coward of him, as he thought of Bella's brother, and as he remembered how completely he had been unmasked before him. In a few moments he had determined upon his answer, and the Goose Creeker rejoiced to find it in the affirmative.

" It's a bargain, then," said Davis—" you swear to it ?"

" I do : I will go with you. Get all things ready, as you have said, and I will fight you whenever you please."

" Well, now, that's what I like ; and I'm glad to find you're so much a man, after all. Keep quiet while I'm gone, and when the horse is clear upon the skairt of the swamp, I'll come to you and set you loose ; all you have to do is to follow—nobody will see us ; but you must be shy how you speak. Only follow, that's all."

Saying these words, Davis departed from the hut. As he emerged from its entrance, he was startled to hear the wild laugh of the maniac Frampton, as he bounded away from the immediate neighbourhood. Frampton had evidently been a listener. But Davis was too much absorbed in the affair before him, to give much heed to an interruption so slight, and hurrying away, without farther hindrance, proceeded to the execution of the devised plan.

The plan had all been heard by the watchful ears of the maniac. Crawling to the hut of Hastings, as once before he had done, when differently occupied, he was about to lift the birch cover from the rear, probably with the same murderous intent which he had before put into execution, when the approach and entrance of Davis had compelled him to be quiet. Concealed in the edges of the hut, and well covered by its shadow, he had lain close and heard every syllable of the preceding dialogue. A strange purpose took possession of his unsettled mind while he listened; and when Davis left the hovel, he ran off howling and laughing with the fancied accomplishment, before his eyes, of that new scheme which, with all that caprice which marks the diseased intellect, had now so suddenly superseded the original object which he had in view. Hastings, meanwhile, with as much philosophy as he was master of, strove to season his thoughts for the events which were at hand.

CHAPTER XXX

" Such the wild purpose of degenerate man,
Vex'd by injustice into greater wrong—
For many sins must ever spring from one "

THE prospect of his revenge before him, Davis hurried away with the view to its accomplishment. The rough countryman had too deeply embarked his feelings in the frail vessel which his more audacious and imposing rival had, to his eyes, so completely carried away, not to desire this object at all the hazards which he was about to incur. He was violating his duty—a matter which, in that day, an inexperienced militia-man was not apt to regard as any very great offence—and was about to peril his life, as well as his honour, for the gratification of his passions. Yet these were too greatly excited to make him regret, or even feel his risks, in the hope of the strife on which he had set his heart. Too burningly eager for this strife, to be at all regardful of the inequality of skill and strength between himself and his enemy, he thought only of the moment when he should confront him with the weapon and the will to slay. Thus excited and eager, he sped across the narrow islet, broken with quagmire and pond and brooklet, with a haste that heeded no obstructions. He had nearly reached the spot, where, as in a pound, the horses of the partisans were all securely tethered. Verily, John Davis was a magnanimous enemy, with all his vindictiveness. He was to free his foe, put weapons into his hands, find him a horse ready saddled and bridled for his flight, and asked nothing in return but the chance of slashing him to pieces in single combat—a gratification for which he was to yield a like privilege to his opponent.

But as he approached the horses, it was necessary to observe a greater degree of caution than he had thus far shown. To remove one of them, without disturbing the sleeping encampment, or the watching sentinels—without causing a *stampede* among the steeds

themselves—was no easy matter; and when he fancied he had
nearly attained his object, he was destined to a sudden interruptio.
When on the edge of the thicket where the horses were kept, and
which skirted a long dark pond, which was fed by numerous sluices
from the swamp, our forester came rather unexpectedly upon no
less a person than Lieutenant Porgy.

What was the fat lieutenant doing in such a situation? What
was the nature of that occupation which he pursued by the precious
starlight, and when most honest men are sleeping? Davis could
not divine the answer to his own questions. It was enough that
the lieutenant was greatly in his way. Had Porgy been sleeping?
No! He was bright enough when he found himself disturbed. But
he had certainly been in a state of very profound reverie when the
unconscious footstep of Davis sounded in his ears. Rifle in grasp,
and crouching low upon the bankside, looking out upon the dark
water which glittered in spots only beneath the starlight, the
philosophic epicure was as watchful as a sentinel on duty, or a
scout on trail. Davis could not say at first whether he lay flat
upon the ground, or whether he was on his knees. To suppose
him to be crawling upon all fours, would be a supposition scarcely
consistent with the dignity of his office and the dimensions of his
person. Yet there was so much that was equivocal in his attitude,
that all these conjectures severally ran through the head of the
woodman. He started up at the approach of Davis, disquieted by
the intrusion, yet evidently desirous of avoiding all alarm. His
challenge—" Who goes there?" though given in very quick, was
yet delivered in very subdued accents. Our woodman gave the
answer; and the tones of Porgy's voice underwent some change,
but were still exceedingly soft and low. They embodied a good-
natured recognition.

" Ah! Davis, my good fellow, you are just in time."

"For what, lieutenant?"

" For great service to me, to yourself, to the whole encampment.
But no noise, my good fellow. Not a breath—not a word above
your breath. He is a fool who suffers his tongue to spoil his supper. As quiet as possible, my boy."

" What's to do, lieutenant?" was the whispered query of Davis, much wondering at the anxiety of the speaker, who seldom showed himself so, and who usually took events, without asking for the salt or sauce to make them palatable.

"What do you see?" he continued, as the eyes of Porgy were straining across the imperfectly lighted pond.

"See!—what do I see? Oh! Blessed Jupiter, god of men as little fishes, what do *I not* see?"

And as he spoke, he motioned to Davis to sink down, crouch close, and creep towards him. Davis, much bewildered, did as he was required, Porgy meanwhile, *sotto voce*, continuing to dilate after his usual fashion of eloquence—a style, by the way, that was very apt to bewilder all his hearers. Davis had never studied in the schools of euphuism; nor in any school, indeed, except that of the swamp. He fancied he knew the philosophy of the swamp as well as any other man; and that Porgy should extract from it a source of knowledge hitherto concealed from him, was a subject of very great amazement. He began, accordingly, to question the sanity of his superior, when he heard him expatiate in the following language:

"We live in a very pleasant world, Master John Davis. Nature feeds us in all our senses, whenever we are willing and wise enough to partake. You breathe, you see, you smell, you taste, and you ought to be happy, Davis; why are you not happy?"

"Well, I don't know, lieutenant; I only know I ain't happy, and I can't be happy in this world, and I don't expect to be."

"Oh! man of little faith. It is because you won't use your senses, John Davis—your eyes. You ask me what I see! Blind mote, that thou art! Dost thou see nothing?"

"I see you, lieutenant, and the dark pond and water, and the big cypresses, and the thick vines and bushes, and just above, a little opening in the trees that shows where the stars are peeping down. I don't see nothing else."

"And what were the stars made for, John Davis, but to show you the way to other things? Look for yourself now, and let me show you the pleasantest prospect, for a dark night, that your eyes ever hungered over. Stoop, I say, and follow my finger. There! See to the lagune just beyond that old cypress, see the dead tree half rolled into the water. Look now, at the end of the fallen tree, —there just where the starlight falls upon it, making a long streak in the black water. Do you see, man of little faith, and almost as little eyesight! Do you not understand now, why it is that I rejoice; why my bowels yearn, and my soul exults? Look, and feast your eyes, Jack Davis, whom they call of Goose Creek, while you anticipate better feeding still hereafter. But don't you utter a word—not a breath, lest you disturb the comely creatures, the dainty delights—our quail and manna of the swamp—sent for our blessing and enjoyment by the bountiful Heaven, which sees that we are intensely deserving, and mortal hungry at the same time. Hush! hush! not a word!"

Here he stopt himself in the utterance of his own raptures, which were growing rather more loud than prudence called for. The eye of Davis, meanwhile, had followed the guiding finger of the epicure, and the woodman nearly laughed aloud. But he dared not. Porgy was evidently too seriously bent to permit of such irreverence. The objects that so transported the other, were such as had been familiar to the eyes of both from their earliest consciousness of light. The little lagune, or bayou, on the edge of which they crouched, showed them, drowsing on the old and half-decayed tree to which Porgy had directed his own and the gaze of Davis, three enormous terrapins of that doubtful brood which the vulgar in the southern country describe as the alligator terrapin—an uncouth monster, truly, and with such well developed caudal extremities as seem to justify them in classing the animal in this connexion. The terrapins lay basking, black and shining in the starlight, their heads thrust out, and hanging over the lagune, into which the slightest alarm of an unusual nature would prompt them to plunge incontinently. Their glossy backs yet seemed to trickle with the water from which they had arisen. Their heads were up and watchful; as if preparing for that facile descent into the native home, a region black as Avernus. Porgy continued—now in a whisper—

"That's a sight, John Davis, to lift a man from a sick-bed. That's a sight to make him whole and happy again. Look how quietly they lie; that farthest one—I would it were nigher—is a superb fellow, fat as butter, and sticking full of eggs. There's

14

soup enough in the three for a regiment; and now, my good fellow, if you will only be quiet, I will give you such a lesson of
dexterity and stratagem as shall make you remember this night as
long as you live. There never was a terrapin trapper that could
compare with me in my youth. We shall see if my right hand
hath lost its cunning. You shall see me come upon them like an
Indian. I will only throw off this outer and most unnecessary
covering, and put on the character of a social grunter. Ah, the
hog is a noble animal—what would we do without him? It's
almost a sin to mock him—but in making mock turtle, John Davis,
the offence is excusable : a good dinner, I say, will sanctify a dozen
sins, and here goes for one."

" But, lieutenant, them's alligator terrapins."

" Well !"

" Well, nobody eats alligator terrapins."

" Nobody's an ass, then, for his abstinence, let me tell you; an
alligator terrapin is the very prince of terrapins."

" Well, he's the biggest."

" And the best ! His meat is of the rarest delicacy, and with
my dressing, and the cooking of my fellow, Tom, the dish is such
as would tickle monstrously the palate of any prince in Europe—
that is, of any prince born to a gentlemanly taste, which is not to
be said of many of the tribe, I grant you. But, there's no time to
be lost. Hold my rifle, and witness my exertions."

Here he forced the rifle into the hands of the Goose-Creek forester,
and prepared for the proposed achievement; which we may venture
to say, in this place, requires a degree of dexterity and pains
taking which few can show, and which no one would attempt, not
stimulated by tastes so exquisite and absorbing as those of our
epicure.

Porgy's agility greatly belied his appearance. You have seen
a heavy man move lightly, no doubt. It requires a certain conformation to show this anomaly. Porgy possessed this conformation.
His coat was off in a jiffy. His vest followed it, and he was soon
stealing away, along the edge of the hammock, and in the direction
of his victims. Davis had become interested, almost to the utter
forgetfulness of his own victim, Sergeant Hastings. He watched

our epicure, as, almost without a sound, he pressed forward upon hands and knees, his huge form, in this attitude, appearing in the dusky light very like the animal whose outer habits he was striving to assimilate.

The terrapins were a little uneasy, and Porgy found it neces sary to pause occasionally and survey them in silence. When they appeared quiet, he renewed his progress; as he drew nearer, he boldly grunted aloud, after the porcine habit, and with such excellence of imitation that, but for his knowledge of the truth, Davis himself might have been deceived. Porgy knew the merit of his imitation, but he had some scruples at its exercise: but for the want of fresh meat in camp, and the relish with which he enjoyed his stew of terrapins, he would have been loath to make an exhibition of his peculiar powers. Even at this moment he had his reflections on his own performance, which were meant to be apologetic, though unheard.

"The Hog," he muttered as he went, "has one feature of the good aristocrat. He goes where he pleases, and grumbles as he goes. Still, I am not satisfied that it is proper for the gentleman to put on the hog, unless on occasion such as this. The pleasures of a dinner are not to be lost for a grunt. He must crawl upon his belly who would feel his way to that of a terrapin."

Thus fortifying himself with philosophy, he pressed forward to the great delight of Davis, who had become quite interested in the performance, and grunt after grunt testified to the marvellous authority which his appetite exercised over his industry. The terrapins showed themselves intelligent. Alas! the best of beasts may be taken in by man. Porgy's grunts were a sad fraud upon the unsuspecting victims. At the first sound, the largest of the three terrapins, having the greatest stake (Qu? steak) of all, betrayed a little uneasiness, and fairly wheeled himself round upon his post, prepared to plunge headlong with the approach of danger. His uneasiness was naturally due to the importance of the wealth which had been intrusted to his keeping. His bullet head, his snaky neck, were thrust out as far as possible from beneath the covers of his dwelling. Like an old soldier, he pricked his ears, and stood on the alert; but he was soon satisfied. His eye took in the form of his drowsy companions, and he saw no sign of danger in the unbroken surface of the stagnant pond. A second grunt from the supposed porker reassured him. He had lived in intimate communion with hogs all his days. The sow had made her wallow beside his waters, and reared her brood for a hundred years along their margins. He knew that there was no sort of danger from such a presence, and he composed himself at his devotions, and prepared once more to reknit his half-unravelled slumbers.

"Beautiful creature, sleep on!" murmured Porgy to himself, in tones and words as tender as made the burden of his serenade, in the days of his youth, to the dark-eyed damsels upon the waters of the Ashley and Savannah. He made his way forward, noiselessly —the occasional grunt excepted—until he found himself fairly astride the very tree which his unconscious victims were reposing on.

You have heard, no doubt, of that curious sort of locomotion which, in the South and West, is happily styled " cooning the log?" It is the necessity, where you have to cross the torrent on the unsteady footing of a spear,—or rather, where you must needs cross on a very narrow and very slippery tree, which affords no safe footing. In plain terms, our fat friend squatted fairly upon the log, hands and knees, and slided along in a style which John Davis thought infinitely superior to anything he had seen. Telling the story long afterwards, John always did the fullest justice to the wonderful merits of the lieutenant, in some such phrase as this:—

" Lord! 'twas as slick going as down hill, with the wheels greased up to the hub!"

" Greased up to the hub!"

Porgy, you may be sure, was never suffered to hear of the villanous comparison.

The anxiety of Davis, at this point of the adventure, made him fidgety and restless. It required strong resolution to keep quiet. But, though himself anxious enough, the stake was too great to suffer our epicure to peril its loss by any undue precipitation. He moved along at a snail's pace, and whenever the huge tree would vibrate beneath his prodigious weight, the cautious trapper would pause in his journey, and send forth as good a grunt as ever echoed in Westphalian forests. The poor terrapins were completely taken in by the imitation, and lay there enjoying those insidious slumbers, which were now to be their ruin.

Nigher and nigher came the enemy. A few feet only separated the parties, and, with an extended hand, Porgy could have easily turned over the one which was nighest. But our epicure was not to be content with less than the best. His eyes had singled out the most remote, because the largest of that sweet company. He had taken in at a glance its entire dimensions, and already, in his mind, estimated, not only the quantity of rich reeking soup which could be made out of it, but the very number of eggs which it contained. Nothing short, therefore, of this particular prize would have satisfied him; and, thus extravagant in his desires, he scarcely deigned a glance to the others. At length he sat squat almost alongside of the two—the third, as they lay close together, being almost in his grasp, he had actually put out his hands for its seizure, when the long neck of his victim was again thrust forth, and, with arms still extended, Porgy remained as quiet as a mouse. But the moment the terrapin sheltered his head within the shell, the hands of the captor closed upon him with a clutch from which there was no escaping. One after another the victims were turned upon their backs; and, with a triumphant chuckle, the captor carried off his prey to the solid tussock.

"I cannot talk to you for an hour, John Davis, my boy—not for an hour—here's food for thought in all that time. Food for thought did I say! Ay, for how much thought! I am thoughtful. The body craves food, indeed, only that the mind may think, and half our earthly cares are for this material. It is falsehood and folly to speak of eating as a mere animal necessity, the love of which is vulgarly designated an animal appetite. It is not so with me. The taste of the game is nothing to the pleasure of taking it —nothing to the pleasure of preparing it in a manner worthy of the material, and of those who are to enjoy it. I am not selfish, I share with all; and, by the way, John Davis, I feel very much like whipping the fellow who shows no capacity to appreciate. I am a sort of Barmecide in that respect, though I suspect, John, you know nothing of the Barmecides."

" No ; I never heard tell of them."

" So I suppose ! Well, I won't vex you by talking of fine people not of your acquaintance.   Now, John, tell the truth,—did I not seem to you very peculiar, very remarkable, and strange—nay, something ridiculous, John, when you saw me crawling after the terrapins ?"

" Well, to say truth, lieutenant, you did seem rather ridickilous."

" Ridiculous ! do you say ?   Well, perhaps !   I forgive you, Jack Davis ; though there are times when to hint such a word to me, would insure you a broken head.   A man of my presence ridiculous !"

" Oh ! I don't mean no offence, lieutenant."

" To be sure not !   Do I not know that !   But, John, think of the soup that we shall get out of these terrapins.   Think of our half-starved encampment ; and do you not see that the art which traps for us such admirable food, rises into absolute sublimity ? Some hundreds of years from now, when our great-grandchildren think of the sort of life we led when we were fighting to secure them an inheritance, they will record this achievement of mine as worthy of Roman fame.   But you don't know anything of the Romans, John."

" Not a bit, lieutenant.   Is it a kind of terrapins ?"

" Yes, indeed ! a kind of terrapins that crawled over the whole earth, and claimed it for their own."

" You don't say so !"

" True, every syllable ; but the breed's died out, John, and such as are left hav'n't marrow enough in 'em for a stew for a single squad.   But, John, it was not the soup only that I thought of when I trapped these beauties.   Did you ever feel the pleasure, John, of chasing a fox ?"

" Yes, to be sure : a thousand times.   It's prime sport, I tell you."

" But you never ate the fox, John ?"

" No, indeed ! the stinking creature !"

" Well, even if I shouldn't taste these terrapins, the pleasure of their capture is a feast.   I have exercised my skill, my ingenuity— I feel that my right hand has not forgot its cunning.   That, John, is the sort of practice that proves the true nature of the man.   He is never so well satisfied as when he is contriving, inventing, scheming, planning, and showing how cunning he can be. Whether it's red-fox or red-coat, John, it's a sort of happiness to chase, and trap, and catch, run down and cut up."

"I reckon that's true, lieutenant. I feel jist so when I'm on a scout, or a hunt, or anything like it;" and John Davis was reminded of his practice with respect to Sergeant Hastings. He began to be impatient of the long speeches of Porgy; but there was no getting him out of the way, except at his own pleasure.

"Talking of cutting up, John, brings up the terrapins to-morrow. You shall see what a surprise I shall give the camp. You shall see what a thing invention is! How beautiful is art! Now I shall dress each of these beauties in a different style. Steaks and soup you shall have, and enough to satisfy, in the old fashion. But I have some inventions—I thought of them as I neared the log; and when the cunning senses of that patriarch there almost found me out, a timely grunt silenced his doubt. With that grunt came the idea of a new dish. It was a revelation. That terrapin, I said, shall be compounded with the flesh of the porker that Joe Witsell brought into camp at noon. There shall be a hash that shall make your mouth to water. There shall be such a union of the forces of hog and terrapin as shall make them irresistible; and you will then learn the great truth—great to us at short commons in the swamp—that alligator terrapin is a dish worthy to be set before a king."

John Davis looked dubiously, but said—

" Yes, I reckon, lieutenant."

" You reckon! well, but whither do you go?" he asked, as he saw the other lay down his rifle and prepare to go.

" I've got to scout for two hours, out here on the skairts of the swamp."

" Very good! But before you go—have you a handkerchief about you?"

" A mighty old one, lieutenant."

" The very one for my purposes. Mine is a new one, John, and meant for great occasions, when I am entertaining some of the big bugs in epaulettes. Let me have it,—and—but—old fellow, won't you help me home with my captives?"

"In course, lieutenant, I'll take 'em all for you." And John soon had the monsters gathered up, and on his shoulders.

"You are a good fellow, John, and must have your share of the hash as well as stew. Be sure, John, that you don't absent your-self to-morrow. I wouldn't have you miss the mess for the world. There's too much at stake; so remember. A day lost to a good stomach is a serious grievance. You not only cannot recall it, but it affects your health the day after. Don't incur any such peril."

And thus talking, Porgy led the way, and the two parties dis-appeared together, taking the backward route to the camp. Davis was beginning to be impatient of lost time. But there was no way to rid the precinct of the lieutenant's presence, but by helping him on his progress, and the epicure was not satisfied to let him off until the spoil had been fairly deposited in safety in the shadow of Porgy's tent. Leaving the epicure to stir up Tom, the cook—for he was not the man to sleep, till all things were discussed and arranged with this able agent of his pleasures—John Davis stole away unseen, and proceeded, without further interruption, in search of his own peculiar prey. He succeeded in detaching his own steed from the group, and in carrying away a couple of heavy broadswords. It now needed only that he should conduct his rival in safety to the spot chosen for the proposed duel.

CHAPTER XXXI.

" What savage man is this ?   What fearful strife
Makes night to shudder in her gloomy halls ?"

THE spot chosen by John Davis for the scene of mortal combat, was well calculated, no less for this than for the conflict of mortal passions. The area was sufficiently large for unembarrassed action with the broadsword, while the trees completely encircled it, and shrouded it from sight of all without. The ground itself was a mere sandbank; such as, in such a neighbourhood, will sometimes rise suddenly out from a swamp, and drink up the still trickling waters of a streamlet running beside it. The starlight gave a sufficiently strong light for the combat, and the moon was now about to rise. Davis surveyed the ground in silence, and with something of grave reflection crowding upon his mind as he did so. His desire for revenge had made him almost entirely unmindful of the possible results to himself of the contemplated struggle; and now that he looked upon the sands, so soon, as he thought, to soak up the blood of himself or his enemy, or both, his reflections were neither so calm nor so pleasant as he could have wished them. Not that he feared death; but the idea had not often forced itself upon him before as a near prospect, and it does not lessen one's bravery, that he should meditate the danger even when he advances to encounter it.

John Davis did begin to think of the prospect before him; but the die was cast, and no useful result could possibly arise from his reflections now, as it was out of the question to suppose that his determination could be changed. That was forbidden by the general sense of society in the quarter in which he lived; and striving heartily to dismiss all consideration from his mind, save that which told him of the injuries he was to avenge, he fastened to a neighbouring tree the horse which was destined for the survi-

14*

vor, and plunging back into the swamp, took his way towards the place where the prisoners were kept.

But the time which Davis had lost in the terrapin hunt with his superior, and in the subsequent removal of the horse and the weapons, had not been left unemployed by others. There was a wild spirit at work and sleepless in the camp of the Partisans, which was even more terrible and threatening than that of our jealous duellist. It has not been forgotten that, in the interview between Davis and Sergeant Hastings, they had been startled at its close by the eldritch laughter of the maniac, Frampton. There was a strange method in the madness of this now savage person. He had eagerly drunk in the language of the parties, and with a calculation and cunning which we are apt mistakenly to suppose inconsistent with insanity, he had treasured the matter in his memory, and prepared to mar the plans and preparations after a fashion of his own. He suffered Davis to depart, and for a time he watched his movements. Satisfied of his absence, if not of his immediate whereabouts, the maniac emerged again from the swamp, and made his way to the hut in which the sergeant was imprisoned. Hastings, anxiously awaiting his rival's coming, had not slept. He looked up in the imperfect starlight, as the huge form of Frampton darkened the entrance. It appeared to him that the form of Davis had suddenly shot into great bulk and height, but he soon dismissed the notion that such was the case, with a feeling of shame, ascribing it to cowardice that he should think so.

" Is that you, John Davis ?"

" Come !" said the maniac,—" come !"

" How can I come, John Davis," was the reply, " unless you cut the cord ? I'm tied, you know, hand and foot, and can't budge a peg."

Without a word, the maniac entered and did as he was required. He divided the ropes with a hunting knife, which he carried at his girdle. He might just as easily have cut the jugulars of the victim ; but he did not, and quietly restored the weapon to his belt.

" Come !" said he.

Hastings rose from his rushes, feeling very stiff and sore. He stretched himself with a painful effort, and wondered how he should ever be able to handle the broadsword.

"A d—d hard bed I've had of it, John Davis, and all my joints feel as if they wanted greasing. A sup of Jamaica, now, wouldn't be a bad thing. I want something to warm me before I fight."

"Come!" was the sullen monosyllable of the maniac in answer.

"Come! Is that all that you can say, I wonder?" growled Hastings in reply; something wondering at the sullenness and unsociability of one whom he was about to indulge with a fight. But he did not oppose the wishes of his visitor, and, of a sudden, appeared to think it prudent to forbear further speech to so moody a companion. Stretching himself accordingly, with infinite yawnings, the sergeant slowly complied with the requisition of his visitor, and followed him forth from the hut.

Now, but that madness is whimsical in its purposes, the probability is that Frampton would have used the knife upon Hastings, as he had already done upon Clough, in a most summary manner. But the insane man usually exhibits the possession of no little vanity. A diseased self-esteem is apt to be an active condition in the mind of most lunatics, and has contributed not a little to their mental overthrow. The madman's vanity is delighted when he can show you that he schemes and contrives. He loves to startle you. He anxiously seeks to extort from you acknowledgments of this character, and would seem to be pleased with complicating his own purposes, if only to compel your admiration. The lingering reason still strives to maintain some of the shows of its authority —of its presence, at all events—in the brain of the unhappy man, in which it harbours, like the fiery volume in the core of the volcano only for explosion. Feeble, wilful, and deprived of all its best auxiliars of steadfastness and judgment, it still seeks, if not to establish, to assert its supremacy. How it plans, with what effort; how contrives; how chuckles over its contrivances; and with what grotesque ingenuity it will combine and create! This cunning of the madman is, perhaps, the true key—if there be any—to his disorder. Properly studied, and you may find in it the clue to his secret, and in some degree the suggestions for his guidance.

Now, Frampton had shown himself thus cunning and wilful.

after a whimsical fashion, when we first found him squat, watching behind the hovel where Hastings was imprisoned. He had made his way to that spot with the full purpose of destroying the prisoner as he had destroyed Clough, in the same situation. The approach of Davis had compelled him for the moment to forbear and to lurk in waiting. As he listened, and heard the proposed plan of the duel, as suggested by our Goose-Creeker, the mercurial fancies of the madman adopted the affair as his own. He had watched, accordingly, till Davis had gone to effect his preparations, and had then chosen his time, as we have seen, to complete for him what he had so well begun. We see how far he has succeeded. Still unknown by the prisoner—for he avoided all unnecessary speech, and the obscurity of the place did not allow of his detection—the maniac led the way at once through the creek, taking a route different from that which would have been pursued by Davis.

"Come!" he cried impatiently to Hastings, as the latter floundered slowly and with difficulty through the mire and water. "Come!"

The sergeant did his best to keep up with his conductor, but he found it no easy matter. Familiar with the swamps—a wild dweller in their depths—Frampton strode away almost as easily as if upon the solid land. He picked no path—he availed himself of no friendly log, offering sure footing and an unimpeded path through the slough; but dashing in, through bad and good alike, he led the luckless sergeant over a territory the worst he had ever in his life travelled. Occasionally, the maniac would pause, as the other lingered behind, to utter the expressive monosyllable—"Come!" a thrilling, half-suppressed sound, which, from his lips, had a singularly imposing accent in the ears of his destined victim.

The fatigue of this progress served in some degree to excite the apprehensions of the captive sergeant; particularly as the dimensions of his guide seemed so much larger than those which belonged to Davis. How had the latter grown? He shook off this thought as well as he could, ascribing it to his own imbecility, and trying to account for the apparent size of his enemy, by ascribing it to the exaggerative medium of the imperfect light through which he beheld him. Still his imagination was painfully impressed, and he half wished himself fairly safe from the encounter. But when he thought of the brother of Bella Humphries, and his superior rights. and superior power for vengeance, he plucked up courage, and congratulated himself on the choice which fortune offered him between the two enemies. He toiled forward accordingly, with most praiseworthy perseverance, at the bidding of the maniac, who still kept ahead, until they reached a hammock—a solemn-looking place enough—closely embowered with the highest pines, and almost isolated by the long and sinuous lagune, through which Frampton had already scrambled. The sergeant shuddered to behold the black-looking water, the depth of which seemed immeasurable. But Frampton stood upon the hammock, tall, seemingly, as one of its pines, and waited for the victim, and welcomed him with a wave of the hand, and still that stern monosyllable—" Come !"

The prospect disquieted the nerves of our sergeant, already considerably disordered.

"Ugh!" he cried, with a shudder, as he looked at the lagune, and thought of its depth and blackness. "Am I to go through this? It will take me to the neck."

The maniac waved him forward impatiently.

"Surely," thought Hastings, " he will give me time to rest for awhile. He will not be for the fight right away. I have scarcely any breath."

" Come!" cried his enemy to him across the lagune. It was with a feeling akin to desperation that the sergeant plunged into it, and soon found himself in a bed of mixed mire and water, which closed round him instantly, almost to his middle. There was no help but to struggle forward through the ooze into which, while stationary, he continued to sink. With unsteady footing he scrambled through the slough, and drenched and dripping, chilled and breathless, he at length stood upon the bank, confronted by the person who had led him thus far through perilous ways. At the moment, a wild and terrible laugh,—a shrill demoniac screech gave him welcome; and he recoiled from the sound and from the strange person who now met his eyes, with unmitigated horror.

" Who—who are you ?" demanded Hastings in feeble inquiry " Where's John Davis ?"

"John Davis?   Ha! ha! ha!   John Davis!   Yes!   John Davis.
Come! come!"

Such was the response of the madman.

"Oh! you are to lead me to him?" said the other, but imperfectly reassured.

"Come!" was all the reply.

"But he told me he would come for me himself."

"Come!" in a voice of thunder; and like a fierce spirit of wrath,
the maniac waved his arms aloft, in the direction of the deeper
and darker woods—a forest wall, dense and dark, which spread
away impenetrably before them. The nerves of Hastings were not
in a condition to enable him to resist the command. The action of
the stranger awed him. The terrible tones of his voice seemed to
paralyse all the faculties of the victim. He went forward passively,
as a bullock to the slaughter. The maniac led the way without
looking behind him. He seemed to think that the other must
follow. More than once the sergeant found himself measuring the
size and estimating the powers of his conductor. Had he been
weaponed, it might have been easy to spring upon his guide, and
strike him down without resistance. But Hastings could not
bring his will to co-operation with his thoughts. Besides, this was
not his man. "Were it John Davis or Bill Humphries now!"
was his muttered conclusion as he went forward.

The two penetrated the thick forest, and passed through a dense
copse of some fifty paces. Suddenly, the scene opened before them,
upon a space, and into a degree of light, that, emerging as they did
from the darkness, seemed really to blind and dazzle the prisoner's
eyes. The hammock was here quite bald, showing somewhat like
what the western men call the "Door Prairie,"—that is, they come
upon it as through a door in the woods. Such it was upon a
small scale.

Hastings looked upwards. The deep vaults of heaven were bare,
and spread clear before him, without a cloud, and flowered with
its profuse myriads of stars, looking down upon the two with a
loving softness, as if there were no crimes to be wept over in the
wide world of humanity. The moon, too, had sent up in the east
a faint glory, the harbinger of her own coming, which spread itself

afar like a gauzy veil, clearly distinguishable from the starlight which it now began to supersede.

The wild man paused, looked briefly upon the rich assemblage above him, turned back to beckon his companion, and once more, with a waving hand, led the way over the prairie. Hastings followed like a tame dog. In a few moments they had gained a tree—a huge cypress which stood on the opposite side of. the hammock—and there the maniac paused. Acquiring confidence as he came up, Hastings approached his conductor, and was about to speak to him, when, with a finger upon his lips, he silenced the forthcoming speech by a look, while he pointed to his feet. The sergeant looked down upon the spot, and started back with something like astonishment, if not terror, in his countenance.

They stood before a newly made grave—the clay freshly piled above it, and the whole appearance of the spot indicated a recent burial. The maniac did not heed the expression of the sergeant's face; but after a moment, seemingly of deliberation, he prostrated himself before the grave.

Much wondering at what he saw, Hastings awaited in silence the further progress of the scene. Nor did he wait long. The maniac prayed—and such a prayer—such an appeal to a ·spirit supposed to be then wandering by, and hearing him, was never before uttered. Incoherent sometimes, and utterly wild, it was nevertheless full of those touches of sublimed human feeling which characterise the holiest aspirations of love, and which, while they warm and kindle, purify at the same time, and nobly elevate. His prayer was to his departed wife. He prayed her forgiveness for a thousand unkindnesses,—a thousand instances of neglect—of querulous rebuke—of positive injustice, with all which he bitterly reproached himself. Then followed a tender and really exquisite description of the humble and secret pleasures which they had known together—the joys of their childhood and youth, and the enumeration of many little incidents of domestic occurrence, of which he now reminded the hovering spirit. Tears poured from him freely as he repeated them, and, for a few moments, the wild man was absolutely softened into calm; but the change was terrific which described her cruel murder; how, stricken down by the brutal soldiery, she lay trampled upon the floor, dying at last in torture, with her infant, yet unborn, adding its prayers to that of its mother for the vengeance to which he had devoted himself.

This brought him to the point when the trial must come on with his victim. He started to his feet, and rushed madly towards Hastings. The sergeant, to whom the latter part of the prayer had taught his danger, prepared to fly in terror. But the swift foot of the maniac was after him, and his strong arm hurled him backward upon the grave, over which the victim stumbled headlong, sprawling hopelessly upon his face. His heart entirely failed for the moment. He cried out aloud in his desperation, as he beheld the maniac bounding towards him. He cried aloud, and the echoes only replied ; and a white owl that hooted from the cypress over the grave, moaned mockingly in answer to his cry. The fierce executioner seized him with a grasp which defied and disdained all resistance. He dragged him to the grave—stretched him out upon it, placed his knee upon his breast, and with that dreadful screech which fitly accompanied his movements, he drew the always bared knife from the belt which contained it.

"Mercy ! mercy !" implored the sergeant, while his shout of terror—a voice beyond his own—rang wildly through the swamp and forest, craving mercy, and craving it in vain.

"You showed her none !—none ! You struck her down—your foot was upon her, and she died under it. Come—come !"

The maniac was impatient for his prey, and he yelled scornfully at the impotent struggles of his victim. At that moment a loud voice was heard calling to them from the swamp. The wild man, with all the caprice of insanity, sprang to his feet as he heard it ; and, seizing that moment of release, the sergeant also started up, and rushed away to the wood in the direction of the voice.

The maniac looked at the fugitive scornfully, and for a brief space did not offer to pursue ; but the delay was only momentary. In another instant, Hastings heard the bounding tramp of his heavy feet—he heard the ominous screech of his enemy, speaking death to his imagination ; and a fresh speed came to him from his renewed terrors. He shouted ever, as he flew, to the approaching person, and had the satisfaction to find that his cry was responded to by the voice nearer at hand. He rushed into the little wood which separated him from the mire, through which he had groped his way before with so much difficulty. The wretch prayed as he ran—probably for the first time in his life—and the cold sweat trickled over his face as he uttered his first fervent appeal to his God.

The prayer was unheard—certainly unheeded. The maniac was upon him, and the first bound which the fugitive made into the mire of the swamp, was precipitated by the hand of the avenger. Rushing into the mud after him, the maniac grappled with him there. Though hopeless of his own strength in the contest with one so far his superior, and only desirous of saving himself unhurt until Davis—for it was ·he who now approached them—should come up to his relief, Hastings presented a stout front, and resolutely engaged in the conflict. He shouted all the while the struggle was going on, and his shouts were chorused by the dreadful yells of his murderer.

"Come to me quickly, John Davis—quickly—quickly—for ·od's sake, come, or I am murdered!"

"Come! come!" cried the murderer, in mockery; and the sound of his victim's voice died away in a hoarse gurgle, as the strong arm of the maniac thrust down the head of the unhappy wretch deep into the mire, where he held it as long as the body continued to show signs of life. Davis at last came up.

"Where is the prisoner, Frampton?—where is Hastings?"

"Ho! ho! ho! See you not—see you not?—he is here—look!" And he pointed him to the legs of the victim, which seemed to move still above the mire.

"Great God! man, pull him out—pull him out, for Heaven's sake, Frampton!" And, as he spoke, the Goose-Creeker, horrified by what he saw, bounded into the mire himself for the extrication of the dying man. But, at his approach, the wild savage thrust the victim still more deeply into the ooze, until it was evident, from the quiet of the body, long before Davis could extricate him, that all life had departed.

"Why have you done this, Frampton?" cried the aroused and disappointed partisan to the murderer; but the maniac only replied by another of his terrible screeches, as, bounding out of the mire, he took his way back to the grave where his wife lay buried. The feelings of Davis were melancholy and self-reproachful enough, as he returned slowly to the encampment. He felt, in some degree, as if he had been the murderer of the wretched captive. He was guilty, in one sense, and might be severely punished for breach of trust and neglect of duty ; but the secret of his error was pretty much his own, and he had not the courage to confess it. The maniac was not the person to reveal it. His insanity made him heedless of the offences which he had no motive himself to punish. Enough for him, that he had done something more towards the satisfaction of the one passion of his life —the avenging of his wife's murder

CHAPTER XXXII.

" Oh, thought may tread that lonely wild,
      And carving on each tree,
   May dream that some, who once have smil'd,
      Will still be there to see :
   The bark o'er former names hath grown,
   Yet there is one remains, alone,
      Whose freshness cannot flee—
   A spirit memory comes by night,
      To make its fading traces bright."

EVEN as the pilgrim, bound upon some long travel, pauses by the wayside to plant a flower, or utter a devout prayer upon the spot once sacred to some sweet affection, which he would not willingly forget; so, gentle reader, ere we depart for scenes of trial and vicissitudes whose issues we may not foresee, let us pause for a moment, and wander aside together into walks of solitude, and regions which are hallowed by powers greater than those of earth. The grave is not simply a monitor; it is a power. Instinctively the heart sinks under its silent spells. We naturally feel a diminution of hardihood and courage, of strength and audacity, when we stand above the little hillock which hides from us the form of him who once trod the earth with a powerful footstep and a swelling heart. And if your mood be contemplative, as it should be, after the scenes of wild strife and savage excitements through which it has been our fortune to conduct you, it will be a pleasing relief, perhaps, to turn aside for a few brief moments from the camp of our partisans, and look, ere we shall have left the sacred precincts, upon the ancient burial-place of Dorchester. As yet, the spot is one in which Death is a fresh empire. Here he dwells in full commerce with the living. The old cemetery, and the village church and spire, are still in the daily use of a populous neighbourhood. It is destined, however, to an early change; and the picture of it that we show you now, will soon be obliterated, leaving few vestiges of what we may at this moment behold. The time will come, and very shortly, when this venerable shrine will be in ruins, when yon old tower will be dismantled and over-thrown, and when these silent graves and solid tombs will all disappear, levelled with the sands, or swallowed up in the vast weeds and dense growth of a new and unconscious forest. Fifty years hence, behold the prospect. We leave the great thoroughfare, and the woods girdle us thickly. The very streets of the village, the scene of so many events, so mirthful and so excited once, are overgrown with triumphant pines and cedars. They crowd fitly here, among the shrines of Death, as trophies of that sleepless con-queror. They shroud from light, and thus shrouding, seem to hallow and to sanctify the spot. You shall pursue your quest, and seek out the few memorials which remain, without dread of the thoughtless jeer of the vulgar, or the heartless laugh of un-sympathising irreverence. Living man disturbs not often this sacred neighbourhood. The spot has no attractions for the hurry-ing crowd. Here nature has thrown up no heights of grandeur. Here she descends in no glorious torrents. The place is a simple plain, overrun with a tangled forest growth, showing for ruin only, or a savage untutored nature. The whole region, to the ordinary mood, is uninviting and desolate enough. Desolating it is, but to us who know something of its history, it is not wholly uninviting. We shall recall many sweet sad histories in this silent ramble. We shall gather something for thought from these mansions of decay ; and Death, bearing the torch for life, shall show us his most secret places and teach us his most solemn truths.

One reflection commonly occurs to us in the survey of the fabrics of ancient times, and while we feel the contrast with our own performances, which is forced upon us by the survey. How much more *solid* than ours, seem to have been the tastes of our ancestors! How earnest did they appear in all their labours! They seem to have built rather for their children than themselves. Now, alas! who is it that plants or builds for other generations than his own ? How sad this reflection, how full of omen, when we regard this change as significant of a change in character—as expressive of a decay of moral purpose, and, accordingly, of **moral** power. In other words, they seem to have contemplated uses Our object is appearances. How nobler, how far less selfish, were their tastes and objects! They honoured death, while rearing such vaults as these. How thick and huge, cumbrous perhaps, but time-defying. Is it a nobler sentiment, a more Christian humility that prompts us, now-a-days, in our forest country, simply to put our dead away from our sight, and so leave the unprotected hillock which covers the sacred remains, that the rains of a single year shall obliterate all earthly traces of the being that we professed to love? We err in deeming it an idle vanity to bestow care and pains and art and beauty on a human monument, set up in the domains of death. Love and veneration delight in such tributes, and are justified by all the affections, and all the charities, and all the humanities of life. Indeed, there is a powerful moral to be adduced from the survey of the noble monument. How impressive is the lesson that teaches us that all the worth, and valour, and nobleness of the being whom we thus honour, were yet unavailing to afford security against the inexorable Fate. The thick and massive tomb seems also well conceived to illustrate those impassable barriers which shut out the living man entirely from him who has already shaken off the coil of mortality. We stand before the tomb, gazing vainly into the blank region of another world which we are soon to enter. And when the vault is rent asunder, as in the one now before us, and we see nothing, may we not infer the ascent upward of the triumphant spirit, throwing aside all the idle restraints, even of the affection that would keep it for ever to itself, and rising, on the transparent wings of an eternal morning, to the fair and wooing mansions of eternal bliss?

And there is the old church, like a thoughtful matron, sitting in quiet contemplation among her children. Their graves are all around her; but she, deserted by those she taught and cherished, without even the tongue to deplore them—dumb, as it were, with her excess of woe—she still sits, a monument like themselves, not only of their worship, but of the faith which she taught. It is a grace-ful ruin, that will awaken all your veneration, if the gnawing cares of gain, and the world's baser collision, have not kept it too long inactive. It stands up, like some old warrior, grey with many winters, scarred and buffeted with conflicting storms and strifes. but still upright—still erect. The high altar, the sacred ornaments, the rich pews, like the people who honoured and occupied them, are torn away and gone. Decay and rude hands have dealt with them, as death has dealt with the worshippers. The walls and roof are but little hurt. The tower has been stricken and shattered, but still more hallowed by the lightning which has done it. Some white owls are in quiet possession of it, but as they are innocent, and seem in venerable keeping with the place, the gentle spirit will hold them sacred from harm ; and may no profane hand drive them away.

Here, to the right of the church, is a goodly cluster of tombs, fringed in thickly by the pine and cedar. The cattle stray here at noonday for the shady quiet, not less than for the rank grass which the spot affords. They are not the least gentle of its visitors. Rude hands, in some cases, have torn away and broken up, in sinful wantonness, the thick marble slabs which covered the vaults, and recorded the history of their indwellers. This was a double wrong—a wrong to those of whom they told, and not less a wrong to those who read, and who might have won useful knowledge from a lesson at the grave. Here, now, is the bone of an arm—a slender bone—perhaps that of a woman. It lies before us, unconscious of its exposure. We will disturb it no further— enough, if what we have seen shall have the effect of persuading us to regard with less complacency the vigour, and the power, and the beauty in our own. Pass on.

Here we may muse for hours, and our thoughts shall be as various as the records we have about us. Some of these tombs belong to history. Here lies one of a man who was killed and scalped at Goose Creek, in the war of the Yemassees, when those brave savages came down in 1715. This stone tells us of another who died at Eutaw in the Revolution, and who was brought here for burial, at his own request. The spot was sacred even then. You, who can " find sermons in stones, and good in every thing," shall be at no loss for matters of thought in the huge volumes of time which death has here bound up together—their leaves closely written upon and every page full of a sweet though sad morality

But, if you will descend with me to the bottom of this little slope, inclining from the burial-ground towards the Ashley, which steals in and out below us, I will take you to one monument, now sacred in our narrative—one monument, the history of which is more familiar to our regards than all the gravestones can possibly make it. The plane descends gradually here, and the young pines crowd upon it thickly. You see a little runnel of water that trickles down its sides. The traveller, who knows where to seek it, draws in from the roadside and drinks of it freely, though he well knows that it finds its source among the dwellings of the dead. At the foot of the hill you behold a little inclosure—a neat paling fence, once whole and white, but now sadly wanting repair. It is in better condition, however, than most of those around it. The seclusion of the spot tends somewhat to its protection. This is the "Walton Burial-place." The old barony has given it many tenants. Here, now, is a solid slab, twelve feet in length, that covers a generation. A long inscription tells us of grandsire, son, grandson—of their wives and children—how they were worthy and beloved in life, and how they were bewept and remembered after death. There are others, equally imposing, at the side of this monument,—a goodly range of graves, each having its memorial in stone. But as we know nothing of them, beyond their names, we need not linger to behold them. They can teach us but the one lesson which the dead everywhere dedicates to the warning of the living. We obey only a common mood of heedlessness when we turn coldly from these unknown sleepers.

But not with such indifference may we pass the slender white shaft to which I now conduct you. Here is a little hillock, grassy and speckled with daisies in the spring. They are proper emblems of the pure, soft, gentle heart of the being who sleeps below. Tread lightly about the spot. It should be sacred to us. It hides one whom we knew and loved in life. There is something in all the natural objects that surround it that seems to be in keeping with youth, and innocence, and beauty. See this infant cedar. Plucked up by the roots, from the neighbouring woods, when the grave was fresh, it was planted at its foot, has taken root vigorously, and is now a beautiful shrub-tree, casting a soft and genial shadow

over the spot.   Shall we read the few words that appear upon the
slender marble headstone?   Stoop with me, while my knife enables
us to discern the inscription.

"E. S.

"Born 7th May, 1763; died 21st June, 1780."

This is all.   No!   There are two words below—but two—and
they declare, as fondly perhaps as words may declare, for the
affections of a noble brother:

"My Sister!"

This is all—the whole story, with what our narrative has
already given, of that sweet suffering creature, whom we knew on
earth as Emily Singleton, whatever may be her accepted name in
heaven.   We may not withhold from these pages the simple
tribute of George Dennison, the rustic minstrel of the Partisans,
made long afterwards, and when we visited the spot together
fondly pursuing the ancient avenues of the graveyard, and deci
phering the old inscriptions:

THE GRAVE OF INNOCENCE.

I.

'Tis a lowly grave, but it suits her best,
Since it breathes of fragrance and speaks of rest;
And meet for her is its calm repose,
Whose life was so stormy and sad to its close.

II.

'Tis a shady dell where they've laid her form,
And the hill gathers round it, to break the storm;
While, above her head, the bending trees
Arrest the wing of each ruder breeze.

III.

A trickling stream, as it winds below,
Has a music of peace in its quiet flow;
And the buds, that are always in bloom above,
Tell of some minist'ring spirit's love.

IV.

It is sweet to think, that when all is o'er,
And life's fever'd pulses shall fret no more,
There still shall be some, with a gentle regret,
Who will not forsake, and who cannot forget—

Some kindlier heart, all untainted by earth,
That has kept its sweet bloom from 't \   ᵈd its birth,
Whose tears for the sorrows of youth snall be shed,
And whose pray'r shall still rise for the early dead.

15

CHAPTER XXXIII.

But, th ... gh we permit ourselves to turn aside occasionally from the highway, to plant or to pluck the flower, we are not to linger idly or long in the grateful employment. The business of life calls for progress rather than repose ; for perseverance rather than contemplation. The repose is needed for renovation, and in itself, as an interval from action, implies the presence of the duty to be done. Contemplation itself is simply an essential to proper action ; preparative wholly, so that design shall not be crudely conceived, and performance rendered rash and incomplete. The play of existence vibrates between two extremes, which yet coöperate in their results. We are not to fly heedlessly and for ever, no matter how much of the race-horse may be in our temperament ; so, equally must it be fatal to proper life, to fling ourselves down beside the highway and only contemplate the performances in which we do not seek to share.

For us, it is enough that we have lingered for a moment, to muse over sacred memories, and restore half-obliterated inscriptions. Contenting ourselves with having cast our tribute flower upon the grave of the beautiful and peaceful, we must hurry away to the encounter with the fearful and the wild ! We must exchange, for a season, peace for war, love for strife, and the beautiful for the terrible and dread ;—striving, in obedience to wild necessities, if not to forget, at least not improvidently to remember. And now to our narrative.

The hot chase over, which Proctor had urged after Singleton, the latter, accompanied by his uncle, now fairly *out*, returned quickly to the shelter of the cypress swamp. The party reached its wild recesses at a late hour of the night, and were very soon wrapt in those slumbers, which were as necessary as grateful after their late excitement and fatigue.

With the dawn, however, Colonel Walton was on the alert. Arousing his little troop, he prepared at once to depart. Unencumbered with baggage wagons or prisoners, movement was easy ; and he resolved to push forward with extra speed, making his way to the borders of North Carolina, where it was his hope to meet with the continentals of Maryland and Virginia, then known to be advancing under the conduct of Baron De Kalb. His own force was quite too small for a distinct command, and he proposed to unite himself with some one of the corps, most deficient in numbers, in the incomplete squadrons of the southern army. His personal services he resolved to volunteer to Gates, whom he had known in Virginia prior to the war, and between whom and himself there had once existed a certain intimacy. He did not suffer himself to doubt, under these circumstances, that he should receive an honourable appointment near the General's person.

The squadron of Singleton was not able to move with such rapidity as that of Walton. It had, in its few days' practice along the Ashley, been accumulating the *impedimenta* of war, baggage and prisoners. There were munitions too, of no small importance to the partisans of Marion—powder and ball and buckshot—a few stacks of extra muskets and some spare rifles—all of which required precious painstaking, nice handling, a strong guard, and comparatively slow movements. Singleton, accordingly, resolved to defer his movement to a later moment. But the preparations for Walton's departure naturally aroused the whole camp, and the troopers generally turned out to take leave of their friends and comrades.

Among those who rose early that morning, we must not forget to distinguish Lieutenant Porgy. But it would be a mistake to suppose that he was stirred into activity at the dawn by any mere sentiment, such as prompts youth, in its verdancy, to forego its pleasant slumbers, in order to take a farewell gripe of the hand of parting friends, and meditate, with no appetite for breakfast, on ruptured ties and sundered associations. Porgy's sentiment took a somewhat different direction. He had survived that *green* season of the heart, when it delights in the things which make it sad.

His sentiment dealt in solids. He might be pathetic in soups **and** sauces; but never when a thinning camp increases the resources of the larder. He rose that morning to other considerations than such as were involved in Walton's departure; though, no doubt, the bustle of that evening had contributed to his early rising. His dreams, all night, had been a mixed vision of *terrapin*. It floated in all shapes and aspects before his delighted imagination. At first, his lively imagination re-enacted to his sight the scene in which he became the successful captor of the prey. There was the picture of the sluggish water, beneath the silent starlight. There, jutting out from the bank, was the fallen tree; and snug, and safe, and sweet in the imperfect light, there were the grouped victims, utterly unconscious, and drowsing to their doom, even as his eyes had seen them, some six or eight hours before. Nothing could seem more distinct and natural. Then followed his experience in the capture. How he "cooned" the log, slowly but surely wearing upon his prey, he again practised in his dreaming mood. How, one by one, he felt himself again securing them, turning them upon their backs, and showing their yellow bellies to the starlight; while their feet paddled ineffectually on either side, and their long necks were thrust forth in a manifest dislike of the fortune which put them in such unnatural position. Porgy experienced an illusion, very common to old fishermen, in being suffered to re-enact in his dreams the peculiar successes which had crowned his labours by day. As the angler then goes through the whole adventure with the cunning trout—beguiles him with the favourite flȳ, dexterously made to settle over his reedy or rocky retreat,—as he plays him from side to side, now gently persuades him with moderate tension of his line, now relaxes when the strain threatens to be too rude, and at length feels his toils crowned with victory, in the adroit effort which spreads his captive on the bank;—even so did the pleasant servitors of Queen Mab bring to the fancies of our epicure a full repetition of all the peculiarities of his adventure.

But the visions of our fat friend were not confined to the mere taking of his victims. His imagination carried him further; and he was soon busied in the work of dressing them for the table. The very dismembering of the captives—the breaking into their houses the dragging forth of the precious contents—the spectacle of crowding eggs and genei ous collops of luxurious swamp-fed meat; all of these gave exercise in turn to his epicurean fancies; nor must we forget the various caprices of his genius, while preparing the several dishes out of the prolific mess before him. He awoke from his dream, crying out "Eureka," and resolved soberly to put some of his sleep devices to the test of actual experiment. Of course, he does not forget the compound of terrapin with pig, which he has already declared his purpose to achieve; but he has other inventions even superior to this; and, full of the one subject, the proposed departure of Colonel Walton, of which he hears only on awaking, provoked all his indignation. He grew eloquent to Humphries, from whom he heard particulars.

"To go off at an hour so unseasonable, and from such a feast as we shall have by noon—it's barbarous! I don't believe it—I won't believe a word of it, Bill."

"But I tell you, lieutenant, it is so. The colonel has set the boys to put the nags in fix for a start, and him and the major only talk now over some message to Marion and General Gates, which the colonel's to carry."

"He's heard nothing then of the terrapin, you think? He'd scarcely go if he knew. I'll see and tell him at once. I know him well enough."

"Terrapin, indeed, Porgy! how you talk! Why, man, he den't care for all the terrapin in the swamp."

"Then no good can come of him; he's an infidel. I would not march with him for the world. Don't believe in terrapin! A man ought to believe in all that's good; and there's nothing so good as terrapin. Soup, stew, or hash, all the same; it's a dish among a thousand. Nature herself shows the value which she sets upon it, when she shelters it in such walls as these, and builds around it such fortifications as are here. See now, Bill Humphries, to that magnificent fellow that lies at your feet. You should have seen how he held on to his possessions; how reluctantly he surrendered at the last; and, in the mean time, how adroitly, as well as tenaciously, he continued the struggle. I was a goodly hour working at him to surrender. To hew off his head cost more effort than in

15*

taking off that of Charles the First. No doubt, he too was a tyrant in his way, and among his own kidney—a tyrant among the terrapins. His self-esteem was large enough for a dozen sovereigns, even of the Guelph family. But if the head worried me, what should I say about the shell—the outer fortress ? I marched up to it, like a knight of the middle ages attacking a Saracen fortress, battle-axe in hand. There lies my hatchet : see how I have ruined the edge. Look at my hand : see what a gash I gave myself. Judge of the value of the fortress, always, from the difficulty of getting possession. It is a safe rule. The meat here was worthy of the toils of the butcher. It usually is in degree with the trouble we have to get at it. It is so with an oyster, which I take to be the comeliest vegetable that ever grew in the garden of Eden !"

"What, lieutenant, the oyster a vegetable ?"

"It originally was, I have no doubt."

"And growing in the garden of Eden ?"

"And if it did *not*, then was the garden not to *my* taste, I can assure you. But it must have grown there ; and at that period was probably to be got at without effort, though I am not sure, my good fellow, that the flavour of a thing is at all heightened by the ease with which we get at it. It's not so, as we see, with terrapin and oyster, and crab and shrimp, and most other things in which we take most delight—which are dainties to human appetite ;—if indeed we may consider appetite as merely human, which I greatly question."

"Well," quoth Humphries, after a short fit of musing, "that does seem to me very true, though I never thought of it before. All the tough things to come at are mighty sweet, lieutenant ; and them things that we work for hardest, always do have the sweetest relish."

"Yes ; even love, Humphries, which considered as a delicacy—a fine meat, or delicate vegetable——"

"Mercy upon us, lieutenant, what can you be thinking of ? Love a meat and a vegetable !"

"Precisely ; the stomach——"

"Oh ! that won't do at all, that sort of talking, lieutenant. It does seem to me as if you brought the stomach into every thing, even sacred things."

" Nay, nay, reverse the phrase, Humphries, and bring all sacred things into the stomach."

" Well, any how, Lieutenant Porgy, it does seem to me that it's your greatest fault to make too much of your belly. You spoil it, and after a while, it will grow so impudent that there will be no living with it."

" There will be no living without it, my good fellow, and that's sufficient reason for taking every care of it. What you call my greatest fault is in fact my greatest merit. You never heard of Menenius Agrippa, I reckon ?"

" Never ; didn't know there was such a person."

" Well, I shall not trouble you with his smart sayings, and you must be content with mine to the same effect. The belly *is* a great member, my friend, a very great member, and is not to be spoken of irreverently. It is difficult to say in what respects it is *not* great. Its claims are quite as various as they are peculiar. It really does all one's thinking, as well as——"

" The belly do the thinking ?"

" That's my notion. I am convinced, however people may talk about the brain as the seat of intellect, that the brain does but a small business after all, in the way of thinking, compared with the belly. Of one thing be certain: before you attempt to argue with an obstinate customer, give him first a good feed. Bowels of compassion are necessary to brains of understanding, and a good appetite and an easy digestion are essentials to a logical comprehension of every subject, the least difficult. A good cook, I say, before a good school house, and a proper knowledge of condiments before orthography. It is a bad digestion that makes our militiamen run without emptying a musket ; and when you find an officer a dolt, as is too much my experience, you may charge it rather upon his ignorance of food than of fighting. A good cook is more essential to the success of an army than a good general. But that reminds me of Colonel Walton. Go to him, Bill Humphries, with my respects. I know him of old ; he will remember me. I have enjoyed his hospitality. If he be the gentleman that I think him, he will find a sufficient reason for delaying his journey till afternoon, when he hears of our terrapin. Be off and see him, lieutenant, and let him understand what he loses by going. Give him particulars; you may mention the dexterity of Tom, my cook, in doing a stew or ragout. And, by the way, lieutenant, pray take with you the buckler of that largest beast. If the sight of what doesn't make him open his eyes, I give him up. See to it, quickly. my good fellow, or you may lose him, and he the stew."

Humphries laughed outright at the earnestness of the epicure. Of course he understood that Porgy had a certain artificial nature in which he found the resources for his jests; and that he covered 'a certain amount of sarcasm, and a philosophy of his own, under certain affectations at which he was quite content that the world should laugh, believing what it pleased. Humphries found no little pleasure in listening to the shrewd absurdities and thoughtful extravagances of his brother officer; and he could sometimes understand that the gravity of Porgy's manner was by no means indicative of a desire that you should take for gospel what he said. But he was this time thoroughly deceived, and was at much pains to prove to him how utterly impossible it was for Colonel Walton to remain, even with such temptations to appetite as might be set before him.

" The fact is, lieutenant, I did tell the colonel what you had for him, and how you were going to dress the terrapin in a way that never had been seen before."

" Ay, ay! Hash, stew, ragout,—the pig. Well?"

" Yes, I told him all, as well as I knew, but——"

" Ah, you boggled about it, Bill; you couldn't have given him any just idea——"

" I did my best, lieutenant; and the colonel said that he liked terrapin soup amazingly, and always had it when he could get it; and how he should like to try yours, which he said he was sure would prove a new luxury."

" Ay, that was it. I would have had his opinion of the dish, for he knows what good living is. There's a pleasure, Humphries. in having a man of taste and nice sensibilities about us. Our affections—our humanities, if I may so call them—are then properly exercised but it is throwing pearl to swine to put a good dish

before such a creature as that skeleton, Oakenburg—Doctor Oakenburg, as the d—d fellow presumes to call himself. He is a monster
—a fellow of most perverted taste, and of no more soul than a
skiou, or the wriggling lizard that he so much resembles. Only
yesterday, we had a nice tit-bit—an exquisite morsel—only a taste
—a marsh hen, that I shot myself, and fricasseed after a fashion
of my own. I tried my best to persuade the wretch to try it—only
to try it—and would you believe it, he not only refused, but
absolutely, at the moment, drew a bottle of some vile root decoc-
tion from his pocket, and just as I was about to enjoy my own
little delicacy, he thrust the horrible stuff into his lantern jaws, and
swallowed a draught of it that might have strangled a cormorant.
It nearly made me sick to see him, and with difficulty could I keep
myself from becoming angry. I told him how ungentlemanly had
been his conduct—taking his physic where decent people were
enjoying an intellectual repast—for so I consider dinner—and
I think he felt the force of the rebuke, for he turned away instantly,
humbled rather, though still the beast was in him. In a minute
after, he was dandling his d—d coach whip, that he loves like
a bedfellow. It is strange, very strange, and makes me sometimes
doubtful how to believe in human nature at all. It is such a
monstrous budget of contradictions, such a diabolical scene of conflict between tastes and capacities."

The departure of Humphries left Porgy to the domestic duties
which lay before him, and cut short his philosophies. While the
whole camp was roused and running to the spot where Walton's
little command was preparing for a start, our epicure and his man
Tom—the cook par excellence of the encampment—were the only
persons who did not show themselves among the crowd. As for
Tom, he did not show himself at all, until fairly dragged out of his
bush by the rough grasp of his master upon his shoulder. Rubbing
his eyes, looking monstrous stupid, and still half asleep, Tom could
not forbear a surly outbreak, to which, in his indulgent bondage,
his tongue was somewhat accustomed.

"Ki! Maussa: you no lub sleep you'se'f, da's no reason why
he no good for udder people. Nigger lub sleep, Mass Porgy
15*

an' 'taint 'spec'ful for um to git up in de morning before de
sun."

"Ha! you ungrateful rascal; but you get up monstrous often
when its back is turned. Were you not awake, and away on
your own affairs, last night for half the night, you might have found
it quite respectable tō be awake at sunrise. Where were you last
night when I called for you?"

"I jist been a hunting a'ter some possum, maussa. Enty you lub
possum."

"Well, did you get any?"

"Nebber start, maussa."

"Pretty hunting, indeed, not to start a possum in a cypress
swamp. What sort of dog could you have had?"

"Hab Jupe and Slink, maussa."

"You will be wise to invite me when you go to hunt again.
Now, open your eyes, you black rascal, and see what hunting I can
give you. Look at your brethren, sirrah, and get your senses about
you, that there may be no blunder in the dressing of these dear
children of the swamp. Get down to the creek and give your face
a brief introduction to the water; then come back and be made
happy, in dressing up these babes for society."

"Dah mos' beautiful, fine cooter, maussa, de bes' I see for many
a day. Whay you nab 'em, maussa?"

"Where you were too lazy to look for them, you rascal; on the
old cypress log running along by the pond on Crane Hollow
There I caught them napping last night, while you were poking
after possum with a drowsy puppy. Fortunately, I waked while
they were sleeping; I cooned the log and caught every mother's
son of them: and that's a warning to you, Tom, never to go to
sleep on the end of a log of a dark night."

"Hah! wha' den, maussa! S'pose any body gwine eat nigger
eben if dey catch 'em? Tom berry hard bittle (victual) for buckrah
tomach."

"Make good cooter soup, Tom, nevertheless! Who could tell
the difference? Those long black slips of the skin in terrapin soup,
look monstrous like shreds from an Ethiopian epidermis; and the

bon*s* will pass current every where for nigger toes and fingers. The Irish soldiers in garrison at Charleston and Camden wouldn't know one from t'other. Tom, Tom, if ever they catch you sleeping, you are gone for ever—gone for terrapin stew!"

"Oh! Maussa, I wish you leff off talking 'bout sich things. You mek' my skin crawl like yellow belly snake."

"Ay, as you will make the skin of other people crawl when they find they have been eating a nigger for a terrapin. But away, old boy, and get every thing in readiness. See that your pots are well scoured. Get me some large gourds in which we may mix the ingredients comfortably. We shall want all the appliances you can lay hands on. I am about to invent some new dishes, Tom; a stew that shall surpass anything that the world has ever known of the sort. Stir yourself, Tom, if you would have a decent share of it. When you once taste of it, you rascal, you will keep your eyes pen all night, for ever after, if only that you may catch terrapin."

"Hah! I no want 'em mek' too good, maussa, eider! When de t'ing is mek' too nice, dey nebber leabs so much as a tas'e for de cook. Da's it!"

"I'll see to it this time, old fellow. You are too good a judge of good dressing not to be allowed a taste. You shall have your share. But, away, and get everything in readiness. And see that you keep off the dogs and all intruders, bipeds and quadrupeds. And, Tom!"

"Sa! wha' 'gen, maussa?"

"Mind the calabashes; and be sure to get some herbs—dry sage, thyme, mint, and, if you can, a few onions. What would I give for a score or two of lemons! And, Tom!"

"Sa!"

"Say nothing to that d—d fellow Oakenburg—do you hear, sir?"

"Enty I yerry, maussa; but it's no use; de doctor lub snake better more nor cooter."

"Away!"

The negro was gone upon his mission, and throwing himself at length upon the grass, the eyes of Porgy alternated between the rising sun and the empty shells of his terrapins.

"How they glitter!" he said to himself: "what a beautifu. polish they would admit of! It's surprising they have never been used for the purposes of manly ornamennt. In battle, burnished well, and fitted to the dress in front, just over humanity's most conspicuous dwelling-place, they would turn off many a bullet from that sacred, but too susceptible, region."

Musing thus, he grappled one of the shells, the largest of the three, and turning himself upon his back, with his head resting against a pine, he proceeded to adjust the back of the terrapin, as a sort of shield, to his own extensive abdominal domain. Large as was the shell, it furnished a very inadequate cover to the ample territory, at once so much exposed and so valuable. It was while engaged in this somewhat ludicrous experiment, that Lieutenant Porgy was surprised by Major Singleton.

Singleton laughed aloud as he beheld the picture. Porgy's face was warmly suffused when thus apprised of the presence of his superior.

"Not an unreasonable application, lieutenant," was the remark of Singleton, when his laughter had subsided, "were there any sort of proportion between the shield and the region which you wish it to protect. In that precinct your figure makes large exactions. A turtle, rather than a terrapin, would be more in place. The city has outgrown its walls."

"A melancholy truth, Major Singleton," answered the other, as he arose slowly from his recumbent posture, and saluted his superior with the elaborate courtesy of the gentleman of the old school. "The territory is too large certainly for the walls; but I am a modest man, Major Singleton, and a stale proverb helps me to an answer: Half a loaf, sir, is said to be better than no bread; and half a shelter, in the same spirit, is surely better than none. Though inadequate to the protection of the whole region, this shell might yet protect a very vital part. Take care of what we can, sir, is a wholesome rule, letting what can, take care of all the rest."

"You are a philosopher, Mr. Porgy, and I rejoice in the belief that you are fortified even better in intellectual and moral than physical respects. But for this, sir, it might not be agreeable to you to have to hurry to the conclusion of a repast, for which, I perceive, you are making extraordinary preparations."

"Hurry, Major Singleton—hurry ?" demanded the epicure, looking a little blank. " Hurry, sir ! I never hurried in my life. Hurry is vulgar, major, decidedly vulgar--a merit with tradesmen only."

" It is our necessity, nevertheless, lieutenant, and I am sorry for your sake that it is so. We shall start for the Santee before sun-set this afternoon. This necessity, I am sorry to think, will some-what impair the value of those pleasant meditations which usually follow the feast."

Porgy's face grew into profound gravity, as he replied—

" Certainly, the reveries of such a period are the most grateful and precious of all. The soul asserts its full influence about an hour after the repast is over, and when the mind seems to hover on the verge of a dream. I could wish that these hours should be left unbroken. Am I to understand you seriously, major, that the necessity is imperative—that we are to break up camp here, for good and all ?"

"That is the necessity. For the present we must leave the Ashley. We move, bag and baggage, by noon, and push as fast as we can for Nelson's Ferry. Our place of retreat here will not be much longer a place of refuge. It is too well known for safety, and we shall soon be wanted for active service on the frontier."

" I confess myself unwilling to depart. This is a goodly place, my dear major ; better for secresy could scarce be found ; and then, the other advantages. Fresh provisions, for example, are more abundant here than in Dorchester. Pork from the possum, mutton from the coon ; these ponds, I am convinced, will yield us cat quite as lively if not quite so delicate as the far-famed ones of the Edisto ; and I need not point you more particularly to the interest-ing commodity which lies before us."

" These *are* attractions, Mr. Porgy ; but as our present course lies for the Santee, the difference will not be so very great—cer tainly not so great as to be insisted upon. The Santee is rich in numberless variet:es of fish and fowl, and my own eyes have feast ed upon terrapin of much greater dimensions, and much larger numbers, than the Cypress yields."

"And of all varieties, major? the brown and yellow—not to speak of the alligator terrapin, whose flavour, though unpopular with the vulgar, is decidedly superior to that of any other? You speak knowingly, najor?"

"I do. I know all the region, and have lived in the swamp for weeks at a time. The islands of the swamp there are much larger than here; and there are vast lakes in its depths, where fish are taken at all hours of the day with the utmost ease. You will see Colonel Marion, himself, frequently catching his own breakfast."

"I like that—a commander should always be heedful of his example. That's a brave man—a fine fellow—a very sensible fellow—catches his own breakfast! Does he dress it too, major?"

"Ay, after a fashion."

"Good! such a man always improves. I feel that I shall like him, major, this commander of ours; and now that you have enlightened me, sir, on the virtues of the Santee, and our able colonel, I must own that my reluctance to depart is considerably lessened. At late noon, you said?"

"At late noon."

"I thank you, Major Singleton, for this timely notice. With your leave, sir, I will proceed to these preparations for dinner, which are rather precipitated by this movement. That rascally head there, major," kicking away the gasping head of one of the terrapins as he spoke, "seems to understand the subject of our conversation—of mine at least—and opens its jaws every instart, as if it hoped some one of us would fill them."

"He contributes so largely to the filling of other jaws, that the expectation seems only a reasonable one. You will understand me, lieutenant, as an expectant with the rest."

"You shall taste of my ragout, my dear major, a preparation of——"

But Singleton was gone, and Porgy reserved his speech for Tom, the cook, who now appeared with his gourds, and other vessels, essential to the due composition of such dishes as our fat friend had prescribed for the proper exercise of his inventive genius.

Major Singleton was one of that fortunately constituted and peculiar race of men who are of all others the best fitted for the conduct of a militia soldiery. The restive, impulsive, eager, untrained, and always independent character of our people of the South and West, requires a peculiar capacity to direct their energies, reconcile them to unwonted situations, hard usage, incessant toil, and the drudgery of a service, so much of which is held to be degrading to the citizen. Singleton possessed the art in perfection of getting good service out of his followers, and keeping them at the same time in good humour with their superior. He could be familiar without encouraging obtrusiveness; could descend without losing command; could wink at the humours which it might be unwise to rebuke, yet limit the mercurial spirit within such bounds, as kept him usually from trespassing beyond the small province of his simple humours. In obeying him, the followers of Singleton somehow felt that they were serving a friend, yet never seemed to forget their respect in their sympathy.

When Singleton left Lieutenant Porgy, it was simply to walk the rounds of his encampment. In this progress, he had his friendly word for all—some words, in every ear, of kind remark and pleasant encouragement. No person, however humble, went utterly unnoticed. The trooper, trimming away the thick hairs from the fetlocks of his horse, or paring down his hoofs; the horse boy who took the steed to water; the camp scullion who washed the kettles; the group of nameless persons—food for powder—huddled together in idle chat, or at some game, or mending bridles, moulding bullets, or, more homely yet in their industry, repairing rents in coat or breeches—all in turn were sure, as the Major of Partisans went by, to hear his gentle salutation, in those frank tones which penetrated instantly to the heart, a sufficient guaranty for the sincerity of the speaker. And there was no effort in this familiar frankness, and no air of condescension. He was a man speaking to men; and did not appear to dream of any necessity of making every word, look, and tone remind them of his authority. His bearing, when not engaged in the absolute duties of the service, was that of an equal, simply. And yet there was really no familiarity between the parties. There was a certain calmness of look and gesture—a certain simplicity of manner about our partisan, too easy for reserve, too graceful for indifference, which always and effectually restrained the obtrusive. He could smile with his followers, but he rarely laughed with them. When he addressed them, he did so with great respect, which always tutored them when they spoke to him. He always rose for this purpose, if previously he had been sitting. His was that due consideration of the man, as a man, that never permitted the same person, as an animal, to suppose that his embraces would be proper to his intercourse. Yet nobody ever thought of accusing Singleton of pride. His gentleness of manner, ease and grace and frankness of speech, were proverbial among his men. Truly, he was the man to be a leader of southern woodsmen. Even now, while his heart was sorely bleeding with fraternal sorrows—fearing all, yet ignorant still of the extent of his loss—he smiled pleasantly with his followers, and spoke in that language of consideration which seemed to show that he thought of them rather than himself. They did not know that the reason why he lingered so long among them, was chiefly that he might escape from himself and his own melancholy thoughts.

Having gone the rounds, seen to all things, and properly prepared his men for the march by sunset, Singleton threw himself down in the shadow of a dwarf oak, beneath which he had a couch of moss, on which he had slept the night before. While he lay here, musing equally over his duties and affections, Lance Frampton placed himself quietly on the other side of the tree. It was some time before the lad attracted his attention. When at length he noticed his appearance, it seemed to him that the boy's face was full of a grave interest.

" What's the matter, Lance ?" he inquired kindly.

" I thought, sir—I was afraid that you were sick," answered the boy.

" Sick ! I ! sick ! Why, what should make me sick ? Why should you suppose that I am sick ?"

" Why, sir, you talked and groaned so, in your sleep, this morning."

" No, surely ! Is it possible ?"

"Oh, yes, sir; I woke before daylight and heard you, and it frightened me, sir."

"Frightened you, boy! That is an ugly confession for a soldier to make. You must not suffer yourself to be frightened by anything. A soldier is not to be frightened, even when surprised But what did I say to frighten you?"

"Why, sir, you were quarrelling with somebody in your sleep, and you swore too—"

"Swore! Did I? A trooper habit, Lance, and a very bad one," said the other gravely. "Surely, Lance, I did not swear. You must be mistaken. I never swear. I have an oath in heaven against the habit."

This was said with a grave smile.

"Yes, sir; but you did it in your sleep."

"Well, I suppose I am not quite responsible for what is done in my sleep; but the fact argues for the possibility of my doing the thing when awake. But are you sure, Lance, you were not asleep yourself, and dreamt the whole matter?"

"Oh! quite sure, sir, for I got up and looked at you. It was just before morning, and the moon was shining right upon your face. I went round and broke the end of the branch—you see where it hangs, sir—so as to make it fall betwixt your eyes and the moonlight, and after that your face was quite shaded. But you swore again, and you gnashed your teeth together, and threw out your hands, as if you were fighting somebody in your sleep."

"A decided case of nightmare; and you would have done me a good service, Lance, had you taken me by the shoulders, and jerked me out of my dream. But I thank you for what you did. You are a good youth, and properly considerate;—and so you broke that twig to protect my eyes from the glare?"

"Yes, sir; but I reckon it was not the moonshine that troubled you, but something in your own thoughts, for you swore afterwards worse than ever."

"It is strange," said Singleton, gravely. "It shows the thoughts to be more wicked than we suspect—I had almost said more wicked when sleeping than waking." And the speaker mused silently after hearing this account. He looked to the broken bush, and the gentle devotion of his youthful protégé touched his heart. Resuming, he said gently—

"I am very sorry, Lance, that I swore in your hearing. I certainly do not swear wittingly. I try not to fall into the foolish habit, which I beg that you will not learn from me, for I detest it. In kindness to me, forget what you heard, and in duty to yourself, never imitate the lesson. To make you remember this counsel, I give you a little token. Take this dirk, and recal my advice whenever it meets your eye. Fasten it there, with the sheath, close by the left side. Let the point come out a little in front, while the handle rests under the arm. Take care of it. It may be useful to you in various ways. It has saved my life once; it may save yours; but use it only when it is necessary to such a purpose. You may leave me now, and for the morning, amuse yourself as you please within the camp."

The boy, made happy by the kindness of his superior, would gladly have lingered beside him, but he quickly saw that Singleton desired to be alone. He disappeared accordingly from sight, finding no difficulty, among the various humours of a camp, in whiling away the hours assigned to him for leisure.

These humours of the camp! But it is time that we see what preparations for his feast have been made by our corpulent Lieutenant of Dragoons. Of course he was busy all the morning. Porgy had a taste. In the affairs of the cuisine, Porgy claimed to have a genius. Now, it will not do to misconceive Lieutenant Porgy. If we have said or shown anything calculated to lessen his dignity in the eyes of any of our readers, remorse must follow. Porgy might *play* the buffoon, if he pleased; but in the mean time, let it be understood, that he was born to wealth, and had received the education of a gentleman. He had wasted his substance, perhaps, but this matter does not much concern us now. It is only important that he should not be supposed to waste himself. He had been a planter—was, in some measure, a planter still, with broken fortunes, upon the Ashepoo. "He had had losses," but he bore them like a philosopher. He was a sort of laughing philosopher, who, as if in anticipation of the free speech of others, dealt with himself as little mercifully as his nearest friends might

have done. He had established for himself a sort of reputation as a humourist, and was one of that class which we may call conventional. His humour belonged to sophistication. It was the fruit of an artificial nature. He jested with his own tastes, his own bulk of body, his own poverty, and thus baffled the more serious jests of the ill-tempered by anticipating them. We may mention here, that while making the greatest fuss, always about his feeding, he was one of the most temperate eaters in the world.

He has effected his great culinary achievement, and is satisfied. See him now, surrounded by his own mess, which includes a doctor and a poet. A snug corner of the encampment, well shaded with pines and cypresses, affords the party a pleasant shelter. Their viands are spread upon the green turf; their water is furnished from a neighbouring brooklet, and Tom, the cook, with one or two camp scullions waiting on him, is in attendance. Tin vessels bear water, or hold the portions of soup assigned to the several guests. The gourds contain adequate sources of supply, and you may now behold the cleansed shells of each of the fated terrapins made to perform the office of huge dishes, or tureens, which hold the special dishes in the preparation of which our epicure has exhausted all his culinary arts.

He presides with the complacent air of one who has done his country service.

"Tom," he cries, "take that tureen again to the major's mess. They need a fresh supply by this time, and if they do not, they ought to."

The calabash from which Porgy served himself was empty when he gave this order. In being reminded of his own wants, our host was taught to recollect those of his neighbours. Porgy was eminently a gentleman. His very selfishness was courtly. Tom did as he was commanded, and his master, without show of impatience, awaited his return. In those days no one was conscious of any violation of propriety in taking soup a second time; and though the prospect of other dishes might have taught forbearance to certain of the parties, in respect to the soup, yet it was too evident that a due regard to the feelings of the host required that it should receive full justice at all hands.

Porgy was in the best of humours. He was conciliated by his comrades; and he had succeeded in his experiments—to his own satisfaction at least. He even looked with complacency upon the lantern-jawed and crane-bodied doctor, Oakenburg, whom, as we have seen, he was not much disposed to favour. He could even expend a jest upon the doctor instead of a sarcasm, though the jests of Porgy were of a sort, as George Dennison once remarked, "to turn all the sweet milk sour in an old maid's dairy." Dr. Oakenburg had a prudent fear of the lieutenant's sarcasms, and was disposed to conciliate by taking whatever he offered in the shape of food or counsel. He suffered sometimes in consequence of this facility. But the concession was hardly satisfactory to Porgy, and his temper was greatly tried, when he beheld his favourite dishes almost left untouched before the naturalist, who evidently gave decided preference to certain bits of fried eel, which formed a part of the dinner of that day.

"Eel is a good thing enough," he muttered *sotto voce*, "but to hang upon eel when you can get terrapin, and dressed in this manner, is a vice and an abomination."

Then louder—

"How do you get on, George?" to Dennison; "will you scoop up a little more of the soup, or shall we go to the pie?"

"Pie!" said Dennison. "Have you got a terrapin pie?"

"Ay, you have something to live for. Tom, make a clearance here, and let's have the pie."

Tom had returned from serving Singleton and his immediate companions. These were Humphries, John Davis, Lance Frampton, and perhaps some other favourite trooper. They had dipped largely into the soup. They were now to be permitted to try the terrapin pie upon which Porgy had tried his arts. They sat in a quiet group apart from the rest of the command, who were squatting in sundry messes all about the swamp hammocks. Let us mention, *par parenthese*, that John Davis had mustered the courage to make a full confession to his superior of his last night's adventure, of his projected duel with Hastings, and how the latter was murdered by the maniac Frampton. Of course, Singleton heard the story with great gravity, and administered a wholesome rebuke to the offender. Under the circumstances he could do no more. To punish was not his policy, where the criminal was so clever a trooper. He had done wrong, true; but there was some apology for him in the wrongs, performed and contemplated, of the British sergeant. Besides, he had honestly acknowledged his error, and deplored it, and it was not difficult to grant his pardon, particularly while they were all busy over the soup of Porgy. If forgiveness had been reluctant before, it became ready when the pie was set in sight. Porgy's triumph was complete. Singleton did not finish his grave rebuke of the offender, while helping himself from the natural tureen which contained the favourite dish. Nothing could be more acceptable to all the party. When the pie, shorn largely of its fair proportions, was brought back to our epicure, his proceeding was exquisitely true to propriety. Loving the commodity as he did, and particularly anxious to begin the attack upon it, he yet omitted none of his customary politeness—a forbearance scarcely considered necessary in a dragoon camp.

"There, Tom, that will do. Set it down. It will stand alone. Did the major help himself?"

"He tek' some, maussa."

"Some! Did he not help himself honestly, and like a man with Christian appetite and bowels?"

"He no tek' 'nough, like Mass Homphry, and Mass Jack Dabis, but he tek' some, and Mass Lance, he tek' some, jis' like the major."

"Humph! he took a little, you mean. A little! Did he look sick, Tom—the major?"

"No, sah! He look and talk berry well."

"Ah! I see; he helped himself modestly, like a gentleman, at first; we shall try him again. And now for ourselves. Gentlemen, you shall now see what art can do with nature; how it can glorify the beast; how it can give wings to creeping things. George Dennison, you need not be taught this. Help yourself, my good fellow, and let this terrapin pie inspire your muse to new flights.

16

Mr. Wilkins, suffer me to lay a few spoonsful of this pie in your calabash. Nay, don't hang back, man; the supply is abundant."

The modest Mr. Wilkins, who was coquetting only with his happiness, was easily persuaded, and Porgy turned to Oakenburg, who was still eeling it.

" Dr. Oakenburg !" with a voice of thunder.

" Sir—Lieutenant—ah !" very much startled.

"Doctor Oakenburg, let me entreat you to defile your lips no longer with that villanous fry. Don't think of eel, sir, when you can get terrapin ; and such as this."

" I thank you, lieutenant, but—yes, I really thank you very much ; but, as you see, I have not yet consumed entirely the soup which you were so good——"

" And why the d—l haven't you consumed it ? It was cooked to be consumed. Why have you wasted time so imprudently ? That soup is now not fit to be eaten. You have suffered it to get cold. There are certain delights, sir, which are always to be taken warm. To delay a pleasure, when the pleasure is ready to your hands, is to destroy a pleasure. And then, sir, the appetite grows vitiated, and the taste dreadfully impaired after eating fry. The finest delicacy in the world suffers from such contact. Send that soup away. Here, Tom, take the doctor's calabash. Throw that shrivelled fry to the dog, and wash the vessel clean. Be quick, you son of Beelzebub, if you would hope for soup and salvation."

The indignation of Porgy was making him irreverent. His anger increased as the tasteless doctor resisted his desires and clung to his eel.

" No ! Tom, no. Excuse me, lieutenant, but I am pleased with this eel, which is considerably done to my liking. It is a dish I particularly affect."

Porgy gave him a savage glance, while spooning the pie into his own calabash. Tom, the negro, meanwhile, had possessed himself of the doctor's dishes, and the expectant dog was already in possession of the remnant of his eel.

" Maussa say I must tek' um, Mass Oakenbu'g," was the apologetic response of the negro to the remonstran:es of the doctor.

"Clean the gourds, Tom, for the doctor as quickly as possible! That a free white man in a Christian country should prefer eel fry to terrapin stew! Doctor Oakenburg, where do you expect to go when you die? I ask the question from a belief—rather staggered, I must confess, by what I have seen—that you really have something of a soul left. You once had, doubtless."

The poor naturalist seemed quite wobegone and bewildered. His answer was quite as much to the point as it was possible for him to make it at any time.

"Really, lieutenant, I don't know; I can't conjecture, but I trust to some place of perfect security."

"Well, for your own sake, I hope so too; and the better to make you secure, could I have a hand in disposing of you, I should doom your soul to be thrust into an eelskin, and hung up to dry in the tropic from May to September every year. Of one thing you may rest assured—if there be anything like justice done to you hereafter, you will have scant fare, bad cooking, and fry for ever, wherever you go. Prefer eel to terrapin! Tom!"

"Sah!"

"Bring me a clean calabash of water, and hand the jug. A little Jamaica, my good fellow, to wash down our Grecians. Prefer eel to terrapin! George Dennison, have you done at last? How these poets eat! Mr. Wilkins, you have not finished? Come, sir, don't spare the pie. It is not every day that happiness walks into one's lodgings and begs one to help himself. It isn't every day that one captures such terrapins as these, and sits down to such cooking and compounding. Tom and myself are good against a world in arts. What! no more? Well, I can't complain. I too have done, a little morsel more excepted. Tom, hand me that tureen. I must have another of those eggs."

The epicure scooped them up and swallowed.

"What a flavour—how rich! Ah! George, this is a day to be marked with a white stone. Tom, take away the vessel. I have done enough."

"Ki, maussa, you no leff any eggs."

"No eggs!" cried the gourmand; "why, what the deuce do you call that, and that, and that?" stirring them over with the spoon

as he spoke. "Bless me, I did not think there were half so many
Stop, Tom, I will take but a couple more, and then—there—tha
will do—you may take the rest."

The negro hurried away with his prize, dreading that Porgy
would make new discoveries; while that worthy, seasoning his
calabash of water with a moderate dash of Jamaica from the jug
beside him, concluded the repast to which he had annexed so much
importance.

"So much is secure of life!" he exclaimed, when he had done.
"I am satisfied—I have lived to-day, and nothing can deprive me
of the 22d June, in the year of our Lord one thousand seven hundred and eighty, enjoyed in the Cypress Swamp. The day is completed: it should always close with the dinner hour. It is then
secure—we cannot be deprived of it: it is recorded in the history
of hopes realized, and of feelings properly felt. And, hark! the
major seems to think with me, since the bugle rumbles up for a
start. Wilkins—old fellow—if you'll give me a helping hand
in hoisting on this coat"—taking it from the bough of a tree (he
had dined, we may add, in his shirt sleeves)—"you will save me
from exertions which are always unwisely made after dinner. So!
that will do. Thank you! It is a service to be remembered."

The camp was all astir by this time. Porgy looked around him
coolly, and chafed at the hurry which he beheld in others.

"Ho! there, Corporal Millhouse, see to your squad, my good fellow. Dennison, my boy, you will ride along with me. I shall want
to hear some of that new ballad as we go. Ah! boy, we shall
have to put some of your ditties into print. They are quite as
good as thousands of verses that are so honoured. They *are* good,
George, and *I* know it, if nobody else. . . . So ho! There! Tom,
you rascal, will you be at that stew all day? Hurry, you sable son
of Ethiop, and don't forget to unsling and to pack up the hambone.
Needn't mind the calabashes. We can get them every where
along the road. . . . What! you're not about to carry that snake
along with you, Doctor Oakenburg! Great Heavens! what a
reptile taste that fellow has! . . . Ha! Lance, my boy, is that
you? Well, you relished the pie, didn't you?"

"*'Twas* good, lieutenant."

" Good! It was *great!* But you are in a hurry. Mounted already! Well, I suppose I must follow suit. I see the major's ready to mount also. Do me a turn, Lance ; help me on with my belt, which you see hanging from yonder tree. It takes in a world of territory. There! That will do."

Humphries now rode up.

" To horse, lieutenant, as soon as you can. The major's looking a little wolfish."

" Ay, ay! needs must when the devil drives. And yet this moving just after a hearty meal upon terrapin! Terrapin stew or pie seems to impart something of the sluggishness of the beast to him who feeds upon it. I must think of this ; whether it is not the case with all animals to influence with their own nature, that of the person who feeds on them. It was certainly the notion of the ancients. A steak of the lion might reasonably be supposed to mpart courage ; wolf and tiger should make one thirst for blood ; and"—seeing Oakenburg ride along at this moment—" who should wonder suddenly to behold that crane-bodied cormorant, after eating fried eel, suddenly twisting away from his nag, and, with squirm and wriggle, sliding off into the mud ? If ever he disappears suddenly, I shall know how to account for his absence."

Thus it was that Lieutenant Porgy soliloquized himself out of the swamp. He was soon at the head of his squad, and Singleton's orders became urgent. Once with the duty before him, our epicure was as prompt as any of his neighbours. In an hour, and all were ready for the start—the partisans and their prisoners ; and, conspicuous in the rear of his master's command, Tom, the cook, followed closely by his dog ; a mean looking cur significantly called " Slink." Never was dog more appropriately named. All negro dogs are more or less mean of spirit, but surly, and cunning in the last degree ; but Slink was the superb of meanness even among negro dogs. He was the most shame-faced, creeping, sneaking beast you ever saw ; as poor of body as of spirit ; eating voraciously always, yet always a mere skeleton, besmeared with the ashes and cinders in which he lay nightly—a habit borrowed, we suspect, from his owner ; and such was the meanness of his spirit, that, having, from immemorial time, neglected the due eleva-

16

tion of his tail, he now seemed to have lost al. sense, and indeed, all capability, for the achievement. There it hung for ever deplorably down, as far as it could go between his legs, and seemed every day to grow more and more despicably fond of earth. Such was "Slink" always in the white man's eye; but see "Slink" when it is his cue to throttle a fat shote in the swamp, and his character undergoes a change. You then see that phase of it, which, more than any thing besides, endears the dirty wretch to his negro master

It was an evil hour for Slink, when, under the excitement of departure, he suffered himself to trot ahead of his owner, and pass for a moment from rear to front of the command. It was not often that he suffered himself to put his beauties of person too prominently forward. What evil mood of presumption possessed him on the present occasion, it is difficult to conceive; but Slink in proper keeping with Tom, his owner, in the swamp, might keep himself in perfect security, as well as Oakenburg. His danger was in passing out from his obscurity into the front ranks. Lieutenant Porgy beheld the beast as he trotted in advance, with a rare sentiment of disgust,—a feeling which underwent great increase when he saw that the dog's spirit underwent no elevation with his advance, and that his caudal extremity was just as basely drooping as before. Porgy summoned Tom to the front, and pointed to the dog. Slink instantly saw that something was wrong, and tried to slink out of sight under the legs of the horses. But it was too late. Eyes had seen his momentary impertinence which seldom saw in vain.

"Tom," said Porgy, "that dog's tail must be cut off close to his haunches."

"Cut off Slink's tail, maussa! You want for kill de dog for ebber?"

"It won't kill him, Tom. Cut it off close, and sear the stump with a hot iron. It must be done to-night."

"But, maussa, he will spile de dog for ebber."

"Not so, Tom; it will *make* him, if any thing can. Don't you see that he can't raise it up; that it's in the way of his legs; that it makes him run badly. It is like a dragoon's sword when he's walking: always getting between his legs and tripping him."

"Slink can't do widout he tail, maussa!" answered Tom with becoming doggedness.

" He *must*, Tom."

" He lub he tail 'twix he leg so; he no hu't (hurt) he running."

" All a mistake, Tom. It's in his way, and he feels it. That's the true reason why he looks so mean, and always carries his head so sheepishly. It must be a terrible mortification to any dog of sensibility when he has a tail that he can never elevate. Cut off the tail, and you will see how he will improve."

" *You* t'ink so, maussa! *I* nebber ken t'ink so. 'Twon't do for cut off Slink tail."

" Either his tail or his head. He must lose one or t'other to-night, Tom. See that it is done. If I see him to-morrow with more than one inch of stump between his legs, I shoot him! By Jupiter Ammon, Tom, I shoot him! and you know when I swear by a Greek god that I am sure to keep my oath. In this way, Tom, I mortify Greek faith! You understand, Tom, with more than one inch of tail he dies! Let it be seen to this very night when we come to a halt."

" He 'mos (almost) as bad for cut he tail as he head, maussa."

" Be it the head then, Tom; I don't care which; and now fall back, old fellow, and whistle back the beast. The sight of his miserable tail distresses me."

And Porgy rode forward; and Tom, whistling back the unhappy cur, muttered as he fell behind:

" Maussa berry sensible pusson, but sometime he's a' mos' too d—n foolish for talk wid. Whay de harm in Slink tail ? Slink carry he tail so low to de groun', people nebber sh'um (see 'em)— nobody gwine sh'um but maussa, and he hab he eye jes whay nobody ebber want 'em for look."

But the last bugles sound shrilly and mournfully as the cavalcade speeds away in a long train through the swamp avenues, and Tom is compelled to forego his soliloquies and hurry forward with the dog, Slink, who, as if conscious of his error, has dropped just as far back in the rear, as before he indiscreetly went ahead. The miserable beast little anticipates the loss that awaits him. Fortunately Tom feels for him all that is proper. He rides forward enveloped in his own and master's luggage, and he too and Slink both finally disappear in the far shadows of the wood. The cypress swamp of the Ashley rests in the profoundest silence, as if it never had been inhabited.

CHAPTER XXXIV.

"The hour at hand, the foeman near
The biting brand, the steely spear,
 The spirit vex'd and warm,—
And these are all the freeman wants,
Who, for the struggle, pines and pants,
 And never knew alarm.
Then let the foeman come and feel
How dread the blow his hand can deal,
 When freedom nerves his arm."

An hour after these movements, and no one would suspect, from the dead silence that prevailed throughout the region, that it ever had been occupied by such wild and roystering fellows as those with whom we have just had dinner. Proctor's scouts might find everywhere the proofs of their occupation, in the beaten ground, the broken utensils, and the embers of recent fires. But of the occupants themselves there were no signs.

Singleton, meanwhile, sent his scouts forward at a scouring pace He led his little command more slowly, but still at a gait which would render pursuit difficult by a force larger than his own, or less admirably mounted. One secret of the success of Marion's men, was in the excellence of their horses, which were always well chosen from the best stables in the country. Our partisan made them show their legs. Aiming to make the Nelson's Ferry road as soon as possible, he struck directly across the country, under the guidance of Humphries and Davis, who knew every turn and twist, short cut and blind path, leading through the forests of this neighbourhood. Speaking comparatively, however, they sped along but slowly, leaving the scouts considerably in advance. They had made no great progress when night began to settle down upon the party. With the approach of darkness, Singleton cast about for a secluded spot in which to form a temporary encampment. This was finally found in a thick wood to which they inclined out of sight and hearing from the road. The scouts had received their instructions to fall back with the setting in of dusk, and report their discoveries; all of which was done. Here, without building fires, they took a brief and supperless rest, until the moon rose, when the troop was again set in motion, and posting forward along the prescribed route.

With the dawn of day, they found themselves, according to the calculations of the guides, within a few miles only of the Ferry road. A little more caution was now necessary to their progress. They were in a travelled region, and the scouts were doubled. The troop entered the road an hour or so after sunrise, without meeting with any interruption or object worthy their attention. In this manner they proceeded for some hours, seeing no human being. The whole route, however, was marked by the devastating proofs of war, which were thick on every side of them. The broken fences, the shattered or half-consumed dwellings, the unplanted and unploughed fields, all in desertion, spoke fearfully for its attributes and presence. But suddenly, towards noon, the scouts were met by a countryman, his wife, and two children, flying from the foe. It was difficult to convince them that they had not fallen in with another; and they told their story, accordingly, in fear and trembling.

They told of a tory named Amos Gaskens, a notorious wretch before the war, who had raised a party and had been devastating the neighbouring country throughout St. Stephens and St. Johns, Berkley.* His numbers were increasing, and he stopped at no excesses. On most of the plantations through which he had gone, every house was burned to the ground, the stock wantonly shot, the people plundered, and either murdered, forced to follow their captors, or compelled to fly to places of refuge the most wild and deplorable. The little family they had encountered had been thus dispossessed. They had only saved their lives by a timely notice, which a friend among the tories had given them of their approach. They insisted

* History has deemed this monster of sufficient importance to record many of his deeds. He was, for some time, the dread of this section of country.

that Gaskens could not be many miles off, and would certainly meet them before noon, as he was on his way to Charleston with his prisoners and seeking his reward.

Singleton determined to prepare for him a warm reception, and having ascertained that the force under Gaskens fully doubled his own, he laid his plans to neutralize this superiority by the employment of the usual cunning of the partisan. According to the account of the flying countryman, there was a beautiful little spring some three miles higher, not more than a stone's throw from the roadside; this was the only good drinking water for some distance, and, as it was well known to wayfarers, it was concluded that Gaskens would make use of it as a place of rest and refreshment. Here, Singleton determined to place his ambuscade; and as it was necessary to reach it some time in advance of his enemy, he pushed his troop forward at a quicker pace. They reached the spot in time, and gliding out of the road, were soon in possession of the desired station.

The spring was one of those quiet waters that trickle along the hollow which they have formed, and with so gentle a murmur, that, though but a brief distance from the road, no passing ear, however acute, could possibly detect its prattling invitation. The water was cool and refreshing; the overhanging trees gave it a pleasant and fitting shelter, which scarcely rendered necessary the small wooden shed which had been built above it by some one of the considerate dwellers in the neighbourhood. War, in its violence, however destructive else, had spared, with a becoming reverence, the fountain and the little roof above it. The whole spot was exceedingly pretty; wild vines and florid grapes clustered over it; a little clump of wild flowers grew just at its porch; while a fine large oak, standing on the brow of the little hill at the bottom of which the fountain had its source, took the entire area into its sheltering embrace. The wild jessamine, and the thousand flaunting blossoms of the southern forests, grew profusely about the place; and in that hour of general repose in Carolina during the summer months— the hour of noon—when all nature is languid; when the bird hushes his fitful note, or only

"Starts into voice a moment, and is still;"

when man and beast, reptile and insect, alike seek for the shade and pant drowsily beneath its shelter—this little hollow of the woods, and the clear stream welling over the little basin around which its dwelling-place had been formed, and trickling away in a prattling murmur that discoursed twin harmonies to the sluggish breeze that shook at intervals the tree above it, seemed eminently a scene chosen for gentle spirits, and a purpose grateful to the softest delicacies of humanity. Yet was its sacred and sweet repose about to be invaded. . War had prepared his weapon and lay waiting in the shade.

Having chosen his ground, Singleton proceeded to his preparations for the due reception of Gaskens and his tories. The troopers and the prisoners were at once dismounted; the latter, with the horses, were escorted to a sufficient distance in the wood, beyond the reach of the strife, and where they could convey no intimation by their voices to the approaching enemy. Here a guard was put over them, with instructions to cut down the first individual who should show the slightest symptom of a disposition to cry out or to fly. A command, otherwise so sanguinary, was necessary, however, in the circumstances. This done, Singleton despatched his scouts, headed by Humphries, whose adroitness he well knew, on the road leading to the enemy; they were to bring him intelligence without suffering themselves to be seen. He next proceeded to his own immediate disposition of force for the hot controversy, and approved himself a good disciple of the swamp fox in the arrangement. The ambush was formed on two sides of the spring, the men being so placed as to possess the advantages of the cross-fire without being themselves exposed to the slightest danger from their mutual weapons. All approach to the waters was thus commanded, and Singleton, trusting to the advantages obtained from the surprise and the first fire, instructed his men to follow him in the charge which he contemplated making, immediately after the discharge of their pieces. In the way of exhortation he had but few words; he resembled Marion in that respect, also: but those words were highly stimulating.

"Men, I have the utmost confidence in you; you are no cowards, and I am sure will do your duty. I do not call upon you to dostroy men, but monsters; not countrymen, but those who have no country—who have only known their country to rend her bowels and prey upon her vitals. You will only spare them when they are down—when they cry, enough. There must be no ' Tarleton's quarters,'* mind you; the soldier that strikes the man who has once submitted, shall be hung up immediately after; 'or though they be brutes and monsters now, yet even the brute has a claim upon man's mercy when he has once submitted to be tamed. Go now, men, each to his place, and wait the signal. I will give it at the proper moment myself. It shall be but one word, and when you hear me say, ' Now !' let each rifle make its mark upon an armed tory. Shoot none that have not weapons in their hands— *remember that ;* and when you sally out, as you will immediately after the discharge and while they are in confusion, let the same rule be observed. Strike none that throw down their arms—none that do not offer us resistance. Enough, now; the brave soldier needs no long exhortation. The soldier who fights his country's battles has her voice at his heart, pleading for her rescue and relief. Remember the burnt dwellings of your country—**her** murdered and maltreated inhabitants—**her** desolate fields—her starving children --and then strike home! Your country is worth fighting for, and he who dies in the cause of his country, dies in the cause of man: he will not be forgotten. Go, and remember the word."

There was no shout, no hurrah ; but eyes were bent upon the ground, lips knit closely in solemn determination; and Singleton saw at a glance that his men were to be relied on.

"They will do," he muttered to himself, as, seeing them all properly sheltered, he threw himself at the foot of a tree, a little removed from the rest, and only accompanied by the boy, Lance Frampton. We have seen the increasing intimacy between the lad and his commander ; an intimacy encouraged by the latter, and earnestly sought for by the boy. He studiously kept near the person of the partisan, listened to every word he uttered, watched every

---

* Tarleton made himself feared and infamous by giving no quarter When, accordingly, the patriots obtained any successes in battle, they were apt to answer the plea for mercy by shouting out—" Ay, Tarleton's quarters," while hewing down the supplicant.

16*

movement, and carefully analysed, so far as his immature capacities would admit, every feeling and thought of his superior. From this earnest and close contemplation of the one object, the boy grew to be exclusive in his regards, and slighted every other. Singleton became one and the same with his mind's ideal, and a lively imagination, and warm sensibilities, identified his captain, in his thought, with his only notion of a genuine hero. The more he studied him, the more complete was the resemblance. The lofty, symmetrical, strong person—the high but easy carriage—the grace of movement and attitude—the studious delicacy of speech, mingled, at the same time, with that simple adherence to propriety, which illustrates genuine manliness, were all attributes of Singleton and all obvious enough to his admirer.

" How I wish I was like him !" said the boy to himself, as he looked where Singleton's form lay before him under the tree. " If I was only sure that I could fight like him, and not feel afraid, when the time comes ! Oh ! how I wish it was over !"

Had the words been uttered loud enough to be heard by the partisan, the mood of the boy would have been better understood by his commander than it was, when the latter heard the deep sigh which followed them. Singleton turned to look upon him as he heard it, and could not avoid being struck with the manifest dejection in every feature of his countenance. He thought it might arise from the loneliness of his situation, his recent loss of a tender mother, and the distressing condition of his father, of whom they had seen nothing since their departure from the swamp. True, the brother of Lance was along with them, but there was little sympathy between the two. The elder youth was dull and unobservant while the other was thoughtful and acute. They had little intercourse beyond an occasional word of question and reply ; and even then, the intimacy and relationship seemed imperfect. These things might, nay, must necessarily produce in the boy's mind a sufficient feeling of his desolation, and hence, in Singleton's thought, his depression seemed natural enough. But when the sigh was repeated, and the face, even under the partisan's glance, wore the same expression, he could not help addressing him on the subject.

" Why, how now, Lance—what's the matter ?   Cheer up, cheer up, and get ready to do something like a man.   Know you not we re on the eve of battle ?"

" Oh, sir, I can't cheer up," was the half-inarticulate reply, as the emotion of the boy visibly increased, and a tear was seen to gather in his eyes.   So much emotion was unusual in one whose mood was that of elastic enthusiasm ; and the pallid cheek and downcast look stimulated anew the anxiety of the partisan.   He repeated his question curiously, and, at the same time, rising from his place of rest, he came round to where the boy was standing, leaning against his tree.

" What's the·matter with you, boy—what troubles you—are you sick ?"

" Oh, no, sir—no, sir—I'm not sick—I'm very well —but, sir—"
"But what ?"

" Only, sir, I've never been in a battle before—never to fight with men, sir."

" Well !   And what of that, Lance ?   What mean you?   Speak !"
The brow of Singleton darkened slightly, as he witnessed the seeming trepidation of the youth.   The frown, when Frampton beheld it, had the natural effect of adding to his confusion.

" Oh, sir, only that I'm so afraid——"

" Afraid, boy !" exclaimed Singleton, sternly, interrupting the speaker—" afraid !   Then get back to the horses—get away at once from sight, and let not the men look upon you.   Begone— away !"

The cheek of the boy glowed like crimson, his eye flashed out a fire-like indignation, his head was erect on the instant, and his whole figure rose with an expression of pride and firmness, which showed the partisan that he had done him injustice.   The change was quite as unexpected as it was pleasant to Singleton ; and he looked accordingly, as he listened to the reply of the boy, whose speech was now unbroken.

" No, sir—you wrong me--I'm not afraid of the enemy—that's not it, sir.   I'm not afraid to fight, sir ; but——"

" But what, Lance—of what then are you afraid ?"

" Oh, sir, I'm afraid I shan't fight as I want to fight.   I'm afraid, sir, I won't have the heart to shoot a man, though I know he will shoot me if he can. It's so strange, sir, to shoot at a true-and-true man—so very strange, sir, that I'm afraid I'll tremble when the time comes, and not shoot till it's too late."

" And what then—how would you help *that*, boy ? You must make up your mind to do it, or keep out of the way."

" Why, sir, if I could only see *you* all the time—if I could only hear you speak *to me in particular*, and tell me by name *when* to shoot, I think, sir, I could do it then well enough ; but to shoot at a man for the first time—I'm so afraid I'd tremble, and wait too long, unless you'd be so good as to tell me when."

Singleton smiled thoughtfully, as he listened to the confused workings of a good mind, finding itself in a novel position, ignorant of the true standard for its guidance, and referring to another on which it was most accustomed, or at least most willing, to depend. The boy laboured under one of those doubts which so commonly beset and annoy the ambitious nature, solicitous of doing greatly, with an ideal of achievement drawn before the sight by the imagination, and making a picture too imposing for its own quiet contemplation. He was troubled, as even the highest courage and boldest genius will sometimes become, with enfeebling doubts of his own capacity even to do tolerably, what he desires to do well. He trembled to believe that he should fall short of that measure of achievement which his mind had made his standard, and at which he aimed.

Fortunately for him, Singleton was sufficiently aware of the distinction between doubts and misgivings so honorable and so natural, and those which spring from imbecile purpose and a deficient and shrinking spirit. He spoke to the boy kindly, assured him of his confidence, encouraged him to a better reliance upon his own powers; and, knowing well that nothing so soon brings out the naturally sturdy spirit as the quantity of pressure and provocation upon it, he rather strove to impress upon him a higher notion than ever of the severity and trial of the conflict now before him. In proportion to the quantity of labour required at his hands, did his spirit rise to overcome it; and Singleton, after a few moments' conversation with him, had the satisfaction to see his countenance brighten up, while his eye flashed enthusiasm, and his soul grew earnest for the strife.

"You shall have the place under my own eye: and mark me, Lance, that eye will be upon you. I will give you a distinct duty to perform, and trust that it shall be done well."

"I'll try, sir," was the modest answer, though his doubts of his own capacity were sensibly decreasing. The time was at hand. however, which was to bring his courage into exercise and trial, and to put to the test that strength of mind which he had been himself disposed to underrate. One of the scouts charged with the intelligence by Humphries now came in, bringing tidings of the tories. They were computed to amount to eighty men; but of this the scouts could not be certain, as, in obedience to the orders of his commander, Humphries had not ventured so nigh as to expose himself to discovery. He computed the prisoners in their charge, men, women, and children, to be quite as numerous.

Singleton, on the receipt of this intelligence, looked closely to the preparations which he had made for their reception, saw that his men were all in their places, and went the rounds, addressing them individually in encouragement and exhortation. This done, he took the young beginner, Lance Frampton, aside, and leading him to the shelter of a thick bush at the head of the little hillock, he bade him keep that position in which he placed him, throughout all the events of the contest. This position commanded a view of the whole scene likely to be the theatre of conflict. The partisan bade him survey it closely.

"There is the spring, Lance—there—in short rifle distance. How far do you call it?"

"Thirty yards, sir."

"Are you a sure shot at that distance?"

"Dead sure, sir;" and he raised the rifle to his eye, which Sin gleton handed him.

"Your hand trembles, boy."

"Yes, sir; but I'm not afraid; I'm only anxious to begin."

"Keep cool; there's no hurry, but time enough. Throw off your jacket—give me your rifle. There—now roll up your sleeves and go down to the spring—plunge your arms up to their pits into the cool water a dozen times, until I call you. Go."

The boy went; and before he returned, Humphries rode in with accounts of the near approach of Gaskens and his tories. Singleton called up his pupil from the spring, and continued his directions.

"Take your place here, by the end of the log; don't mind your jacket—better off than on. Our men, you see, are ranged on either side of you. They can see *you* as easily as you can see them."

This sentence was emphatically uttered, while the piercing glance of Singleton was riveted upon the now unfaltering countenance of the boy.

"Below you is the spring, and in that shade the tories will most probably come to a halt. They will scarcely put their prisoners under cover, for fear they should escape; and they will be likely to remain at the opening there to your left—there, just by those tallow bushes. Now, observe: I am about to trust to you to commence the affair. Upon you, and your rifle shot, I depend greatly. Don't raise it yet: let it rest in the hollow of your arm until you are ready to pull trigger, which you will do the moment you hear me say, 'Now!' I will not be far from you, and will say it sufficiently loud for *you* to hear. The moment you hear me, lift your piece, and be sure to shoot the man, whoever he may be, that may happen to stand upon the rise of the hill, just above the spring, and under the great oak that hangs over it. It is most probable that it will be Gaskens himself, the captain of the tories. But no matter who he is, shoot him : aim for the man that stands on the hillock, and you *must* hit an enemy. You will have but a single fire, as our men will follow your lead, and in the next moment we shall charge. When you see us do so, slip round by the tallow bushes, and cut loose the ropes that tie the prisoners. These are your duties; and remember, boy, I shall see all your movements. I shall look to you, and you only, until the affair commences. Be in no hurry, but keep cool: wait for the word, and don't even lift your rifle until you hear me give the signal. Remember, you have a duty to perform to yourself and country, in whose cause your life to-day begins.'

The boy put his hand upon his heart, bowed his head, and made no other reply ; but his eye glistened with pride ; and as the partisan moved away, he grasped his rifle, threw his right foot back a pace, as if to feel his position, then, sinking quietly behind the bush, prepared himself as firmly for the contest as if he had been a veteran of sixty

CHAPTER XXX;

" And war shall have its victims, and grim death
   Grow surfeit with his prey. The signal soon,
   That marks the feast prepared, their ears shall note
   A sound of terror—and the banquet spread,
   Shall call the anxious appetite that see?
   And gloats upon its garbage from afar."

SILENCE and a deep anxiety hung like a spell above the ambuscading party. The woods lay at rest, and the waters of the
fountain trickled quietly, as if Peace lay sleeping in their neighbourhood, and Security watched over her. So well had Singleton
made his arrangements, and so cautiously had his plans been executed, that no necessity existed for bustle or confusion. Each
trooper had his duty as carefully assigned him as the boy Frampton ; and all of them, taking direction from their gallant leader,
lay still in the close shadow of the thicket, silent as the grave, and
only awaiting the signal which was to fill its unfolding jaws.

They waited not long before the advance of the tories appeared
in sight ; then came the prisoners—a melancholy troop—men,
women and children ; and then the main body of the marauders,
under Gaskens, bringing up the rear. In all, there was probably
over a hundred persons ; an oddly assorted and most miscellaneous
collection, with nothing uniform in their equipment. They were
not British, but tories ; though here and there the gaudy red coat
probably a tribute of the battle field, was ostentatiously worn by an
individual, upon whom, no doubt, it conferred its own character,
and some of that authority which certainly would have been possessed by its owner were he a Briton. The present troop of banditti
—for, as yet, they could be styled by no other more proper epithet
—was one of the many by which the country was overrun in every
direction. Banding together in small squads, the dissolute and the
wicked among the native and foreign thus availed themselves of the

distractions of the war to revenge themselves upon old enemies, destroy the property they could not appropriate, and, with the sword and the rope, punish the more honest, or the more quiet for that pacific forbearance which they themselves were so little disposed to manifest. In every section of the province these squads were continually forming. In one night, ten, twenty, thirty, or more, would collect together, and by a sudden and impetuous movement, anticipating all preparations, would rush with fire and sword upon their whig neighbours, whose first knowledge of the incursion would be the brand in the blazing barn, or the bullet driven through the crashing pane. They shot down, in this manner, even as he sat with his little circle at the family fireside, the stout yeoman who might have defended or avenged them. The arm of the law was staid by invasion, and the sanction of the invaders was necessarily given, under all circumstances, to the party which claimed to fight in their behalf. The tory became the British ally, and the whig his victim accordingly; and to such a degree were the atrocities of these wretches carried, that men were dragged from the arms of their wives at midnight, and suffered for their love of country in the sight of wife and children, by dying in the rope, and from their own roof trees.

Of this character was the body of tories, under Amos Gaskens, now rapidly approaching the place of ambush. They had formed themselves on the Williamsburgh line, chiefly the desperadoes and outcasts from that quarter, and had chosen among themselves an appropriate leader in Gaskens, of whom we are told by the historian, that even before the war he had been notorious for his petty larcenies. From this quarter they had passed into St. Johns, Berkley, marking their progress everywhere with havoc, and stopping at no atrocity. Such employment was not less grateful to themselves than to their new masters, to whom they thought- it likely, and indeed knew, that it must commend them. Gaskens aimed more highly, indeed, than nis neighbours. He had already been honoured with a British captaincy—he desired a still loftier commission; and the recklessness of his deeds was intended still further to approve him in the sight of those from whom he hoped to receive it. If the atrocities of Tarleton resulted in his promotion and honour, why not like atrocities in Amos Gaskens? Reason might well ask, why not since, in cruelty, they were fair parallels for one another.

The prisoners brought with Gaskens were chiefly taken from the parish of St. Johns, Berkley. One family, consisting of a man named Griffin, his wife, and daughter, a tall, good looking girl, about seventeen, were closely watched, apart from the rest of the captives, by a guard especially assigned for this purpose. The taking of this man had cost the tory two of his best soldiers, and he had himself been wounded in the arm by a stroke from Griffin's sabre. Griffin had fought desperately against his captors; and an old grudge between himself and Gaskens had stimulated them both, the one to desire his capture, the other to resist, even unto death, the effort of his enemy. The result, so far, has been shown. Griffin tried to escape at the approach of the tory, but the back track to the neighbouring swamp had been intercepted by Gaskens, who knew the route, and three of his men who went there in advance to watch it; while the main body of the troop pressed forward to the cottage. It was there that the flying man encountered them, and the fight was desparately waged before they conquered him. This did not happen until, as we have said, two of his dastardly assailants had fallen beneath his good sword and vigorous arm. He pressed Gaskens himself backward, and would have probably slain him and escaped, but for the aid of other tories coming on him from behind.

Though not seriously wounded in the fray, Griffin had been much chopped and mangled. A large seam appeared upon his thigh, and there were two slight gashes over his cheek, not so deep as ugly. Conquered at last, his hands were bound, and, with his family, he was made to attend his captors on foot. The manly resistance which he had offered to his enemy, instead of securing him respect, exposed him only to the most torturing irritations in his progress with them. Before his eyes, they hurled the brand into his little cottage, and he saw the fierce flames in full mastery over his little homestead, long before they had left the enclosure. In spite of his wounds and injuries, the sturdy fellow maintained a stout heart, and showed no sign of despondency; but, bearing

ANTIPATHY. 383

himself as boldly as if he were not the victim but the victor, he defied the base spirit of his conqueror, and with an eye that spoke all the feeling of the fiercest hatred, he looked the defiance which, at that time, he had no better mode of manifesting.

Nor was the feeling of Gaskens towards his prisoner a jot less malignantly hostile than that of Griffin. There was an old grudge between them—such a grudge as is common to the strifes of a wild and but partially settled neighbourhood. They had been neighbours—that is to say, they dwelt on contiguous plantations — but never friends. For many years they lived in the same district, seeing each other frequently, but without intercourse. This was entirely owing to Griffin, who disliked Gaskens, and studiously withheld himself from all intimacy with him. Griffin was an industrious farmer—Gaskens the overseer for the Postell estate. Griffin was a sober, quiet man, who had been long married, and found his chief enjoyment in the bosom of his family. Gaskens loved the race-turf and the cockpit, and his soul was full of their associations. It is the instinct of vice to hate the form of virtue, or that habit which so nearly resembles her, as to desire no exciting indulgences, no forced stimulants, no unwonted and equivocal enjoyments. Griffin sought for none of those pleasures which were all-in-all to Gaskens, and the other hated him accordingly.

But there were yet other causes for this hostility, in the positive rejection of his proffered intimacy, which Griffin had unscrupulously given. Though but a small farmer, with means exceedingly moderate, the sense of self-respect, which industry brought with it to his mind, taught him to scorn and to avoid the base outrider, and the dishonest overseer of the neighbouring plantation. Words of strife, more than once, had fallen between them, but not with any serious rupture following. Gaskens, finally, removed to another plantation somewhat further off, and all acquaintance ceased between them. There he pursued his old courses; and at length, left without employ, as he had lost the confidence of all those whom he had served heretofore in his capacity of overseer, he had become the regular attendant of the tavern.

The arrival of the British forces, the siege and the surrender of Charleston, with the invasion of the state by foreign mercenaries, presented him with a new field for action ; and, with thousands of others, to whom all considerations were as nothing, weighed against the love of low indulgence, unrestrained power, and a profligate lust for plunder, he did not scruple to adopt the cause which was strongest, and most likely to procure him those objects for which his appetite most craved. He became a furious loyalist, mustered his party, and became the assessor of his neighbours' estates. The fortune which threw into his hands the person of Griffin revived the old grudge; and the stout defence made by his prisoner, determined him upon a measure but too often adopted in that saturnalia of crime, the tory warfare in Carolina, to excite much attention or provoke many scruples in the party employing it. With a spiteful malignity which belongs to the vulgar mind, he.had ridden along by the side of his captive; and finding, as he rode, that the presence of his wife and daughter was a consolation still, he ordered them to the rear with the other prisoners, not permitting them to approach, or even to speak with him. As thus he rode he taunted his captive with low remark and insolent sneer at his present fortune, compared with his own, and with the past. The wounded man, with his hands tied behind him, could only demonstrate his scorn by an occasional sentence from his lips, while his eye, gleaming with the collected vengeance of his heart, spoke well what the other might expect, were they only permitted a fair field and equal footing for contest. It was when they had reached the immediate precincts of the spring, that the intercourse between them had reached the extremest point of savage malignity on the one hand, and fierce defiance on the other.

" Yes, you d—d rebel," continued Gaskens, " you see what's come of your obstinacy and insolence. You fly in the face of the king and refuse to obey his laws; and now you have your pay. By G—d, but it does my heart good to see you in this pickle."

"Coward! if I could lay hands on you but for two minutes— only two minutes, Amos Gaskens—and by the Eternal, chopped up as I am, you should never have it in your power to say again to an honest man what you have said to me."

" Two minutes, do you say ?" said the other—" two minutes ? You shall have two minutes, Griffin—two minutes, as you ask; but they shall be for prayer, and not for fighting. I remember you of old—I have forgotten nothing—and you shall pay off to-day a long score that's been running up against you. You remember when I was overseer to John Postell, and you gave me to know you didn't want to see me at your house, though that was a log-house like my own? I wasn't good enough for you, nor for yours, eh? What do you say now?"

"The same. I hold you worse now than I did then. And then I didn't despise you because you were poor, for, as you say, I was poor myself; but because I thought you a rascal, and since then I know'd it. You are worse now."

"Talk on—I give you leave to talk, you d—d rebel—and that's a mercy you don't deserve; but I have you in my power, and it won't be long you'll have to talk. I wonder what your pride comes to now, when I, Amos Gaskens, who wasn't good enough for you and your daughter, have only to say the word, and it's all dicky with both of you. You yourself—you can't stir a hand but at my orders; and look there—that's your wife and daughter—and what can you do for 'em, if I only gives the word to the boys to do their likes to them?"

"Oh! villain! oh! monster! If I only had my arms free and a we'pon in my hand!" cried the prisoner, vainly struggling with his bonds. But he writhed in them in vain. The tyrant looked down upon him from his horse with a grin of delight which completed the fury of the victim, until he rushed, though with a fruitless vengeance, against the sides of the animal, idly expending his strength in an innoxious and purposeless effort against his persecutor. A blow from the hilt of his sabre drove him back, while, as he reeled among the troop, a shriek from the wife and daughter in the rear, at the same moment, announced their consciousness of the whole proceeding.

"Two minutes you shall have, my boy—two minutes, as you asked for them," said Gaskens to the prisoner, as they now approached the spring.

"Two minutes—for what?" he inquired.

"For prayer—and quite long enough for one that's passed so good a life as you," was the sneering reply.

" What do you mean ?" was the farther inquiry of the prisoner

Gaskens pointed to the huge oak that surmounted the spring,
and at the same moment a corporal approached with a rope, the
running noose of which—as this agent was frequently in requisition
—was already made, and now swung ostentatiously in his hands.

"Great God ! Amos Gaskens, wretch as you are, you do not
mean to murder me ?"

"May I be totally d—d if I do not. You shall hang to that
tree in two minutes after I say the word, or there are no snakes."

"You dare not, ruffian. I claim to be a prisoner of war—I ap
peal to the troop."

"Appeal and be d—d. My troop know better than to disobey
the orders of a lawful officer in commission of his majesty ; and as
for your being a prisoner of war, that's a lie. You are a murderer,
and I have proof enough of it. But that's neither here nor there.
I will answer for all I have done to the commander of the Dorchester post, and if you can make him hear your voice at this distance, you have a better pipe than my rope has touched yet—
that's all. So, to your prayers, while I take a sup of this water.
Here, boy, hold the bridle."

The wretch descended, and the boy reined up the steed, while
Gaskens strode onward to the spring. The corporal approached
the doomed victim, and was about to pass the loop over his head
but he resisted by every effort in his power.

"Great God !—but this is not in earnest ? Hear me, Amos
Gaskens—hear me, man ! Monster ! are you not ashamed to sport
in this way with the feelings of my poor wife and child ?"

Gaskens looked round contemptuously, but still strode onward,
as he replied—" Do your duty, corporal, or blast me but I run you
up, though I have to do it myself. You shall know, Wat Griffin,
whether I am not good enough for your d—d log-cabin now, or not.
Two minutes, corporal—only two minutes, and a short cord—remember—two minutes, I say—no more."

With the assistance of two of the tory squad, Griffin was thrown
upon his back, and lay struggling upon the ground, while the rope
was adjusted to his neck.

"My wife ! my child !—let them come to me, Amos Gaskens—.

let them see me, Gaskens—man or devil! Will you not suffer them to come to me?—let me see and speak to them, I pray you!"

"They will see you better when you are lifted up! Be quick—say your prayers, man, and lose no time. One minute is almost gone already. Make the most of the other."

The ruffian spoke with the coolest indifference, while mixing a gourd of spirits and water at the spring. This done, he ascended the hill, bearing the liquor in his hand, and bade the execution proceed. They hauled the victim by the rope up the little rising, and towards the tree, almost strangling him before he reached the spot. In the meanwhile the air was rent with the shrieks of his wife and daughter in the rear, who were pressed back with the other prisoners, the guard keeping them back from any approach to the doomed man, then about to be separated from them for ever. He cried to them by name, in a thick, choking voice, for the rope was now drawn, by the party hauling him along, with a suffocating tightness.

"Ellen!—Ellen, my wife! Oh, Ellen, my poor child! Amos Gaskens—God remember you for this! Oh, Ellen! God help me! Have you no mercy, monster—none?" He screamed to his murderer, in agony—and in vain!

"Father, dear father!" cried the girl.

The mother had simply stretched forth her hands as she beheld the threatened movement, and, overpowered by her emotions, had fallen senseless in the effort to speak. The daughter strove to rush forward, but the strong-armed sentinel rudely thrust her back with a heavy hand, and pressed her down with the rest of the prisoners, who had been made to file into the grove of tallow bushes, which the prescience of Singleton had already assigned them.

Gasping, but struggling to the last, the victim had been already drawn up by his executioner within a few feet of the broad limb stretching over the spring, which was to serve the purpose of a gallows; and the brutal leader of the party, standing upon the little eminence —the liquor in hand, which he was stirring, yet untasted—had already declared the time to be elapsed which he allowed to the prisoner for the purposes of prayer, when, distinctly and clear, the voice of Singleton was heard—above the shrieks of the daughter—above the hoarse cries of the prisoner in parting to his wife—above all the bustle of the transaction. The single word, as given to the boy Frampton, was uttered ; and, in the next instant, came the sharp, thrilling crack of the rifle, fatally aimed, and striking the legitimate victim. The body of Gaskens, between whose eyes the bullet had passed—the word unspoken—the draught in his hand untasted—tumbled forward, prostrate, immovable, upon the form of his reprieved victim, whom—still struggling, but half strangled—the corporal had just dragged beneath the fatal tree.

CHAPTER XXXVI.

'Too long a laggard, he hath stood,
Until the hearth w~~ drenched in blood,
Until the tyrant grew
All reckless, in his bloody game;
The cities proud, he wrapped in flame,
Their brave defenders slew."

THE young partisan, Frampton, to whom Singleton had intrusted
so leading a part in the enterprise, had well fulfilled the duty
assigned him. He put himself in readiness with the first appearance of the marauders; and, with a heart throbbing with anxiety
all the while, witnessed impatiently the progress of the preceding
scene, until broken by the emphatic utterance of the signal, and
his own prompt obedience to its dictates. Then, with an instinct,
which in that moment silenced and stilled the quick pulsations of
his breast, he raised the deadly weapon to his shoulder; and, with
a determined coolness that arose, as it were, from a desire to convince himself, not less than his commander, that he could be firm,
he twice varied his aim, until perfectly assured, when he drew the
trigger, and most opportunely singled out a different victim from
the one whom Gaskens had contemplated for the fatal sisters, in
the person of that foul murderer himself.

There was a moment of dreadful pause after this event. The
rope fell from the hands of the executioner, and his eyes, and the
eyes of all, were turned in doubt and astonishment upon the quarter from whence the deadly missile had proceeded. The condemned
man seized the opportunity to throw from his body the lifeless
carcase of the slain tory; and not doubting that further aid was at
hand, and looking for a closer struggle between the parties, in
which his condition did not suffer him to hope to share, he crawled
along the hill for shelter to the neighbouring tree. His effort was
interrupted; for, in the next moment, another and another shot

17

selected their victims; then came the full volley; and then the loud voice of Singleton, as, plunging through the copse, he led the way for his men, who charged the confused and terrified tories on every side.   They scarcely showed sign of fight.   One or two offered resistance boldly, and with as much skill as resolution; but they were soon overpowered, as they received no support from their comrades, who were now scampering in the bushes in every direction.   The surprise had been complete; not a man was seriously hurt among the whigs, while every rifle, fired in the first of the fray, had told fatally upon its victim.   Seven were slain outright, a few more sabred, and some few were made prisoners—the rest took the back track into the woods, and though pursued, contrived, with few exceptions, to make their escape.

The boy, Lance, meanwhile, had well performed the other duty which had been given to his charge.   The conflict, pellmell, had scarcely begun, when, slipping noiselessly round to the hollow where the prisoners were confined, so as not to arouse the notice of the two sentinels having them in custody—and whose eyes were now turned in surprise upon the unlooked-for contest—he cut the cords which bound them; and, prompt as himself, they were no sooner free, than they seized upon their guards and disarmed them. The ropes were transferred to other hands than their own.   This was all the work of an instant; so, indeed, was the affray itself; and the first object that met the eyes of Singleton as he returned from the charge to the spot where it first began, was the person of the boy, Lance, bending over the man he had shot, and curiously inspecting the bullet-hole which he had made through and through his forehead.

"Ha, Lance!" said Singleton; "you have done well—you have behaved like a man."

Lance Frampton looked the picture of the personification in the ode of Collins, where Fear

> "— recoils, he knows not why,
> Even at the sound (*wound*) himself hath made."

"What do you wonder at, Lance?" demanded Singleton.

"Oh! sir, I can scarcely believe that this was the same man"—

pointing to the body—" who was swearing so dreadfully but a minute ago; and it was *my* rifle that made this awful bullet-hole !"

" A good shot, Lance, and at the right moment!"

" Ah ! sir, but how terrible to think ! He was swearing dreadfully at the very moment when I pulled trigger, and it was my hand that stopped his mouth, full as it was of curses; and he's gone—gone where ? Oh ! sir, I do feel so strange !"

" The thought is a sincere and solemn one, Lance, that of sending a fellow creature to judgment, while his mouth is full of curses ! But how else could we have saved his worthier victims—the poor captives—the wretched father whom he was about to hurry out of life ?"

" Yes, sir, that's true ; and how fearful I was lest you wouldn't say the word ' now' soon enough to let me save him. Oh ! I felt so eager to shoot; but I'm afraid it was a wrong feeling. It makes me feel very strange, sir, to feel that I have killed a man—and one so much older than myself. What would poor mother say, if she was alive and knew it !"

How many secret avenues to the boy's nature, and his mother's training, were laid open to Singleton's eyes, with these words of boyhood. But the time was not favourable to philosophy.

" Enough, now, Lance, that you have done your duty, as you were bid—that you slew this miserable creature in a good cause, and for the safety of more innocent people. Let that content you. You will soon get over all that is strange in your emotions. One rifle shot will cover another. Go now, put on your jacket, and think no more of the matter."

" Ah !" murmured the boy, upon whom new and only half revolting experiences were rapidly dawning,—" ah ! I can't help thinking of it ! I have taken the life of a man ! What would mother say, if she was alive and knew ?"

He moved slowly to the copse where he had thrown down his rifle and jacket, his thoughts wandering wide from his immediate objects, while, to his eyes, the whole atmosphere, sky, and wood, seemed bathed in a deep crimson dye, that showed the sort of passion that was taking possession of his brain. Ah ! how rapidly may the pure young soul of innocence—the path once open, the first step taken—become bloody with sanguine tide, from a heart whose billows but too quickly rise, and swell above the brain, and. sweep away all its landmarks of justice, and love, and mercy! That first lesson in the work of strife—that first blow struck, which tears the life away from the heart of the victim! Alas! how easy afterwards to wade out deep in the sea of battle, and find a tumultuous joy in sounding through its red and raging billows, forgetting, so easily, with what reluctance and horror, at first, we prepared for the deed, and approached to the performance of the fearful work of death.

But we are not permitted to linger only on the gloomier and more revolting aspects of the picture. It has other scenes, which justify the work, if they cannot wholly reconcile us to its more fearful results. Let us turn, with Singleton, to another quarter of the scene of this little skirmish. The group which now meets his eyes amply compensate, by the innocent joy which they feel, by the glad sense of escape which they share together, for all that has been painful and oppressive in the trial he has just gone though. There we see the freed captives, rescued by the blow which destroyed the murderous tory, and dispersed his band— there rise the wretched prisoners, trembling but a moment before with terrors worse than death, to the consciousness of life, safety, and liberty! The beaten and bound man stands erect. He has shaken off his pangs of body, in the feeling of his new sense of safety for himself and kindred—his wife and little ones. Oh! what compensation to the gallant soldier is that cry, that cheer of joy, and thanks, and gratulation, from every lip, of that recently doomed and trampled circle! They hail their deliverer—they cling around him—tears are in their eyes, the most expressive utterance of their joys; and murmurs and shouts, on all sides, attest the new consciousness of delight and freedom which they feel.

Conspicuous among these poor captives, in the sudden revulsion of their feelings, growing upon the new and fortunate change in their condition, is the family of the brave but greatly suffering man whom Gaskens had singled out as the especial victim of his malignant power. He had escaped the halter, but how narrowly! But where is he now! Scarcely had the strife ceased, when the wife ot Griffin, whom the tender cares of the daughter had recovered from her swoon, was seized with new apprehensions and anxieties. She had been told that the seasonable ambush of Singleton had rescued her husband from the rope; but a new terror filled hei soul, as, when the skirmish ceased, her husband did not appear. She ran through the crowd of captives and partisans, crying aloud his name. For a moment, a silent dread filled all hearts, as the woods returned no answer. Wildly the woman was about to rush away into the thickets, the daughter following, when she felt a pair of strong arms thrown around her. Blinded by her tears and fears, she could see nothing; but she heard a voice—but a single word, and her arms were thrown around the neck of the brave man, and she sobbed convulsively.

'Oh! Wat! oh! Wat! I haven't lost you, Wat."

" No! no! Ellen! no! Not this time."

And the girl clung about him, with her one word also—thrice and thrice repeated—" Oh! Father! my dear, dear father!"

Singleton was a strong man, not much given to the melting mood, but the tears, spite of himself, grew into his eyes as he surveyed the simple, touching, wordless embraces of these poor, fond people, and beheld the deep sorrowful sweetness of the rapture they enjoyed—the rapture which is kin to agony—the pleasure which grows into a very pain, in the extreme of its intensity.

" Oh! are you indeed safe, my husband? Tell me true, Wat Griffin, is there no more danger?"

" Safe! safe! Ellen! Thanks to these brave men. We are all safe from this danger."

" And you—you are not hurt badly?"

" Spurred only—riled a little, back and sides; but sound at the core, and tough enough to do mischief to the enemy when they give me but a chance."

" And that cruel Gaskens!" said the woman, with a shudder, looking round her as she spoke, as if still dreading the power of the tory.

" The wretch is on his back. God bless the bullet that came in time, and the true hand that sent it."

" And we are free, my father; free to go home again—to our own home ?" said the daughter, as she took the hand of her father in both of her own.

" Home ! where is it ?" he exclaimed fiercely, and with the same savage expression with which his eyes had regarded Gaskens, even in the moment of his greatest danger. " Where is it ? Did you not see the blaze through the trees, as we looked back ? Did he not throw the torch into the loft with his own accursed hands ? and yet you ask for our home   We have no home, girl "

" But we are free, my husband, we are free. You will go to work—we will soon have another in the old place, we can build a log-house in a short time."

" Never, never ! I do no such folly. What ! to be burned down again by other tories ?—no, no ! I am chopped already—I cannot be chopped much worse, and live ; and if I must suffer, let me suffer with those who will help me to strike, too, and to revenge my wrongs ! I will burn too ; I will kill too. I will have blood for what I have lost, and the sufferings of others shall pay me for my own and yours."

Singleton approached at this moment, and the prisoners, so lately freed, gathered around him. Each had his own story of affliction to tell, and each more mournful than the other.

"They chased me, it mought be a matter of three miles, 'fore I gin up, captain, and they wore out a bunch of hickories on my back, becaise I run—jest see the marks," was the complaint of one. Another had his tale of petty treachery : his neighbour who had eaten a hundred times of his bacon and hoecake, had come in the night time, shot down his cattle, and, finally, led the tories to his door to butcher him. Another had his wife shot in her bed, in mistake for himself, while he was traversing the swamp to make his escape. And so on—one with a tale of simple cruelty, one with a burning, another with a murder, and some with even more atrocious crimes—each of the prisoners had his own and his family's sufferings, at the hands of the bloodthirsty tories, to narrate to their deliverer.

Singleton administered his consolations, and put arms into their hands. The greater number of them joined him ; those who did not, receiving the upbraidings, in no stinted measure, of those who did. The lately doomed prisoner, Griffin, seized upon a broad-sword—a massive weapon, which had fallen from the hands of a huge-limbed tory—and proffered himself among the first. His wife laid her hand upon his arm—

"Oh, husband, you are not a-going to join the soldiers? You are not going a-fighting?"

He looked sternly upon her, and shook away her grasp with indignation.

"Ay, but I am! you shan't keep me from my duty any longer. I wanted to come out six months ago, but you tried the same game over me, and I was fool enough to mind you, and see how it's turned out. Our cattle shot—the house burnt—the farm destroyed —and me chopped up, and almost hung; and all owing to you."

The woman sank back at the reproach. The girl came between them. She only said :

"Oh, father!"

The tearfully bright eyes of the girl did the rest. He felt their reproach; and more deeply when the girl turned to the sad and stricken mother, and with arms about her neck, murmured—

"He don't mean it, mother; it's only because he's wild with the fighting. He don't mean what he says."

But there was a truth at the bottom of Griffin's reproaches, though the blame was rather his than his wife's. If the fears of the woman kept him back unwisely from his duties, the weakness was his. But without meaning unkindness, and only desiring to declare his new resolution, Griffin answered the apologetic speech of his daughter in a rough fashion.

"I do mean it! I do mean it! She whined, and begged, and cried, and kept me back, until the bloody varmints overcrowed us at every turn. She shall keep me back no longer. I say to you, major, here's an arm, and here's a sword. To be sure the arm's chopped, and the owner is ragged with cuts and scratches; but no matter, they're true blood, and, by G—d, it's at your service for old Carolina. Put me down in your orderly book as one of your men, as long as the troop holds together. Wat Griffin is one of your men, and one of Marion's men, and one of all men that are enemies to the tories."

The man was resolute, and his wife spared all farther speech. She knew how unavailing was the woman's pleading against the stern will of the man, once determined upon. She clung to his arm, however ; and it could be seen, in that moment of reserve and of doubt, of trying adventure and long fatigue rising up before them, that the firmness of her resolution to share his fortunes was equal to that which had determined him upon them.

An hour's labour buried the bodies of the men who had fallen in the conflict. The recruits were well armed from the hands of those who had perished and become prisoners ; and, with a troop now grown to a respectable size from the acquisitions of the morning, Singleton prepared for his farther progress. The men were soon mounted, some riding double—as the number of horses was not now equal to that of the partisans. The prisoners were driven along before them ; and rather more slowly than they otherwise would have marched, not thus embarrassed, our little corps of patriots was soon in motion. Singleton led the march at a gentle pace—the boy, Frampton, as had latterly been his wont, taking his place and keeping close alongside of his commander.

CHAPTER XXXVII

" And subtle the design, and deep the snare,
And various the employ of him who seeks
To spoil his fellow, and secure himself "

CERTAINLY, man is never so legitimately satisfied, as when in the realization of his own powers. The exercise of those attributes which make his nature, is the duty that follows his creation; and it is only when he exceeds the prescribed limit, and runs into excess, that he suffers and is criminal. How various are these powers— how extensive their range—how superior their empire! Creative, destructive, perceptive—all co-operating for the same end—the elevation of his own capacities and condition. They are those of a God—however subordinate—and they prove his divinity. Balanced duly, each in its place, and restrained as well as promoted by its fellow, he deserves to be, and most probably will be, happy. But, whether the balance be preserved or not, the discovery, on his part, of any one of these powers, must have the effect of elevating him in his own thought, and giving him pleasure accordingly. Sometimes, indeed, to such a degree does its realization delight him, that he maddens and gluttonizes in its enjoyment—he gloats upon it: and, from a natural attribute, cherished for a beneficial purpose, and forming a necessary endowment, it grows into a disease, and preys upon its master.

Such is that love of enterprise which sometimes leads to ungenerous conquest; such that stern desire of justice which sometimes prompts us, in defence of our own rights, not to scruple at unnecessary bloodshed. In the pursuit of both, the original purpose is soon lost sight of. We gauge not our revenges in measure with the wrongs we suffer; and the fierce excitements which grow out of their prosecution, become leading, if not legitimate, objects of pursuit themselves. The conquest of new countries, to this day, at

17*

whatever expense of blood and treasure, is scarcely criminal in the eyes of civilize⁂ and Christian man ; and where conscience does suggest a scruple, the doubt is soon set aside in the gracious consideration of those vast benefits which we assume to bring to the people, whose claims we despise, and whose lands and lives we appropriate. Yet is the enterprise itself legitimate, according to our nature ; and the sense of resistance to injustice and oppression is a virtue that could not be dispensed with. They form vital necessities of our condition, but only while we keep them subordinate to our virtues and necessities. The misfortune is that we pamper them, as we do favourite children, till they rise at last into tyrants, and change places with us.

The boy Frampton had undergone a change which did not escape the eye of Singleton as he rode beside him. The lively laugh had left his countenance, the gentle play of expression had departed from his rich, red, and well chiselled mouth, and in place of them the eye was kindled with a deep glare of light, lowering and strong, while the lips curled into a haughty loftiness becoming the lord of highest station. A vein that crossed his forehead was full almost to bursting, and his brow lowered with an expression that indicated feelings, even then warmly active with the brief scene of strife through which they had so recently passed. The boy was a boy no longer ; he had realized one of the capacities of manhood ; he had slain his man ; he had taken one step in revenging the murder of his mother ; he had destroyed one of the murderers ; but, more than all—he had taken human life.

Something of a higher feeling than this was at the same time working in his bosom. Though previously untaught, he had learned too much of the struggle going on in the colonies, not to have acquired some knowledge of the abstract question upon which it depended ; and though his thoughts were all vague and indistinct on the subject, the rights of man, the freedom of the citizen, and the integrity of his country, he had learned to feel should all be among the first considerations, as their preservation was always the first care, of the true patriot. The furious popular discussions of the five preceding years had not been unheard by the youthful soldier · and its appeals were not lost upon one, who, in his own

family, had beheld such a bloody argument as had long since
taught him to illustrate by the real and actual those lessons which
otherwise might have floated through his mind as only so much
spirited declamation. His country entered into his thoughts, therefore, in due connexion with his feeling of the individual wrong
which he had sustained; and that personal feeling which prompted
the desire of revenge, was lifted higher, and rendered holier, by this
connexion. It became hallowed in his bosom, where it contemplated, not only the punishment of the wrong-doer, but the protection of the cottage-home—his own, and his people's—from the
injustice and the violence of the invader. It grew into a solemn
principle of action thus associated, and the moral abstraction over
which the unassailed citizen might have dreamed through a long
season of years, without duly considering its force or application,
became purely practical in the eyes of young Frampton—a feeling
of his heart, rather than a worked out problem of his understanding.
The thought grew active in following out the feeling; and Singleton, as the boy rode abstractedly beside him, revolving a thousand
new and strange sensations that were running through his mind,
regarded his countenance with a glance of melancholy rather than
approval. He saw that in his glance, which taught him the leading activity of his new emotions. The boy had a new sentiment
in his bosom, the contemplation of which made it eminently more
familiar. He could destroy—and he could do so without his own
rebuke. He could take the life of his fellow—and good men could
approve. He had penetrated a new world of thought, and he was
duly enamoured of his conquest ; and, even as we all desire to renew
the novelty, and partake a second time of the strange pleasure, so
the heart of the boy panted for a repetition of that indulgence
which had lifted him into premature manhood. The passions grew
active without the least countenance of reason to uphold them, and
this is the dangerous point in their history. Crime was made legitimate to him now, and the fruit once forbidden, was forbidden no
longer. He could now pluck with impunity—so he began to
think—and his mind was on that narrow eminence which divides
a duty from an indulgence—which separates the close approach of
a principle to an appetite—which changes the means into an end :

and, identifying the excuse for violence with an impelling motive
to its commission, converts a most necessary agent of life into a
powerful tyranny, which, in the end, runs riot, and only conquers
to destroy.

Singleton regarded his charge with a close attention, as he surveyed the unsophisticated emotions of his heart, plainly enough
written upon his face.   He read there all that was going on within ;
and his own heart smote him at the survey.   He thought of his
sister Emily, of her prayer for peace, her denunciation and her
dread of war ; and though he knew not yet of her death, the
thought that she might, even then, be a silent watcher from the
heavens, was enough to persuade him to an effort to quiet the fierce
spirit at work within the bosom of the boy.   He spoke ; and his
voice, modulated by grief into a tone as soft as that of a girl, smote
strangely upon the ear of his companion.   It was so different from
the wild strain of thought with which his mind was crowded.   A
note of the trumpet—the shriek and shout of advancing foemen—
had been far less discordant ; and the boy trembled as he heard
the simple utterance of his own name.

"Lance—Lance Frampton."

For a moment he was incapable of all reply.   The eye of Singleton was fixed upon him ; and when he met, and felt the look, he
seemed to understand the rebuking mood of his superior.   His
lips, which were rigidly compressed before, now separated—though
it was still with seeming difficulty that he answered—

"Sir !"

"Your father is not with us, boy ?"

"No, sir—I have not seen or heard him.   I don't think he'll
come out of the swamp, sir ; he loves the Cypress : though I reckon,
if he only knew we should have had some fighting so soon, I'm
sure, sir, he would be glad to come.   He loves to fight with the
tories, sir.   He always hated them, and more since mother's death
—them, and the dragoons."

"And you too, boy, seem to have acquired something more of
fondness for the sport than you had before.   You have learned also
to love to fight with the tories."

The words of Singleton were cold—rather stern, indeed ; and his glance was not calculated to encourage the stern passion which was growing so active in the breast of the boy. Lance felt the meaning of Singleton's tones and glances, and the disapprobation they conveyed; but the excitement in his bosom was too great to be brought into immediate subjection. His eye flashed and lightened, his lip quivered, closed firmly, then parted and quivered again, and his hand twisted convulsively the bridle of his steed.

"Oh, sir, I'm not afraid now. I know I shan't be afraid. I didn't know at first how I should feel in shooting at a man; but now, sir, I'm not afraid. I wanted to run in, sir, when you told the men to charge, but I had to go round and cut loose the prisoners; but I watched you all the time, sir; and I clapped my hands, sir—I couldn't help it—when I saw your sword go clean down through the tory's arm and into his head, in spite of all he could do. It was a great blcw, that, sir—a great blow; but I couldn't handle a sword so heavy."

There was something of a desponding earnestness in his tones, as this last regret was uttered, and Singleton surveyed, as some curious study, the face, so full of transitions, of the boy beside him. After the pause of a moment, in a calm, subdued voice, he said to him—

"You shall have a sword, Lance—a small one to suit your hand. But remember, boy, war is not a sport, but a duty, and we should not love it. It is a cruel necessity, and only to be resorted to as it protects from cruelty; and must be a tyranny, even though it shields us from a greater. It is to be excused, but not to be justified; and we should not spill blood, but as the spilling of blood is always apt to discourage the wrong-doer in those practices by which all men must suffer, and through which blood must be spilt in far greater quantity."

The boy looked on the speaker with an expression of astonishment which he did not seek to conceal. Singleton noticed the expression, and continued with his lesson. But it is not the youthful mind, full of spirit, and resolute in adventure, which will draw such nice distinctions as the partisan insisted on. The duty would be performed, doubtless, while it continued a pleasure; but when the pleasure to the mind survives the duty, it is not often that the

unregɩlated impulse can be persuaded to forbear. The boy replied
accordingly—

"Ah, sir, and yet I watched your face when you were fighting,
and you seemed glad to cut down your enemy, and your eye was
bright, and flashing with a joy, and your lip even laughed, sir—I
saw it laugh, sir, as plainly as I see it now : and then your shout,
sir, and your cry to ' charge'—Oh ! sir, it was like a trumpet."

"Still war is a duty only, and should not be made a pleasure,
Lance. It has its pleasures, as every duty must have ; but they
are dangerous pleasures, and not the less so because we can smile
when indulging in them. It is a sad reflection, boy, that we can
laugh when taking the life of a fellow-creature, and taking the life,
too, that we can never restore."

"Yet, sir, where can be the harm of killing a tory ? They don't
mind killing our people, and burning their houses, and driving off
their cattle. I wish I could kill a thousand of them."

Singleton looked again on the boy, and saw that he was nevei
more in earnest. He thought once more of his sister's pleadings,
and her fine eloquence in defence of humanity, while considering
this very subject. What a contrast ! But the one was on the
verge of the grave and of heaven, and her spirit attuned to the
divine and gentle influence of the abodes of bliss. The other was
on the verge of life—its storms yet to go through, and by them to
be purified, or never. No wonder that the mood was sanguinary.
The trial and the path before him seemed to call for it.

"Alight, boy," said Singleton, "and bring me a gourd of that
water, while the troop is coming up."

A branch ran across their path, and an opportunity was suggested to the partisan for a useful lesson to his charge. With
alacrity the youth alighted from his horse, and went to gather the
water, while Singleton waited the coming up of the long cavalcade
of troop and prisoners, women and children, behind.

The boy stooped over the clear streamlet which trickled without
a murmur over the road ; it gave back his features from its untrou-
bled mirror, and he started back from their contemplation. He
had never before seen that expression—the expression of triumph
in war, and a sanguinary desire for a renewal of its fierce and

feverish joys. The blood-shot eye, the corded vein, the wild and
eager expression, were all new and startling as new, to him who
had been the favourite of a mother, gentle to weakness, and foster-
ing him with a degree of sensibility almost hostile to manhood.

He dashed the gourd into the water, and hurried away with the
draught to his commander. Singleton barely looked upon him,
and the eye of the boy was turned instinctively from his gaze—but
for a moment, however. His firmness was soon restored, the strong
fire again filled it, and once more it met that of his superior
unshrinkingly. Singleton gave him back the vessel, and from that
moment felt assured of his nature. He saw that courage to desperation, and a love of the fight—that rapture of the strife, which
was the Hun's passion—were all working with a fiery ardour,
which no immaturity of strength, no inexperience, could keep
down or diminish. He waited till he was again mounted, and at
his side ; and he himself felt, in despite of his own exhortations, a
feverish sort of pleasure at seeing, so clearly depicted as they were
upon the face of the boy, the emotions of so bold and promising
a spirit.

By this time the lengthening files of the cavalcade had all contracted, and had overtaken the advance, where it had rested with
Singleton. Humphries, who had given his attention hitherto chiefly
to the prisoners and the rear, now rode up to his commander.
They conferred upon the subject of their next proceeding, and as
the evening was at hand, and there could be little prospect of their
reaching the Santee that night in time to cross it, burdened as they
were with baggage and prisoners, they had almost resolved to lie by
with the coming darkness ; but while they spoke, Davis, who had
been sent on ahead with the scouts, rode in with intelligence which
partially altered their determination.

" There are outriders, sir, that hang on our skirts, all well
mounted. We have had a glimpse at them through the bush, but
not to overhaul them. Once or twice, sir, we saw men peeping
out from the woods, sir, but though we pushed hard, they got shet
of us mighty quick, and we lost 'em. I only rode up to put you
on your guard, for I reckon there's more of 'em that we don't
see."

" 'Tis well: put out again, Davis, and do not let them escape you now if you can help it. We shall see to the troop."

Davis rode away, and Singleton proceeded to arrange his men for all circumstances.

" Close up, Humphries, and bring your prisoners into the centre see that they do not straggle, and let your men look to their arms. Put them in preparation for any chance."

Then calling to the front a squad of the better armed and mounted, the partisan extended his line on the advance, so as to throw a few troopers, on either hand, into the woods that skirted the road. It was not long after this that Davis, with the scouts, who had more than once detected a pair of keen eyes watching them from the distant copse, now came suddenly upon a country-man, who sat mending a bridle upon a log at the road-side. He did not seem much startled at their appearance, and his whole features wore an expression of the most approved simplicity and sang-froid. He made no movement until the scouts had actually surrounded him, then blurted out his astonishment with the cool est composure.

" Why, hello! now; but you block a fellow in, mighty like as ef you wanted to look at his teeth. What mought your wish be, stranger ?"

Thus addressing Davis, the countryman rose, and with an air half of doubt and half of defiance, confronted the new-comers. The Goose-Creeker looked on his big bones with admiration, for the man was huge of limb, though uncomely ; and the contrast between him and Davis was calculated at once to command atten-tion. The lieutenant, however, did not long delay his answer.

" Well, now, friend, our wish aint mighty hard to come at ; and the first question 1 hev to ax you, is after yourself. What may your name be, and what's your business ?"

The man chuckled incontinently for a moment, then recovering, and looking grave, he replied.—

" Look you, stranger, I never let a man poke fun at me twice on the same day ; so I give you fair warning. I'm all hell a'ter a varmint, and no tree your eyes ever looked on will come at all uigh to hide you, if I once sartainly set out to hunt you up. So.

now, you'll see it's a mighty ridiculous notion you have if you think to poke fun at Thumbscrew without paying for it."

" Well, Mr. Thumbscrew, if so be that's your true name, I'm much obliged to you for your civility in warning me about your ways. I've no doubt you're thought a big man in your part of the country; but I'm thinking they'd look at you for a mighty small one in mine. But that's not the business now. Big or little, Mr. Thumbscrew, there's too many upon you now to give you much chance, so the best way for you is to bear one dry scraping kindly, and that'll save you from two."

" What! won't you give a fellow fa'r play? Well, that's not so genteel, stranger. Fa'r play's a jewel, all the world over; and, man for man, or if so be you mought like it better, I'm not scrupulous to take two of you for a bout or so on the soft airth; but more than that'll be a leetle oncomfortable."

" We haint got time for that, friend," was the careless reply of Davis; " and all that we wants from you in the way of civility is jest to answer a few questions that we shall ax you."

" Well, ax away," was the half-surly reply—" ax away; but it wouldn't take too much time for a lift or two on the soft grass, I'm thinking."

" You say your name is Thumbscrew?"

" Yes, my boy-name; but at the christening they gin me another, that aint so easy to mention. The true name is John Wetherspoon, at your sarvice; but Thumbscrew comes more handy, you see, and them that knows me thinks it suits me better."

" Very well, Mr. Thumbscrew, or Wetherspoon—now, will you tell us what you're doing here in these parts at this time of day?"

" Well, that's jest as easy to larn now, sence you see I'm mending my bridle, and looking arter my critter that's been stolen, I reckon, by some thieving soldiers—saving your presence, and axing your pardon."

" What soldiers?"

" Why, how do I know! Sometimes they're one thing, and sometimes another; now they're whigs, and now they're tories. One time they're Gainey's, another time they're Marion's men, just as the notion suits 'em."

"And what are you? Are you a whig or tory?"

"Neither, thank God, for all his civilities and marcies. I'm a gentleman, and not a soldier, no how, I'll hev you to know."

"And where do you live when you're at home?"

"In the Big Bend, by Red Stone Hollow, close to the Clay Church. and right side of Black Heifer Swamp. My farm is called Hickory Head Place; and the parson who does our preaching is named Broadcast—he preaches through his nose, and has a way with him."

"What way?"

"Margery Way, what does his mending; all the parish knows her."

"Well, but I don't know any of these places or people you've been telling me about," said Davis.

"I reckoned as much. They say, though I've never been in them parts, that you folks, from low down by the sea, are most unmarcifully stupid."

"Humph! and how far are we here from the river?"

"A small chance of a run, if so be you mean the Santee. This morning, when I left it, it was ten miles off, but it's been running ever since; and God knows, stranger, I can't tell how far it's got to by this time."

"I'm jub'ous, Mr. Thumbscrew, that you're playing possum with me, after all; and if so be I find you at that work, I'll hang you, d—n my buttons, if I don't, by your own bridle, and no two ways about it, old fellow—how far is the Santee?"

"Well, now, you're mighty like getting in a passion, and that'll be quite too ridiculous. The Santee, now, if it stands still, you see, is jest about ten miles away to the right. It mought be more, and it mought be less, but it's tharabouts, if it stands where it ought; but I tell you it runs mighty fast; and thar's no knowing whar you may catch up with it, the next time you happen to find it."

"Ten miles—and what have you seen in the shape of men and soldiers about here? Have you secn any tories or any whigs? Marion's men, they say, are thick along the swamp."

"It's a bad business that, stranger, hunting after sodgers. I knows nothing about them. If I could only find Nimrod, now, stranger, you can't count up how little I'd care about all your big sword-men, tories or whigs, red coats or blue. Thar all the same to Thumby. They've stolen the nag, and may he ride to the ugly place with the rapscallion that straddles him, drop him fairly inside the door, and come back a minute after to Red Stone Hollow."

In this way, until Singleton's approach, did Davis seek, in vain, to obtain his information from the stranger. He communicated his ill success to his superior, and the incorrigible Thumbscrew was brought before him. The partisan surveyed him closely, and saw at a glance that the fellow, in southern phrase, had been "playing possum," and knew much more than he delivered. But the key was at hand, and the first words of Singleton unsealed the mystery.

" How are the owls, Thumbscrew ?"

" At roost, but ready for the moon," was the instant reply ; and every feature was full of awakening intelligence. Singleton ordered his men back, and conferred with him alone.

" The swamp fox is at hand—not moving ?"

"He waits for Major Singleton, and prepares for the continen tals ; but must lie close for the present, as the tories under Pyles, Huck, Tynes, and Harrison, are all around him."

" And how far are we now from Nelson's ?"

" Just nine miles, and the road clear, all but our scouts. Horry, with twenty men, scours to the left, and ten of us skirt the track to Nelson's, partly on the look out for you, sir, and partly for the tories."

" 'Tis well—you have a horse ?"

" Ay, sir, close in the wood."

" Shall we be able to reach the Santee before dark ?"

" Impossible, sir, with all your men ; but a detachment may, and nad better ride on to prepare for the rest. Colonel Marion is fast transferring the boats to the other side, and as the road is clear, sir, you would do best to spur forward with a few, while the ieute-nant brings up the remainder."

Desirous of securing the passage, Singleton adopted the counsel, and singling out a dozen of his best horse, he led the way with his new guide, and left Humphries to bring up the cavalcade.

CHAPTER XXXVIII

————— " thick woods,
Strange aspects, and the crowding things tha/ rove,
Peopling their deep recesses."

THE little force led by Singleton, in advance of his main body continued to make acquisitions at every step of its progress. The scouts of Marion, lining the woods at convenient intervals from each other, were soon notified of the approach of friends by the peculiar whistle which Thumbscrew employed; a whistle shrill in itself, and singularly modulated, which Marion's men were all taught to understand. They came out, one by one, from the bush; brought out their hidden horses, and each, answering to his *nom de guerre,* as it was called out by Thumbscrew, took his place along with the advancing party. There were Supple Jack and Crabstick, Red Possum and Fox Squirrel, Slickfoot and Old Ben; all men of make and mettle, trusty and true, and all of them, in after years, winning a goodly reputation in the land, which the venerable tradition, in sundry places, will " not willingly let die."

The river was now at hand, and Thumbscrew was required to give the signal to the scouts who were at watch along its banks. He did so, and the effect was admirable. From one bush to another, cover to cover, they all gave back the emulous sounds. The old cypress had a voice from its hollow, the green bush from its shade, and the shrill echoes rollingly arose from the crowding leaves of the thick tree that overhung the river, reverberating far away along its bosom. The signal was but once repeated, and all was still for a moment. Suddenly, the approaching troop heard the plash of paddles, the plunge of a horse in the water, and a quick, lively blast from the common horn, the sounds seeming to arise from the swamp on the opposite shore. Pushing his steed forward, and followed by his men, Singleton rode up to the bluff of the river, just as the last gay glimpses of the setting sun hung like so many rose-streaks upon its bosom, trembling to and fro like so much gossamer on the green edges of the gathering foliage.

And what a sight, in addition, was before their eyes! The surface of the river was strewn with boats of all sorts and sizes. A dozen or more, filled with the men of Marion, were in progress from one side of the stream to the other, while they towed behind them as many more, laden with live-stock and provisions—a large assessment having just been made upon the farmsteads of the neighbouring tories.

They had reached the centre of the stream, when the signal of the scouts struck their ears; and the quick command of their leader, the renowned partisan—for it was Marion himself who led them—arrested their further progress. He stood erect when the troopers rode up to the bank; and the eye of Singleton soon distinguished him from the rest.

Yet there was little in his appearance, to the casual spectator, to mark him out from his compatriots. His habiliments were not superior to theirs. They had borne the brunt of strife, and needed, quite as much as those of the rest, the friendly hand of repair and restoration. His person was small, even below the middle stature, and exceedingly lean and slender. His body was well-set, however, with the exception of his knees and ankles, which were thick, incompact, and badly formed. At this time, he rested almost entirely upon one leg—the other being at ease upon the gunwale of the boat. He still suffered pain in one of his limbs from a recent hurt; and in walking, an unpleasant limping movement was readily perceptible. His dress, as Singleton now beheld him, was one rather unusual for a commanding officer from whom so much was expected. It consisted of a close-bodied jacket, of a deep crimson colour, but of coarse texture. His smallclothes, of the fashion of the day, were badly conceived for such a figure. The free Turkish trowsers might have concealed those defects which the closely fitting fashions of the time rendered unnecessarily conspicuous. His were of a blue stuff, coarse like the jacket, and made with exceeding plainness, without stripe or ornament of any description, beyond the frog of his sword, the small cut-and-thrust which hung rather low at his side. A white handkerchief about his neck, wound loosely accorded strangely with the rest of his dress, and did not seem in its disposition, to have tasked much of the care of the wearer His uniform, if so it may be styled, was completed by the round leathern cap, forming a part of the dress which he wore when an officer in the second South Carolina regiment. It bore in front a silver crescent, with the words, "Liberty or death," inscribed beneath. He wore no plume, but in its place a white cockade, which was also worn by all his men, in order that they might be more readily distinguished in their night actions with the tories. Such was the garb and figure of the famous guerilla—the Swamp Fox—of Carolina.

The features of his face did not ill accord with the style of his garments. His skin was dark and swarthy; his eyes, black, piercing. and quick; his forehead, high, full, and commanding; his nose was aquiline; his chin bold and projecting, though not sharp; and his cheek sunken and deeply touched with the lines of thought. He was now forty-eight years of age—in the very vigour of his manhood—hardened by toil and privation, and capable of enduring every sort of fatigue. Cool and steady, inflexible, unshrinking; never surprised; never moving without his object, and always with the best design for effecting it, Marion, perhaps, of all the brave men engaged in the war of American liberty, was the one best calculated for the warfare of the partisan. His patriotism, wisdom, and fearlessness moved always together, and were alike conspicuous Never despairing of his cause, he was always cheerful in vicissitude and elastic under defeat. His mind rose, with renewed vigour, from the press of necessity; and every new form of trial only stimulated him to newer and more successful efforts. His moral and military character, alike, form the most perfect models for the young, that can be furnished by the history of any individual of any nation.

The paddles of the rowers were lifted as Singleton appeared in sight. The boats rested in the centre of the river, and, shading his eye with his hand, Marion closely noted the troop as its several members wound out of the woods and gathered along the bank. He did not need much time in the survey, before his keen eye singled out the persons of such of the new-comers as he had before known. His voice, strong, regular, and clear, though at the same time subdued and musical, was heard immediately after.

" Ah, Major Singleton, you are as prompt as ever. I rejoice to see you. You come in good season, though you seem but poorly accompanied."

A few words from Singleton explained the cause of his apparent weakness, and the orders of Marion were promptly given.

" Lieutenant Conyers, throw off the empty boats and put back after me in your own, leaving the spare ones. Take the whole of them, for the squad of Major Singleton will doubtless fill them all. McDonald, convey the rest to the camp, and let Oscar* bring Ball † with him. It may be difficult otherwise to get the strange horses over, and there is no flat."

With these, and a few other instructions, Marion led the way back to where Singleton with his troop awaited him ; and a few minutes only had elapsed when they stood once more together in close conference. The brief history of past events was soon given, and the major was delighted to meet with the unqualified approval of his superior. He learned from Marion that Col. Walton had gone forward to join with Gates only a few hours before his arrival, having being anxious to find active service at as early a time as possible. He had not endeavoured to dissuade him, as his was an independent commission ; though the determination of Marion himself, was to proceed with the same object in the same direction. His force, with the recruits brought by Singleton, was now something more respectable in numbers, if not in equipment. In arms and ammunition, not to speak of clothes and the usual equipages of camp and horse, they were miserably deficient; but with the hope that the continentals were provided well, and with a surplus, this matter gave the partisan but little concern. The small supplies of arms and ammunition which Singleton had succeeded in picking up and bringing from the neighbourhood of Dorchester, were gratefully welcomed ; and, with a new hope from this seasonable arrival of his men, Marion determined earnestly to press his advance to

* His favourite servant—called "Buddy" in the family.

† Ball, his horse—a noble animal, that always led the advance in swimming the rivers.

a union with the powerful army supposed to be coming on with Gates.

To Singleton he partially unfolded his determination, though he entered into no particulars. He had not yet determined as to the time and route of his purposed movement. It was necessary that he should first ascertain the precise position of Gates; and, again, he had the duty yet to perform, in part, which he had voluntarily undertaken, of destroying all the boats upon the river at the various crossing-places, which might otherwise be employed to facilitate the progress of Lord Cornwallis to the assistance of Rawdon at Camden; upon which place it was now understood the first effort of the approaching southern army would be made. There was little doubt that Cornwallis would soon be apprised, if, indeed, he was not already—of the necessity for his presence at Camden; for, though Singleton had arrested one courier, and Marion himself another, it was not to be expected that others would not succeed in passing with intelligence, where the line of country to be watched was so extensive. To retard the movements of the commander at Charleston—to keep him back until Gates should be able to strike his first blow, was an object quite too important to be foregone or given up but with great effort; and an understanding between Sumter and Marion had assigned one of the two leading routes, to the designated ground of battle, to each of the partisans.

Marion had done much already towards his object. He had destroyed more than two hundred boats on both sides of the river, sparing neither canoe nor periagua. All within reach had been broken up, save the few which he still employed for his own purposes in the swamp, gathering provisions, and for the facilitation of his own progress. Another day, and Singleton would not have found it so easy to

"Swim the Esk river, where ford there was none."

That night, as soon as the whole party had come up, the passage was effected, and without any great difficulty. The horses swam beside the boats, secured by ropes and bridles, while their riders, for the time, occupied a more secure seat within them than they might have done upon their saddles. Ball, the famous horse of Marion, led the way for the rest, and he went through the water as freely and fearlessly as a native-born of the element. The rest followed with some little shivering and restiveness, but, with the boats, they soon reached the shore, and were then mounted and ridden through the river-sedge, over the fallen tree, and safely, at length, into the island thicket which formed the hiding-place of the Swamp Fox on the Santee.

The boats, filled with the women, children, and prisoners, under a small guard, had a more tedious, though more secure and easy passage to the same spot. Soon as they left the current of the river and got within the foliage, the swamp-suckers, with an old experience, seized upon their long canes, twenty feet in length, to the end of each of which a prong of the deer's antlers, and some times a crotched stick of some hard wood, had been tightly fastened. With these, catching the overhanging limbs and branches that fenced in a crooked creek that led to the island, they drew themselves along. Without dip of oar or plash of paddle, silently and still, as if endued with a life of its own, the boat swept through its natural abode, a familiar tenant of its depths. Torches flashed along at intervals upon the banks to guide them, but they were perfectly unnecessary to the frequent dwellers in the swamp. They who steered and led the way could have travelled by night and day, unfearing, and unswerving from their designated path, with the ease of a citizen along the high-road. The rapidity of their move ments, through scenes only distinguishable when the torch flashed over them, delighted and astonished the men from the low country, who now traversed them for the first time. Porgy was absolutely overcome with anticipations. He could not refrain—such was the good-humour which the novelty of their progress inspired—from addressing Doctor Oakenburg, who sat beside him in the boat, on the subject of his musings.

"This, Doctor Oakenburg," said he, "this is a region—so Major Singleton tells me—which, in the language of Scripture, may be said to flow with milk and honey."

The doctor, terrified before into silence, was now astounded into speech.

18

"Milk and honey!" he exclaimed, with wondering.

"Ay, doctor, milk and honey! that is to say, with fish and terrapin, which I take to mean the same thing, since nobody would
desire any land in which there was no meat. The phrase, milk
and honey, simply means to convey the idea of a land full of all
things that men of taste can relish ; or we may even go farther in
this respect, and consider it a land teeming with all things for all
tastes. Thus, yours, Doctor Oakenburg—even *your* vile taste for
snakes and eels—has been consulted here not less than mine for
terrapin. Along the same tussock on which the bullet-head
reposes, you will see the moccasin crawling confidently. In the
same luxurious wallow with the sow, you will behold the sly alligator watching the growth daily of her interesting little family. The
summer duck, with its glorious plumage, skims along the same
muddy lake, on the edge of which the d—d bodiless crane screams
and crouches ; and there are no possible extremes in nature to
which a swamp like this will not give shelter, and furnish something to arouse and satisfy the appetite. It is a world in itself,
and, as I said before, with a figurative signification of course, it is
indeed a land of milk and honey."

"Land indeed !" said one of the troopers ; "I don't see much of
that yet. Here's nothing but rotten trees and mud-holes, that I
can make out when the lightwood blazes."

"Never mind, my lark," said one of the conductors in a chuck
ling reply ; "wait a bit, and you'll see the blessedest land you ever
laid eyes on. It's the very land, as the big-bellied gentleman says,
that's full of milk and honey ; for, you see, we've got a fine range,
and the cattle's a plenty, and when the sun's warm you'll hear the
bee trees at midday—and such a music as they'll give you ! Don't
be afeard now, and we'll soon come to it."

"I doubt not, my good friend," replied Porgy, with a singular
gravity of tone and aspect—"I doubt not what you say, and I rejoice that your evidence so fully supports my opinion. Your
modes of speech are scarcely respectful enough, however ; for,
though a man's teeth are prime agents and work resolutely enough
for his belly, yet it is scarcely the part of good manners to throw
one's belly continually into one's teeth."

" Oh, that's it,' said the other; " well, now don't be skittish, mister, for though I am Roaring Dick, I never roars at any of our own boys, and I likes always to be civil to strangers. But it's always the way with us, when we don't know a man's name, to call him after that part that looks the best about him. There's Tom Hazard now, we calls him by no other name than Nosey; 'cause, you see, his nose is the most rumbunctious part that he's got, and it's a'most the only part you see when you first look on him. Then there's Bill Bronson—as stout a lark as you've seed for many a day—now, as he's blind of one eye and can hardly see out o' t'other, we calls him Blinky Bill, and he never gets his back up, though he's a main quick hand if you poke fun at him. So, stranger, you must not mind when we happen to call you after the most respectable part."

" Respectable part! I forgive you, my friend—you're a man of sense. Dr. Oakenburg, your d—d hatchet hip is digging into my side; can't you move a jot farther ? There, that will do ; I am not desirous of suffering martyrdom by hip and thigh."

" Now we're most home," said Master Roaring Dick to his little crew. " One more twirl in the creek, and you'll see the lights and the island; there, there it is. Look, now, stranger, look for yourself, where the Swamp Fox hides in the daylight, to travel abroad with old blear-eye—the owl that is—when the round moon gets out of her roost."

And very picturesque and imposing, indeed, was the scene that now opened upon Porgy and the rest, as they swept round the little bend in the waters of the creek, and the deeply embowered camp of the partisan lay before them. Twenty different fires, blazing in all quarters of the island, illuminated it with a splendour which no palace pomp could emulate. The thick forest walls that girdled them in were unpierced by their rays; the woods were too impenetrably dense even for their splendours; and, like so many huge and blazing pil-lars, the larger trees seemed to crowd forward into the light with a solitary stare that made solemn the entire and wonderful beauty of the scene. Group after group of persons, each busy to itself, ga-thered around the distinct fires; while horses neighed under conve nient trees; saddles and bridles, sabres and blankets, hung from their branches, and the cheery song, from little parties more remote, made lively the deep seclusion of that warlike abiding-place.

The little boat floated fairly up to one of the fires ; a dozen busy hands at once assisted the new comers to alight, and a merry greeting hailed the acquisition of countrymen and comrades. Boat after boat, in the same way, pressed up to the landing, and all in turn were assisted by friendly hands, and saluted with cheering words and encouragement. It was not long before the strangers, with the readiness which belongs to the life of the partisan, chose their companions in mess and adventure, and began to adapt themselves to one another. Lively chat, the hearty glee, the uncouth but pleasant jest, not forgetting the plentiful supper, enlivened the first three hours after the arrival of Singleton's recruits, and fitted them generally for those slumbers to which they now prepared to hasten.

" Well, Tom," said Porgy to his old retainer, as he hurried to his tree, from a log, around which his evening's meal had been eaten in company with Roaring Dick, Oakenburg, and one or two others—" well, Tom, considering how d—d badly those perch were fried, I must confess I enjoyed them. But I was too hungry to discriminate ; and I should have tolerated much worse stuff than that. But we must take care of this, Tom, in future. It is not always that hunger helps us to sauce, and such spice is always a monstrous bad substitute for cayenne and thyme. How about the dog, Tom ?"

" I cut he tail, maussa, as you bin tell me."

" Well, how did he like the operation ?"

" He bleed bad. He no like 'em 'tall. I don't tink he can ebber run like he been run before."

" Poh ! poh ! I've no doubt he'll run a thousand times better for it, besides being able to carry his head more genteelly. He'll be a little sore for a few days, but a sore tail is a cure for a sore head, Tom ; as an ulcer is a relief to a troubled liver. Let me see the dog in the morning. You left him but an inch, Tom ?"

" Jis' about, maussa."

" Well, only tie a pine-burr under the stump, and that inch will stand out with proper dignity. Did you sear the wound with a hot iron, boy ?"

"Jis' as you tell me, maussa. A'terward, I put some pine-gum on de cut."

"No use, Tom ; but no man is quite free from quackery of some sort, and where water is a good wash of itself, the fool fancies it still needs salting. Make yourself clean to-night in the Santee, Tom, before you sleep, and 'Slink' needs a dipping also. Take him with you. Here,—help me off with this coat."

With Tom's assistance, the man of girth proceeded to strip for the night. He was helped out of his coat, the dimensions of which seemed daily more and more to contract; and after certain examinations of his belt, which needed to have a few extra holes opened, to admit of freer use, Porgy prepared to lie down for the night; when the examination of the place assigned for his repose aroused his discontent anew.

"This will never do, Tom. The bed is as hard as a bed of ra coon oysters. You must get me a good armfull or two of rushes and pine straw, though you rob some other man's sleeping quarters for it. Stay ! What is that hanging from yonder beech ? Isn't it—bless my soul, Tom,—isn't it a blanket ?"

"Da blanket for true, maussa. 'Spec' (expect) he b'long to somebody."

"Very likely, Tom; but God knows I'm somebody—I have some body, at least, to take care of and provide for : so bring it hither. It shall help to smoothe the rough places among these roots."

The blanket was brought, Tom remarking, as he spread it according to the directions of his master—

"Ha ! de man wha' claim dis blanket will sartin to be feel 'bout you to-night, maussa !"

"Will he, then ? Well, you may let the whole swamp know that I sleep with sword and pistols, and, if waked too suddenly, that I am sure to use them. Do you hear ? But you needn't roar about, you rascal, of what materials my bed is made ?"

Tom chuckled, while the epicure rolled himself up in the borrowed blanket, and in such a way as to leave no ends free to meddling fingers. His saddle formed his pillow, and all things adjusted to his satisfaction, he bade the negro take himself off, and, take care of himself. Ten minutes had not elapsed when the proprietor of the blanket came to look after his property. Porgy had already become an old soldier. Never did nose insist more sonorously upon its owner's slumbers than his. The intruder looked upon the apparently sleeping man, and saw how comfortably he was enveloped. In the dim light of the camp-fires, he fancied the blanket bore a resemblance to his own; but our epicure lay in it, calm, assured, confident, as if he were the real proprietor. The man doubted—retired, plucked a brand from the fire, and waved it over the figure of the sleeper. Meanwhile, the hilt of our lieutenant's sabre, and the muzzles of his big horseman's pistols, had been made to protrude from the covering, convenient to his gripe. The stranger was duly cautioned. Still he looked and lingered. Porgy's nose, at this moment, sent forth an emphatic and prolonged snore. The man began to meditate. The night was tolerably warm and pleasant. He really did not know that he should need the blanket, to which he yet felt ready to make oath. No doubt the usurper of his goods had only made a slight mistake. There is something cruel in disturbing a man in a profound sleep after a long journey, only to correct a mistake; and so the good-natured proprietor of the stolen goods resolved to forego his claim, for the night at least; and retired quietly, to the great relief of our cunning epicure. Scarcely had he gone from sight, when Tom heaved himself up from the opposite side of the tree, and, with a chuckle, cried out—

"Hah! maussa, you snore de man out o' he blanket dis time."

"Ah! rascal, are you watching me?" answered Porgy, in good-humoured accents. "Well, remember to restore the blanket to the fellow in the morning, and give him, with my compliments, a sup of the Jamaica. He has the bowels of a Christian, and will relish it. Meanwhile, Tom, let this be a lesson for you. Always fall asleep when the lion's in your path. When your conscience don't feel easy, make your body easy. And now, begone, for I must do some real sleeping, if I can."

CHAPTER XXXIX.

"'Tis some time yet,
To the grey dawning ; but we move betimes,
And our impatience ushers in the day."

THE stars were yet shining, when the slumbers of Major Singleton were broken. His page, Frampton, stood beside him, where
he slept in the shadows of the greenwood tree, his hand gently laid
upon his shoulder.

"How now, Lance ; what's stirring ?   What disturbs you ?"

Such was the demand of Singleton as he started into consciousness. But he needed no answer to his own question. His senses,
completely awakened, took in sounds of stir from every side. The
partisans were stirring all about, rousing from sluggish dreams,
and filling the woods with bustle ; and the shrill voice of Marion
himself, a few rods distant, brief and emphatic, was heard in accents
of command. The Swamp Fox suffered nobody to surprise his
people but himself. But he beat up their slumbers frequently
enough. He was preparing for one of his rapid movements. His
policy was—here to-day—to-morrow where ? on the wing,—not to
be traced, not to be pursued ; not found by his enemies, except at
moments when his presence was not wanting, and far less than
grateful. Singleton soon comprehended what lay before the brigade, and was on his feet and in armour in the twinkling of
an eye. Lance Frampton already had his horse in readiness.
Meanwhile, the buzz of preparation everywhere went on. Horses
were heard approaching from the upper edge of the swamp ; below
other steeds were in motion also. Above all other sounds, wild,
shrill, and sudden, came the quick, significant whistles of the scouts
coming in. The bugle sounded soon after and Singleton hastened
to join his commander.

"You are prompt, major, and as I would have it," said Marion as he rode up. "Make your own men ready—still keep their command, till our disposition may be made more uniform—and put them into a column of advance. Horry is just coming in with his troop, from which your lead will be taken. Our scouts are all in, and one brings me a courier with news from the army. De Kalb is now on the way, in rapid march from Salisbury, with two thousand continentals; Colonel Porterfield, with Virginia horse, is moving to join him; and General Caswell, with the North Carolina militia in force, arming for the same object. Though better provided than ourselves, as well in arms as in numbers, we must not hesitate to show ourselves among them. General Gates will doubtless bring a force with him; and it will be hard, if our boys, ragged though they be, should not win some laurels and blankets together."

Alas! for these fond estimates—these famous promises of Congress and continental generals. De Kalb's force consisted of only *one*, instead of *two* thousand regulars, and Gates joined his command without bringing any accessions of force. But of these details hereafter. The present movement of our Swamp Fox was to join his little squadron to the grand army. His proceeding was that of scores of partisan leaders besides, each of whom made his little contribution of militia-men, swelling the nominal strength of the conqueror of Burgoyne with additions which, in their unfed, untrained, unarmed, and naked condition, added little to his real capacity for action. One of Marion's best military virtues was celerity. He roused his people with the view to a timely junction with the continentals, while yet they were on the march, and within the limits of North Carolina. He had a wild region to traverse before he could attain this junction, and every league of ground was in the possession of certain enemies or very doubtful friends. To work his way through these, demanded all his caution, and required that he should lose no time. As soon, therefore, as his advices brought him positive intelligence of De Kalb's progress, he set his troop in motion. He had no reserves with Singleton, and readily told him all that he had need to hear. Our hero soon set his own little command in motion, and was as promptly on the ground as any of the rest. But we must not so summarily dismiss from notice the routing up of certain of our *dramatis per-sonæ.*

Porgy *had* slept, and still slept, with the profound wisdom of a soldier, who will always secure every opportunity for the performance of this duty. Porgy valued sleep too well to abridge its enjoyment unnecessarily. Whenever this necessity occurred in his case, it impaired the serenity of his temper. Now, his colleague, Lieutenant Humphries, had kindly dispatched a sergeant to awaken his brother officer. The sergeant was a rough, untutored forester, who usually adopted the most effectual processes for effecting his object. In the present case, he had seized forcibly upon the ends of the blanket in which our epicure was still comfortably wrapped, and had hauled away with the energies of a person whose muscles were perpetually claiming to be employed. Under his very decided action, one of Porgy's arms was nearly twisted from its socket, and one of his legs was dragged out from beneath the covering, tossed over its fellow, and let to fall with an emphasis which effectually tested the sensibilities of the other member. Porgy opened his eyes in the dim light of the morning star, with a soul full of indignation.

"It is scarcely civil, young man," he cried, endeavouring to unwrap himself from the thrice twisted folds of blanket in which he slept—his anger increasing with the increasing difficulties of the effort. "Scarcely civil, young man, I repeat! What if the blanket is your property"—the idea of its adroit appropriation by himself, the night before, still running in his head—"suppose it true, I say, that the blanket is your property, is this the way to seek for it? I have never denied it, sirrah, and a polite demand for it would have at once obtained it. But to disturb, in this rude and insolent manner, the repose of a gentleman! It's a foul offence—an offence which shall have its punishment, by Hercules, or I'm not the man to thresh an impertinent. Let me but unwrap. I'm a pacific man. My temper is not harsh, not irritable. I'm slow to take offence. I'm of forgiving nature. But there are some things which mortal patience cannot bear, and which, by Jupiter, I will not bear. To disturb one's slumbers, which are so absolutely essential to the digestive functions of a large man, is an offence not to be forgiven."

18*

By this time he had extricated himself from his wrappings, and stood erect. What would have been his next proceeding, it would be difficult to say. The sergeant, who aroused him, was evidently bewildered by his evident indignation. Porgy advanced upon him, and with sabre in hand, though scabbarded, he would, in all probability, have laid it heavily on the shoulders of the offender, but for the happy interposition of Humphries, who now showed himself.

"What's the trouble, lieutenant?" demanded this third party. "What vexes you?"

"This rascal—I but wrapt myself in a strange blanket, which, I suppose, belongs to the brute—I say this rascal has been pulling me to pieces, dislocating my legs and shoulders, and depriving me of a glorious morning nap, and a most delicious dream; and all because of his d—d blanket."

"Pshaw, that's a mistake; I sent the sergeant to wake you."

"You did! and why the devil did you take an improper liberty, I pray?"

"Why, man, don't you hear the bugles—don't you see all the camp in motion? Don't you know that the Swamp Fox is for an early start, before daylight? It was a kindness, lieutenant, to have you wakened in season."

"It was d—d unkindly done. Hark you, my good fellow,"—to the sergeant—"remember, hereafter, when you waken a gentleman, that it is scarcely necessary to pull him to pieces to effect your object. I forgive you this time, as you meant well; but see that you sin no more in the same manner. You were, no doubt, a blacksmith before you became a soldier. Forget your old vocation hereafter when you deal with me. If you seek to make a vice of your fingers, you will find something more than vicious at the end of mine!"

The sergeant moved off much wondering.

"Now, bestir yourself, lieutenant, and get yourself in harness," quoth Humphries.

"Take that fiery faggot from my eyes, Humphries, unless you wish to blind me eternally. What blasted folly is this of moving daily and loading the troops with such an infinity of broken slumbers! Are you dreaming, or I? Do you really mean that we are to leave the swamp?"

" Even so."

" Why, we have just got into it. I haven't seen it fairly, and know nothing of its qualities. Major Singleton assured me that it was boundless in its treasures of fish, flesh, and felicity. He spoke of its terrapin as superb. To leave it without tasting! This is shocking. I had hoped to have had a rest here of a few days to have compared its products with those of the cypress."

" You're to be disappointed, nevertheless. I'm sorry for your sake, old fellow, that it is so! But the major's orders are to breeze up as fast as possible. You mustn't delay now for trifles."

" What do you call trifles? Life, and that which feeds it, are no trifles. The tastes which enter into the dressing of food are among the best essentials of life. Who presumes to call them trifles? I trust, Lieutenant Humphries, that it is you who are the trifler now. There is surely no movement now on foot?"

" As sure as I'm a sinner, it's truth; and you must stir up. Let me help to brace you. The major's on horse a'ready. The Swamp Fox, as the people here call Marion, has been about and busy this hour. Look at him yonder—he that has his cap off—standing where those dragoons are in the saddle. He's talking to the men, and they say he talks seldom, but short and strong; and we ought to be there to hear him. Hurry yourself a bit now, or we shal. lose it all."

" There's no policy so vicious. Never hurry, John Humphries. Keep cool, keep cool, keep cool! These are the three great pre cepts for happiness. Life is to be hoarded, not to be hurried. Hap piness is found only in grains and fractions, and he who hurries finds none. It is with pleasure, as with money-making—according to that cunning old Pennsylvania printer—take care of the pence, and the pounds will take care of themselves. Take care of the moments, and you need never look after the hours. That's my doc trine for happiness—that is the grand secret. Hurry forbids all this. You skip moments—you skip happiness. Why do you sip rum punch? Why, indeed, do you sip all goodly stomachics?— simply to prolong the feeling of enjoyment. It is your beast only that gulps, and gapes, and swallows. It is only your beast that hurries. Happiness is not for such."

"But we must hurry how, Porgy, if we want to hear what he says."

"I never hurried for my father, though he looked for me hourly I will not hurry for the best speech ever delivered. Do oblige me with that belt; and lay down your torch, my good fellow, and pass the strap through the buckle for me. There—not so tight, if you please; the next hole in the strap will answer now; an hour's riding will enable me to take in the other, and then I shall probably try your assistance. Eh! what's that?"

The pitiful howling of a negro, aroused from his slumbers prematurely by the application of an irreverent foot to his ribs, now called forcibly the attention of the party, and more particularly that of Porgy.

"That's Tom's voice—I'll swear to it among a thousand; and somebody's beating him! I'll not suffer that." And with the words he moved rather rapidly away towards the spot whence the noise proceeded.

"Don't be in a hurry now, Porgy; remember—keep cool, keep cool, keep cool," cried Humphries, as he followed slowly after the now hurrying philosopher.

"Do I not, Humphries? I am not only cool myself, but I go with the charitable purpose of cooling another."

"But what's the harm?—he's only kicking Woolly-head into his senses."

"Nobody shall kick Tom while I'm alive. The fellow's too valuable for blows;—boils the best rice in the southern country, and hasn't his match, with my counsel, at terrapin in all Dorchester. Holla! there, my friend, let the negro alone, or I'll astonish you."

The soldier and Tom, alike, became apparent the next moment the former still administering a salutary kick and cuff to the growling and grumbling negro. Porgy soon grappled the assailant by the collar, and shook him violently. The latter, taken by surprise, and seemingly in great astonishment, demanded the cause of this assault. He was one of that class, some of whom are still to be found in the country, who, owning no slaves, are very apt to delight in the abuse of those of other people. Porgy had his answer in his usual fashion.

"That's the cause, my good fellow; that's the cause,"—pointing to the negro,—"an argument that runs upon two legs, and upon which no two legs in camp shall trample."

"Da's right, maussa," growled Tom, indignantly. "Wha' for he kick nigga, what's doing not'ing but sleep? Ax um dat, maussa."

The soldier grew ruffled, in spite of Porgy's uniform, and answered savagely—

"His dog stole my bacon, cappin, and when I chunked the varment, the nigga gin me sass. He's a sassy fellow."

"Ah! he's a saucy fellow, is he? That may be, but I'll let you know that I'm the only one to take the sauce out of him. As for the dog—so, Tom, your dog stole this man's bacon?"

"He say so, maussa, but I ain't sh' um (see um). De dog hab shinbone, but how I know whey he git um? Slink never tief we bacon, maussa."

"Ah ha! Slink never steals our bacon, you say? That shows him to be a dog of discrimination—that knows where his bread is buttered—what we can't often say for wiser animals. But did he ever steal bacon before to your knowledge, Tom?"

"Nebber, maussa."

"Then, Tom, it's all owing to that cutting off his tail. You see he plucks up spirit, you rascal; for a certain amount of spirit is necessary to a thief. His enterprise grows the moment that you take off the miserable appendage that kept down his spirit. The only misfortune is, that in exercising his new quality, he has not been trained to distinguish between the *meum* and *tuum*. Now. that's your fault, Tom."

"Wha' you mean by *meum* and *tuum*, maussa?"

"Well, Tom, as far as concerns us, who have no goods to lose, the distinction is not of much moment; but the lesson is not the less valuable for Slink to learn, in a camp where other people possess ham bones, in which they claim special rights. See to it, hereafter. As for you, my good fellow, you must see that the dog had no felonious intentions. The *animus* makes the offence. He did not steal—he simply appropriated. Do not suffer yourself, my friend, to indulge again in the defamation of character. The rising spirit of the dog must not be kept down because you have a shin bone of ham. Do you hear that ! And further, let me tell you, that any second attempt to kick that fellow—who is decidedly the best cook in the Southern army—will subject you to the chance of being kicked in turn. As it is, I let you off this time, with a simple shaking."

The soldier grew savage and insolent. He was tall and vigorous ; did not seem to regard the epicure's epaulet with any great degree of veneration ; and, as he replied with defiance, Porgy again took hold of his collar. The affair might have ended in the soldier's tumbling our fat friend upon his back, but for the timely approach of Singleton on horseback, at sight of whom the soldier stole away, pocketing his hurts of self-esteem for a more advantageous occasion.

"To saddle, Mr. Porgy, to saddle," was the command of Singleton. "Be ready, sir, for a movement in five minutes. The Colonel has already given orders for a start, and I would not that any of my command should occasion a moment's delay."

"Nor I, Major Singleton—nor I. Honourable emulation is the soldier's virtue, and though I would never hurry, sir, yet I would never be a laggard. The golden medium, major, between hurry and apathy, is still to be insisted upon. It is a principle, sir, which I approve. But haste, sir, hurry, is my horror. Slumbers once broken—visions rudely intruded upon—seldom return to us in their original felicity. Here have I had my sleep torn in twain, as I may say, just when the web of it had become precious to body and soul. Just as the one was at perfect repose, after a toilsome march, and just as the other had become refreshed with a dream of delights which almost compensated for an empty stomach "

"It is a hard case," was the reply of Singleton, who knew the humours of our friend, " but you must allow for circumstances. Perilous necessity is a despotism, Mr. Porgy, to which it is only wisdom to submit with as much resignation as we may.   Necessity overrules all laws, as well of stomach as of soul."

"A manifest truism, Major Singleton ; and in its recognition, I will even hasten to obey our present orders. But you err, major.

in speaking of soul and stomach as independent organizations. Be assured, sir, the relation between them is much more near than is vulgarly supposed. For my part, I would not give a sixpence for any human soul without a stomach."

Singleton waited to hear no more, but putting spurs to his horse, repeated his request that Porgy should follow soon. The latter turned to Tom.

" So, Tom, that fellow has bloodied your nose. There is an ugly abrasion of your left nostril."

" He feel so, maussa. He feel berry much as ef he been breck (*break*—for broken)."

" 'Pon my soul, you're right. The bridge is broken. It was ugly enough before ; it is scarcely *passable* now. You are disfigured for ever, boy. Fortunately, the nose, however essential to the lungs, is hardly of importance to the genius. You are no doubt as good a cook as ever. Were it likely to affect your skill in that department, I should deem it a duty to have that soldier up at the halyards. Well ! I don't see what we can do for it. Wash it as often as you can. Meanwhile, tighten that girth, and bring up the horse. Lead him to that stump. One's own girth is greatly in the way of his steed's. By the way, Tom, you're sure that Slink has not made off with our ham as well as the soldier's. If he has, he's a dead dog from this moment. You have it in the buckskin safely ? We shall need it to-morrow, old fellow, for our hard riding promises nothing better."

Tom's assurances in respect to the ham-bone and Slink's fidelity, were promptly given, and, talking to himself or others as he rode, Porgy soon joined himself to his command, where he found the several squads of the partisans already assembled, prepared to see and hear " The Swamp Fox," whom many of them were now to behold for the first time.

Under that forest canopy, in the cold light of the morning stars, now rapidly paling in the west,—amid waving torches and prancing steeds—Marion unfolded his plan, and briefly informed his men of the condition of things, not only as they affected the colony, but as they concerned the confederation. He read to them a resolve of Congress, in which that body had declared its determination to save each and every province that had linked its fortunes with the federal union ; particularly declaring its resolution, in the teeth of a report to this effect, which the British and tories had industriously circulated in South Carolina and Georgia, not to sacrifice these two colonies to the invader, on any terms of peace or compromise which they might make with him. Such a resolve had become highly necessary ; as the great currency given to the rumour of such a compromise, and on these especial terms, had produced, in part, the results which had been desired by the enemy The patriots, drooping enough before, had begun to despair entirely while the tories were encouraged to perseverance, and stimulated to the most adventurous and daring action. This statement read— and the formal resolution as it had been adopted by Congress was in his hand for the purpose—Marion then proceeded to recapitulate, not only the information which he had been enabled to obtain of their own army, but of that of their enemies. His information, gathered from various sources, was comparatively extensive ; and while it taught his men the full extent of the danger with which they were to contend on all hands, it also served greatly to increase their confidence in a commander, whose knowledge of passing and remote events seemed intuitive ; and whose successes, though small, had been so unbroken, as to inspire in them a perfect assurance of his invincibility.

The military force of the British then in Carolina, was distributed judiciously throughout its entire circuit. The 23d and 33d regiments of infantry, the volunteers of Ireland, the infantry of the legion (Tarleton's), Brown's and Hamilton's corps, and a detachment of artillery under the command of Lord Rawdon, hutted in and about the town of Camden. Major McArthur with the 71st regiment was stationed at Cheraw, near the Peedee region, covering the country between Camden and Georgetown, and holding continued correspondence with the rank and thickly settled tory region of Cross Creek, North Carolina. With the approach of the continentals, this regiment had been ordered in, to a junction with himself, by Rawdon ; and they left the passage open for Marion through the country where most of his warfare was to be carried on. In Georgetown, a large force of provincials was

stationed. The chain of British military posts, to the west of Camden, was connected with Ninety-Six by Rocky Mount, itself a strong
post on the Wateree, occupied by Lieutenant-Colonel Turnbull of
the New York tory volunteers and militia. Lieutenant-Colonel Bal-
four, and subsequently Lieutenant-Colonel Cruger, commanded at
Ninety-Six. The troops there consisted of battalions of Delancy's,
Innis's, and Allen's provincial regiments, with the 16th regiment
and three companies besides, of light infantry. Major Ferguson's
corps, with a large body of tory militia, traversed the country between the Wateree and the Saluda rivers, and sometimes stretched
away even to the borders of North Carolina. Lieutenant-Colonel
Brown held Augusta with a large force of British and tories;
Savannah was garrisoned by Hessians and provincials under Colonel
Alured Clark ; Charleston contained the 7th, 63d, and 64th regiments of infantry, two battalions of Hessians, a large detachment of
the royal artillery, and several corps of provincials under the immediate command of Brigadier-General Paterson. The legion dragoons
(Tarleton's) were employed in keeping open the communication
between the several cantonments. In addition to these, there were
the posts of Fort Watson, Biggins' Church, Dorchester, and many
others, which, as the whole colony lay at the feet of the conquerors,
were maintained with small bodies of men, chiefly as posts of rest,
and not likely to be perilled by assaults in the present condition of
the country.

Having narrated, at full, the amount of the British force distributed thus throughout the colony, Colonel Marion did not scruple
to present, without any exaggeration, a true picture of the strength
of that power which was to meet and contend with it. He painted
to them the depressed condition of Congress, the difficulties of
Washington, and taught them how little was to be looked for, in
the shape of succour and assistance, apart from that which he
insisted was in their own hands—in their own firm determination,
fearless spirits, and always ready swords.

" I take up the sword, gentlemen," said he, " with a solemn vow
never to lay it down, until my country, as a free country, shall no
longer need my services. I have informed myself of all these difficulties and dangers—these inequalities of numbers and experience

between us and our enemies—of which I have plainly told you
Having them all before my own eyes, I have yet resolved to live o
die in the cause of my country, placing the risks and privations ol
the war in full opposition to the honour and duty—the one which
I may gather in her battles, and the other which I owe to her in
maintaining them to the last. I have told you all that I know, in
order that each man may make his election as I have done. I will
urge no reasons why you should love and fight for your country,
as my own sense of honour and shame would not suffer me to
listen to any from another on the same subject. Determine for
yourselves without argument from me. Let each man answer,
singly, whether he will go forward under my lead, or that of any
other officer that General Gates shall assign, or whether he will
now depart from our ranks, choosing a station, henceforward, of
neutrality, if such will be allowed him, or with the forces of our
enemy. Those who determine with me, must be ready to depart
within the hour, on the route to Lynch's creek, and to the continental army."

The piercing black eye of Marion, darting around the assembly
at the conclusion of his speech, seemed to look deep into the
bosom of each soldier in his presence. There was but a moment's
pause when he had concluded, before they gave a unanimous answer. Could they have had other than a single sentiment on such
an occasion? They had not—and no one voice hesitated in the
utterance of the cheering, soul-felt response—

" We will all go!—Marion for ever!" and from the rear came
up the more familiar cry—

" Hurra for the Swamp Fox!—let him take the track, and we'll
be after him."

A single bow—a slight bend of the body, and brief inclination
of the head—testified their leader's acknowledgment; and, after a
few directions to Horry, he ordered the advance. With a calm
look and unchanging position, he noted, with an individual and
particular glance, each trooper as he filed past him. A small
select guard was left behind, who were to conduct the women and
children to the friendly whig settlement of Williamsburg. The
partisans were to follow, after this, upon a prescribed route, and

meet with the main body at Lynch's creek. An hour later, and the silence of the grave was over the dim island in the swamp of the Santee, so lately full of life and animation. The brands were smoking, but no longer in blaze; and the wild-cat might be seen prowling stealthily round the encampment which they had left, looking for the scraps of the rustic feast partaken at their last supper by its recent inmates.

"A devilish good speech," said Porgy to Humphries, as the latter rode beside him, a little after leaving the island—"a devilish good speech, and spoken like a gentleman. No big words about liberty and death, but all plain and to the point. Then there was no tricking a fellow—persuading him to put his head into a rope without showing him first how d—d strong it was. I like that. I always desire to see the way before me. Give me the leader that shows me the game I'm to play, and the odds against me. In fighting, as in eating, I love to keep my eyes open. Let them take in all the danger, and all the dinner, that I may neither have too little appetite for the one, nor too much for the other."

"Ah, Porgy," said Humphries in reply, "you will have your joke though you die for it."

"To be sure, old fellow, and why not? God help me when I cease to laugh. When that day comes, Humphries, look for an aching shoulder. I'm no trifle to carry, and I take it for granted, Bill, for old acquaintance sake, you'll lend a hand to lift a leg and thigh of one that was once your friend. See me well buried, my boy; and if you have time to write a line or raise a headboard, you may congratulate death upon making the acquaintance of one who was remarkably intimate with life."

CHAPTER XL.

"Sound trumpets—let the coil be set aside
That now breaks in upon our conference."

MEANWHILE, the hero of Saratoga—a man who, at that time, almost equally with Washington, divided the good opinion of his countrymen—arrived from Virginia and took command of the southern army. The arrival of Gates was a relief to the brave German soldier, Baron De Kalb, who previously had the command. The situation of the army was then most embarrassing. It lay at Deep river, in the state of North Carolina, in a sterile country, filled either with lukewarm friends or certain enemies. The executive of the colony had done but little to secure aid or co-operation for the continentals. Provisions were procured with difficulty, and the militia came in slowly, and in unimportant numbers. The command of the state subsidy had been intrusted to Mr. Caswell ; a gentleman who has been described as being without the qualities which would make a good soldier, but with sufficient pretension to make a confident one. He strove to exercise an independent command, and, on various pretences, kept away from a junction with De Kalb, in whom his own distinct command must have been merged. Even upon Gates's arrival, the emulous militia-man kept aloof until the junction was absolutely unavoidable, and until its many advantages had been almost entirely neutralized by the untimely delay in effecting it. This junction at length took place on the fifteenth day of August, nearly a month after Gates's assumption of the general command. We repeat here what was the army criticism upon Caswell ; but this should be taken with some grains of allowance. Caswell had previously shown himself a man of merit, and had done good service.

A new hope sprang up in the bosoms of the continentals with the arrival of a commander already so highly distinguished His noble appearance, erect person, majestic height and carriage, and the bold play of his features, free, buoyant, and intelligent in high degree, were all calculated to confirm their sanguine expectations. In the prime of life, bred to arms, and having gone through several terms of service with character and credit, every thing was expected by the troops from their commander. Fortune, too, had almost invariably smiled upon him ; and his recent success at Saratoga—a success which justice insists should be shared pretty evenly with Arnold—the traitor Arnold—and others equally brave, but far more worthy—had done greatly towards inspiring his men with assurances, which, it is not necessary now to say, proved most illusory. Nor was De Kalb, to whom General Gates intrusted the command of the Maryland division of the army, including that also from Delaware, without his influence in the affections of the continentals. He was a brave man, and had all his life been a soldier. A German by birth, he was in the service of the King of France, and was already a brigadier, when transferred to America in the revolutionary struggle. Congress honoured him with the commission of a major-general, and he did honour to the trust—he perished in the execution of its duties.

The command given to Gates was so far a shadowy one. With the Maryland and Delaware regiments, it consisted only of three companies of artillery under the command of Lieutenant-Colonel Carrington, which had just joined from Virginia, and a small legionary corps, of about sixty cavalry and as many foot, under Colonel Armand, a foreigner. But the general was not to be discouraged by this show of weakness, though evident enough to him at the outset. He joined the army on the 25th July, was received with due ceremony by a continental salute from the little park of artillery, and received the command with due politeness from his predecessor. He made his acknowledgments to the baron with all the courtesy of a finished gentleman, approved and confirmed his standing orders, and, this done, to the surprise of all, gave the troops instructions to hold themselves in readiness to move at a moment's warning.

This was an order which manifested the activity of their commander's mind and character ; but it proved no little annoyance to the troops themselves, who well knew their own condition. They were without rum or rations—their foragers had failed to secure necessary supplies in sufficient quantity—and nothing but that high sense of military subordination which distinguished the favourite line of continentals under De Kalb's direction, could have prevented the open utterance of those discontents which they yet could not help but feel. De Kalb ventured to remind Gates of the difficulties of their situation. A smile, not more polite than supercilious, accompanied the reply of the too confident adventurer.

" All this has been cared for, general. I have not issued orders without duly considering their bearing, and the unavoidable necessities they bring with them. Wagons are on the road with all the articles you name in sufficient quantity, and in a day or two these discontents will be all satisfied. Your line is not refractory, I hope ?"

" Never more docile, I beg your excellency to believe, than now. The troops I command know that subordination, not less than valour, is the duty of the soldier. But human nature has its wants, and no small part of my care is, that I know their suffering —not from their complaints, sir, for they say nothing—but from my own knowledge of their true condition, and of what their complaints might very well be."

" It is well—they will soon be relieved ; and in order to contribute actively to that end, it is decided that we march to-morrow."

" To-morrow, sir ! Your excellency is aware that this is impracticable unless we move with but one half of our baggage, for want of horses. Colonel Williams has just reported a large deficiency."

With evident impatience, restrained somewhat by a sense of politeness, Gates turned away from the baron to Colonel Otho Williams, who was then approaching, and put the question to him concerning the true condition of the army with regard to horses. The cheek of the old veteran, De Kalb, grew to a yet deeper hue than was its habitual wear, and his lips were compressed with painful effort as he heard the inquiry. Williams confirmed the statement, and assured the general, that not only a portion of the baggage, but a part of the artillery must be left under the same deficiency in the event of a present movement.

"And how many field-pieces are thus unprovided, Colonel Williams?"

"Two, sir, at least, and possibly more."

Gates strode away for a few moments, then returning quickly as if in that time he had fully discussed the matter in his own mind, he exclaimed:

"They must be left; we shall be able to do without them. We must move to-morrow, gentlemen, without loss of time, taking the route over Buffalo ford towards the advance post of the enemy on Lynch's creek. We shall find him there, I think."

Gates seemed to think that nothing more was wanting to success than finding his enemy, and his eye declared the confident expectation of youth, unprepared for, and entirely unthinking of, reverse. Flattered by good fortune to the top of his bent, she now seemed desirous of fooling him there; and his eye, lip, look, and habitual action, seemed to say that with him now, it was only to see, to conquer.

De Kalb turned away sorrowfully in silence; but Colonel Williams, presuming on large personal intimacy with the general, ventured to expostulate with him upon the precipitate step which he was about to take. He insisted upon the necessity of horse, not only for the baggage and artillery, but for the purpose of mounting a large additional force of the infantry, to act as cavalry along the route. But Gates, taking him by the arm, smiled playfully to his aide, as he replied:

"But what do we want with cavalry, Williams?—we had none at Saratoga."

Perhaps it would be safe to assert that the game won at Saratoga was the true cause of the game lost at Camden. The folly of such an answer was apparent to all but the speaker. With a marked deference, careful not to offend, Williams suggested the radical difference between the two regions thus tacitly compared. He did not dwell upon the irregular and broken surface of the ground at Saratoga, which rendered cavalry next to useless, and, indeed, perfectly unnecessary; but he gave a true picture of the country through which they were now to pass. By nature sterile,

abounding with sandy plains and swamps, thinly inhabited, nothing
but cavalry could possibly compass the extent of ground over
which it would be necessary that they should go daily in order to
secure provisions. He proceeded, and described the settlers in the
neighbourhood as chiefly tories—another name for a banditti the
most reckless and barbarous—who would harass his army at every
step, and seek safe cover in the swamps whenever he should turn
upon them. Williams, who knew the country, ably depicted its
condition to his superior, and with a degree of earnestness only
warranted by the friendship existing between them. It was, nevertheless, far from agreeable to his hearer, who, somewhat peevishly,
at length responded :

" Colonel Williams, we are to fight the enemy, you will admit ?'
He will not come to us, that is clear. What next ? We must go
to him. We must pit the cock on his own dunghill."

" It will be well, general, if he doesn't *pit* us there. Though we
do seek to fight him, there's no need of such an excess of civility
as to give him his own choice of ground for it ; and permit me to
suggest a route by which we shall seek him out quite as effectually,
I think, and, with due regard to your already expressed decision,
on better terms for ourselves."

" Proceed !" was all the answer of Gates, who began whistling
the popular air of Yankee Doodle, with much *sang-froid*, even while
his aide was speaking. The brow of Williams grew slightly contracted for an instant ; but, well knowing the habits of the speaker,
and regarding much more the harmony of the army and its prospect of success than his own personal feelings, he calmly enough
proceeded in his suggestions. A rude map of the country lay on
the table before him, on which he traced out the path which he
now counselled his superior to take.

" Here, sir, your excellency will see that a route almost north-
west would cross the Peedee river, at or about the spot where it
becomes the Yadkin : this would lead us to the little town of Salisbury, where the people are firm friends, and where the country all
around is fertile and abundant. This course, sir, has the advantage
of any other, not only as it promises us plenty of provisions, but as

it yields us an asylum for the sick and wounded, in the event of a disaster, either in Mecklenburg or Rowan counties, in both of which our friends are stanch and powerful."

The suggestion of disaster provoked a scornful smile to the lips of Gates, and he seemed about to speak, but perceiving that Williams had not yet concluded, he merely waved his hand to him to proceed. Williams beheld the smile and its peculiar expression, and his manly and ingenuous countenance was again slightly flushed as he surveyed it. His tall, graceful figure rose to its full height, as he went on to designate the several advantages offered to the army by the suggested route. In this review were included, among other leading objects, the establishment of a laboratory for the repair of arms at Salisbury or Charlotte—a depot for the security of stores conveyed from the northward by the upper route— the advantage which such a course gave of turning the left of the enemy's outposts by a circuitous route, and the facility of reaching the most considerable among them (Camden), with friends always in the rear, and with a river (the Wateree) on the right. These, and other suggestions, were offered by Williams, who, at the same time, begged to fortify his own opinions by a reference to other and better informed gentlemen than himself on the subject. Gates, who had heard him through with some impatience, only qualified in its show by the manifest complacency with which he contemplated his own project, turned quietly around to him at the conclusion, and replied briefly—

"All very well, Williams, and very wise—but we must march now. To-morrow, when the troops shall halt at noon, I will lay these matters, as you have suggested them, before the *general* officers."

Laying due stress upon the word general, he effectually conveyed the idea to the mind of Williams, that, though he had received the suggestions of a friend and intimate, he was not unwilling to rebuke the presumption of the inferior officer aiming to give counsel. With a melancholy shake of the head, De Kalb turned away, jerking up the hips of his smallclothes, as he did so, with a suffi- ciently discontented movement. Williams followed him from the

19

presence of the infatuated generalissimo, and all parties were *cool*
busy in preparation for a start.

The next morning, the journey was begun ; the army setting
forth, unmurmuring, though with but half its baggage, and with no
present prospect of provisions. Gates, however, seemed assured of
their proximity, and cheered his officers, and through them, the
men, with his assurance. At noon the army came to a halt, and
here they were joined by Colonel Walton, bearing advices from
Marion, and bringing up his own skeleton corps, which was incorporated with Colonel Dixon's regiment of the North Carolina militia. The services of Walton, as, indeed, had been anticipated by
him, were appropriated at once by the general in his own family
No conference took place at this halt, as Gates had promised Wil
liams. After a brief delay, which the men employed in ransacking
their knapsacks for the scraps and remnants which they contained,
the march was resumed : the waggons with provisions not yet in
sight, and their scouts returning with no intelligence calculated for
their encouragement.

The country through which their journey was to be taken,
exceeded in sterility all the representations which had been made
of it. But few settlements relieved, with an appearance of human
life, the monotonous originality of the wild nature around them ;
and these, too, were commonly deserted by their inhabitants on
the appearance of the army. The settlers, dividing on either
side, had formed themselves into squads to plunder and prey upon
the neighbouring and more productive districts. They were Ish-
maelites in all their practices, and usually shrank away from any
force larger than their own ; conscious that power must only bring
them chastisement.

The distresses of the soldiery, on this sad and solitary march,
increased with every day in their progress. Still, none of the provisions and stores promised them by the general at the outset, came
to their relief. In lieu of these, they had the long perspective, full
of fertile promise, set before them. There was the Peedee river at
hand, the banks of which, they were told, exceedingly fertile, held
forth the prospect of abundance ; but hour after hour came and

passed, without the realization of these promises. The old crop of
corn, along the road, had been long since exhausted, and the new
grain was yet in the fields, unripe and unfit for use. But the necessity was too peremptory, and not to be restrained. The soldiers
plucked the immature ears, and boiling them with their lean beef
which herded in the contiguous swamps, they provided themselves
with all the food available in that quarter. Green peaches were the
substitute for bread ; and fashion, too, became a tributary to want,
and the hair powder, so lavishly worn by all of the respectable
classes of that period, was employed to thicken the unsalted soups,
for the more fastidious appetites of the officers. Such fare was productive of consequences the most annoying and enfeebling. The
army was one of shadows, weary and dispirited, long before it came
in sight of an enemy.

It was on the third day of August that the little army crossed the
Peedee, in batteaux, at Mask's ferry, and were met on the southern
bank by Lieutenant Colonel Porterfield, of Virginia, with a lean
detachment of troops, which he had kept together with much diffi
culty after the fall of Charleston. A few hours after, and while the
army was enjoying its usual noon-day halt, the little partisan corps
of the Swamp Fox rode into camp.

His presence created some sensation, for his own reputation had
been for some time spreading ; but the miserable and wild appearance of his little brigade was the object of immense merriment on
the part of the continentals. They are represented by the historian
as a most mirthful spectacle, all well mounted, but in wretched
attire, an odd assemblage of men, and boys, and negroes, with little
or no equipment, and arms of the most strange and various assort-
ment.

Colonel Marion was at once introduced to the marquee of the
general, but his troops remained exposed to the unmeasured jest and
laughter of the continentals. One called them the crow-squad, from
their sooty outsides ; this name another denied them, alleging, with
a sorry pun, that they had long since forgotten how to crow,
although they were evidently just from the dunghills. A third,
more classical, borrowed a passage from Falstaff, and swore he
should at once leave the army, as he wouldn't march into Coventry

with such scarecrows; but a fourth said that was the very reason that he should stick to it, as Coventry was the only place for them.

The fierce low-countrymen did not bear this banter long or with patient temper. As they sauntered about among the several groups which crowded curiously around them, sundry little squabbles, only restrained by the efforts of the officers, took place, and promised some difficulty between the parties. Our friend Porgy himself, though withal remarkably good-natured, was greatly aroused by the taunts and sarcasms uttered continually around him. He replied to many of those that reached his ears, and few were better able at retort than himself; but his patience at length was overcome entirely, as he heard among those engaged most earnestly in the merriment at his expense, the frequent and boisterous jokes of Colonel Armand, a foreign mercenary, who, in broken English, pressed rather rudely the assault upon our friend Porgy's equipment in particular. Armand himself was lean and attenuated naturally. His recent course of living had not materially contributed to his personal bulk. Porgy eyed him with wholesale contempt for a few moments, while the foreigner blundered out his bad English and worse wit. At length, tapping Armand upon the shoulder with the utmost coolness and familiarity, Porgy drew his belt a thought tighter around his waist, while he addressed the foreigner.

"Look you, my friend—with the body of a sapling, you have the voice of a puncheon, and I like nothing that's unnatural and artificial. I must reconcile these extremes in your case, and there are two modes of doing so. I must either increase your bulk or lessen your voice. Perhaps it would be quite as well to do both : the extremes meet always most readily : and by reducing your voice, and increasing your bulk at the same time, I shall be able to bring you to a natural and healthy condition."

"Vat you mean?" demanded Armand, with a look of mixed astonishment and indignation, as he drew away from the familiar grasp which Porgy had taken upon his shoulder.

"I'll tell you; you don't seem to have had a dinner for some time back. Your jaws are thin, your complexion mealy, and your belly—what there is of it—is gaunt as a greyhound's. I'll help to

replenish it. Tom, bring out the hoecake and that shoulder-bone,
boy. You'll find it in the tin box, where I left it. Now, my
friend, wait for the negro; he'll be here in short order, and I shall
then assist you, as I said before, to increase your body and diminish your voice: the contrast is too great between them—it 's
unnatural, unbecoming, and must be remedied."

Armand, annoyed by the pertinacity, not less than by the manner of Porgy, who, once aroused, now clung to him tenaciously all
the while he spoke, soon ceased to laugh as he had done previously ·
and, not understanding one-half of Porgy's speech, and at a loss
how to take him, for the gourmand was eminently good-natured
in his aspect, he repeated the question—

" Vat you sall say, my friend ?"

" Tom's coming with ham and hoecake—both good, I assure
you, for I have tried them within the hour; you shall try them
also. I mean first to feed you—and by that means increase your
bulk—and then to flog you, and so diminish your voice. You
have too little of the one, and quite too much of the other."

A crowd had now collected about the two, of whom not the
least ready and resolute were the men of Marion. As soon as
Armand could be made to understand what was wanted of him,
he drew back in unmeasured indignation and dismay.

" I sall fight wid de gentilmans and de officer, not wid you, sir,"
was his reply, with some show of dignity, to the application of
Porgy. A hand was quietly laid upon his shoulder, as he uttered
these words, and his eye turned to encounter that of Singleton.

" I am both, sir, and at your service, Colonel Armand, in this
very quarrel; though, in justice, you owe the right to Mr. Porgy,
who just asserted it. You waived your own rank, sir, when you
undertook to make merry at the expense of the soldier and the
simple ensign, and thus put yourself out of the protection of your
epaulet. But conceding you all that you claim, I claim to be your
equal, and beg to repeat, sir, that I am at your service."

" But, sare, who sall be you—vat you sall be name ?"

" I am a leader of the squad that has provoked your laughter.
I am Major Singleton, of the Brigade of Marion. He will answer
for my rank and honour."

"But sare,—*honneur*, I sall not laugh at de gentilmans and de officers."

"The officer and the gentleman protects the honour of his followers. Will you compel me to disgrace you, sir ?" was the stern demand of Singleton, who had felt quite as keenly as Porgy the ridicule of the foreigner.

It is difficult to say what might have been the fruit of this little quarrel, had not an inkling of the truth reached the main force of the General. Armand's corps, meanwhile, had clustered about their colonel. They consisted chiefly of foreigners, and this fact would have told fearfully against them, had the parties come to blows. Singleton, in like manner, was soon supported by a handsome levy from his own squad, fierce fellows from the Cypress and the Santee swamps. There were the potential Porgy, and Bill Humphries the cool, and Jack Davis the stubborn, and young Lance Frampton, eager with finger already on the cock of his rifle. Swords were already half drawn, and restless fingers were working at the knife handles in the belts of their owners, and warm work was threatening, while each of the opposing parties seemed already to have singled out his foe. But at the perilous moment the loud voice of command from general officers was heard, the drum rolled to quarters, and Gates, with De Kalb and Marion, appeared among the hostile parties; and they retired from the ground, like so many machines, at the simple will of the maker. The affray was thus prevented, which, a moment before, had seemed inevitable. Such is military subordination. The soldier, in fact, is most a soldier, when most a machine: but this very fact requires that the will which governs him should be that of a born master. Gates, with his officers, again returned to their conference, which, before this interruption, had become highly animated and important. Porgy was quite soured that Armand had gone unwhipt. Somebody mentioned that this personage was, in fact, a Baron.

"Did you know that he is a foreign Lord, Lieutenant, a Baron de la Robbery or something ; and would you whip a Lord ?"

"As the Lord liveth," was the seemingly irreverent answer, "I should have whipt him out of his breeches !"

CHAPTER XLI

The evening clouds are thick with threat of storm;
The night grows wild; the waters champ and rave,
As if they clamoured for some destined prey."

THE reader will scarcely believe, knowing as he does the great achievements of General Marion at the South throughout the revolution, that his proffer of service on this occasion was met with indifference by General Gates. Yet so we have it, on the authority of history. That gentleman partook largely of the spirit which circulated so freely in his army; and the uncouth accoutrements, the bare feet, and the tattered garments of the motley assemblage of men and boys, half armed, which the Swamp Fox had brought with him to do the battles of liberty, provoked his risibility along with that of his troops. The personal appearance of Marion, himself, was as little in his favour. Diffident even to shyness, there was little that was prepossessing in his manners. He was awkward and embarrassed in the presence of strangers : and though singularly cool and collected with the necessity and the danger, he was hardly the man to command the favourable consideration of a superficial judge—one of mediocre ability, such as General Gates undoubtedly was. The very contrast between the two men, in physical respects, was enough for the latter. Built, himself, on a superb scale, the movement, the look, the deportment of Gates, all bespoke the conscious great man. Marion, on the other hand, small in person, lame of a leg, with a downcast eye, and hesitating manners, was a cipher in the estimation of the more imposing personage who looked upon him. And then the coarse clothes—the odd mixture of what was once a uniform, with such portions of his dress as necessity had supplied, and which never could become so—altogether offended the nice taste of one rather solicitous than otherwise of the symmetries of fashion. Nothing, therefore, but a well regulated sense of politeness, formed closely upon the models of foreign service, prevented the generalissimo from laughing outright at the new auxiliaries now proffered to his aid.

But, though he forbore to offend in this manner, he did not scruple to lay before Marion his objections to the proposed use of his followers, on this very ground. The shallow mind could not see that the very poverty, the miserably clad and armed condition of Marion's men, were the best pledges that could be given for their fidelity. Why should they fight in rags for a desperate cause, without pay or promise of it, but that a high sense of honour and of country was the impelling principle? The truth must be spoken: the famous Partisan of Carolina, the very stay of its hope for so long a season—he who, more than any other man, had done so much towards keeping alive the fires of liberty and courage there, until they grew into a bright extending, unquenchable flame—was very civilly bowed out of the Continental army, and sent back to his swamps upon a service almost nominal.

"Our force is sufficient, my dear colonel," was the conclusion of the general—"quite sufficient; and you can give us little if any aid by direct co-operation. Something you may do, indeed—yes—by keeping to the swamps, and furnishing us occasional intelligence-picking off the foragers, and breaking up the communications."

"My men are true, your excellency," was the calm reply; "they desire to serve their country. It is the general opinion that you will need all the aid that the militia of the state can afford."

"The general opinion, my dear colonel, errs in this, as it does in he majority of other cases. We shall have a force adequate to our objects quite as soon as a junction can be formed with Major-General Caswell. Could you procure arms, and the necessary equipments,—proper garments, for example, and attach your force to his—"

"I understand your excellency," was the simple answer, as Gates hinted his true objections in the last sentence; but, save the slight compression of his lips, which were usually parted otherwise, no trace of emotion besides, appeared upon the countenance of the speaker

"My men," he continued, "are some of them, of the very best families in the country; homeless now, they have been robbed of all by their enemies. They are not the men to fight less earnestly on that account, nor will their poverty and rags hinder them from striking a good blow, when occasion serves, against the invader to whom they owe their sufferings."

Gates was sufficiently a tactician to see that the pride of Marion was touched with the unjust estimate which had been made of his men, and he strove to remove the impression by a show of frankness.

"But, you see, my dear colonel, that though your men may fight like very devils, nothing can possibly keep the continentals from laughing at them. We can't supply your people; and so long as they remain as they are, so long will they be a laughing-stock—so long there will be uproar and insubordination. We are quite too delicately situated now to risk anything with the army; we are too nigh the enemy, and our troops have been too stinted. To deny them to laugh, is to force them to rebel; we can only remove the cause of laughter, and in this way, defeat the insubordination which undue merriment, sternly and suddenly checked, would certainly bring about."

Gates had made the best of his case, and Marion, with few words, yielded to the opinion, from which, however, he mentally withheld all his assent. He contented himself, simply, with stating his own and the desire of his men to serve the country by active operation in the best possible way. Gates replied to this in a manner sufficiently annoying to his hearer, but which had subsequently its own adequate rebuke.

"Any increase of force, my dear colonel, would be perfectly unnecessary after my junction with the troops I daily look for. Caswell will bring me all the North Carolina subsidies, and General Stevens, with a strong body of Virginians, will join in a few days. My force then will be little short of seven thousand men, and quite sufficient for all contemplated purposes. We shall therefore need no aid from your followers."

"I hope not, general; though should you, my men are always ready to offer it for their country. Have I your excellency's permission to retire?"

"You have, Colonel Marion; but I trust you will still continue operations on the Peedee and the Santee rivers. One service, if you will permit me, I will require at your hands; and that is, that you

19*

will employ your men in breaking up all the boats which you can possibly find at the several crossing-places on the Wateree—at Nelson's and Vance's ferries in particular. We must not 'et my Lord Rawdon escape us."

It was now Marion's turn to smile, and his dark eye kindled with an arch and lustrous expression as he heard of the anticipated victory. He well knew that Rawdon could not and would not endeavour to retreat. Such a movement would at once lose him the country. It would have stimulated the dormant hopes of all the people. It would have crushed the tories, by withdrawing the army whose presence had been their prop. It would destroy all the immense labours, at one blow, by which the invader had sought, not only to realize, but to secure his power.

The weakness of Gates amuse I the partisan, and the smile upon his lips was irrepressible. But the self-complaisance of the general did not suffer him to behold it ; and, concluding his wishes and his compliments at the same time, he bowed the Swamp Fox out of the marquee, and left him to the attention of the old baron, De Kalb. The veteran was gloomy, and did not scruple to pour his melancholy forebodings into the ears of Marion, for whom he had conceived a liking. When they were about to separate, with a ludicrous smile, he reminded Marion of the employment which Gates had assigned him in the destruction of the boats.

"You need not hurry to its execution, my friend," said he ; "it is a sad waste of property, and, if my thoughts do not greatly wander, I fear an unnecessary waste. But God cheer us, and his blessing be upon you."

They parted—never to meet again. The partisan led his rejected warriors back in the direction of his swamp dwelling, on the Santee, while the veteran went back with a heavy heart to his duties in the camp.

In an hour, the onward march of the army was again resumed. The troops went forward with more alacrity, as they had that day feasted with more satisfaction to themselves than on many days before. A small supply of Indian meal had been brought into camp by the foragers, and produced quite a sensation. This gave a mess to all ; ard the impoverished beef, which, hitherto, they had eateu either alone or with unripe fruit, boiled along with it, grew particularly palatable. With all the elasticity which belongs to soldiers, they forgot past privations, and hurried on, under the promise of improving circumstances, which were to meet them at every step of their farther progress.

This spirit was the more increased, as the commanding officer, aware of the critical situation of the troops, unfolded himself more freely than he had hitherto done to Colonel Williams, who acted as deputy adjutant-general. The show of confidence operated favour ably on the troops, who were at a loss to know why General Gates, against all counsel, had taken the present route. He said it had been forced upon him ; that his object was to unite with Caswell ; that Caswell had evaded every order to join with him ; that Caswell's vanity desired a separate command, and that he probably contemplated some enterprise by which to distinguish himself.

" I should not be sorry," said he, " to see his ambition checked by a rap over the knuckles, if it were not that the militia would disperse and leave this handful of brave men (meaning the continentals) without even nominal assistance."

He urged that the route was taken to counteract the risks of Caswell, by forcing him to the junction he seemed so desirous to avoid ; and, at the same time, to secure some of the supplies of provisions and other necessaries, which he asserted, on the alleged authority of the executive of North Carolina, were even then in the greatest profusion in Caswell's camp. He, moreover, suggested that a change of direction now would not only dispirit the troops, but intimidate the people of the country, who had generally sent in their adhesion as he passed, promising to join him under their own leaders. These were the arguments of Gates; and whatever may be their value, he should have the benefit of them in his defence. To these were opposed, in vain, the poverty and destitution of the country, and the perfidious character of the people along the route they pursued. The die was cast, however, and the army went forward to destruction. But we will not anticipate.

On the fifth of August, in the afternoon, General Gates received a letter from Caswell, notifying him of an attack which he meditated upon a post of the British, on Lynch's creek, about fourteen miles from the militia encampment. This increased the anxiety of the general to advance, fearing lest Caswell should involve himself in utter ruin; and he eagerly pressed forward the regulars. While urging them still upon the ensuing day, a new despatch was received from the general of militia, stating his apprehensions of an attack from the very post which, the day before, he had himself meditated to assault. Such a strange mixture of boldness and timidity alarmed Gates even for his safety; and he now hurried forward to relieve him from himself, and with more rapidity than ever. On the seventh of August, by dint of forced marching, he attained his object, and the long-delayed junction was safely effected, at the Cross Roads, about fifteen miles east of the enemy's most advanced post on Lynch's creek.

The army was now refreshed; every thing was in plenty; for amid the greatest confusion, and in spite of all his difficulties, Caswell had contrived to keep a constant supply of wines, and other luxuries on hand, with which the half famished continentals were pleasantly regaled. After the junction, which occurred about noon in the day, the army marched a few miles towards the advanced station of the British. On the next day, pressing forward to the post, they found the field their own; the enemy had evacuated it, and had retired back, at his own leisure, to a much stronger position on Little Lynch's creek, and within a day's march of the main post of Camden. There Rawdon commanded in person, with a force already strong, and hourly increasing from a judicious contraction of the minor posts around him, which he effected as soon as apprised of the approach of the continentals.

Still, the army pressed forward, in obedience to command, ignorant of its course, and totally unconscious of the next step to be taken. The commander, however, began to take his precautions, as he saw the danger of encountering an enemy—encumbered as he now was with unnecessary baggage, and the large numbers of women and children, whom he had found with Caswell's militia. Wagons were detached to convey the heavy baggage, and such women as could be driven away, to a place of safety near Charlotte; but large numbers of them preferred remaining with the troops, sharing all their dangers, and partaking of their privations

Exhortations and menaces alike failed of effect; they positively refused to leave the army on any terms.

Relieved, however, of much of his encumbrance, Gates proceeded to the post on Little Lynch's creek, to which the enemy had retired. Here he found him strongly posted. He was in cover, on a rising ground, on the south side of the Wateree; the way leading to it was over a causeway to a wooden bridge which stood on the north side, resting upon very steep banks. The creek lay in a deep muddy channel, bounded on the north by an extensive swamp, and only passable (except by a circuit of several miles) directly in front of the enemy.

" To attack him in face, would be taking the bull by the horns indeed," was the conclusive remark of Gates, as he reviewed the position and examined its defences. " We'll go round him!"— and, for the first time, the commander prepared to take the *least* direct road to the enemy. Defiling by the right, having cautiously thrown out a flanking regiment under Colonel Hall, of Maryland, the army pushed on by a circuitous course towards Rawdon.

This movement had the effect of breaking up the minor post of the enemy which Gates had been compelled to avoid, and its commanding officer, with some precipitation, fell back, with all his garrison, upon Camden. The post at Clermont, Rugely's Mills, was also abandoned at the same time; and, on the thirteenth of August, it was occupied by the American general with his jaded army.

The movements of Gates had been closely watched by the enemy, who was vigilant in the extreme. The precautions taken by Rawdon—who, up to this moment, had been the general in command opposed to him—were judicious and timely. But the command was now to be delivered into yet abler hands; for, with the first account of the proximity of the southern army, Cornwallis, with a portion of the garrison from Charleston, set forth for Camden. His march communicated, like wildfire, the business of his mission to the people of the country. through which he was to pass; and it was with feelings in nowise enviable, that he saw the exulting looks of the disaffected whenever they met with him on his progress. At Dorchester, where he paused a day, and by his presence controlled somewhat the restless spirit of those in that quarter, who, otherwise, were willing enough to rise in mutiny, he could almost hear the muttered rebellion as it rose involuntarily to the lips of many. Standing lustily in his doorway as the glittering regiments went through the village, old Pryor growled out his hope for their destruction.

"Ay, go! ye glitter now, and look d—d fine, but Gates will roll your red jackets in the mud. He'll give you a dressing, my lads, ye shall remember. Ay, shake your flags, and beat your drums, but you'll have another guess sort of shake and tune when you're coming back."

The stern and lofty earl, erect and tall, inflexible and thoughtful, moved along upon his steed like some massive tower, before the dwelling of the sturdy rebel; who, uttering no shout, waving no hat, giving no sign but that of scornful hate, and a most bitter contempt, gazed upon the warrior without fear or shrinking.

"Go, d—n you, go; go where the drum that beats for you shall be muffled; go where the bugle that rings in your ears shall not stir you again in your saddles; go where the rifle shall have a better mark in your bodies than it ever found at Bunker's and at Lexington."

And as he muttered thus, his old eye rekindled, and he watched the last retreating forms in the distance, repeating to himself the fond hope, which was then a pregnant sentiment in the bosom of thousands, who had felt long what they could not resent, and now rejoiced in the belief, confidently entertained, that their enemies had gone to a battle-field from whence they never would return. The hour of punishment was at hand—so they fondly thought— and Gates's was the avenging arm sent for its infliction.

On the night of the fifteenth of August, without any conference with his officers, Gates bade his army advance from Clermont on the route to Camden. What was his hope? What, indeed, we may well ask, was his object? He literally had no intelligence in respect to his enemy; he had omitted most of those precautions by which, in armies, intelligence was to be procured. The suggestions of his own friends were unheeded, and he deigned no general consultation. Colonels Williams and Walton, both ventured to emind him, in general terms, of the near neighbourhood of the foe, doubtless in force; for, on the subject of their numbers, no information had yet been received. On the same day, an inhabitant from Camden, named Hughson, came to head-quarters, affecting ignorance of the approach of the Americans, and pretending a warm interest in their success. He was a Marylander, and was disposed to be very friendly with his countrymen, the continentals. He freely gave his information to Gates—information which was true, so far as it went; but which was given in just sufficient quantity to promote the precipitation of the American commander and the purposes of the British. Gates readily believed all that was told him; and though suspicions arose in the minds of some of the officers around him, the credulity of the general himself underwent no lessening from the more prudent counsels of his subordinates. The spy—for such he was—was actually suffered to leave the camp and return to Camden, not only with the fulfilment of the purpose for which he went, but possessed of the more valuable information with which he was permitted to return. Besotted self-confidence had actually blinded the American general to the huge and fearful trench which he had been digging for himself, and which now lay immediately before him.

A few hours only divided him from his enemy; yet, strange to say, he knew not that it was Cornwallis, himself, who stood opposed to him. That brave commander had hurried with all possible celerity to the scene of action. He knew how greatly the fortunes of the colony depended upon the present contest. Marion was even then busy along the Santee, and so effectually did he guard the passes by Nelson's and Watson's, that his lordship, though commanding a fine body of troops, veterans all, fresh from Charleston, and superior far to any force of the partisan, was compelled to take a circuitous and indirect route in reaching Camden. Marion had greatly increased his force with a number of insurgents from Black river. Sumter, too, was in active motion, and watched the Wateree river with the avidity of a hawk. On the success of this battle depended every thing; for, though to gain it would not necessarily have secured the conquest of Cornwallis in Carolina, *not to gain it* would most probably have been the loss of all. He knew this, and his desire was for early battle before the troops of

Gates were rested; before the militia could come in to his relief; and before the spirit of revolt, throughout the province, should distract, by various risings and simultaneous enterprises. No general was ever more ready than Cornwallis to carve his way out of difficulties with the strong arm and the sword. Policy, and his passion alike, persuaded him now to the adoption of this stern arbitrament.

At the very hour that Gates moved from Clermont in the route to Camden, the British general set out from that station to attack him in his encampment. Yet Gates had no intelligence of this: he knew not even that his lordship had reached Camden. He neglected every means of intelligence, and the retributive justice, which, in one moment, withered all the choice laurels of his previous fame, and tore the green honours from his brow, though stern and dreadful, must yet be held the just due of him, who, with a leading responsibility of life, freedom, and fortune depending upon him, forfeits, by the feebleness of a rash spirit, all the rich triumphs that are otherwise within his grasp. Vainly has the historian striven after arguments in his excuse. He is without defence; and in reviewing all the events of this period, we must convict him of headstrong self-confidence, temerity without coolness, and effort, idly expended, without a purpose, and almost without an aim. It was the opinion of his officers, and, indeed, of all others, that the delay of a **few** days, with his army in a secure position, was all that was necessary towards giving the American an immense superiority over the British commander. Provisions would have been plenty in that time, and the native militia, once satisfied of his presence, would have crowded to his camp. But the fates were impatient for their prey, and he whom God has once appointed for destruction, may well fold his robes about him in preparation for his fall.

CHAPTER XLII.

THE American general at last began to exhibit some consciousness of the near neighbourhood of foes; and that day, the 15th
August, after general orders, he prepared the following in addition
—Colonel Williams, acting adjutant-general, Colonel Walton, and
one other member of his family being present:—

" 1. The sick, the extra artillery stores, the heavy baggage, and
such quarter-master's stores as are not immediately wanted, to
march this evening, under a strong guard, to Waxhaw. To this
order the general requests the brigadier-generals to see that those
under their command pay the most exact and scrupulous obedience.

" 2. Lieutenant-Colonel Edmonds, with the remaining guns of
the park, will take post and march with the Virginia brigade
under General Stevens. He will direct, as any deficiency may
happen in the artillery affixed to the other brigade, to supply it
immediately. His military staff, and a proportion of his officers,
with forty of his men, are to attend him and await his orders.

" 3. The troops will be ready to march precisely at ten o'clock,
in the following order, viz :—

" Colonel Armand's advance—cavalry commanded by Colonel
Armand ; Colonel Porterfield's light infantry upon the right flank
of Colonel Armand, in Indian file, two hundred yards from the
road ; Major Armstrong's light infantry in the same order as Colonel Porterfield's, upon the left flank of the legion.

" Advance-guard of foot ; composed of the advance-pickets, first
brigade of Maryland, second brigade of Maryland, division of North
Carolina, division of Virginia ; rear-guard—volunteer cavalry upon
the flank of baggage, equally divided.

" In this order the troops will proceed on their march this night.

" 4. In case of an attack by the enemy's cavalry in front, the light infantry upon each flank will instantly move up, and give, and continue, the most galling fire upon the enemy's horse. This will enable Colonel Armand not only to support the shock of the enemy's charge, but finally to rout him. The colonel will therefore consider the order to stand the attack of the enemy's cavalry, be their number what it may, as positive.

" 5. General Stevens will immediately order one captain, two lieutenants, one ensign, three sergeants, one drum, and sixty rank and file, to join Colonel Porterfield's infantry. These are to be taken from the most experienced woodsmen, and men every way fittest for the service.

" 6. General Caswell will likewise complete Major Armstrong's light infantry to their original number. These must be marched immediately to the advanced post of the army.

" The troops will observe the profoundest silence upon the march, and any soldier who offers to fire without the command of his officer, must instantly be put to death.

" When the ground will admit of it, and the near approach of the enemy renders it necessary, the army will, when ordered, march in columns.

" The artillery at the head of their respective brigades, and the baggage in the rear. The guard of the heavy baggage will be composed of the remaining officers and soldiers of the artillery, one captain, two subalterns, four sergeants, one drum, and sixty rank and file, &c.

" The tents of the whole army are to be struck at tattoo."

Such were the general orders for the march. Colonel Williams and the adjutant-general, Colonel Walton, and Major Thomas Pinckney, were in conversation at the entrance of the general's marquee, when, with a smiling and good-natured countenance, he brought the paper forth, and called for he adjutant-general's attention.

" Colonel Williams, you will be punctual in the transmission of these orders to the several commands, so that there be no delay.

Look also at this estimate, which has been made this morning of the entire force, rank and file, of the army. It would seem to be correct."

Williams took the paper, and glanced rapidly over the estimate, which startled him by its gross exaggerations.

" Correct, sir !" he exclaimed, with unfeigned astonishment ; " impossible ! Seven thousand men !—there are not four thousand fit for duty."

" You will see, and report on this," said the general, coolly, and at once turned away o the tent, in which, a moment after, he was lost from sight.

" Pinckney," said Williams, " come and assist me in this estimate. Colonel Walton will keep in attendance—you will not be wanted."

The gallant young soldier, then a tall, fresh and vigorous youth, noble, and accomplished by European education, as were few native Americans at that period, immediately complied with the request, and the two moved away upon the contemplated mission. Availing himself of his orders, which were to bid all the general officers to council in Rugely's barn, Williams called also upon the officers commanding corps for a field return. This he required to be as exact as possible ; and, as neither himself nor Pinckney was required to attend the deliberations, they devoted themselves to a careful abstract of the true force of the army for the general's better information. This was presented to him as soon as the council had broken up, and just as Gates was coming out of the door, where Williams and his aides awaited him. He took the paper, and with clouding brows examined its contents.

" How ! what is this ? what is this figure, Colonel Williams ?" he inquired, dashing his forefinger hurriedly upon the paper.

" A three, sir," was the reply.

" A three ? And you mean to say that there are only three thousand and fifty-two men, rank and file, fit for duty ?"

" I do, your excellency—scarce a man more."

" Impossible ! There were no less than thirteen general officers in council, and our estimate gave not a man less than seven thousand, rank and file."

"Your estimate of the general officers is correct enough, sir," said Williams, firmly, "but mine of the men is not less so. The disparity between officers and men, in our battles," continued the speaker, innocently enough, "has always been rather remarkable."

A quick motion of Gates's head, a sudden shooting glance of his eye, intimated his own perception of the sarcasm, and apprised Williams, for the first time, of the equivocal character of his re mark. His cheeks grew to scarlet, as he perceived its force, and his confusion would have been evident to his superior, but that the general relieved him by turning away, with the paper crumpled up in his hands, simply remarking as he left them—

"Three thousand—that is certainly below the estimate of the morning; but they are enough—enough for our purpose."

Williams longed to ask him what that purpose was, but prudence restrained him. The only farther remark of Gates on the subject was uttered as he was retiring—

"You have delivered the orders, sir?—see them obeyed. There was no dissent from them in council."

True it is that there had been no dissent from them in council; but they were scarcely submitted for examination. There had been no consultation, and their promulgation, *out of council*, at once provoked the most unrestrained animadversion. The officers generally insisted that all opinion or discussion had been silenced by the very positive terms in which the orders had been expressed; and, indeed, there could have been little doubt, from all the context, that General Gates did not conceive it necessary that any reference should be made to the opinions of those around him. The council was simply the creature of a certain sense of military propriety, and was yielded by Gates rather to general notions of what was due to courtesy, than as a matter necessary to the great cause and deep interests in which he was engaged. The elder officers said little when the orders were conveyed to them. The veteran Baron De Kalb, presuming on his age and services, however, and the usual respect with which Gates had treated him hitherto, sought an interview with him, which was not denied. He suggested to him the diminished force of the army, so infinitely inferior, as it was found to be, to the estimate

...nch had been made of it in the morning. This he held a sufficient reason for changing the present resolution of advance for ...ne less hazardous. There was another and more forcible reason yet.

" Two thirds of our army, your excellency is aware, are militia— men who have never yet seen service, and have scarce been exercised in arms together."

" True, baron, but that is an argument against using them at any period. They must begin some time or other."

" Yes, your excellency; but our first experiments with them should be easy ones. By these orders, we are not only to march them, but to require them to form column, and to manœuvre, by night, in the face of an enemy, and probably under his fire. This is the work of veterans only."

" The danger seems to increase in magnitude, baron; does it ...t ?"

The old soldier drew himself up with dignity—his manly person, ...longer bowed or bent, his fine blue eye flashing, and his cheek ...ddening as he spoke: he replied :--

" I know not what your excellency's remark may mean ; but in regard to the greatness or the littleness of the danger, I, who have been forty years a trusted soldier of the King of France, should care but little to encounter it. Were the question one affecting my life only, it were easily answered. 1 came to fight the battles of your country, sir, and am prepared, at all hours, to die in them."

The rebuke had its effect upon the commander, though he did not acknowledge it. His self-esteem was too great for that. Nor did he allow the suggestions of the baron to have any weight upon his previous determinations. With a commonplace compliment, the conference was closed, and De Kalb went back to his command —doubtful, pained, and justly offended. In camp, the dissatisfaction had rather subsided, with the single exception, among the officers, of Colonel Armand. He took exception to the positive orders concerning himself, as implying a doubt of his courage; at the same time he objected to the placing of his cavalry in front of a line of battle—certainly a very injudicious order, particularly as the legion of Armand was most heterogeneous in its formation, and such a disposition of cavalry had never been m... ...

complained that Gates had placed him there from resentment, on
account of a previous dispute between thèm touching the use of
horses.

"I do not say," said he, in broken English, "that General Gates
intends to sacrifice us; but I do say, that if such were his intentions, these are just the steps which he should take for it."

Still, however, as it was not known that the enemy was posi
tively in force before them, all the parties grew more satisfied, after
a while, to proceed. The army moved on accordingly at the
appointed hour.

The two armies met at midnight. They first felt each other
through the mutual salutation of small-arms, between their several
advance-guards. The cavalry of Armand's legion were the first to
reel in the unexpected contest. They recoiled, and in their retreat,
flying confusedly, threw the whole corps into disorder. This, with
a similar recoil, fell back upon the front column of infantry, disordered the first Maryland brigade, and occasioned a momentary
consternation throughout the entire line of advance. But Colonel
Porterfield advanced from the wing, agreeably to first orders, threw
in a prompt fire upon the British van, and his men gallantly cheering
as they advanced, restored the general confidence.

The British, seemingly no less astounded than the Americans,
fell back after the first shock, and both parties seemed to acquiesce
in a suspension of all further hostilities for the night. Prisoners
were taken on both sides in this rencontre, and the intelligence
gained by those brought into the American camp, was productive
of a degree of astonishment, in General Gates's mind, which found
its way to his countenance. He called a council of war instantly.
When the adjutant-general communicated the call to De Kalb, the
old veteran's opinion may be gathered from the response which
he made to that officer—

"Has the general given you orders to retreat the army, Colonel
Williams?"

"He has not," was the answer.

"I will be with you in a moment, then, but will first burn my
papers;" a duty which he performed, a short time after, with
scrupulous promptitude.

Assembled in the rear of the army, General Gates communicated the intelligence obtained from the prisoners just taken ; and then for the first time, proposed a question, implying some little hesita-tion on the subject of future operations.

" What now is to be done, gentlemen ?"

For a few moments all were silent, until General Stevens of the Virginians, after looking round for some other to speak, advanced in front of the commander, and put his own answer in the form of a new inquiry.

" Is it not too late, *now*, gentlemen, to do any thing but fight ?"

Another pause ensued, which, as it seemed to give assent to the last words of Stevens, General Gates himself interrupted—

" Then we must fight : gentlemen, be pleased to resume your posts."

They all moved to their stations with the promptness of soldiers, but with the thoughts and feelings of men also, who could not approve of what had been done, and who had nothing consoling in the prospect before them. Gates moved hurriedly for several moments up and down the little tent which had been raised for him within the hour. His manner was subdued, but cool. Once or twice he looked forth from its cover with an air of anxiety, then turning to Williams, and the aides in attendance, he remarked—

" This is a quiet night, gentlemen, but it promises to be a tedious one. What is the time, Colonel Walton ?"

" A little after one, sir," was the reply.

" You may leave me for an hour, gentlemen—only an hour ; we must prepare for daylight."

Walton and Major Pinckney, together, strolled away, not re-quiring repose. The thought of Colonel Walton was with his child—the one—the one only—who could fill his heart—who could inspire painful anxiety at such a moment in his mind. How fervent were his prayers in that hour for her safety, whatever fate in the coming events of the daylight, might award to him !

CHAPTER XLIII.

"Then came the cloud, the arrowy storm of war.
The fatal stroke, the wild and whizzing shot,
Seeking a victim—the close strife, the groan,
And the shrill cry of writhing agony."

IF every thing was doubtful and uncertain in the camp of Gates, the state of things was very different in that of Cornwallis. That able commander knew his ground, his own men, and the confidence and the weakness alike of his enemy. That weakness, that unhappy confidence, were his security and strength. His own force numbered little over two thousand men; but they were tried soldiers, veterans in the British southern army, and familiar with their officers. The troops of Gates—two thirds of them at least—had never once seen service; and the greater number only now for the first time knew and beheld their commander. They had heard of his renown, however, and this secured their confidence. It had an effect far more dangerous upon his officers; for, if it did not secure their confidence also, it made them scrupulous in their suggestions of counsel to one who, from the outset, seemed to have gone forth with the determination of rivalling the rapidity, as well as the immensity, of Cæsar's victories. To come, to see, to conquer, was the aim of Gates; forgetting, that while Cæsar commanded the Roman legion, Horatio Gates was required *first to teach* the American militia.

Cornwallis seems perfectly to have understood his man. They are said to have once seen foreign service together; if so, the earl had studied him with no little success. He now availed himself of the rashness of his opponent; and, though inferior in numbers, went forth to meet him. We have seen their first encounter, where Gates, contrary to the advice of his best officers, commenced a march after nightfall; requiring of undrilled militia the most novel and difficult evolutions in the dark. Having felt his enemy, and per ceived, from the weight of Colonel Porterfielc's infantry fire, that the whole force of the Americans was at hand, Cornwallis drew in his army, which had been in marching order, when the encounter began ; and, changing his line to suit the new form of events, proceeded to make other arrangements for the dawning.

The firing was still continued, in the advance, though materia.ly diminished and still diminishing, when Cornwallis gave the orders to recall his forces. The order was a timely one. In that moment the advance of Porterfield was pressing .heavily upon the British van, and driving it before them. The mutual orders of the two generals, both dreading to risk the controversy on a struggle so unexpectedly begun, closed the affair for the night.

Dismounting beneath a clump of trees, Cornwallis called around him a council of his officers. The tall, portly form of the earl rose loftily in the midst of all, with a cool, quiet dignity, that indicated command. His face was one of much expression, and spoke a character of great firmness and quick resolve. His features were bold and imposing ; his cheeks full and broad, nose prominent, forehead rather broad than high, his lips not thin, but closely fitting. His eye had in it just enough of the kindling of battle to enliven features which otherwise would have appeared more imperious than intelligent. His carriage was manly, and marked by all the ease of the courtier. Standing erect, with his hand lightly resting on the hilt of his sword, and looking earnestly around him on his several officers as they made their appearance—a dozen lightwood torches flaming in the hands of the guards around him—his presence was majestic and noble. Yet there was a something in his features, which, if not sanguinary, at least indicated well that indifference to human life, that atrocious hardihood of deed, which a severe justice would describe as crime, and which marked too many of his doings in the South. His looks did not belie that callosity of soul which could doom his fellow-men, by dozens, to the gallows—the accusation unproven against them, and their own defence utterly unheard.

Beside him, conspicuous, though neither tall nor commanding in person, stood one to whom the references of Cornwallis were made with a degree of familiarity not often manifested by the comman-

20

der. His person was of the middle size, rather slender than full, but of figure well made, admirably set, and in its movements marked alike by ease and strength. He was muscular and bony —though not enough so to command particular attention on this account. The face alone spoke, and it was a face to be remembered. It was rather pale and thin, but well chiselled; and the mouth was particularly small and beautiful. Its expression was girlish in the extreme, and would have been held to indicate effeminacy as the characteristic of its owner, but for its even quiet, its immobility, its calm indifference of expression. The nose was good, but neither long nor large: it comported well with the expression of the mouth. But it was the eye that spoke; and its slightest look was earnestness. Every glance seemed sent forth upon some especial mission—every look had its object. Its movements, unlike those of the lips, were rapid and irregular. His hair was light and unpowdered; worn, singularly enough, at that period, without the usual tie, and entirely free from the vile pomatum which disfigured the fashionable heads of the upper classes. His steel cap and waving plume were carried in his hand; and he stood, silent but observing, beside Cornwallis, as Lord Rawdon, followed by the brave Lieutenant-Colonel Webster, and other officers, came up to the conference. The warrior we have endeavoured briefly to describe, was one whose name, for a time, was well calculated to awaken in the souls of the Southern whigs, an equal feeling of hate and dread. He was the notorious Colonel Tarleton, the very wing of the British invading army: a person, striking and commanding in aspect gentle and dignified in deportment, calm and even in his general temper; but fierce and forward in war, sanguinary in victory, delighting in blood, and impatient always until he beheld it flowing.

Webster, equally if not more brave than Tarleton, and certainly a far better officer, bore a better character for mercy in the southern warfare. His worth to his own army was equally great, and there is no such odium coupled with his exploits, as shaded and stained the very best of Tarleton's. His celebrity with the one, never obtained for him any unhappy notoriety with the other.

"The enemy is in force before us, gentlemen," said Cornwallis, abruptly—"so our prisoners tell us. These confirm the reports of the Marylander, Hughson. The rebels come, as we could wish them, fairly into our clutches."

"The fact would seem to be fully confirmed, my lord, by the severity of their fire from the infantry on the left. Such an advance guard would at once speak for the presence of their entire army."

This was the remark of Webster. There was a pause of a moment, in which Cornwallis appeared to consult a memorandum in his hand. He spoke at length to Tarleton.

"What horse was the report of Hughson?"

"Armand's only—some sixty-five, your excellency."

"And their late reinforcement of Virginians?"

"A perfect, but single regiment."

"'Tis odds, gentlemen, large odds against us, if these reports be true. The lines of Maryland and Delaware—good troops these—the Virginia troops, the North Carolinians, and native militia, make up five thousand men at least—full five thousand—for the rebel army. Ours is not three."

"But quite enough, my lord," was the prompt but measured language of Tarleton. "The rebel militia are mere carrion, half starved ; and, De Kalb's continentals alone excepted, will not stand a second fire. We shall ride over them."

"Ay, Tarleton—you will ride over them when our bayonets have first given you a clear track," said Webster.

"Which you will soon do," was the equally cool but ready response of the other. "They have come into our clutches, to employ the phrase of your excellency ; it will be our fault if we do not close our claws upon them. Half starved, and perfectly undrilled, they will offer little obstacle. The novelty of situation, alone, is always terror enough for these militia. It is such a terror as they never get over until the third trial. This is the first, with at least two thirds of this hodge-podge army. We must see that they do not get to a second."

"There spoke the sabre," said Rawdon, playfully.

"It should never speak twice," responded Tarleton, without a smile ; "dead rebels never bite."

" No, but they howl most cursedly before they die, as you should know, Tarleton above all others. We hear the echoes even now from the Waxhaws, where your sabres told upon Buford's regiment," said Rawdon.

" Ay, that was a sad business, Bannister, though, to be sure, you could not well help it," was the additional remark of Cornwallis, who yet looked approvingly upon the person whom he thus partially censured. Tarleton simply smiled; his thin lips slightly parting, and exhibiting a brief glimpse of the closed teeth, as he replied—

" Better they should howl than hurt : their bark is music; their bite might be something worse. I am content to bear the reproach, so long as our good sovereign reaps the benefit ; and will always prefer to amputate the vicious member that we cannot so surely heal."

"Our wish is for the fight, gentlemen," said Cornwallis ; "my own opinion insists upon it as the preferable measure. They outnumber us, it is true; but I feel satisfied we can outfight them. Whether we can or not, I think, at least, we should try for it. We gain everything by victory; delay increases their force ; and even without defeat, makes the difficulty of conquest with us so much the greater. The suggestion of Tarleton is one also of importance. The rebels are half starved men ; their provisions have been unequal to their wants, and unsatisfactory, for some time past. Disease, too—so we learn from Hughson—has thinned them greaty ; and in every possible aspect, our condition imperiously calls or fight. This is my opinion."

"And mine," responded Tarleton slowly, letting down his sabre, which rattled quiveringly in the sheath with the stroke. The same opinion was expressed by Rawdon, Webster, and the rest ; the resolve for fight was unanimous. Cornwallis then proceeded to arrange his army in order of battle. They displayed in one line, completely occupying the ground, one flank resting on a swamp, the other on a slight ravine which ran parallel with, and near it. The infantry of the reserve, dividing equally, took post in a second line, opposite the centre of each wing. The cavalry, commanded by Tarleton, held the road, where the left of the right wing met the volunteers of Ireland, a corps which, thus placed, formed the right of the left wing. On the right, Lieutenant-Colonel Webster was placed in command. To Colonel Lord Rawdon the left was assigned. Two six and two three-pounders, under Lieutenant M'Leod, were placed in the front line, and two other pieces with the reserve.

The arrangement of this force, though at midnight, so perfectly drilled and well experienced had they been, was the movement of machines rather than of men. Every step was taken under the eyes of superior officers—every cannon found its assigned place with a niceness, admirably contrasting with the confusion which is supposed to belong to battle. Each soldier, before the dawn had his supply of rum provided him; and officers and men, resolute and ready, held their places in order of battle, anxiously awaiting the approaching daylight.

The American army was formed with similar precision, and at the same hour. The second brigade of Maryland, with the regiment of Delaware, under Gen. Gist, took the right; the brigade of North Carolina militia, led by Caswell, the centre; that of Virginia, under Stevens, the left. The first Maryland brigade was formed in reserve, under General Smallwood. Major-General Baron De Kalb, charged with the line of battle, took post on the right, while Gates, superintending the whole, as general-in-chief, placed himself on the road between the line and the reserve. To each brigade a due proportion of artillery was allotted; but the wing of an army—the horse—was utterly wanting to that of Gates. The cavalry of Armand, defeated at the first encounter of the night, is thought, by some of the simple countrymen who witnessed their rapidity, to be flying to this very day.

Gates's line of battle has been criticised, with the rest of his proceedings, in this unhappy campaign. His arrangements placed the Virginia militia, an untried body, which had never before seen service, on the left, a disposition which necessarily put them in front of the enemy's right, consisting of his veterans. The better course would certainly have been, to have thrown the continentals, our regulars, upon the left; by which arrangement, the best men of both armies must have encountered. This was the plan of Lincoln in previous events, and certainly that plan most conformable to, and indeed called for by, the circumstances of the case. The flank of the American, like that of the British army, rested upon a morass; and, thus disposed, it awaited upon the ground, and in the given order, for the first glimpses of daylight and the enemy.

With the dawn of day the British were discovered in front, in column, and on the advance. This was communicated to the adjutant-general, Williams, who soon distinguished the British uniform about two hundred yards before him. Immediately ordering the batteries to be opened upon them, he rode to General Gates, who was in the rear of the second line, and informed him of what had been done, communicating his opinion, at the same time, that the enemy were displaying their column by the right; but still nothing was clear enough in the proceedings of the opposite army for certainty on either side. Gates heard him attentively, but gave no orders, and seemed disposed to await the progress of events; upon which the adjutant-general presumed upon a farther suggestion.

" Does not your excellency think that if the enemy were attacked briskly by Stevens, while in the act of deploying, the effect——"

" Yes, sir," said Gates, hurriedly interrupting him ; " that's right —let it be done, sir."

These were almost the last orders given by the unhappy commander. Quick as thought, Williams seized the commission, and, readily obedient, General Stevens advanced with his brigade to the charge ; all seemingly in fine spirits. But the instructions came too late—the evolution of the enemy was complete ; they were already in line, and prepared to receive the attack.

But this did not alter the determination either of Stevens or the adjutant. Assigning a force of fifty men to the latter to commence the action by firing from the cover of trees as riflemen, in the hope to extort the premature fire of the British, Stevens cried out to his brigade, as he saw the enemy's column moving down upon him in front—

" Courage, my men, and charge—charge home ! You have bayonets as well as they."

His words were drowned and lost in the wild huzzas and the

fierce onset of the opposing British, who fired as they came on, with their pieces in rest for the charge of bayonets. The militia was seized with a panic, and, in spite of all the efforts of the gallant Stevens, could not be persuaded either to stand the charge or to return the fire. A few only stood with their leader. The great majority, throwing away their loaded arms, fled in every direction ; and, catching from them the unworthy panic, the North Carolinians—a single regiment under Colonel Dixon alone excepted—followed the shameful example.

In vain did Stevens and Caswell endeavour to stem the torrent of retreat. The fugitives were not to be restrained; and sought, in desperate flight, for that safety which flight seldom gives, and which it most certainly denied to them. They broke through the line, leaving the right still firm, and pressing down upon the reserve, disordered them completely while passing through the ranks, which were already partially demoralized. Panic is one of those indescribable things upon which comment is usually wasted. Its contagious operation is sufficiently understood, if the cause be unexplainable. Gates was sufficiently experienced in war to under stand his danger. He beheld it at a glance. His blind vanity had led to the disaster. It no longer deceived him as to its conse quences. From the place where he stood he beheld the disaster with emotions, wild, staggering, humbling in the last degree, and which almost left him wholly without resource. He had only the native courage of his heart to fall back upon ; he could only seek now to lead them into the thickest waves of danger. His hair withered to the very roots as he surveyed the rout. Through the crowd, the torrent of confusion, with head uncovered and grey locks flying in the wind, he darted headlong, and his voice hoarsely rose over all the sounds of battle, as he strove, with incoherent cries, to arrest the flood, and bring back to order his panic-borne and broken battalions.

"Stand !—stay—turn ! Whither would you fly—why fly, men of Virginia? Am I not here to lead you back—to lead you to victory? Turn, cowards, for shame's sake, for the sake of your country. There is no danger. The battle is yours, if you will but make a single effort. Back with me. Shame not yourselves, your s'ate, your country! Shame not these grey hairs, my countrymen. entreat—I implore—I command you, turn, and strike but a single blow—deliver but another volley. Behold! I myself will lead you to victory!"

He might as well have spoken to the winds, wild and headlong in the autumnal equinox. He might as well have spoken to the floods, loosed from the bonds of the deep, and mounting in foaming mountains above the shores. They heard not—they heeded none of his exhortations—his cries, his entreaties, his curses. He threw himself amidst the fugitives. He smote fiercely among them with bared sword, striking as if among foes only, and all in vain. Never were efforts more honestly, but idly made, to compel the flying militiamen back to the ranks which they had broken, and the standards which they had dishonoured. Then, too late, were the evil effects beheld of that recklessly forward march which had considered none of their necessities,.and had allowed its commander no time to win the confidence of his people. His was an *unaccustomed* voice; and in this lies half the cause of militia panics generally. The voice of a favourite leader would not have been unheard at such a moment; and even then the field might have been recovered—the victory might have been won. But Gates's was not the voice to effect this object. He shouted, implored, raged; and was never heard. In his fury, smiting down a refractory soldier who offered much more defiance to his general than he had done to the British bayonets, he vented his indignation in a torrent of oaths.

"Villains! cowards! wretched cowards! Why will you fly? Turn for shame! For your country, for me, turn upon your enemy, and deliver but one fire—strike but one blow. Turn about, I say—turn, you d—d rascals, turn!"

His exhortations and oaths were equally in vain. The panic had become a madness—drunk, deaf, delirious, insensible to all influences but the one governing terror which beheld danger on all sides, without the resolution to encounter it on any. The torrent bore the unfortunate general along with it; the rush of numbers was no longer resistible; and as, despairing at last of bringing them back, he sought to turn about himself, in order, with the resolution of despair, to throw himself into the thick of the struggle, where it was carried on still between the continentals and the British, a tall sergeant who was hurrying away with the rest, and who had just coolness enough to endeavour to oppose a courage greater than his own, did not hesitate, with one slash of his sabre, to cut the bridle of Gates's horse, and set the animal free to a flight which he naturally followed with the fugitives. Free from all control, the fiery steed of the general, spite of all his efforts, and seeming to share in the common panic, darted along upon the route, pursued by the flying mass, as madly as the rest. Gates had now seen al of the battle which he was destined to see. His hair whitened as he flew. The sting of shame was in his soul—his sense was bewildered—maddened. He would have thrown himself from the horse, but he was prevented by those about him ; and overwhelmed with despair and humiliation, which clung to him ever afterwards through life, to its weary close, the unfortunate general was borne away from the conflict which no generalship now could possibly retrieve.

Meanwhile, the battle still raged fiercely in certain portions of the field. The British were not suffered to sweep the plain without paying the price of honourable victory. Flushed with the successes which they had won, they rushed forward on all hands to lay the final sickle to the harvest ; but their onward course of conquest was arrested for a season by the steady front and unyielding nerve of the continentals under De Kalb. The main battle was yet to be fought. Accustomed to previous encounters, the brave division which was led by the German Baron had too frequently smelt gunpowder to be greatly moved by the panics of militiamen ; and their courage rose in due degree with their isolation. They beheld the rout with little or no emotion, save that of indignation. The panic touched not them. As for the sturdy veteran at their head, it only brought out his best resources, and in showing him the extent of his danger, elevated his soul to a due sense of the resolution which was needed for its encounter. He saw that the field before him was that of his last conflict ; that it would be impossible, with his small division, to make head against the concentrated attack of all the forces of the British : but he was firm
20*

in his decision to exact from his enemy the fullest price of con
quest.

"Stand your ground, my brave fellows," he cried, as, with uncovered head, he rode calmly along through the smoke and danger
—"stand your ground, brave men, and do no shame to your
officers. You have a name to preserve unsullied, and a country to
save from tyranny. Be resolute for both, and we may yet win our
best laurels from this day's struggle!"

They received his speech with cheers.

"Colonel Dixon," said he, addressing the officer in command of
the only regiment of North Carolinians who kept their places in
the line—"Colonel Dixon, close up and feel the Maryland regiment."

It was done handsomely. Surveying the prospect as he rode, in
one of those pauses of the storm that indicate the accumulation of
the masses for new thunders, and seeing that his flank, which had
been exposed by the desertion of the militia, was now partly
covered, the noble veteran prepared to take the initiative, and to anticipate, by his own, the charge of the British. His orders to this
effect were delivered with the tone of true valour. His decision
was the only course left him for comparative safety, and was that
of a sound experience. To have simply received the assault, with
the full momentum upon him of the rushing masses of the enemy,
would probably have been the annihilation of his division. He
alighted from his horse, resolved to share with his infantry the
full perils of his next movement, and turned the beast loose in the
rear, to seek safety where he might. The well trained charger
wheeled about with the platoons, and subsequently went into the
charge with the rest, as if his bridle had been governed by the will
of a rider.

De Kalb, meanwhile, took his place in the ranks with his men ;
then with clear shrill voice, his sword stretched and flaming out
along the pathway to be traversed, he gave command for the last
terrible movement.

The loud, clear order to "charge bayonets !"—uttered in the imperfect tones of the foreigner--was heard distinctly along the line.
It ruled over all the sounds in the confusion of the strife. It found

its generous echo in the hearts of all the brave fellows in that devoted phalanx. They seemed to have caught his spirit—they certainly shared in his resolution. Without a moment's hesitation, the whole line advanced as a single man. Shouting with wild hurrahs as they pressed forward, the little space which separated them from the enemy's left, commanded by Rawdon, was soon compassed; and, once more, the opposing torrents were mingled together in the shock of battle. The rival muskets were crossed, their bayonets linked, and for a few seconds the opposing armies reeled to and fro, like so many limb-locked and coherent bodies; but the rush, and the enthusiasm of the charge of De Kalb, were, for the moment, irresistible, and Rawdon fell back beneath it.

"Where is the commander-in-chief?" cried De Kalb, in a fierce voice, as he beheld the adjutant-general, Williams, advancing with his own, the 6th Maryland, having actually driven the enemy out of line in front.

"Gone!" was the single word with which he announced to the old soldier the isolation of his continentals.

"On, then, on!" was the immediate shout of De Kalb; "look not to the right, nor to the left, brave men—but on! You are alone: your own steel must work out your safety. Charge! on! Press them out of the field! Ha! Ha! Cold steel, my brave fellows. Cold steel!"

And as the brave division, with serried arms, rolled forward upon the receding foes, the baron murmured—"Oh! for another column, to keep what these fine fellows have won!—Charge! Cold steel! Cold steel! Give them no time to breathe!"

A group—officers and soldiers—British and American—was seen struggling in front. An officer was down; a squad of soldiers were seeking to despatch him, and two others were unequally contending against them with their swords. The wounded officer was an American.

"Again—once more, my brave fellows—once again—through hem to the hearts of the enemy—charge—charge!" was the fierce order of De Kalb, in his imperfect English; "through them, and stop for nothing!"

"But the officers are ours—they are aides to the general," cried

Brigadier Gist, in the hope to arrest the desperate charge of De Kalb, and save the Americans.

"And we are men!" was the response—"what are these officers to us? Onward! over them, brave men—once more to the hearts of the enemy!"

The group sought to disperse; the assailing soldiers fled away, leaving the wounded officer, and those who had been fighting in his behalf, alone, before the charging squadrons.

"Hold!" cried Colonel Walton, for it was he, advancing as he spoke—"hold, I pray you, Baron De Kalb! we are your friends—"

"On then—to the enemy!" cried De Kalb, unheeding the exhortation; and, filled with his own fury—the fury of desperation—the advancing line resolutely obeyed him The wounded man, and those who stood beside him, must have been crushed, or gone along with the pressing line; and the moment was, therefore, full of peril to the group. Presenting his sword to his advancing countrymen, Colonel Walton cried to the wounded officer, who lay almost senseless at his feet—

"I will share your fate, Pinckney, if I cannot divert it. I stand by you to the last. Hold, Americans! What madness is this?— we are friends—would you trample us down?"

"On with us, then!" fiercely cried De Kalb, "on with us, if you be friends! We know you not otherwise."

"He is too much wounded," cried Walton, pointing to the insensible officer.

"This is no time, sir, to regard the dead or the wounded. The field is covered with both; shall we lose all for one man—officer or soldier? On with us, Colonel Walton—there is no help else. On!"

It was the last command of De Kalb, who was already severely wounded. In that moment the fierce onset of the continentals was arrested. A new obstacle, in a murderous fire from the right, restrained their progress. This was from Webster. Having thoroughly defeated the American left, he was now free to turn his strength upon the isolated continentals. This small, resolute, and now compact body, had moved forward irresistibly. The fierce spirit of its commander seemed to have been shared equally with his men; and, though eve.y step which they took was with the loss of numbers, they had ceaselessly continued to advance—the fire of the British left and centre still telling dreadfully upon them, but without shaking the inflexible and reckless charge.

The sudden movement of Webster upon their flanks first arrested their progress. He turned the whole force of his infantry, together with the twenty-third regiment, upon the exposed flank of the first, or Smallwood's brigade. This had been commanded bravely by Colonel Gunby, and other of its officers, the general himself not being available for some time before. The shock of Webster's charge upon this body was irresistible; they reeled and broke beneath it. They were rallied, and once more stood the assault. They stood, however, but to perish; and it was found impossible to contend longer with the vastly superior and fresh force from the British reserve which was now brought to bear upon them.

This shock, and the effect of Webster's assault, at this critical moment, saved the life of Walton and that of his wounded friend, Major Pinckney. The fierce command of De Kalb was no longer obeyed by the flank regiment, now compelled to combat with another enemy. They faced Webster; and Walton found himself on the extreme left, instead of being in front of the body which, a moment before, had been ordered to pass over him. In another instant, the line reeled beyond him; he saw the enemy pressing on, and he rushed to the front of the retreating division of Americans. Again they were brought to a stand; again the impelling bayonets of Webster drove them backward; and while they yet strove bravely, at the will of their officers, to unite more compactly together for the final conflict, the shrill voice of Tarleton was heard upon the left. Then came the rush of his dragoons; the sweeping sabre darting a terrible light on every hand, and giving the final impetus to that panic which now needed but little to be complete throughout the army.

"Spare! oh, spare the Baron De Kalb!" was a cry of anguish that went up from the centre of the line. It was doubly agonizing, as the accents were uttered evidently by a foreign tongue. Walton looked but an instant in the direction where lay the old veteran, feebly striving still to contend with the numbers who were now pressing upon him. The Chevalier Du Buysson, a faithful friend, stood over him, vainly endeavouring to protect him by the interposition of his own body. His piteous cry—" Spare the baron! spare the Baron De Kalb!" had little or no avail.

Eleven wounds already testified to the reckless courage of the veteran, and the earnestness with which he had done battle to the last for the liberties of a foreign people. The bayonet was again ifted above him to strike, when Colonel Walton pressed forward to his relief. But, with the movement, he was himself overthrown— himself exposed to the bayonet of the enemy. He threw up his sword and parried the first stroke of the weapon, which glanced down and struck deeply in the grass beside him. Another pinned him by his sleeve to the spot; and his career in the next moment would probably have been ended, but for the timely appearance of Colonel Tarleton himself. His order was effectual, and Walton tendered him his sword.

" You have saved my life, sir: my name is Colonel Walton."

The lips of Tarleton wore something of a smiling expression, as, returning the weapon, he transferred his prisoner to the guardianship of two of his troopers. The expression of his face, so smiling, yet so sinister in its smile, surprised Walton, but he was soon taught to understand it.

The battle ceased with the fall of De Kalb. It had been hope less long before. Turning his eyes gloomily from the thick confusion of the field, Colonel Walton moved away with his conductors, while Tarleton, with his eye kindled with fight, and a lip that seemed quivering with its pleasurable convulsions, led his cavalry in pursuit of the fugitives, marking his progress for twenty-two miles from the field of battle with proofs of that sanguinary appetite for blood, which formed the leading feature of his character, according to history and tradition, in all the fields of Carolina.

CHAPTER XLIV.

"A stubborn knave, you may not trust or tame
Go, bear him to the block! The biting axe
Shall teach him quiet hence."

THE victory was complete in all respects. The army of Gates was dispersed—that general, a melancholy wanderer, hopeless of fortune, and with a proper self-rebuke, dreading the opinion of his country. The loss of the Americans in this battle was heavy. Of the continentals but six hundred escaped; and as their number was but nine hundred in all, they necessarily lost, in killed, wounded, and prisoners, one third of their entire force. The whole number slain of the American army must have been six hundred men —a large proportion, in a small body of three thousand and fifty-two. The loss admitted by the British commander was three hundred killed and wounded—an amount certainly unexaggerated, and showing conclusively what must have been the result of the contest had the militia done their duty,—had they but stood the first round,—had they but returned the fire of the foe. The continentals alone bore the brunt of the conflict, and they were victorious until isolated and overborne by numbers.

The prisoners, among whom is included Colonel Walton, were roped by the command of Tarleton, and formed not the least imposing portion of the triumphal procession of the victor, on his return to Camden. De Kalb died a few days after in the arms of Du Buysson, his aide. His last words were those of eulogy upon the gallant troops whom he had so well trained, and who, justifying his avowed confidence in them, had stood by him, in the previous struggle, to the last.

"My brave division!"

These, in broken accents and imperfect English, were his last words. While expiring, his eye blazed up for a moment, as if the

ardour of the strife were again burning in his soul, and then its
light went out for ever. His name can never be erased from the
history, nor his memory forgotten by the people in whose cause he
perished.

A different fate awaited the other prisoners, to many of whom
a like death would have been a glad reprieve. The vindictive
feelings of Lord Cornwallis were yet to be satisfied. The banquet
of blood which the late battle had afforded, had quickened and
made ravenous the appetite, which, at the same time, it had failed
to satisfy. There was much in the circumstances of the period to
provoke this appetite in the British commander, though nothing to
justify its satiation to the gross extent to which it carried him. He
had seen much of his good labours in the province entirely over-
turned. Deeming the country utterly conquered, such had been
the amount of his communications to his king. The work had
now to be begun anew. The country, so lately peaceable and sub-
missive, was now everywhere in arms. The swamps on every side
of him began to swarm with enemies ; and his own victory over
Gates and the continentals, though unqualified and conclusive, was
burdened with tidings of the performances of Sumter on the
Wateree, of Marion on Black river, and of many other leaders, not
so distinguished as these, but highly promising for the future in
the small successes of the beginning. These tidings gave just
cause of irritation to the mind, which, having first flattered itself
with an idea of its complete success, now discovers that all ts
labours have been taken in vain. He grew vindictive in consequence, and, persuading himself that a terrible example was necs-
sary, if not for justice, at least for his cause, he ordered a selection
to be made from among the prisoners in his possession, who were
doomed to expiate the guilt of patriotism upon the gallows.

The streets of Camden were filled with lamentations the day
upon which this determination was made public. This was three
days after the battle,—time enough, surely, having intervened for
the subduing of his sanguinary temper. Twenty victims were
chosen for the sacrifice, and among them was Colonel Walton.
They were chosen either for their great popularity, or for their reputation as special malignants. The former class was selected in

order that the example might be an imposing one; the punishment of particular offences was the ground upon which the others were "to be justified." Yet reasons, if "plenty as blackberries," were not readily furnished, or cared for, on the occasion. Even the trial which preceded their execution was of a most summary and nominal character. The stern commander himself presided, with a general officer on either hand. The prisoners were brought before him singly.

"Why has this man been chosen?" was the inquiry of Cornwallis to Lord Rawdon.

"Violation of protection, my lord: this man is one Samuel Andrews, who was quiet and pacific enough—full of professions-until the rebel army came to Lynch's creek. He was taken on the field."

"Take him away, marshal," was the immediate order. "To the tree with him!" The man was removed. "Who are these?"

"Their names are"—Lord Rawdon, in reply, read from a paper which he held in his hand—"Richard Tucker, John Miles, Josiah Gayle, Eleazar Smith, Lorimer Jones——"

"No more," cried Cornwallis, interrupting the reader. "Enough of that. They are all brought up under the same charge—are they?"

"All but one: the man Gibson, there, in the blue stripes, is little better than an outlaw. The charge against him, in particular, is, that he shot Edward Draper, a soldier in the 'Queen's Guards,' across the Wateree river, and was subsequently taken alone, without connexion with any military body whatsoever."

"The insolent outlaw! Advance him, guard—bring him forward."

The man was singled out from the group. His arms were lashed behind him with cords, but he moved forward as if perfectly unbound, and no figure could have been more erect. He had on neither coat nor jacket; his shirt was torn, bloody, and open at the breast, displaying beneath the fair bosom of a youth, but the full muscular development of the man. He approached the table unshrinkingly, striding boldly forward to where Cornwallis sate, and, with an upward eye, met the stern glance of his judge, intended to be an overwhelming one, with a corresponding look of defiance.

"Stand where you are, sir !—we desire you no closer," cried his lordship. "You hear the charge against you?"

The man did not stand where he had been ordered, but continued to approach until the table only intervened between himself and his lordship. The latter repeated his inquiry.

"You hear the charge against you?"

"I do—it is the truth. I shot Edward Draper, a corporal in the Queen's Guards, across the Wateree."

"With what purpose?"

"To kill him."

"Ay, we suppose that—but what did you propose to gain by it?"

"Justice."

"Justice!—what had he done?"

"Beaten my mother."

"Why did you not apply for justice at the first station, instead of taking it into your own hands?"

"I did ;—Lord Rawdon, there, will tell you why I took it into my own hands."

"Well."

"He denied it to me."

"It is false, my lord," exclaimed Lord Rawdon ; "Draper was severely reprimanded."

"My mother was beaten, and the man who beat her was—reprimanded! I did not think that enough of justice, and I shot him."

The evident discrepancy between the original wrong and its punishment by Rawdon, could not but appear evident to all parties ; and Cornwallis himself was almost disposed to look favourably upon the offender. But example—a terrible example—was supposed to be necessary to keep the Drapers of the army from being shot on all occasions ; and, with this belief, he was determined to shield no victim from his fate, who exhibited any thing like a strong and decisive character. Still, as the offence was rather of a private than of a public nature, the commander proposed to the prisoner the usual British alternative of safety at that period, and under like circumstances.

"If I pardon you your crime, Gibson, will you at once take arms for his majesty ?"

"Never !" was the quick and firm response ; "I'll see him d—d first."

"Take him forth, marshal, with the rest. See that they suffe· instantly. Away with him !"

The stern voice of Cornwallis rang like a trumpe. through the assembly ; and, as the sounds died away, another voice, yet more thrilling, sent forth a scream—a woman's voice -a single scream, and so shrill, so piercing, so woe-begone and sad, that it struck through the assembly as something ominous and unearthly. A woman rushed from behind the group, and threw herself before the merciless commander. It was Gibson's mother.

"My son—my only son—he is all I have, my lord ! Oh ! spare him—spare him to his widowed mother ! I have none on earth but him !" was all she said,—her eyes bent upon Cornwallis, while her finger pointed to the tall and manly youth beside her.

"Take him away ! It is too late, my good woman—you should have taught him better. Take him away !" was the stern and only answer.

The prisoners were hurried forth ; the woman, doomed so soon to be childless, clinging to her son, and shrieking all the while. There was yet another victim. Rawdon whispered the commander, and from an adjoining apartment, Colonel Walton was brought before his judge. Cornwallis rose at his approach with a show of respectful courtesy, then again quietly resumed his seat.

"Colonel Walton, I am truly sorry to see you thus—truly sorry," was the considerate speech of his excellency, as the prisoner approached. Walton bowed slightly in return, as he replied—

"I am grateful for your lordship's consideration, but cannot withhold my surprise that you should regret your own successes. The fortune of war has made you the victor, and has given me into your power. The prisoner of war must not complain when he en-counters the risks which should have been before his eyes from the beginning, no more than the victor should regret the victory which he sought as the fruit of war."

"The prisoner of war! I am afraid, Colonel Walton, we cannot consider you in that character."

"Your lordship will explain."

"Colonel Walton, a subject of the King of Great Britain, found in arms against his officers, is a rebel to his authority, and incurs the doom of one."

"No subject of the King of Great Britain, sir! I deny the charge. I am not his subject, and no rebel, therefore, to his authority. But this is not for me to argue now. To what, may I ask your lordship, does all this tend?"

"The consequences are inevitable, Colonel Walton—the traitor must bear the doom—he must die the death of the traitor."

"I am ready to die for my country at any hour, and by any form of death. The prisoner, sir, is in your hands. I will simply protest against your decision, and leave it to the ripening time and to the arms of my countrymen to avenge my wrongs."

"I would save your life, Colonel Walton—gladly save it, would you but allow me," said Cornwallis earnestly.

"My dissent or assent, my lord, on such a subject, and under present circumstances, is surely unnecessary. The mockery of such a reference is scarcely agreeable to me, and, certainly, not becoming on the part of the conqueror. The power is in your hands, my lord, to work your pleasure."

"We will speak plainly, Colonel Walton, and you will readily understand us. As you say, mine is the power to command your instant death: and whether I do so in error or in right, it matters not; it will avail you nothing. I would save you, as your life, properly exercised for the royal cause—for the cause of your king, sir—will serve us much more materially than your death. Your influence is what we want—your co-operation with us, and not your blood. Twice, sir, has a commission—an honourable and high commission—in his majesty's service, been tendered to you from me. Twice has it been rejected with scorn; and you are now taken in arms against his majesty's troops, having violated your solemn pledge to the contrary, which your protection insisted upon."

" Wrong, sir !" exclaimed Walton, interrupting him-—"wrong, sir! The contract was violated and rendered null by the proclamation of Sir Henry Clinton—not by me."

"This is your opinion, sir; and I need not say how incorrectly entertained. But, as I have before said, whether justly or unjustly you fall a victim, will avail you nothing. The hanged man heeds nothing of the argument which proves that he was hung by mistake. I have the power of life and death over you in my own hands; and, believe me, Colonel Walton, in opening a door of safety for you, I am offering you the last, the only alternative. You shall die or live, as you answer !"

"I am ready, my lord. You somewhat mistake my character, if you think that I shall fall back from the truth, because of the consequences which it may happen to bring with it. Ha ! What is that ?"

He was interrupted by a sudden blast of the bugle, a confused hum of voices, and then a shriek. Another, and another, wild and piercing, rose from the court in front. At that instant, a soldier entering the apartment threw open the doors, and gave an opportunity for those within to behold the awful tragedy that had been going on the while. A single tree in front of the place bore twenty human bodies; the limbs were yet quivering in the air with their agonizing convulsions, and the executioner was not yet done.

"Close the door, sergeant," said Cornwallis calmly. Then, continuing his exhortation to Walton, he made use of the awful circumstance which they had just witnessed, the more earnestly to impress his desires upon the mind of the hearer, and produce in him a different determination.

"An awful doom, but necessary. It is one, Colonel Walton, from which I would gladly save you. Why will you reject the blessings of life ? Why will you resist the mercies which still seek to prevent the purposes of justice ?"

"Justice !" was the scornful exclamation of the prisoner, and all that he deigned to reply.

"Ay, sir, justice! The cause of the rightful monarch of this country is the cause of justice; and its penalties are incurred by disloyalty before all other offences. But argument is needless here."

" It is—it is needless," said Walton, emphatically.

" And, therefore," Cornwallis proceeded—" therefore, sir, I confine myself to the brief suggestion which I now make you, by the adoption of which you will escape your present difficulties. Though you have twice rejected his majesty's terms of favour, he is reluctant to destroy."

" That tree attests the reluctance. It bears its own illustration, my lord, which your assertion, nevertheless, does not need. I hear you, sir."

Somewhat disconcerted, Cornwallis, with a show of rising impatience, hurried to a conclusion.

" Once more, sir, he offers you safety ; once more he tenders you an honourable appointment in his armies. Here, sir, is his commission—take it. Go below to the Ashley and make up your own regiment ; choose your own officers, and do for him what you have hitherto fruitlessly sought to do for his enemies."

" Never, sir, never !" was the conclusive reply.

" Yet, a while, bethink you. You know the doom else—death —the gallows."

" I know it ; I have thought : you have my answer."

" Then, you die—die like a dog, sir, in the scorn of all around you."

" Be it so. I hope, and fear not, to die like a man. My country will avenge me. I am ready !"

" Your country !" said Cornwallis, scornfully. Then turning to Rawdon, he gave his order.

" My Lord Rawdon, you will instantly detach an especial guard for the prisoner, in addition to that which has been designated to conduct the prisoners of war taken in the late action to the Charleston provost. He shall go with them to Dorchester."

" For what ? with what object ? why to Dorchester, my lord ?" was the anxious inquiry of Walton.

" You shall die there, sir, as an example to the rebels of that quarter. You shall suffer where you are most known—where your loss would be most felt."

" Let me die here, my lord ! I pray you for this mercy. The mere place of execution is of small importance to your object. Not there—not there—almost in sight of my child

"There, and there only, Colonel Walton. Your doom is sealed; and, refusing our mercy, you must abide our penalty. Make out your orders, my Lord Rawdon, to the officer of the station, Major Proctor; I will sign them. Say to him that the rebel must be executed at the village entrance, within three days after the guard shall arrive. Take him away!"

Such was the British jurisdiction; such was the summary administration of justice under Lord Cornwallis. These items are mostly historical; and fiction here has not presumed to add a single tittle to the evidence which truth has given us of these events.

CHAPTER XLV.

" What sad despair is this, that braves the storm,
Would battle with the whelming tides that heave,
And pant to close around, and strive 'o cling,
And keep the victim down ?"

IT was a fine, but warm summer afternoon, in August. The
Santee river ran smooth and shining like a polished mirror in the
unclouded sunlight, and all nature appeared to revel in the same
luxurious repose.   Our old acquaintance, Porgy, stretched at length
along the banks of the river, lay half concealed in the shelter of
the brush around him.   The spot which gave him a resting-place
and shelter, shot out, at this point, from the dead level strip of
shore, boldly into the stream ; which, seemingly vexed at the interruption, beat with a pettish murmur upon its upward side, as if
vainly struggling to break through it in its downward progress
The jutting piece of land, thus obtrusively trenching upon the
water, was of no great extent, but, being well covered by the trees
and luxuriant foliage, it formed an excellent hiding-place for one
desirous of watching the river on either hand, without danger of
exposure.   Sweeping around the point, both above and below, the
spectator, thus stationed, might see for a few miles, on both sides,
the entire surface of the stream, commanding, in this scope of sight,
one or two of the usual crossing-places at low stages of the water.
The river was probably a mile wide at this point, not including the
swamp, which, in some places, extended to a width three or five
times that of the main body of the stream.   From this dead level
of swamp, it was only now and then that the banks of the river
rose into anything like height or boldness.   The point now
occupied by Porgy was one of those places most prominent of
elevation.   On the upper or northern side of the river, directly
opposite, there was another bold ascent to a bank, from which the

boats usually started when putting across the stream. This bank was easily beheld by the spectator opposite. The trees were but few upon it; and its baldness, the natural result of the frequent use made of it, contrasted, not unpleasantly, with the otherwise unvarying wall of woods that formed the boundary of the main current. The trees crowded thickly down into the river until their bending branches met its embraces; and their tops, sometimes, when the freshet was great, rested like so many infant shrubs, depending, without root or base, upon its swollen bosom.

The afternoon sun streaming from the west along the river's surface, its beams mingling in an even line to the east with its current, still farther contributed to the softness of the picture. A warm flush, tempered by the golden haze that hangs like a thin veil over the evening midsummer prospect in the south, subdued pleasantly the otherwise blinding effulgence of the day. The slight breathings of the wind, only equal to the lifting of the lightest leaf, whispered to all things—the bud, the flower, and the insect—of that dreamy indulgence and repose which our well kept epicure, who felt always and appreciated such an influence—had stretched himself off to enjoy—lying at length under an overhanging tree, lazily watching the scene around him, and with a drooping eye, that seemed to say how irksome was the task which he yet found himself bound to execute.

He was on special duty even then. The men of Marion were all around him in the swamp on the southern side of the river. The partisan chief was full of anxiety, and his scouts and guards were doubled and spread about on every hand. He looked hourly for intelligence from Gates and the continentals. Not that he hoped for much, if anything, of the army, or of good in the news which he anticipated. He had not been persuaded—in the brief interview which had been vouchsafed him by the American general, and in what he had seen of his command—to look for or to expect much from the then approaching conflict. Marion was the very opposite of Gates in nearly all respects. Modest, yet firm, his reliance upon himself arose not from any vague confidence in fortune or in circumstances, but in the timely adaptation of corresponding means to ends, and in the indefatigable industry and zeal

21

with which he plied all the energies, whether of himself or of his men, to the successful attainment of his object. Gates, he had soon discovered, was afflicted with his own infallibility—a disease that not only forbids precaution, but rejects advice and resists improvement. How should he receive advice who is already perfect? Such a malady is the worst under which generals or philosophers can labour; and Marion needed no second glance to perceive the misfortune of Gates in this respect. His confidence in that commander was lessened duly as he beheld this failing; and he returned from the camp, if not full of forebodings, at least warmly anxious on the score of approaching events.

He had partly fulfilled the duties which Gates had assigned him; he had traversed the Santee and Peedee, breaking up the boats, dispersing the little bands of tories as they leagued together and came in his way, and contributed largely to the overthrow of that consciousness of security, on the part of the British, which they had hitherto enjoyed, but of which they were deprived, in' greater or less degree, from the moment that Marion rose in arms, and led what was called the Black river insurrection. He had now, in pursuit of the same objects, brought his brigade again to the Santee, occupying those positions along that river by which he would be sooner likely to receive intelligence, assist his friends, or harass his enemies.

Lieutenant Porgy, on the present occasion, held the post of a sentinel. This duty, at such a juncture, was special and complimentary, and Marion employed his best officers upon it. A good watcher was Porgy, though the labour was irksome to him. Could he have talked all the while, or sung, with no ears but his own to appreciate his melodies, he would have been perfectly content; out silence and secresy were principles in the partisan warfare, and tenaciously insisted upon by the commander. Porgy looked east and west, north and south, without relief. The banks lay beautiful before him, in a deep quiet, on both sides of the river. Near him ran a dozen little creeks, shooting into the swamp—dark and bowery defiles, whose mouths, imperceptibly mingling with the river, formed so many places of secure entry and egress for the canoes of the warriors. Stretched along the grass, he might be seen to survey one of these little bayous, with an increasing heedfulness which indicated some cause of disturbance. Then might you see him carefully rise from his luxurious posture, and take up his rifle, and look to the priming, and put himself in the attitude to take aim and fire; when, presently, a shrill whistle reached his ears; and quietly returning the signal, he crawled along the bank towards its edge, and looked down to the little creek, as it wound in, behind him, from the river. The signal which he had heard proceeded from that quarter; and from the recess, a few moments after, a little "dug-out" shot forth, propelled by the single paddle of Lance Frampton. Concealing the boat behind a clump of brush that hung over the mouth of the creek, the boy jumped out, and scrambling up the sides of the bluff, was soon after alongside of the pursy sentinel.

"Harkee, young man," said Porgy, as the youth approached him, "you will pay dearly for good counsel, unless you heed carefully what I now give you. Do you know that you had nearly felt my bullet just now, as I caught the sound of your paddle, before you condescended to give the signal? A moment more of delay on your part would have given us both no little pain, for truly I should have sorrowed to have shot you; and you, I think, would have been greatly annoyed by it."

"That I should, Mr. Porgy; and I ought to have whistled, but did not think."

"You must learn to think, boy. That is the first lesson you should learn. Not to think, is to be vulgar. The first habit which a gentleman learns, is to think—to deliberate. He is never to be taken by surprise. The habit of thinking is to be lost, or acquired, at the pleasure of the individual; and not to think, is, not only to be no gentleman, but to be a criminal. You will suffer from the want of such a habit. It is the vulgar want always, and, permit me to add, the worst."

"I try, sir, to think, for I know the good of it; but it takes time to learn everything, sir."

"It does; but not so much time as people usually suppose. The knowledge of one thing brings with it the knowledge of another; as in morals, one error is the parent of a dozen—one crime, the

predecessor of a thousand. Learn what you can, and the rest will
come to you; as in fowling, you inveigle one duck, and the rest
of the flock follows. Talking of ducks, now, boy, puts me in mind
of dinner. Have the scouts brought in any provisions ?"

"No, sir—not yet; and no sign of any."

Porgy look.., with a woe-begone expression, towards the sun,
now on the decline, and sighed audibly.

"A monstrous long day, Lance—a monstrous long day. Here.
boy, draw this belt, and take in another button-hole—nay, take in
two ; it will admit of it."

The boy did as he was directed—Porgy stretching himself along
the grass for the purpose of facilitating the operation—the boy
actually bestriding him ; the slender form of the latter oddly
opposed to the mountainous mass of matter that lay swelling and
shrinking beneath him. While engaged in this friendly office, the
boy started, and in a half-whisper, pointing to the opposite shore,
exclaimed—

"Oh! Mr. Porgy, look! the deer! What a beautiful shot! I
could kill him here, I'm sure, off-hand. I could lay the bullet
betwixt his eyes, without damaging the sight!"

"You'll damage mine, if you show me such sights very often!"
murmured Porgy, as he let the rifle drop heavily to the ground.
He had started at Frampton's words, followed the guidance of his
fingers, and seizing the rifle, had taken aim without a word ; but
immediately after he remembered his special duties, and was
compelled to forego his prey. Well might he be mortified. Before
him, on the opposite bank, his whole figure standing out beautifully in the sunlight, in perfect relief, was a fine buck of the
largest size. The young horns were jutting out like great spikes,
giving promise of the glorious antlers which he would wear by
Christmas. Now he tossed his head in air, now seemed to snuff
the breeze; at length he bent his nose to the stream, prepared to
drink, and anon suspiciously lifted his head to listen—in all these
changes of attitude, the spirit and grace of the beautiful creature
furnishing a fine study for the painter not less than the gourmand.

"Master Lance Frampton," continued Porgy, "you will certainly
be the death of me You show me a deer, yet deny me a dinner

Why, boy, the beast is nearly half a mile away, and you talk of shooting him through the head! I could sooner pitch you on his back."

The boy laughed.

"Don't laugh, boy; it is too serious a matter, quite. It is too provoking. D—n the beauty! look at him—he seems to see us, and to know our mortification—mine, at least. Now could I be tempted to send him a shot, if it were only to scare him out of his breath. He looks most abominably impudent."

"He looks scared, sir," said the boy, as, starting to one side of the bank, and towards the thickening swamp on the right of it, the animal seemed to show alarm, and a desire for flight.

"Yes: something has frightened him, that's clear; and what troubles him, may be equally troublesome to us. Lie flat, boy—draw that brush a little more in front of you, and take off your cap. You can see through the leaves well enough."

At this moment, a whistle behind them announced a friend, and Humphries joined the two a little after.

"What do you see, Lieutenant?"

The gourmand pointed to the deer, which now, in evident alarm, bounded forward a few paces into the stream, then, swimming a few rods up the river, sought a cover in the swamp thicket to the right. His alarm was unequivocally clear to the partisans, and Humphries, following the example of the two, squatted down beside them; taking care so to cover his person behind the brush, as, while seeing everything, himself to remain unseen. He had scarcely done so, when the cause of the deer's alarm was made evident in the approach to the very spot upon which the animal had been standing, of a man, in the common dress of the woodman. His appearance was miserably woe-begone and unhappy. His garments, tattered and dirty, consisted of the coarse stuffs worn by the poorer orders of the country. He had no arms—no apparent weapons at least, of any kind; and his movements, sluggish and without elasticity, seemed those of one greatly fatigued. He threw himself, a moment after his arrival, at length along the bank, with that air of listless self-abandonment which indicates exhaustion.

" Poor devi ! he seems wearied and worn, Humphries."

" He is one of our men. Ten to one he brings us news from camp."

" Bad news, then : he looks like anything but the messenger of good. But stay—what is he about ?"

The stranger, while they spoke, had arisen ; and, leaving the edge of the bank, went back to the wood, from which, a few moments after, he emerged, bearing in his hands a couple of common fence rails. These he bore with difficulty to the edge of the water, and, though no burden to a man in ordinary strength their weight, in his fatigue, seemed to demand more than ordinary effort.

"Why, what's he going to do now ?" said Porgy.

The fugitive threw off his jacket and shoes, and taking a ragged handkerchief from his pocket, inclosed them within its folds, then placing them over the two rails, which he laid side by side for the purpose, he lashed them strongly together. This done, he advanced to the stream, taking the bundle in his hands. For a few moments he paused, looked up and down the river, and seemed to hesitate with a due sense of caution ; then, as if ashamed of his fears, he rushed to the water, and throwing the rails before him, boldly plunged after them into its bosom.

" The ridiculous booby, he will certainly drown ; he can never resist the current in his present state !" said Porgy, half rising from his place. Humphries pulled him down and bade him be quiet.

"But we must not let the poor devil drown, Bill."

" We must do our duty—we must not expose ourselves if we can help it, Porgy. His life is nothing to our own ; and we don't know who comes behind him."

" That's true : d—n the fellow—let him drown ! – who cares ?"

Meanwhile, swimming feebly, striking with one hand while the other derived a feeble support from the rails, the stranger moved forward. But it was soon evident that his strength was that of a child, in opposition to the current. He strove desperately to keep a direct course over the water, but every movement carried him out of his line, and the sweeping stream resisted, and rendered futile, the feeble dash of his hand, with which, striking with ex-

hausted muscles, but no little will, he laboured, as earnestly a..
vainly, to make his way across. As he advanced further within
the current, he found himself still less able to contend with it ; and
the partisans, from their place of watch, could now see that his
almost powerless hand was just raised above the water, dropping
into it feebly, at long and increasing intervals, without impulsion,
and taking no purchase from the stream. He certainly ceased to
advance, and his movement now was only with the current.

"We must help him, Humphries, my dear fellow, or he will
drown and be d—d," said Porgy.

"Oh, yes, sir—do let us help him !" exclaimed Lance, who had
watched the scene with an anxiety that kept him starting anxiously,
with every movement of the swimmer.

"If it must be done, Porgy," said Humphries, in reply, " there's
only one of us that can do it. The ' dug-out' won't carry more, and
I'm the best hand at the paddles. So, keep cool and quiet—don't
cry out, for we don't know but the tories may be after the fellow,
or maybe the British ; and if they guess at Marion's men being in
the swamp, it'll break up all our schemes. Lie close, and if the
chap can keep above water till I get to him, I'll save him."

With the words, descending quickly from the bluff, Humphries
took the skiff ; and the little canoe, under his powerful arms, soon
shot from the concealing bush where Lance had left it. It was
not long before the swimmer saw him, and he shouted joyfully, but
very faintly, at the sight. The tones were so feeble that the boat-
man threw all his skill and strength into his paddle, sparing no
effort to reach him, as he felt assured that the man could not long
continue the struggle with the heavy setting current of the river.

"Keep up, keep up," Humphries cried out to him in encouragement ; "keep up for a little while—only a few minutes more, my
poor fellow, and I'll fish you up like an oyster."

Words, but so faint as to be undistinguishable, reached Humphries from the swimmer in reply. The sounds only were audible,
but none of the syllables. The canoe, light as a feather, was sent
more rapidly than at first towards the speaker, as Humphries felt
more and more the necessity of speed. It whirled on nearer and
nearer, and Lance started up. and clapped his hands in delight, as

he beheld the swimmer throwing aside his frail support, and grasp
ing firmly the gunwale of the little bark that had so opportunely
come to his assistance. Supported, without effort on his own part,
by holding upon its little sides, the man was brought safely to
shore ; Humphries, with all the dexterity of the Indian, having
trimmed and propelled his frail canoe, even though thus encumbered, with little fatigue and apparently as little effort. The exhausted swimmer was carried into camp, and soon recovered sufficiently to unfold his intelligence to the commander of the partisans
in person.

CHAPTER XLVL

"Now let us follow in the quick pursuit."

COLONEL MARION examined the fugitive himself. He was one of the little squad of Colonel Walton, and had susta ned the battle in the regiment of Colonel Dixon, to whose North Carolina regiment—the only one that had stood the fight—he had been attached by Gates. He had seen the first and last of the battle, and had been fortunate enough to reach one of the swamps which lay on the flank of both armies, where he found shelter until the victor had departed. He gave the whole gloomy story of the defeat in broad colours to the partisans ; and though he could say nothing as to the fate of Gates himself, and the several officers touching whose safety the inquiries of Marion and of Singleton were made in parti cular, he yet knew enough to assure them of the utter dispersion of the army, and the slaughter, according to his account, of at least one half of it. His farther intelligence was important, and suggested opportunities which were yet available to our partisans. He had seen, and with difficulty had escaped from the British guard, which had been despatched by Cornwallis, having custody of the continental prisoners, destined for the provost, or common prison in Charleston. That guard, he informed the partisan, had pursued an upper road, and would, according to all probability cross the Santee at Nelson's, a few miles higher up the river.

Burdened with baggage and prisoners, they might not yet have reached the river ; and, with this hope, giving his signals with the rapidity of lightning, Marion collected his squad, reso'ute to try all odds, however inferior in number, with the detachment in question The rescue of one hundred and fifty continentals—for that was tl least number of captives—would be an important acquisition to the cause ; and a successful stroke so soon after such a defeat as

21*

that of Gates, might have the beneficial effect of restoring confidence, and giving renewed hope to the paralysed Carolinians.

Himself undespairing, Marion adopted his plan with due determination. Dividing his force into three parties, he gave one to Colonel Hugh Horry, another to Singleton, and the third he led in person. The signal sounded, the men rose from their hiding-places, and gathered around their different leaders; and within an hour after the receipt of the intelligence just given, and while the sun yet shone rich, and like a sovereign, in the west, the partisans were all mounted upon their fleet steeds, and dashing up to the spot where they hoped, and prepared to receive their enemies. Silence resumed her savage empire in the swamp, and the grey squirrel now leaped fearlessly over the island retreat, which, an hour before, he had trembled but to approach.

As the partisan drew nigh the designated point, he obtained intelligence that the guard with the prisoners had not yet crossed the river, but had marched to the Great Savannah, a little above it. He was particularly informed as to their number, and that of their prisoners, though nothing was yet known to the partisans of the peculiar condition of some among them—the doom to which they were destined, or of those who had already been sacrificed to the vindictive spirit of the British commander. All this they were yet to learn.

Moving now with greater rapidity, Marion soon crossed the river with all his force; and, as the enemy could not be very far off, he proceeded more cautiously. He sent out his scouts, and as they severally came in with intelligence, he prepared his farther plans. Night came on, and he was advised that the British would most probably lie by, on the main road, at the public-house which was kept on the edge of the Great Savannah. The opinion seemed probable, as travelling by night in the southern swamps was no part of the British custom; and to cross the river after dark would have been a risk of some magnitude. This, however, was Marion's favourite mode of warfare; and calling in his parties, he gave directions to Colonel Horry to make a circuit round the savannah, and, lurking on its lower edge, gain the pass of Horse creek, and keep close in cover until he should receive a communication how to proceed from him.

The reckless and ready officer in question immediately went off in obedience to his commander. To Major Singleton a similar station was intrusted on the other side of the road, where the woods were open, and where he was compelled, as the sheltering cover was thin and imperfect, to bury his party more deeply in its recesses than would otherwise have been considered necessary. A third, and the largest division of his force, which Marion reserved to his own command, occupied both sides of the road above the designated house; while a detachment of selected scouts traversed the whole line of road, bearing intelligence to the commander as promptly as t was required.

Unsuspectingly, the British guard marched on; and duly informed at every step in their progress, Marion suffered them safely to reach the house at which they were determined to stop for the night. A scout of the partisan looked in at the window, disguised and unobserved. He carefully watched the progress of the supper, saw the disposition of the soldiers and the prisoners, and left, in safety, his place of observation.

A little before daylight in the morning, while it was yet quite dark, an officer of Marion communicated to Horry the instructions of the commander. Promptly moving forward as directed, Horry led his men to the house, and had almost reached it without interruption, but, as he threw wide a little paling gate that opened from the garden, through which he came to the court-yard of the dwelling, he was challenged by a sentinel. Horry not answering, but advancing at the moment with alacrity, the sentinel fired his piece unsuccessfully, and was immediately cut down by him.

The alarm was given, however; and though the surprise was effective, it was incomplete. A pile of arms before the door was seized upon; but the great body of the enemy, partly armed, made their escape through the front entrance, and immediately pushed down the road.

It was then that Singleton charged upon them. He was promptly met. The guard rallied with coolness and in good order, and the small force of Singleton was compelled to give back before them But Horry, who had lingered to release the continentals, now came up, and the contest was resumed with vigour. The British, slowly

moving down the road, held their way unbroken, and fought bravely
at brief pauses in their movement.   They were still in force quite
too great for the parties opposed to them, and the advantages
gained by the latter were those chiefly of surprise.

While they fought, the guard divided; a portion of them car
ried Colonel Walton, with such other prisoners as had been subjects
of special judgment and particular care, to the cover of the savannah, while the rest, now unencumbered, continued the fight valiantly
enough.   But, by this time, the troops of Marion, all fresh men,
rushed in, and falling upon the enemy's rear, they soon finished the
contest.   The fight lasted, however, for an hour at least, and the
loss of the British was severe.   The partisans not only rescued all
the continentals, one hundred and fifty in number—all of the Maryland line—but they took besides twenty-two regulars of the 63d
regiment, including their captain, and sundry other prisoners.   But
the small guard, carrying with it Colonel Walton, and the other
South Carolina prisoners, had gone clear ; and, hurrying under good
guidance to the Santee, while yet the fight was going on, they seized
upon some of the boats of Marion, and were safe upon the other
side of the river, and speeding upon their way, before the conflict
was half over.

What was the horror of Singleton, when, at daylight, the released
prisoners gave intelligence of the destiny of Colonel Walton, and
the perfect escape of the guard having him in custody !   He immediately rushed to his commander with the melancholy narrative.

"It is unhappy—dreadfully unhappy, Major Singleton," said the
commander—" but what are we to do ?   It is now scarcely possible
that we should overtake them ; they have the start too greatly to
'eave us any hope of a successful pursuit, and, beyond that, I see
nothing that can be done.   If they do indeed execute our citizens,
we shall only be compelled to retaliate."

"That, of course, we must do, Colonel Marion," was the rejoin-
der; " and ! am willing, sir, that my name should be the first on
the list which pledges our officers to the practice, and incurs the
risk which such pledge involves.   But, surely, we must do something to save, not less than to revenge our countrymen.   I believe,

Colonel Marion—nay, I am sure, I can overtake the detachment
Give me, sir, but twenty men—the men I brought with me from
the Cypress. They will volunteer in the service, they will risk their
lives freely in behalf of Colonel Walton."

Marion regarded the earnest speaker with a melancholy glance.
He shook his head mournfully as he replied—

"They are too far on the start—some hours the lead upon you.
It is impossible, Major Singleton, that you should overtake them."

"Our horses are superior—"

"But not fresh—no, no! It is a bad business; and I fear we
cannot mend it."

"You will not suffer a brave man, a good citizen, to perish.
Pardon me, sir—pardon me, if in my earnestness and anxiety I seem
to overstep the bounds of propriety and privilege. Pardon me, sir,
but hear me. Permit *me* to make the effort—let me save him if I
can. Think, sir, he is a man of great influence in his parish; one
highly valuable to our cause; he is brave and virtuous—a good
citizen—a father!"

"All—all these I grant; but, look at the prospect, Major Singleton—the great risk to all—the little hope. After this defeat of the
continentals, the region to which you propose to go, will be one of
certain doom to you. We shall now, ourselves, have to hurry farther from the Santee; and I have already prepared orders to march
our little brigade back to Lynch's creek, though I leave you and the
force you propose to take with you, to certain destruction."

"Not certain, not even probable, Colonel Marion; for, believe
me, I will do nothing rash."

Marion smiled.

"Your blood even now is boiling, Major Singleton; the veins
rise upon your forehead—your cheek burns—your lips quiver. You
are in a feverish impatience which will hurry you into fight with
the first opportunity."

"Oh no, sir—no! I am feverish—I am thirsting, I grant you, to
strike the enemy at all hazards; but I know the risk. I have esti
mated the danger. The section to which I go has been exhausted
of troops to supply the army of Cornwallis at Camden. A small
force, scarcely superior to the little one I brought with me, is all

the garrison at Dorchester. The army of Cornwallis will press the pursuit of Gates into North Carolina; the results of so great a victory will not be neglected by the British commander. This movement will leave the country free for some time; and they have not men enough below to find me, or rout me out of the Cypress."

But Marion thought differently as to the probable course of Cornwallis. He knew the weakness, not only of the British army, but of the footing upon which their cause stood in the country. He knew that Cornwallis had quite enough to do in South, without exposing his army in North, Carolina; and he shook his head in reply to the arguments of Singleton, as he suggested his own doubts of their validity.

"But I know *you*, Major Singleton," he continued; "and your claims to serve and save your relative, if you can, should be considered. What force will you require for this?"

"Twenty men, sir; twenty will do."

"Take thirty, sir, if you can get as many to volunteer from the force brought with you. I give you no instructions. I will not fetter your courage or good sense with any commands of mine. But I counsel you, sir, not to forget, that neither your own, nor the lives of your men, are at this period your or their property. You belong to your country, Major Singleton; and it is only as one of her sons and defenders, that I am now willing to make the effort to save Colonel Walton. Proceed now with what speed you may; and if safe and successful, you will seek me out, with the old signals, somewhere near Black Mingo. Go, sir; and God speed and prosper you."

The acknowledgments of Singleton were hearty, though made in haste. He hurried to the men of the low country, and in few words made known the circumstances. Humphries, Porgy, Davis, the two Framptons—indeed, all of the original party from the Cypress—volunteered instantly. He could have had a dozen more for the enterprise. Black Tom was permitted, after some difficulty, to attend the party, the obstinate negro swearing he would *not* be left: and with this addition to his limited number, Singleton was soon in saddle, and pushing fast in pursuit of the enemy.

CHAPTER XLVII.

" Then bring me to him. He shall hear from me,
How much I fear—how much I dare to hope."

THE chase was unsuccessful. The pursuers reached the Cypress without having overtaken the enemy. The fugitive guard, with their captives, reached Dorchester in safety. So did our Partisans, —a little after them. Once there, having discretionary power, Singleton proceeded earnestly to do what he could towards the rescue of his uncle. The good sense, the skill and partisan qualities of Humphries, all came into excellent exercise, and were found immensely important at this crisis. With him, Singleton conferred closely, and immediately after his arrival. The result of the conference was the departure, that night, of Humphries alone, for the village of Dorchester.

Meanwhile, the individuals of the party in the Cypress resumed their old places and habits. Porgy was quite at home, and not the less pleased that the eel-loving Oakenburg had forborne to volunteer. He soon set the peculiar talents of black Tom in requisition; and a little foraging furnished the scouts with a sufficient supply for the evening feast. Of this we need scarcely say that Singleton ate but little. He was eminently wretched; and as he wandered gloomily along the edge of the island, he was not unpleasantly aroused at hearing the wild laugh, and at meeting the wolfish visage, of the maniac Frampton immediately beside him.

"You are come," said the wretched man—"you are come to see him. You *shall* see him; he is there," pointing with his finger. "I have put him to watch her grave, and he watches well; he never leaves it. The owl and he—they watch together, and one hoots while the other sleeps. Come—you shall see."

Singleton could only conjecture the meaning of his speech; the scattered rays of reason illuminating the vain obscurity of his language, even as the faint flickering of the twilight lighted up imperfectly the crowding blackness and the strange cluster of objects around them in the swamp. The firelight fell on the cheek of the madman, and showed Singleton its squalid and miserable, not less than maniacal, expression. He had evidently suffered from hunger as well as woe.

"Come with *me*, rather," said the partisan, losing for a moment the feeling of his own wretchedness in that of the unfortunate being before him. The man followed quietly enough, and Singleton led him to where the rest were busily engaged at supper. Porgy, in an instant, made room for him on the log on which he himself was sitting: at the same time he broke the hoecake before him, and gave orders to Tom, who was standing conveniently by, to produce the remnants of certain chickens, in the procuring of which one of the neighbouring plantations had suddenly suffered assessment. But the wild man did not for a moment notice the invitation. He seized Singleton by the arm, and with a gentle pressure, carried him through the circle to the spot where his younger son was sitting. The elder rose at his approach; but him he did not regard for a moment. But when he looked upon the younger, and beheld the sword at his side, he burst into one of those dreadful laughs which seemed to indicate, as they invariably accompanied, every occasional symptom of his mental consciousness. The boy stood up before him, and the hand of the maniac rested upon his head. His fingers, for a few seconds, played with the fine long hair of the boy; but, as if satisfied, in a little while, he dashed away from the spot, and hurried back to the supping-place of the rest.

"Poor fellow—he doesn't seem to have eaten for a month," said Porgy, as the maniac voraciously devoured the meat set before him. "No wonder he's mad—I should be mad myself, I doubt not, were I to go without eating even a day. I felt something like it on the Santee, one day, when required to deliberate and not dine. An empty stomach justifies insanity."

The maniac ate on, heedless of remark or observation; but sometimes he would pause, and indicate, by a slight chuckle, that some faint gleams of perception had come into his brain. To the surprise of all, he did not depart as soon as he had eaten, as had been his usual custom heretofore; but, throwing himself under an old tree, he seemed disposed to follow the example of several of the rest, who had resigned themselves to sleep.

Humphries, meanwhile, had reached Dorchester in safety. The night was favouringly dark, and he trod the street in which his father dwelt, in perfect safety. He penetrated, with cautious steps, and with the utmost circumspection, into the inclosure, and successfully, and unseen by any, made his way to the stables. Here he remained quiet for a while, until the hour had fairly arrived at which the tavern was usually closed for the night. He then ventured out of his hiding-place, and went towards the dwelling. But the "Royal George" was still open, and still full of guests. A couple of British soldiers were drinking at the bar; and there were some four or five of the villagers. The old landlord had been listening to some narrative which had greatly awakened his attention. It could be seen that he was in that awkward situation, when a man finds it difficult to laugh, and when it is yet expected that he should do so. The efforts of old Humphries in this way were very unhappy. His laughter died away in a hoarse chuckle; a gurgling, gulping sound filled his throat; and the poor fellow turned away to conceal tears.

"And when will he be hung?" asked one of the villagers.

"Friday—Friday next," replied one of the soldiers, gruffly; "and that's giving him a d—d sight too much time for any prayer that he can make. I'm for having it soon over. Just the same with other people as with myself. No long-winded speeches, say I."

"Only three days!" continued the villager. "Well, it's a great pity, for he used to be a mighty good man, and quite a gentleman. And then there's his daughter, Miss Katharine—poor girl, I wonder if she knows it?"

"I reckon she does," said another of the villagers, "for I seed the family coach drive in not an hour after the guard brought him; and, though I didn't see who was in it, yet I s'pose it couldn't be nobody but her."

"Yes, she's come," said the soldier who had just spoken, "and she s been to the major, begging him, I suppose, for mercy. But it's all in my eye and Betty Martin—the major can't help her much."

"Yet they did say that Major Proctor had a liking for the young lady. Maybe he might do much on her behalf for the father."

"He can't, even if he would," said the soldier; "the order comes from Lord Cornwallis himself; and it's as p'inted as a baguet, and jist as positive as old Jamaica. The colonel has done all he could. He's let the girl go to her father, and she was with him when I left the garrison. She's going to put herself under guard the same as her father, to be with him all the time."

"Poor, poor girl," muttered old Humphries, hastily turning away. "Bless me, where's Bella? Here, Bella, my dear!"

Taking a parting draught, the soldiers first, and then the villagers withdrew. The old man proceeded to fasten the doors; and when this was securely done, the younger Humphries, who had been waiting and watching, concealed in an inner apartment, made his appearance before his father. It was a meeting of rejoicing as well as regret; for the old man was proud of his son, and loved him not less than his daughter. There were long stories told between them which do not concern this narrative. But all relating to Colonel Walton, his daughter, and the danger before him, was drunk in by the son with a greedy interest. He ascertained the place of the colonel's imprisonment; and found, to his great regret, that it was within the walls of the fort itself. It was there, and there only, that Katharine could see him. It was there that she watched and wept with her father now; and the soul of the proud-spirited girl, mortified in many respects, was humbled to the dust as she contemplated the degrading doom which he was destined to undergo. Death on the battlefield would have been honourable death, in her estimation; and though, even now, he was to perish in the cause of his country, that cause, sacred and lofty as it was, could not lessen her horror of that disgrace which such a mode of death brought with it. The infamous hangman, the defiling rope! The aristocratic education, the proud, unbending spirit of the noble girl, revolted whenever she thought upon it. She shuddered to survey the picture which her imagination continued to describe before her. She shuddered and lay convulsed at the feet of her father.

She was permitted to remain with him throughout the day, but was compelled to leave him at a certain hour every night. This was an indulgence of Major Proctor, who sympathized with her sufferings with all the feelings of a man, and the courtesy of the honourable gentleman. He deplored and disapproved of the judgment of Cornwallis; but, according to that strict military etiquette, upon which no officer insisted more rigidly than Proctor, he forbore any utterance of opinion in respect to his superior's proceedings, and only, while he resolved to obey them rigidly, prepared to temper his severity with all the softening indulgence which was left discretionary with him. Katharine felt, and looked her gratitude—her consciousness of his delicacy and forbearance. Still, it pained her pride to be dependent, even to a degree so small, upon her country's enemy. She felt this humiliation also, but, with a proper good sense, yielding to circumstances, she showed no sign of such a feeling.

Humphries gathered these particulars from his father and sister. He learned that even at that moment Katharine was at the garrison ; that, as the gates were closed at ten o'clock, she would then be compelled to leave it ; and readily conjecturing that she had made arrangements for remaining at Dorchester during the night, he now felt desirous of finding out her place of residence. There was, however, but one ready mode of making this discovery, and as the night was dark, and the object worthy the risk, with a bold determination, he made his arrangements to lurk around the gate of the fortress, until she should make her appearance. He could then follow her at a safe distance, and thus find out her abode.

No sooner determined than acted upon. He sallied forth, and, by a circuitous route, reached the point of observation. Here he waited not long before the old family coach made its appearance ; and, in half an hour after, two ladies, escorted by as many officers, appeared from the entrance. The ladies were assisted into the carriage, the officers returned, the gates were again closed, and the vehicle wheeling about to pursue its way, when Humphries, who

504 THE PARTISAN.

had sheltered himself behind a tree close in the neighbourhood, now boldly leaped forward, and mounting behind the coach, was carried along with it.

They alighted, as he had anticipated, at the lonely dwelling of old Pryor. The sturdy landlord himself came forth, and pushing aside the negro, assisted the ladies from the carriage. They entered the house, and, watching his opportunity, Humphries followed them. The moment that Pryor was disengaged, the partisan sought him, and, in private, unfolded himself to the pleasantly astonished landlord. A few moments more gave him an interview with Katharine and her aunt. The guise, garb, and expression of the latter, were stiff and old-maidish, as usual. Not so with the former. Her eye was wild, her hair disordered, her cheeks flushed, and her step quick and convulsive, while her lips frequently quivered with the thrilling thoughts that were present and working in her mind. She hurried forward to meet Humphries upon his entrance; seized his hand with unstudied and earnest warmth, and hailed him as a friend—as one sent from Singleton.

"I cannot talk to you yet," said she, brokenly, "I must wait for breath; but I am glad—oh, very glad to see you."

"Sit down, Kate, my love," said the old lady; "you fatigue, you afflict yourself, my dear."

She sank obediently into the chair; but again immediately started up, and approached the partisan.

"I cannot sit—I am in no want of rest, and have no time for it. Oh, Mr. Humphries! tell me—speak to me—say what is the hope you bring me?"

"Major Singleton—"

She interrupted him.

"Ay—Robert—I look to him to save me—to save my father. Where is Robert now?"

"In the Cypress, Miss Katharine—I come from him now!"

"Thank God! He has not deserted me—he will not desert me!"

"Never, Miss Katharine, I'll answer for it; the major is never the man to desert you, or anybody—never."

"I know it—I know it, Mr. Humphries. You do his noble heart only justice when you say so. He will not desert me—he will not desert my father. But I must go to him—I must see him, this very night. He must tell me what he can do—what he will try to do for me—in this horrible necessity. He must show me that he will save my father."

And as she spoke, she hastily retied the strings of her bonnet; and her whole manner was that of one full of resolution.

"Why, what would you do, my child?" asked her aunt.

"Go to Robert Singleton."

"My child, don't think of it—remember, you're a lady—"

"A woman—a daughter!" she replied, almost fiercely. "I have no fears—I should have no scruples. If there be danger or reproach, I will risk it all for my father. You fear not, Mr. Humphries, to conduct me to your leader?"

"It's an ugly road, Miss Katharine, for a lady—mud and water bog and bush, and mighty crooked."

"Is that all! shall such things keep me back from my duty, when all depends on it? Oh, no! These are trifles—your difficulties I fear not." Then, turning to her aunt, who had now risen and seized her arm persuasively—"Oh! scruples, aunt, scruples. Do you think I see and feel these things, when I see death and dishonour both sitting on our hearth! I must go!"

"The major will be mighty glad to see you, Miss Katharine, I'm certain; and no harm can come of your going. I can guide you to the spot, dark or daylight, just the same; and I'm close and cautious enough about danger. But you'll have to ride horseback."

"I can do it—I can do it," she cried eagerly; "that will be no difficulty."

"Then we must get you a saddle from Pryor—that's easy enough too; for I know he's got one, and he'll be quick to let you have it."

"See to it—see to it at once, Mr. Humphries, I pray you. Let there be no delay."

Humphries hurried off. The aunt strove to change her resolve, but the fearless girl was inflexible.

"Robert Singleton knows *me*, aunt—thank God! I know him. If I did not, I might listen to you now. Knowing him, I freely confide my name, my life, my honour to his keeping. I have no fears—none. But since he has come—since I have heard his name, and seen his messenger—I have hopes—many hopes--good hopes—sweet hopes. He will save my father—he will try with all his soul, and with all his strength ; and God must—God will—prosper him !"

Such was the strain with which she rejected her aunt's entreaties, and persisted in her determination. When Humphries reappeared with Pryor, announcing his; determination to depart, the old lady, finding she could not change the resolution of her niece, was for going along with her in the coach ; but Humphries resisted the suggestion as impracticable.

"We can't run the old coach into the bush, if an enemy pops into the road, ma'am ; and it's a chance we may have to do that before we get to the Cypress, even at this time of night. The fewer, the easier to hide; the smaller the bundle, the less the hole to cover it. It won't be an easy journey, ma'am, no how, I tell you."

The old lady was soon discouraged, and consented, though with great reluctance, to the arrangement which separated her from Katharine. The latter was soon ready, and carefully muffled up ; she was conducted by Humphries to the edge of the wood where his own horse had been concealed, and to which spot Pryor had promptly carried that intended for the maiden.

They rode with spirit, and soon reached the swamp. Humphries carefully chose a path, which, if more direct, and more exposed to detection, was, at least, far more easily travelled than that which he usually pursued. He conducted her into safe concealment along the little rising ridge of sand which Davis had previously chosen for his proposed fight with Hastings. Here he persuaded her to remain, until he should go to the camp and conduct Singleton to her. She did not hesitate to do so ; the arrangement was more agreeable to her in many respects, as it spared her the toilsome journey through the worst portions of the swamp, at the same time that it promised her that privacy in her interview with Singleton, which, as we shall see, was absolutely necessary to its progress.

In leaving her, Humphries saw no impropriety. He knew not of any danger in the swamp to her ; and she was quite too much absorbed in the thought of her father's danger, to think for a single instant on the subject of her own position. The spot, too, upon which she stood had nothing terrific in its aspect. The trees were few, and not gloomy like those of the swamp. The stars shone down freely over the bank, and the light was sweet, though faint, as it fell glistening over the white sands upon which she stood, and was freely reflected from the glazed green of the leaves that hung circling about her. Alighting from her horse, her trusty companic. fastened him to a hanging bough, and promising to return quickly, rode onward to the camp.

He had not been long gone, when she heard the rustling of the bushes behind her. She turned towards the spot, and beheld a gigantic figure emerging from the copse. The intruder was the maniac Frampton. His fierce habits, wild aspect, dismal shriek, and soiled and tattered garments, were enough to startle, not a timid maiden only, but a bold-spirited man. Katharine might have been alarmed even more than she was, had he appeared to her as he usually appeared to others. But a singular change seemed to have come over him. His step was irresolute—his manner shrinking—his countenance full of awe. He continued, however, to approach ; and, though really apprehensive, the maiden firmly held her ground, looked steadily upon him, and neither screamed nor spoke. But, as he continued to advance, though slowly and respectfully, she gave back before him. He then addressed her in a strain which confounded and astonished her.

" Fly me not, sweet spirit—leave me not in darkness—hear me —scorn not my prayer—I kneel to you—I pray you for pardon—have I not loved—have I not revenged you ? You know it—you feel it—you have seen it—fly me not—I will do more—I swear it on my knees. Look."

The maniac was prostrate before her—his face prone in the dust —his hands clasped above his head—his tones, when he spoke, subdued, and full of humility. She was more terrified at what she saw, as it was now evident that she was alone with a madman.

In this way crouching towards her, he continued to rave, address ng her as an angel—as one departed—and reminding her, as his wife, of the happiness which they had known together—the love they had borne each other, and which he prayed her still to cherist for him in heaven. Approaching footsteps startled him just as he had partly risen to his knees, and while he was still imploring her after this fashion. The noise brought to him a momentary consciousness. He seemed, at once, to realize his mistake; and, with his fearful laugh, bounding away, he was sheltered in the neighbouring bush before Singleton and his comrade had yet reached the spot where the latter had left the maiden.

Humphries kept aloof, while Singleton met his cousin. The scene was short between them, but how full of all that was sadly sweet—all that was exciting to both! She rushed towards him as soon as his person was distinguished.

" Oh, Robert! I have come to you a beggar—a woe-begone beggar. I have no hope but from you—no confidence but in you. To you—to you only—I bend my thought—I turn my eye—I look for life—my life, my father's life—all. Save him—save me!"

" For this, Katharine, have I come. If I can save your father, even though at the hazard of my own life, I shall do so. You have my pledge for this."

" Thanks, thanks, dear Robert! my heart thanks you. But what is your hope, your plan?—Tell me all, that I may calculate on your chances, that I may note their progress, that I may pray! that I may assist, if assist I can, in a work which calls for men— for manhood only."

The question troubled Singleton. What could he tell her? He himself knew little as yet of the true condition of things in Dorchester. No time had yet been allowed him to devise a scheme or take a step in its execution. He told her this, and she heard him with impatience.

" But something, dear Robert, must be done, and quickly. Do not be cold, I pray you—do not deliberate too long, or nothing will be done. Hear me, Robert—hear me but a while. You came to me a suitor—you said you loved me, and I believed you, Robert."

He took her hand She continued—

" I believed you, and I was pleased to believe. My pride and my heart both rejoiced in my conquest: but this I said not—th. I showed not to you. I did not reject, though I did not receive your prayer. Now, hear me—my hand is in yours—it *is* yours—I give it to you in love, in pledge, in true affection—it is yours, and *I* am yours for ever. Only save my father—say to me that you will save him; and here, in this solemn place—these dark trees, and the spectre-like stars, only looking wanly down upon us, and bearing witness—I avow myself your wife—yours, at any moment after, that you shall name, to bind me such for ever."

He carried her hand to his lips—he kept it there for a moment—then releasing it, replied—

" And does Katharine Walton think to buy me to the performance of a sacred duty ? Am I not come to save your father ?—to save or perish with him ? This was my resolve when I sued for leave to pursue the guard which brought him to the village. Even your love will fail to add anything of strength or spirit to my determination. It is an oath in heaven, Katharine, and my life for his, whether you love or hate, whether you receive or reject my prayer."

" Noble, unselfish !—true friend, brave cousin ! You will do all for me; you are determined to make me and mine your debtor. You will not be bought by the hand which I have placed in yours —which you have sought for years—as you would leave me free still to any choice upon which my heart has been set. You are too proud, too noble to take advantage of my necessities. But I will not be outdone thus. I will now become the suitor in turn ; and, Robert, if the poor charms and the humble virtues of Katharine Walton be not all gone, in the eyes of her cousin, she offers them all—all, without pledge of service, without hope of recompense, without anything in return, but the noble heart and the true hand which he once proffered to her."

Singleton caught the high-minded and beautiful woman in his arms: the first sacred embrace, the first mutual kiss of requited love, hallowed and terminated the scene between them

He rode forth with her on the way to Dorchester, taking a circuitous route in his progress, and leaving her to the conduct of

22

Humphries as they came in sight of the village. On their way, he gave her a certain message which she was to bear to her father —containing advice and instructions for his government. He also suggested—more to satisfy her impatience than with any certainty of their adoption—various plans of rescue. Having a perfect reliance on the skill and courage of her lover, not less than upon his affections, she became more soothed and satisfied by what she had heard. Her hopes grew active and warm, and her sanguine thought already beheld the freedom of her doomed sire, obtained by the powerful arm of her adventurous lover. Let us not, however, anticipate events.

CHAPTER XLVIII.

" God speed the good endeavour ! for it stands
An earnest of success ; thus virtue strives
Still hopeful, when most hopeless."

THE next night found Singleton himself in the village. He could not be persuaded by Humphries to keep away. The house of old Pryor, who was ready for any uproar, received him ; and there, concealed even from Aunt Barbara, he contemplated the prospect before him, and devised more fully his plans for the rescue of his uncle. His fair cousin was in the same dwelling, and he engaged her company at such brief moments as he could steal from his labours, and she from the presence of her aunt. Humphries was in the village also, having his hiding-place in his father's stable-loft. Obeying his instructions, Davis came to him there late the same night, and once more found himself in the presence of the fair coquette, Bella. The Goose-Creeker turned upon her an unfriendly shoulder, and, humbled as she had been by circumstances, of which Davis knew nothing, his conduct distressed her to a degree which she could not conceal. She turned away to conceal her tears, and the heart of the trooper smote him.. When she retired, Humphries bluntly asked Davis why he was so rough to his sister. The subject was a delicate one ; but the person addressed was a plain-spoken fellow, who did not scruple at any time to speak what he thought. Accordingly, he went over briefly the whole course of difficulty between them, and particularly insisted upon the preference shown to Hastings.

" But he's a dead man ; there's no fear of him now."

" I never was afeard of him, Bill ; but then I didn't love him, and the girl that did can't love me, for there's nothing alike between us."

"Oh, pshaw man ! but she didn't love him, you see," said the

other. " I know all about it. A girl's a girl, and there's no helping it—she will be foolish sometimes. There's none of them that
don't like a dozen chaps hanging at their skirts—that's the fun of
the thing with them; and Bella is just like all the rest. But the
girl is good stuff after all, you see; for though I did think when
Hastings was dancing about her that she had a liking for the fellow, I soon found out that she liked somebody else all the time."

" You don't say so ! Who ?" demanded the other, violently
and hurriedly, as if taking the alarm anew at 'the prospect of a
rivalry, which, whatever might be his cause of anger with the
girl, he had no desire to hear of.

" A man," replied Humphries coolly.

" Oh, speak out, Bill. I'm sure I don't care. I shouldn't quarrel with him for it."

" No, I reckon not when you know him. His name's Davis."

" What Davis ?"

" John."

" Who—what—why, you don't mean me ?"

" You're mighty dull, John Davis, for a man that's seen so much
of the world. That's you, for certain—gospel-true, now, as I tell
you. Bella Humphries, my sister that is, has really a greater
liking for you, in your way, as a man, and a good swamp-sucker,
than for any other man body that I know of."

" But Bill, old fellow, you're joking now; it's all fun and fool-
ishness. How do you know, now? what makes you think so ?"
and chuckling and sidling close to his companion, Davis wound
his arm affectionately round the neck of Humphries as   listened
to this narrative, and put his doubting inquiries in reply.

" How do I know ? I'll tell you."

Humphries then proceeded to give a brief account of the dialogue between Bella and Mother Blonay, prior to the assault of
Hastings upon the former. We need not describe the joy of Davis on the recital. That very night an interview between the coquette and her lover put all things right between them.

" But you were cross, Bella, you know; and then you took such
pains to please that fellow."

" Yes, I was foolish, John ; but you know you had no patience·

and if I only looked at any other body than yourself, you were all
in a blaze, and spoke so angry that you frightened me more than
once. But you won't be angry with me again, and I promise I'll
love you always, and you only."

Davis made similar promises, and both, perhaps, kept them
With this, however, we have nothing now to do. Enough that
the Goose-Creeker and his sweetheart were put in requisition for
the contemplated rescue. Other persons in the village, known
whigs, were also entrusted with parts of the general performance;
and, in the brief space of time intervening between the arrival of
Singleton in Dorchester, and the day of execution, a bold scheme
had been prepared for the rescue of the destined victim. The partisan discovered that the whole force of Major Proctor at the garrison scarcely exceeded the command of a captain; sixty regulars
was the estimated number given him by Humphries. The greater
part of these would, in all probability, form the escort of the solemn
procession ; and these were too numerous, too well armed, and too
well drilled for Singleton's little force of thirty men, unless he could
form a scheme of surprise, by which to distract their attention and
defeat their unanimity. The plan was suggested by old Pryor,
and its boldness won the confidence of our hero.

"Here's the road, Major Singleton, you see—here's the red clay
hill, and here's the blasted tree that's borne better fruit than was
ever born on it. Here comes the red-coats, d—n 'em, I say. Now,
look here—here's the bush, thick enough on both sides to cover a
troop quietly. You fix your men here, and here, and here; and
the guard comes ; and here's the captain—he's in the centre.
What do you want then ? Something to make a noise and a confusion, is it ? Well, you must begin with the crowd ; them that's
got nothing particular to do, and that goes only to look on :
there'll be enough of them. Begin with them, I say ; only get
them frightened, and when once the fright begins, it goes like
wildfire in dry grass—it goes everywhere. First the people, then
the soldiers, all get it; and them that don't scamper will be sure
to be very stupid. When that's done, all's done. Then you
tumble among 'em, now on one side, now on the other, cutting up
and cutting down, shouting and screaming all the while, till you've

done as much as you think will answer. That's what you want, is it ?"

" Yes, let us once create the panic without breaking our own little force for the purpose, and we will then take advantage of it. The odds then will not be so great, and the prospect of success no longer doubtful."

Such was the reply of Singleton, whose previous suggestions Pryor had only adopted and reiterated in his long and prosy speech. The old man, hitching up his waistband with a most provoking gravity, approached the chair where the partisan sat, and whispered a single sentence in his ear.

" Can you do it—will you do it ?" was the quick inquiry of Singleton.

" I can—I will.

" Then set about your preparations directly, and I shall prepare for the rest."

There was no time for delay, and that night, after the return of Katharine from her customary visit to her father, Singleton sought her in private. She was hopeful, but doubtful. The manner and the words of her lover strengthened and assured her.

"Katharine, I have strong hopes—very strong hopes, though we depend greatly on circumstances. We have many agents at work, and you, too, must contribute. You must go to 'The Oaks' tonight, and provide horses, as many as possible, and of the fleetest. We shall probably want them all. Have them sent, by daylight to the little wood, just above the—"

He paused, and his cheek grew pale. She understood the occasion of his pause. But her spirit was strong, greatly nerved for the necessity ; and, at the moment, masculine in the highest degree.

" The place of execution—the gallows—you would say. Go on, go on, Robert. Let me hear—let me do."

" Yes ; there—in the little wood above—I shall station trusty men to receive and dispose of them. This you must do—and do quickly ; and this is all—all that you will be required to perform. To me, and others, you must leave the rest. Go, now, Kate, and"
-he passed his arm about her, and his voice grew tremulous—" I

shall not again see you, Kate—my own—my love—until it is all over. If I fail—"

"You must *not* fail," she cried, hurriedly, starting from his embrace, and looking almost sternly into his countenance. "You must not fail, Robert; rather than that—hear me—my father must not die in shame—the gallows must not pollute him—the rope must not dishonour his neck. There is an alternative—a dreadful alternative, Robert—but still an alternative." She put her hand upon the pistols at his side, as she concluded the sentence, wildly, but in a voice subdued to a whisper, "If he must die, there is another mode—another. Only do not hesitate, Robert; if you cannot save him from death, you may from dishonour. Fear not to spare him the shame which is worse than death to his spirit, and quite as dreadful to mine."

She threw her arms around his neck, and sobbed audibly for an instant.

"And if I fall, Kate—"

"In life or death, Robert. I am only yours." She had withdrawn her face from his bosom as she spoke. Her glistening eyes, with a holy earnestness, were fixed upon his own, and truth was in all their language. How holy, how sweet, how ennobling, how endearing, was the one kiss—the last embrace they took that night! That night, preceding a day of so much—of such an awful—interest to them both. A hurried word of mutual encouragement—a parting prayer, sent up in unison to Heaven from their mutual lips and united spirits—and they separated—the one to pray for that success for which the other was appointed to fight.

From this conference, the partisan proceeded to another with his coadjutors, Humphries and Davis. The whole plan was then matured, and Bella was made a party to the labour by her brother. His instructions to her were simple enough.

"Bella, you're not afraid to go to the church, just before daylight?"

"Afraid, brother William! No, I'm not afraid; but what am I to do there?"

"Listen. Go there by daydawn, and go up to the steeple."

"But how am I to get in?"

"Through the window; the door will be locked fast enough, and no getting the key out of old Johnson's hands. Get in at the window, which you can do easy enough, and keep quiet until you see the soldiers marching off with the colonel."

"Well?"

"Watch them—you can see everything easy enough from the tower. Look to the red hill, and when you see them arrived at the foot of it, set the bells a-going as hard as you can, as if you were ringing for dear life; and ring away until you can't ring any more,—you may then stop. That's all you've got to do. Will you do it?"

"But what's it for—what's the good of it?"

"No matter—I can't tell you now; but it must be done by somebody, and you're the best one to do it. Will you promise me?—now come, be a good girl, Bella, and I'll tell John Davis all about you."

The girl promised, and the conspirators then proceeded to other preparations, which were deemed essential to the complete success of their enterprise. They had all returned to the swamp long before the daylight opened upon them.

CHAPTER XLIX.

" 'Tis the last trial, and the strife must come,
Soon to our peril. But the heart is firm—
The rigid muscle set—the steel prepared,
And the thought hopeful of our full success.
The gods befriend and aid us, as we serve,
And battle for the right ! "

THE day dawned beautifully and brightly. The sun rose without
a cloud darkening his upward progress, and the richly variegated
woods gladdened in his beams. The air was balmy, and the wind
silent. The quiet, slumberous day of the intense summer, unbroken
by warning or discordant sounds, and alive only in the cheering
scream of the bird, and the drowsy hum of the insect, seemed but
indifferently to accord with the bitter and the gloomy purposes
of man. It was the day of purposed execution. How little did
the spirit of the unconscious and thoughless nature harmonize with
that, having an immortal hope and destiny, yet so bent upon earthly
strife, so busy with its foolish passions! Alas! that man should
take so few lessons from the sweet ministers of God—the bird and
the flower—sent for his pleasure and his profit, and which, ministering innocently, by song and sweet, to his happiness, should yet so
commonly fail to teach him innocence.

A sad scene was going on in the cell of the destined victim.
His daughter kneeled beside him at daylight in his prison. She
had cheered his solitude with the sunshine of her own sweet and
gentle thoughts — she had whispered hope in his ears when he
himself refused to hope. She had forgotten her own griefs while
ministering to his — and this is the reward which virtue always
brings to duty. How happy was she thus to minister! how point-
less was the shaft of fate to him, while thus he listened to, and felt
her tribute ministry! In that hour, if he did not hope, he at least
felt free from all the humiliating emotions of despair. What if the

22*

doom came—what if he suffered the cruel indignity and the painful death—had he not heard—did he not feel, deep in his soul, the prevailing force of those prayers which the lips of his innocent child sent up for him momently to Heaven?

"Yet, do not flatter yourself too much, my daughter," he said to her, in reply to one of her uttered anticipations of relief from Singleton. "You must not persuade me, at least. I must be prepared; and though I shall certainly contribute all in my power to coöperate with Robert in any effort which he shall make, I must not the less prepare to encounter the last trial as unavoidable. Robert will do what he can, I feel satisfied. But what of that? His force is small, inferior to that which guards me, and desperation only may avail in in what he attempts."

"And he will be desperate, father; he will not strike feebly, or heartlessly, or hopelessly. Oh no! I know he will not. He is resolved with all his resolve, and you know his spirit. He does not say—he will not tell me what he intends; but his eyes are so earnest, and he looks! Could you but have seen him, father, when he promised me to save you, your hope would be like mine; you would not, you could not, doubt that he would do it."

"I do not doubt, my child, that he will try—"

"And if Robert tries, father—"

He interrupted her sanguine speech and the implied tribute to her lover, folding his arms about her neck, as she knelt beside him, and placing his lips upon her forehead.

"You are a devoted girl, and Robert may well love you, my child. Tell me, Katharine—it will do me good to know that his affections are yours, and that you have not been unmindful of his worth."

"How could I—how? Have we not known him long enough, my father?"

"God bless you, Kate—God bless you! This, if I perish, would still be a redeeming pleasure, as I should then know him to be well rewarded, and be sure that I leave you with a protector. Your loves, my child, are hallowed with my blessings, with the prayers for your good of one who, in a few hours, may be in the presence of God himself."

She clung to him like a despairing infant.

"Speak not thus, my father—let me hope—do not make me doubt that you will be saved—that the bitter cup will pass by us."

"Hope—hope on, my child—it is your duty. Hope is one of life's best allies—the first to come, the last to desert us. But I need not tell you to hope. You cannot help it. Hope and virtue are twins, and inseparable; the one never flies until the other deserts the heart. There is no despair for the good."

"I believe it—I trust—and you, too, hope, my father, if this be true. I feel it in my soul, even as if, at this moment, I beheld it with my eyes. A good spirit at my heart—God's spirit—is there to assure me of my hope."

Thus cheered and cheering, the two, interrupted only occasionally by the entrance of the colonel's sister, conversed together from daylight until the approaching noon. But, as the hour drew nigh assigned for the execution—when the danger began to assume, as it were, a bodily form and pressure; the thoughts came thick to the mind; the doubts grew strong and oppressive about the heart; the fears seized upon the flickering fancies; and imagination, painting in vivid colours the dreadful circumstances of the approaching time, to the mind's eye of the maiden, greatly served to overthrow all the stability of her resolve—all the fine soothing of her hope. She moaned aloud as she clung now to the neck of her father. In that moment, the nature of the man grew active, and the contrast between the two would claim the art of the painter to embody to the eye; and the strong imagination, only, could depict it to the mind of one not beholding it. He, who had wept with her before, was now erect and strong. If it was not hope that strengthened, it was the courage and high resolve of fine moral character, strong in conscious integrity—strong in resolve—that lifted up spirit and form alike, defyingly, in the face of death. It is a noble picture, that of a brave man looking out upon danger, and fearlessly preparing for its approach. It is a painfully sweet picture, that of the frail woman,—storm-beaten, storm-broken, like a flower stricken to the earth, and, in its weakness, compelled to rest upon its bosom; but still smiling, still cheering, still giving forth love and worship, even as the flower gives forth perfume, and ready to share the fate which it dreads, but which it has not the strength to avert.

Such was the picture in the dungeon of Colonel Walton. The masculine spirit was already composed for the final trial—the last struggle of life with its uncompromising enemy. The man was prepared to meet death with unshrinking resolution; the gentleman, with grace and dignity: and when, entering his dungeon, Major Proctor came to his prisoner—his own eyes suffused, and his deportment that of one, himself a victim—a victim certainly to humiliation and grief—to announce the arrival of the hour, he met the unshaken glance and carriage of one who seemed rather a conqueror than a condemned.

"Leave us, but a few moments, and let my servant, Cæsar, be summoned, if you please. He, only, will attend me."

Proctor bowed, and departed. "Father—oh! my father—it is not the hour—it is not time yet—do not go—not yet! Robert may not be ready—not quite ready. He has to come from the Cypress —he has a great deal to do, and will want all the time he can get."

She clung to him, as if to keep him back. Her eyes were starting from their sockets, bloodshot and wandering. Her words came chokingly forth—her frame was convulsed and shivering; her whole manner that of one in whose mind reason and opposing apprehensions were earnestly at strife for the ascendency. He lifted her from the floor as if she had been a child—his own nerves untrembling all the while. He lifted her to his lips, and calmly kissed her cheek. The act itself told more than words. He had treated her as a child, and she understood the gentle form of that rebuke. She tried to compose herself, and her words, though equally broken and incoherent, were far more subdued in their utterance. How tender—how holy was that brief communion!

"Katharine, be firm, my child—be firm for my sake. Be firm to pray—to pray for my rescue; nor for that alone—you must be firm to act."

She grasped his hand, and looked inquiringly.

"Robert," he continued, as she listened—"Robert, with that good sense which distinguishes his proceedings always, has told you nothing plainly of his present plan. He knew that you could not well comprehend military particulars, and that you would better be satisfied with his own general assurance, than if he had undertaken to show you those arguments which you must yet fail to appreciate. To teach only a part of his design, would be to leave the inquiring mind doubtful of the rest. I can conjecture the design which he has in view, in part at least—and the horses which you were required to send him, he has doubtless prepared in readiness for me along the road, in the event of his rescuing me. It is for you to contribute something to the same object. He could not venture across the bridge, and he therefore made no arrangements in that quarter, should it suit me to shape my flight to that side of the river— a desperate man, most desparately bent, I may be disposed to push through my enemies, even where they are thickest. In that event, there should be horses there also. You must see to this, for your aunt has none of the necessary energy. Your firmness must do this, even now. Take the carriage there, and there remain with it. It may be all to me, and the trust is now with you."

The object of Walton was not expressed to his daughter. He had no real idea that he should need any such assistance; but he well knew that, by the employment of her mind at the most perilous moment, in a labour of seeming necessity, he should divest it in reality of its own griefs. Throw reponsibility upon the young mind, if you would seek to strengthen it. This was his design; and its effect was instant. The belief that on her resolution and action, now, so much was to depend, alone restored and strengthed her. Yet she could not so soon recover, and, taking her last embrace almost in a convulsion, she was hurried away by her aunt from the mournful dungeon, a few moments before the officer appeared to conduct the prisoner to the place of doom. Major Proctor himself forbore to attend the execution. He assigned the task to an inferior officer, his duty not requiring his personal presence. A strong guard was detached from the garrison, and the sad procession emerged at midday from the gates.

Major Singleton had well devised his plans, and prepared, as fully as in his power, for the due execution of his purposes. He had brought his troop before daylight to the spot assigned them. To

those who know the ground, his arrangement will be readily comprehended.   To those who do not, a few words may be necessary, and
will certainly suffice for explanation.   The road at the point of execution was on the easy ascent of a small clay hill.   The woods were
thick on either hand.   On the eastern side of the wood, a few yards
below the gallows, a small track—a common wagon or neighborhood
road—wound into the forest, making a turn within a few paces from
the main path, which effectually concealed it at that distance from the
sight.   In this sheltering place, one-half of Singleton's troop, well
mounted and ready for the charge, lay concealed.   On the opposite
side of the main road, closely hidden in the wood, some thirty paces
above, another portion of his force, similarly posted and prepared,
stood in waiting for the signal.   Three chosen riflemen were assigned
trees at different points of the wood on either hand, commanding the
scene of execution.   They were closely embowered in the foliage ;
and the trees intervening, effectually secured them from sight, even
though the report of their pieces indicated the direction in which they
harboured.   Their horses were hitched to swinging boughs in the
wood behind them, ready for their flight the moment their task
should be finished.   Singleton himself led the party destined to make
the first charge.   To Humphries the other body was assigned.   No
instructions were omitted, necessary to bring about concerted action ;
and the minutest directions—aye, even to the rifleman who was
required to lead the fire—were insisted upon by the young but
thoughtful partisan.   Such being the preparation, there was no danger
of the plan failing from hurry or want of coolness.

The little coquette, whom the restoration to the good regards of John
Davis had made the most obliging little creature that the village had
for sometime known, did not forget the part which had been assigned
her in the duties of the day.   Clambering over the graves, with some
little feminine trepidation, she made her way into the church, and
from thence into the steeple, while the stars were yet shining palely
in the heavens.   She had her dread of ghosts, for she had heard a
thousand stories of their nocturnal habits ; but then, she recollected
John Davis, who had given her a parting admonition to do ably the
task assigned her.   John Davis stood to her at that moment in the

place of a principle; and, like many thousand others of both sexes, she always understood her duties best when they came through certain lips, and were insisted upon by a certain preacher. Man-worship, in those times, as at present, was not uncommonly mistaken for the most profound worship or God.

Here she watched patiently and long. Day came, and from the tower looking forth, she beheld his rising light with a feeling of relief, if not joy. The first faint blush that drove away the stars from the east, almost won her worship on this occasion; not only because it relieved her gloomy watch, but because of its own beauty. How natural is the worship of the sun! How idle to wonder at the pagan who sees in it the embodied god of his idolatory! He speaks for a God in all his aspects, and is worthy of homage, not only as he so greatly ministers to man, but as he is worthy of the Creator.

Patiently, hour after hour, until the approaching noon, did the girl continue close concealed in the steeple, awaiting the moment which should call for the execution of her duties. And it came at last. The painful and mournful notes of the military music reached her ear, and the gloomy procession emerged from the gate of the garrison beneath her eye. First came a small guard, then the prisoner, attended by a clergyman, and then the main body of the guard marching on either hand. As the fearful notes resounded through the village, its inhabitants came forth in groups, joining the melancholy march, and contributing by their numbers to its imposing solemnity. The prisoner was much beloved in the village and its neighbourhood, even by those who had taken sides with the invader; and the knowledge of this fact alone made the hope more strong and active in the bosom of Singleton, that his plan must be successful. He felt assured, that, in the event of a commotion, none of the natives would interfere to prevent the rescue of Walton or assist in his recovery.

The heart of Bella Humphries thrilled fearfully as she watched the procession. The imposing martial array, the georgeous uniform of the British, their fine regular movement, close and well arrayed order, and gleaming bayonets, struck terror to her heart, while they aroused all the enthusiastic admiration of her mind. Her task was to watch until the cavalcade should reach a certain point, which, from her elevated position, she could easily behold over the trees. She was then to sound the tocsin, and thus furnish the expected signal to all the conspirators. Firmly, though tremblingly, she looked forth upon the array, which she could readily distinguish in all its parts. There was the prisoner, seated in the degrading cart; there was the priest beside him; there the different bodies of soldiers; and there, hanging upon the skirts, or crowding upon the sides of the melancholy procession, came the villagers and country people. She could even distinguish Blonay, and his hag-like mother, trudging along, at a hurried pace, in front of the procession. The old woman hung on the arm of her son, who seemed but partially disposed to carry such a burden. The savage had not lost a single feature marking his old identity. He was the same lounging, shuffling, callous wretch that we have before known him; and his slow, indifferent movement—for here he had no mischief to perform—was the subject of rebuke with his own mother.

"Come now, Ned, my boy—move a bit faster, will you? The people are coming close behind, and we shall see nothing if they get before us."

"Why, what's to see mother? Adrat it, there's nothing so much in a fellow hanging. I've seen more than one, and so have you."

"That's true, Ned; but still I like it, and I don't care how many of these great folks they hang up among the trees. I hate 'em all, Neddy, boy; for all of them hate you. They keep you down, my son—they trample upon you—they laugh at you, and their best word to you is a curse. God curse 'em for it; I hate 'em all.

"Adrat it, but you can't hang 'em; and so what's the use to talk about it?"

"If I could!" she muttered bitterly between her closed teeth. The son replied with a laugh, concluding the sentence—

"The trees would be full of such fruit."

"Aye, that they would; and I've tried for the power—I've asked for the power over them but it hasn't come to me. I've got out of my bed at midnight, when the night was blackest, and I've called upon the bad spirits to come to me, and help me to my revenge on them

THE OLD HAG'S DESIRE. 525

that have scorned you, and spit upon you, and called you by scornful names; but I had no learning, and so the evil ones came not to my aid, though I've looked for 'em, and longed for 'em, and wanted 'em badly."

She spoke in a language of disappointment; her looks and manner both corresponding with the chagrin which her words expressed. Yet she complained unjustly. The spirits of evil had been serving her to the utmost extent of their power; but with the vulgar mind always, the power must have a body and a sign to the external senses, before its presence will be recognized or understood.

The ill-favored son chuckled at the disappointment she expressed, and, with a taste differing from her own, congratulated her upon their indulgent absence.

"Adrat it, mother, but they would have been ugly company if they had come; and I'm mighty glad they didn't listen to you. They would ha' made the cabin too hot to hold us."

"Fear not; for they say that the person who calls them can keep them down, and make 'em only do what's wanted. I wasn't afraid; they wouldn't have seen me tremble if they had come, even at mid night, when I called them. But there goes another that ought to be strapped up too. He's another great man, too, and has scarlet cushions in his pew at church, while I must sit on the bare bench in the aisle, as if in God's house some are to be poor and some rich.

"Adrat it, mother, hush, or they'll hear you. Come this side, out of the way of the crowd—here, to the left."

"Don't carry me where I can't see. I want to see everything, and you must get me a place on the hill."

"Why, that will be close by the tree."

"That's what I want. I want to see his mouth when the cart moves off."

"D——n my heart, if I stand there with you; I'll go higher up; and so must you. You'll only be in the way, mother, to go there."

"But there I will stand, for my eyes are bad, and I can't see farther off. You can leave me, if you don't like it. I can stay by myself."

"Adrat it, so I will. I can see very well at a hundred yards; thats nigh enough for me; and I don't like to go too nigh when people's in the notion of hanging. It ain't safe."

He hurried the beldam to the hill assigned for the place of execution. A few paces only separated her from the fatal tree; and she saw all the desired points distinctly. The procession moved on; the crowd gathered; the tree was before the doomed victim; and the officer in command riding up, ordered a halt before it, and proceeded to make his arrangements, when the bell sounded: a single stroke and then a pause—as if the hand grew palsied immediately after. That stroke, however, so single, so sudden, drew every eye, aroused all attention; and coming immediately upon the solemn feelings induced by the approaching scene in the minds of all the spectators, it had the effect of startling, for an instant, all who heard it.

But when it was repeated—when the painful clamour grew quick and violent, and the rapidly clashing metal thundered forth a reckless, unregulated peal, varying, yet continuous—the surprise was complete. In that moment a new terror came, close following upon the first. The signal had been heard and obeyed by the other conspirators, and wild cries of men, women and children, coming from Dorchester, aroused in painful astonishment those forming the procession, soldiers as well as people. The cause of the alarm, in another instant, seemed explained to the wondering multitude as they looked towards the village. A sudden rush of flame—a wide, high column—rose from its centre, and ascended into the calm atmosphere like a pyramid. Another and another body of flame, in different directions, and the now distinguished cry from the village, announced it to be on fire. The crowd—each individual only thinking of his family and household goods—broke on every side through the guard clustering around the prisoner; heedless of the resistance which they offered, and all unconscious of the present danger. In that moment, while the alarm was at the highest, and as the officer struggled to keep his ranks unbroken, the rifle of one of the marksmen in the tree-top singled him out as a victim, and he fell beneath the unerring aim which the rifleman had taken.

It was then that the bugle of Singleton sounded—a clear, quick and lively note. That of Humphries, on the opposite quarter, responded and the charge of the partisan followed close upon it. The officer next in command to him who had fallen, however surprised, cooly enough prepared to do his duty. He closed his men around the pris-

oner with the first appearance of danger, and when the rushing horses
were heard trooping from the woods, he boldly faced in the direction
of the expected enemy.

All this was the work of an instant. The brands had been well
prepared under the direction of old Pryor; and, with the feeling of a
true patriot, his own dwelling had been chosen by him the very first
for destruction. He had piled the resinous and rich lightwood in
every apartment. He had filled it with combustibles, and had so prepared it, that the blaze must be sudden, and the conflagration complete. Three other houses were chosen and prepared in like manner;
and, once ignited, their possessors rushed away to the place of execution, crying their alarm aloud, and adding to the wild confusion,

Their cries resounded violently, with a new and more emphatic
burst, as, coming out of the village, they appeared upon the road, just
as the bugle of Singleton had sounded for his charge. The brave
partisan had bent all his energies to his purpose, and he now gave all
his spirit, and all his strength, to its manful completion. His first
plunge from the coppice placed him in front of a presented bayonet.
Quick as thought, he wheeled his steed to the right, avoiding the
lunge which carried the soldier forward. While the fore feet of the
animal were yet in air, he, as suddenly, wheeled him back again, and
his hoofs were beaten down, with all his weight, upon the body of
the soldier, who lay crushed and writhing under his legs.

This movement had broken the bristling line, in the centre of
which the strong-limbed partisan now found himself. He did not
stop to calculate. In action, alone, lay his hope of safety or success.
He was penetrating the square in which his uncle was a prisoner. The
fatal cart was before him, and this was enough to give new vigor to
his effort. Right and left, his heavy sabre descended—a sweeping
death, defying the opposing steel, and biting fatally at every stroke.
He was well supported by his men, and, though not one-half the
number of his enemies, he had already gained a decided advantage,
and made some progress toward his object, when the charge of
Humphries followed up his success. The lieutenant hurried over the
ground, cheering and shouting. An old woman, feebly tottering to
the roadside, stumbled along the path, but he did not pause in his
progress. Indeed, he could not. The troop followed him—horseman

after horseman went over the prostrate body, grinding it to the earth, until there was as little human in its appearance, as there was in the heart of its owner. She gave but one cry—a dreadful scream. It chilled the heart of the brave trooper, as the hoofs of his steed went down upon her breast. He knew the voice—he heard the words—and, hag as she was, foul and malignant, the appeal to her son, in the last accents of her lips, was touching in the extreme. It was his name that she cried in her death struggle—and Blonay heard the cry. He emerged from the bush where he had been sheltered; but, when the contest was clear before him, he again sank back. He was cool enough to see that nothing could save the beldam—he was calculating enough to risk nothing in an effort so hopeless. Stealing along the wood, however, he unslung his rifle, freed his knife from the sheath, and prepared to take any possible advantage which the progress of circumstances might afford him.

The fight grew fearful around the cart in which the prisoner sat. The clergyman leaped into the crowd, dreading that conspicuousness in the affray which the situation gave him. Colonel Walton, alone, remained within it. He had arisen, but his hands were tied; and, though his feet were free, he yet felt that his position was much more secure, as long as the sabre only was employed, than it would be, without weapons, and having no use of his hands, in the *melée*, and under the feet of the horses. But he shouted encouragingly to Singleton, who, indeed, needed now no other encouragement than his own fierce frenzy. The fury that impelled him looked like madness. He seemed double-armed and invulnerable. More than once had a strong combatant opposed him, and hopelessly. He had ploughed his way through the living wall, with a steel and strength equally irresistible.

"Courage, uncle—courage! Can you do nothing for yourself?" And striking as he spoke, down went another soldier.

"I am tied," was the reply, as quickly. In the next moment, leaping from his horse into the centre of the vehicle, Lance Frampton applied his knife to the cords.

"Hurrah !" was the cheering cry of the partisans, as the prisoner clapped his hands in the air, showing their enlargement. A soldier seized the horse which drew the cart, by the bridle, and turning his head among the crowd, sought to lead him off. But the sabre of Singleton — seemingly aimed at the soldier, who dodged it by sinking down while yet holding upon the bridle — was adroitly intended for the horse. It went resistlessly through his neck, and falling among the crowd about him, the animal struggled in the agonies of death, still farther adding to the confusion.

Walton at this moment sprang from the cart, and the partisans gathered around him. The guard, considerably diminished, now collected for a charge; but the pistols of the partisans, which they could now safely venture to employ, were brought to bear upon them. They recoiled, and in the moment, Colonel Walton gained the cover of the wood; another found him mounted; and, rushing forth, with a wild shout, he gave the enemy an idea of the presence of some fresher enemy. This was all that was wanting to the completion of the confusion. They gave back — at first they merely yielded — then they broke; and, as the partisans beheld their advantage, and pressed on to avail themselves of it, the dismembered guard fled down the road in the direction of the village.

"Back—back!" cried Singleton to his men, as they were preparing to pursue. "Enough has been done for our purpose — let us hazard nothing in pursuit."

Then turning to Colonel Walton, in a few brief words, he congratulated him on his rescue, but urged his immediate flight.

"Humphries," cried he to that officer, "conduct Colonel Walton to the Cypress instantly. I follow you with the men. Nay, linger not for me; there is more to be done if we delay. I will collect the troop."

They would have paused, Colonel Walton in particular — who seemed determined to share all the risks to which Singleton was subjected; but the latter at once put on the authority with which he was invested, and sternly commanded immediate and implicit obedience to his orders. There was no farther delay. Walton was soon out of sight, while Singleton, collecting his scattered troops, followed hard upon his footsteps. They fled in season — just as Major Proctor, who had now become familiar with the cause of alarm, and sallied forth with all the remaining garrison, emerged from the village.

The Briton found only the remnant of the defeated guard; and it was not his policy to pursue, with so small a force as that under his orders, an enemy, of whose strength he knew nothing, and who was flushed with recent victory.

Thus terminated the battle of Dorchester. The victory was with the partisans, but they paid dearly for it. Five of their men were slain outright, and an equal number wounded. The battle so long as it lasted, had been sanguinary in the extreme; nor did it terminate altogether with the actual conflict. The flames which had ushered in the conflict continued to rage long after it was over; and one-half of the beautiful town, by close of day, lay in ashes.

How sweet was the meeting of the father with his child, the day of peril now safely over, in the deep recess of the Cypress Swamps! There, on the first tidings of the advantage gained by her friends, she had repaired in the hope to meet him. Nor had she sought him there in vain. He himself bore her the first tidings of his safety; and, convulsive with joy, and almost speechless, she hung upon his neck, feeble and fainting, with not strength enough to speak her emotions. But when she looked round and saw not her lover, the thought of his danger — the doubt of his safety — awakened all her anxieties anew, and brought forth all her strength.

"Tell me that he is safe—Robert."

"He is, and will soon be here."

They had not long to wait. He came, guiding her to the spot where her first pledge to him had been given—where the first kiss of true love had been exchanged between them. The pledge, under better auspices, was gratefully renewed.

"And you are now mine—mine for ever, my own Katharine."

"Yours—yours only, and for ever."

The eye of a father looked on, and sanctioned the fond embrace which rewarded the partisan for his peril, and the maiden for her firm and filial devotion.

"But this is not a time for dalliance, my Katharine. It is enough that I am secure of your affections—enough that you are mine—we must part now. Your father is not yet safe—not till we get him into the camp of Marion. Be satisfied that the immediate danger is withdrawn; we must try and keep him from a renewal of it; and can only do so by throwing the Peedee between him and his enemies. We must part now."

"So soon!"

"*Too* soon. But we may not linger here with safety. We are still in danger. This blow will bring Tarleton upon us; who rides like a madman. Come, I will lead you to your carriage, and——"

He bore her away through the copse, and no eye beheld their parting; but it was sweet, and it was holy. Her last kiss hung upon his lips with an enduring sweetness, for the long season which intervened between that period and the hour of their final union. He returned in a few moments to the Swamp, and there found the maniac Frampton standing upon the edge of the swamp, in curious observation of the men. He would have carried him along with the party, and spoke to him to that effect; but the other appeared not to heed him: and the only glance of consciousness which he seemed to exhibit was when his fiery eye rested upon the features of his youthful son. Singleton approached, and while persuading him to remove with his party from the Swamp, laid his hand upon the shoulder of the insane wretch. The effect was electrical. He bounded away with his demoniac laugh, and plunging through the creek, fled in the direction of his wife's burial-place. The partisan saw that nothing could possibly be done with him, and bidding his youthful charge, Lance Frampton, beside him, he put his band in motion, and hurried forward, once more to unite with Marion in the long and perilous warfare of the Swamps—kept up as it was, until, step by step, beaten to the Atlantic shores, the invader fled to his ships and left the country. But these events are for other legends. Our present task is ended.

THE END.